PENGUIN BOOKS

NEWFOUNDLAND

Rebecca Ray lives anywhere and everywhere. She is enjoying a happy, healthy retirement.

Newfoundland

REBBECCA RAY

PENGUIN BOOKS

PENGUIN BOOKS

Published by the Penguin Group
Penguin Books Ltd, 80 Strand, London WC2R 0RL, England
Penguin Group (USA) Inc., 375 Hudson Street, New York, New York 10014, USA
Penguin Group (Canada), 90 Eglinton Avenue East, Suite 700, Toronto, Ontario, Canada M4P 2Y3
(a division of Pearson Penguin Canada Inc.)
Penguin Ireland, 25 St Stephen's Green, Dublin 2, Ireland
(a division of Penguin Books Ltd)
Penguin Group (Australia), 250 Camberwell Road,
Camberwell, Victoria 3124, Australia (a division of Pearson Australia Group Pty Ltd)
Penguin Books India Pvt Ltd, 11 Community Centre,
Panchsheel Park, New Delhi – 110 017, India
Penguin Group (NZ), cnr Airborne and Rosedale Roads, Albany,
Auckland 1310, New Zealand (a division of Pearson New Zealand Ltd)
Penguin Books (South Africa) (Pty) Ltd, 24 Sturdee Avenue,
Rosebank, Johannesburg 2196, South Africa

Penguin Books Ltd, Registered Offices: 80 Strand, London WC2R 0RL, England

www.penguin.com

First published by Hamish Hamilton 2005
Published in Penguin Books 2006
1

Copyright © Rebbecca Ray, 2005
All rights reserved

The moral right of the author has been asserted

Set by Rowland Phototypesetting Ltd, Bury St Edmunds, Suffolk
Printed in England by Clays Ltd, St Ives plc

ISBN-13: 978-0-140-28609-0
ISBN-10: 0-140-28609-8

Contents

This book is for my family and for
Wales

Autumn

She found the deaf girl smashing bottles on a garden path. That was how it started. The town was called Ynys-morlan and she knew no one. She had come here to change her life.

It was the first day that she came down to the place itself, her third day in the house. You could see it from the edge of her garden, little buildings in distant sunlight. Two long, thin rows of houses stretched along the coast. They held their backs to the shoreline and to the floodplain on their other side, a reach of flat land laid like pages all the way from the mountains' feet out to the sea.

Gentler mountains, dark in the mornings, shadowed like a memory. They'd be touched along the ridges with sudden sun. She had spent a long time just looking. The grassed slopes were almost yellow, the stretches of bracken tinted rose. They seemed to hold the clouds away, dusky, a still storm behind. It was right to be alone in a place like this.

There was silence in the mornings. She'd thought, coming here that first night, that she might hate the morning's quiet, but she loved this too. Only the sound of the gulls and the light on the walls of her home.

The third day. The people who lived in Ynys-morlan didn't own the mountains or the sea. She thought she would keep that in mind. And anyway, she didn't think she'd speak to anyone.

She applied a little make-up. She stood in front of the mirror, touched her hair and the lines around her mouth. She picked the right coat and the right bag. Small things like this were important, a proper impression. She sat in the hallway before she left, wearing the right coat, holding the right bag. She looked at her bare hands and at the door.

The lane led down a small hill from which she could see the

town drawing closer. The houses were all tipped angles from here: corrugated roofs and slate and salt-worn wood. She saw lines of washing, moving slightly, and a rusted weathervane in the shape of a dragon, that was still despite the wind. It wasn't a temporary place but it felt that way. The buildings looked like a line of driftwood that had been piled here by the sea.

Charlotte Weyland walked with her head up and her back straight. She passed a gift shop with closed doors and dusty windows, a blank concrete space outside. It was October now, the end of October and the summer had gone.

Ynys-morlan was quiet in the cold. Wheeling birds and a vacant street. The houses had small windows, very deep-set windows where the light met only the few little things left near the glass to be seen: model ships and trophies, things like that, and only shadows behind. In this silence, she could hear her own shoes walking and received the sound of every step. She looked out and past and over, like she wasn't going into the town at all, but going through it, heading on.

Charlotte held her bag. In this new, hushed street she saw the little girl.

Two years old maybe, three at the most. Brown hair cut into a thick fringe and very pale skin, very dark eyes. When she shifted, the hair fell across her face. And there was something – Charlotte paused. She didn't hear her feet stop. There was something – in the expression on the girl's face, in the way she stood. She looked at nothing around her. She was so concentrated, removed. Charlotte stood in the stillness. For a moment, she forgot about the bag she was holding, she forgot about the mountains and the sea; that this was her home too. She saw the expression on the little girl's face and felt memories rise in cold threads.

She was holding the bottle, holding it outstretched. Her arms were straight, as though balancing. It was a milk bottle, Charlotte saw. And then she saw the others, a line by the girl's feet. More milk bottles, Bell's whisky here and there. Her small hands were blanched around the glass. Her knuckles were red.

The child's shadow was draped across short grass and perfect flower beds, curving over the stones of the garden's low wall. And she dropped the bottle. The noise was violent in an empty day.

My God, she wasn't sure if she thought the words or if she said them and she looked around, she looked down the street for someone else and there was no one. Standing on the garden path, the girl stared down at what she had made. Charlotte should have walked away.

'Oh God, Nia. Nia, no.'

And then the front door was open and Charlotte saw the woman. Saw her run down the path, saw brown hair just like the girl's.

'Nia,' the woman said, but her voice was very low. She had one shirtsleeve rolled up to the elbow.

This is private, Charlotte thought. And the little girl just stood, gazing intently at the ground about her feet.

'Don't do that, Ni, what are you doing? Don't.' As though she spoke to herself. And Charlotte didn't walk away. Clearly, slowly, the mother shook her head, strain overwritten on her face. 'Nia . . .'

Charlotte saw her try to smile, crouch down, her face caught momentarily by the light – and watched as she gathered up the bottles, held them to her chest with small sounds. All of them in her arms, the woman didn't stand. Glass pressed to her, she just remained there, looking at the broken scoops and the shards, the soft spots of light they cast, and then closing her eyes.

Motionless. At rest in the sun and the sharp air, her daughter stood taller than her. They looked like a painting, Charlotte thought. The girl reached out and she touched her mother's hair.

And Charlotte didn't turn as they stirred, stood up, or as the woman lifted her head. They saw each other. Bottles clinked together, glass against solid glass. Behind, fallen leaves moved on the road.

Tight and still and ready, though she didn't want to be, Charlotte waited for the ugly words. What sort of person was she to stand staring at people over garden walls?

'I'm sorry,' the woman said, though. She gave a big, distracted smile. 'Don't worry, we're just mad, don't worry about us.' She stepped forward, laughing, saying, 'Oh we just like to break things, bottles, furniture. We do it on Thursdays.' Trapped by the collection in her arms, her fingers moved, they fluttered. She put the bottles down while Charlotte stood without answering. She reached over the wall to shake hands.

'Ruth Lewis.'

The touch was cold.

'My name is Charlotte. Charlotte Weyland.' Hearing the sound of her own voice, she wanted to walk away. Finally she said, 'I heard a noise.'

'Yes, well.' Ruth Lewis gave a playful schoolma'am frown, said, 'That'll be this one. Little mischief maker, she is. Little Dennis the Menace.' She reached for Nia, drew her gently forward. 'This is the culprit.'

Charlotte looked at the girl's quiet face.

'Can't keep track of her half the time, she's inside, she's outside, I think she does it just to wear me out. What can I do next? she's thinking.'

Reaching her hand out again, she began for the child, 'I'm Charlotte.'

And then Ruth said, 'She's deaf.'

There was a silence.

She asked Charlotte if she was on holiday. She said that really the season was over now but that she'd never understood why people only wanted holidays in summer. 'I think it's nicer here in autumn than it is in mid-July,' she said.

'It's lovely.' Charlotte turned from the girl's face, nodded and cleared her throat.

'Mind you,' Ruth went on, 'I think if I was American, I'd have to go for holidays in Florida. Take Nia to Disneyland maybe. I bet it's hot in Florida all year round, I bet it's lovely there.'

'I've never been.' Charlotte smoothed her coat, she didn't look at Nia. 'I've lived in London since I was twelve.'

'Oh well . . . you've still got the accent, that's all.'

'I'm not on holiday,' Charlotte said. That's how I look, she thought. 'I've bought a house. It's on the hill there . . .'

'Really?'

'You know it?'

'Yes . . . well, I knew it'd sold. Course, it's been on the market for years now, since I can't remember when. And you bought the garden too? The walled garden, I mean.'

'That's right.'

She could have said a lot of things. She could have told the woman that she'd bought the property only because of the garden. She could have said that the house was fine but really it was the garden – really it was only the garden. She looked away and didn't see the expression that passed across Ruth Lewis's face.

Goodbyes would sound natural now. Sometimes it was easier just to walk. Coming or going, it didn't matter.

'It must be very derelict.'

'It needs work, yes,' Charlotte answered.

Now the woman was looking at her in a different way. 'I'd love to hear about it . . . Maybe, have you got time for a cup of tea?' And then she said, 'You could probably do with a cup of tea, lots of sugar and milk, what with Nia scaring the life out of you. You could probably do with one.' She gestured to the little house at the end of the path. 'Have you got the time?' she asked.

It was small and pink and pebbledashed. It had perfect little curtains and was surrounded by the year's final flowers. The woman could have been saying, just step over the shattered glass.

This was the day, the 27th of October, when Dai Meredith found his mother dead. Half an hour before, he sat doing a crossword puzzle. He liked to fill in the little blank spaces in crosswords with circles or sometimes with squares. When he was at home and he had colouring pens, he always did the circles yellow and squares red; had a feeling that squares should be red. Here in the café, he only had a biro though, and had to leave the colours in his head. It was three twenty-eight in the afternoon, and he didn't think that life could be like that, that you could just be sitting with your crossword puzzle and drinking your hot chocolate and then you could find your mother dead.

The café wasn't busy, just a few regulars. Bethan's mum called them regulars, she said that he was one and when he came in she always smiled. She said, 'The usual?' like that. There was Mr Edwards in the corner by the window, with his newspaper and his magnification sheet. His mother had a magnification sheet but she kept it away in a drawer and she called it 'that wretched thing'. Mr Edwards's magnification sheet caught the sunlight and made Dai feel ill.

There was Bethan's mum, Patty, behind the counter with the tea-maker and the milkshake flavour bottles, hung upside down. And there was Bethan, sitting here with her friend, Bethan holding the baby. Dai looked up at her but only for a moment. The sun lay across the table and his crossword puzzle. There were cooking sounds, the smell of vinegar and tea and something stale. He listened to Bethan's voice.

She always sat in the same place, the table by the counter. Had done all through the last part of being pregnant and then, when she'd come back with the baby, she'd started sitting there again. She liked to get all her things arranged around her: the cigarettes and the ashtray, the coffee, her magazines. Sometimes she just stared out of the window. His mother said, 'Sometimes I sits and thinks and sometimes I just sits.'

Now she wasn't reading her magazines or looking out, but listening to her friend talk. She had the baby on her knee.

'It's on at the rugby club,' her friend was saying. Dai kept his head down. 'Saw the sound system, they had it set up yesterday, speakers like a fucking cliff face. I'll be deaf for a week. I'll hit the top note and break every window in Aber. Ultrasonic, it'll be. People'll think the bomb's hit, and all their dogs'll have bleeding ears. You wait, you'll read it in *The Star* the day after, like: shell-shocked Labrador found wandering in street . . .'

Bethan snorted a laugh, she was quieter. 'What are you doing then? Decided?'

'I'm doing "Search for the Hero Inside Yourself". M People.'

'That's inspiration, like. I hear that song, it's as much as I can do to hold myself back from going parachuting.'

Dai looked at his puzzle, half finished. The paper rustled under his hands. It was three thirty-two and fifteen seconds. His mother had bought him the digital watch – he'd picked it out himself, the blue one. He needed to go home now. He looked out through the window at the tarmac, the low-lying afternoon, and didn't want to.

This was where he came every day after work. Outside he could see the cart, sitting quiet on the shadowed pavement. He liked to have hot chocolate after work, at the same time. Regular.

'I'm doing the curlers tonight, the lot.'

Dai looked up, he saw Bethan move the child on her knee, he saw her nod and not look at her friend. 'Yeah,' she said. 'Well, don't drink any cider and black. Some poor bastard's got to clean up the stains the next day and whoever it is, they've got my sympathies, like. I could tell them from personal experience, Vanish Mousse won't work, never mind what the advert says: "Pasta? Red wine?" No, actually, vomit. Got anything for that?'

'Haven't drunk cider and black for a year and a half now.'

Bethan still didn't look up. 'Well, just don't start again.' Her hands fussed around the baby's clothes. After a moment, she said, 'You've not got college tomorrow?'

Dai got up slowly from the chair.

'We're only doing electrolysis at the moment. Hair removal,' she said. 'I mean, it's complicated, got to be done right. I don't need to go in, though. Claire said I've got it down pat already.'

Bethan nodded. 'Yes,' she said. 'But then you've had a lot of practice.'

Between them, there were empty tables, little menus like open books, salt and pepper and sugar. They changed the menus at twelve o'clock, you could come in here and always know what time it was, even if you didn't have a digital watch. Changing the menus took the morning away from the afternoon.

Dai folded his paper slowly, he put his pen in his overall pocket and his feet scuffed against the checked floor; a large man, too tall when standing.

'Have a good time anyway,' Bethan was saying. She brushed the baby's fluffy hair. Her own was long and blonde and flat. Sometimes when she sat down, she caught it under herself.

The café was quiet without their talking. They saw him there.

'Afternoon,' he said. 'Afternoon, Bethan.' She looked up, maybe smiled, and then turned to the baby again. Sometimes she did that, she used the baby not to talk to him.

'How are you, Bethan?'

'I'm fine, Dai. I'm always fine,' she said. Then she looked up at him and suddenly said, 'How are you? You all right?'

Dai felt a smile like butter. 'Very well, really well. You know, I had a cold. But that went away.' He came forwards. There were dummies, rattles, things like that lying across the table. 'Mum's still ill.'

'Reckon she's ill enough to forget about my rent then, Dai?'

'Oh no. No, I don't think she's that ill. No.' The baby on Bethan's knee jiggled as she held it. 'You look nice with it,' he said.

Bethan smiled, she looked briefly into the baby's face. 'Think she looks like me?'

'Looks like you. No. I wouldn't really say that, like, that she looks like you.' He watched Bethan tickle her.

'Got my double chin, though, haven't you,' she said.

He stood in front of them, not knowing what to say now. He wanted to tell her she looked nice with the baby again. He wanted to explain to her why. Every day, he came into the café and she was almost always here. He wanted to tell her that gradually, over the months, you could watch the baby getting bigger. Like she'd got bigger before having it. Always here and changing a little bit each day. You could see time in her and in the baby. You didn't say that sort of thing to people, though. Instead he just told her, 'It's grown.'

Bethan laughed, a little snort. She looked like she was judging a sheep.

'Feels like I'm carrying a bag of cement around these days. I swear, by the end of the year, you'll see me on telly: world's strongest man competition. Fucking tyre-dragging's nothing to this. You know what it is,' she said then, and she looked up at Dai. 'Breast-feeding,' she said. 'Two months of it at the start. I reckon the stuff's so full of calories she's still getting fat on it now.' She smiled up at Dai, stuck with the baby between the immovable table and the immovable chair, all her things spread round. She smiled. 'Breast-feeding,' she said. 'That's a funny feeling, Dai. I tell you.'

He stood still in front of her.

And then her friend laughed. He looked up with the sound of it and, after a moment, Bethan turned away, the smile gone from her face.

'Hey, Dai,' she said. Something lacking in her voice as well then. 'You want to hold her?'

'Oh no. No. I don't think I'd want to do that, no. But thank you.'

But Bethan said, 'Go ahead. You won't break her. Bounce her on the floor a few times.'

And she lifted the baby from her knee with effort, held her out across the table. Dai cleaned his hands on the legs of his overalls. The baby had its back to him.

'I . . .' he said. But she was giving it to him. Careful, he thought now. Very very careful. He reached out and took the baby from her, careful, like he'd put his mum's back against the pillows when she told him to move her.

The baby was heavy.

'It's heavy,' he said.

From the corner of his eye, he saw her draw her arms back across the table and rest them there. He thought very quickly, all in a moment, that she looked changed without the baby, suddenly like a whole different person.

It moved slightly.

'It's moving,' he said, and then he laughed. He said, 'You can't tell how much it moves till you hold it. You just can't tell.' He shook his head.

'She's a "she" not an "it",' Bethan said quietly. 'And her name's Chelsea. You know that. I've told you.'

Dai didn't answer. The baby was almost looking at him. He could feel the nappy, bulky and plastic under her clothes. He could see the pink in her cheeks, tiny little fat cheeks. Tiny little nose. She made a sound.

'Oh,' he said.

Her arms moved above his hands.

'It's like being a giant,' he quietly told them.

He wasn't sure how long he held her for. He knew how time moved so well, he always knew how much time was passing. But the baby shifted. It was tiny and alive and stopped time from being noticeable.

Dai Meredith felt the warmth of the café around him, he smelled all its memories. Outside, beyond the closed door and its little ringing bell, the sun was a thin wash across the street. But here he stood, Bethan's baby held in his hands.

He thought that he wouldn't forget this. He thought he would make sure by recalling it every day. The baby's hair looked so soft. It didn't even cry.

'Thank you,' Dai said. And Bethan gave a smile that passed over her face.

'This used to be my mother's house,' she told Charlotte. She moved a lot as she was speaking, took things from cupboards and held them in her hands, seemed always to be doing something. 'Lennie and I moved in . . . it must have been four years ago. It doesn't feel like that. Married in September . . . must've been four years. September's a lovely time to get married. I always thought that I'd marry in spring, you know?' She shrugged.

Charlotte smiled. She watched the woman move from the sink to the kettle. She had a gap between her teeth.

'Probably don't keep it as well as my mum'd like.' She put the cups down on the counter.

The room was perfect, a place for everything and everything in its place. She had pots labelled Tea, Coffee, Sugar. She had them facing slightly in towards each other, like a little group of friends. An oilcloth on the table, a small bunch of flowers in a vase, each chair tucked in neatly and every surface clean.

'It's lovely,' Charlotte said. The bottles stood on the counter by the window. 'Better put them out of that one's reach,' Ruth Lewis had joked. A line, and the light stretched through them, cast glass shadows across the floor.

And now Nia stood near to them, she kept her back against the counter and her eyes on Charlotte. She twisted both hands in the hem of her jumper. Charlotte had never seen a deaf child before. She wondered if the girl could feel the difference between conversation and quiet. And how this room seemed to her. She watched as Nia's hands moved against each other in the wool. So lonely, she thought.

She made a small smile at Nia's staring face. But the girl didn't know her, maybe felt afraid.

'Is she watching you?' Ruth said, laughing. 'She's got some stare on her, bet she wins the staring competitions at playschool.' Ruth made a glaring face and Charlotte smiled, looked down at the tabletop. 'Did you ever do that in school? Sit there staring till one of you laughs or looks away or something. I was always the loser, only have to look at me to make me laugh. I tickle from a distance.'

The woman put tea bags into the cups and Charlotte watched her, thinking that she seemed very young, thinking that she seemed to let go of every thought she had. But people liked that, of course, openness. Ruth Lewis must make a lot of people feel comfortable. In Charlotte's lap, her hands were still, intertwined.

'She's so good at playschool, never makes a fuss.' Ruth ruffled her daughter's hair. 'You're good aren't you?'

'She doesn't have an aid,' Charlotte said. 'Or an implant?' She found herself looking at Nia again. The child's silence drew the eye.

'No, well.' Ruth turned, she watched the kettle click off. 'She's only three now, bit little for us to make a decision like that, an implant. And it's only in the last year that it's really been . . . noticeable, you know. Two-year-olds can be very quiet, even hearing two-year-olds can be. And she passed her IDT at six months. Infant distraction test, that is.' With her back turned, Ruth poured the water. 'Bit of a long name for banging a drum out of sight. Lennie says the only reason they call it that is so they can give people the job of making up the name.' She put the kettle down. Charlotte saw her push a strand of hair behind one ear. 'But anyway, she passed that. A lot of children develop hearing problems in the first five years, though. Meningitis sometimes, not that Nia's had that but . . . But anyway, they do a

cochlear echo, that's what they did on Nia. They put a little micro-
phone into the ear.' She stirred the tea. 'Tiny little thing. They listen
to the sounds that the ear makes, the response. And a deaf ear gives
no echo.'

Charlotte looked at her back across the room.

Ruth turned round, a cup of tea in each hand.

'Is it too weak? Sorry, I'm a dishwater-tea kind of person.'

'It's fine. Thank you.'

'Was my mother's china, this, so no juggling, all right? No playing
frisbee with the saucers.'

Charlotte smiled again, she tried to think of something to say and
couldn't, something that would make Ruth laugh, put her at ease. She
picked up the cup and sipped.

'Anyway, I'm babbling on about myself. I do that, I talk people into
the ground . . .' Ruth moved her hands around the cup. 'The house
must've needed a lot of work, been empty for a while . . .'

'There wasn't that much.' The questions would come now. Her
cup made a tiny sound as she placed it in the saucer.

But Ruth only said, 'The garden must be . . . a ruin.' She looked at
Charlotte, waiting for an answer.

'Not a ruin.'

'No?'

'It only needs work. You see it from outside, it could still be
functional . . . I'll get it done obviously, but it'll take time. I may have
to get someone in for part of it.' She cleared her throat.

'So the brickwork's still all right.'

'You've been there,' Charlotte said. It had never even occurred to
her, that someone from the town might have. People had lived there,
people had moved in and out of course. But still the place was – it
had no sense of that. It was hidden.

'I used to go up there . . . Yes, you know, a long time ago.'

'You knew the people that lived there?'

'Well, I mean, it was empty then. Was a long time ago, donkey's
years. Why do we say that, donkey's years?' Ruth watched her own
hands, drinking. The liquid shifted.

'A lot of people know it then?' Charlotte pictured the walls, the wooden door. Not so secret.

'Well, I wouldn't think "a lot". I went there a few times with people, you know, other kids. They got bored there, though. Not so much to do, I suppose. I never understood it though. It's lovely.'

'It's a very beautiful place.'

'I used to push pennies into the walls. You know, in between the bricks, make holes. You could put your little finger in.' She laughed then, as though it was silly, though her expression looked full of the past, sad.

It stalled Charlotte. 'It's hard to get inside now.' She thought of the walls, which still looked strong in the sunlight or rain. The red bricks darkened. She'd watched them yesterday. They were ivy-trailed. 'You can open the door.'

'It's still there?'

'It's . . . yes, it's still there.' There was no handle now, only a hole in the wet wood. You had to bend to walk inside. 'There are no paths, though,' she said. 'Just overgrowth.'

'There are paths. I mean, I'm sure they're grown over. They were almost gone even back then.'

'Where? Do you know then, what it looked like when it was still in use?'

'No. I mean, not really. It was such a while ago. You could work it out, though . . . It must be very bad if you can't even see the paths. It's been neglected for a long time then.' She waited, watching, and Charlotte realized it was a question, that the woman wanted her to say something else. To say again that it only needed a little work, a little time, a person. She opened her mouth to answer. In another room, a telephone rang.

Ruth Lewis moved. She said something like, 'I'll get that,' or, 'I'll only be a minute.' But for a moment, the smile was gone from her face, the talking and the motion and the jokes. When she wasn't laughing she was somebody else.

Charlotte watched her leave the room and looked down at her tea. She wondered how old Ruth had been when she'd seen the garden. She thought of the brambles and could imagine her there, making holes with pennies.

In the other room, Ruth's voice said, 'Lennie.'

Charlotte shifted on her chair.

' – no, I'm fine. I'm fine.'

She saw the oilcloth and her thoughts grew diffuse.

' – I know. I miss you. Nia misses you.'

She felt the unfamiliar kitchen and the unfamiliar rooms around. From the corner of one eye, she saw something shift.

With her back to the counter, still watching Charlotte, Nia was edging sideways.

'I'm sorry,' Ruth said.

Charlotte didn't move. In the daylight, on the counter, the bottles stood in a line. Nia took one hand from her jumper's hem.

'Nia . . .' Charlotte said. 'Nia.' The girl's fingers reached upwards.

Charlotte almost stood. She looked back at the kitchen door, wedged open, but she could only hear Ruth's voice.

'Nia, don't,' she said. 'Your mother won't want . . .'

The girl's hand touched a milk bottle, she just stared at Charlotte's face. Skin that became almost translucent as she stepped into the sun.

Ruth said, ' – I will. No, I will. Really.' And Nia grasped the bottle's neck.

Charlotte took a step back from the table, her chair scratched against the slate floor.

' – well I love you, Lennie.'

In the room, the autumn sun was weightless, a dusting on the air. It touched the edge of the bottle, gleaming. The girl's hands only reached halfway round.

'Nia . . .' she said.

She reached out and she put her own hand round the glass, suddenly felt its cold and the girl's small grip give out. In another room, Ruth said goodbye to someone. Charlotte heard the phone replaced as Nia stepped away from her and ran out through the open door.

And then she was standing alone in this family's kitchen. Standing here with their biscuit tins and closed cupboard doors. Charlotte held the milk bottle. It was dirty inside, still whole, as she placed it gently on the counter again.

Ruth watched the woman walk away through the kitchen window. She was wrapped up in her coat again, the velvet scarf swept over one shoulder. Ruth saw her dark hair, the long white streak, running from above her temple, all tied back into a bun.

'Well, Dalmatians watch out,' she said. The kitchen was empty. Charlotte Weyland walked like she was somewhere else, like the path didn't touch her feet. A little street in London, Ruth thought. The sun was warm through the window. A little street, clean pavements and wrought-iron railings. She watched the woman pass the real houses by. There would be trees. Maples, she thought.

The Weyland woman walked with her head up; even steps.

This ice-cream pink house was small, needed repainting. Mismatched slates on the roof, from which the old stone of the chimney rose.

Ruth swept up the broken glass outside, pausing only once, when she was almost finished. She looked out at the hill that framed this side of the bay, and at the lane, branching from the main road, tree lined. She couldn't see the house, white stones.

She thought that later she'd put Nia on the sofa and they'd watch something on telly, maybe a video. They had a lot of Busby Berkeley musicals on video. Maybe one of those. Nia loved them, would gaze at them for hours. Sometimes Ruth loved them herself. The costumes were beautiful, matching. The girls moved past each other on the screen in a pattern, like a huge kaleidoscope. They danced and changed until they didn't look like girls at all but like some lovely complex design that you could get lost in. She and Nia could draw the curtains, she thought.

Dai Meredith began the walk home, rolling the cart slowly, happy with the sound of its wheels on the pavement. The day was lower now and soon the sun would push through the alleys between the houses on the seafront. The bus would be here with the people from school, coming in with the noise of engine and brakes, dropping them in bunches with their messy uniforms to talk and walk and move away and leave the street quiet again. He tried to take everything in as he strolled, the little sounds, the smells. Days like these were the good days and it was nice to hold on to them. On days like these, he wasn't confused, didn't need to think about time or the museum.

It was closed up now, the museum. Boards and polythene and peeling paint. It had been closed for a long time, sometimes it still made him sad. He didn't know what the museum looked like inside, now that the day didn't come through its windows. If the glass cases still lined the walls, settled in dust, or if the photographs still hung there.

He often needed to remember the museum. On days when he felt like everyone was watching him, or things were happening and happening, when he walked with his hands gripped very tight around the handles of the cart. There had been photographs of the town from a long time ago. The houses hadn't had porches on them then, or windows that stuck out from the roofs, there'd been no cars in the street. In the pictures, the houses seemed bare and there were people in caps with grey faces. But it was the same place, the same long road. When he felt bad it helped to remember this. Little things throughout Ynys-morlan, changing like the dunes.

He passed the bus shelter. No seats, just a little roof and a map. 'Go further!' the map said, though Dai couldn't read it. It had a lot of lines, all moving away from Ynys-morlan. It said, 'Look how far you can go!'

Dai glimpsed the curve of the hill, where he'd walk now. Just a silhouette. He made his decision as he passed the last few houses, which faced the evening with their stones and dark glass. He would give Bethan one of his hedgehogs. He thought about it as he walked up Brynheulog Lane, the road that Charlotte Weyland had taken a while before. He thought about it as he left the town behind, and was smiling as finally he came into his mum's yard. Full of dust and shadows it was, the sound of birds. It might still have been summer here.

He had thirty-two hedgehogs in all, little beanie-bag ones and puppet ones. But he thought he might give her the best. His best hedgehog was as big as a very big cat, it had long fluffiness for its spines and its face was pink felt. She would like that one most, he thought. Chelsea would like that one most. And when she kept it in the café, on the table by her side, people would ask her where it came from.

Dai opened the back door to his house, to the little windowed porch where he left his cart. He sat there on the bench, untying his laces, with a reddening sky reflected in his eyes. It darkened the shoes and coats, his mum's gardening basket. Trowels and little forks and things, her gloves laid ready over the side.

It was quiet as he walked into the house.

There was a structure to coming home and there was nothing he did that evening that did not fit. On the landing at the top of the stairs, his mother's door was closed. The slate floor was cold, walking around in his socks. He went into his bedroom and took off his overalls. He stood next to the kitchen window and he put the kettle on.

He always made tea for her. The kitchen clock made its sounds. Before his mum had started being ill, he had taken the tea into the living room. They'd sat there and talked with the night growing outside. These days, he took it to the bedroom. It was a change he didn't like. It wasn't the room, his mum had a chair by the bed, they could still talk. She'd sit up with all her pillows. It wasn't the change he minded, it wasn't even that he was worried about her being ill. It was something else.

It was laziness to lie in bed too much, it was a waste of time. He remembered all the days she'd called up to his bedroom when he had slept in late. 'The birds are up,' she'd say. And if he didn't get up then, she'd knock on his door. 'Come on now, Dai,' she'd say. 'Time's time.' When she was working, she'd work herself out. 'My feet are clay,' she'd say when she'd finished. 'They'll crack.' Now, she was almost always in bed. It was wrong. He'd look at her big face and hear her loud voice. He'd think, you don't like people lying in bed. The thought sat there like a little hitch between them, it tainted everything.

He looked at the dry tea bags in their cups. On the gas, the noise of the kettle rose.

He was so careful as he carried the tea up. He watched the liquid slip gently from side to side, ready to talk. The steps creaked very softly. Upstairs, the landing was cold. There was nothing he'd done differently that evening. There was nothing he had done wrong.

Dai said her name as he opened the door. He said it quietly, 'Mum?' Because she might be asleep. And he moved into his mother's bedroom, where there were no lamps on. Where there was only light from the little window, that touched the covers on her bed and fell, soft as autumn, over the lines of her face.

There were stains on the bedside table from other cups of tea they'd drunk.

'Mum?' he said.

He put the cups down gently. He thought that she'd have to drink the tea soon or it would get cold. She didn't like it cold. That was particular about her tea. She liked two sugars in it. He reached out and touched her hand. He liked to measure them very carefully, spilling out grains of sugar from each side of the spoon and back into the pot. Exactly the right amount. He was thinking this and her hand was very cool.

In the evening light, he touched her. Her skin moved. Nothing else about her moved, not her hair on the pillows underneath her, not her slightly open mouth, nothing. Dai bent over her in the quiet room and looked at her, not moving, not warm.

For a long time, he didn't touch any other part of her. She didn't like to be touched like that, it wasn't OK to touch her like that, prod her, push her, shake her. She would hate that. For a long time, as the tea cooled on her nightstand, he just moved his hand on hers. He waited. He said her name many times.

He didn't hear the sound of his voice change until it was too loud. Until he realized that he was almost shouting at Mum, in her own bedroom. And then he took his hand away and only stood there. His voice dropped into quietness. Her face was still. 'Come on now,' he said.

Very slowly, the daylight moved out and away from the room. It left her bed and her hand in greyness. After a while, he stopped asking her to talk to him. He sat down on the edge of her bed as the tears started. He reached out very slowly, hesitating, and he stroked her hair. Several times, his mouth opened as though he had something to say. He wanted to have something.

He thought about the word 'death' and knew it with no understanding. His hand moved like another shadow. All her expressions had been taken away from her.

He cried for a long time as the room grew colder. At some point, he heard the noise of the central-heating boiler start downstairs and it made him cry again. Below him, in the fading kitchen, the little red light was on. It sent the first gradual flow of hot water to the radiators in other rooms. There was a while when Dai tried to lie down with his mum, to get very close to her. He tried to hold as much of his body as he could against hers, while the boiler worked on downstairs. It warmed the house very slowly, though none of the lights were on.

Before he left, Dai pulled the bedspread up around her. He went down the stairs and he opened the front door. He walked out into the yard and the wind. He stood there for a little while and then he began again, through the gate and down the lane. He walked until he was standing on the path of a lit and pretty house. A large house with two parked cars in the driveway and a nameplate on the door. The house belonged to Emyr and Gwen Morgan. It was the right place to go. He knew because Gwen had told him. Talking to him in his mother's kitchen, she had taken things out of her shopping bag. She had cleared a little space on the counter and put them out in a line. Bread. She had nodded at him. 'Right down the lane,' she said. 'Any trouble at all, you come to us.' It had been raining that day, he remembered it. Upstairs, his mother had been asleep.

Dai stopped walking now and only stood there as he started to cry again.

Their house looked very warm to him, standing there on the road as around him the night congregated. It all seemed warm to him, the little diamonds in the window glass, the bright spill that came from the kitchen and settled on the ground. He shivered.

It was so pretty. He could see the kitchen table where they'd be having a nice dinner soon. They might be having roast lamb, with roast potatoes and peas and gravy. He wanted dinner. He stood looking and the guilt was very heavy, he wrapped his arms around his tummy. He wanted dinner and being in there. He couldn't see their sofa but it must be nice. It must be very comfy and perfect to lie down in, lie down with all the lights on and sleep. That was all he wanted, to just be in there and sleeping. He wanted someone to put a duvet over him, he just wanted to close his eyes, have someone touch his face. He didn't want to go home.

Behind, all about, Dai heard the trees wend and sway. He looked at the Morgans' brass doorknob. Above him, the sky had lost the day.

Behind the front door and through the carpeted hall, where people took off their shoes, the lounge was tranquil. The three-piece suite was cream coloured. Gwen had chosen it at Leeke's last year. Now, she sat at one end with her ankles crossed and a cup of tea on the table beside her. Every so often, she reached and picked it up and sipped, then settled her hands back on her knees. 'Emmerdale' was on the television and Emyr sat across the room in the armchair. He was reading a book on industrial architecture. Lamplight from the upright standard touched his square glasses when he shifted and when he cleared his throat, following the lines on the page with his finger. Their two little King Charles spaniels were stretched out and asleep.

There were two walls between this room and the night. The walls were painted cream as well, they glowed.

Gwen didn't hear any sound, there was no ring at the bell. She was moving for her tea when Lucky rolled over, sat up and looked suddenly at the door to the hall. She stopped her reaching hand. Lucky's ears were lifted, she saw Baby sit up.

You didn't need to be an experienced dog trainer to create two intelligent dogs. She spent a lot of time with them. She talked to them and, when they looked into her eyes, she saw understanding and obedience that other dogs just were not capable of. Now, they sat staring at the hallway.

She saw Lucky stand up. She said, 'Are you expecting anyone, Emyr?' He wasn't expecting anyone, she knew. It would have been one of the first things he had said, walking through the front door.

Emyr was holding his place on the page with his finger.

Gwen watched the dogs move toward the hallway together. 'Emyr . . .' she said, but she didn't look at him. She could hear them now, growling. She got up slowly, smoothed the front of her skirt and glanced towards the door. 'Emyr?'

The soft strains of this lamplight lay over the carpet and brushed reflections across her husband's framed steam train prints, hanging evenly along the wall.

She said, 'They don't growl for no reason. Lucky's sitting there.' She moved towards the hallway. 'He's sitting by the front door.'

Crouching, with his hackles raised.

'Well, for God's sake,' Gwen said suddenly. She walked into the hall.

She was a small woman with a small nose and small lines. Her hair was short, ash blonde and moussed into waves. It cost fifty pounds per fortnight, she had it done in Aberystwyth where the girl who served the tea never needed to ask what she wanted. Now, looking at the door, she moved a curl from her forehead with one finger, coral-nailed. There was someone standing outside, she felt sure of it. And what sort of person stands outside a front door and doesn't knock? In the small pane of glass at the top of the door, the world seemed very dark.

Gwen stood without moving, stiff and straight. She always carried herself this way. Sometimes in the evening, lying in a foam bath, she found that there was a pain in her back that wouldn't leave her. She took very long baths, often an hour, she rested her hands on the dry sides and listened to Emyr moving in the other rooms. She would try sitting up, lying down but there was nothing that would make the pain go away and sometimes when the bath was finished, she would stand and watch the water and the scented bubbles sink slowly into the drain. It was typical, she would think, that good posture could give you such a bad back.

Lucky's bark was suddenly loud. She heard the wind outside. What sort of a person would only stand there? It was a ridiculous thing to do. She reached out but her hand paused, hesitation, before she opened the door. Later she wouldn't remember.

She would remember the way she saw him, though: standing on her doorstep, looking down at her with the dark behind. She would remember the look on his face, the wetness she saw there, and pain. His matted hair blown every which way.

For a moment Gwen was caught without words, her mouth was open. She felt the cold touch her face and her throat.

'Dai –' she said.

She saw the motion as Lucky rushed out to his feet, barking, jumping. Dai was crying. His face was beaten by the cold. Lucky's noise sharp between them, 'Dai,' she said again. She said, 'Lucky, stop it now. Dai, what on earth . . . ?' Her hand held tightly to the door's brass handle. 'What's wrong? Why didn't you ring the bell?'

Standing on her doorstep, he didn't answer. His face seemed broken. He wasn't wearing any shoes.

'What is it?'

She saw him wipe his sleeve across his face. Scrubbed at the skin. He stared out to her, where she stood on the warm cream carpet, in the bright light of her hall.

'She's dead.' His voice was raw.

Gwen felt Baby touch her ankle, move past.

'She's dead,' he said. And then a sound came from his mouth.

Gwen faltered. 'Oh God . . .' she said. 'Oh, Dai.' She tried to clear her throat and felt her own hand, her soft palm, on her mouth. Somewhere behind her in the hallway now, Emyr was talking. She didn't hear the words. 'Come in,' she said. 'Come in now.' She held the door open for him as he stepped into her house.

'Thank you,' he said, the words sounding strange where nothing had been strange only just before.

He stood there, large and dirty between the clean walls. Around his feet, the dogs were moving and she saw his glinting tears.

'Come into the lounge now, Dai,' she said. And when she turned, she saw Emyr standing in the doorway in his shirt and ice-cream pink jumper. He looked as if he'd had notes prepared for this and perhaps had lost them. She felt anger pass through.

The television was playing in the living room, the closing credits of 'Emmerdale'. The voice that came on over the music told her that it would be shown at the slightly later time of eight o'clock next week. She looked at the cup of tea on the table. And felt uprooted, confused.

Somewhere around her, Emyr was standing. That would be his solution. She touched Dai's arm, she pressed him towards the sofa.

He sat like there was no point in standing. He stared at the carpet, hunched as though he would curl into himself. Gwen's hand moved on his arm and on his shoulder. 'Shh,' she said. She felt him hitch. 'It's all right now, Dai.' He looked so pitiful, for a moment she wanted to hold him. 'Dai,' she said. 'Tell me what happened. Come on, it's all right.'

There was silence then and the sound of Dai's breathing below his meat-red eyes. His weight sunk the sofa cushions.

'Just go and make a cup of tea for him, Emyr? Will you do that?'

'I'll phone the doctor,' he said.

'I'm dying,' the woman had told her. Gwen remembered.

A year ago, Eirian Meredith had still been hands-on at the gift shop, settled in like some queen insect behind the counter or moving between the shelves with that way she had, that fat and stately way. Only a year. And then bedridden and growing more bitter each day. Of course, Gwen would never have said that to anyone. But it was true, she had seen it: more bitter and more hateful, 'Stewing in her own juices,' Gwen's mother would have said. And if anything, Gwen had seen it coming. If you were going to take the kind of attitude that Eirian had taken – well, you could only expect the worst. Of course she had seen it coming. Only the other day, she had said to Siân

Humphries what a terribly sad thing it was. Standing in Spar with her handbag settled over her shoulder, she remembered. She had said that and she'd shaken her head. Obviously, she hadn't told Siân what it was really like, the things that Eirian Meredith had really said – the way she had said them, wetting her lips beforehand like the taste of them was something to anticipate. She'd spoken with nothing but mercy for the woman, sadness for her situation. Memories of Eirian had seemed better to her then, talking over the counter.

'Just bed to fire, it is for her now. Poor woman, it's a terrible thing.' Compassion in the face of insult, she'd shown.

So Eirian Meredith was dead, she had got what she'd wanted, and now Dai sat here on Gwen's settee. She listened to the story through long minutes when the carriage clock counted Dai's breaths, and she thought how random it was, with anger. Someone had given birth to Eirian Meredith once, had named her. That baby had grown and become an adult and given birth to Dai. And Dai had loved her. Randomly named, she thought, randomly birthed. And the love that grew, like some blind plant between them, was enough to break this man.

Across the room, Emyr gave some smile, the tea in his hand. Perhaps it was meant to be condolence. She looked at the blank television screen and felt a sense of fear, a sense of loss that settled inside.

He told her that his mother was still in bed. He told her how he had taken up tea and how she hadn't spoken. The story had walked a mile almost, to come into this gentle, evening room and make changes that you could not touch.

'I'm going to take care of it,' she told him quietly.

She stood in the hallway with Emyr before she left. The door was pulled to between them and the living room, they spoke in hushed voices. She held on to a smile when he touched her arm.

'Are you sure about this now?' he said. His face was pale, he hadn't had time to arrange it. His shadow was soft on the hall carpet.

'There's nothing to be unsure about, Emyr. It has to be done, that's all.' She shifted her scarf. She cleared her throat. Her hands were empty and she had nothing left to do.

'I'll go, Gwen. Let me go. It's cold outside.'

She glanced away. 'Poor Dai,' she said. 'To find her like that . . . Awful. She should have gone to the hospital a month ago, two months ago. I told her. What a thing to put him through, really. It was a thoughtless, thoughtless thing. Stubbornness goes before a fall, I've always said.'

Emyr nodded. The overhead light picked out silver hairs on his head. Behind him, the steam train prints were regiment-neat, and there was no neatness left in him. She remembered, a foreign thought, how he'd told her once that he would have liked to have lived in that era. 'That was a time,' he had said. 'That was a time to make a mark.' She remembered just how he had said it.

Their home seemed full of endings suddenly, where before – the lamps, the television – there had only continuance. Gwen held an image of what she would see when she came to Dai Meredith's house.

'You don't have to go.'

'Of course I have to go, Emyr. There will be things that need arranging. Do you think Dai wants some stranger walking into his home while his mother's still there in bed? Do you think that's what he wants? Someone he's never met, while the tea's still sitting there on the bedside table. Like someone walking into his life. For God's sake . . .' she said. 'Really,' she said. And then she turned away.

She opened the front door and here was the night. She stepped out of the warmth. It was three minutes' walk to Dai's house.

Emyr stood for a moment after she left, just looking out through the glass in the door. Whatever she had needed hadn't been in his face.

Nothing had changed really in this bright, blank hallway. He saw the pictures now, the small table he always seemed to kick by mistake. Half an hour ago he'd been thinking about a whisky before bed. He wondered how, when no object had been altered, it could feel suddenly as if the place was full of props. Theatre props. Dai had walked in through the front door like a stranger wandering onstage.

In the living room, the man was sitting motionless. Emyr could just hear his breath.

He imagined Gwen taking a piece of this room's now glass-edged normality and carrying it with her inside there, like Dai had brought sadness, dereliction here. Things were exchanged, he thought, were displaced.

He felt now, looking towards the lounge, like he was caught in the moment before the tide, washed here and waiting for the next wave to come. John Evans had been having dinner when he'd called.

He would have liked to have told Gwen how he felt – if she'd still been here though, would not have been able. But abruptly needed to. He wanted to just hold her hand, tell her that he felt like everything was imperceptibly changed; less definite somehow.

The yard was small, held by shifting lines of trees against a veiled sky. Gwen could hear them, branches and brown falling leaves, her own footsteps. She had come here before, in spring and summer and evening, she'd come with shopping bags full of bread and pints of milk. The house had never looked like this.

In September, in the last of the sunlight, the high slate roof cast shadows down over the walls. The ivy climbed like a stain over paint and wood and windows. It was an old house: cornices and window ledges peeling, a dirty mat next to the door. The summer had taken the last sense of people from it. Now it stood unlit.

She had watched the house, draining to dry like this, each of her three days per week. She had talked lightly about repairs. Gwen knew quite well that Eirian had the funds, the whole town knew that she had the funds. Upon refusal, she had offered to water the garden, which was now nearly dead, herself. Eirian must have looked out at it many times, standing at that shaded window in her huge white nightdress, her thin hair all a mess. She must have watched it wither from there; flowers she had planted herself.

She had been different around her son, though. She had owned another kind of laugh for him. Had always listened to him patiently, concentrated, as she had never done to any other. He was thirty-six now. Gwen had once watched him sit with no embarrassment as his mother wiped dirt from his face, tenderness in her fingers, calmness in his eyes.

He hadn't understood that her death had already begun. Maybe he hadn't seen the life go from his home.

Gwen stood in front of it now. It was very still here. It blocked the wind.

As she stepped towards the door, light hit her like a siren. Flooded her arms and face. She saw the huge terracotta pots that lined the path – bleached pale, bleached out and full. She saw the spider lines of brown plants inside them, and the sudden shadows, everywhere.

'My God.'

She covered her mouth. Her jaw was tight.

Above the doorway hung the little floodlight. The front door's boards were roughened. She thought of Dai, back home, back behind her. There were blankets in their closet upstairs.

Under her shoes, the mat was soft as she opened the door and stepped in. The outside light clicked off behind her.

She knew what was here, though now she could see nothing. Eirian had lived in this place for more than fifty years. Her possessions had gathered here, on pegs and shelves and across the floor, like a sediment soaking into the walls. When Gwen had once organized a jumble sale for her playschool, she had asked Eirian for any objects she might contribute. The woman had offered to make a cash donation.

Eirian had leaned back in her chair, and with a small smile had said, 'Do you know, forty-six years I've lived in my old house. Forty-six years of little things I've bought, all the little gifts I've had for Christmas, so many things, it is. House gets more full every year. I've never once sold one single thing, never thrown things away. I have a cupboard upstairs,' she'd said, 'where I keep all the clothes that Dai's worn. Little things I've got, from when he was only tiny. I've got his school uniform there.' She'd unfolded her arms, placed her hands down on the counter. 'I don't let things go, Gwen,' she'd said. 'All my memories are in them. I know you can understand that.'

Gwen herself had had three bags of clothes to donate, two boxes of ornaments and tableware. She liked to throw things out and replace them. Often, she liked to walk around her rooms and imagine the other ways they could be.

Now, standing blind, she wondered if Eirian's things were hollowed and had become only objects again. The low sound of the central-heating boiler came, its tiny thermostat somewhere else in the house. There might be a sale now, an emptying. In front of her, the hallway was unfelt.

She reached carefully towards the place she knew the light switch to be. She touched it. It won't work, she thought. It did.

In the hallway, there were bags that had been left against the walls, there were shoes and she saw Dai's coat, hanging from a peg. She saw the pictures, some hung, some only leaning with their faces hidden and dust across their frames. No different to when she had last been here.

Only objects now, she had thought. But she saw them and nothing had bled away: the Toby jugs with their fat red grinning faces, hanging askew on their hooks, the chairs pushed with their backs against the wall and their seats piled with papers and mail. Gwen let her hand fall away from the switch. The carpet on the staircase's risers was worn. She wondered how many times in the last few months Eirian might have climbed those stairs. There were two doors on the landing, the new light touched their boards. Both were closed. It was the nearest that led to the woman's bedroom. The last time Gwen had been here, she'd been carrying Eirian's post.

As she reached the top, her hands were empty. She told herself that she would check the woman. She would make sure that everything was decent. She would cover Eirian's face. Between the two doors on the landing stood a grandfather clock with dust across its face. She could hear it now, ticking. Gwen remembered the sound of hate in Eirian's voice, last time she had opened this door.

It moved softly, let the hallway's light stretch out across the floor, touch the edge of the bed and travel upwards, the mattress, a sheet. She saw hair.

Gwen held herself and she was ready, rising breath in her chest like the strength of a wave.

*

Eirian Meredith lay in her bed, huge and regal still. On her back as though sleeping, there was a blanket pulled up over her chest and arms and gathered at her neck. The light was yellow on her, almost delicate on the creases of her face.

Those little, mean blue eyes were closed, they wouldn't ever open again. She looked almost composed, Gwen thought; felt fleetingly useless, deceived. Like everything had just been waiting here for her to open the door.

She wished that there was someone else now, Dr Evans, Emyr, anyone. She would rest her hand gently on their arm, she would say, 'Well that's good, anyway. Thank God for small graces.'

It was only natural for her to have expected worse. But no, she lay like that. Perfect, just so. Gwen stood in the doorway and around her, above her, the house was nearly soundless.

She looked down at Eirian's face. The lines around the eyes had softened, free of squinting and laughing and staring. Looking at them before, while the woman's voice had been hitting her, Gwen had thought of what she often said to the children: the wind will change and your face will freeze like that. But the lines were nearly gone. Gwen herself felt naked.

She had wanted to find Eirian's nightclothes showing. She had wanted to come here and move through the final mess and make it proper; could have covered the woman's words as she had covered flesh. Now the blanket lay like silence. And what Eirian had said to her remained hanging in this room, without challenge.

'Why do you come here, Gwen?'

'I would have thought that was obvious,' she had replied. 'I come here to help you, Eirian.'

She had just finished tidying this bedroom, moving dirty plates and cups. She had stood there with everything finished, not looking at the woman's face.

Now, she turned away in one movement. She saw the blue shape of the window. I should leave now, she thought. There's nothing to do here.

But she didn't leave. She only stood there, staring towards the square of sky, feeling the corpse behind her. And she could see the faint lines of furniture, the chair, the desk, she could see them in the night just like she had seen them in daylight. When Eirian Meredith spoke, her words would slap at you.

'I come here to help you, Eirian.' Her own voice had been civilized.

It had started with the will. But it had been only natural for Gwen to mention it, only sensible for her to mention it, with the things that Eirian had been saying. She'd been talking about dying again, she'd been talking about God. Gwen remembered her, the way she'd sat propped up there, the way her arms had spread and her eyes had been bright with sickness. The last afternoon light had been grey on her skin.

Gwen remembered the sound of the birds in the dry yard outside.

Eirian had said, 'I've been thinking. Really thinking now. I've been working it through.' And Gwen had seen that look, that small curl around the mouth, baiting her. Oh, she was sure it had become quite a little game for Eirian, she wasn't blind. But that was all right, it must have been a very hard thing to become like this, bedridden like this, waited on. Terribly hard for a woman like Mrs Meredith. Gwen had seen her leaning on the banister, teeth gritted, final and stubborn, as she opened the grandfather clock.

'Do you think,' Eirian had said, 'if you lose your faith before the end, that you'll be punished for it? Or do you think that it might be more like putting money in a bank?'

'I hardly think that money in the bank is a good way of putting it, do you?' Gwen had picked up a plate from the nightstand, toast crumbs all over it. She'd put it down neatly on the table by the wall, dusted her hands over it.

'Well now, a good way of putting it? Save it up, is all I meant. You know that rhyme, Gwen? I'm sure they sing it in the playschool, I'm sure they do.' And then the woman had started to sing, her voice rising as her body lay bogged down in her covers. '"Jesus puts his money in the Westminster bank, Jesus Saves, Jesus Saves, Jesus Saves."' The singing changed to laughing then, and the laughing fell to a coughing fit. It had pulled at Eirian and her shoulders had shaken, quivering.

Gwen had moved across the room, patted the wide, heaving back. 'There now . . . there now.' Seen spittle come from the woman's mouth.

No memory now; Gwen stood again in a different day.

Eirian's breath rattled out and for a moment she only stayed like that, leaning forward away from Gwen's touch.

'I don't believe any more,' she said.

Gwen drew back her hand. 'Well, it seems you're determined that this is . . .' She took a breath and moved away from the bed. 'Have you organized everything then?'

'Organized everything?' The woman raised her head, her face was pale but her eyes fixed on Gwen. 'Organized what now?'

'You know very well what I mean.' Gwen saw the toast plate, and the window's dim reflection in it, crumbs that had fallen to the table. Behind her back, her hands held each other.

'Think you'll be getting a little, is that it? Maybe that's why you've been coming round here so much. A little help here, a little shopping there. That what you think, Gwen?' She gave a weak laugh.

'No, Eirian.'

'I know,' she said, looking through the window. 'You don't think that, of course.' Pale lashes, sags under her eyes. 'Of course. Not you.' And Gwen, seeing a ghost of something new there, wondered how Eirian might have looked at the age of twenty or at thirty. She kept no photographs of herself out. Perhaps there was a drawer.

'I only meant,' Gwen said, 'that you've organized someone to take over the shop, the property. I'm sure you have.'

Eirian turned to her. She was hunched in the bed and there was no smile on her face. She said, 'Dai will take over the shop. And the property. Who else would it be?'

'Yes, but someone to run it, I meant.'

'Dai will run it.'

'Obviously, though, you'll –'

'I think you've clogged your ears with that hairspray, Gwen. I told you that Dai will run it.'

Eirian was very still as she looked at her, no movement in her face or in her wisps of hair. Gwen said, 'If I remember right, up until a few years ago, Dai wanted to work in the shop. I remember talking to him about it once. He said he'd asked and he'd asked and he said that you'd refused him. You wouldn't let him stack the shelves then, you wouldn't even let him make the soft ice creams. Am I wrong in remembering that?'

Eirian watched her for a long time. Finally, unmoving, she said, 'I doubt you're ever wrong in remembering anything. I wouldn't be surprised if you wrote it down.'

Gwen looked down at the floor. 'So he'll run the shop then. Keep the books, check the stock, empty the till. Employ a girl to come in on Saturdays.'

Eirian's voice was as quiet as the failing season. 'Tell me why not, Gwen?' she said.

'You know that Dai can't do all that.'

'Why? Tell me, why can't he do that?'

'Eirian,' Gwen said smoothly, her eyes still on the floor. 'It was you yourself that said he couldn't work in the shop, couldn't even stack the shelves.'

And then the woman's voice struck at her. 'Go on! Say it then! Say the words, why don't you? Have you not said them before, Gwen? Can you not get them through your mouth? You say them: simple, dull. Come on. Retarded, backward. Say them.'

Gwen swallowed slowly, she didn't look up. She thought, this is what the woman's become. She thought of Siân, asking about Eirian's welfare. Of course, she couldn't tell Siân this.

'Quick to judge, aren't you, Gwen? Good at it. Good at deciding what can and what can't. I'm sure you've spent long enough already discussing it, over your tea and your sandwiches, deciding should and shouldn't.' Her smile was almost kind then. 'And I bet you haven't said them, either. I bet you've never once used one of those words.'

'I've never been a gossip, Eirian.'

'Gossip's a common word, Gwen. I'd never use it for you.'

There was silence between them then. Gwen let the woman's words move through her. Finally, she opened her mouth. She used her voice slowly.

'You've been building up that business a long time, Eirian. It's more than ten years. And I'll be honest with you, my father had doubts that it would work. I remember when he signed the deeds, he said it, the shop was nothing but empty and still confetti on the floor.'

'Well then,' Eirian said softly. 'Nostalgia, is it now?'

Gwen looked up at the woman's face. Behind her back, her hands were still. She remembered the marks all their shoes had left on the floorboards, she remembered cutting the cake. 'My father said that and he was wrong. I'm the first to admit it. He would have been the first. You've not stopped work in that shop for a decade, more. Surely you didn't do that just to let it fall to ruin, Eirian.'

The grey light shaded the folds in the woman's face, her eyes were very bright. 'I remember your wedding,' she said. 'I remember you standing there pouring the wine, checking everyone's faces. You know they have a joke about you, Gwen. It isn't very original and it isn't very funny, but oh, they like to tell it. You drive into a garage with Emyr, just out shopping, something like that. And you see the man who's filling the cars, standing at the pumps. You say to Emyr, ' "You'll never guess. That man used to be my boyfriend."

'Emyr smiles and he shakes his head. "Just think," he says. "If you'd kept on with him, you might have been married to a petrol pump attendant."

' "Don't be silly, Emyr," you say. "I would have been married to the Town Mayor."

'Heard that joke in three different places from three different people. Nostalgia? I don't really think so. Don't try to pretend you care about four walls and a roof just because you had your wedding reception there.'

She stood without speaking and her throat was dry. The woman in the bed was smiling.

'For your information, I have very fond memories of that building,

Eirian. I'm not deaf and I'm not dull. I know very well that you'd rather I didn't come here and I've kept coming despite it. If you want to act this way towards me then that's your choice. If you want to dislike me, then that's your choice too. It isn't for my sake, Eirian, that I'm discussing this with you. If you leave the gift shop to be run by Dai, if you leave him to look after the property . . . it isn't me you'll be hurting. It's your own son you'll be hurting.' She stopped for a moment, just the right length of time. 'How do you think Dai will feel when the gift shop runs down? When he can't keep track of what's coming and going? When it has to be boarded up? I'll tell you how he'll feel, Eirian. Like he's failed, that's how. Like he's failed you and everyone else. I know you don't want that. Why don't you take a moment to think?'

Eirian smiled, a small grim smile. She looked out at the evening's descent.

'So it's for Dai, is it, that you're so worried? For Dai's sake? What a caring person you are.'

'You don't want to think about it then. I see,' she said. 'I see.'

'Think about it? I don't want to think about it? Now that is funny, Gwen. That really is . . . quite funny. I don't believe that you've ever had a thought in your life. I don't believe that it's possible to squeeze a thought through all that righteousness that you carry around under your skin. A real thought? A proper honest thought? I don't believe it. So just how would you know what it is I want to think about and what I don't? How dare you. How dare you tell me I can't leave my own business to my son. What exactly do you think it is that gives you the right? The fact that you click in here in those tacky shoes of yours three afternoons a week?' The woman stopped. In the half-light, her face was brutal, her old mouth whistled out the words. 'Why do you come here, Gwen?'

'I would have thought that was obvious. I come here to help you, Eirian.'

'I don't need your help. I don't want your help and you know that. So if you want to think about something, why don't you think about this? Why do you come here, Gwen?'

'Eirian . . .' She could feel her own face, composed. She told herself that the more abusive Eirian became, the easier it got. She said, 'I've continued to try and help you through what I can only describe as rudeness, rudeness that I'd never have expected from a woman of your . . . But I've continued to come, for Dai's sake. And to give you help that you need.'

Eirian sat there, huge like a quarry face. A pile of disused stone. She said, 'That's not why you come here. Why don't you just be honest? Know how long I've waited to tell you your joke? Thought about it on every single occasion that I've had to talk to you. It feels good to say it, Gwen. It feels good to tell you that every time you open your mouth I have to take a good deep breath just to keep me from telling you to shut it.' She sat so still there, hair like fallen leaves. 'I'm dying. I don't care, not now. You can't imagine how that feels. So why don't you tell me? Why do you come here? Pick up my dirty plates and bring me food. You could tell me the real reason. No one will ever know. Go on, Gwen, tell me what you think of me.'

A bullfrog of a woman.

'Tell me now,' she said.

A dinosaur. Great bones and loose skin.

'What are you thinking, Gwen?'

Evil, Gwen was thinking, almost helplessly.

'I'm dying!' Eirian crowed. 'You know what that gives you? Chance for honesty. You may never get another one, never. So you tell me now! You tell me what you're thinking.'

Would she like to hear her say, 'I hate you'?

I hate you. She touched at the words.

In the dying yard, the birds were loud. The covers were sprawled across the woman's legs and the only other sound was of her breathing.

A chance, she thought. She could hear the sound of the grandfather clock in the hall. 'I hate you.' The words were clear and very simple.

And Dai's mother was staring at her. She could almost see the way she would look to Eirian: her careful make-up, her clean skirt, her hair. She felt confined. She tried to level her gaze at the woman in the bed; tried to feel the pity that she spoke with.

'I wonder how it came to be that so much hate built up in you, Eirian.'

In the new stillness of the house, Gwen wanted to reach out and set Eirian's hands; a cross on her chest. There was no one here, no one to speak to. She could hear her own shifting and felt bare, looking at the woman in the fall of yellowed light from the door.

A shame, she thought. And she wanted to say it, a terrible shame. A pity.

She was hardly going to stand here in an empty house and talk to herself. Ridiculous and naked like a lie.

She only stood for a long time, feeling the deep sleep of this room. In the hallway behind her, the grandfather clock marked the moments just for her.

'Well, that was your chance, Gwen. Did you see it? There! It's gone!' She laughed and slapped the covers and Gwen looked whitely away. 'Fat, you could have said. Fat and ugly and dying.' She shook her head with that laughter. 'Bitch, though. Think that would've been my favourite. Oh, I'd have liked to hear you say that. "You're a fat, dying bitch, Eirian Meredith."' The laughter seeped away as thin water. 'You missed your chance.'

Gwen adjusted her clothes. 'I wanted to speak to you about organizing matters that are more than important, Eirian . . . vital. Obviously now isn't the right time to have a reasonable conversation with you. I'll leave. I need to get home anyway.'

Eirian didn't answer, she didn't even blink. 'So I'll tell you instead then,' she said.

Gwen moved towards the door. She could see it, slightly open. She could imagine how quiet the hallway was and the yard outside, how far away from Eirian's voice.

'I'll take this plate downstairs but I'm afraid I have to go.'

'You come here because you've got nothing else.'

Gwen turned. She couldn't stop herself, it happened without any thought. 'Well,' she said, 'if that's what you think –'

'You've got nothing but your coat and your bag and that make-up on your face. Maybe that's why it's all you ever see, Gwen. Maybe that's why it's all anyone sees.'

'I'm sorry, Eirian –'

'I haven't finished. Don't you dare walk out on me, because I haven't finished yet. Polite person like you doesn't walk out in the middle of someone talking, do they? Only kind of person that walks out while someone's talking is the kind that doesn't want to hear. Why wouldn't you want to hear, Gwen? When all you've got for me is pity.'

They looked at each other, from the bed to the doorway.

Gwen didn't answer but she raised her head. She didn't walk away.

And then Eirian spoke quietly, she spoke slowly, sitting there, in the dirty litter of her bedsheets and pillows.

'You've got your bag and you've got your make-up and you've got that look on your face. Years, you've spent perfecting that look, though I saw it on you when you weren't more than five. Took Emyr's appointment to really bring it out, though, and I remember that day as well. I remember your smile. You thought that day was the end of it, didn't you? Thought you'd never have to hold your head up again, just like the air would do it for you. Thing is, Gwen, that look you keep on your face, that takes an awful lot of maintenance. And it wasn't the end when Emyr got that big gold necklace to hang outside his coat. No. You've got to do all kinds of things to keep hold of a look like that. You've got to teach a playschool, you've got to hold raffles and jumble sales and you've got to go round and visit old women, old women dying in their beds. That's why you come round here. Because if you didn't, you might lose that expression you try so hard to keep on your face, and you might lose all that expensive make-up you varnish it over with. And then what, Gwen? What would people see when they looked at you then? What would you talk to your husband about when you got home at the end of the day? Be an awful lot of silence at the dinner table then. You'd disappear without that look, I think. That's why you keep coming here.

'You think it makes you a good person too, don't you, Gwen? And even better with the way I talk to you, now that's just icing on the cake. Poor Gwen, taking all the strain, day after day and never once saying a word. What a martyr to keep coming back. Think it makes you a good person to look after me? Or traipse around town for that little trollop that lives in my property and the fat baby trollop she birthed? It doesn't make you a good person just to do good things. You aren't a good person. You've never been.

'When you die, Gwen, when some woman just like you finds you dead, they're going to hold a great funeral for you. Oh, they'll all be there. So many eulogies, there'll be, you won't be able to open your ears without hearing the praise. I can see it now. And they'll have just the same expressions on their faces as you'll have when you stand by my grave. "It's such a terrible shame," they'll say and every one of them will be a liar.

'They hate you, Gwen. More than I do. They hate you for your nice bag and your quality shoes, and for every good thing that you do. When you tell them how poorly I am, when you pick up that fat little Hughes child, when you ask for money for a good cause and a good cause and a good cause, they hate you. Do you see? No good thing you've ever done has made you a good person. And they hate you for doing them anyway.

'But the funny thing is, they'll never say it. That's the funny thing. They'll talk well about you every day like their own health depended on it, and when you die they'll talk even better. That's the funny thing. Because they're just like you, Gwen. So maybe everything you do is worthwhile after all. You go on pretending to be a good person and they'll go on pretending to like you. Maybe that even balances, being empty on both sides. But I'd just hope, if I were you, that nothing *real* ever happens. Nothing that'd ever catch you in your stride . . . nothing that'd catch them in their lies.

'I'll be leaving the gift shop to Dai, Gwen, I'll be leaving him every piece of property I own. And they'll fail, of course they'll fail. I'm not a stupid woman. But I'm going to tell him that before I die, and I'm going to tell him that it doesn't matter. I don't care, you see? I don't care. I'm going to tell him that he can turn that place into a shop full of hedgehogs, if that's what he wants. Into an Elvis Presley museum, I don't give a damn. At least that'll be something real for him. And I hope to God that when you all walk past it, it catches you all in your stride. I hope to God that you all sit around and try to talk about why it happened without mentioning any of those nasty words. Any of those words like simple or retarded or dull. I wish I could be there to see you try.

'And when you walk past it, Gwen, I want you to think about what I said. I want you to ask yourself why you care about that place at all. Why it made you so happy to see a nice little gift shop there, and why it'll make you so damn unhappy to see Dai's choice there instead.

'Ynys-morlan's dying, Gwen. My returns have gone down every year and next year they would have been worse. You look at the peeling paint and the cracks in the pavements and you try not to see it. It's dying, see. Just like me.

'So there won't be anybody hired to look after the gift shop. No one but Dai. It's an irresponsible thing to do, isn't it, Gwen? Unreasonable and irresponsible, that's what it is. But then, why should I be responsible? Why not do just what I want – before I'm not here to do anything any more. That's the question, isn't it, Gwen? Why not?'

Gwen had stood and listened to the woman speak that day because she would not run away. She had not shouted out to try to stop her, or even answered her. Hadn't opened her mouth for even that. And later on, maybe that day, maybe another, she had said to Siân in the Spar that, sad as it was to say, she didn't think Eirian could have too long now. She'd been handing Siân a loaf of Kingsmill to pass through the till.

Now she remembered. With Eirian's body behind, laid out so perfectly, so right, she remembered the last thing that the woman had said and felt a thin flowering in her chest. She stared at the window.

'I feel like a child, Gwen,' Eirian had said. 'Do you remember what it was like to be a child?'

Charlotte Weyland did not remember. She did not have to, she had the diaries. Thirty-one volumes and many thousands of pages. She had drawn a curtain of words across her past.

They were large books, each bound in red leather. There were diaries from Massachusetts, from school in England. Every year's volume looked the same in its leather. She sent them away one by one to be bound before the beginning of each next year. She sent them away while the pages were still blank inside, thick against each other and soft against the fingertips. Beautiful still. Anyone could write inside them. They seemed full of hope this way.

When they came back, they could only have been hers. They were delivered to her in presentation boxes, from which she took them, hardly looking. Mahogany, silk-lined, the boxes were disposed of. There was nothing beautiful about the journals' coverings. It was necessary that they match.

Bound, each spine was pressed against another, faceless. The gold leaf ran along them in one even line and every book was just the same width. They filled almost four shelves now. Volume after volume, they held each other tightly and nothing but the year told of any change throughout them.

This had been the rhythm. They had lined the shelves in Cheyne Walk, undisturbed.

Charlotte Weyland had used diaries since she was eight years old. She had not looked back at any of the words.

These were the recent events in her life: two thousand miles away, at home like Eirian Meredith, Charlotte Weyland's mother had died. Charlotte had finally booked the London to Boston flight. She had returned to Hedera and its rooms, had organized the sales. The house's contents had been individually lotted and auctioned on a day when Charlotte had left to stay in a hotel. The estate apportioned and privately sold. The house and the grounds left to it had been bitterly fought over, she was told. Hedera was split from its memories and land.

It was two months since she had returned. She had sat during the flight, unable to sleep, the sight of that empty house fixed like metal in her mind. The blank corridors, the silent rooms. Her mother's suite, bare. She had sat with her jaw clenched and her eyes closed, one hand on each rest beside her, knowing she couldn't stay in London. There had been years. She had told herself at times that freedom would come with this moment. But when it had finally arrived, she'd feared grief.

The money lay in an account from which a withdrawal had not yet been made. The sale of the leasehold on her apartment beside Cheyne Walk, which she had accepted from her father at the age of nineteen – and not reconciled herself with until far later – had bought this house, and its garden, with ease.

Maybe she had known before seeing the garden. Maybe, sitting in the passenger seat while the estate agent talked and talked, looking at the low building and its white-painted stones, the overgrown grass, maybe she had known already. The front of the house caught the morning and the windows were sombre in contrast. It felt good, it felt as though it had been empty a very long time, as though it needed someone. The door was small and it creaked when it opened, she liked the little sound it made.

There was a low hallway with a small wooden staircase, a large kitchen with an Aga and oak counters, where her heels clicked against the slab floor. There was the study. And on the western side of the house, running the length of two rooms, there was an old conservatory that looked out on the garden's walls. She'd stood there for a while, with the estate agent's noise behind her, smelling dust and geraniums in the empty room. Looking out, she had seen the brickwork.

'That's the kitchen garden there, that you can see. As I said, though, not in perfect repair . . .'

Ivy, she saw, in the wind. A path in the grass that had been roughly cut, the rest growing up at the walls. She saw the worn panels of the door where the ivy crowded in. It was stained by the rain.

'I'd like to see the garden now.'

Walking down the path, the smell of cut grass had still been there. The bricks were dusty, soft, and that ivy fluttered over their highest edge. Charlotte had stood, with her light coat catching in the wind, looking at the wooden door.

She had known, watching him work at pushing it open. There was no latch, just a pale hole in the wood. It was only a house, she thought, only a garden, there was nothing magical or special here. But she wanted them. All she needed was a house, somewhere to keep the things she owned and to wake in the morning.

He'd said, 'The people who lived here before –'

And she'd said, 'I'm not interested in the people who lived here before.'

The door had moved inwards, catching, held back by what was inside. She had put her hand on its wet dirty wood. Only a quarter open, she couldn't push it any further. She might have been able to squeeze through, she didn't try, only held the door like that and looked inside.

The garden had grown over itself. Held inside the high brick walls and sheltered, the growth was old and very great: brambles, climbing over each other, dead and living, with their soft leaves everywhere. Tall nettles that would have moved in any wind. There was no wind, they were hidden from the wind, and when she breathed in, she could smell them, bitter and summery. She saw other plants, high purple fireweed, thinning with autumn. There was grass in every empty place. The sunlight lay across the far wall and it was warm in here. It still felt like summer here, and the ground was wet.

Left alone in the weather, it had healed itself. It was beautiful and full of weeds.

On her first day in the house, she watched the three boxes being moved to the study, she told the men where to put them down. They sat in shadow in the corner of the room. Packed and taped in London and now laid here on this cold slate floor. Inside those boxes there was no light.

At Cheyne Walk, she'd been beside the river. She had sat there sometimes, some mornings, unable to sleep. The traffic had passed behind her, rumbling, while she'd watched the first sun touch the Albert Bridge in pink and gold. That road was busy, even before the start of the day, always loud. People had walked past her. She'd felt very still then in the centre of a city waking. Around her, people walking to work, behind her, driving cars. She had sat there in the midst of others' lives.

Here there was no one. Charlotte thought about old statues, bramble-covered under the old growth. She could uncover these things slowly, as though cleaning clear glass, a mirror. Perhaps on days when she wanted to write, she could walk in there instead.

She unpacked the journals herself, after the removals men had left. Underneath her hands as she cut the tape, the first line of light was drawn across leather. She moved them one by one to the shelves of her new study and, dusting their bindings clean, did not open their covers.

On her third evening in the house, remembering her first sight of Ynys-morlan, she sat with her hands carefully placed and planned what she would do; how the garden could be revealed. Around her, rain moved slowly down the conservatory's glass and she listened to music play.

It was the opening of Rachmaninov's second piano concerto and she felt it clearly inside her as she looked out at those brick walls. She felt the first chord strike, almost in her mouth and her throat. It was gone. She felt the space in between like a breath, she gave it back like an answer. She sat this way, with her chair rocking very slightly against the brick floor and the grey light withdrawing from the room.

Another chord, another. She knew them like somebody's touch. She waited for them. There were the strings. Simple, tender strings and a turning in her chest. There were hard chords; the piano's rising.

Inside the garden, the plants would be still in the rain.

Her third day; a place she hardly knew, where she had come only so the one before would be left behind.

Evening gathered in the air. Charlotte listened to the music for a long time, wordless. The notes like hands.

Eirian Meredith lay dead in the half-light, arranged. Her arms were straight and her eyes were closed. She had wound the grandfather clock before lying down.

Outside now, there was a small sound, growing. Engines working on the slight hill that led to the yard, wheels, scraping on gravel. Headlights washed over the walls of her house, weak in the dark, over terracotta flowerpots.

Soon, there would be footsteps in her hall. For this moment, though, she lay alone. The clock chimed twice. Her heavy face was composed, her expression peaceful.

One mile away, on the empty, wind-driven beach, Tom Humphries stopped walking. He saw her, a small black figure, holding her bag and her clothes against the wind. His foot came down in loose sand.

The beach was blue, and the line of the quiet sea far from him now. The woman was facing out towards it but there was no way she could see it, not in this light. She stood very straight with her head up, looked like she'd been left behind. Cold now, his collar flapped against his face. He saw, and didn't know what to do.

Behind him, the stretch was black, a shoreline stained by the lines of the groynes. He'd stumbled on stones, walking. He was tall, hunched, hands bunched in pockets, cold with almost an hour out here. He'd passed the backs of houses, the Lion, and now the buildings were crammed against each other, no windows lit. They kept from the beach the streetlight that pushed through dirty windows, touched chequered floors on their other side. It was two o'clock in the morning and everyone was in their dreams. Bethan Hughes in the flat above the launderette. In the next room, in a handmade cot, the baby Dai had held. Ruth Lewis, lying next to her husband, a space between them even in sleep. The houses remained, still in wind that hit them as a wall. Tom had given up walking in the street a long time ago.

On nights like this, he couldn't sleep. The caravan shook and he had to keep the windows closed. Nights like this, he found he had to walk all the way out here just to get tired enough to close his eyes.

When he'd first moved into the van, felt it rocking like some cat box, he'd walked in the street for the light. This time of night, no matter how well you knew it, it looked almost derelict. You couldn't even see the houses' colours. Tom had lived here all his life, knew pretty much every person. Still it would look like no one lived here. Like his mum's house: the concrete cracked, the plants black. All the bits of work that people did on their homes just cheap mends. His mum would be asleep by now.

Tom stood, caught in the wind, the sand shifting under him.

The woman was less than twenty yards away, staring straight out, as though she was looking something right in the eye. And he knew her, that way she stood, and still he couldn't place her. He didn't know how many times he'd walked out like this but he'd never seen anyone else. October too, two o'clock in the morning.

Far behind him, the cramped little caravan would be unlit, in the middle of a hundred others. They were set in rows beside their tarmac paths like a buried pharaoh's army. All empty now with the tail of the year.

He knew her. Currents of air from the sea pushed at him. He saw her shifting her arms, trying to hold her coat down against the same wind.

Emyr Dowie Morgan was an orator, a facilitator, a man of plans and meetings. He could remember Gwen's father telling him this very thing once, and he'd still been greener than seawater then. After they'd passed the application for the gift shop it had been. Of course, it hadn't been planned as a gift shop, it had been planned as a cash cow and it had worked well enough as one. Gwen's father had made a great deal when Eirian had put her name to the papers, and Emyr had not played any small part in that. Her father had shaken his hand when the approval had come. 'You talked it right through,' he'd said. 'A talent for speeches,' he'd said.

It did him no good tonight. He had heard the carriage clock chime two. Gwen had not returned. And there were no words, or plans, through which Dai might have found himself now.

*

Just a silhouette, but Tom must have seen her pretty much every day of his life, must have talked to her a million times and seen his mother with her more. They liked to sit together and agree. She was the kind of woman you only ever saw in the daytime.

There was a rhythm to Ynys-morlan. Like working in the café. Like the old boys that always stood on the corner where there'd been a garage a long time ago. Like Bethan in the café every day or Lennie Lewis in the Lion. What Tom saw trailed from that rhythm like a loose thread.

He could turn back right now and it would be like it had never happened. Maybe he'd see her tomorrow, in the daytime, passing. He wondered at her. He wondered what reasons might be on her face. He didn't think anyone had seen him out walking like this, not ever. If anyone on any night had looked down at him from a window, they'd never called out.

Emyr Morgan was thinking about responsibility as he sat with Dai, thinking that he'd always prided himself on being a good person. He wasn't a large man, forty years old and grey already, growing a paunch. Not so very long ago, he'd been good looking behind his glasses. Social functions, the Rotary club, things like that, Gwen had used to tell him to take them off. They seemed to fit with his face more now. She didn't tell him any more. He was the sort of man who always liked to give people a smile, a man who always liked to wear summer colours, even when the summer was past. He'd been married to Gwen for eighteen years now. Often, he liked to tell her that it didn't feel that long.

He was a good person. And there was only a thin line between good people and bad, he believed. He believed that the difference came up every day with the little decisions you made.

'Where is Gwen?' Dai asked again.

'It's natural for her to be this long,' Emyr told him.

In Eirian Meredith's bedroom, where she had lain for seven hours, a man slowly straightened and gave a small nod.

And distant, in dimness, Tom Humphries's face was bruised with the cold.

'Gwen . . . ?'

Through the navy dark, her head turned quick. He took another step and somewhere on his right, a wave came down against the sand.

'Tom?' she said. 'Tom –'

Her face was ruined. She only turned towards him for a moment but he saw, there were make-up stains.

'Well,' she said. She looked away from him and wiped at her skin. She was crying. Gwen Morgan. 'I certainly wasn't – certainly wasn't expecting to see anyone. Out this late . . .'

He stared at her, thinking of her busy goodbyes, her normality. The wind pushed her hair away from her face. She looked like she'd been cracked open.

'I'm sorry . . . I just . . . saw you from a distance. Didn't know if you were all right.'

She smiled at him. He saw it twist her face and her voice was thin as oil. 'Oh, I'm fine. Just fine. I'm sure you weren't expecting to see me either. Two o'clock in the morning.' She turned blind eyes back to the unseen tide. Wet, her skin had a sheen. 'Well . . . Now I don't know what to say.' She sniffed, like she could draw the tears back in, like she could just draw everything back in.

He hesitated then said, 'How's work?'

Gwen nodded, laughed, but he watched the laugh fall quick into something else. 'Yes,' or 'How's Emyr?' she said. She looked down at the sand. 'Do you know something, Tom? It's – what is it now? – ten past two.' Her voice was light and he wondered how long she might have been standing here. 'I think it must be about two years since I was out this late at night. I was just thinking that. Two years. New Year's Eve, there was, Emyr and I went to a dinner . . . Alone, though,' she said, 'out alone this late . . . I can't even remember.'

'You're not missing much, like.' And then he said 'Must've been out here fifty times, more.' He tried to smile at her. 'Rather be asleep any day.'

'Out for a walk . . .' she said, like walking was different when he did it. 'I would have thought it'd be nice. Someone your age, no responsibilities . . . No one telling you what to do.'

Her mascara made murkier smudges under her eyes. Seeing her, he thought of all the other people he knew, nodded to in the daytimes. Thought of the way that they left their homes and shut their doors behind them, having to smile then.

She said, 'Eirian Meredith passed away a few hours ago. It's been a very difficult evening.' As she said it, she nodded. 'It's an awful thing. For Dai, for everyone. It's been a long night is all. I've been . . . trying to take care of everything, arranging everything. She . . . she didn't leave anything in order, anything at all. Dai found her this evening. He found her,' she said. 'He came to our house.' She wiped at her face with her hand, looked for a moment like a girl. She nodded again. 'It's been a very difficult night.'

'I'm sorry,' he said. 'Is Dai all right . . . ?' A picture, he had; an afternoon picture of the man with his council road-cart. The image burst when he thought of the old woman's death. Like maybe Dai, so ill-equipped to handle anything, would now just cease to be.

'No,' she said. 'Dai is not all right. I should be with him. It's my responsibility. I'll place a piece in *The Star* tomorrow. You know, it's a funny thing. My name won't be on it, but I'll tell you, everyone who reads it will know it was me.'

He didn't know what to say. She was trying to swallow, she was clearing her throat, her face turned away from him.

'It's my responsibility. Emyr won't know what to say to him.' In the vague light, Gwen's hair was blown back from her face. 'She's left everything to Dai. The shop. She wanted it to fail. Wouldn't have had it any other way, and I ask you, what sort of person . . . ?' she shrugged, held her hands out as though to show him, as though she'd made her point, so fundamental that it lay all around them. He saw a bracelet tinkle down her wrist. She nodded to herself but she didn't move. 'I should go home . . .' she said. 'I'll have a cup of camomile tea.' As if it would be a new day. She kept nodding. She looked towards him for a moment.

He touched two fingers up to his face. 'Your make-up's . . . run a bit.' He would have looked away but he saw her put her hand up too, mirroring him. She looked very bare, doing that. Nothing like the person who stood outside the community centre, ringing the bell for the children to come in. Seeing her now, touching her own face in the dark, there seemed to be no sure footing.

'Run?'

'Just a bit, like. Here . . .' He showed her on his own skin. He could have told Rhys this, a midnight story, and Rhys would've pissed himself. But Gwen Morgan pressed her lips together and looked down as though gathering herself.

'Well,' she said. 'Well that's wonderful.' She turned away so he couldn't see her any more. 'I can't, I can't walk through town with make-up all over my face. Oh for God's sake.'

He ran his tongue over cold lips. He tried to tell her that it wasn't too bad.

'If it "wasn't too bad", you wouldn't have said anything.' She was still turned away.

'I can't – I'm sure you think it's very stupid –' Her hard voice rose and fell a little. 'But then you wouldn't understand. I can't walk through town like this.'

'There won't be anyone up. I should know.'

But she wasn't really even thinking of people, she couldn't explain it to him. It was a long walk and there were a lot of houses to pass, the pavement would be vacant.

'I can't go home like this. How am I supposed to talk to Emyr with make-up running all over me?' She pushed hair from her face, the collar of her blouse flapping against her neck. The frequent falling waves overran her voice. 'Do you know, the first time I put make-up on was with your mother. I remember it.'

He watched her. Couldn't picture her as a child.

'Your grandmother was out, we sat at her dressing table . . . I'm sure everyone has a story like it. We tried everything on, her mother used to wear red lipstick. We had the pan-stick and the powder. When she came home, we heard her come home, you could always hear the front door open, and we ran into Siân's bedroom, you know, so she wouldn't see. Siân wouldn't stop laughing and I was trying to shush her. We locked the door and tried to wash it off. It got everywhere,' she said.

'Can't imagine her doing that . . .' Sometimes he'd see her put on blue mascara, for the shops a few times. It made her eyes look smaller, made the bags underneath them worse. 'She doesn't use much now . . .'

'I know she doesn't,' Gwen said. And then she continued quietly, 'It grows on you. Not even because it makes you look better.' It didn't make her look any better now, she knew it. 'All you've got is that make-up,' Eirian had said. In the mornings now, it took her half an hour to apply. At night, she put cream on before going to bed, after she'd brushed her hair.

She looked away from Tom as though she could look away from herself. 'I can't just walk through town like this.'

'Where is she? I don't want her here soon, I want her here. She'd said she would be! "I'm here," that's what she said.'

'You told her that you wanted things taken care of. Now, you said that to her. She's had to go and do it. She'll be back . . .' Emyr felt like an object, awkward, all corners. On the mantelpiece the carriage clock ticked and ticked. 'She'll be home soon,' he repeated. He could hear his own voice, as full of bluster as the wind. 'Look,' he said. 'Look.' And he pointed at the clock face. 'Eight minutes past two it is now . . .' He heard Dai's sniff and how it tapered off. 'Eight minutes past two . . . I'll tell you what, we'll watch the clock, OK now? We'll just sit here and watch it and if she's not back by half past two then . . .'

Dai looked up at him in the soft light of the lounge. There was something very ugly on his face, his eyes stared out. 'If she's not back by half past two then . . .' He swallowed and he raised himself up and Emyr saw the stubble on his neck. '. . . then she isn't my friend any more.'

'She is your friend, Dai. Now, you know she is. She's doing every-thing she can to –'

But Dai only said it again. His tone was outraged but he looked like he was holding on. 'I decide who's my friend and who's not. I want her as my friend. If she isn't, it'll . . . it'll be as bad for me as for her. But if she's not back,' he looked at the clock and shook his head, 'then I can't help it.'

He saw a familiar expression on Dai's face: judgement that was out of his hands. Just as it had always been with his mother. He wondered how much the man really felt it, and how much he was trapped by it, without seeing that really it was not his.

Emyr rubbed the palms of his hands against each other slowly as though he could tease out what he tried to say. 'Gwen's got a good reason. As soon as she can come home, she will come home.' He looked up at the subtle shine across that clock's face. A pretty thing, silver. A wedding present to them both from Gwen's mother. And he thought of the gift shop, soon to be sold again. Its time sounded softly between framed photographs.

'Nineteen minutes past two,' Dai uttered eventually. The skin around his eyes was weathered earth. Only a few years younger than Emyr.

'It's all right, Dai,' he said. He wondered at the state Eirian must have been in for Gwen to take so long; what Dai must have seen. In bed, he had said, just that. Emyr heard the dogs shift in their box, one growl briefly at the other.

For a little while after Gwen had left, the man had just sat and cried with Emyr beside him. Just cried, not speaking words. Emyr had tried to say a few things but there were no right things. He had needed to wet his mouth often. He'd wanted to tell Dai to be calm but the man's shoulders had shaken, rising and falling as though, with every sound, he could drive out what he felt. Emyr wondered how many times he would have to cry like this before he was empty. Let it out, Gwen had said as Dai had told his story, but watching Dai, he couldn't see any end to this outletting. Emyr had sat with his hand on his arm, feeling him every time he moved. It was a brutal thing, a physical thing. Dai was wounded.

After a long time, it had seemed to fade to exhaustion. Emyr had listened to him, breath hitching like a child. How many times, till the childhood was gone?

Now Dai said softly, 'It'll be morning soon. Everyone'll get up and go to work. Bethan'll be in the café and everything.'

'Dai, if you don't want Gwen and I to go to work tomorrow, I'm sure we can stay.' He felt himself give some kind of a smile. 'If that's what you want.'

Dai wouldn't look at him, though. He said, 'Tomorrow, tomorrow, then the day after tomorrow. She's dead.' He couldn't explain, whether or not they worked tomorrow, a day would come when they would work, when everything would resume, and at the centre of it all, where his mum should have been, there'd be nothing. He turned to Emyr then and for a moment really seemed like a man. 'I can't,' he said. Slowly the words came. 'Last week, when Gwen came round to bring Mum all the shopping. After, she . . . she came downstairs and she said, did I have any clothes? You know like, dirty clothes, for the wash.' He stopped, he didn't know how to say it. 'So she washed them for me. I watched her put them in the machine and that. I said to her, like . . . No one told me how, that's all it was. Mum likes to do that kind of thing. The cooking . . . and the washing up and . . . You know?' he said.

Emyr frowned, breathed silence to the floor. 'They're easy things, Dai. Things like that, they won't take you five minutes to learn . . . I don't know how the washing machine works,' he said. He looked at the man.

Dai didn't take his eyes away. 'That's only a few things.'

After a stretching second Emyr answered, 'It always takes time . . . to learn things like that. It's not . . . I won't lie to you, Dai. You might find that some things are hard. But Gwen and I will be there. And people have . . . fortes. You know, they have strengths and weaknesses, they have to learn to capitalize on their strengths and . . . play down . . . accept . . . not worry too much over the things that aren't their specialities. Gwen and I, we'll be with you.'

Dai was watching him, watching.

'It'll be hard but . . . it'll be worth it. When you learn to do something for the first time and you do it well, there's a . . . a satisfaction,' he said, nodding. 'And that satisfaction is better, far better than having someone else do it for you.' He smiled at Dai. He said, 'It's a process every one of us must go through at some point.' He studied the man's face, waiting to see what would come.

Dai watched him just as clearly. In the quiet, he slowly articulated, 'She's given me the gift shop. The gift shop and the flats and everything. All of it.'

Emyr didn't answer that.

Tom Humphries looked very young. She kept thinking this as she followed him, very young, with his hard face, the way he winced into the wind. She wanted to tell him that she knew this make-up running down her face was nothing. She wanted to explain to him that it wasn't about being pretty, being beautiful. It was only that she had spent years wearing it on her face and when it ran – she had seen it on other women – it was a parody, grotesque.

She talked about Siân and about the past, vague things, their friendship.

She said, 'When your father died, and you were only a tiny thing, I stayed with her. I must have stayed with her for two months, more. I might as well have moved into the house.' But he only told her that his mum didn't talk much about that, he said he knew that she'd been there.

'It'll only take me a moment, just to clean my face,' she said. 'I'll be out of your way.'

'It's fine.' He looked at her when he said it and she thought again: young, with Siân's old eyes.

'I'm sorry,' she said.

They walked through the empty caravan site, down the small lanes. Each van was set in its row and shade-grey, their footsteps very clear. Plastic windows were opaque, the caravans' white sides indistinct. A silent maze of them, hibernating, curtains drawn, their small doorsteps all removed.

'How long have you been living here?'

'A year maybe, year and a half. It's all right,' he said. 'It's fine.' But when he had walked her through most of the site, right to the end where his touring caravan stood spaced on the grass as if ready to be towed away, he looked embarrassed; touched the door with the tips of three fingers. 'Here it is.'

He opened it, pulled at a light switch she couldn't see and held it for her to pass in.

It was full of everything. Food cartons on the counter and the sheets across the floor, there was a newspaper and beer cans, there were cigarette butts lying in saucers and in mugs, wan light that touched everything. She took two careful steps inside, she held her coat in place.

At the other side of the caravan, only eight feet away, there were clothes on hangers. They were suspended up above the mess, trousers and neat shirts. She saw two dry-cleaning bags. He gave a sort of smile.

'Never saw the point in looking scruffy,' he said. He moved around the tiny space and his head was bent. 'School, like, everyone had their shirt all pulled out and their tie fucking everywhere. Never saw the point in that. Uniform's a fortune.' He moved a beer can from the bed to the small kitchen counter. There was a sink the size of a plate with a dishtowel lying in it. 'Can't seem to do it for the housework, though.' He rubbed a hand through his short hair and he looked away from her. 'The mirror's there.' He gestured for her to sit, if she liked, on the bed.

She didn't move towards it, though. Just stood looking at it all. She thought about Siân. She took her bag from her shoulder and placed it carefully on the mess of sheets. She saw the lights flicker as Tom stood in the cupboard kitchen. Bent-backed against the wall, he took a packet of cigarettes quickly out.

The wind hit the caravan's side.

'I should be at home now. I don't know –' And then she stopped speaking.

He said, 'If you want, you don't have to, like . . . If you want, you can tell me about it.'

But he was looking down at the floor when she turned to him. Even now, out of the wind, his face looked hard. He'd had his hair cut very close round the sides, she could see the scalp through the stubble; long at the front, hanging in his eyes. Siân wore her hair short now and had done for a while.

There were magazines overturned on the floor, a bottle of something, aftershave. His shoes were lined up on the only shelf.

Moving slightly, Gwen reached past him and opened one of the tiny drawers, to pull from it a carrier bag she saw the edge of.

'You don't have to do that –' But she wasn't looking at him any more. The make-up had spread, black and transparent over her skin, tracking tears that were now gone. Her eyes were pale as she turned to him, naked: wanting to tidy up, without humour at the strangeness they both could see. As she looked away she said, 'At home, I have everything tidy, there's hardly anything to do. Have to redecorate just to stop it from seeming finished.'

She found a carrier bag and then she started moving. She started walking around and picking things up and putting them into it. Food cartons, she put in it, and beer cans, and she emptied ashtrays.

She said, 'Emyr and I had our wedding reception in that building. Everyone came. If Dai decides, just on the spur of the moment, to fill the place with stuffed toy hedgehogs, then he can do exactly that. You know . . . you know what she said to me? She looked me right in the face and she said: "Ynys-morlan's dying." Emyr's worked his whole life to get to a position where he could . . . could take care of this town. Just as simple as that . . .' She looked at Tom. Seeing him stare like that, she could almost feel the make-up drying on her. She said, 'Eirian told me that I should . . . when Dai has done whatever he intends to do with the shop, that I should go and stand outside and ask myself . . .' She shrugged. 'Ask myself why it matters to me.' She held the full carrier bag between her hands. The light shone on its red plastic. 'There,' she said. 'The place looks better already. Doesn't it?'

*

'Mum told me yesterday, how I should do whatever I want with the shops. One day, she said. When they're mine. Everyone would want to give me advice and I shouldn't listen to them. Whatever I want.' Dai looked at Emyr, determination held on his face like the last inch of thread. 'Maybe I'll . . . maybe I'll just let them sit there. Maybe the gift shop'll be empty. She shouldn't have given it to me.'

Emyr stared at the bright floor. He pushed his glasses slowly back up his nose. 'If you don't want it, Dai, you can sell it. You know that. All of them.'

'She said she wanted them to be mine . . .'

Emyr sat quiet for a moment before answering. When he did speak, he moved his hands, palms open, as though he was giving Dai things. They sat close to each other on the sofa.

'Dai . . . I can see why you'd be . . . upset about this.' He smoothed his hair carefully. 'Your mother has given you a lot of responsibility. And I can see why you're worried. There are decisions to make but . . . everyone has to make decisions. Gwen and I have to make decisions every day. Some little ones, some big ones. That's . . .' he pressed his hand to his mouth, deciding. 'That's what all adults have to do.'

Dai watched. Emyr could see the look on his face, searching for the condescension.

'Sometimes I wish that I could just be . . . young, and not have to worry about choices. But I'll tell you something, Dai, I wouldn't really be happy like that. Because the greatest happiness comes from responsibility. You're going to be able to make decisions for yourself, to choose whatever you want. And, Dai . . . making the right choices . . . is all of life.'

Emyr nodded to prove his point, he held his hands out to show him. On the other side of this double-glazing, they both could hear the wind.

Gwen moved slowly from place to place. She picked up the things he had left lying all over his floor, the things that were scattered on his bed. The oddity of it as weightless as their shared silence.

Finally she said, 'It shouldn't make any difference to me . . .' She said, 'I've got photographs of us there, Emyr and I, and the cake, the presents. It's just a building, it's just four walls and a roof, covering up a piece of ground.' She looked around Tom's home. A year, living in this place, she thought. He wouldn't glance up at her.

She took the things that he had used as ashtrays, his cups and his plates, and she put them in the little sink. It did look better. She moved over to his bed. Quiet, he stood and listened to her, staring down at the cigarette pack that he held in his hands, unmoving.

'Never wanted anything grand, do you know that? Siân and I used to talk about it, I remember us talking about it, what kind of houses we'd have. I always wanted . . . what I've got now.' She watched her own hands and very slowly the expression on her face broke apart like pieces of ice in a thaw.

Tom saw her put her arms around herself. His face raised, the expressions that had played across it could be seen. He moved towards her, stood in the small space, three feet away still. He moved his hand out and then back. He didn't know what to say.

Gwen held out her wrist to show him the gold bracelet that hung round her hand. She said, 'Do you know, Tom, I've had this . . . oh, had this since I can't remember when.' It was a gold chain, little gold objects hanging from it that sounded with each movement of her hand. 'Used to get a charm for it, every birthday and every Christmas, you know.' Her voice skated over what was on her face. She said, 'My mother used to tell me that every one you put on it meant something different.' She showed him. It was a tiny gold kettle, it shone pallid as she moved it in the low light. 'This one means home,' she said, as though it were a list. 'They're supposed to represent your hopes. This one means home.' She turned it. There was a miniature gold book. 'This has a . . . it has a pound note folded up inside. It means money. This one . . .' She turned it to show him a small heart-shaped padlock. 'Obviously, this one means love.' She showed him others, there were a lot on the chain. She turned it round and she tried to speak slowly but more and more she had to clear her throat, and when she'd come to the end of the bracelet her eyes were closed. He saw her unclasp it and throw it past him to the floor.

There was a laugh from her. Then silence.

'Well . . .' she said. 'Well that was a silly, childish thing to do, wasn't it . . .' She shook her head and she tried to look around for where it had landed, but her eyes closed again.

Beside her he could see the places where her hands had smoothed the sheets. Her thin shoulders moved.

He tried again to draw closer to her. 'Don't –' he said. 'Look –'

She didn't look, though. She covered her mouth. When he stepped near, to touch her arm, she was smaller than him. 'Gwen –' he said. And then, when she turned her face up, when she dropped her hand, he kissed her.

She sat motionless. Her mouth was almost closed and her skin was damp. He kissed her. With the walls very close on either side of them. In the wind, this caravan moved, the two bags that held his rubbish lying beside her feet.

'They've taken her away now. From the house,' Dai said.

'I think . . . yes, they've probably taken her away now.'

Dai nodded and when the clock on the mantelpiece chimed only a few moments later, he didn't look at Emyr, but he said, 'Thank you.' He wiped his nose. He stared out at time's face. On either side, the photographs gave muted gleams.

'Half past two,' he read.

There were things that Emyr could have said to him but he didn't answer.

Gwen broke away from Tom, took two steps away, stumbling steps. She turned her face from him and pressed steadying hands to her hair. Her movements ran out as he watched her.

'I have to . . . Well, I have to go now, Tom.'

'I'm sorry,' he said. Like he could blink away what he'd done. He tried to reach for her arm again. 'I'm sorry, like. I –'

'No. No, it's fine.' He watched Gwen Morgan come back like this, watched her expression reform and though her hands were moving and she looked around her, he could see it cover her completely, a dust sheet. 'You were very sweet,' she said. 'Offering me a mirror and everything, coming to see if I was all right. Very sweet,' she said. Her eyes didn't once light on his face.

'I'm sorry.'

'Don't apologize. You've nothing to apologize for.'

He took a breath. 'Fuck –'

'*Please.*' She had her hands and mind organized for leaving. She had the collar of her coat pulled around her throat.

'I'm sorry,' he said.

She only looked down, at the space between her and the door. She said, 'I have to go home now. Emyr will be waiting for me, there are things I have to do. I'm sure that I'll see Siân tomorrow and . . .' She talked like this.

'Sure,' he said. And then he moved out of her way, back into the tiny kitchen where the dirty cups that she had emptied lay piled up in the sink. He heard her take a step towards the door, picking up his cigarettes and taking one out.

He felt the cold when she opened it and the kitchen window shook in its frame. He stood there, not hearing her, not seeing her, cigarette in his mouth. He waited to feel the wind die away, so he could strike a match.

He didn't strike it. He stood in the silence of the empty caravan, bleary light on the sheets, the pillows, the clothes hanging at the end. He was staring downwards. He was looking at the small gold bracelet that was lying on the caravan's floor. Thinking about how cold it was outside, about the night street that he knew. He couldn't hear her footsteps.

After a while, he went across to the bracelet and he picked it up. It was heavy and its weight moved between his fingers. He turned around, he opened a cupboard above the sink. He put the bracelet down next to a tin of spaghetti hoops and then he gently shut it away.

*

Some distance from him, from everyone, in Eirian Meredith's silent house the central-heating thermostat turned itself off.

It was Emyr who convinced Ruth Lewis to go back to the garden. He found himself doing so, his hand on her arm, the day after Dai had come to their door.

He went in to tell her about Eirian's passing. There was no need, really he didn't have time, but it was raining that morning. Walking beside the road, he saw Lennie's cab parked there. Huge and ugly, it looked like a giant toy, broken without the trailer. Water trickled on the metal, every surface.

He thought about all the things he needed to do. Everything was grey: the low sky behind, reflections on the wet garden path. He looked through the kitchen window and saw the light that was on.

It wasn't a large house: two windows set into the rose pebble-dash of the ground floor, three above. Ruth had lived here all her life. Every morning her mother had swept the front step, the path and the pavement here. The rose bushes which still lined it had been hers. And although the door was painted now, much was the same.

Behind that door, the hall was clean. There was a small table by the kitchen doorway with a vase of dried flowers, the telephone. All carpeted now, only the kitchen still showed its slate floor. Ruth kept all the doors wedged open. Anyone who came inside could look up and see into every room. In Nia's, toys had been piled in the box in the corner. The pens and pencils on her little desk had been put in their holder. Eeyore the donkey lay there. Grey light touched the flowers on the wallpaper and the bare mattress on Nia's bed.

Ruth was a small woman, pretty now. She smiled a lot, a sudden smile which looked no different than it had done when she'd been young, when the gap in her teeth had been big enough to fit a ten-pence piece in. She was five years younger than him. They were cousins. He remembered her, all smartened up in her school uniform, neatly brushed hair, and she'd smile at something and just break the neatness open. He thought, seeing her perfect, clipped garden, the spotless hallway when she opened the door, that the house looked effortlessly tidy, and that the work only showed in her face.

He said his hellos and how-are-yous. In the quiet they could both hear the rain patter on his anorak.

'Well, come on then,' she said. 'Come in.'

'You're not busy?'

'Busy?' She laughed. 'Doing the laundry.'

'You know something.' He gave her a smile he only kept for women. 'I don't even know how to use a washing machine.' Dai Meredith sat on the settee in the Morgans' home and Emyr failed to leave thoughts of last night behind.

'Well,' Ruth put her hands on her hips and led him into the kitchen. It was brighter here, with the weather outside. 'It's a very complicated thing, Emyr. Which is why men take so long to pick it up.' She picked up a bottle of Comfort and said, 'I've added the powder, so now the softener goes in. Lenor is better at softening but then Comfort transports you to a magical world of freshness, so.' She watched the wall and said, 'Should see the Alps about now.'

He smiled, sat down at the table, he took his anorak off. Removing his glasses, he saw raindrops on the lenses. They were quiet for a moment and then, not really looking at her, he began to tell her about Eirian. He shook his head slowly over Dai. She watched him smile as he finished, looking up at her, as though saying there was nothing they could do. But all the time, he moved his glasses in his hands and when he glanced back out of the window after they had stopped speaking, he didn't really look like he wanted to leave.

She said, 'You know what you need, I can see. I can read you like an open book with big print. You need hot chocolate.'

'Well, I won't say no to that. Never look a gift hot chocolate in the mouth.' He shifted the glasses round. Seeing him like that, she almost spoke again, almost asked him.

Moving over to the kettle, she said a lot of little things, talked for a while about Lennie, chatter over silence like the rain against the windowpane in Nia's room. In the washing machine, wet sheets tumbled over.

She was thinking about Eeyore the donkey, lying on the little desk. This morning, Nia had wanted to take it to playschool again.

She'd held on to it very tightly, standing in the hall by the front door.

'He's tired,' Ruth had said. 'Look.' She'd put its head on one side, closed her own eyes. 'I'm going to put him to bed.' Nia's fingers had gripped it. They had both held it, between them. Ruth had seen her face tighten up, like she was drawing in everything she needed, to cry, to kick. She'd had to let go of it, to hold her daughter instead.

Ruth's fingers stirred as she talked. She turned around and she put it down in front of him. She said with a smile, 'Take that look off your face now. God helps those who help themselves to hot chocolate.'

'I'm fine,' he said. 'I'm fine.'

'Good,' and she kept smiling. Through the glass behind him, the sky was coal.

'Gwen says Nia's coming on well. She said that only last week.'

'Had a fight with a boy in class on Friday, though. And gave him hell. Got him a good one in the mouth from what I hear. Wham. Bam.' She laughed. 'I bet that boy's never been so embarrassed in his life, beaten ragged by a girl. I bet –' she said. And then she started over, 'Anyway, he's not going to be picking on a Lewis again.' It had been on that afternoon that Gwen had told her Nia couldn't take the toy into class any more.

'I don't think it's a good idea.' Careful voice.

And Ruth had told her: 'It was hardly Nia's fault. Wasn't her fault at all if he took it off her. It's his fault,' and, saying this, she'd felt as young as the boy. 'I don't think it's fair to punish her.' Nia had been outside the community centre then, playing. Ruth didn't know what sort of games she might play.

Gwen held the playschool in the community centre's largest room. From outside, you could see shapes of crêpe paper stuck in the windows. Inside, when it was sunny, they cast colours across the floor. Gwen had examined them for long moments.

'I'm not punishing her, Ruth,' and had held her hands out, palms open.

Seeing her face, Ruth had wanted suddenly to say, 'Well maybe you're right, and it's time. Maybe she can't take her toys in for ever.'

She'd wanted to say it as though they were on the same side and she could put her hands on the desk as well and they could just talk this out between them.

She'd kept her hands in her lap. 'I don't think it's fair to Nia.'

'None of the other children are allowed to bring their toys in.' Speaking oh so gently, 'They've been taught that they come here to learn, not to play. They see Nia with it . . .' She'd looked at Ruth.

The boy had taken Eeyore from Nia's table when Nia had been looking the other way. Then, when she was looking again, he'd beaten its head against the side of the desk.

This morning, she'd driven Nia to the playschool through the rain. She'd sat in the back, stock still, hands on her lunch box. She hadn't moved much at all after Ruth had taken Eeyore away. Holding her in the hallway, Ruth had felt her go heavy; she had carried her out to the car.

Now she watched Emyr drinking. They talked for a while longer about Dai, about Eirian. He told her when he thought the service would be.

Last night, Gwen had come home at a quarter past three and he'd been in bed when he'd heard her footsteps in the hall. She had gone to the bathroom first, she'd spent a long time in there, but when she'd come into the bedroom, she'd only said that she was fine. She had undressed, invisible. He'd asked her if she was all right, but whatever it was that she had felt in the house with Eirian, she hadn't wanted to tell him. She had lain down next to him and, for all the things he'd said, he might as well not have spoken. He remembered her profile, dun-coloured in the dark. He hadn't known what she was feeling. He'd thought of her alone in that house and he'd tried to touch her arm. Really, he'd only wanted her to turn to him.

He said to Ruth, 'Gwen'll take care of Dai and everything else. She must just do a million and one things when she's not with me. And I haven't been around a lot. Getting things done. Not exactly sure what half those things are but they seem to take a long time anyway.' He laughed and then lifted his cup and drank the rest.

Ruth looked at him, remembering. Picking the dishtowel up from the counter, she hung it on its hook and said, 'D'you remember, ages ago this was, we used to go out to the house up the top. You know, past yours and Gwen's? Walled garden out at the back.' She wiped her hands on her trousers. 'I met the lady that's bought it yesterday. Came in for a cup of tea. Said she's been there a couple of days.'

'You met her then, did you?'

Ruth turned. 'She came in. She was nice.' She nodded, thinking of the woman, the way she'd reached up every now and then to adjust the scarf on her shoulder. 'Why?'

Emyr had been the one to take her there first. Lumbered with her, probably, trailing after him and his friends. She remembered them all sitting in a line against the wall, drinking Dandelion and Burdock out of the glass bottles it had come in then. Emyr with a stick in his hand, prodding the grass. Mostly she'd just played alone. And then after, when they had stopped going, she'd continued to.

He gazed levelly at her now. 'Do you know how much money she's got?'

'Yes because that's the first thing I'm going to ask, isn't it. My name's Ruth and how much money have you got? Emyr . . .'

He shrugged, smiling, held his hands out. 'I'm not a gossip, only heard. Can't help hearing things, that's what happens when you've got ears.' He folded his arms on the table but he was still smiling. He looked better, she thought. 'I know someone at the agent's that handled the place. You know Glyn? They check the bank records . . .'

He didn't say it and she didn't ask. After a moment, they both laughed. She looked very young when she did. He said, 'Four and a half million.'

'God.' Ruth put her hand up to her mouth for a moment, and then she dropped it and said, 'I thought her scarf looked nice.' She laughed and then she looked at him, sitting there with his glasses off, his arms resting on the table. She said, 'I was going to ask her if maybe Nia and I could go round. I'd like Nia to see it. *I'd* like to see it again, before it's done up.'

He shrugged. 'Call her. Number's probably the same as when the Douglases had it. It'll be in the book.'

'She told me yesterday, she might be getting someone in. You know, she said it had grown up a lot. Some help.'

'Then you should definitely call her.'

She laughed and when the laugh had faded said, 'I'd be too nervous to get a word out whole. You know what I'm like, go from normal to nervous in under two seconds, and back again just as quick.'

He didn't say anything.

'I probably hold the Guinness world record, nervous and fine and nervous again. Like a sheep: "Oh my God! It's a great big wolf thing! Oh, look at that, some grass . . ." I'm not going to ask her for work, Emyr. She wasn't even sure she was going to get anyone in. I wouldn't. If it was mine. I'd keep it all to myself and if cute little children came in to play, I'd shout at them and wave sticks.'

Behind her, the washing machine kicked into spin.

He said, 'Why not?' He gestured a hand to the garden outside, which was growing bare now, but in summer brought comments from tourists, when the lobelia spilled and the pansies fluttered. Emyr had seen them point to it. 'Why not?'

He'd always liked to start his speeches with questions. Gwen had told him once that his best speeches included little apart from questions. 'It forces interaction with your audience.' He remembered her saying it. He thought of the way she'd said his name last night, lying in the bed beside him, a foot away.

'Why not?' she echoed. 'A hundred thousand million different reasons, so you won't be wanting to go into them, will you?'

She made as if to get up but looking at her like that, he found himself saying, 'Can't do any harm to call her. Think about it at least.' Outside the rain hit. 'Promise?' he said.

She had been thinking about it constantly though. The night before, looking at the ceiling, the streetlight had pushed between the curtains and she'd remembered sun on dry brick walls. On nettles, on paths which almost showed through the grass.

Now she smiled. 'Brownie's honour,' she said, 'though I was a terrible Brownie. Used to steal the badges. Only Brownie ever to go through a full court martial.'

He laughed, they both did, but she sat with her arms drawn across her stomach while behind her quiet resumed in the room.

She let Emyr out into the rain, pulling up his anorak hood. A car drove past on the wet road behind him.

'So,' he said. 'Are you going to say goodbye to me in sign language then?'

'No I am not going to say goodbye to you in sign language.'

'Oh go on.'

So she held up her hand and she waved.

The door closed after him, and left her in that quiet. Upstairs, the edge of Nia's desk and the Barbie poster on the wall could be seen. She had stripped the bed up there already, wiped the chest of drawers, done the ironing and put the board away. She couldn't see the wardrobe through her own bedroom door. It was pine and had a loose handle on one side. Pairs of shoes stood guard in there, a carrier bag behind them: four thick books on sign language, with a slim layer of dust, a receipt still tucked under one cover.

Outside, halfway between the front door and her garden gate, Emyr was standing still in the rain. He was looking down, underneath the rose bushes that Ruth had weeded clean. Raindrops hit his anorak. In the soil beside the edge of the path lay a piece of broken glass.

She stood with the receiver cradled to her ear, her other hand touching the dried flowers.

'I'm fine, thanks for asking. Oh yes, she's fine, she's well. And how's the garden looking? Well, I mean, it's raining today, so . . . Probably be in mud right up to your elbows.' She laughed. 'You're probably wondering, I'm calling you . . . I was just remembering, you were saying yesterday that you were thinking that you might, you know . . .' And she laughed again. '. . . That you might hire someone . . . no,' she said. Her hand fell away from the edges of the flowers. 'With the rain and everything, of course. I was just going to say, if you did decide . . . I'd like to see it again. I was thinking how much it must've grown since I was there, and you said the paths were covered. I could show you, at least, where they are under it all.'

It had been raining on the last day Ruth had seen the garden. She'd come home with mud on her legs and on her cheeks, with her dress torn, and her mother had held her by the shoulders and shaken her, said things into her face. When her mother hadn't really been like that at all, had never shaken her. She'd liked to brush Ruth's hair in front of the mirror.

Now Ruth stared at the front door's frosted glass. Somewhere, only up the hill and round the lane, Charlotte Weyland would be standing, maybe gazing out through one of the windows that Ruth had only ever seen blank.

'Perhaps I could just come round for one day, I could bring Nia. And then, you don't want to hire anyone . . . wouldn't matter.' She said, 'I'd just like to see it again.'

It had been raining and the young Ruth had stood in front of the house, trying to see which room her mother was in. But her mother never put lights on in the daytime. If it was thundering, she wouldn't put the lights on. There could be a total eclipse and her mother would just walk around with her hands held out in front. Ruth remembered very clearly that the welcome mat had been taken in from the rain, and the tiles underneath the living room's bay window had been stained by the drops running down.

She had tried to creep inside, looked down the hall. There'd been these paintings of flowers above her, their Latin names in flowery letters, pulsatilla, delphinium, under glass.

As they were today. For a few moments now, Ruth only stood listening. She lifted her hand to touch her hair but it stopped, midway. She almost smiled. She said, 'Really?'

Charlotte opened her mouth and she told Ruth that she could come. She heard herself, 'As I said before, I'm not sure I want to hire anyone. We'll try it for one day, shall we?' And after a while, when they had arranged a time and said the other things they had to say, Charlotte put the telephone receiver back in its cradle and thought of impoliteness, of imposition, though it was really fear she felt. The sound of her low heels on the slate floor fell with regularity – a clock's moments – walking back into the conservatory.

That long ago, similar day, Ruth had tried to tiptoe here, but open doorways let through every sound. And her mother had heard things even through closed doors, she had heard things under people's breath. From the living room she'd come. Smiling as she'd emerged. Ruth had felt the mud on her like shame.

'I fell over.' She'd held her arms out like a doll. 'Bang.'

The hallway grey as clouded water. Her mother's skin grey too.

Ruth had said, 'I'm going to fix the dress now. I was going up to fix it now.'

'My God. My God, look at you. Where?'

'In the garden.'

'Outside?'

'In the garden . . . up the hill. It was the brambles, I caught my foot.' She'd shown her mother her shoe. 'Went over my foot, like that, in a loop, and I went to put my hands out . . . in the garden,' she'd said. She had watched her face fall, like something had just been taken from her.

'You walked home like that.'

'I –'

'Where's your coat? You didn't put your coat on even? Where is it? Did you wear it home?'

'It was sunny this morning, it looked nice.'

Her mother had moved towards her in the hall, touched the hem of her dress, held it in her hand.

'So you just walked home like that. With mud up to your knees and your elbows like you've been crawling in it and a great big rip in your dress, some gypsy. Right down the street.'

'I had to come home.'

'I know you had to come home, don't talk to me in that voice as though I'm some bully. I know you had to. But you didn't have to fall over in the middle of some mudslick and paint yourself all over with it. You didn't have to go there in the first place. Look at you! Have you seen it? Have you looked in the mirror?' And she'd picked up Ruth's hand and walked her to it. A chest of drawers in the hallway then, an oval mirror. She held Ruth by the tops of her arms.

There'd been dirt at her throat, drying, and her hair had been flat against her head. Her dress was yellow cotton, a very pale, pretty yellow. Like bruises, its stains.

'Well?' And the fingers around her had jerked a little. 'You tell me what you think you look like, because I'd love to know your opinion.'

Standing behind, her mother had looked into her eyes through the reflection. She'd had short curly hair, her mother, not tight curls but soft brown fluffy curls. Ruth's hair had come from her dad, it was straight. In the mirror, there'd been rainwater on it. Her mother's face had been angry, open, desperate.

'You tell me,' she'd said.

Ruth had seen her own mouth move and all her expressions had looked like lies. 'I look like I fell over. Bang.'

She'd turned Ruth around, stared into her face, her eyes had asked questions. 'But you know what people would think seeing *you* like this? Poor Ruth, they'll think. Poor Ruth!' And then she'd shaken her. She'd moved her hands and stared down and Ruth had seen that she didn't want to do it, seen it in her face. 'Poor little Ruth and they'll nod and they'll tut. "No surprise," that's what they'll say.' And, shaking her, she'd knocked against the table behind her. The vase of dried flowers that her mother had always kept there had rocked and settled again. Her voice had parodied others in a way that others never spoke. '"What can you expect after what she's been through? Walking down the road, she was, mud all over her like something dragged back from the tip. Still living in that house."' In the hushed and ashen hallway, she'd been very loud. 'I've got two jobs, Ruth. Got a day job, I've got a job in the evening. One afternoon a week I've got to myself. And you've seen me. How do I spend my one afternoon a week?'

'Cleaning,' she'd said.

'Why do you think I do that?' And she'd kept looking, kept on, and Ruth had kept thinking about the dirt that was on her, wanting to wipe it off, set her hair and set her shoulders. Her mother's hands had held her. 'Why do you think? Because I won't live like there's something wrong with us. Do you understand?' She'd taken her hands away from Ruth, she'd said, 'When I ask people round here, for tea, for dinner, they see us and they see our house . . . and it's nice. I won't live like there's anything wrong here. And they sit down and they say, "Oh, such and such is lovely." And every time they say something like that, it gives me just a little bit back, just a little bit of pride. Do you understand?'

Ruth had nodded.

'And I'll tell you what, they give grudgingly. They look, I've seen them, through the doorways, all upstairs. They search. My friends, and they search. My sister. Something that'll tell them how awful it is for us. Is it awful? Is it awful for you?'

'No, it's not awful.'

And then she'd said softly, 'Well, they can look. All the doors are open. They can see.'

But that had not been true, though Ruth wouldn't have opened her mouth to say so. Not all the doors were open. Ten feet from them, at the end of the hallway, in the shadow cast by the stairs, there was the door which was not. And Ruth had thought then that really they lived around a hole.

Her mother had looked at her. She'd said quietly, 'Then they see you walk down the street like that.' Her hands had fallen to her sides like pieces of wood.

'I'm sorry. I'm sorry, I didn't –'

'Did I bring you up blind? Every day for ten years, two jobs. Do you think I do it so I can go out on spending sprees? Nice clothes, restaurants, is that what you think? I've bought us back our home. Every week, a picture . . . a little ornament, something. I buy a little back.'

'I know,' she'd said. 'I know you do.'

She didn't remember but the story was very old. She'd only been two, or younger even. Her mother had scoured the house. She'd taken many things. She'd taken them down from walls and out of cupboards, from the shelves and the mantelpiece. She had put them in one room and then closed the door. At the end of the corridor, you never needed to pass by. Since then, she had graced the house with new things.

'Beautiful, ugly, it doesn't make any difference. I don't do this for myself. I'm trying to explain it to you.' She'd looked down but had been unable to find the words. When she'd slowly led Ruth down the corridor, she'd taken her by the wrist, into the room where she only went once a week, to dust, to pick things up and put them down again.

Standing in her own hallway, Ruth remembered the walled garden. Moving through its tiny door. The things her mother had said had not all been true. She hadn't kept this house perfectly only for the people who came and looked. It had been for herself. For, when she'd walked downstairs in the morning and thought about the day before her, there had been a calm. Ruth knew it now.

Lennie Lewis spent his life driving, or trying to shed the miles. Shut his eyes and rid his head of them. Sometimes after a run, just sitting in the cab outside his front door and waiting for the feel of the engine to leave his hands, he'd see broken white lines. In silence, in stillness, would want to change gear for every turn. Like his body was the machine, sometimes his fingers would shake.

Every run's last moments: finally driving in past his old man's flagpole at the edge of town, past the sign that read Ynys-morlan. Ruth and Nia closer by the metre. They'd stand in the hallway when they heard the cab, big eyes and Ruth with enough questions for them both, 'How was your day?' Like he was meant to give them a commentary on how the Midlands looked through his windscreen. He'd watch the house getting closer, the flag, raised there almost forty years ago, shaking in the wind. It flew over a small grass space, its pole set in concrete. There was no plaque on the base, no date, though they'd had a plaque commissioned for it. His father had described it to him when Lennie had only been young. It had been brass, his father had said. Good engraving. 'They could've had kittens when I walked in and told them they couldn't set it.'

Lennie's father had taken them all to see it in a morning, had stood with them while they looked on. Not just a great hole in the ground as it had been the previous evening but a full concrete plinth with the pole's base set. 'Mouths dropped open like they had no hinges.'

The concrete was blank. Four feet wide and four feet long and, around it, the grass was high. In the summer, in bright sunshine, you could see through to the sand-gritted earth. Around the base, there was often litter now. Days came when Lennie took a bag and ridded the place of it.

Ynys-morlan's street – through the windscreen as he parked. In the quiet left by the engine, everything seeming to vibrate. The roofs of parked cars through the clear swipes the wipers had left. After a moment – winding the window down. Gulls outside in the voiceless road, where exhaust fumes dried the air.

It was a beautiful town this, a beautiful setting, right next to the sea. Mountains on the other side. His town like it had been his old man's. Lloyd had walked down the street and it had taken forty-five minutes to get from one end to the other, all the people that stopped to talk. And nothing had changed. He knew every person that lived here by name. Far down the street now, the old boys, Garwyn and Edward Evans, standing in overcoats, talking. Rows of houses under the cloudy sky. Slate roofs, slate roofs. If you saw them in sunshine from a distance, the light would catch on them. The houses' faces would shine, made white, made wet it almost seemed. Porches, extensions, bay windows, the pebbledash in yellow, blue and pink. The weathervane on the roof of the Davises', unmoving.

His father had built half the extensions in this town, most of these dormer windows. Glass stacked up ready against the walls of houses, his old man working with his shirt off. Lennie remembered the sound of that work, always going on in one part of town or another.

And this was now the walk, as if he hadn't just driven a twelve-hour stretch, across and back again, three hundred and fifty miles of pure shithole.

The whitewash on the windows of Owain's. The sign above the door, still 'Owain's Family Butcher' but the glass dirty with its smears and streaks and circles. Close up, his face to the pane, trying to see through his own grey reflection. Unlit inside. Patches of shadow on the floor, the meat counter now empty. With his fingers cupped around his face, Lennie saw the fake green grass still lying there, in old refrigerators that were unplugged.

It felt like he brought a little bit of those shitholes back with him every time he came home. Each time, this place seemed smaller. Everything outside crushing it down into something frail.

Birmingham, Dudley, Solihull. Places where people didn't need rubbish bins because the ground did them just as well, places where kids had to write their names on the walls just to remind themselves that they still owned a little bit of where they lived. Just driving, he wanted to lock the doors. He wanted to put his foot right down on the pedal and drive into whatever pile of bricks happened to be in front of him. People couldn't live in places like that, he didn't see how people could live, huge and sprawling, one just running into another, there was no end to them at all.

Lennie Lewis was a big man, handsome as bare ground, no smaller now that some of him was running to fat. When he walked down the street, he walked with his hands in his pockets and his head up, looking out. He'd never had anything to hide. What he was, people saw in his face and he'd never been scared to show it there: quick-tempered but as quick to laugh, and to make others do so.

It was eleven forty-five in the morning. Somewhere behind him, in the small pink-painted house, Ruth was looking down at Nia's freshly remade bed. Past her, past the Spar where Siân Humphries stood next to the till and looked out through the glass, the flag was shaken against its pole.

Lennie walked beside houses and shopfronts and windows, paint peeling. Something in the atmosphere maybe. It wasn't lack of care. Lack of money perhaps but not of care. Something in the atmosphere, like too few ten-pound notes floating down. As though it was sunny, he kept his head high.

He saw Garwyn with a Woodbine hanging out of his mouth, Edward Evans with his stick.

'All right you two?'

'Can't complain at all,' Evans answered. He leaned on the stick like it was the only thing between him and lying down. 'Had to go down the doctor's about the knee, like. Man would not shut his face. I'm damn good.'

Garwyn wracked in another breath. 'Can't complain.'

'Good, good.'

'And Ruth and your girl now?'

'Not so bad.' Across the road behind him, Owain's whitewashed windows, a puddle of rainwater before the door, spoke of days when they'd all been better. 'Seen that then?'

Ted snorted, 'Fishing shop before. Tobacconist's before that. Pipes racked up at the back there. And it was a grocer's by here.' Standing on the pavement, he shrugged. 'Goes round,' he said.

Lennie looked up at the clouds, felt a slight rain on his face for a moment. He nodded them goodbye but, standing here, where the garage had come and gone, they looked more permanent than the street, and when he settled himself again, the loss he felt was buried. He'd take Ruth out for dinner at the Lion here, take her tonight, and Nia. Would surprise them with it.

He was twenty feet from the door when he saw Rhys at the bus stop. Next to the map of the coastline, under glass, with all its lines moving away from Ynys-morlan. Lennie pulled one hand from his pocket, squinting through a peppered wind.

'Rhys! All right?'

Across the road, the boy looked up.

He was leaning back against the shelter's wall, moving one foot slowly against the ground. He had hair almost shaved to the scalp. Close up, you could make out a slight scar in one eyebrow, pockmarks on his skin.

'Oi!' Lennie said, and that smile was on his face again. 'Get over here!'

A car drove past between them.

Eighteen he was probably, and Lennie must have known him for pretty much all those eighteen years. His father was a good man, though a busy one these days.

'What's a pretty girl like you doing in a place like this?' The smile on the boy's face could have been Lennie's own. People had used to ask him with a grin if he'd never shared an hour or two with Rhys's mother.

'Waiting for my white knight, like,' the boy said.

They turned away from the bus shelter and the rain together. He pushed Rhys in front of him till they were inside, and let his hand fall from the boy's shoulder. The plaster lion above the door, big and rough-cast, stared out over the street for them while they were gone.

Some way behind, Ruth was picking up the telephone.

Lennie shouted for Bill but it was high heels he heard. The pool table had been covered. Every so often, the slot machine in the corner made little Las Vegas sounds. There were names scratched into the wooden table. Outside, it came down hard now.

In the dilute light, Lennie could see the stubble on Rhys's chin. Hand around his drink, his head was leaning against the back of the bench, there were shadows on his face and a bruise underneath his jaw.

'Someone got you,' Lennie said. 'Been giving your mum lip again?'

There was a silence.

'Got him in the face. Bottle,' Rhys said finally. 'Didn't do much good, like. Teach me not to drink Babycham.'

Lennie smiled. He looked down at his own hands round the glass. He shifted. 'Here,' he said. He held them out in the window's grey light. 'Here.' He showed Rhys three scars. 'Here.'

After a moment, droplets moving down the window behind, their slight, distorted shadows on Rhys's face, he said, 'Your old man all right? Works those fucking hours, I never see him. Making a bit, is he?'

Rhys smiled. 'Like he'd tell me.'

Lennie added, 'And that little girl of yours? She well?'

He watched Rhys shrug, drinking.

'Go on then. How is she?'

'She's all right, like.'

In the corner, the slot machine talked to itself.

'You don't know how she is.'

Rhys rubbed his hand over his scalp. 'She's all right. I said.'

'Really? She standing up yet, then? Said any words or what?'

'I don't know if she's said any fucking words. I've seen her . . .'

'Seen Bethan?'

'I've seen her. She's in the café every fucking day, hard not to see her. She's got her mum and everyone in there, Gwen Morgan . . . She's got a whole fucking gaggle of them set up. Loves it, I reckon. Never had so much fucking attention since she won carnival queen. I've seen her.' He looked out at the wall. 'They used to tear chunks out of her for opening her legs. She opens them and a baby falls out, suddenly they're all over her.' He lifted his glass.

'Shit a bowling ball and tell me you don't want some sympathy.'

'Know what she called her? Chelsea.' He laughed. 'Chelsea. Believe that, like? Never been to London once in her fucking life.' He was still laughing, wiping his hand across his mouth. He was shaking his head.

After a moment, Lennie said, 'Liam.' He nodded. 'That was the name I wanted. I said it right from the start.'

'Oh yeah, that's nice. Really pretty, that is. "Meet my little girl, Liam."'

Lennie looked away. He snorted, shrugged again.

He'd said Liam right from the beginning. He wasn't even sure where it had come from but he'd known the first time he uttered it. He hadn't wanted to know if it was a son or a daughter though. Ruth had said she didn't either. The name Nia hadn't come until after. Ruth had spoken it, lying in bed and holding her, staring down at the girl. Standing by, seeing them, he had nodded.

Now he said, 'You picked her up? Once?'

'Bethan doesn't need me round. I don't blame her. Don't want to see her either.'

'Well, I tell you, you want to pick her up and look at her before she gets big enough to start looking back at you. Before she starts with the questions, all that.' He thought of Nia, her mouth always closed, or stoppered up with her thumb. He remembered two years ago, imagining all the questions that would come. Questions every minute, his dad had said once. He'd wondered over it, when Nia hadn't even been walking, before Ruth had taken her for the tests. 'Hope you've been giving her some money.'

'She doesn't need my money. Parents have got the café.'

'I don't know what thing's going on between you and her,' he looked at Rhys, 'but you give her some money. You make sure, if she wants to go out and buy Chelsea a dress, she's got that money to do it. Or a pram or a fucking cot or a dummy. Doesn't matter what it is, it's no one's job but yours. If you don't want to be in there every day, don't want to go and pick her up, all right.' He held his glass with both hands, looked into it. 'You do the right thing. You give her some money. Every week.' He nodded, 'I'm bringing Ruth out for dinner tonight, bring her here, and Nia. Last weekend, she went down to Aber and she bought herself some clothes.' He looked at Rhys and he nodded again, showing him. 'That's your responsibility,' he said. 'And then later, like, you can look back and you can fucking say to yourself, you did the right thing.' He saw Rhys, the cuts across Rhys's knuckles. He thought of the sound of Ruth's voice in their hallway, and Nia's silence. 'The right thing.' He nodded one last time and then, seeing Rhys, he said, 'You're only young.'

Heart in mouth was the phrase. Ruth went back to the garden. She glanced often at Nia in the rear-view mirror as she drove. People said that, she thought, to describe fear, when really it should mean something far softer. Heart in mouth.

The rain had passed over. Blown by western winds, the clouds had moved from the coastline over the floodplain and gathered on the mountains' other side; a dim caul behind the sunlit ridges there and the reaches of old grass. It left a clear sky above Ynys-morlan – the town small behind them, in glimpses.

Ivy was drying, leaves turning in waves with the wind. On the path that led to the garden's small wooden door, the puddles of rainwater had drawn gradually back until they gathered in shade round the rotted panels' feet. Charlotte could see through her kitchen window. This morning she'd walked through the house, checking things.

People said that you should never go back to places, because they were different or maybe, Ruth thought, because they were the same and you couldn't be. She'd never gone back to anywhere before, because she'd never gone away.

Driving the hill's steep corners slowly, there came spaces between the trees. Ruth saw the grass stretching down, the rock outcrops, heather and gorse. A white sea.

'You know what it's like, Ni?' But in the back seat, with shade moving over her face, Nia was looking out of the window. She was holding Eeyore, Ruth saw, cradling it as the view moved past. Ruth did not continue.

They parked on the lane's verge, the car canted slightly, one tyre sunk into a dip and the road beside them empty. Soundless when the engine died. Ruth got out, opened Nia's door and undid her seat belt. Bending, she rubbed her nose against Nia's. Cool skin, silky smooth, the smell of baby shampoo.

'Eskimo kiss,' she said, 'butterfly kiss.' And taking her from the car, turned around.

Standing at the gates, she only stared at the house in front of them: two low storeys of painted stone, the shaded door, the eaves. Huddled in the stonework, the windows gave no clues. But it wasn't empty now. Ruth saw full, black plastic bags lying close. She saw that the door to the small shed was standing open, through which this sunlight almost reached. But they were only touches. The polished look of the doorknob, clean window glass. Only touches. Out of place, she thought. Nia was still beside her hand, and it was all just the same.

She said aloud, 'Well, I don't know what we're doing here, when Gwen'll mark you absent on that register she's so in love with, got the red pen for it specially and everything. And it goes on your record of achievement, all that, probably mar your career for ever and you'll end up cleaning toilets. Or probably . . .' she said. '. . . And I tell you, I had things to do.'

She looked at it, the same sunlight, the same. She felt quiet fall on her. She thought of Lennie, now nearing the border.

She said, 'I feel like I'm going to walk into a picture.'

Charlotte Weyland knew the events of her life. No close memories came with the knowledge though, no sense of how it had been. She had written over them, pasted words across like new skin. The years 1969, 1978, 1986 belonged to no one. As the garden's memories seemed to. She knew the course of her life but that knowledge was

empty rooms and corridors. I arrived nine days ago. This was still a home. Today Hedera is bare. I've waited for this all my life — or since I first understood. I've expected — I don't know, relief maybe, some kind of sense of justice. I don't feel it. What she did to me here has stolen the foundation a person needs to feel reparation.

I touched down at four p.m. Everything there unfamiliar, everything new of course. And for the first time — in the car, leaving the airport — it came to me that

Hedera may have changed, may have **been** changed.
Almost thirty years now, and all the countless
recollections, and this thought's never crossed my mind.
You know why? The building was always stronger.
Always older than me, pre-contrived - its nature has
always been changelessness.

I don't know if I was scared of difference or hoping
for it. In truth, it didn't matter. The journey was two
and a half hours. And the landscape is just the
same - as is Hedera.

The elms have survived. I'd read that the disease had
spread the whole state, but there they were again.
Marching men I used to think of them. Guards. It
was drawing down to nightfall when we reached the
gates. I was a fossil in the back of the damned car,
I swear. I was sick to my stomach. Scared.

Could see the edge of the formal garden and just the
same - **just the same**. There it was, just passing by
my window, and on the right then I was looking and the
Ride is **unchanged**. There were the stables - down in the
distance and the barns. Could see the sidings. All
white now, or I wouldn't have been able to catch sight of
them with the evening coming down. I ran that drive once.
I'm sure I did - remember writing an entry over it.

No one came to meet me, of course. The Green, the
entrance stair, the porticos, they were empty, everywhere,
as we drove in. The house stood there. Every window
looking down - and seeing me - outside its doors again.
Goddamn house always knew I'd come back. But no
prodigal daughter of the place. No daughter at all.

The air was cold. I carried my own luggage up as
the car left. I don't believe I was thinking clearly. Must
have been simple once I was standing on the steps. To
put my cases down. To open the doors. No locks, bolts
or latches, no change. Why would they need to secure

the doors? Someone always sees. When has Hedera been empty? They met me in the hall.

She was gone. Of course she was. The parlour-table days ended years ago. She was gone – and there was her life, left behind. I stood in it. Christ, I heard her voice. Echoing right back to me, every inch of oak, every doorway. Looked up at the balcony. Heard her.

Names then, in a clutch, and I couldn't remember them. Judgement on all their faces, oh so skilfully carved. And I believe I stood there like a child again. I believe I looked around with my baggage in my hands like I was twelve years old and I'd never left. We spoke, or they did. They'd made up the north suite.

The mirrors are gone from it, though. Perhaps she sold them. Perhaps she broke them, I don't know. You'd never feel the difference, a thousand years of bad luck in this place.

Ate in the kitchen that first night. They left me to. Should have stayed in the suite but couldn't keep from wandering. I sat at the long table again – looking through those three windows out across the kitchen garden, all the uplights shining out there, and the statues staring back. Cried. In weakness. Broke my own promises.

Nine days from there to here. I'm sitting in the nursery. She kept it. Self-validation. Self-delusion. She must have liked to stand, I can imagine her – crying too maybe.

All that time, **all that goddamn time**, how did she get away with it? When **every one** of them knew, every one of them saw me and **understood** what she was doing and **still** it went on. All her friends and the staff and Daddy. And him. No. No, it took **me**, it took a twelve-year-old **child**, **took a little girl to draw the damn line and leave** – how did she get away with it and no one –

*no one helped me but Nancy. That's money – that's what wealth means, **that's** POWER. No one tried to tell me, no one rescued me.*

I'm sitting in the nursery – but none of the rooms have functions any more. When I opened the door, it was all here. When I opened the door, the rocking horse was right there in the corner and every toy and every doll displayed. She lived a curator's life. No room is distinguishable now. ~~Dealers~~ like carrion eaters. Hedera is

empty.

Charlotte remembered the Lewis woman's daughter, small hands and pale face. No curiosity in her expression at all, Charlotte thought, just a wariness, which was almost hostility.

She had told Ruth they could come. She remembered what the estate agent had said, standing with his arm out, showing her trees and views and past the tall grass, the old walls of her home. A retreat, he had called it. A beautiful retreat.

The driveway opened to lawns, grass not yet mown before the house. Their footsteps scraped on the gravel. And when she knocked on the door of this building she'd only ever seen empty, when Charlotte opened it to them, her heart retreated. She found nothing to say. Yes people talked about how you should never go back to childhood places. Once, the quiet here had been filled by Ruth – imagining her future.

'We're late, aren't we? Always like to be late on the first day, just to make the right impression. Are we late?'

Charlotte's hair was pulled back into a bun, as when Ruth had first seen her. Strands of grey loose at the side of her face.

'Well, it's quarter past. It doesn't matter, I was busy.' She looked at the woman and child on her doorstep. It was always like this. Small, cold things occurred to her while speaking, like edges which she must step over. 'Come inside. We'll have some tea, if you'd like.'

She watched: in the hallway, Ruth staring around her, looking through the doors into each room. She opened her mouth to move them through to the kitchen and then saw Ruth's face: not nosiness but almost a girl's curiosity. Small smiles at a place she'd often wondered about.

Charlotte was not an open person – and this house contained personal things. Private things, she thought. She had not asked them to come for a guided tour. The thoughts ran on, despite her silence.

The first minutes were difficult, and Ruth Lewis used her daughter, Charlotte saw. So that it seemed as if Ruth herself was the younger.

'Earl Grey or Assam?'

'Anything's fine. Thank you.'

'Would Nia like a drink?'

'Milk maybe? She'll probably get her own, wait and see. Three going on thirty, she is. Getting dressed by herself. Pretty soon I'll be coming home and finding a casserole in the oven, she's so tidy.' And she bent down and poked at Nia's nose, she smiled and turned to Charlotte so that Nia would look too. The girl sat, holding a soft toy.

Through those first minutes, Charlotte found herself watching the child more and more. Perfect little nose and rounded cheeks, her fringe hanging near to her eyes. Every so often, she reached at Ruth with her fingers and pulled. The rest of the time, she only held the toy in her hands, in just the same way she had held that glass bottle.

Ruth said, 'No, I wouldn't swap her for a Hotpoint dishwasher.' She patted Nia's head. 'I don't deserve her. It's true what they say about kids being a gift, absolutely true. A curse as well, of course . . . you are, you're a curse . . . But it's true. I don't.' She talked over the girl's silence. Some kind of double act. Ruth knew it herself and could not stop.

They sat drinking their teas.

Charlotte told her slowly about moving in, about small refurbishments and things she had bought. She heard her own voice, moving from word to word as though they were stepping stones. She showed Ruth the Welsh dresser in the corner, remembering the purchase as she spoke. Handing over the cheque. Passing it crisply from her hand to the shopgirl's, not looking down. She had bought all her things this way; so clearly that nothing could be wrong.

'I'm nervous to see it, after all this.' Ruth nodded to no one. 'Ridiculous, isn't it?'

'I'm sure there's nothing to be nervous about.'

'It's going to be a state, though, the whole place. Twenty years, whatever it is, and no one looking after it. It'll look like the triffids have landed.' She drew Nia to her, putting expressions on her face for the girl. 'Can't look the same but I feel like I'll walk back in there and see the footprints I left yesterday.'

Charlotte watched her and asked herself what it was on the woman's face.

'Well, do you want to? Shall we go and see?'

She stood, and held her hand half out for them, showing them the way.

Even after the memories, though, and the nervousness, Ruth wasn't prepared for how she felt. And when she saw it, she looked away from Charlotte, smiling, embarrassed, knowing it showed on her face. It reduced her expression.

The walls were ten feet high, pale in the sunlight against the ivy's dark leaves. On either side of the garden wind moved the tallest branches of the trees. Ruth stood, laughing once at her own silence, looking at the wooden door, now overhung with trailing leaves. Standing on the path, the wind struck her. The walls cast shadow over the grass. The terracotta tiles that lined their ridge were broken and tangled with moss.

'It doesn't look so different.' She felt like she had lost something. When this was a gift, surely that.

'Well? Shall I?' Charlotte wanted to see what would pass across her face when she opened the door.

Past the last of Ynys-morlan, between the community centre and the first vans of the caravan site, the beach widened into dunes. Only small, covered here and there with marram grass that rattled in the sea wind, caught the sand between its stems. High enough to hide the two of them, lying down. Rhys had hollowed a small groove in the sand near to their faces, to rest the rifle barrel in. It was morning, wind and high sun.

'It's coming for us, Tom. Look at it! Hideous fucking freak of nature: half vulture . . . half chicken. Train the sights on it. It's coming! Look at that, poison dripping off its beak, like, eyes of a shark.'

'It's a seagull.'

'Look, it's not a fucking seagull. Do you want to do this sensibly or what?'

'I'm just saying, looks like a seagull to me.'

'Tom, like. I'm not going to play this game if you're acting like a fucking child.'

'You're right.' He nodded, hunched. 'It's a fucking . . . half vulture half chicken monster.'

He adjusted himself, cold ridges shifting under him, the toes of his shoes digging in. Rhys watched him line up the sights, squinting against the slight blow of sand. His hair was in his eyes.

'Fucking now, Tom! What in God's holy name can it be? Like, created in the filthiest holes of hell . . .'

'OK, all right.' He talked around aiming, trying to see against the sky. Very quietly, moving his finger a fraction, a fraction, Tom told himself, 'Pull.'

They watched the bird fall, both of them in silence. It dropped, turning like a coin through the sky.

You only noticed how it flew, he thought, once it had started to fall. He wondered now how its shadow had moved. It had been circling, slow arcs above the sand. Long, lazy curves of flight. Now it dropped. No moment had lain between.

Even from that height, it only took an instant. Tom let go of the gun, moved it away. He could see the small shape of the bird on the sand. It had been too quick.

He nodded at Rhys. 'It was a seagull,' he said.

'You know, my friend. I think you might be right.'

He sniffed, pulling himself up, shaking sand out of his trousers. The wind rippled his jacket and flattened it to him, but it hadn't moved the bird. The bird had fallen straight.

There was only a shoreline, stretching out with the day's first low tide. And the sea that would soon return, a faraway line.

They walked across the shore towards the small shape of it, talking more slowly now. Rhys carried the gun by his side, he swung it while he walked. Looking at him, Tom thought he seemed tired. He'd been working a lot, a lot of hours, taking on other people's. He'd been working a lot for almost a year now.

Rhys only looked out across the beach in front of him. The wind was in his face.

'Good shot anyway though,' he said.

Stepping into the shade, the wind lessened. Ruth let her hand fall from her hair.

The door scraped, caught in grass, pushed against overgrowth. After a moment, Ruth came and put her hands against the wood as well and they pushed together. She felt ivy brush against her cheek and thought suddenly of the dried flowers, touching the back of her hand as she'd picked up the telephone. Standing there, she could smell the damp bricks, the wood. She cleared her throat, looking at the hole where the latch had been a long time before. The door had swung open freely then. Ruth looked at the ground, the grass round her feet. Somewhere here, the latch would be lying in soil. Dirty now and rusting, somewhere here. She looked up at the tarnished oak again as the door gave very slowly.

Behind them, still in sunlight on the path, Nia stood with Eeyore the donkey held in both hands. She watched their backs.

As Ruth had thought, it was almost windless. Every angle was overhung with quiet growth. She saw it for the first time, so still.

It was briar that had kept the door closed, she couldn't move inside for it. Brambles twisted over each other, wet from past rain. Leaves and blackberries and grass. The berries overripe, she saw, falling. There would be more on the ground. Reseeding there.

Those nettles had grown very tall against the brickwork, some bending with the weight of themselves. In places, ivy trailed on to them from the very tops of the walls. They looked like strands of spiderweb, Ruth thought. Everything was softened. She could hear each tiny sound.

'Well . . .' Charlotte said.

'Well.' She laughed at herself. She said quietly, 'An hour or two weeding . . . should have it sorted out in no time.' She laughed again, looked down at the wet couch grass, it had grown to the height of her knees. She raised her head. 'I don't think . . . I don't think it's as much work as it looks to be.'

It seemed so sad, though. It forgot so easily.

'That's where we used to sit, over by that wall there.' She pointed. 'Ground was always drier there.' Under the leaf mould and earth, the memories were no longer warm. She looked like she would carry on but instead said, 'It's like it's hidden itself. Twenty-five years or whatever it is, no one coming here. Like it's hidden itself away.'

Charlotte didn't answer. She had thought this, something very close to this, the first time she had seen inside. She could smell the nettles, sharp and summery, though the autumn was growing full now.

Ruth would have liked to describe this to her mother, this slow neglect: the way the ivy would lengthen its tendrils and the grass rise through briar. She thought that she could have taken the hem of her dress away from her mother's hand and said it all. Looked into her face. Shown her the way it would be. It was pity Ruth felt, so strong and unexpected. She stared at the trails of still, wet life and wanted it all to be hers. She had played hide and seek here, the weeds, the slow dereliction, breaking already around them while they hadn't noticed.

She turned to Charlotte, half a smile cast on her face, and saw that Charlotte had been watching. What she felt must have shown then.

'It's a sad place, in a way,' Charlotte said.

'I just haven't seen it for a long time is all. And it didn't use to be like this.' She felt a touch on the back of her leg. She glanced down and saw Nia, Eeyore hanging from one hand as the other tugged her.

'How did it look then?' Charlotte asked her.

Ruth raised her face. 'How did it look? Looked like childhood to me.'

The caravan site lay behind them, row on row of white and peppermint vans.

Rhys said, 'We still on for Friday then?'

'If you promise to wear the black dress.'

'You don't remember.'

'Uh . . . Yes?'

'Not yes. Fucking no is what you mean. Friday? The museum?'

'Oh right, yeah.'

'Half twelve, like. I'll meet you round the back.'

'Synchronize watches,' Tom said.

'I've got a crowbar for the boards. Looking at them the other day, like, I don't reckon we'll need it. But I've got it.'

They'd organized it weeks ago, walking past, seeing the polythene flapping on the windows. Go in, have a look round, take some beers and a torch. They'd laughed a lot, talking about it, Tom remembered. Rhys had tried to pull the polythene back, get a glimpse inside. He'd put his hands in his pockets, saying wooden boards weren't any match for someone as incredibly fucking hard as he was. He'd had to go to work after that. Tom had left him sitting in the bus shelter, waiting, looking out at the road. Rhys had raised his hand but Tom remembered how his expression had seemed to grow more distant.

'I've got like a camping light, like lantern thing. I'll bring that. You bring your sister.'

'Whatever.'

'And she's got to wear, like a bikini and heels. You can do that, right?'

Tom didn't answer. He'd had dinner with them last night, his mum and his sister, sitting round the table in the kitchen. They'd had extra, his mum had said.

Stacey had been bleaching her hair again, had it up in a plastic bag. He'd tried to eat, listening to them talk, but all he'd been able to smell was her hair dye. Piss. She'd had a crop top on and Tom had been able to see the muscles in her pale skinny stomach. A crop top and a plastic bag.

His mum and her had talked about school, him pushing the food round his plate, smelling her peroxide, trying to be hungry. After ten minutes, his mum had turned and stared at it. 'It's not extra for wasting,' she'd said.

After a while, she'd asked him, 'How's the work going then?'

'Lot of it. Even with no one in the café, like.'

'Don't complain about too much work, if it's there, you go ahead and you take it.'

Stacey had said then, 'You know what I'm going to take, like? They've got a course going in Aber, evening class.' The light had shone off the plastic bag as she moved. 'It's not too much, like, I'll pay for it with the round. Voice coaching.' She'd nodded. She had too much make-up round her eyes and he didn't like it. 'Voice coaching, like for accents.'

Mum had looked up at her across the table, the fork very still in her hand. 'You don't need any voice coaching. Got a lovely voice, you have. Always had a lovely voice, in choir and everything. What are you talking about, voice coaching? Your problem isn't your voice, I tell you, it's half the rubbish you spew out with it. Voice coaching, good God.' She'd shaken her head slowly, not knowing what could possibly come next.

'You don't need anything done on your voice,' he'd said. 'Fucking voice is fine.'

Stacey had pushed her potatoes around for a minute, looking down at them. She'd made fork patterns in the margarine that was scraped on the edge of her plate. 'How many actresses and actors you know with a Welsh accent? You know a lot of those?' She cut through him when she talked like this. She said things in a way she never used to say them.

'You think putting questions at the end of everything you say makes you sound cleverer?'

'You think you could shut up and let me eat? There's none,' she said. 'Simple as that.'

Looking down at the table, Tom said. 'There's the bloke, lives with Hugh Grant in *Notting Hill*.'

She'd looked at him like he was a Labrador. 'He's a comedy extra. You think I want to be a comedy extra? You can have a Welsh accent if you're a comedy extra.'

'Anthony Hopkins. He's from Swansea, somewhere round Swansea.'

'Exactly. You've just gone and proved my point exactly, haven't you? Anthony Hopkins doesn't have a Welsh accent. Hannibal Lecter wasn't Welsh, was he?'

'Look.' Siân had turned to them, she'd put her fork down on her plate.' If you want to get voice lessons, you get them. Just as long as I don't have to *hear* your voices talking about *this* any more. You get them. I don't care.'

Later, Tom had sat in the low chair in the living room. He'd had a can of beer in one hand, a cigarette in the other, glancing occasionally at his mum's face. The light from the TV had flickered on her, blonde hair up in a bunch. Behind her, a little light had been on. He'd remembered the things Gwen Morgan had said. Stacey had gone up to her room by then. They'd sat, just watching together.

'How's work at the moment?' he'd asked her. 'Is it OK?'

'Quiet.'

He had sat up then, reached into his pockets and pulled out the three ten-pound notes. He'd folded them carefully there, fresh and crisp from the cash point. 'Here,' he'd said. He'd not looked at her really. 'Brought this for you.'

He hadn't heard her answer, the adverts had come on loud. He'd seen her smile though, before she'd put them in her pocket and leaned back on the sofa, into the TV's shadows and the shaded orange light.

Now walking with the wind in his face, he could see the form of the bird. It was lying on the beach alone. The other birds, he saw, had moved away from the place where it had fallen. It lay on empty sand. In the distance, he could see the long curve of the town. Another twenty feet, thirty, bootprints trailing out behind them in two uneven lines.

The bird was broken. Its wing was ripped, almost all the way off its body. The other lay crooked beneath it. Most of its feathers were still white. Its head lay on the sand. Tom saw it blink, slowly, staring somewhere past them. He hadn't known that birds had eyelids.

They stood there for a while in silence, heads bent over it in the wind, with the sound of the ocean far away. The bird's eye was very black, just a tiny pinpoint of light, a reflection of the sun. On either side of it, their shadows stretched across the sand. There was no one else out here. No one else, not on the whole beach, that Tom could see. Just the two of them and this dying bird.

He crouched down beside it, feeling grains of sand hit his face. It couldn't last very long now.

Quietly, above, he heard Rhys say, 'Ashes to ashes.'

Beside his feet, the seagull tried to move its neck. It couldn't move its neck, though. It was dying. That was when he reached out to touch it. He didn't even want to touch it. Diseased things, they were, vermin like rats, they'd eat rotting meat if they found it lying on the sand. Now, though, he reached out his fingers. He could see its feathers shake, the tiniest movement.

They were very soft when he touched them. They were softer than he'd thought they would be. It had tendons stretching from its body to its wings, that would hold them out, catching the air as it flew.

After a moment, he looked away from it. He drew his hand back. It was dead.

'Well,' he said. 'Now I'm a hero.' He didn't see the expression on Rhys's face behind him; a fascination, low and sad. The laughs of before had fallen from it as quickly, as naturally, as the bird itself had dropped. They hadn't come here really for the laughs.

He didn't see that, or the way that Rhys's gaze caught and wavered then, on the thing around his wrist. Tom stood slowly as behind, Rhys's eyes were widening.

He turned. 'What?' he said.

Picking each word in this quick wind, Rhys said carefully, 'What the fuck is that?'

'What the fuck is what?'

'Oh let me see now, like … That huge gold fucking bracelet hanging round your wrist.'

Tom drew his hand back. He drew it back, even knowing that his sleeve was already hanging down, already covering it. He turned his face away and then back, his other hand over his mouth. He sniffed. 'Well what the fuck does it look like?' he said.

'It looks like the kind of bracelet my aunt might wear. Obviously, she'd think it a bit flashy, like. Go on, give me a look.'

'No.'

'Well don't be embarrassed of your nicest new buy. Been shopping a lot recently, have you? Well I like it. I reckon it's you. Anyone tries to tell you different, you just don't listen to them, Andrea.'

'Right.'

'Really . . . Because there comes a time, like, in every teenager's life, when things can get a bit, you know, confusing. Maybe you're in the showers after PE . . . And it's nothing to feel ashamed about.'

'I've got to go.'

'What? Hey, come on. You tell me where the thing came from. You're wearing a gold fucking bracelet round your wrist.' He grabbed at Tom's hand then, he grabbed and Tom tried to pull away. Their coats flapped in the wind. He'd never been as strong as Rhys, not when they'd done pull-ups, seven years old, hanging off his mum's back porch, not when they'd jump-started Rhys's dad's car, pushing it down the slight hill outside the edge of town. He'd never been stronger. Taller. Just that.

He pushed Tom's sleeve up and he looked at the bracelet. After a moment, Tom gave up struggling. He let his arm hang there, in Rhys's hand.

He'd told himself not to put the fucking thing on, two days running, he'd told himself. Yesterday, though, bending over in the café to reach out a pan, it had fallen out of his pocket and on to the chequered floor. Falling out like that, you could lose it anywhere. You could drop it in the road and not know the slightest thing about it until you got home and found it gone. This morning, picking it up off the counter in the little kitchen, he'd held it in the palm of his hand for a long time before he'd put it round his wrist.

Rhys's fingers went loose round his hand now. He looked up from the bracelet to Tom's face, that grin spread all over him.

He said, 'You think I don't know whose it is.'

'Look. You want to know whose it is? I'll tell you whose it is, all right? It's my mum's. Is that enough?'

'That's good,' he said. He laughed suddenly and Tom saw something in his face that he'd never seen there before. Never seen, at least, when Rhys was looking at him. He thought of the way he'd stared out at the beach as the bird had still circled. 'That is really fucking good, actually. Your mum's, like.' Rhys didn't stop talking, the collar of his coat prancing at his neck in this wind as he grinned little broken rocks. 'That's good,' he said. 'Course, it's total fucking shit. That's not your mum's. You think I don't see whose it is?'

He was silent, waiting now. He looked from Rhys, out towards the town, but he didn't see it as Rhys's voice changed.

'Sly fucker . . .'

'What?'

But Rhys was only shaking his head, moving very slowly, his mouth open with that shocked smile. 'You sly bastard. I don't believe it, I really do not fucking believe it. You think I wouldn't recognize it, like? I've had it waved in my face enough fucking times . . . set of pink fingernails.' He kept shaking his head, the most wondrous surprise spreading. 'That's Gwen Morgan's.'

Tom said, 'Maybe I found her bag.'

Rhys made as if to turn away but came back, smiling more. He couldn't turn away, Tom thought.

'You didn't nick it off her. Even if I believed for one second – known you all my fucking life, like – even if I believed you'd ever nick anything off anyone, you think I'd believe you'd nick it off *her* and then walk round with it hanging on your wrist?'

'I didn't say I nicked it. I said maybe I found her bag. Look . . .' But he didn't have anything to put after the first word.

'If you found her bag, you'd return it, that's what you'd do. If you found a fifty-pence piece on the floor of the pub, you'd stand up and shout if anyone'd lost it.' He twisted his voice into some high-pitched imitation. '"I brought you up better than to steal and beg, Tom Humphries. I brought you up better than that."'

'Rhys.'

He was silent for a moment, looking at Tom's face. Above them, they heard a gull cry. He said suddenly, 'I'm going to ask you this once, like. I'm going to ask you this once, and if you lie to me then you kiss goodbye to eighteen years of me paying for your pints. Once.

You ready?' He looked Tom in the eyes and he said, 'Are you fucking Gwen Morgan?'

'What d'you mean am I fucking her? No I'm not fucking her! You need to be locked up, you think she'd let anyone . . . or I'd fucking *want* to.'

'All right. Now I'm going to explain to you that this could be the best piece of news I have ever heard in my whole fucking miserable life, like, and I'm going to give you twice. You listening, Tom? Are you fucking Mrs Emyr Morgan?'

Standing there, the empty beach on either side of him just as it had been that night, Tom opened his mouth and didn't know what to say. Later, he'd tell himself that he hadn't had any choice. Later he'd think that there was nothing else he could've said. Standing on the wind-scattered sand right then, though, it didn't feel that way. Even though there were no other explanations in his head.

Tom said, 'Don't want to tell you about it yet.' With a knowing look. With a smirk. Because what kind of person wore someone's jewellery when they weren't fucking them? He might as well have said yes.

'No. You sly fucking cunt.'

'Look –'

'Don't you "look" me, like! *You're having Gwen Morgan –*'

And then he did the strangest thing. He put his arms half up in the air and he did some kind of dance on the beach. He turned around and he did it again. He took Tom by the shoulders and he shook him. Once. Twice. Hard. He said, 'I've had that bracelet shaken right at me. I've had her fingernails. D'you do it from behind? You tell me and you tell me now. You do it from behind? Please God, tell me you did her up the arse. Please God.' He looked at the sky and he put his hands together.

And Tom could only turn away from him. Rhys's face was no different than it had ever been but it had never looked so foreign. He thought of Gwen standing by the sink in his caravan, holding a bag full of the rubbish that he'd left lying across his floor, make-up running down the sides of her face. He saw Rhys. Rhys had always made him laugh, when he laughed you couldn't help but laugh with him. He fucking danced. Coat blown out on either side of him, he stood and danced on the shore.

Now he took Tom by the arms and he said, 'You tell me now.'

And it was the only thing he could reply with. Only thing he could have done, to lead him on. How would Rhys's grinning face have looked if Tom had told him that he'd held Gwen Morgan and kissed her like some awkward twelve-year-old? And then he'd stood and watched her leave and when he'd found her bracelet lying on the floor, he'd kept it. He'd taken it to work. Looking at Rhys, he wondered how those words would sound.

He grinned, some kind of smile – was it that? – on his face. He said, 'Next Friday,' and he heard himself.

'Next Friday what? What the fuck does that mean? Next Friday?'

'Tell you then . . . The museum, you can wait. I reckon you can wait.' That was what he said.

'The path runs straight from where we're standing.' She moved her hand to show the brambles. 'It's here.' Sheltered, she saw, silent. 'I think . . . if we can get something, a fork, find the edges of the path here, we'll know how wide a space to clear, then . . . the shears. We'll have to cut as much as we can and drag it out.' She said, 'Underneath, the path is . . . all made of bricks. We should be able to pull up the loam, it should come clear from them.'

Charlotte nodded, she stared out over the mantle of growth. 'We ought to take a photograph,' she said. 'I don't have a camera. I won't remember.' She thought that she could write it into her diary, try to describe its detail. But she'd never read it. She thought that she seemed always to move past things in this way, leaving them behind her, no longer visible.

She had bought a lot of tools; had the delivery men stack them on the dry floor of the shed, lean them against the walls. They walked back around the house, Nia and Ruth hand in hand.

'My God. You could open a gardening centre.'

'It's better to have the things and not to need them than to need them and be at a loss, surely.' Forks and spades and trowels and shears, stacked in shadow, flowerpots of every size and two trellises against the back wall, bags of compost. There was a lawnmower, a strimmer. She didn't look at Ruth as she took out a fork and a pair of shears. One thousand, two hundred pounds, forty-eight pence. She picked up the tools.

'I know you probably have to be home. We should get as much done as we can in the time.'

Ruth nodded. She offered to help carry the tools but Charlotte told her she was fine. She watched the woman's straight back as she struggled with them towards the garden.

It was a magic trick, the way the wind died as you stepped through. Final rainwater was caught in the leaves of the ground's lowest growth.

'Well,' Ruth said, 'I think you should be the one to make the first cut, pronounce the garden open for a change.'

After a pause, looking at the first snarl of bramble, Charlotte said, 'I've never seen the paths. I don't know where to start.'

Ruth smiled. She looked at the sixty yards of briar and tangled weeds laid out in front of them. 'I don't really think it matters,' she said.

She held the shears awkwardly in both hands, manoeuvred the blades around the first blackberry branches. The sound of their closing was clear, and the sky above clearer. A perfect blue, framed by these walls.

Charlotte laughed once at her ineptitude. From behind her, Ruth said, 'Now that's the first time I've heard you laugh.'

Charlotte stopped, she didn't turn. After a moment, she moved the shears again. 'I apologize,' she said, 'if I've been dull company for you.'

'I didn't mean that.'

But Charlotte didn't answer. She opened the shears and cut.

Ruth said, 'You know I didn't mean that.'

Caught between words, Charlotte moved instead of speaking.

'I'm sorry,' the woman said to her back.

Ruth disarmed her. There was nothing in the way she spoke that Charlotte could hold on to, no reason for saying the things which were in her mind. Quiet, angry things, that would have been easier than this unguarded silence. It *was* a reason, she realized, or an excuse, that she was looking for. Her hands were still. 'If I cut for a while, and you could drag them outside.' She turned to Ruth and tried to give a smile, troubled.

They worked quietly, Charlotte breaking with difficulty through the tangles, close to the ground, stepping back for Ruth to pull them free and form a ragged pile with them across the path outside. Where she bent, Charlotte could smell the wet earth, the slight tang of sap. The sun was warm. Every time she stooped, she felt it on the back of her neck, on her hair. Through the brambles' shadow, first, small patches of light touched the earth.

It didn't take them long to clear a space, perhaps three feet, cut bramble on each side. She put the shears down for a moment, stood looking upwards, seeing the trees' outside, their higher branches moving in the wind she couldn't feel. The leaves were turning against each other. Somewhere here, under the mess of weeds and loam in which she stood, there were bricks. They were russet-damp. But sometime later, sometime soon, would be cleaned. These long-quiet weeds would open on to flowers, lawns perhaps.

She looked out now over it all, unchanging in the sunlight. She had to wince a little against the brightness. Flying back from Boston, it had been a day like this. She remembered sitting, wine glass before her. It had been a day like this, she'd seen the clouds from above, glanced at them before pulling the window blind. Like landscapes, and Massachusetts just like an atlas, as though, if you could have looked further, you might have been able to see the whole continent there, stretched out, see the way that it lay on the world.

Standing in the small space they had made, loose hair touched Charlotte's face. It was a privilege really to be able to see the clouds from above. Really, it should move you.

Nia had sat out on the path for the last little while, holding her toy very tightly, stroking it. Half an hour before, Ruth had found her eating blackberries from the severed branches and had scolded her with jokes. 'Can't eat them now . . .' Charlotte had heard her say, 'Devil pees on them in October, don't you know anything?' She had turned to watch Nia drop them, hesitating, to the ground, only for Ruth to pick them up and give them back to her.

Now Ruth was taking from her jacket pocket a pair of miniature gardening gloves.

With Eeyore still clamped in one fist, Nia had been drawing out a bramble branch. She'd put her fingers carefully between the leaves and the thorns, pulling at it with thick concentration.

'Well, it's about time,' Ruth was saying. 'About time, with us working in here all morning and you out there, lounging around. You're just the Queen of Sheba, you are. Decided to join us . . .'

Passing Eeyore from one of Nia's hands to the other then, Ruth put the gloves on her. 'So cute they're sickening,' she remembered saying to the woman at the jumble sale a year ago. They were hard to get on, she had to hold Nia's hands by the wrists. She didn't hear the sound of the shears stop.

'Come on you,' she was saying. 'You've got too big hands, that's your problem. Big slabs of meat hands, you've got.'

For the last few months, the summer, the gloves had been shut away in a drawer. Nia stood very still, letting her. Looking at her face now, there was no trace of what had been there that last time.

She'd only been trying to show her, pulling weeds out. Little bits of grass, holding them up so that Nia could see. She had turned her face from Ruth, she'd sat on the lawn and twisted away, and Ruth had said things, 'Come on now.' Nia's gloved hands had pushed a bland rejection at her face. But she'd kept trying. That expression had risen out of nothing, made her ugly, fringe in her eyes. The pansies, it had been, small and delicate, shallow-rooted. There'd always been pansies in that corner of the garden, near the front door. They were brightest for longest, her mother had used to say. Nia had torn them out. She'd wanted to hurt them, as many as she could. It had come from nothing, Ruth had thought. But really, that wasn't true. She'd just been unable to see it form, it had come from under silence.

'Nia!' she had shouted. She remembered shaking her. 'You just look at what you've done!' But she hadn't let her look. 'Do you know how long we've had pansies there? Do you know? Do you even know *why* they're there?' She had shouted things that Nia hadn't heard, that she herself couldn't remember now – only the way she had felt, seeing the flowers dug through dirt. Guilty, she remembered. As though she'd done it herself.

Now, outside the ivy-covered doorway, beside the still growth of years, Nia was docile while she crouched. She kept trying to pull the gloves down around her fingers.

Charlotte watched them, the shears still held in her hands. She saw Ruth smile and speak. She seemed always to be close to something. Even laughing, she seemed open, as bright as saltwater. And thinking this, Charlotte realized: it was tears.

She had never been able to endure people crying. But seeing them now, she only felt mired. And like this, thoughtless, a memory came to her. It came cold and complete. She had written it. People cry for others' pity and when they cry alone it's their own pity they cry for. She remembered. The night they'd called from Hedera.

Here, watching them, she wanted to turn away.

'Well,' Ruth was saying. 'Well.'

Charlotte hadn't tried to put her mark on any part of this new house. The quiet inside was now traced with the edges of their outdoor voices.

It was static in its age, as if it would remain unchanged whether she came or went. It wasn't a home. She had never needed one. She had moved through, she was always moving. The diaries had been placed in different bookcases, they had lived under her bed. Pages pressed together in shadow, each entry beginning 'Dear Charlotte', they stood in her new study now. Between many red leather bindings, the

words were a façade. She was crying, can you believe that? My God. But mother's already explained to her what my response will be. Crying goddamn it and behind

the girl's voice there was a picture. Came so clearly.
Even as she began to tell me, her **first** words, I knew
what she'd called to say. I saw mother: lying in her bed.
Irises, she loves. Pale colours for her furnishings. Yes
– clearer than if I had stood in the doorway, seen her
turn to me, clearer than if our eyes had met. She is
dying. Bedridden, no more than days. I picture her
surrounded by photographs.

So is she crying now as well? The girl said 'asking
for me'. The girl said 'alone'. It is me she really wants
now? But then what state is her mind in? There are
questions I should have asked. I could call back.
First time dialling the number in how long? Maybe in for
ever. I won't call back. I won't just **lie down**, I won't
just **buckle**. Isn't that why she's had me informed?
Give me a final chance to crawl back to her. How much
of her reasoning is hate these days? How much has she
changed? An old woman now.

It's seven years, now I count, since her last attempt
at contact. I remember justifications – holding the letter
and feeling that old nausea, they were so **slight**, so
goddamned **offhand**. But it was punishment of
course. And now maybe with all her flowers and her
memories, she begins to understand what she denied my
father.

Asking for me. In my mind she's still young, no image
of her that can be true any more. Irony. And those
photos – though I could be wrong, and she was nothing
if not bullish, maybe she's sitting there now without
a picture in the room, spending her last hours with
her own bloodyminded will, but I imagine – **I imagine** –
regret. She's had her staff make contact. And
once upon a time, her collection of photographs was
great.

I picture her inside an imprecise circle of them, on

tabletops and on the piano, the window sills. I wonder, if I saw them, her picnics and her Christmases, all the Thanksgivings, the endless childhood portraits she had taken, complementary-colour backgrounds, little blue-eyed smiles, I wonder if I'd be able to tell which were of myself. I wonder if she can.

I've watched this coming, imagined the moment so many times. Since before Dad. I think — I'm sitting here now, trying to look back — I remember believing I'd be free after this. But she's playing me again. Maybe through the years has known, if I ever went back to her it would be now. So she gives me this last chance, so I can regret too. Spend years wondering like she did. What might we have said to each other? Would she finally admit, if I went to her? Tell the truth to me. Would she ask me to forgive?

Maybe she was good once. Maybe before '54 she was full of love and care. No lies in her. Maybe she was happy then. In truth, I think it must be the case. I saw that love. Like you can see, in a person's abstinence, the addiction they've had. Like you can see the shape of a life in the hole bereavement leaves.

Far away from me now, she is still alive. She is sitting up in that bed maybe, digesting whatever précis the girl took back to her.

Yes, her words were well-schooled, a mask. Mother had already warned her that I would not come.

Maybe confession is what she hopes to end her life with. I will not give her that.

Tears now when she doesn't deserve them. Maybe she knows I'll be crying. Like we were never separated, you can't tear people from each other. I won't ever cry for her again, not at her funeral, not in remembrance, **not in loss**. People cry for others' pity and when they cry alone it's their own pity they cry for.

*I heard sadness in that girl's voice. I believe it was
even genuine. Mother's surrounded herself with staff
then, drawn them to her like a blanket, not caring who they
are. She never did. They are all she has left. If she
wants family she can paint family faces above their
throats. I will go to her funeral. I will be her daughter
when I hear the*

words were lost to her. They sat, gathering new dust where afternoon sunlight came through the window and painted bright squares on the slate floor. The desk was blank, only a little vase of flowers and a chair beside it.

Inside the lowest drawer, within a black box file, Charlotte Weyland's account books lay untouched, a small clip of money beside them. She had tried to estimate the price of each day that Ruth would spend with her.

A small clink and the fork would not go down. They were searching, pushing into the loam – the garden dry now. The western wall's shadow covered half its space, lying in the silence of a day almost gone.

This carpet of deadfall pulled upwards cleanly. Damp, matted, it tore away from what was beneath. Ruth tugged – the first piece – and they saw bricks. As dark as Charlotte had imagined. As though with rain that had fallen years ago. She looked up at Ruth and there was a smile, this scent suddenly strong, discovered. The path's beginning was three feet wide. The brickwork laid in a herringbone.

He'd left his caravan under the white and windswept evening sky. The gulls had been flying high in that wind. Standing on the van's step for a minute, he'd watched them, remembering the one that he had brought down. He'd put Gwen's bracelet thing back in the cupboard. It would sit there. Maybe for a day or two, it would sit. He'd give it back to her the next time she came to the café. He'd say, in front of Pat, in front of the customers, that he'd found it lying under one of the tables, he'd say that it must have fallen from her hand.

There were a lot of people in the Lion that night, the slate floor was crowded with footsteps, the air crowded with smoke, the sounds of pool balls knocking each other, loud hellos and laughter. Tom stood, watching Rhys work his way round the table, a cigarette sticking out of his mouth, frowning through its haze. The smoke would be getting in his eyes, Tom thought, it would be stinging like a bastard. Looking at him like that, he smiled a little bit.

Near to them, at the quiet end of the bar, the old boys talked to the girl who was serving. She had her hair up, must have spent a long time, done like Sharon Stone's in *Basic Instinct*. Wasn't quite long enough, though. It made him smile in this small way. She'd had to use a lot of clip things, now she kept pushing loose strands back, pushing like she wasn't thinking about it, as she nodded at Ted. She was thinking about it, though.

'So you know what that bloody doctor says? Not more than bloody fifteen years old and he says, "Q fever" is what I've got like. "One in a hundred thousand chance, like," that's what he says. Tests came back. And I'm saying, if it's one in a hundred bloody thousand chance then you've not seen it before, have you? How in the hell'd you know to tell if it was Q fucking fever. Excuse me. Bloody fever.' Tom watched the coughing take over again. 'Get it from hay, on the wind apparently. Comes in from hay.'

Nearby, he saw Jeanette. She was leaning back, laughing so hard, sitting with her vodka tonics and her husband – always laughed like that. Sitting there, with her crunchy perm and her bloody lipstick. His mum would be watching telly, down the street. She'd have the curtains closed against the fading sky.

'It's four,' Rhys said, standing now.

'What?'

'Look about a million fucking miles away. Thought you must be trying to work it out again. Told you before. Two and two. It's four.'

He smiled as Rhys nodded to the table. 'Fouled,' he said. 'That's it then.'

There was a slight blow of colder air between them. Rhys looked towards the door.

She wasn't fat, as Rhys often said, not really. Pleasantly plump, his mother would've called it. Course, she would have meant it even more nastily than 'fat', but it was true: pleasantly plump. She had long hair, blonde and not dyed either. Not as pretty as she had been once, and with a harder look these days. Had caught it off Patty maybe, and his own mum, spending so much time there with them.

He'd known Bethan since they'd gone to playschool together – as long as Rhys had known her, only he still knew her now. They'd used to go out to the beach a lot, the three of them, a few years ago. A blanket and cider, long evenings. Summer was always passing, it was always a memory.

She was different now. Sometimes, the few times that Rhys ever talked about her, his voice hard with something, contempt, Tom thought he wouldn't sound that way if he knew how much she'd changed. But then maybe it'd changed Rhys as much. You could see it underneath his expressions sometimes. Stones underwater. He hid it.

Now, having glanced at her, he looked back at Tom with nothing on his face. 'Two bloody shots,' he said. He stepped back, blowing a stream of smoke out at the table.

Tom watched him for a moment then he said, 'Two shots, my arse. I'll clear the table with this.'

They played the game out and Rhys stood back, leaned his cue against the wall and drained his pint.

He said, 'Don't want to see you making any sharp exits either. I believe I'll do you one last time before your mum tucks you in.' He put his empty glass down on the beer-wet table and said again, 'You'll stay, like? Ten minutes.'

He glanced at Rhys over the rim of his own. 'Sure, yeah.'

She was perched on the bar stool, arse spread nicely on every side, Rhys thought. He saw her hair hanging down. He saw it had been cut a little. Putting his empty down, he didn't look at her, only at Claire, serving. 'Carling. Pretty please sugar on top.' He took his hand from his pocket, rested it on the bar, and he turned to her. 'All right,' he said.

She laughed. Just a little one, but a laugh nonetheless, with that expression stained all over her face, that little twist of a smile. She looked out past the bar, into nothing for a minute. Then she turned back.

'Hello then, Rhys. Wondered if you were going to say hi. I can always tell when you're going to say hi, see. You take half an hour to put fifty pence in your jeans pocket. You know when you're going to say hi? When you look like you're about to walk off, that's when.' She smiled slightly. 'You look well then.'

'And you.'

'Well thank you,' she said, and didn't take her eyes from him. 'Look like you've been working a lot.'

'Better than hanging round here.'

'Now, that is true.' Her skin was pale. She picked up her drink but only held it for a moment. It was wine, he saw. Red.

'Thought wine was for "girls that don't know anything except that they're better than everyone else".'

Bethan smiled, looked at her glass. 'Well,' she said. 'Maybe I'm one of those. What are you up to, Rhys?'

He shrugged. 'Working a lot. Like you said. Good pay. Yeah, I'm down in Aber a lot now.'

'That's nice for you.'

He glanced up, couldn't see anything on her face, though. 'Yeah. It is. Probably be moving down there soon.'

'Yeah?' She didn't seem to need to look at him. And he wasn't keen on it; she didn't know what was on his face. Always thought she'd known him inside out, and she'd always been fucking wrong.

Rhys left his drink on the bar and he turned to her properly. He put his hand in his pocket and took something out so that she couldn't see. 'What about you?' he said.

'A bit of work here and there. Looking after Chels'.'

'How is she then?'

Bethan looked at him and gave a soft smile. She said, 'About two feet long. Arms, legs, a head.' She turned away and said, 'She's almost walking. Standing, she is, kind of wobbly, holding on to things. Got this look on her face like, "May have my hand on this chair here, see, but I don't really need it."'

Rhys nodded, nodded – after a moment, opened his hand, pushed what was in it towards her. 'Well,' he said. 'Thought you might want this, anyway. Like I said, I'm working all the time and the pay's good . . . Have rent to pay soon enough. Not right now though.'

Bethan looked from his face, down to the crumpled mess of notes that were lying on the bar. He didn't draw his hand back from the space beside them.

'Not anxious to lose it?' she said. 'Or worried I might forget who left it there.'

'You always were more than ready to pick holes in things. It's your mother that taught you. Pick pick pick,' he said quietly. 'Brought it to give you, Bethan. I'm sure you could do with something extra.'

'That's kind of you.' But she didn't move her own hand anywhere near.

He picked up his pint. 'Buy yourself some new clothes or something.'

'I just went shopping actually,' she said. 'Went yesterday. Bought this top.'

'Yeah, well. It's nice like.'

'I could tell you liked it. Saw you noticing it five minutes ago. And two minutes ago. And thirty seconds ago.' She moved her glass very slightly on the bar. Behind them, around them, the noise of others was loud. She sat quiet in its centre. When she spoke again, it wasn't anger in her voice. 'What made you think to do this suddenly?'

There was some shout behind them that Rhys didn't really hear. Before he answered, and without moving them towards her, Beth opened the notes on the bar; spreadeagled them.

'Watch it,' he said, nodding at the rest of the pub.

She turned to look up very slightly. 'I don't reckon anyone in here's going to take your money.'

'I know they're not going to take it . . .' He shrugged. He remembered the first time they'd come in here – together anyway. He'd held her hand, and he remembered the way she'd looked around. Head up, because she knew these people, but maybe too far up to be friendly. She had moved her fingers in his, dry. Now, she counted out the notes. Looked like she'd never been so comfortable as she was now, in this noise.

'Well,' she said quietly. 'Fifty pounds.'

'There you go.'

'Rhys,' she said, 'I don't need any money.'

'Well, you can put it away then, can't you. Start a little kitty up.'

'I don't need a kitty. Café's doing as well as it's ever done. My rent's paid.' Picking up her glass, she sipped. 'Thanks anyway.'

'You can't tell me you don't need it. What did that top cost you? A fiver? You're not working, I've seen you.'

'Have you? Been looking?'

'What's the point of staring a gift horse in the mouth, Bethan?'

'Take it back, Rhys,' she said gently, and she stared out over the bar. She didn't have a thing to be gentle about. He didn't need her gentle voice.

'I'm trying to do you a favour here. Do yourself one. And Chelsea.'

He saw her turn slowly like she wasn't sure what she'd heard. Her mouth was open slightly, polished with lipstick.

'I don't think you are trying to do me a favour. Are you, Rhys, really? You're trying to do yourself a favour, I think. Always were better at that. I tell you what, you want to do something for us? Put that money in a little kitty for yourself. You can use it to get a few photos taken, just those passport ones, they'll be good enough. You send us a few back, like. One a year.' She turned away, picked up her wine and did not drink. 'Truth of it is, I don't need any money. But thank you. It was a sweet thought, Rhys. And I've enjoyed this. Little catch-up.'

Rhys only stared at her face for a moment. He only stared and saw no memories there – like sand after the tide, Bethan Hughes. He took the money and he turned away from her. He pressed it back into his pocket where it belonged. And in the noise of the place she didn't hear him walk away, leaving the drink he had bought, still half full, standing next to her in an empty space on the bar.

She'd been drunk the night that she'd taken Rhys into her bedroom and told him she was pregnant. She'd saved up, her mum paying her for weekends. That day she'd gone into Boots in Aber and spent twenty pounds on pregnancy tests. She'd had thirty-five in the bank. The rest she'd spent on two bottles of cider, one bottle of blackcurrant and two packets of Benson and Hedges. She'd taken them home like a carrier bag full of treats. Like a Christmas stocking in her bedroom.

Laid them side by side on the dressing table. She'd had pictures cut from magazines stuck to the mirror then. Eyeshadow and foundation pictures, showing you how to apply. Stuck up with Blu-Tack, she remembered now. Sometimes at night, with all the lights off, she'd been able to hear them, softly falling from the glass on to the tabletop.

Two tests. Three bottles. Two packets of cigarettes. She had gone downstairs to get a glass. She'd poked her mum in the bottom and smiled at her. Her mum had been cooking.

The television playing, she remembered. 'Neighbours', as she'd poured the first drink. 'Family Fortunes' by the time that Rhys had stood there in her bedroom, picking things up and putting them down again, a lot of things, like each was different after it had been in his hand. Waiting for her to tell him why she'd called.

Les Dennis's voice had risen up through the floorboards. *'You said wine. Our survey said . . .'* And she'd been unable to stop laughing.

Bethan remembered nights, standing, holding Chelsea, only a strip of light laid across the floor from the hallway door. Nights at her parents' flat. Chelsea crying. Not even crying, screaming. The sound of it hitting her face. She remembered calling out to her mum.

Her mother standing at the doorway there, soaked in sleep, rubbing her hair with one hand.

Asking her, 'I'm sorry, mum. Will you? Please?'

And Patty saying, 'Bethan . . .' Just an outline against the light. 'You've got to do it yourself sometimes . . .' and leaving her.

In her arms, Chelsea had been hot with screaming.

Rhys had said to her, that evening of cider and black and pissing on medical sticks, that evening of fighting and her laughter, that she wasn't fit to be a mother. After a while, Chelsea would stop screaming, her sounds would soften, Bethan walking with her or only still, and Rhys's words would be wrong.

'Now, I won't disturb you for too long, I know you're busy.' It was ten forty in the morning. There was no more than a handful of people in the Shoreline Café. 'I just wanted to ask you if you'd seen something . . . might have been lying on the floor. I have a horrible feeling I dropped it.'

She had stepped out of the car while Bethan watched through the window, smoothing her skirt as she stood, reflections bright and cold across the Xantia's bodywork. Emyr Morgan had sat with his hands on the wheel, telling her – mute sounds to Bethan – that he'd only be ten minutes.

Gwen Morgan, Siân Humphries, her own mother, they made a circle around Chelsea and herself, every morning. Today Gwen only raised her hand, though, passing to stand at the counter with Patty and call through to Tom behind.

'A bracelet,' she said. 'I've looked everywhere at home, been through the house, top to bottom and I can't find it. I can only think I must have dropped it.' Outside sunlight caught on Emyr's car as he drove on down the road, out of sight. 'I always said that the clasp was too loose. I told the jeweller when he fixed it three years ago, and the man wouldn't listen. What can you do?' She nodded at Pat. They nodded at each other. 'Hate to say it but they're not honest people.

And now I've lost the thing. I don't know if you've seen it? It's very important to me. I'm sure you can imagine.'

'No, like . . . I can imagine,' Tom said. He stood in the kitchen's doorway, a cake slice in one hand and the memory of what he'd said to Rhys fading to stone as he saw Gwen's morning face. 'No, I've not seen it.'

'No . . .' Patty was saying. 'And you've had it so long . . .'

'Yes I have, yes I have.' Gwen only glanced at her. 'And, not that it's the most important thing, but it's worth a sum of money. Mostly the sentimental value but . . . Anyone who picked it up could sell it.'

'I don't think anyone would do that, Gwen, not sell it off. No one who comes in here would do that,' Patty said.

And Tom added quietly, 'There's no thieves in here.'

It was the last Bethan heard of it.

She sat with Gwen and her mother for a while, listened to words about the Meredith funeral, then to Pat talking about pre-school again, how important it was to social development. It seemed that the kind of development they spoke about was finding a place, a space that was the shape of your future, and fitting into it. She listened till they heard the Xantia pulling up outside. Until they looked up and, seeing Emyr there, fell silent. The bell above the café's door tinkled. He stood unmoving. He stared at them, mouth open. His grey hair lifted once in a breeze.

So shocked, he looked; like he'd lost sight of every landmark. For an instant, the time of day, the time of year, everything around him seemed to have migrated.

Rhys had taken the spray-paint from his father's garage that morning; had shaken it and heard the ball bearing rattle. Away from the morning sun, he had been cold.

He was sick. It had grown on him. With no plan, he'd taken the spray-paint can. With no plan, walking off, walking out of Ynys-morlan, passing the community centre, he had stopped. The light was hard, October-cool, fading the pavement and the clean brick walls.

Sick of this place and sick of the faces he passed. Sick of their expressions when they talked to him, or when they didn't even say hello. Two years, he'd seen it really, he'd heard it in their voices when they asked him how he was. Like the word 'Chelsea', unspoken, was linked to his fucking name. And he'd not cared; had ignored it. This morning, he was tired of that.

He could have called Tom, maybe got him to take the day off. Rhys kept thinking of him in the Lion last night though. Rhys hadn't looked at him as he'd left but Tom would have been watching him with Beth. He didn't want to talk, see sympathy.

He stopped walking, feeling the wind at his neck. Very new, that brickwork. And all the coloured cut-outs in the windows, pink and green and blue. It was four or five years old now, the community centre. Two pillars outside the main doors, like it was some kind of palace and a person would be privileged to get in there. He remembered acidly, Gwen Morgan spouting her shit, and that bracelet, the revelation. It was quiet out here at the end of town. The car park was empty. It was ten forty-five.

The place might as well have been made of paper. How much had it cost? Tens of thousands? Hundreds? Just so Mayor Morgan could bring the councillors round, they could sit and have meetings to plan other meetings when they'd make arrangements for their annual meeting. Sitting round the table in this giant fucking Wendy house.

He imagined Gwen Morgan, bent over that table, Tom behind her. He thought of the day when she'd stood in front of him, right out on the street, back when Bethan's stomach had started getting fat. Phantom pregnancies it had made him think of. He'd seen it on telly once. Bethan had looked like she was bloated out with morals and nothing but. And Gwen Morgan had stood in front of him, right out on the street, and asked him if he'd seen her. He'd wanted to say yes. He'd wanted to say that she was swelling so fucking fast that it was hard to miss her now. It had been two years ago, though. He'd been different then. He'd made some excuse and said he had to go. He remembered the sound of that gold bracelet jingling, cold and gold and heavy. And yesterday, the light shining off it as it hung from Tom's wrist like a trophy. Was it true? Could it be?

He'd wanted to say to Gwen that day: You know what she did? Got a good fucking screw is all. The very words would have shocked the woman silent.

Rhys glanced both ways before he stepped into the car park; he looked down the road in each direction. As he turned his head, Emyr was parked outside the café. Gwen was smoothing her skirt.

He walked around the community centre, past the row of white-framed windows. Inside, he could see, it was unlit. His footsteps scraped against the black tarmac as he turned the building's corner.

He shook the spray-paint can for maybe a minute, considering, looking at the wall. He held it out in front of him, arm's length just like it told you on the tin. He walked along beside the wall very slowly, moving his arm in small and gentle shifts while the letters on the bricks fell jagged.

Twenty feet long. He walked it twice. He took his thumb off the can and looked carefully at the indentation there, white at first, turning slowly to red as the blood flowed back, into his hand, his stomach, his mouth.

The white letters stumbled, crawled across the brickwork as if they were clinging on. Two lines of them and he didn't smile. Felt hollow. What a pretty building, the letters said. And underneath that, Ynys-morlan suck my cock.

He wanted to say them out loud. He wiped a hand across his mouth. They'd clean it off in twenty minutes.

When he heard the first footstep, standing there, still, some kind of gladness came before the fear. It was quick so that it was forgotten, but for a moment it flared in the quiet sunlight, to strike himself and the wall and this town. Quick, so that he'd be able to tell himself later, like Bethan's morals, it had never been there. From twenty yards away, it sounded. He turned towards the noise. Another quiet scraping. Past the doors, he thought, to hear it so clearly, past the doors. He could have run then. He looked in the other direction, the building's next corner, shining tarmac, black. A wall there, he saw, easy enough to jump over. He could have.

But he kept thinking of Gwen Morgan. The white letters that he'd scrawled across the wall were dripping, drying in the sun. Gwen's pursed lips and that look on Bethan's face last night, so close she must've studied. It was a stupid thing, a stupid thing to write, but he wouldn't run away from it, stumbling over that wall the way he'd stood in front of Gwen and stumbled over his own tongue.

Standing there, the sun was in his eyes as he watched, heard the footsteps drawing closer. He squinted into it, wanting to put his hand up for shadow, not doing so. The car park was silent. Wind touched his face.

Emyr Morgan walked around the corner and into Rhys's stare. He saw the graffiti. He saw in a moment what was happening here. In a moment, knew all.

'God . . .' The word slipped out of him as though he was only breathing.

The boy stood before him without moving, thick eyes, head almost shaved of hair. Emyr saw his expression, scrawled on his face and held up there, brazen and ugly as the writing.

'My God,' he said, his voice sounding more quietly than he'd intended as he stared at Rhys. 'You did this. This is you?' He stuttered over it, turning from the boy's face to the wall, back again. 'Come on then! Answer me? Did you do this? This . . . disgusting!'

The can was here in his hand. Rhys looked back at him.

'Vandalism,' Emyr found the right words – if not the tone, 'a prosecutable offence. Do you realize that? An *offence*. I could take you to court. Something like this, I could take you to court, no problem at all.'

Rhys looked: Emyr Morgan's face open with shock. He couldn't believe it, Rhys saw. Couldn't fathom it. They stood three feet away from each other, nothing but sun and spit between.

Emyr had looked back at his wife, driving away from the café, seen her straightening her shoulders before walking in. Looking after Dai, all her time had been bought up. The playschool. Eirian's house. Last night, he'd sat on the sofa with her, asked her, 'If there's anything on your mind, Gwen, because this has been difficult . . . if there's something you'd like to talk about, talk to me.'

'There isn't anything, Emyr,' she'd said. She'd looked up at him but only quickly; just, he'd thought, for the time she needed to. Dai had been sleeping in the guest room and all their home had been filled with dreamless quiet.

Thirty seconds ago he had parked at the roadside, forgetting which telephone numbers he'd come out for. He seemed full of some kind of indecision. Each time Gwen spoke to him, he felt it. Into this drift of worries and notions, the boy came. The boy had sprayed profanity across this wall. A dog, cocking its leg. Words like these, he didn't have the right to use the English language.

He stood before Emyr in some kind of over-jacket. Some utterly ridiculous puffed up thing, his trousers dragging on the ground.

Emyr's fist opened and closed at his side and he didn't notice. His own mouth so full of words now that they jammed behind his tongue.

'I know exactly who you are.' His voice caught in the breeze. 'If you think that I'll let something like this pass . . . let me tell you, you've got another think coming. I don't let a thing like this pass.'

Disgusting, he wanted to say again. He wanted to take the boy by his arms and shout it into him so that it would pierce through that expression.

Rhys said, throwing these stones in his eyes with each word, 'I don't give a shit.'

The man could've been wearing his chain of honour, this look on his face. He remembered Gwen, and her husband was just the same. Couldn't look at what was written there. It would stain his eyes. Right then, standing in silence in the car park, he could have taken Emyr Morgan.

'Children come here . . .' He shook his head, without comprehension. 'Children come and play here every day. Three-year-olds.'

'So?' He tried to think but couldn't. It was all that would come out of his mouth. 'So they can fucking read it then, can't they? They can . . .'

'You ungrateful little . . . bastard.' Emyr held his hand out, his finger. Like he could point to the wall and this boy would suddenly see it for what it was. 'Do you know how long this place took to build? Do you even have the slightest idea of how many hours, how much of people's time went into constructing this? A *community* centre. You know what that means? Community? You even recognize the word? My God, your parents' taxes paid for this! I bet that didn't even occur to you when you thought you'd just . . . Like some dog! Your parents, out working so that – '

'So you can build a great big fucking hall to have your meetings in,' Rhys said. He tried to find something to hold on to in the empty air. 'No one even comes in here, you know when my parents came in here? Jumble sale, fucking jumble sale! And they weren't buying stuff either. They were selling it.' He wiped the back of his hand across his mouth again. 'You've got no right to talk about my parents, like. Bet you don't even know who my parents are. You don't know your arse from your tit. Go on then. You tell me who my parents are.'

'I know damn well who your parents are. And I can tell you something, they'll be the first people I'll call. I think they have the right to know first that their son will be going to court.'

Rhys looked at him, his pale face and his pale hair, his pale fucking clothes. Behind his glasses his eyes had widened like just standing here was stretching him, and Rhys found his voice too loud. 'Names!' he said. 'Go on! Fucking names!'

The man turned his head away. 'I don't need to speak to you.' He wet his lips, the boy not running, nor even speaking now, only grinning. 'You don't deserve to *be* spoken to. People like you don't deserve a place in this community!'

'You can stick your community up your fucking arse if you think I want a place in it – ' his voice came cold, his hands were tight. He couldn't find the words he needed. Knew them and couldn't find them as Morgan turned back, some kind of loathing on his face.

'People didn't work to build this so that someone . . . who's so stupid, so downright thick that they can't think of any better way to spend their time than *ruining* it, what those people achieved . . . they didn't work so someone like you can live in their town. Spraying your profanity all over it!'

'Think you're so holier than thou, don't you?' Rhys shook his head. 'Think just because you walk round with a big chain of fucking medals round your neck you're better than anyone else. You and your wife!' He saw morals on the man's face but Morgan didn't know what morals were. Rhys could feel his own. They weren't easy fucking patterns. They were clouds. 'I don't want anything to do with your fucking town, your *community*. I'll be moving out quicker than you could push me. I hate you,' he said. He wanted it to ease what he felt. He wanted to spit out these feelings with the words but could not.

He looked at Emyr and didn't see the way the man's hands shook. Ten minutes ago he had sat in his car, looking at his wife, trying to say the right things. Now he stood, locked and motionless. He could have struck the boy.

Beside them both, the wet paint ran and dripped on the bricks. A beautiful building, Emyr thought. He had made out the plans for it. He and Gwen had found the funding, pound by pound. He wanted to tell the boy just what he'd done.

'You've no idea of decency, have you?'

'Fuck your decency.'

'I can see it in your face, you've got no clue. No respect. You're too . . . you're too ignorant to even know the difference between decent behaviour and . . . immoral.' He finally found the word himself, used it, used it. 'Immoral!' And then it came to him, dawned. 'I know who you are,' he said. 'I know exactly who you are! You're the one with the child, Bethan Hughes's child! Oh well! I've heard then! I don't need to say anything else. We know what you're capable of! This is how you spend your time, so. Writing dirty words on the wall like a little boy with Bethan looking after your child. Pathetic!' He said it again, saw Rhys's expression changing. 'Pathetic . . .'

Rhys strained to see him through the sun. 'Shut up.'

'What? Touched a nerve, did I? Well maybe you shouldn't give yourself the name if you're not prepared to wear it. Pathetic. Immoral.' Could have bullied it into the boy. He felt flooded with it. He looked at Rhys, only eighteen but a hulking, ugly eighteen. By his sides

Emyr's fingers twitched. And knowing then that he'd said it all, knowing he had made every point, he repeated it anyway. It seemed the first thing for days that was really clear to him.

'Shut up, why don't you?' Rhys asked him quietly. 'Shut your fucking mouth. You don't know about me, nothing. No fucking right to ride your high horse.' And then he took a step forwards, he moved like he could push his face into Emyr's, like he could grind his face in. Two feet apart now, he spat the words instead. And, even saying it, he knew it was wrong. He knew it before it came out of his mouth. 'You've no fucking right. You want to talk about immoral, like? I'll tell you about it.' It came out of him. He wanted to hurt the man, that was all. 'I'll tell you about immoral,' he said. 'How about your wife?' He heard his own voice. 'Your wife who walks round town like she just bought it, like she's too good to let her nose drop in case she smells everyone else. I'll tell you something you don't know, you know so fucking much. Know what your wife does between telling everyone else how they should run their fucking business? She gets into bed with an eighteen-year-old, that's what she does. I know him. I know him! How about that? *You like to talk about fucking immoral?*' He wanted to make Morgan see what he saw himself. Injustice.

But Emyr only said, 'What?'

'You *heard* me! You heard every fucking word I said!'

'What are you talking about?'

'*You fucking heard me!* Your wife! So don't you preach to me! Don't you try telling me what's moral and what's not! *You've got no right!*'

Emyr turned away. He turned back. 'Do you think for one minute I'm stupid enough to listen to your disgusting lies?'

Simple words which hung like strands between the gusts of wind.

'I know . . . well enough what comes out of your mouth. Only have to look at what you've done to this wall, see what sort of thing comes out of your mouth. That sort of lie . . . it's the last resort for you, isn't it? I know the level you'll sink to.'

But Rhys nodded with him, striking the rhythm of his words – they were nothing but defence.

'I'll tell you something . . .' the man went on. 'You go round talking lies like that, they'll be the last things you say, understand me? I'll have you in court, I'll have you in prison so quick you won't know what day of the week it is. Do you hear me, do you hear?' He looked like he would say something else. He didn't speak.

Rhys said, 'I wouldn't spread lies about you. Think I've got nothing better to talk about than you? I'm not a gossip like your wife.' His voice dropped low, though everything in him seemed to float now. 'You don't have to worry. I'm not going to tell.'

Emyr laughed, too loud.

'You don't believe me,' Rhys said, 'too stuck up to even think about it, aren't you. I tell you what. Why don't you ask your fucking wife where that pretty bracelet of hers has got to. You'll notice it's not round her wrist. I know who's got it. Wore it on his own the other day, he did. She gave it to him, nice little memento to remember her by. Why don't you ask her?'

Emyr only stood, he moved his hand, he pointed. He said, 'You're a specimen, you are. If I find her bracelet missing, I'll know just who's taken it. Liar. Have you up for theft as well as vandalism.'

'Your wife, she's the liar. Not me. *Not me!* You ask her!' And then, fists clenched with all the things he wanted to let go of, Rhys said, 'When did she last open her legs for you? Huh?' He heard his voice crack, he swallowed, turning away. 'When d'you last fuck her?'

Emyr didn't speak, he raised his hand. Truly, he could have struck him. Could have walked towards the boy, raised his fist, brought it down on his mouth. He looked at the size of him, though, only two feet away. He saw the hate in the boy's eyes. His hand only fell to his side.

'You little bastard,' he said. He tried to fill it with the emotions he saw in Rhys. He stood motionless in the fragile sun.

Rhys stared at Emyr Morgan, empty though nothing had left him. He saw the words he'd put on this wall. 'Don't talk to me,' he said, wooden-voiced. 'Don't ever talk to me again. You're the one . . . the disgusting one.' He looked at Emyr's face, one last moment. Found nothing else to say.

He turned away then, from Emyr, from what he'd written here in paint. He didn't look up again. Hollow and sick. He couldn't be here any more.

'Come back! Come on! Come back here then!'

But he walked away. Emyr's words drifted around him. He watched the ground move underneath his feet. Not running but walking.

'Come back here –'

But Emyr didn't go after him. Only watched him pass away across the tarmac. He didn't take even one step. Beside him, the white spray-paint ran down the bricks like spit.

'Little bastard . . .' he said. His voice trembled in the quiet. He swallowed. Above his head, he heard a gull call out. He stood there in the sunlit car park and his hands were shaking.

'Emyr . . . ?' she said.

She sat at a table with Patricia Hughes. And Emyr saw the boy's ex-girlfriend, and his daughter, there beside her. Their conversation trailed away, as insubstantial as the scents of cooking, chips and fish and beans, that escaped through the open door.

The street was quiet. He stood looking at the shadows' ruler lines, pale pebbledash, old chimneys now caught with the morning sun. He'd told them he'd had a call from Dai. That Dai had called him and they needed to go home now. Washing lines and rubbish bins, shaded front doors. He saw these few walking people. It didn't seem like his town. No it did not. When it had always seemed that way.

'I'm sorry.'

'Well don't be sorry. What did he say? Is he all right?'

Emyr got into the car. The buildings were glassy. The road waited.

Driving slowly then, always under thirty, always checking his mirrors, he told her the beginning of what had happened. He told her how he had walked around a corner and how the words had run down the wall. He spoke gradually, moved from point to point as though these were delicate questions. He could feel the adrenaline drain from him, his hands.

He kept looking at her. 'You know him,' he said. He said that it was the boy who'd left Bethan Hughes. 'You know his name,' he said, wanting her to repeat it; wanting them to be speaking about this together.

'Rhys.' She looked out through the windscreen.

'You wouldn't believe the filth. Where the children play. Where they play hopscotch, for God's sake. You wouldn't believe it,' he said, glancing at her.

'There are people like Rhys in every town, in every place in the world.'

'And then the lies started,' he went on. 'People like that fall back on lies, they retreat to lies. Lies about you,' he said. His voice was matter-of-fact, you could expect nothing else from a boy like Rhys. Emyr's tone was almost like hers.

They passed the gift shop as the houses thinned on either side, wide concrete spaces in the sun. Some way off, down the main road, he saw the flag flying, bright. 'The lowest shot he could take, of course. I tell you,' he said, 'if you gave that boy some slime to crawl through, he'd be down on his belly quick.' He looked at her.

Her hair was neat, washed and curled, her make-up perfect. Even looking after Dai these last few days, even up in the night, she found time to take care of herself. And to take care of him too, still cooking and cleaning. She had an ability to cope. She was the calm in the storm. He looked at her and remembered the things that Rhys had said. He reached out with one hand, touched her shoulder gently.

'Lies about me I could take. I don't care what someone like that says about me.'

'That's sweet of you to say, Emyr.' She nodded, looked away from him. The trees blended their fading leaves in passing. His hands were still now on the wheel.

The sound of their engine paled from the street as they drove out of Ynys-morlan. It left the dust and gravel settling, catching in the wind and scattering between houses which were quiet in the morningtime.

'What did he say then?' Gwen was asking him.

*

There was a sense of openness to this place, empty or crowded in the summer: a town that people moved through like this strew of dry sand. The houses, as close as though their spaces had eroded, held gardens full of debris. Guarded from the pavement by low stone walls, their furniture and toys, things abandoned since summer's end, grew slowly dirtier. All front doors huddled beneath their guttering from the rain – autumn, winter or spring.

Ruth Lewis's front door was hidden behind the red cab on the roadside, large and unbalanced without its trailer, the sky painted on its bodywork in many shades of red.

He'd driven yesterday, coming slowly back into Ynys-morlan with the worn-away evening and the wind. Walking towards the door, he'd looked at the roses on either side of Ruth's path that talked to each other of nothing but growing. And when he'd gone inside, seen Ruth getting up from the table, he'd said the words to her, 'Sick and tired,' as he'd moved past, towards his room, feeling relief.

His quiet room. A different silence, though, than in the rest of the house. Nothing ever changed in here, Ruth didn't come in here, to pick things up, move them. This room was static. Its window looked out over the bend of the main road that led out of Ynys-morlan. A few trees, growing less visible under yesterday's evening, the flagpole.

Bronze figures and their motionless kicks surrounded him, silver figures with wreath leaves and rugby balls which never flew. There were photographs of Nia and Ruth, framed. There were photographs of his mother and his father, his hand on her.

He could look out of the window and watch the flag; a ship's sail. He remembered standing there and staring at it with his father, his old man pointing down at the concrete base. Already worn by then. Already seventeen years old, and Lennie far younger. He remembered: 'See that there.'

The work had been planned for several of them, it had been planned for a couple of days, the plaque to be set in on the last. Lennie's father had done it in the space of one night and he'd done it alone. Lennie remembered squinting against a grey sky behind, as his father had told him why. Grass that had grown up, to draw it into the ground.

Lennie had climbed that flagpole on the night he had first gone out with Ruth. At the end it had been. They'd had a good fucking time that first night. He'd made sure of it; the best time. He'd asked her if she'd come to watch the match and it had been one of the best nights he'd ever played, his knee had been good round that time. He'd been a fucking bulldozer round that time. An Indian summer, long twilight. They'd gone out after with the rest of them. A lot of them, and when it had got too loud for her, he'd put his arm round her shoulders and he'd shouted at them to shut up in the presence of ladies. She'd laughed. That night he'd only had to say the smallest thing and she'd laughed. At the end he'd sat her on his knee and bounced her up and down in the middle of all that noise, and she'd only sat and held on to his shoulders, laughing, afraid to fall.

He had climbed the flagpole while she stood watching from the ground. They'd been alone by then, in only streetlight. He remembered looking down at her and seeing a pale shape, a pale face turned up, her arms around herself.

'I'm not going to catch you if you fall. I'm just going to move out of the way.' She'd shouted something like that. But it had been very quiet up there, just the sound of his own breath and the creak of the pole.

'My father put that up,' he'd said before.

'I know your father put it up. I've lived here all my life.' She'd smiled, showing that gap she had in her teeth. 'You just haven't noticed.'

'I've noticed.'

After a moment she'd said, 'Why did you ask me out, Lennie?' her voice all conversational, like she wasn't talking about herself. 'It's the question on everyone's lips,' she'd said.

'Why d'you think I asked you out?' He'd heard the sound of the flag's cloth shaking.

He remembered how the laughter had left her voice, those white arms of hers about her knees. 'Doesn't matter, forget it.' She'd looked at him like there was something underneath what she said: 'I had a good time.'

But it had mattered, it had bothered him. Sitting there next to her, he'd felt the way she'd gone all cold. Her posture had kept him away. 'I like you,' he had said. 'You don't believe me.' He'd laughed in the quiet and, when she had only nodded, reached out with his hand and turned her face to him, his fingers on her cheek. He'd wanted her to see it. 'I'll prove it to you.'

'I don't want you to prove anything. For God's sake,' she'd said. 'I just wondered. I was just asking.' She'd been embarrassed but he hadn't been.

'I'll fucking prove it to you.' He'd looked back at the flagpole. 'I like you a lot,' he said. The words hadn't come easily but he'd needed to say them. 'I will. I'll fucking prove it.' He'd pointed in the dark, his arm a ghost. 'D'you know how high that is? That's thirty feet, that is. Thirty-one actually . . .' And he'd got up, not even knowing what he was doing really. He'd wanted to look down at her from the top, call her name out from there. He hadn't wanted to sit there discussing things, stupid questions. He'd been drunk and he hadn't wanted to answer. Actions spoke louder than words.

'Lennie,' she'd said. 'For God's sake, I don't want you to prove anything. How are you going to prove anything by climbing up a flagpole? Lennie –'

He'd put his hands up and got a good grip on the metal, very cold beneath his palms, shadow-white. Around them the trees had shifted, black leaves moving. The town had been behind, people sleeping. Houses clustered. 'You watch,' he'd said. 'I've never done this for anyone. You'll see.' But he hadn't really known what he was trying to show her.

He had put his body against the metal and clamped the sides of his boots against it. He had climbed with the sound of his breath. It had been hard.

His father had been dead by then. By then, his father had been five years dead. It had felt good to climb the thing, the first edges of the town spread there in front of him in light and darkness. High up the pole the wind had bent it like a sapling and he'd held on as Ruth had grown smaller.

He had climbed past the leaves and his hands had been sweating. A foot at a time. Six inches at a time. The pole slimmer.

'Fucking see that!' Lennie had said. Loud enough that people sleeping might turn. 'Fucking see that . . .'

Below him, on the ground, Ruth hadn't answered. She'd stared up at him. He had seen the gift shop, the Spar, the first rows of houses stretched there. Pulled himself higher. And above the trees then, above it all, he'd touched the flag's cold cloth.

'See that,' he'd said. But there'd been no way that she could hear as he had clung on like a child. Distant from Ynys-morlan the land had been faceless-black and, far away, farther, against the slight sky, he had seen the mountains.

'Ruth!' he'd called. He hadn't known if she'd heard him. She hadn't answered or her voice had been lost.

As Emyr drove past the house that day, not looking at their front door or at the dusty cab outside, Lennie was remembering. He was thinking that he loved Ruth. The door was closed. The windows were closed. There was sunlight on Ruth's mother's roses.

Lennie was sitting on their bedroom floor. Memories recurring, as accusations, he was looking at what he had found.

Gwen's voice was normal because she could expect the worst from someone like Rhys. He could hear that in it. He opened his mouth several times.

He should have been relating this, calmly condemning it. It should have been something he told her later perhaps, over dinner, when they could have had the same expressions on their faces. Dai was in their house, though. He would be sitting with the television on, as it had been on for several days now. Formula one racing. A documentary on sparrows. Disney's *Anastasia*. He would sit forward always as if he could drag the television's pictures into his eyes. The blanket they'd given him on that first night would still be lying across his knees. When Emyr spoke, and he had to turn away from the programme, there was desperation in him as though, beneath his face, foundations were broken.

Emyr put his feet down gently: gently, clutch and brake. He drew to a stop.

She was wearing a blouse of silk and a silk tie at her neck. A pink colour which had always suited her. It was long-sleeved and he couldn't see her wrists.

'Emyr?' she said, in the quiet of the idling engine.

There was sun across her face, he saw, its light distorted by the window's glass.

'You're right. There are people like that in every town. You're always right.' And he shook his head, laughing a little for her. 'Why don't I always listen to you?'

'What did he tell you?' she asked again. 'Why are you looking at me that way?'

'Just looking at you is all.'

'You are not "just looking at me", Emyr. And you're lying to say that now. You must be the worst liar that I've ever seen.'

He looked away, touched the steering wheel. 'Yes well, there's no percentage in being a good liar. If I was the worst liar that'd ever lived, I wouldn't be ashamed.' He was edging towards it. Over the engine's low noise he could now hear the birds. 'I always tell you everything. It's just a difficult thing to say, that's all. So nasty, it's difficult to repeat. I'm not going to hide it from you, though. If you meet this boy in the street, I won't have you talking to him without knowing what kind of a person he is.' Emyr took a breath. 'The lies he resorted to . . . were the worst kind. You'd expect that from him, of course. The worst kind . . . sexual.'

He looked at Gwen, wishing she'd say something, touch his hand or something, make this easier. She was so small really, fragile underneath her neat clothes, her neat hair. She carried herself in this way, but she was tender underneath.

'Rumours as well as lies,' Emyr said. 'Because I'm sure he'd have no qualms about spreading them. Rumours about you. And a boy.'

Outside, through the glass, the wind turned branches. On the road in front of their idling car, shadow patterns moved.

'It took me by surprise. Going out to get some phone numbers, nice sunny morning. And then this.' He remembered telling her once that she had an aristocratic bone structure. Like a princess, he'd said. He hadn't told her things like that for a long time, complimented her that way. He thought suddenly that he took her for granted now. He reached across the small space to touch her hand. He felt it and it was cold. She took it away from him.

'I'm sorry,' he said.

'For what now?'

'Barging in on you . . . dragging you off. Taking this too seriously.'

She didn't look at him, though. She stared through the glass. 'That's not what you're sorry for at all. At least be honest with me. You're going to talk about honesty, at least be honest. Why don't you just come out and ask me?'

'Ask you what?' Emyr's hand left behind, lying where hers had been, they sat in the quiet. 'I've got nothing to ask you,' he said. 'I resent that.'

'You resent it.' Gwen nodded slowly. She held herself carefully. 'Myself and a boy. This rumour,' she said, 'you were going to ask me if it was true.'

'No,' he told her. 'No.'

The little wooden box had flowers painted on its lid. Pink and yellow roses. He had given it to her when Nia was born, for keeping mementos in. Now it lay upside down on the carpet. It lay open and empty.

Below this room, Ruth was moving.

She couldn't have reached that far under the bed. She must have taken something, a broom. He looked at what he'd found and he thought of the way she'd smiled twenty minutes ago, talking about lunch.

He got up very carefully from the floor. He picked the wooden box up.

He'd had it wrapped properly in the shop with a gift tie. He'd handed it to her, lying in the hospital bed. 'To remember this by,' he'd said. Her face had been hot and pink and swollen. He had seen Nia, little red thing, frowning in a way that looked almost grown-up.

He had thought for such a long time about the right way to celebrate this. He remembered how she had smiled back and the sterile smell of the ward.

Lennie stood for a moment in the corridor, looking at Nia's open doorway, and then he reached out carefully, moved the doorstop with his foot and swung it shut without looking inside at her.

Hidden under the bed, he thought. Hidden. The word seemed new, an alien object. This house was so tidy, so homely, so clean – she would walk around polishing – there couldn't be a hiding place in any one of these rooms. The open bathroom door, he saw, the washing basket in a splash of sun. He moved past, knowing nothing about the dirty clothes balled up inside, in pillow cases, touched by the tiny spots of sunlight that reached through the wicker weave. Their open bedroom doorway left behind him, sunlight motionless there too: across the bed, the wardrobe's wooden doors. Lennie moved down the staircase, not recollecting any more the books which, still wrapped in their carrier bag, were now kept down there in shadow. But he looked at this box and he could feel the lies forming, in these walls he could feel them, revealing themselves.

Standing outside the kitchen, he watched Ruth's back. She was making sandwiches, he saw. She had three little plates, all laid out.

'Ruth,' he said. He watched the way she turned around and gave that broken jigsaw smile of hers. The way it faded as her eyes trailed down to what he held.

'Lennie –' But she didn't say anything else, her mouth fell closed and he was glad because he didn't want to hear lies coming from her lips or see them in her eyes now.

He showed her the box that he had given her to remember Nia's birth. He showed her the money he had found inside it, hidden under his bed.

'Ruth,' he said. His voice was quiet and he looked at her, standing in the streams of sun that fell, all the miles down here, to pass through their kitchen window. The table was between them. He moved so the table wasn't between them. 'Ruth,' he said, holding his palms out.

*

'You hedge around it as though you're trying to trap me into saying something.'

'That's not true, Gwen . . .'

'It is true. That dog face, as though you can't bear to say the words.'

Emyr opened his mouth. 'Please,' he said.

'Well don't ask me "please". Looking down at my wrist every five seconds –'

'What?' Emyr said.

'I . . . Staring at me, that's what!' She moved her hands, she moved under his stare. 'Looking me up and down, checking to see if anything's changed . . .'

'What did you say?'

'You heard what I said. You wanted to ask me, you were just building up to ask me. All that talk about lies, about rumours, and you don't trust me yourself. That's why you drove me out here, isn't it? Isn't it?' She kept talking, she pushed the words out through her teeth and her gaze didn't touch on him once, nor even the shifting trees at which she stared.

All these words, as if, one after another, they could cover what she had said. And he only sat. He only looked at her.

'That's what,' she said. 'That's what.'

He saw how clear her anger was, the way she gripped her bag. Like she could turn on him. Like she was afraid she would.

Around them the car shuddered and died. He spoke slowly. 'Looking down at your wrist, you said.'

She sat rigid in the passenger seat. Her mouth might have been moving, framing every word she thought of and rejected. There was only the sound of the birds.

'Why did you say that?'

'Well that's what you were doing, wasn't it? Looking for something, obviously. You kept doing it.'

He heard himself say, not quite believing it. 'Did you lose your bracelet?'

'My bracelet? What has that got to do with anything? What are you talking about?'

Her face was bare with it, though. 'You're lying.'

'Lying? I didn't even say anything! I asked you what you were talking about.'

'You look so angry,' he told her.

'I'm not a liar!'

Emyr turned from her. He put one hand over his mouth as though he would decide something now. They were only a few minutes from the door. He looked at the wheel, the ignition key hanging loose. He had a wooden keyring there with his name on it. He could turn the ignition key now, he thought. Just take off the handbrake and drive home to where Dai would be sitting on the sofa. He could be silent, not speak to her at all, until there were fine, normal things to say.

He almost reached for the keys. His hand fell to his lap. He looked at her and didn't even recognize what was in her expression. He thought of the way he'd stood outside the café, looking at the street as though it wasn't his.

'What is this?' he said.

But she just talked.

'Be honest with me,' he said, and could not remember ever saying that to her before.

'I think it was stolen,' she said. 'I may have lost it but I think it was stolen.' She lied to him like he was a stranger. He thought of the way he'd lain in bed next to her on the night that Eirian had died. She had moved away from him, not telling him the way she felt, not wanting him to help her. She'd come home hours too late and she'd been angry with him.

'Stop talking like that,' he said.

'Don't tell me –'

'You're lying to me. I can tell. Just stop it. Just stop it.'

Those moments then, he'd never wanted to touch her so much. As if only by reaching out she would be herself again.

'The boy . . .' He couldn't speak Rhys's name now. 'You know what he said? He said that you've been with someone. He said you gave your bracelet to . . . this person. That he saw it round their wrist. A memento, that's what he said.' There was silence. 'Can you believe that?'

'Not, "Can you believe that?"' she said quietly. 'What you mean is, "Is it true?"'

Autumn scattered its breaths along the lane and, in the car here, left them untouched.

'Finally it comes out,' Gwen said, 'the question. Well does it feel better to have it off your chest? You've been trying to ask it for half an hour. Feel better? What would you like me to say?'

'I'd like you to say the truth. I'd like . . . I don't know,' he said. She sat far away from him, the very edge of her seat. She could not have moved any further. 'Tell me it's not true,' he said. 'Tell me what's wrong. Just look at me.'

'For God's sake, Emyr! It's not true.'

'Then why can't you look me in the eye?' She was angry and still seemed so calm. She knew exactly what to say, knew everything, and she sat there and kept it to herself. 'You hate liars. You're . . . you're a moral person, you have principles.' Things which sounded trite, things so important to him. 'It's one of the reasons,' he said, 'and there are lots of reasons . . . why I love you. I've never met anyone who cares about what's right and what isn't like you do. You hate liars.'

'You don't need to tell me what I believe. I'm not lying. I never have lied, especially not to you.'

He didn't speak, his mouth was wet.

'That boy is a liar,' she said. 'I would never do anything . . . even approaching what he said.'

Awkward she sounded, though. Trying to fit her words around something unsaid. Staring out through the glass, she rearranged her hands, and he realized that she wasn't calming her anger, but struggling.

'I . . . simply wouldn't do it,' she said. 'Regardless of you, I wouldn't.'

Emyr felt hollow. These were the words she used in her difficulty: regardless of you.

'But I won't lie to you,' Gwen said quietly. 'And I won't shirk the blame either, I've never done that, never believed in doing that.' She cleared her throat. 'I'll take blame, in that I put myself in the situation. It was no one's fault but mine . . .'

'What situation?'

And he watched her then; taking that blame and so absolving herself. Looking out through the glass as though she'd brought him here to tell him this. Unflinching. The leaves shifted and he heard those birds, a cloud passed over the sunlit car.

She said, 'On the night that Eirian passed away, I was very upset. We were all upset, but I was especially . . . especially. There were things she said to me before she passed away, that had no reason behind them. Hateful things. I don't mind saying that. It's true. I'm not sure why she'd bear a grudge against me. I said it to her, I'd done nothing but try to help, never criticized her in any way at all, never . . .' She finished this with a nod. 'When she passed away, I was sad as anyone else. I was also left remembering everything she'd said to me. The manner . . . and I'm not immune. I'm sure there are people like Rhys who are quite happy to believe that I don't have any feelings at all . . . She criticized everything about me,' Gwen said suddenly. It fell from her. 'Every little thing. Oh, there wasn't any part of me that she left out. She must have been thinking up the speech for days before she had the chance to say it to my face. Do you know what she told me, Emyr? She told me people hated me. Yes. She told me she hated me. She said . . .' Gwen took a breath, she looked downwards, gathering herself. 'She told me that I had nothing. How do you like that? Nothing – and that that was the reason I looked after her, nothing better to do than . . . traipse after her. I was very upset. I went . . . to the beach. I walked a long way, I suppose I needed to think, I kept remembering . . .' She turned to him and for a small moment looked like she was close to breaking. She was so still, all the time, so still. In that moment, only sitting and staring at him, she looked like things might overrun. If she had ever been this way before, she had never shown him her face.

'Gwen –'

'Let me tell you, Emyr. At my own pace. I was crying. I'm sure that people like Rhys don't believe I'm capable. But I'm just as capable as anyone else. I was crying. I was in a state.' She talked as though she were reading a list. He watched her fall into this and he didn't say her name again, or anything. She talked that way until she'd finished. She told him that she had been crying, that a boy had come to her.

She said that he hadn't been intending anything, only asking her if she was all right. Folding her hands in front of her, she told him how she had lost her bracelet. Describing this, her voice faltered, as it did in no other part. She had thrown it to the floor. "Upset," she said again. She continued. The boy had kissed her. For a moment, she had let him, not knowing what to do. She had let him kiss her. She had left.

'Nothing but a kiss, Emyr,' she said. 'And I was hardly the one to . . . to initiate it. It was a small thing,' she said. 'A kiss.'

He said nothing.

'I left. It happened very fast and I left.'

He saw her: she was remembering.

'For God's sake,' she said. 'Do you think I would have an affair? Me? How many years have you known me, Emyr?' She looked away from him and her voice was transparent. 'Me, of all people. I'd hardly be the one.'

Emyr stared at his hands as these things filtered through him. They fell through water, turning slowly, and he lost them as the light faded.

'For God's sake, Emyr. It was a kiss. A small thing.'

'It's not a small thing,' he said slowly. 'Sometimes . . .' He didn't want to tell her. He wanted to give her a chance, though, to understand. He settled his voice. 'Sometimes I try to kiss you and you don't want me to. You turn away or you say something to . . . break the moment. Do you know what I mean? You do that a lot. It's not a small thing then,' he said. He looked at her as though, with a clear enough gaze, he could give her understanding. She seemed so cold, though. She moved her hands. She was so sure of what this meant and he didn't know how she could be. 'It's not a small thing.'

'Yes it is! Think! Think, will you?'

Emyr turned away from her.

Those trees moved.

'It was nothing,' she said.

'How long did it last for?' he asked her.

'It doesn't matter –'

'How long did it last for? Did he kiss you . . . did he kiss you deeply? Did he try to touch you? Did he hold you like that? How long?'

'Emyr . . .'

'You sound so fine,' he said.

She told him that she sounded fine because there was nothing to be troubled over. She said that there was nothing to be troubled over because it had meant nothing. He saw her, so logical. One thought leads to another, that to another, and at the end there was nothing for him to feel hurt over. When she had sat with Dai on the sofa, telling the man it was all right, she had looked nothing like this. There was glass in her face now.

Emyr said, 'How old was he then? A boy. What was his name?'

'You don't know him. I didn't know him.'

'Tell me,' he said, he tried to raise his voice, 'tell me the details then. Why don't you do that? Tell me if he touched you . . . If you ran away. Did you just stand there? Tell me something! Can't you just look at me and tell me something? Can't you be upset now?'

Perhaps he didn't really want to know, though. Perhaps he only wanted her to turn to him, to speak and have her voice break, to cry. He couldn't have remained as she did now. Seawater cool as sunlight drifted down around them.

'You don't even care.'

'Of course I *care* –'

Of course.

'What do you mean anyway? *"Care?"*' she said.

He looked into her face and had never felt so remote.

'I feel like I don't know you,' he said.

'You know what I just thought? Standing here, I just thought, I wonder if she'll lie to me. And I can always tell, Ruth, you know that. Watch her face, I thought to myself. First expression . . . I don't know what this is.' He raised the money upwards. 'I don't know why you hid it from me. But I know guilt when I see it.'

Gwen made them lunch as Emyr watched her. She seemed to gain from everything around her, standing at the counter, taking out bowls from the place where she kept them, spoons. She cleared the table in front of him and arranged bread and butter and salt and pepper in the centre like a still life there.

Every time she caught his eyes, she was trying to give some of her normality to him.

She put a bowl of soup down in front of him. 'Do you want some bread now, Emyr?' She put it down beside the bowl of soup because he didn't answer. French bread cut into rounds.

Emyr said quietly, 'Do you remember when you got the flu? You were lying in bed all weekend and I made you soup. Do you remember? I burned the bottom and you said I could burn water.' He remembered: her face, soft and pale in the curtained light, her hair a pillow mess. Every morning, taking her temperature. She was very rarely ill.

She picked up another two bowls and brought them to the table. 'Yes, I remember.' She called out for Dai. 'It's lunchtime, Dai. Come and eat it at the table now,' voice gentle for him. She stood with the sound of the television, not looking at Emyr, only into the living room.

'Gwen – Gwen, come here,' Emyr asked her.

'We're going to eat lunch, Emyr . . . Dai?'

'Just for a second. Give me a kiss?' he said. 'Yes?'

'Emyr, I'm not going to kiss you now.'

Dai came in to sit down. He was wearing the same clothes as when he'd come to them that night, though she had tried to give him Emyr's. His hair stuck out, flattened to his head in other places where he'd pushed it down. He sat in front of them, and the carefully laid meal, wreck-eyed as he picked up the spoon. And the room, Emyr felt, was full of silence.

Gwen said, 'Do you like the soup, Dai? Tomato? Is that all right for you?'

'It's nice. Thank you,' he said.

Gwen was eating now, taking her own spoon to her mouth and then buttering bread. She reached for the salt-shaker from the centre of the table. He wondered how she might respond if he asked her now, over lunch and before Dai Meredith, whether she still loved him. Something like that could not be said. In the gentle turn of midday, the seasons passing slowly outside their window, he might shout, strike the table, and the noise of his voice or the violence in his hands wouldn't even touch these things.

'Look at you,' Lennie said, 'I can almost see the gears working: what should I say? will he believe that? I can see it, Ruth. I gave you this box when Nia was born. I thought for weeks of what would be the right thing. I had all these ideas, like photograph albums and a camera. But they weren't the *perfect* idea. I remember when you were packing your hospital bag, like, I was trying to think of it . . . And now I find it hidden under the bed with seventy pounds in it. I counted it. Seventy. I don't know –' he said, and he stopped to adjust the tone of his voice. 'I don't know where you'd get seventy pounds.'

Ruth stood in the kitchen, half-made sandwiches across the counter-top, the butter knife still in her hand.

'I can see why you'd hide a bit from me, like. Get a bit of money without your husband knowing, put a bit aside for some shopping every now and then. That what you were doing? Saving up to go shopping?' Last week, he had given her thirty pounds extra. Get something nice, he'd said. He'd pulled it out; crumpled tenners. The notes he held now were very flat, they'd only been folded once. 'You've not got on anything new,' he said. 'I got that jumper in Aber for you, got those trousers from your cousin last birthday.' He moved his hand conversationally, holding the ten-pound notes. 'Been shopping yet then? Or were you saving up?'

'I haven't been shopping,' Ruth said to him. 'I haven't spent any of it, that's all there was. Seventy. I wouldn't just get seventy pounds and go and spend it on shopping, Lennie. I wouldn't do that. We haven't got the money to do that . . .'

'What d'you mean, we haven't got it? You reckon that, but you get seventy pounds and you hide it from me.' He watched her mouth move, deciding what to say, and he could see her trying to lie, trying to pull the pieces back together, gather them over herself.

'I didn't say that we've not got enough money, I didn't mean that.

I haven't spent any of it. I was saving it. Seventy pounds, that's all there was. And I wasn't hiding it from you.'

Lennie held his hand out, and the money, very straight. Close to her but he moved closer. The kitchen counter was behind her and she had no place to retreat to.

'Look,' he said. 'Look at it then, look at it.' Between the wall and the money he held there was room for her lies still. She pulled her eyes away. Tried to keep a gap between them. 'Where did you get it? Why did you hide it?'

'I was saving it, I told you. I wanted to wait and then we could spend it on Christmas, I was waiting until I had some more –'

'More?'

Outside, wind tossed in the flower beds, the weak nasturtiums. It rippled through the lawn. Ruth looked pretty in the sun. Caught like this, she looked suddenly different. Her face was frozen and despairing. She looked beautiful.

'I won it on a scratch card, and I know what you think about them, but I couldn't resist it. I was just standing in Spar and it was there. And I thought: what if? And I just bought it on an impulse, I don't do it all the time because I know what you think and I think the same, you know? They're a waste of money. They wouldn't sell them if they weren't the ones making it all. But I just thought: what if? And I won.'

'More, you said. Waiting till you got more.'

'Well, if you can win once.' She shrugged and gave him something, a laugh. Like he couldn't see her, couldn't hear her tone. Was blind.

'I don't believe you.'

'It's the truth.'

'You think I'm stupid.'

Upstairs, above their heads, they heard a small noise. Nia moving in her room.

'I won it,' Ruth said.

Lennie turned away from her and closed his eyes like they were stones.

'Last week, in Spar.'

She did it like this, repeating.

'You look ugly when you lie,' he said. 'You sneak around like a fucking child. And I won't be lied to by my own wife when I'm holding the proof in my hand. Like a fool, do you understand me? Don't turn away from me! Don't turn away!'

'*Please* –'

'Please what?'

'*I'm sorry!*'

'I shouldn't have to tear the truth out of you! I'm your husband!'

He watched her raise her face to him, pale in this sun. 'You're right,' she said. And she was trying, he could see that. 'You're right. Let's sit down. I'll leave the lunch and we can sit down, I'll make some tea. Lennie, I don't want to lie to you, OK? I love you.'

'I'm not going to sit down, like.'

'We can talk about it –'

'We can talk about it right now. Tell me.'

She gestured with her free hand, the other, hanging by her side, still held the knife as though she'd turn round in a moment and start making lunch again.

'It's nothing really. I met this lady –' she said, and told him.

Lennie was silent. Holding the money, his hand felt heavy.

'It was stupid not to say to you, but I didn't know if it would work out. I didn't know if she'd change her mind. You know what people are like. And I didn't want to go round crowing about it and telling everyone and then have her say, you know, that's it. Thanks for your help but I don't need it.' She laughed, a shifting breeze. 'You know me,' she said.

He looked away from her in the quiet, at the ten-pound notes. He tried to imagine her, having this chat with this woman and then his own return, her silence. They must have talked about things that night. He tried to imagine Ruth changing her clothes to go off to this place, after he'd left the house, unknowing. He thought of the way that he'd sat in the Lion and told Rhys to give that girl some money.

'You didn't just not tell me,' he said.

Ruth stood, her head down, only six inches from him, from his hand. And when she finally turned her face up to him, something was lost from it. Her words dropped like scraps of paper to the floor. 'I love you.'

Quiet fell in the day's light across his hands. Held out to her like she could help him. 'Ruth,' he said.

Holding her then, he said other things.

The kitchen doorway behind him was open. Dried flowers on the hall's little table there. Light beige carpet leading up to the second floor. The stairs were empty in shadow. There was the sound of Lennie's voice. The noises he made drifted up to the landing, and then Ruth's voice as well. The doors were open, their bedroom and the bathroom, spaces vacant in these unbalanced sounds. Flower paintings hung there neatly. Wild geraniums and poppies under glass.

Nia's door was still closed. She was sitting on the floor of her bedroom, the walls covered with their floral paper. They'd been white when this room had been Ruth's, but this pattern, chosen specially, was brighter, warmer. In places, Ruth had stuck up the pictures Nia had drawn: stick people on green grass, looking out, side by side. The sun was passing now. Nia's hair was tidy. Ruth had brushed it half an hour ago.

Now Ruth's voice made a sound. The noise settled through every room like dust, like a year's worth, on the carpets she'd vacuumed this morning. Nia had her legs crossed, one wet strand of hair in the corner of her mouth, concentrating. From down here the room looked different: the bed above her, the desk above her. From down here it was a room of heights. Nia watched Eeyore walk past her knees. She turned him slowly and watched him walk back again as the noise fell around her, as it settled, like dust would on her hair.

'She wouldn't take it,' Rhys told Lennie Lewis that afternoon.
'Wouldn't take it?'

'That's right.' He didn't glance at the man.

'She's got some pride on her. I've seen her.'

'Fuck her pride. She chose to stay here. She wants to act like that
makes her a martyr, so holy, fuck her. Nothing's holy about this
shitheap.'

'Let me tell you something, Rhys. You're nothing but eighteen so
I'll forgive that. Let me tell you something about what matters in this
life. Ynys-morlan's your home.'

'So what? What does that mean? Means nothing.'

'You want to live in some place that doesn't know you?' Lennie
asked him. 'Your home, your family, those are the things that make
you. The things that let you know who you are.'

'She's no family of mine. And the kid she's had? That kid's a choice,
like. Might not ever have been here. There's nothing in this place that
lets me know anything, anything about myself.'

Lennie was silent for long moments, the day's first pass of rain –
the sound of it against the window behind them – like a distance. 'I'll
tell you a story about family,' Lennie said. The sun was gone now. It
was three o'clock. Only that. In the Lewises' kitchen, Ruth sat alone
and quiet like this day's easiest ending. 'I'll tell you,' Lennie said, 'a
real story about family.'

There was no cosy hearth here, no horseshoes hung on the walls,
polished to glow sepia-toned and false as memories. Bill wouldn't
buy the old signs; the antique tools that came by the yard and meant
nothing more than that you could charge seven fifty instead of four
seventy-five for a fisherman's pie. Nets you could get, he'd said to
Lennie once, that had never seen saltwater. Half-boats you could buy,
to jut from the wall like some tourist's daydream.

Lennie picked up his drink and wet his mouth. Rhys's hands, as he
watched him, cupped his glass, touches of spray-paint white around
his nails and nothing open in his eyes.

'My mother was nineteen,' Lennie said, 'when my father proposed, six months older than you but she'd been engaged before that. She'd been engaged and she'd been given the ring, though by the time my old man asked her, that ring was sitting in a box by her bed, not on her finger any more. Cheap thing, it was, he said.' He laughed a little, was silent. 'She was lovely, my mother. And you don't need to take his word for that, you can have mine because I've seen the photographs. She could have won a beauty contest, she could. Could have won Miss United Fucking Kingdom, and I'm not exaggerating now. Can look at my ugly face and say you don't believe me but it's true. Fucking beautiful, and he'd had his eye on her long before that ring came off her finger. He'd had his eye on her while she was talking about setting a date. She wasn't from here. Llan-y-bont, she was from. And the boy she was engaged to.

'My father was older now, twenty-six he must have been, twenty-seven. Working hard by then and not labouring either. Had four or five men himself. Can-do attitude, he had. By the time he first saw my mother, he was getting the council jobs already. Getting ready to put that flagpole up. You know it, outside town. "Don't say can't if it's won't." By the time he saw my mother, that attitude was well set in, I bet.

'Said he saw her on that boy's arm to start with. He wasn't the sort of man to change the little details in stories. Keen on the truth. I won't have people lying with me and it was him I got that from.' Lennie nodded, he drank and held the glass in front of him. 'He saw her on the boy's arm, and I say "boy" like he did, but he wasn't a boy at all. Built like a brick shithouse. They were the words my old man used.' He laughed. 'He saw them together, this boy showing her off like he'd bought a new motor. Ugly bastard, my father said, and God knew what she was ever doing with him. He saw the ring she had on, though. Was two weeks after that, he said, he bumped into her when she was on her own.

'He fell in love with her. Didn't know what hit him, he told me. Went up to her and they got talking. Thirty seconds with her, he said, and he couldn't take his eyes away. Except to look down at that ring. Blonde hair down her back. Curly hair.' Later in her life she'd never worn it long, that Lennie could remember. He took a last swallow, Rhys watching him through the smoke that moved between. 'Most fantastic thing that God had seen fit to mould up with his hands, my dad said. Was everything about her. The way she moved, the way she smiled, him telling joke after joke just to get that smile to come up again. Said he could have fallen in love with her just for the way she held her change, counting out money he'd given her for the drink. It's what love does to you, like.' He smiled. 'Makes you fucking mad. Madly in love, that's what they say, isn't it? Madly,' he held his smile for a long time before it broke away. 'Said he could've just held on to her arm so she couldn't leave when she got up to. He saw the look on her face, though, like she was starting to get guilty. And he didn't want her to feel that, or she wasn't going to be meeting him again. He let her go, after she'd promised to see him. After she'd set a time and place.

'Three times, they met up, and he said it was two times longer than he needed to know that he had to have her. He told her. He told her a lot of times.'

Rhys nodded, watching him, nodded slowly.

'They'd set a date, though, her and this boy. Three months' time, and she was getting the dress ordered. They were talking about fucking colours and invitations by then.

'"Put it off," he told her. "Cancel it," he said. And she gave him every excuse under the sun. She didn't want to marry the boy but she wouldn't cancel it. Not by then. So my father just nodded. The last time he saw her, just nodded. He told her, if that was the way, that was the way he'd live with it.

'He went back to work, doing that flagpole's foundations. They'd had that plaque made ready. He went back to Llan-y-bont, though. Like I said, can-do attitude. Once he'd set his sights on something, he didn't let it go.

'Took a while before he saw the boy again. He waited round the pub, got to know the landlord, like, got to know a lot of people. And once people met my father, they liked him, simple as that. Told them he was doing a job outside town and he was in that pub most nights for a while. And when the boy did come in, my father got to know him too. Only one night it was, but like I said, once people met my old man, they liked him. Didn't even need a whole night for it.

'Got him going on the rings, my father did. Not for money, not at first, but he had the money on him. He'd been paid that night, you see.' Lennie smiled. 'The job he was doing just outside Llan-y-bont was over, he said to them, and he'd just got paid.'

'Rings.'

'Yes, rings. Don't need them now, like, since landlords got pool tables and realized they could charge a quid a fucking game. Rings.' He made a circle with his hands. 'Know what a ring is, don't you? They had a box, six-inch nail sticking out of it, like, and a few holes behind that. You can work the rest out for yourself: a nail and some rings.' Looking out at the stone wall, Lennie saw memories which were too old to be his. 'He won a few games but he lost most. He made sure that he lost most, and not so you'd notice it. Then they started playing for money, him and this boy, and my father winning just enough to keep in. But losing really. Steadily.

'He was a nice enough boy, that's what my father said. I told you he was no liar. Would've been easy to say to me the boy was a cunt. Could've said the boy was mean, had a loose tongue, talking about my mother, dirty mouth, like. That wasn't the case, though. The boy asked him if he was married.

'"I wouldn't be in the pub, playing rings right into the evening if I was married," he said. And then my father asked the boy if he was. Just to see what he'd say.

'"Almost. Almost, like." Said he was engaged to marry the most beautiful girl he'd ever seen. He said they'd set a date for a couple of months' time. Said my father could come.

'So the boy goes to go home. It's ten o'clock, like. He's got a job. He says, "That's it."

'And my father goes to him, "Well give me a chance to win my money back."

'The boy says, "Haven't got another whole night."'

Lennie smiled, he looked at Rhys.

He said, 'Once, my father told me this. Only once. I've got the whole thing up here, word for word. This is how he told it.'

The pub was empty around them now, the bandit made empty winning sounds.

'He bet five quid on the next game. Doesn't sound a lot now, like. If the boy didn't have all night then he'd win it back in one game. Smiling while he said it. He had this fucking grin. Must've been the grin that convinced him because there was no way their bets had added up to five quid through the night. Must have been the smile.

'They played for five quid. My old man'd been losing all night, can't blame the boy for thinking he'd lose again. Didn't know him. My old man won.

'So now the boy's down, and not just down by a bit. He's down by enough to play another game. "Five pounds again, like?" my father says, and then the boy's ten down. He gets down to twelve before my father starts letting him win again, down to twelve, he goes, then right back up again. Back up to my father owing him thirty-five quid. Near a week's wages.' Lennie spoke quietly, 'They're pissed by now, and it's late enough that other people are picking up coats. He says thirty-five quid down is enough for him in one night. "You see that?" he says to the landlord. "See that?" And then they leave to get the money.

'Cold night, he said. See your breath. They talk about a lot of stuff, walking out to the van, because the van's a way out of town. Not that the boy notices after what he's drunk. Not until he gets there anyway and then he tells my father that they've just walked a fucking mile and what's the van doing out here? He says the job's out here. Or it was out here. Being as it's over now.'

'It's a lay-by, a little lane, nothing bigger. Not enough of a road to have cars driving past this time of night. He said the boy stood with his hands in his pockets while he opened up the doors. Van had a light in the back. I remember it myself.

'And my father says, "I have to tell you something." He says, "I don't like to be lied to. Hate it, in fact."

'The boy says, "I haven't lied to you, like –"

'But my father just shushes him. He says, "I know you haven't. And if you listen instead of bursting in, then you'll know what I mean." He leans against the open door. He says, "I know you're not a liar, I can see it in your face and it's a shame. Tell you the truth," he says, "I wish you were. I like you," he says. And the boy doesn't butt in again, this brick shithouse boy, because he's standing in an empty road, a mile from town, and he might be a big ugly bastard but I tell you something, my old man's just as big. He doesn't butt in again.

'"I can see you're no liar, I'm the one that's been lying. See, I know you," he says. "You told me your name earlier and I pretended like I didn't know it, but I did. I came out here for another reason than to give you your money, like. You can have the money. But I came out here – brought you here – to ask you a question too. Like I said, you can have the money. If you answer the question right." Standing like that, looking at the boy in the light from the van, he says, "You ready? Here's the question. Will you call off your wedding?"

'He says, "What d'you mean, call off the wedding? What are you talking about?" He says, "I don't know what this shit is, your asking me that. I'm not going to call off the fucking wedding. Don't know what you're talking about." That's what he says.

'"All right. I'll tell you what I'm talking about. I'm talking about the woman you think you're marrying. I don't want you to marry her because I'm going to ask her myself. That's what I'm talking about."

'The boy turns away. The boy can't believe what he's hearing, and he doesn't know what to do. But he says no. That's the thing, like. Because he must have been afraid. But he said no. That's the thing about love.'

They sat together in the close and smoke-strewn quiet as Lennie told him.

'It was the boy that threw the first punch. He got a good one in, my father let him get that. Then he took him down on the tarmac, he put his knees over the boy's shoulders and he held his arms down that way. He hit him on one side of the face. The same side, each time. Other side was dark,' Lennie said quietly, remembering just how his old man had told it. 'Just that one light from the van. Hit his nose, his cheekbone, got his head up by the hair and took it down against the road. Sitting on his shoulders.

'The boy got him over once, got him on to his back, and that was the only time he was scared. Sitting on him like that, the boy could have reached into the back of the van. There were a lot of things in the back of the van that he could have used. He didn't do that, though. He was drunk and he was hurt. Maybe he didn't think to look.

'He got the boy in the stomach, though. Just once, with his knee. And it was only a moment, only a moment that the boy let go. He put his hands into his collar, he pulled him off and he rolled him back on to the road. He held him down under the van's door. Said he could hear his breath, so quiet. There wasn't screaming, there wasn't anything like that.

'He had to spread his legs to hold both the boy's shoulders down. That was how wide he was. And he hit him in the same place, used the heel of his hand because his hand was broken by then. He got him under the arms and he dragged him up on to the edge of the van, his head and his neck, over the edge and then his shoulders. He got in, got behind him, dragged him the rest of the way inside. Then he was laid out like that, all of him under the light, in between the tool boxes, the spades, the spare tyre, all that. Bags of cement, sand. My father was crying by then, laying him out. He said he couldn't stop. It was falling out of him. That was the most noise there was, he told me.

'He turned the boy's head over, on to the side. He took a blanket, put it over him. Looked once before he laid it down, he said. Could see the broken bones clearly. You shouldn't do a thing like that and not be able to look. So he covered him. He took a shovel, used the handle. He finished it.

'He said he stopped crying, driving back. He said he couldn't remember when it happened but he started feeling different. He got excited. After it had all happened, started getting excited and laughing. He was seeing stupid little things and he couldn't stop laughing, the sort you'd never laugh over. Couldn't stop moving like he had ants under his fucking skin. Said he'd never felt anything like it. Fucking blood pounding, fucking heart beating, like nothing else. Everything goes the other way, like. You should be guilty. It goes the other way.

'By the time he got here, though, he was serious by then. Because that was when the work started up. They'd dug the hole the day before. More like a trough it was really, long and thin, like. Flagpole doesn't need that much width but it needs a lot of depth.

'He said he drove to the edge of town that night, and he'd driven into town at night a lot of times. It had never looked like that, though.'

Rhys saw Lennie blink slowly as he stared out at the bare stone wall.

'He said the lights were so bright they were fucking blurred. Huge circles round every one of the street lamps. Beautiful orange things, he said. From the edge of town like that, he could see them through the trees. Sunflowers. Like sunflowers those lights, that's what he said to me – and what a sight,' Lennie finished softly, 'that must be.'

He had sat on their bed, boots in front of him on the carpet before leaving for the Lion. Silence from downstairs that had seemed to seep up through the floor. There'd been the slight creak of the bed as he'd reached to pick the first up. The sound of his own heavy breath. Hadn't taken it in his hand, though, only listening.

No sound of plates being cleared away, no footsteps on the slate below. He'd looked out through the open bedroom door at the flower pictures hanging on the long stretch of wall. Painted petals bending with their own weight. He'd remembered when she had taken all those flower pictures down, a couple of weeks after the honeymoon. He had found her standing at the bottom of the stairs, holding a stack of them, and more piled on the floor. She'd been looking at the wall where the pictures, hanging there for so long, had left dark, rectangular places, the real colour of the walls. For a while, the flower paintings had been stacked up in the attic. And with the new pictures, no matter where she'd hung them, some of the dark rectangles had shown. She'd talked about repainting but after some long time, he'd come home to find the flower pictures back up. She'd not said a word to him about it, but there they'd been, hung in their lines again. Sitting on the bed this afternoon in the settling silence which always followed, always came, he had stared at them.

Lies, he had thought, looking at the money that he had gathered up from the kitchen floor. Lies in the hush. Lies in the daylight. Their only sign this emptiness. He was looking at those painted flowers when Nia walked through her door. Coming slowly up from the kitchen ten minutes before, Lennie had opened it again.

She moved through her doorway, wearing her blue dress, blue tights wrinkled round the ankles. She walked without any sound.

Lennie had sat motionless, watching her, ten feet away from him. She gave him ghost stories. She had her donkey toy tucked under one arm. She didn't seem to touch the floor and the expression on her face took in nothing that wasn't held in her own hands. She was the sort of child, he thought, that you saw playing on alone after school.

Nia and Eeyore had walked on to the landing. He himself heavy as stone. She passed beneath the line of painted flowers, thumb in her mouth. Sitting in the reach of sun that had lain across their bed, he had wanted to call out to her.

'Nia. Hey you. Hey you.' He would pat the bed beside him there, help her up on to it, lift her under the arms. 'Nia!'

He had watched her move away from him like she might break if she just brushed the door frame. He didn't get this often: wanting to say things to her. He didn't need to talk. He could still hug her, ruffle her hair. Actions spoke louder than words.

There was no sound of footsteps as she passed down the corridor, far away from where he sat. Above the fragile curl of her fingers, her brown eyes had laid silence across the walls. If she'd turned and seen him, would he have gestured for her to come closer? She walked into the bathroom, she pushed the door shut, the last sun on his hands, as warm as cloth.

As Lennie had left the house, not looking into the kitchen, Gwen had been settling herself in the passenger seat. She saw tarmac now, standing in the cold outside the community centre, and could almost hear Eirian's words. She saw the brick wall. What a pretty building, the words said. And underneath that, Ynys-morlan – and then the obscenity. They were scrawled across the brickwork, the letters rough with anger, or with excitement. Her short hair was blown back from her eyes as she looked.

Disgusting, she thought, disgusting, remembering Tom's touch on her arm. And she thought of the way they must have sat together, he and Rhys, close enough to kiss. Smiling over the words they spoke about her; wetting their mouths with them.

She wanted to turn away but she wouldn't. She would look at it, take it in so that she would never be in doubt again. She had stood and she had let him kiss her. Looking at these words now, she could feel the shame all over her, each inch of her skin. She remembered the filth spread across his bed.

What a pretty building. Ynys-morlan suck my c---. Repulsive. And she wished that Tom was here now, that she could open her mouth and drive what she felt into him. She would have stepped so close that there was nowhere else for him to look, his eyes caught. She would take him by his collar and grip him.

Gwen's fingers fluttered, tightened. It was right to be ashamed of her own part in this. She had stood there while he'd moved his body closer. As she'd said to Emyr, she would not shirk the blame. Crying, she had followed him that night.

'Repellent,' she said, her voice clear as a raindrop in this quiet that had been Emyr's enemy. And the first rain itself touched her skin, moistened her cheeks, as she read the words again to absorb them.

'And is it true? Is it true or what?' Rhys asked him.

'It's true.'

'You're fucking kidding me.'

'I'm not kidding you, like.' There were things he wanted to say but for a moment, he didn't speak, only watched Rhys's face.

'I'll have to, like . . . make some inquiries.' Rhys was grinning, the first smile Lennie had seen today.

'You won't be making any fucking inquiries, you won't be asking around. And you won't be telling that to anyone else, hear? You listen to me, Rhys. It's eighteen years since I heard that story, like, and you're the first person I've told. You get me? You're the only one.'

As he had stepped out through his front door and felt that coming rain, he'd watched the thing in the wind. The way the cloth caught. He had seen the vague grey of lichen on the concrete – and the grass, not cut for a month now, trying to hide it in its hands. He'd remembered the pale touch of Ruth's face down below – night-time – staring up towards him.

'My father went back to Llan-y-bont,' he said quietly, 'four days later, like. He went into the pub, gave five quid to the bloke behind the bar. He'd not had it all that night, he said, to give the boy. When he next saw him, could he pass it on? And the landlord said yes.

'He killed a man for her.' He nodded slowly as though only now, in repeating, could he understand himself. 'To have her, like, have a family with her. Have me.' He looked out at the stone wall, at nothing, and it was his old man's face he remembered. His profile, hair moving in the wind as Lennie had watched him.

His father had said, 'That's how much I fucking love her.' Not looking at Lennie but only upwards. 'That's how much,' he'd said.

Lennie nodded at Rhys again, whose eyes were walled no longer but looked out. He saw promise in the boy's face, a rare thing in these times. 'That's what family should mean,' he said.

He remembered Nia's eyes, her tiny, curled fingers. Had she been older, had she been able to hear the story, he thought, still he couldn't have spoken it to her.

The noticeboard stood outside the Spar, half dulled in the shade of its eaves. Green paint was peeling. There were the prints of children's hands in still dances across the shopwindow behind. A cork board with a wooden frame. Two months ago, Dai had found the glass screen smashed in pieces on the pavement and had swept it away, Siân Humphries standing in the doorway with her green smock and nametag, shaking her head. People tied their dogs there.

Stray raindrops had curled the paper notices: a car boot sale sign from three weeks before. Others, older, where the drawing pins had rusted. Ynys-morlan town council meeting, a date, brittle paper.

The notice at the bottom was fresh, straight and well pinned down. The same words as had been printed in local newspapers, a black border around the edge.

> Thursday 2nd November
> Llanfihangel Ynys-morlan –
> Church of St Michael, Ynys-morlan
>
> Remembrance Service for Eirian Meredith
> Worthy member of our community
> who will be greatly missed
>
> Held by the Reverend Evan Thomas
> 11 a.m.

This house, built of stone and wood and slate, was made for a family, Ruth thought. It was old, it creaked or settled in any wind and it rattled, she'd said in that first year, without kids running and banging and talking. There were too many little rooms without them.

This place in the kitchen, where twisting wooden beams held the stone, was the place where her mother had stuck her well-loved lists. Shopping lists, things to do, bills to pay. Here at the kitchen table she'd sat and made them out, cut flowers always in a vase, sometimes the radio playing. Nia's pictures were pinned up in the kitchen now, in the wooden beams where those many tiny holes could be made out. Stick families with big heads and Ruth would say, 'Look at that, see? I love her to bits, always draws me as a size ten.' The stick people stood and held hands and stared out of the picture and into Ruth's home.

Here, by the fire in the living room, this was the place where she'd come in and first sat down with Nia in a carrycot. She'd wanted to show Nia the house, wanted to carry her through all of the rooms and say to her, 'This is the kitchen, this is your room, what do you think? Do you like the colour?' She'd been too tired to do it right away, though, she'd just sat. Nia had been wrinkled, asleep. Leaning her head back, she had remembered: her mother had stood with a screwdriver in one hand, working and working at where the old shelf brackets were fixed and when she hadn't been able to un-screw them, shoving the screwdriver under, trying to wrench them out, trying to lever them out, grunting with the effort. Not speaking at all, as Ruth had come down the stairs and stood behind the sofa watching her, shoulders all tensed up with the effort, her expression misshapen with it. A long time ago, an old memory, soft as the shadow that had lain over the wall as Ruth had sat with one hand on the carrycot.

And here, at the end of the hallway, the closed door. She'd used to say that she didn't want to go in, that she didn't care, but for all her thoughts about it, she might have been there every night, her hands in the piles of things, rooting, holding them and turning them over like she could soak up what they'd been before. All those silent things that must say something, if she were to wait and listen long enough. The house had been full of questions she could never ask.

Nine years old maybe, she couldn't remember. Maybe a year since she'd last seen the garden. She'd got off the bus, walked to her front door and unlocked it, same as she'd always done. And she'd seen it straight away, at the end of the corridor, past the chest of drawers and its shadowed, oval mirror, the closed door had stood open. A lump of quartz rock on the floor, holding it. She remembered dropping her bag, so clearly could she summon up the image, walking past the wooden staircase. Afternoon light had come from inside the room and lain across its threshold. Her mother still out at work. The house had always been silent, coming home. Always empty. She could have gone in there, any day. It would only have taken a few quiet paces. But her mother, who crossed her thin arms over her chest and knew the world, would see Ruth's invisible footsteps like a trail of broken glass. And it was funny because she'd been no less scared, seeing the door wedged open like that. She remembered that afternoon light; had never seen anything look more like a trap.

The door would speak to her, a light daytime voice: Come on in, come on, why don't you?

The house had seemed full of dust that could never settle, moving quiet in the air. Her mother had set the door that way, knowing well enough which of them would be home first.

With her bag left behind her on the hallway floor, she'd passed the chest of drawers, passed under the shadow of the stairs and walked from it into the doorway's radiance.

She'd looked into the room, and the room had been bare. There had been carpet, the same carpet she'd stood on maybe a year before with her mother's hands moving like sticks as she'd showed her: 'Look at this, you see?' There'd been carpet, and there'd been four walls and there hadn't been anything else. With that sunlight, the room had felt warmer than any other in the house.

She'd seen vacuum marks fresh like a lawnmower's lines. The glass in the windows had been clean. And she'd looked at the stonework and the beams. Halfway up the farthest wall, there'd been a picture hook: a little brass thing, dusty, gleaming.

Nothing to pick up. No marks where those things had been. Her mother had scrubbed and scraped. Standing there, she'd tried hard to remember the place she'd seen a year before, as if she could lay those memories across this room where she was now free to stand or move.

It was the picture hook which she thought about, the day after Lennie found the box. Nia was in the bathroom. She was brushing her teeth by herself these days. Ruth had watched her do it, she was careful and very slow and had almost made Ruth smile. On the bedside table, the little wooden box sat underneath a lamp, where its circle of light would be cast. No light on now, in the morning. Its lid was open and the ten-pound notes were folded carefully, replaced inside.

Maybe it was only the timing of it. Maybe if the telephone had rung five minutes later. Because she'd practised the things she was going to say to Charlotte. 'I had a lovely time, really a lovely time.' But she was thinking about the garden, about their work in its silence, and thinking of that old brass picture hook. Like a draught through cracks, the past came. Three times, the telephone rang out, four. It might have only been the timing.

Charlotte Weyland's voice: touched with its foreign accent, its foreign history.

Ruth said, 'I'm fine. Nia's fine, you know. Up to her usual tricks, not smashing anything at the moment, though,' she held the phone to her ear and she laughed. She laughed, she told her that Lennie was well. 'Off to work again,' she said, 'but he's well. He's well.' She stood next to the phone table and heard the bathroom door open above her, and she didn't look up, didn't even glance.

'I was in the garden just now,' Charlotte said.

'Really? That's nice,' she said. 'How's it looking? Is it looking good?'

'It's looking good. The bit of path is drying out.'

'That's good,' she said. 'That's nice.' She had all the words prepared. Into the receiver, she said, 'You haven't cut any more?'

'Not yet, no I haven't. I think I probably need Nia, she seemed to get more done than me.'

And Ruth laughed again in the hallway, to the dried flowers on the table, to the open kitchen doorway, to the awkward wordless moment on the line. You stand there lying to me, he had said.

'So, I was wondering when you might . . . bring her here again.'

Her fingers shifted and she stared out. She said, 'Charlotte, I'm . . .' She thought of the way Nia had walked with brambles dragging on the ground, her face white as paint in the sun.

Lennie had spoken her name over and over, as if the one word could not hold all he needed to release. Do you hear me, Ruth? he'd asked her.

'Why don't you come?' Charlotte said. 'Come today, unless you're busy.'

They stood in the thin shadow of the doorway. Mrs Lewis had a smile, Charlotte saw, already painted. They were hand in hand.

'Well, here we are.'

So similar, Ruth and her daughter, they might have stolen and been holding pieces of each other.

'How are you?'

'Fine. Thank you, fine.' Behind them, wind moved through the high front lawn.

Charlotte heard a great deal on that second day. Ruth told her story while she listened with her own silence.

The house was quiet as sleep. Charlotte had bought biscuits and set them on the table. They passed the uncarpeted staircase, its rail dulled where people had placed their hands over and over again. Looking out at its walls while the garden stood sheltered and waiting, they drank tea again.

Inside, reaching perhaps six feet from the tiny doorway, brambles forming its end, the path's dry brickwork ran to nothing. Willowherb against the walls now seeding as cotton, high stinging nettles in the sun – ivy spilled down into them.

Ruth's hand trailed over Nia's shoulder as she stood there again, remembering Lennie's voice. She'd stepped out over a drop, it seemed, and had fallen here between these well-remembered walls.

Through the early afternoon they searched and cut and pulled the wet loam from their slow-growing road between the weeds. Charlotte Weyland heard much.

'Used to sit over there, over there with their sticks and poke the ground. What is it with men and sticks? Ground dips down a little by there. Used to find buttercups, you know, when you hold them under your chin, if you like butter . . . Did you do that?'

Charlotte shook her head.

'See, even then, people used to say I was a tomboy, my mother used to say that, and hated it too, I don't know why it is people feel the need to say things they can't stand. And then repeat them, just in case no one heard. I wasn't a tomboy, though. They'd be poking the ground.'

It spilled from Ruth Lewis; the sort of person who could not prevent it. Expression . . . or Charlotte did not know the right word. Below the things she said, emotions ran like water. The minutes passed, as would the hours, at ten pounds each. Ruth had needed to come. She saw it clearly.

'And then I kept walking up here afterwards. October. Used to just wander around, sit down, think.' She remembered the scraping sound of her shoes, walking in little circles, round and round. 'Came here all the time on my own, up till my mother found out.' She laughed, 'Put a stop to that, quick smart. I don't think she was too keen on the idea of me going off without an escort.' She watched Charlotte reach in awkwardly and pull the branches free.

'I'm amazed she let you come here with the escort.' Her voice was colder than she'd meant it to be. She didn't know what sort of tone she should have.

'She didn't let me,' Ruth said, that little smile back on her face. She looked younger. And Charlotte could see it then, that it was true: how Ruth must have looked, nine years old, smiling that smile every chance she got, coming here at every opportunity.

'Used to send me off with Emyr but she didn't know that he'd bring his friends. No, I don't think she would have taken too kindly to that. She was set enough on me getting a boyfriend but I don't think she'd have been too keen on four. Not that I . . . you know.' She watched Charlotte hand some of the branches to Nia, hesitating. And Nia, with no hesitation at all, took them and walked with them outside. 'I'd probably be just like her now, throw a fit if I found out Nia was going off with four boys at ten years old. But my mother wasn't averse to boys. Mad-keen on me getting a boyfriend, asking if I'd got any valentines. And I had to disappoint her every year on that one. Wouldn't let me make any for them, though. Might as well have suggested we go shopping naked, the expression on her face. Nothing makes you look more desperate than sending a valentine to a boy.' She nodded as though teaching a lesson. 'No, she fell in love with the idea of my wedding before I was old enough to be a bridesmaid. And I mean, I wasn't blind to it, even then. You'd have had to be blind not to see it, after my dad. It was sweet really. It was sad.'

She watched Ruth set to work again, like she could leave behind every single thing she said. In the clear sunlight, the slight rustle of the leaves, Charlotte was silent, looking at her. She wanted to ask her: 'After your father?' She wanted to ask her a lot of things. And behind them, she heard Nia's footsteps walking through the doorway, as though the girl's silence lay over her, old, deeply rooted as these weeds.

'No . . .' almost speaking to herself. 'She was all right with me coming up here with Emyr, she'd arranged that and everything. It was me on my own that she'd never arranged.'

She looked at Ruth's back, her movements in the sunlight, listening and wanting to speak. She hacked at the weeds and Charlotte wanted to ask, 'What's wrong?' Only that.

'You can't keep a hand on someone's thoughts when they're off God knows where. Told me in no uncertain terms that I wouldn't be coming back. Probably it was a good thing anyway. Not like I was having any fun here by then. I was just walking around.' She cut at the briar. 'I'm not even going back,' she had said, and Lennie had agreed. 'I was just making myself miserable by then, coming here, raining every day, and me walking around in it. But then –' she said it like she was telling a joke, Charlotte thought, '– you don't know the history, do you. I should tell you the history. The Story Of My Dad. Everyone knows it, bigger news than Elvis's death. And everyone knowing, that was it for my mother. And everyone talking about it, that was worse. I'll tell you the history.' She looked at the weeds.

Gwen Morgan sat with Dai, her husband's quiet study like a small stone behind them, the occasional sound of his cough, and tried to explain the ceremony which tomorrow would commemorate his mother's disappearance from his life. Something had disappeared, Emyr thought, from the fabric of the house. From underneath everything.

Lennie Lewis drove, working over and listing the many absences in Ynys-morlan now. The lack that had grown, and for no reason, above foundations that were strong. It was a town of erosion. This stretch of coastline, it was empty under autumn air, as if every season had worn it thinner. A town of disappearances, as for Ruth it had always been.

'The family saga. And you won't feel left out then, when people are gossiping over it. They still do, I swear. There you go, you see: my mother, never wrong. "Do you remember . . . ?" they say. Honestly, you get a small town, life's slowed down by about a thousand per cent. Something happens in nineteen hundred and two, and they're still working it over now. Boring life, you see.' She smiled. 'I reckon there's a little space in everyone, set aside just for gossip. Even if nothing happens in twenty years, still got to fill that little space. They can't even help it. Like a bodily function, gossip is, and I'm no different, I'm sure.'

Rhys took his break, smoking cigarettes on the seafront in Aberystwyth, the pier empty, the pier silent. He imagined great fucking distances but tonight, like Lennie, he'd return home. He imagined street lights like sunflowers but for him all the lights in Ynys-morlan had gone out years ago.

And Tom Humphries, outside the Shoreline Café – on his break too, smoking too, imagining – glanced in at Bethan Hughes's face behind the glass and at her baby. Saw this street again: all three's home. Imagining Gwen Morgan in tears and in the middle of the night. Yes, imagine that. A lot of widening holes in the weave of this place – yes, he thought – which crossed each other and became all there was.

On every side of Ruth, the ivy trailed from dry walls. The nettles, pale yellow, nodded their heads, drowsed in the sun, and the willowherb seed was catching.

'I don't know what year it is, I'm bad with years, can never remember.'

'Yes,' Charlotte said, 'I'm the same.'

'It was a Tuesday, though, I know that much, must have heard her say it a hundred times. I was an infant, a toddler, you know.'

She cut all growth from the line where their forks had touched the clinking bricks, the path continuing. Back in the Lewises' home, the hours accumulated slowly – in the Aga's warm air, gently touching Nia's drawings, travelling slowly through each room – the hours of their absence. Lennie would stand in the doorway tonight and would sense it, not knowing what it was that he felt.

'They had me a year after they were married, and they were happy and everything, she said. Perfectly happy. My dad had a good job and they were setting themselves up. He worked a lot, she said, Saturdays. Sundays too, sometimes. But anyway, it was a Tuesday, this day. My dad went off to work in the morning, same as always. He kissed her at the door. He used to say, you know, going to work: "You have to still be pretty when I come home. Promise?" Like that. That's what she told me. And he said it that day, as he left – she was specific on that point.'

Ruth gave a smile, down at the brickwork, and Charlotte saw how many times she'd told the story, like she could just settle into the words, like it wasn't even her own voice.

'Only he didn't come home that night. Not at half past five when he was meant to. He didn't come home at six o'clock. Or at seven, and my mother's going frantic by then. Because he's not called.'

Charlotte watched as Nia walked her silence between them, put her gloved hands into the brambles.

'By then, she's calling the hospitals,' she said. 'I can imagine, you know. She's calling his work. She phones them up and the people that he worked with, they told her. He left at five, same as always. They don't say anything else, of course. They don't say, if something's happened, it must have happened *after* he left. But that's what she's thinking, and she's calling up the hospitals. But the hospitals don't know anything, they haven't got his name. There haven't been any accidents on the road he'd always use to drive home.' Ruth smiled again. 'So she sits, she waits up for him, you know. She said I was screaming that night but maybe that was just what she said. She didn't go to bed, she sat and listened to the radio right till morning, sat with the phone.'

The herringbone path grew from the doorway where Charlotte stood; from her feet to the edge of the woman's story. She hadn't wanted anyone else to see this garden, she hadn't wanted Ruth Lewis or her overflowing memories. But she hadn't truly known what she wanted; in coming here at all, or in trying to change her life.

Ruth said quietly, 'My mother woke up that next morning so she must have slept a little, on the sofa. She said she'd never woken up so fast, from dreaming to standing up in under a second, she is. But the house is quiet. I'm sleeping fine upstairs by then.' Ruth pushed hair from her face. 'She runs up but there's no sign of him, there's nothing.' Ruth cut. 'She phones the hospitals again. By then, they must have known her name, just from the sound of her voice. She was like that, she'd get on to something and she wouldn't stop. Couldn't sit and wait. I'd be the same, I'm sure.' She drew a quick breath, smiled, standing up to let Nia take the branches away. Quiet enough here that the child's movements could be heard. 'She calls the hospitals,' Ruth said, 'and then, come nine o'clock, she calls his work again because it's the only thing she can think of to do. But he hasn't got into work and he doesn't get into work all day and by that time . . .

she doesn't know what to do. So she tells people. She tells everyone. Walking up and down the street and knocking on doors. Because she thinks something's happened. One house after another, like a door-to-door salesman, asking everyone to call whoever they can think of, that might know where he is. You ask people in town, you ask anyone who's older and they'll remember the day my mother knocked on the door. I swear, people who weren't born that year remember the look on her face. She told everyone. She called the police. But they wouldn't do anything then, not with him only gone for the night. "Did you have a fight?" they asked . . . And it didn't matter what she told them: that he wasn't that kind of person, that he'd never been home late in his life without calling her to check first of all. She told them that he was responsible like that because he had a daughter, a family. She told them they were happy.'

There was the low sound of wind outside these walls, a rustling. Charlotte could not feel it.

'So she can't sit and wait – she hasn't got anything else to do, though. Do the ironing, you know.' Ruth laughed as she worked. 'So she puts me with a friend, in the house next door . . . She said she went in raving over it, over the police not helping, you know. She was going to hire a car out in Aber because he'd driven theirs to work. She said she didn't know really, what she was going to do, just drive, search. She went down to the post office to get the money from the savings account for it, but she couldn't get the money because the savings account was closed and all the money had gone.'

Charlotte looked at her. 'He'd left,' she said.

Ruth smiled. 'He'd left. And how.'

There was a moment of quiet before she asked, 'And what happened then?'

'She came home and she got me from the neighbour's again. She said she'd changed her mind, that she'd wait in case the hospital called. She said something like that. She went back to their house – her house. Whichever.'

'He didn't come back. There was no message.'

'She went into his room and looked through his drawers, and she was never one to do that. She was specific on that point too. It looked normal, she said. He had papers out all over them, same as always because he'd never been organized. She'd always had to tidy up after him. Probably one of the things she liked about him most.' She smiled again and looked away. 'There was his stuff, his papers and photos of her and all that. A pen lying there, she said, like he was just in the middle of something and he'd had to put it down. Like he'd pick it up again that evening. But there were things missing, she had to hunt to see what but after a while, she started seeing the gaps in what looked normal.'

'What had he taken?' Charlotte heard her own voice etch between Ruth's continuing words.

'Things he'd need later on. In a year's time, or ten. Passport, birth certificate, bank books. Marriage certificate.'

Charlotte looked at her, the weeds unmoving around them. 'What did she do?'

'There wasn't much she could do. She waited. She looked after me, she kept the house. And when she couldn't wait any more, she got a job, got two jobs in fact. But really, I don't think she stopped waiting even then, because there wasn't any ending to it. Things need an ending. She never got a call or anything like that. She just kept on. She was living in their house, you know. She was dusting his things.'

'She kept his things? Even after she knew?' Charlotte looked away, speaking slowly. 'That's ridiculous. You can't move on like that.'

'She didn't know what else to do. She started taking them down after a while, she told me. She changed the place. Painting and everything. She'd go out to get new bits and bobs, but she kept his things, yes. She took them all down off the walls, and the things they'd bought together, put them in cardboard boxes. Like he was moving out, you know? Put the boxes in his office.'

There was a pause. 'I don't see why someone would do that,' Charlotte said quietly. 'To themselves or to their child.'

'I don't know.' She laughed suddenly, and the noise fell away as though caught in every soft leaf, every dry branch that covered the garden. 'It was like I got to live with him anyway, her keeping it all.'

She gave some smile. 'He was in the air. He was in all the rooms. I swear, sat between us at dinner every night.'

Ruth remembered standing here with the rain, walking here with the rain, going round in her circles. Sun shone down on them now, warm as water, as she dragged branches free and clear, to pass to Charlotte, to be held and nothing more. Charlotte's own memories heard and gave no answer.

'The oddest thing, like it was always for show. She had the tables and the chairs all set up, you could see them coming in through the front door, but you could see that we never sat in those chairs, or when we did, sitting down on our own, it was still only for show. Like you could pull all the things you saw away, like a dust sheet. And there'd be something else underneath.'

Charlotte's nod was her only response, and Ruth's back was turned to her.

'She was stubborn. You know what she did? A fortnight after she'd last seen him, it was. She walked out of the house and she knocked next door, stood on the doorstep like she'd done that first day. And she told them. Just like that: handbag over arm.' Ruth smiled again. 'Told them about the savings account and the things she'd found gone. And when she'd told them, she walked down the road to the next house and she told every single person she knew, standing on their doorsteps like that.'

'I can't imagine,' Charlotte said again, 'why someone would do that.'

'Give herself that ending, I think. Because you need to have it.' The grasses looked as if they'd been parted, surrounding this path and the three of them, chest-high. 'She took back a bit of pride. It's not had an ending, though . . . You see it now, I don't know that it's any different.' She laughed again, sunlight whitewashed her eyes as she looked up at Charlotte. 'I want to keep the place nice, you know. My mother used to say about him, that he went and walked out on all his responsibilities.' Ruth's smile didn't leave her face. 'Responsibilities don't just up and float away when someone leaves, though. Everyone else has got to . . . take up the slack. You can feel them, like. Still feel them. Monstrous little ghosts they are, but it's a beautiful house. You've seen it. I love it so much, you know? I couldn't have . . . just emptied it. That's what you have to do, isn't it? If you're not going to live there, you have to empty it. Well it's full still.' And then she said suddenly, 'Feast on the quiet, responsibilities do. Lennie's not happy. I can see it. I don't know how to ask Nia if she's all right.' Ruth gestured to her, a soft hand. 'She could be crying, I don't know how to ask. I try, you know? Don't know how to make Lennie feel better. Don't know . . . how to go up to him, I can't hold him,' she said. She looked at Charlotte, all the smiles mixed together there, like this was her; when you took the words away, this was how she looked. 'He's not happy,' she said. 'I don't know what I'm meant to do. I see it in his face every day, he comes home and he won't talk to me. Can't force him to talk to me, can I? If he doesn't want to tell me what's wrong, I can't force him.'

'I'm sure that's not true.'

Nia came between them to draw the brambles away and Ruth took her up, a briar strand hanging from the girl's hand. She gave her a hug and turned away with the flooded smile which Charlotte now recognized. Nia put her arms around her neck. In the sunlight, everything was clear and every sound was loud: Ruth's catching breath as the thorn scratched her cheek. The noise she made as she pulled away. Everything clear: the thin line of blood that rose there as she put one hand up to touch it, as Nia raised her face and saw. Small hands were motionless.

And for a moment the child looked normal, Charlotte thought. Not still as usual, pale as usual, but normal. There were spots of colour on her cheeks, staring at Ruth's face. Shocked like a little princess, just slapped. In that one moment, her eyes seemed for the first time truly open. And Charlotte began to speak, to say to Ruth, don't move, look at her. But it was then that Nia changed.

Clarity in the wordless garden like slowing time. Charlotte saw the girl's expression tighten, she saw the hand that was in Ruth's hair, a fist.

'Nia fach,' Ruth said. 'It's fine.' Ruth's mouth moved quickly, her face animated. The slim line drawn down her cheek was beading into tiny drops.

'Ruth?' she said. 'What's wrong? Is she all right?'

Charlotte thought later, sitting at her desk in the lamplight, her diary open in front of her, that it was the silence which made it so strange. No sound at all, only the girl's face.

Nia's hand bunched in Ruth's hair, her other arm tightening until it was stretched out straight, like she would hold Ruth away from her. Her eyes were wide. Ruth said the same things, again and again.

'Baby, Nia fach, it's fine. OK?' Smiling. 'OK?'

Nia slapped her. A slight movement, no effort, not so much harder than if the girl had been trying to stroke Ruth's face. In Ruth's hair, Nia's fingers gripped. It came again, not a stroke but some loose blow. In this quiet it was distinct as a breaking branch.

Ruth own hands moving now, gripping Nia's shoulders as the girl hit her again, as if the blood was Ruth's fault and she should make it stop. Stumbling, Ruth tried to hold her. Charlotte saw a flash of the child's face, sunlit as her hair fell over it, contorted.

'My God –' Charlotte spoke but lost her own voice.

'Nia, no. It's all right. It's all right!'

No words as her hands came down. Charlotte watched. Ruth put both arms around her daughter. It might have been an embrace, crouching there in the mist of weeds. Nia kicked at her, she kicked. Words screamed out of the girl's hands. They cried and pattered out, Ruth's voice the only sound.

'Let me help,' Ruth said. 'Let me help, Ni.'

There was no view from here, no shoreline, no town. There were no sounds that didn't come from them or the overhanging trees. As though the weeds, the dry branches and blades of grass, caught every noise, and held them, refusing to let them sift gradually down to the ground.

That afternoon Ruth found a bottle amidst the brambles. 'Well look at that,' she said. 'This, I'll have you know, isn't any bottle. This is a Dandelion and Burdock bottle, circa . . . Mid-Nineteen Seventies?

Good for digestion, joint pain, vitamins.' She held it out, grimy in the light. She said, 'Was also Emyr Morgan's favoured tipple. Before he discovered Scotch, that is.'

She passed it to Charlotte across the few feet between them, and Charlotte held it, looking at the earth. Sediment, filled day by week by year, washed in with the rain maybe. The neck was chipped.

'There you go,' Ruth said quietly. The smile she always gave was clear sky.

They took the loam up in the last of the sun. Outside the walls, the wind swelled into an early dusk.

The garden was divided through its centre by this herringbone brickwork; the first part dry, tinted orange in the late light, the last part still wet from the earth.

Ynys-morlan, place of missing persons, saw the school bus, the bus from Aberystwyth and a slow trickle of cars draw in, evening slowly bringing back the people who still called this town home.

June 14th 1995

Dear Charlotte,

I found Mother's letter again today. I sat and I reread it. Ten days after the Tribune and she was well aware. She waited until it had been published - she timed it.

Sat with it for an hour maybe. At first could not believe that I'd kept it, couldn't imagine any reason. But slowly realized. Forgetting - which just flows over you so naturally, over me, so easily - it's too close to forgiving.

I wasn't old enough back then to see their behaviour. Too many other parts to assimilate, ones that left no room. But I see it now. Reading this again. She hated him.

These are the words she chose: 'It could not have

been deemed in your father's best interests.' As if life were an equation and its solutions unchangeable. Comprehended properly only by her. But I see under the language now - of course could not in '92. Why use those words? Underneath their precision, do you know what I can hear? Confusion. Guilt. Hate.

Because I remember. I remember when callousness was not her reaction. I remember a house that was full of her sadness like the rooms were under goddamned water. How everything revolved around a lack. There it was, in all the echoes. Every time a door stood closed, that absence was behind it.

Wherever I wasn't, there it lay.

But she had the chance to heal. She could have found solace in me. I was a blank page once. I was a baby, Christ there must have been one day, at least **one** when I was unnamed. She could have written a future. Disregard blame - I know what it's like to feel that hole and never be able to fill it - my God she gave me nothing if not an understanding of what she'd been through - but had **I** been given the chance - at **any** point in my life, to let it go, for happiness, for change, I would have taken hold of it with **every** damn strength in me. I swear to God. And thirty-six years ago, I was that chance for her.

Instead, I have these memories. Her screaming. Breaking things - and how she locked her door. She could have gotten better. She had me, she could have **grown**. I remember how she used to hold me. She could have mended herself through me. I remember how she never wanted to let go. How she'd tell me she loved me, over and over.

It was the night before Eirian Meredith's funeral. On Gwen and Emyr Morgan's sofa, Dai was sitting now. Gwen had told him, explained in slow words with a hand on his shoulder, the things that would happen tomorrow. There was a purpose to them, she said. That purpose lay in the words 'to put someone to rest'. Afterwards, she said, you felt better. It was a chance to celebrate a life, a thanksgiving, a chance to say goodbye.

As Charlotte opened drawers to wander through figures and columns, through familiar numbers and feelings, Dai had the blankets up round his face and the television's bright reflections in his eyes. The volume was turned down very low but he could hear it; couldn't quite make out the words but felt its sound. He was waiting.

Upstairs, in their bed, Gwen and Emyr slept from half past ten through the night, his face bare as a child's without his glasses. He wore pyjamas, red with silk trim, that Gwen had chosen from a catalogue. Lying on her side, her eyes showed no lines. In sleep, forgetting, he moved closer to her.

There were no stars that night, the sky was black and the wind rocked Ynys-morlan with the new season's fickle switches. Under the soft light from the street lamps, it tore through the road, caught sand and litter from the bins, from the gutter, skittering. At the edge of town, the flag slapped against its pole. And the houses were still inside it, they were hunched as it rattled black window panes.

His mum's clocks would be running down to their last hours now. Dai looked toward the hallway's open door: shadow where his coat hung. And finally, he thought, it was safe. He looked at the blanket and the messy sofa where he'd sat for a lot of hours now. After a moment, standing, he picked the blanket up and he folded it.

Outside, down the long and twisting road, the wind buffeted roofs. On the Lewises', it worked under slates. Beneath the edge of one, broke it free, it came falling. Between the rose beds and the lawn it shattered itself across the paving slabs and, lying in bed, Lennie's eyes started open. He saw the ceiling. He listened to Ruth's even breath. Dai Meredith left the Morgans' house with his shock of hair dancing over his collar, listening to the trinket sounds of his own keys, and Lennie didn't move. From the wardrobe's door, a dulled shape, his suit hung. Neat and careful. It had been cleaned, there wasn't a mark on the thing. His black tie was strung through the hanger.

The paint peeled from signs and window frames, as if all the times that Lennie Lewis remembered had been only decoration. Standing outside the gift shop's double doors, Dai could see his own yellow reflection.

It was quiet with those doors unlocked and closed again behind him. Through their glass the concrete forecourt was laid out: dully gleaming light across it, as if on water. Dai didn't move at all. On every side of him, he could feel the shades of things stacked up against the walls.

This was the place where Gwen had stood, dressed in white with those glass doors open, ushering people inside through the breeze. Her coral-coloured shoes had shifted on the floorboards with confetti underneath.

Dust now – he smelled it.

Siân, she had said, Siân come in, come in, it's up the stairs. And she'd touched their shoulders.

Dai reached one hand out but did not move forward. His mother had stacked these things here, all these things he couldn't see. Their growing musty smell did not belong to him.

'Dai,' Eirian had gently called. 'Come here now, come sit on the bed here. I've got a gift for you.' She had given him this bunch of clinking keys, which weighed when he held them in his hand, each key for a lock, for its own door. 'Come here,' she'd said. 'Come on.' She'd taken him in. 'You,' she'd said. 'You're so good, you know that, Dai? Of all the people I've ever met, you're the best. There's no harm in you.' She'd said, 'You know what you've been doing, you've not seen it, even I've not seen it, but you know what you've been doing? Waiting, Dai. You've been waiting for such a long time.' She'd told him to look at the keys, to turn each one over in his hand. 'The flat that Bethan Hughes lives in,' she'd said. 'The launderette underneath.' They'd been silver-cool as he'd held them. 'Our house, you know that one.' And then she'd said, 'The gift shop.' Three for that, as small and sharp as teeth.

Dai remembered the sound of his mum, the feeling of being close to her, but she was gone. His hand brushed a shape. He heard it, heard it rock in front of him and he reached out to try and steady it. Couldn't find it again.

People slept or spent the hours. He stood and looked around him: the vague outlines. Buckets and spades, there'd be, plastic windmills, jelly shoes and mugs with Ynys-morlan on their curves.

Lennie lay with the noise of this wind. He had the sudden feeling, the sudden fear, that he could make a sound now and it wouldn't come out, he could say something, and Ruth wouldn't wake and Nia wouldn't hear, and it would be lost to his own ears.

Dai spoke in the gift shop's silence, to hear his own voice. It came more quietly than he'd intended and didn't feel like it belonged to him. He listened, alone, as his sounds lay down in the dark between all these summer things.

The church stood alone above the town, Llanfihangel Ynys-morlan. Grey stone on short grass, yellowed with the past season. Leaning graves in the shadow of the yew; a huge, low tree that laid its shade-hands over half the graveyard. Here, at the top of this hill, you could look out and see the ocean far down a reaching rugged slope. If not for the trees, you could have seen the houses, dotted here and there on the hill's other side; the low, white-painted stone of Charlotte's home, Emyr Morgan's with its clean bricks and double garage, and the house where Eirian Meredith had lived. The lane wound between.

Birds landed and took flight between the marble graves and the older, slipping stone. Near the wrought-iron fence they moved, flitting from the turf to the shoulders of loose earth on which canvas sheeting had been laid.

In the distance there was the low sound of cars.

Charlotte heard the first pass at half past ten, sitting at the kitchen table, eating breakfast, the window open. The engine was quiet, she didn't look up. She was drinking a cup of coffee with slow sips, not thinking, not really. It wasn't until the third or the fourth vehicle that she began to notice. She could have counted on the fingers of her hands the cars that had passed here since the day she'd moved in. She'd started to recognize them: a small blue Fiesta that drove by in the morning, a Land-Rover at about five every afternoon – up the hill, then back, an hour or so later. Once, she'd waited on the doorstep to watch him, not wondering who he was or what he did, only liking the way she knew his passing by. An old face, rough as quartz, like a part of the evening.

When she heard the fifth engine pass slowly, she put her coffee cup down on the table and walked into the hall. Last night, she had written four pages. Letters so small that the lines touched each other. Her pen had moved in little ferocious jolts, her face close to the page. Finishing, she had pushed her chair away from the desk and it had been late – morning, night no longer. She was tired now, the sunlight hurt her eyes as she opened her front door.

Between the branches, the cars shone. One, another. She watched them pass and for a moment could see the faces. She turned to look up the lane towards their destination, whatever it might be, but the trees abreast did not allow her to see.

Charlotte steadied the door gently, walked a few steps on to the path. An old white car, rusty, with the window down. An older woman with her hands set on the wheel, a young man in the passenger seat. The next, a man and his wife unspeaking, the leaves' shadows sliding over their faces. The wind had fallen but even without it, even in the sunshine, it was now cold. The trees were ochre.

And then, just a glimpse as the small car drove past, Charlotte saw Ruth. She took two further steps towards her gate. She saw Ruth looking out, her pale face like a map behind the glass. Tiny continents of reflection, staring back to the house as the car moved by and on, disappearing.

For a time there was no traffic. The lane was still. She folded her arms across her chest to keep out that cold. How many cars? Fifteen? And she could hear more now, coming closer as they laboured slowly up the incline. A different engine, heavier like a tired old monster. Charlotte watched the lane. She saw a glint through the trees and there were black cars in her memories.

The hearse was long and low, across its bodywork a half-blue sky. She heard its tyres crackle on loose dirt. She stood, motionless but not stiff now, not straight-backed. She stood as though lost.

Hours she had written last night, until the memories that had struck her like Nia's fists falling on Ruth were gone. Until they were colourless with words. Now she could have laughed, standing here in the high lawn's stillness. They came again. A thousand pages couldn't force them to rest in peace.

She had come here to change her life. Though she failed, she was trying each day not to write. She'd moved away from everything she knew, to a place where she could wake every morning and see no one, and this was what she found: they waited, the memories, in any country's silence.

★

Cars parked side by side and canted, silent now, lined the road. The church's grey stone rose. The oak doors were open, shadow across the entranceway like a tiny lapping shore.

They stood on the grass, gathered in small circles, moving carefully, slowly around each other. Black coats, black hats, white shirts, they walked between the graves, around the church. Their voices blended, men and women of all ages. Their hands were behind their backs and the grass seemed vivid against their dark clothes. They nodded, different faces, good-mornings, in accordance as though assuring each other. 'Yes.' 'True enough, true enough.' They had come here on appointed days, winter, summer, spring. 'That's right now.' And each time there was a sense that everything else they did was only time between these days.

Edward Evans with Garwyn beside him, his face the colour of liver, coughing into cold air. 'Emphysema, they said. Man's fallen in love with the word, amount of times he uses it. No, I can't complain.'

By the church's open doors, Bethan Hughes stood with her mother and Siân. She looked at the doors, swung wide, and could see just the edge – patterned sunlight falling from high windows – of the stone rim of the font where Chelsea had been christened, screaming.

'Gwen'll be here soon now,' Siân said and nodded, arms folded over ironing-board chest. It was her house afterwards of course.

Sun touched the people's backs and the shoulders of their coats. From this distance, the pale sea was motionless.

Tom Humphries's lean face, calm and speaking when he felt it was all right to speak. Patty Hughes, with her arm hovering, almost to touch Bethan's shoulder. An older woman, bent on two walking sticks so that she seemed always to be looking upwards, saying that she'd known Eirian when Eirian had been a girl, that they'd sat together in embroidery class and Eirian had always made jokes, jokes all the time, nothing but.

Limousines they had been. They had filled the wide, circular drive in front of Hedera. Tinted windscreens. She remembered. And she had stood, looking out of the window and down, her hands folded like she could hold some other barrier between her and the glass. She'd left the view, walking down the empty stair. At the wide entrance, dressed in cold black, she had looked at the cars without seeing. Now, unprepared and open, Charlotte could only watch. In the back of her mother's hearse, the arum lilies had been strewn over each other.

A grey sky that day, clouds so low. A grey sky softened by that limousine's window, leather seats that could rock you to sleep with the engine's quiet hum. Only eighty dollars per car, to filter your grief through polarized glass. A clean and perfect parade, shining and on short lease.

Charlotte didn't turn away now, the lane empty. She raised a hand, an unfelt gesture, to her face. She was gone: all the posture that held her. She wanted to see it. Even only to stand outside the gates, to stand where she couldn't be noticed and see the ceremony. She wanted to hear the words they'd say and watch them stand together in the sun. They would all know each other there, they would watch the coffin lowered in each other's silences.

Lennie stood with his hand on Ruth's back, he had come to her now after talking to others; as though guiding he touched her.

'That's right enough,' he said. 'Yes,' he said. He was waiting.

He watched the graveyard, no one alone, and the sober set of his features as his gaze moved said that what he saw was right.

Not a breeze, through the grass or the leaves not a breath. And the birds had taken to the trees. The sound of the engine came first. Between the graves, the talking pattered to nothing.

The hearse and the first car to follow pulled up beside the gates. And from the church's steeple, high over their heads in the sky, the bell rang. Doors opened slowly on that car and Dai's feet came down on the path. Filling every space between every person, filling the silence, the dim swarm of the organ began.

Lennie watched the man stand up and slowly raise his head. And he put his arm around Ruth then, not touching but holding. Dressed in a black suit that couldn't have been his, cuffs didn't reach quite to his wrists, Dai's hair was moulded to his head. With lines around his brown eyes, he looked at them all, his footsteps lost in the organ's music. Gwen stepped from the car. She was wearing a long and simple black dress, coat over it. The make-up on her face was thick. A small black hat, new and perfectly matching. At a distance, hidden in between the others, Tom Humphries saw her. He watched her as she moved quickly to Dai. Her arm around the man's waist, he stooped for her, staring at the people waiting behind the gates.

From this distance, in this music, they couldn't hear what she was saying to him but she was pressing it in gently with her fingers on his arm. The organ swelled. Reaching the gate, she looked at them. She took in the faces. She gave one nod, all was fine.

There was a shifting as they moved towards the churchyard, as if they wanted to give Dai room or perhaps come closer, they milled as Gwen led him on to the path.

'It's all right,' she said. 'It's all right.' He could hardly hear her voice, though.

'Dai,' Siân Humphries said, nodding her head in acknowledgement. 'How are you?' His eyes were wine-coloured.

Tom watched them pass, words that he'd had already fading. She might have moved her eyes to him. There would have been no recognition.

'Dai,' he heard Pat Hughes say.

He was stepping on to the stone, between the doors, glancing back at the woman who served him hot chocolate every afternoon.

' – I'm so sorry, lamb.' She nodded gently at Gwen, saying her name as Gwen took him through the doors, into the cold shade. And as he moved out of the sunlight, Dai felt a brief touch on his arm. He raised his face. Lennie was standing on the stone step beside him, stationary. They looked at each other, just a moment through the shuffling people, and Lennie's voice was lower than them all. 'Well done, Dai.' Though the man should have walked behind, following the pallbearers, instead of standing inside already and staring down at the stone.

Emyr got out of the car and the sound of the closing door was lost in the organ's swell too. From the church's railings, he could see Gwen's hair, the back of her neck in the last moment's light.

Lennie wiped his hands at his sides. No one to follow the bearers now. He said to Ruth, quiet-voiced, 'We'll walk behind the coffin, you and I. Come and stand with me at the gates.'

'Are you sure Dai would want that? Not next of kin . . . ?'

'I'm sure he'd want it a lot better than no one there at all.' He cut her off without a glance. And, looking out across the churchyard, his gaze flicked over faces as suited men stood at the hearse's back doors. Gwen Morgan would know enough to take him to the right pew at least. Lennie took Ruth's hand and moved between the groups of people. They stood at the church gates.

'It's not so bad, is it? To have no next of kin? I don't want to offend, we're not family.'

'D'you not think there's a reason for people to follow the bearers?' He looked away. 'Obviously, they'll be making special arrangements for Dai, like. I see now. We'll try and keep it as close as we can to the way it's meant to be.' Over the fence, fifteen feet from them, Lennie watched as the first door of the hearse was opened. 'A thing like this,' he said. He saw a flower fall on to the path. 'A thing like this, each part's got a reason behind it.' He searched for the right word. The sun cast clear silhouettes on his face. He said slowly, 'It's the rites, like. Last rites.' He couldn't have explained how important this was, not only for Dai but for every person: to bring them together, to do this in the way that it had always been done. More than important now, at a time like this, when everything was going so dry. He couldn't explain to Ruth how it felt to try and hold on to something that was changing even in your hands.

The coffin's wood was touched by this clear light as the men lined either side. There was no sound of footsteps yet. He watched the weight settle on the bearers' shoulders before they began to move. Brass fittings sparking their little glares.

Emyr stood, his clothes, his thinning hair, all still without a breeze. After this, in their home, the people would move from room to room and Gwen would weave between them. Always nodding, always speaking, smiling. In their kitchen and living room, she had laid out food this morning, put plates on every clean surface. He'd seen sausage rolls and small cakes and sandwiches that she must have made when he'd been away.

The bearers stepped on to the path, two by two.

Gwen watched them come. Unmoving, she remembered.

'They'll hold a great funeral for you,' the woman had said. Black wood, she saw. The Reverend Evan Thomas was waiting. The church's hue, across his face, his robes, was grey. The morning, through each stained-glass window, was cast across the stone. Dai saw colours, red and greens there.

'They'll tell each other what a great loss it is,' Eirian had said, 'and every one of them will be a liar.'

Gwen could feel him shifting. Her face was hard. Walking behind the bearers, where family would have been, she saw Lennie and Ruth Lewis, her own expression settled on his face as well.

'Gwen . . .' Dai said. 'Gwen.'

Past the massive organ, through the sunlight's broken colours.

She told him to stand with her. She told him when to open his mouth and sing. She looked at his face and saw that tears had fallen loose. The reverend met the bearers and led them along the aisle, between the rows of oak pews and, reaching Dai and Gwen, turned aside. He stood in the transept and looked out as they placed the coffin down behind him, slowly as they could. He held his hands to his sides.

At harvest festival, children walked down this aisle, out of the late summer heat, carrying fruit or vegetables, organized into lines by Gwen, knowing what to say. They placed the things they were carrying down, where the coffin lay now. The stone held echoes. The organ's music died.

'The Lord be with you.'

They spoke, their voices low and complete.

'And with thy spirit.'

'Let us pray.' The reverend said, 'Lord have mercy upon us.'

Lennie uttered the words as though unafraid. 'Christ have mercy upon us.' He heard their voices with his.

'Lord have mercy upon us.'

They spoke The Lord's Prayer together.

'Thou art the King of Glory, O Christ.'

'Thou art the everlasting Son of the Father.'

'When thou hadst overcome the sharpness of death –'

'– Thou didst open the kingdom of heaven to all believers.'

'Thou sittest at the right hand of God in the glory of the Father.'

'– We believe that thou shalt come to be our judge.'

The reverend looked at them, 'We therefore pray Thee, help Thy servants –'

'– Whom Thou hast redeemed with Thy Precious Blood.'

Dai moved his mouth without speaking the words, unsure what he was supposed to say. He didn't make any sound in case someone heard him and, hearing, realized. But he moved his lips as he stared towards the coffin. He remembered her patting the bed. He mimicked the ceremony with his sounds.

The reverend said, 'Make them to be numbered with Thy Saints –'

Dai felt Gwen's hand.

'– In glory everlasting.'

The graveyard was empty when Charlotte came to it. Her footsteps sounded on the road outside the gates as she moved between the two black vehicles. She heard the birds. It had been nothing like this.

It had been raining, hard spring rain that beat in puddles over the grass. The sodden ground had given under her heels. Standing without any other sense, her umbrella had closed the world to a small space around her. Until there had been nothing but the clenched pain in her jawline and her silence, like justice. She remembered.

Here, sunlight touched the pale headstones. She stared through the iron railings. There was no anger on her face now; it had left her. Everything had left her, lost and shaken. Wrought iron was cold between her fingers. The church's doors were open, she saw.

Maybe some long time ago, her mother had begun to understand. Maybe not, maybe she had only accepted. At twelve years old, Charlotte had left for London and had not gone back. She hadn't called or written and when the letters from her parents had been given to her, she had thanked the house mistress politely and had placed them, unopened, under her bed. Usually, she would collect four or five there before disposing of them.

And she had wondered sometimes if her mother and father sat and talked about it alone, asked each other why. They must have, she thought. They must have realized. Maybe at some point, when they had spoken all the other possible reasons, they had left themselves in silence, looking at each other.

She had kept that silence. Over her mother's grave had held the words inside like her last chance at pride. Standing here, pride had left her too. From the church's darkened doors she heard their voices start to sing and she could almost picture them.

Questions filled her journals, every volume. No word left the page, though. No fear of answers. Their song, disembodied in the graveyard, left her without any words now. Perhaps there came a time, one that couldn't be prevented. It was a breaking that she felt.

Dai stopped mouthing words. Under the high stone ceiling, there was silence.

A chance to grieve, Gwen had said. And after grieving you could begin to heal again.

Dai looked at the coffin. His mother was in there. He didn't know what clothes she was wearing, they had dressed her. He hadn't been back to his home. Had they taken her clothes from there? Had they gone into her cupboards and chosen for her? She couldn't have stopped them – no choices in her now. There couldn't have been any expression on her face, even that. She didn't have them any more. She couldn't.

'Gwen . . .' he whispered, but her hand was soft and her glance said no.

Outside, that sunlight lay across the grass without memory. Charlotte could hear the words. They faded in the air. Past the church, the ground was bare as it led down to the coast. Beneath a bleached sky, the sea's horizon was just a line, darker. From such a distance it seemed almost like land. Charlotte

was fine. No loss to me. How could there be? Grief for my father but not for her. He kept it from me, kept me in the dark but he didn't create it, that was her. Today I watched her put into the ground. At the end I felt this hand. I looked up and someone was passing me a rose. I threw it in. ~~Deep enough to be dark.~~ *I*

watched the shadow shift inside. They came into the sunlight, the reverend leading six pallbearers dressed in identical suits. Faces strained, looking out, with the weight of what they were carrying. It rocked gently. They stepped on to the path between the headstones. Charlotte stared: a woman and a man. Her arm around him like an oversized child, his wet hair slipping forward and his gaze cowed by the sun. Charlotte could see his hands at his sides, stretched open, unnoticed, as though they wanted

anything from her, never asked for anything. I made a goddamn promise and I never broke it. Wouldn't take a thing from that woman. She didn't love me and I never wanted

something to hold.

Now they came, line by line. They carried coats and belongings as if walking towards a new home. Ruth looked out from the procession, Lennie's hand grim on her arm, and between the trees she saw a figure. In the cold and quiet air, the pallbearers stood around the grave. Dai's footsteps slowed. The hole was shapeless. There was a net drawn across it, there were ropes.

Ruth glanced back and yes, it was Charlotte. Standing on the railings' other side, her face was white as mirror glass.

Dai stopped, and they fanned out around him, a wave breaking on his back, unfelt. The new spademarks cut through the turf, he saw. She was in that box and could not speak.

'It's all right now, Dai,' Gwen said, as Emyr moved to stand beside her. 'You know what's going to happen now,' low-voiced as she saw Tom, standing opposite. He was looking directly at her face. Plain as day, he was standing there, plain as day staring at her. She could feel Emyr settling as Tom's expression lay open.

In the quiet, the Reverend Thomas raised his head. He held the book open with his fingers though there wasn't any wind.

'Dearly beloved, let us turn to . . .'

My God, Gwen thought. She saw Tom's mouth move.

Are you all right?

Standing next to his mother. In front of them all. After passing her name between them, he and Rhys, like it was just some little dirty treasure.

They heard Dai make a sound, as though his voice could ripple out like lakewater, packed so close, so still as this.

They sang.

'O anfeidrol rym y cariad,

' – Anorchfygol ydyw'r gras –'

Green ground, brown earth, deep enough to hide from the slanting sun. She would be lying on her back maybe, under this thin layer of wood, under these shades of the sky.

Gwen sang but Tom was staring. Was it some kind of empathy in his expression? So that Emyr must be able to see? Their paper songbooks rustled in the pauses of their breath.

' – Digyfnewid yw'r addewid –'

They stood gathered on the grass. Surrounded by autumn-toned beeches, their backs were turned to Charlotte and to the quiet cars. From where she stood, she could see only those shoulders and hats, black, each one of them, and the white shape of Ruth's face. Turned to find her.

February 25th '92

C,

dad is gone. died. already buried. In the last week while I was working. She didn't tell me. Here – the obituary. The Tribune. It's been months

'– A bery byth o hyn i maes –'

Dai cried out.

Moving to stand beside the man, hearing his shout and seeing Gwen's eyes elsewhere – negligence – Lennie placed his hand on Dai's shoulder.

'It's all right,' he said.

Charlotte was crying. Ruth saw it.

'– Hon yw f'angor ar y cefnfor –'

Dai spoke under Lennie's hold. Gwen, glancing, said quickly in the sound of their song, 'It's all right, Dai. It's fine now.' But the words sounded like lies to her, caught this way with Tom's eyes on her face.

'Stop it,' Dai said.

Lennie Lewis let his hand tighten on Dai's shoulder as he bent close and whispered. He could smell the man, thick aftershave, sweat. Could feel his shaking movements as their voices rose up in the still air.

People were glancing at Dai. His sounds grew. 'Stop it, stop it, stop it,' he was telling them.

'Look, Dai, you see all these people, like, see them all. All here for you. Look at them. All here to help you, so you just be quiet now. You see?'

'– Na chyfnewid meddwl Duw –'

The pallbearers were bending down, reaching for the pegs; men Dai didn't know.

'*No!*' Dai's voice lashed out between the lines of song.

Lennie turned to search for help, for Ruth, but her eyes were far away. Her eyes were staring out towards the trees behind them. She had no mind for what he was trying to hold together now but was in another place.

He almost spoke her name, saw her turning back to him, her head moving in a tiny silent arc.

Dai wrested himself away and Lennie grasped him. He pulled coarsely, violently, and under his hands Dai fell as Ruth looked from Charlotte's distant figure – the railings' shadows thrown across her clothes – to see her husband bending over his struggling shape.

Their voices rose. 'Fe addawodd na chawn faru –'

'*STOP IT!*'

Dai's shout was a moment in their silence. He looked up at all their faces and in the breath that came, Lennie's fingers were still clamped in his collar.

And Gwen's, touching Lennie's sleeve, fluttered. Drew back, away. She raised her eyes to the circle of figures too.

'Get up man,' Lennie said, his words like smooth iron cogs. 'Get up and show some pride for these people here.'

They each looked back, every figure, every face.

Lennie spoke into Dai's ear. 'You can cry.'

In the chiming silence everyone opened their mouth and raised their voice and the song was resumed.

' – Yng nghlwyfau'r Oen y cawn ni fyw.'

Under the cast of the yew Charlotte stood, arrested, watching, as birds rose from the yellowing trees.

Eirian Meredith had laughed, her eyes black as money.

'Ynys-morlan's dying,' she had said.

Crouched in her bed, the light from the window had been grey. Reaching through the glass from her lifeless garden, it had pooled in the bedclothes which she'd drawn over herself.

The houses faced each other across Ynys-morlan's single road, they kept their backs to the sea, blanched to its horizon, and to the wide floodplain that led marsh grass and scrubland to the mountains. Vehicles passed, returning from the churchyard: between the rows of worn shops, the plaster lion's chipped and ugly face, the museum, where sunlit polythene rustled in the spaces which windows should have filled. Doors here that had once stood chocked open were now peeling. That polythene caught in the backdraft after each car. There had been a collection box at the door. The glass display cases that had lined the walls had been full of fossils and antique tools, photographs framed over them.

Dai had used to walk here. Without reading the plaques, he'd looked at the town as it had been. Houses that were now plastered with porches, extensions, dormer windows. You could see the same stone chimneys. In the photographs, the houses' colour had matched the sepia sky's. Pictures of people working, of church groups, sitting in lines outside the doors of Llanfihangel Ynys-morlan.

Hanging there in shadow, Dai had stared at photographs of the storms. Nineteen thirty-eight; they had started in November and by January had broken down the Aberystwyth cofferdam. His mother had read this to him, a long-past afternoon. The photographs of Ynys-morlan had shown waves that burst against the beach, the low seawall, and reared up over the houses. Windows whose views now belonged to people he knew. He'd stood looking for a long time. In them, the waves were brown, they drenched chimneys. So old, though, so still, they weren't frightening.

There were pictures of this street as it had been the next morning. The road that Dai cleaned every day had been buried beneath sea stones. They had filled the town, they had lain in drifts against the houses' faces and swept all across to cover the road itself. The pictures showed men standing amongst them, holding rakes. The storm had filled their town with stones.

Dai had loved the photographs. He'd loved the way they pictured the headland beyond, just the same, just the same mount that could be seen in far-off daylight now, if you were to hold the polythene back and step outside again through the museum's derelict window frame.

The cars parked and sat in silence. Drivers removed ignition keys. Away from Ynys-morlan, sapped, now voiceless, Dai thought of the museum, and of his own home, envisaging his mother's stopped clocks.

'What's wrong with you?' Ruth said. Soft as a whisper the words came into the house.

They had driven to pick Nia up and returned here. Nia had gone into her room. Since her footsteps, this was the first sound.

He sat, his expression made of cinders. Their own bedroom was filled with the sun. She saw how he was stopped by the question like something he'd never touched before. She saw him stumble, when he never stumbled.

'What's wrong with *me* . . . ?' he said. '*What's wrong with me?*' His tie in his hand, white shirt collar open, the light seemed to lessen him. There was anger in his face but it was only the surface. Things grew under it, she saw, and began to rupture what he was trying to hold there. 'Where were you, Ruth? Did you see me trying to hold it together? And you, staring off! Where were you? In some other fucking place! Like you didn't give a shit, about me, about the service, about any fucking thing other than what was flitting through your head!'

He stared at her as she stood lifeless near the doorway. He wanted to reach his anger out but she saw him; he was unable. Dai Meredith's face filled her thoughts, and the face of silence that had covered every person though they'd opened their mouths to sing.

'It was a farce,' he said, stone-voiced. 'The man screaming like he didn't even know how to behave. No better than a child. Screaming. What did he want to do? Pull her back out of the fucking ground? A farce! Reverend couldn't even get his words out between that man's shouting. And I'm there . . . I'm trying to hold it together with my bare fucking hands . . . Do you know how important today was?'

Ruth looked at him and could not answer. He seemed to speak to the walls instead.

'You only have to look at this town, only have to look down the street to see how fucking important that service today should've been. Everyone there, the two of us there. Should have been something *decent*! Should have been something with fucking dignity!' He took a breath and this light just dried his words. 'There was no fucking dignity there. Parade of clowns. Nothing decent about today. Should have been a chance to . . . should've been . . . You know what it felt like? Felt like the fucking end.'

Her eyes followed what he said.

'Look at this place.' He raised his hands from the bed and held them out, and she didn't know if he meant the house, if he meant their home, or everything. 'It's falling apart. Little pieces. Look at it. What's wrong with *me*? Look outside! Do you think anyone gives a shit about this town any more? People used to care, no one cares now. Every shop shut down, graffiti on the fucking walls like this is some sprawling city shithole. Litter on the road. Whole street's a rubbish bin so what should it matter? Right?' He stared at her. '*What should it matter?*' He shouted into the quiet. '. . . My old man spent twenty-five years working on this town. Bit by bit. A job here, like, a job there. Keeping it *whole*. Twenty-five years. Half his life as it turned out. They're falling to ruins, the jobs he did. Could walk up and down this street and list the things he made, wouldn't see a single one of them wearing a fresh coat of paint. Looks like the scrapings could fall off and there'd be nothing but fucking bones . . .' He turned from her as though there was no help – and he no longer had the strength to even want it. 'Only new paint in Ynys-morlan these days is the whitewash that covers the shop windows.' His words ran faster, like he couldn't sever them. 'Every day, looks worse to me. If nothing's changed, it looks worse. Every day I drive, like, sick of the sights I look at, hour after fucking ... industrial estates, fucking council estates, houses so ugly they might as well knock them down and live in the fucking ruins. And I come back here ... and this place, this place, looks more like them every time. What's wrong with me?'

He couldn't move from the bed. Only three feet from him, she was beyond his reach.

'What's wrong with me is seeing it like this. Dirtier. Dirtier every fucking evening and smaller.' He turned to her, his staring eyes defeated. 'Don't ask what's wrong with me, there's nothing wrong with me! I have to see it! Just a shitty little town. It looks like nothing!' His voice ran out and in one breath left him: only sitting here on their sunlit bed. Silence waited in this house, he thought, after every word. 'There's nothing wrong with me ...' he told her.

She didn't move towards him. What she saw, she'd never seen. She was standing, her blouse open, her everyday clothes lying on the wicker chair beside her, ready to be put on again. Over the stripe of her white-shown skin, the edge of a bruise could be seen and Lennie sat now like the last way he had to release what he felt had been taken.

Ruth was crying but he didn't see. Old tears and, looking at him, she didn't feel them.

'What's wrong with you?' she had asked. Soft as spring the words had come into their home.

DEATH OF BOSTON PAPER GIANT
SPOTLIGHTS END OF TRADING ERA

Charlotte,

he suffered with cancer of the bowel for three years and passed away on the 21st. I was at work. Obituary says he fought it hard, took two years more than doctors gave him. In the picture he has a beard. Taken in '88. It's clearly him - unmistakeably but I don't recognize him. My father's dead and this portrait shows a stranger. Did he need me? **She let him die three goddamned years and sent no fucking word** he's gone. Should have tried - what is it? thirty years? - should have tried to change the picture of him in my mind - the person I love hasn't lived since I was twelve years old. I've read the column over and over. So much in it I didn't know. And at the end it says he leaves behind a wife.

This was her punishment for me. Maybe for him. My god, I would have gone to him. I would have told him - I didn't blame him. I can't. She knew it.

She suspected he'd told me maybe I don't know. I wish he'd had the strength. decency. She **must have** suspected, **must have** - deep down in whatever passes for the little bit of honesty left in her, she must have admitted to herself - my God, **did she expect to hide it from me all my fucking life?** but she did. Believed she could. And I remember, far back, and they're so vague now, all the past so cursed dim, but the memories I have - I know she blamed him. She built a house of cards and called it her life. She took ghost stories and turned them into her memories. She blamed him for knowing the truth.

Why did he stay with her? All the bitterness between them. That July fourth and I can picture looking down at them, him drunk and her shouting. They were a joke for God's sake and everybody knew it. Why didn't he leave her? He could have looked in my face the day I left America, he could have seen. I know he felt guilt, I know he was sorry, I saw it in his eyes when we stood on the steps but he didn't speak it. I remember. holding my chin. just kissing me once. He could have chosen me.

The estate goes to her. I don't want it and I'm still trapped by it. Tangled up in their fucking expectations all my life and letting it happen. It's in the corner of my eye every damn day. I've done nothing, in my life achieved nothing. It's a rope round the neck. I say I'll never take it and it's still there.

I look at this picture of Dad's face and it's careworn. It's just ragged with the years he spent. decades.

The obituary says he didn't leave the board till two months ago. It says. 'acumen defined by the takeovers in '55'. But by that point I suppose he had nothing left except the businesses and his grief. I imagine. remember. try to make a whole out of the two. Why did he stay with her? Why did he go along with the deceit? The question lives in me, what happened that August?

No word from her yet.

Where does this leave me? A person's meant to have a future by the time their past is gone. Children. A career. The gallery isn't mine. I have a home where I walk in the door and inhale the same breath I left behind that morning. Where would I find a life now? I imagine some group goddamn therapy. Meeting an 'understanding' man. A 'Philip' an 'Anthony.' I imagine a late, out of date, third ring for him kind of wedding. Having a child. I can imagine that. Not being able to pick it up. Not being able to go near it. fear. And even these things are make-believe. Where am I? I want to ask my father but he's left me. Where am I? I died at three years old.

She came alone today. Charlotte waited for her, the decision she had made lying like a spectre over her features as she sat before her mirror, one mile from the town.

Between Ruth's house and Charlotte's, the leaves were turning. A fine tracery. There wasn't much between autumn and winter; a gust of wind strong enough to take them down. She had dropped Nia at playschool.

It was being judged that Ruth was afraid of. She drove the car, waited on the doorstep, she stood in Charlotte's kitchen, and the excuses she could give for Lennie, for Ynys-morlan, circled in her mind. Miss Weyland's face would be cold like air, she had imagined – and she'd feel small, deserted in it.

But Charlotte was quiet that morning. Behind every pause, her choice waited.

Ruth didn't go to the table when she gestured, filling the kettle without looking back.

'Are you all right?' Turning the tap, drawing water. 'How is your husband?'

She sat finally, a carrier bag in her lap, her hands softly covering it. 'I'm fine. I'm good actually. I'm good,' she smiled at Charlotte as she turned. 'We talked,' she said. 'Talked a lot. He spoke to me, after the service.' She pushed the hair from her face. 'He cried,' she said.

Charlotte lit the gas ring with a long kitchen match and did not answer.

'I know what you must think. Seeing Lennie and – me the day before, blubbing all over the place. I know how it looks. I don't want you to think the wrong things. How would anyone know how to handle that? No one would. Dai – he's a wild one. No one could anticipate, you know?' Though Ruth had only seen him, cart out front, walking, silent.

Charlotte only said, 'I'm sure I don't know what you must think of me, just for going there.'

Ruth saw her, the woman tearless now and poised again. 'I think we're a pair . . . All of us,' she remembered their faces, that loose

half-circle of song, 'all of us, one big pair. I don't know what to
think . . .' She remembered Lennie's hard hands and the silence they'd
shared over the lowered head of Eirian's son.

'And the man, Dai? Did he get home all right? Someone took him
home?'

'Of course. Course someone took him home, the Morgans. Emyr
and Gwen, they're looking after him.'

Reaching into the cupboard, Charlotte glanced out of the window
at the garden's far wall, seeing again the way that man had cried,
buckled over. Her eyes were fixed on something, on the ivy or the
red brick. Such a lot of crying. And in the study her black box file lay
open, and it seemed a simple, quiet thing. Just waiting.

She said, 'Does he always act – with such little empathy?'

'Lennie? He's not a bad person. He'd never be so . . . so unthinking,
so quick to . . . you know, normally. He's not happy.' She looked at
Charlotte's back, her hair drawn and tied up. 'He talked to me, after,
you know? And he never talks to me, so. People can't work things
out without speaking to each other.' And then she told her, 'I've never
seen him like that before.'

She wasn't sure if Charlotte nodded.

'I mean, he gets angry, always been the type to go off. Vim, my
mother used to say. "Well, the girl's full of vim and vigour, have to
give her that." . . . You couldn't hold him back and I'd never have
tried . . . The rugby, and he used to get in a fair few fights.' She looked
at Charlotte, wished she'd turn. 'He's full of life,' she said. 'With a
good glossy coat . . . He's like a bulldozer when he's happy, you can't
stop him. He carries you along. First night he took me out, I said two
words to him and suddenly he was climbing up a bloody flagpole . . .
Really, you can't not love it,' she said.

Charlotte was quiet, as she looked away from Ruth her eyes lost
focus. For a moment they both seemed stranded in their own silence.

'He used to come home, the first year, before Nia – he used to walk
in the door and tell me we were going to go up on the headland to,
you know . . . And I'd be saying to him, it's only April for God's sake.
I could never keep up with him.'

'You shouldn't need to keep up with anyone.'

Ruth saw her in the window's light: silhouetted and still. Quiet for too long. 'Are you all right?' she asked suddenly.

Charlotte reached, took tea leaves from their pot and then stopped and only rested her hands on the counter's edge. 'Yesterday – was a difficult day for me.' She spoke, the noise of the kettle rising behind her, laying her words slowly down. 'I would say – that my mother died six months ago. I would say that, except that sounds as if I were grieving, and that isn't the case.'

'What then . . . ?' Ruth watched and saw again how Charlotte had looked through the railings.

'I don't know. Regretting . . . maybe.' She gave a little sound, a laugh.

'You miss her.'

'I don't miss her, no.' Behind her the kettle whistled out. She turned and spoke while she took it from the heat. 'We hadn't had any contact since I was young.'

'I'm sorry.'

'You've nothing to apologize for.'

Ruth looked away, said with a quiet, flavourless smile, 'I know. Just like to apologize here and there. Scatter them round like sweets.' After a moment, her gaze settling on the blank slate of the long kitchen floor, she said, with no light in her voice, 'I miss the talks. With my mum. That's what I miss most of all. Having someone to tell when you've got news. No beating round the bush when she gave you advice but she used to listen. I remember telling her when I started with Lennie. I used to come home and she had the room upstairs. I'd go up and tell her if I had some good news. Takes the ring out of anyone's good news if you've got no one to go home and tell it to. I used to go up.'

Charlotte could see it clearly: medicines at the bedside, remnants of activity spread over the covers, all in hand's reach, a calm eiderdown sea. She could imagine Ruth there, twenty-three or twenty-four, picking up those remnants, knowing them as well as her own.

'It's good,' she said, 'to have such close relationships in your family.'

Ruth nodded.

'Few people are lucky enough,' she said.

'I agree, yes.'

'It seems to me, very few families perform the function they were meant to – take advantage of that . . . bond. That trust,' she said. 'The home should be somewhere you can speak about everything that matters to you.'

Ruth was quiet as Charlotte stopped, and slowly replied, 'I used to miss a lot of things when I was younger. All the nights out, friends, you know. Think lots about the things I was missing. I never really saw till I was older, it's a special thing to have. I always had this idea that there was a way to be some perfect family. Like it was behind all the other doors, you know? Like it was in all the other towns. Seemed a bloody crazy thing to me when I started to see . . . friends' mums talking in town and they'd be saying, "He's doing this and that in Leeds and his course tutors are like this." And you could hear how sad they sounded. I mean, proud. Obviously proud but – you could hear, they had these four or five little facts. The course is sociology and the girlfriend's name is Laura, he's got a job in Tesco Metro at night and he wants to save up at the moment to try and get himself a car. They're proud but . . .' She didn't finish, only said, 'I was surprised, you know, when I started realizing.'

'You're lucky to be so close to Nia.'

Ruth looked away, nodded. 'She trusts you . . . She likes you, and she doesn't take to many people, I can tell you that.'

'She likes the garden here, she probably associates it with me . . . She loves you very much anyway. I can see how she trusts you. You pick her up . . . She'll get older and that trust will always be a foundation.'

'I am glad for it, all the time I am.' But she didn't look up, only at the cracks between the black slabs.

She wondered if Charlotte saw the strength she had herself, needing to rely on no one. She took the carrier bag from her lap as the woman turned to sit, and pushed it across the table. 'I'm glad you were there yesterday. I know you were upset, I . . . I would've tried to help.' She took her hand from the bag. 'I'd help now. Or try to. But I'm glad you were there.' She looked uncomfortable, as though it was something else she was trying to say. 'I brought you a book,' she finished, 'to look through, think about the planting. You know, sit round and fantasize a bit, when it'll be more than a blackberry patch. And you can marvel over my wonderful wrapping technique.' She lifted her hand from the bag. 'It's a reprint of a flower album, Victorian. I collect them, you know, books on flowers, not that I'm a secret librarian or anything. They're drawings, man called Henry Terry drew them for his children; eighteen seventy-three, so there you go. Borrow it. Read it through.'

Charlotte only looked at her, not knowing really what to say.

Ruth had collected them since she was little, arranged on the shelf in her room where Nia's soft toys played motionless games now. She'd used to pore over them, sitting on her bed. She would hear her mother, footsteps on slate. People said, 'A man's home is his castle.' Her mother had moved through the house like a miniature kingdom, and always preparing for winter. Between the sounds, Ruth had turned pages.

A Victorian Flower Album was slim, it had a loose wreath of wild flowers painted around its cover.

Her mother would be cleaning the difficult bits in the window frames; lichen would grow like mould if it was allowed – it wasn't. Summer, the dividing page would say, and there'd be drawings of honeysuckle, spiraea, lavender.

And then, though Ruth couldn't see, it would start downstairs. Seeds which had been lying just under the grass of her mother's perfect garden would be changing in the soil. They'd sprout upwards in slow seconds and, if she'd been down there, she'd have been able to see them: up, through the neatly cut lawn or between the roses' twisting roots. Her fingers on the page, Ruth had almost felt them gripping. Round the first inches of the pebbledash in minutes, throwing out new leaves. Honeysuckle, and even though it wasn't blooming, not yet, Ruth would smell it, thick and heavy and rising. As she had sat on the bed, it had grown, strong and mindless, struggling over the other flowers. Sometimes it would cover the windows. She'd always know when it had reached the frames because that was when her mother's voice would fall silent for a moment, looking up to see the shade that had come into the room.

Weekend memories put a quietness, a sadness on her face, that Charlotte didn't know the meaning of.

Ruth said to her, 'I think we can clear the path today.'

Charlotte took the book and held it. 'Thank you.' Her smile was brief as sunlight falling on some other place. 'I think we probably can, yes.'

'And you know what comes after the path's cleared?' Above the garden wall, leaves browned and broke free.

Charlotte shook her head.

'We'll have enough space cleared, wall to wall. We can set a fire now that'll burn it right through.'

'Burn it off?'

'Burn it,' she said. She gestured out through the small-paned windows. 'We can't take it all down with shears, all that bramble. We'd be here to next year. We've got a channel through it now. Burn it off.'

'That won't damage the walls?'

'It won't damage them – never suggest it if it was going to damage them.'

Charlotte looked at her, last night's long resolution bare beneath her face. Ruth saw it but mistook it as uncertainty.

'Burn it,' she repeated. 'It's good. A fresh start for the ground. Ash will fertilize it.'

The path broadened to a wide oval. Loam and belligerent bramble trails that revealed, as they cut and hefted and pulled, a circular pattern in the brickwork. And Ruth found, each time they tore away another section, that she remembered that oval space more clearly; the first slips of grass that had grown up through it. She had walked its shape. The sky had been blue and the boys' shouts had chimed between the walls. Kings of the castle and everyone else a dirty buggering rascal.

She and Charlotte worked as the skies grew heavier; rain was threatening. In this cool air, the oval space shone. And as they finished, stood in the doorway, looking, saying nothing for a moment, it didn't feel to Ruth like she had ever been away. Not a breath or a movement for all those years.

'Burn it . . .' Charlotte said. It didn't look like fire could take here. 'It must have taken twenty years to grow.'

The nettles hung their heads, motionless. Only on the very tops of the walls could Ruth see the ivy move.

'Will it even burn?' Charlotte asked. 'It's green.'

'Not underneath, though. We've seen it, pulled it out. The bramble's dead. It grows over itself. All of this,' her gesture was faint, 'this wasn't here when I used to come.'

She thought of her own garden, roses she'd pruned and deadheaded, taken cuttings from to replace any that died. Pansies in winter where the pansies had always been, everything in its place, but not places she'd chosen. And these weeds had grown. Like the honeysuckle that had covered her house, moment by moment as she held her finger on some book's pages. Only year by year. Through the cracks in the path at first, up against the walls where the sunlight was brightest, where the rain gathered when it fell. 'Someone put these walls up to keep out the wind and keep in the sun. It could be lovely,' she said. 'And the fire . . . it'll leave stains, soot. But we can clean it off. We can get some soapy water and a brush, we can clean it off. I'll do it with you.'

Charlotte felt spots of moisture touch her face. The growing clouds had made the sky ember-dark. She wondered if anything could burn under the rain that seemed ready to fall. Finally she said, 'All right. Clear it out then. Clear it all away.'

They set it with newspaper.

Scrunched balls placed under the briar's damp leaves. The paper snagged there on thorns. They pushed it as far into the weeds as they could reach, not speaking any more. Both sides of the long path, they set, and an open circle around the edges of old oval terrace.

They took the box of cooking matches from beside the gas stove and stood, cuffs pulled over cold fingers, the slight edges of newspaper poking out here and there, just visible. By this time they could both feel the rain.

'Well,' Charlotte said.

Ruth smiled. 'Well.'

They looked out. The garden was hushed, it was mute.

Standing by the little doorway, Ruth watched her bend slowly down, saw her face as she struck it and cupped it in her hands.

In the daylight, even this low daylight, they could hardly see the flame. Tiny, fragile thing it was, catching on the match's wood and taking the slimmest hold. The yellow light was faint on Charlotte's sheltered palms, reaching out to the first piece of paper.

She stood slowly then. Watching as it blackened, curled, and then caught into flame. She turned and passed Ruth the matches quickly. 'Do your side then, before it goes.'

Ruth bent down and struck one and held it in between the brambles. They watched the fires catch together.

From the first papers, whispering into the next, they lit in struggling motion. Two lines, the flames a pallid orange, spreading till they formed a border, as flowers might.

'Here it goes,' Ruth said.

But neither of them looked at the other. In the first of the falling rain, the fires began to build.

'I feel like we should make a wish.'

'Make a wish then.' Charlotte smiled and they could hear the sounds of it now, crackling, growing. She was thinking of the way Ruth had looked at her through the railings, knowing nothing about her, saying today that she wanted to help. 'Make a wish,' she said. 'If I could grant them, I'd grant yours over other people's.'

'You don't know what I might wish for.' The sound of the fire was louder in front of them. Her smile faded and she said, 'You know, I used to come here, like, and we'd play hide and seek or we'd play secrets or something, and I didn't even think I was happy then. I don't remember ever thinking once: I'm happy now, this is as good as it gets. I swear, it's like the end of the rainbow, you only see happiness looking back.'

Charlotte didn't answer. She didn't see it.

Ruth said, 'I tell you what I wish. I wish everyone in this town could be as happy as we were, sitting here, playing secrets when we didn't have any secrets to tell.'

They looked out at the garden of weeds, the only things that were moving now were the flames. On each side of the path, they were rising, framing the brickwork to climb with their own rhythm into the hushed, grey air. It was catching deeper.

'Have you got secrets then?' Charlotte remembered her face, shaking hands over the low stone wall.

Ruth saw hanging nettle heads, scorching, blackening until they flared. The fire reached up, five feet and rising as the rain began steadily to fall. 'Hungry flames', wasn't that the term? It was thirst, though, really. Dry, Ruth thought, and striving like that.

'Everyone has secrets.'

'They're evil,' Charlotte said. She stared out at the grasping fires. 'The longer you live, the more you keep. The more you keep, the more precious they seem. They're like money.' She turned to Ruth and Ruth could see moisture from the rain on her face, beading in her drawn-back hair. 'I'm glad I went yesterday. Even . . . I'm glad that I went. I made a decision.' But before Ruth could ask her, Charlotte spoke again. 'Tell me a secret,' she said. In each one of those tiny droplets, she could see orange light.

'I already have. Lots . . . lots of them.'

'Honestly?'

Ruth was stopped by what was surfacing in Charlotte's expression, intense as she had been as she'd cried outside the church. 'Honestly.' Here, in the shade of the doorway together, she saw firelight on Charlotte's small, fine face. 'Honestly.' Not knowing now whether she should make some joke and finding that she had none in her anyway. She watched the woman turn back to burning weeds and could feel their heat on her bare hands and face.

Charlotte didn't speak, only stared out at the garden; at what she'd made. 'Do you want to know a secret then?'

Ruth nodded. Charlotte must have seen it, though she didn't glance.

Because she said, 'There are thirty-three million pounds – thirty-three million, four hundred thousand pounds, today, in an account that holds my name.'

'Thirty-three million . . . ?' She remembered Emyr's face at her kitchen table. How much had he told her then? Four? She couldn't remember. A great deal. But little, because she exhaled empty air now. She didn't have anything to answer with. Finally she said, 'I knew you had some . . .'

Charlotte gave a small smile.

'Someone told me. I didn't ask them. It's a small town.'

'Shall I tell you another then?' She nodded, though still she didn't look at Ruth. The heat was on her skin now, in her eyes. She said, 'I don't want it any more.'

'What?'

'I've bought this house, the things inside this house. Nothing else . . . not now, not for myself.'

'What are you talking about? My God.'

But Charlotte didn't take her eyes from the blaze, felt the raindrops hit her face and her voice was quiet. 'It shouldn't have been mine.'

'Why not? Why shouldn't it? Better yours than anyone else's surely. Right?' She tried to laugh but she was struggling. She could smell the burning. Looking at the woman beside her, she thought, I don't know you at all. '. . . And do what with it?' she asked her. 'Charity?'

Charlotte turned and Ruth saw she was smiling. Before them, the herringbone path was only a dark stretch between the flames. Most of this place was now hidden from their fire-dim eyes.

'I don't know.' Her smile was a sharp thing. 'Would you like some?'

In the warmth, Ruth opened her mouth. 'No.' She laughed. 'No! I don't want any.'

'Why not?'

'Because it's not mine, that's why not, I don't want any.'

'Better yours than anyone else's. That's what you said, isn't it? I'd give you some, if you'd like.'

'If you're going to give it, my God, it's your decision, but if you're going to give it away, give it to . . . somewhere it'll make a difference.'

'It wouldn't make a difference to you?'

'I don't want your money. I wouldn't – I wouldn't know what to do with it, how to spend it.'

'You'd do something good with it.'

'I'd go out and frivel it away on eclairs.' She laughed again and immersed in the noise, it sounded small, unreal. 'I can't believe you,' she said. 'I don't understand you. I don't –' she shook her head and the temperature coated her face. It came to her that she had seen a smile like this before, small and fierce like this, on Nia. The expression of a three-year-old girl. 'Why would you want to give it away? Why would you want to do that?'

'Because my mother shouldn't have left it to me. And I don't want it.'

It, she said, like it was singular. But really it was them, Ruth thought, all those pounds, the millions of them, all together.

'Because it won't make me happy.' Determined she looked, as if she had only now made the decision that she deserved that.

Ruth watched her, flushed, her blood rising to her skin to protect it. She looked like she could beat the fire down, or make it rise, or any damn thing she wanted, Ruth thought. She remembered the woman crying.

'But she wanted you to have it.'

'I don't care what she wanted.'

Charlotte remembered Hedera. Coming to the place and finding it full of her mother. Everywhere. All of it left lying. Mrs Weyland gone already by the time she'd arrived, they'd been things to clear away by then. Charlotte remembered how it had looked when she'd finished. She'd not gone back to the northern meadow, as though there had never been a family. An eye for an eye. Her mother dead, it had been too late to go back.

Now she said, 'I'm going to give it away. All of it away, piece by piece.'

'If that's your decision . . .' Ruth stopped and started, 'then it'll be a wonderful thing. To make a difference like that, a wonderful thing. The amount of money . . . it's a lot of difference to make.' She laughed suddenly, couldn't have stopped it if she'd tried. 'Thirty-three million pounds, my God, that's a lot of difference.'

'It's not like that.' She stared out, and Ruth didn't know what she saw. Through the doorway in front of them, the flames moved through every branch and leaf.

'You wouldn't even have to give it to a charity. One that's already set up, I mean. Every pound they get, they spend fifty pence on boardroom tables and twenty-five on coffee and cakes. I heard –'

'It's not like that. You think it's generosity, it isn't. I don't want anyone's gratitude, I told you. It isn't mine to earn gratitude from.'

'Whatever way you want to see it,' Ruth looked at her, 'to have that money and then give it away . . . that'd be a good thing to do. Good deed like that,' she said, trying to make a smile, 'if that doesn't buy you a place in Heaven then God just isn't on the take. Whatever way you want to look at it, it'll be a wonderful thing to do. First hand, you can do it, see where every pound goes. And any charity you want, any cause or lots of them. I'll be jealous to see you do it . . . Dip your conscience in milk.'

'No.' In front of her it blackened brick and she looked at Ruth like she felt nothing.

'That isn't how it'll be. Not at all. I don't have the right to do that any more than to spend it on myself.' She could have told Ruth, she had sworn an oath. A stupid promise, once, a long time ago.

Any day before today she would have said nothing at all, but some part of this, she knew, was over. She could feel it now. Maybe it had been over for a long time, but she had been too lost in it to see.

'They told me she was dying. They called me and told me. I was in London. They said she was asking for me. I didn't go.'

Ruth only stared. In the noise of the fire, she heard herself say, 'Why not? You didn't go? And you knew?'

Charlotte nodded, as though Ruth would see her clearly now. 'Not until they called to tell me she was gone. There. I'm sure the situation looks different now.'

In her bedroom, the room where she'd passed away, there had been many pictures, as she'd imagined, photographs.

Ruth was silent. There was the blaze of collapsing branches. She felt the rain on her face and hair. Above the walls, the sky was sad with it. She said, 'I don't see what she could've done, don't see what anyone could've done to make . . . to make someone else that angry.'

Ruth saw her turn, vicious-quick. The woman's expression was open and feelings moved across it like she didn't even know: that determination on her face, Ruth saw, like poison.

'She wasn't any mother to me in life. It doesn't change a thing like that, to be dying, to be –' But then she only turned away, looked out. Her eyes were bright. Reflections.

She thought of the bed. Standing in that room again, she had wondered how it must have looked to her mother. That view through the picture window. The formal garden. And the door, opposite that bed directly. Her mother would have faced every person that entered the room, and every one of them a stranger, every time no word from her, until she must have known. In those last few days, Charlotte thought, her mother's mind must have turned to the meadow beyond the lake. In those last few days she must surely have admitted.

It was over. Looking out, Charlotte thought of Nia, standing on the path outside a small and pretty pink house, little curtains and a beautiful garden, old rose beds. A house that needed new slates and a new coat of paint, that looked like it had had a hundred new coats already. And Ruth had run out, a glance thrown to the doorways either side as she tried to gather up girl and glass and bottles. Ruth had held out her hand over that wall, never looking down.

'What would you do with the money?' Charlotte said. 'If it was yours.'

'I don't know . . .'

She only looked at Ruth, pale skin lit. 'What would you do with it? Tell me.'

'I don't know.' She looked away, shaking her head.

Through the doorway, the fire filled the garden with noise and motion, as perfectly as the weeds had filled it with silence. She watched Ruth, both their faces wet now with the rain.

'Tell me.' Charlotte was still, eyes that might have been hiding something or offering everything they had.

Ruth didn't speak. Nothing came, though her mouth opened.

'I'll give it to charities if that's the only way. Not through generosity or kindness but because I don't . . . want it in my name.' Charlotte Weyland's voice was still like water, 'I'm asking you, what would you do if it was yours?' She didn't take her eyes from Ruth. The branches were skeletons, slender as paper now. 'I'm offering it to you,' she said.

Ruth saw it in her face: this was the truth. And she didn't know what might be behind Charlotte's words. Because nothing came free. She thought unclearly, this is how it feels to stand on a cliff, this is how it feels. If Lennie'd let go of that flagpole, just taken his hands away and started to fall, one simple movement, this is how it would have been.

Her mouth was dry as the air. 'Don't offer it to me again because I'll take it. I don't even know you. You might've . . . seen me cry, but you don't know me. You offer it again, I'll say yes.'

The smile didn't quite touch Charlotte's face.

In the silence that seemed to fill the Morgans' house as thickly as air freshener, Dai Meredith sat alone. He filled the sofa, staring at the clock on the mantelpiece like he was seeing it for the first time.

While Gwen Morgan stood at the head of the community centre's hall and read to the small faces from her book on Mardi Gras across the world, card and pens ready to be handed out for the making of Halloween masks, while Nia watched her face move and the council worker Emyr had brought in now slowly scrubbed paint from the rain-wet bricks, Dai Meredith blinked, he stared. Alone and in soft-growing shock.

His face was wet because he had been crying and really was still crying now – hitching, tapering away – no longer thinking about the tears, though. Only looking at this clock. Through the gentle, Ambi-Pur silence, he could hear its ticking.

It was beautiful. He looked at it in the rain's grey light as the tears dried on his skin. Tightening up there like one of his mum's facial masks. He'd tried one of those once. Never again. This clock had a creamy-white face and its numbers were Roman numerals. He didn't need numbers at all to tell the time, though; knew their shapes and directions by heart. This clock's hands were delicate, made of gold. Its rectangular edging was gold and the tiny little pillars each side of its face. Looking at it now, even with the guilt of remembering his mum's grandfather clock or the digital watch she'd given him, Dai thought that it must be the most beautiful he'd ever seen. Wet-eyed, he was reading it again.

He'd been thinking of his mum, all things about her. Not just lying in her bed like she had been this summer, but before. Shopping with her, picking things out, or gardening when he'd hold the basket. She'd bend over with the little fork or a pair of scissors. He'd been seeing it, perfectly clear. Eating dinner with her. How good it had been, not even doing anything. He'd been crying. Same as every day before today – worse, after how he'd ruined the funeral. He hadn't meant to. As he'd seen the coffin he'd thought of her like she was still alive. She wasn't alive. The things she would have wanted weren't the right things any more.

Sometimes it seemed like he cried for a long time, sometimes for no time at all. A few moments. Yes, it seemed that way. But he hadn't been watching the clock.

The recent days that had wound away from Dai, they'd been days in which he'd hardly seen time at all. He must have glanced, though. Must have. Because on several occasions, crying through those days, he'd seen that ten minutes had passed in tears.

Beautiful white and gold, so fragile. Like you could knock and it would never tell the time right again. He was staring, really staring. Ten minutes had passed. Ten minutes, exactly, before the tears had tapered away.

On the mantelpiece, it ticked its moments.

He'd used to think when he was younger that they'd invented seconds because nothing came exactly on the minute. He'd told Mum. She'd said it wasn't true, seconds and minutes had been invented at the same time, not one after the other. He hadn't believed her though. Nothing was exact, he wasn't stupid, he could see it everywhere. And every time something didn't fit, Dai had reasoned, people made up another, smaller way to measure things. By the time he was old they would've invented one smaller than seconds, to make seconds more exact. He had stopped this train of thought, though. If they invented that, they'd also have to invent new clocks and watches, to show them on. If everyone had new clocks and new watches then all the old clocks and watches would be thrown away. And he'd been able to imagine that: a great big landfill site with the gulls arcing over it in the sky, and nothing in the dirt but clocks and watches: grandfather clocks like his mother's, carriage clocks like this one, old-fashioned watches that hung on chains but could still be used, even now. Digital watches like his own, still blinking in the middle of all the muck. He'd stopped thinking about it after that.

On the windowpane, rain was now falling. He didn't hear it; heard nothing but this beautiful timepiece's minutes. At ten to twelve he'd begun to cry. Yes, remembered seeing it. It was twelve now, and the tears had left him.

There was a rhythm. Ten minutes. A rhythm. Realization came and slowly filled Dai. Throughout his stomach, all his body. He stared.

Since Mum had died, he hadn't been watching the clocks. But the clocks had been watching him.

If it hadn't been Gwen and Emyr's clock, he would have taken it. It would have fitted in one of his overall pockets, they were big. Wouldn't even have cared for how wrong stealing was. Fine gold hands. Lovely round white face. It had counted the rhythm of his sadness every day. Even at the church maybe, standing over that hole, shouting things that were wrong, knowing nothing – this clock had sat on the mantelpiece and had counted for his tears. Had it been ten minutes over the grave? He was sure now. It had.

Everywhere, time was the same. This clock might not have existed, but it was ticking on others. Maybe every person had their own rhythm. As smoke passed outside this window, Dai saw his own reveal itself before him. Felt a presence, everywhere.

The house was empty about him but, in this dawning, didn't seem it. All around there was something, he realized. There was time.

'I'm afraid to say yes.' She felt laughter bubbling. 'I'm afraid to.' Rain beat against the ground. 'Everyone in the world must've sat and fantasized, the lottery or something . . .' Drops trickled down between the yellowing leaves. 'I bet nobody thinks they'd be afraid.'

'Will you take it then?' Charlotte asked. 'Say yes.'

She tried to clear her throat so it would be spoken well. Something like this, it was important. 'Something like this,' she thought blankly. In her mind, the words floated.

She said it, just as simple as taking one step. 'Yes,' she answered.

For a moment there was no sound between them but the burning.

'My God.' Ruth's voice was low.

'My God,' Charlotte repeated quietly.

'Feel like I could shout it, you know that? Just to get it out of my throat,' she put her hand below her jawline. 'Right about here,' like she could swallow down the rift she felt. 'That amount of money,' she said, 'could buy all the wishes you could think of.'

Charlotte didn't answer but only said, 'And what would you wish?'

'I . . .' But nothing seemed to be properly still. She thought of Lennie, sitting on the bed like he wouldn't look at her unless forced. 'I know what's wrong – with Lennie, with everyone. You can see it.' She nodded. 'Ynys-morlan,' she said. 'It's the place. That's what's wrong.'

Charlotte's eyes didn't leave her, the firelight was dying.

'He can't bear to watch his home fall apart, no one could bear to see that, could they? Like looking at bones, he said. Like the paint could come off and there'd be nothing underneath. He grew up here. No one could be happy, seeing that.'

Watching, Charlotte slowly shook her head, though Ruth couldn't see if it was agreement or only lack of knowledge.

'You put everything into your home, spend all your time when you're little, planning how it's going to be, drawing pictures. Every-thing goes into it. Memories . . .' she looked at Charlotte, who held the answer in her empty hands. 'You only have to walk down the street to see what's happening here. People trying to keep their homes up to scratch, and it doesn't matter how hard they try because the place is dying anyway. There's no trade, there's no money. People leaving . . . There's nothing more important than your home. You see on the television, on the news, when hurricanes go tearing round. See the pictures, people standing in the ruins, families, picking up things that used to sit on the mantelpiece. And you can see the looks on their faces, they're lost. They were a family, like, with a home and a life. Standing in the rubble, that moment, they're not even a family any more. Just three people, like they don't even know how to be.'

Underneath the furnishings of Hedera, the antiques, the silver, the photographs, books and mementos, only walls and vacant floors. You could whisper and hear the words come back to you.

'I used to draw these pictures . . .' Ruth said. 'Houses and gardens. You plan it all your life. But you can see it on all our faces here, walking down the street like the end of the season's the end of us. Might as well just leave. You know how it'd look? No one living behind the windows. Spar empty and the gift shop empty and tables in the café with no one sitting at them.' She saw it through someone else's eyes, through past years. In a rear-view mirror she saw it.

Smoke rose through the black and leafless ivy trails. Above the walls the wind caught and stole it.

'Ynys-morlan's dying, Lennie said. But it doesn't have to be that way.'

And whatever it was that had been emerging in her eyes was full there now, bright as pennies, Charlotte saw. Bright as pounds.

'We could start a fund,' Ruth said softly.

'Go on. A fund.'

'A fund for everything. To stop the rot setting in. It could be a beautiful town, this. It could be full of beautiful buildings, enough to make people want to visit just because it feels good to walk down the street. That kind of town,' she nodded. 'Full of shops, not just shops for the tourists, for the people who live here. Could be the kind of town that people want to move to, start a family, a business, a life. Not just a town for three months a year.'

'How would you change it?'

'You see the street, you see Spar . . . pebbledash that looks like it's been rained on so many times, it's turned as grey as the bloody weather. Or the gift shop, great big lump of breezeblock and concrete, more concrete outside just for good measure. The houses,' she said, 'peeling paint, like they're falling apart, missing slates. The museum closed up, boards and polythene on the windows. But those things aren't a lot of work. They're all on the outside. The buildings, they're beautiful underneath. Underneath, they're all stone cottages. You can see where the chimneys still stick out. It wouldn't even take a lot. To strip that render off, pebbledash. Strip out the rotting wood. Re-slate, repaint, you know? It's all on the outside.' She looked with hope into Charlotte's face. 'A fund,' she said. 'We could actually do it. It could be renovated . . . Regenerated. It could be beautiful.'

Charlotte Weyland watched, as though these things were shown in Ruth's eyes, small and perfectly recreated there.

Bethan Hughes sat before a streaming windowpane, running cloth through her hands, through the sewing machine, and looking out across the street at the café's sandwich board. A fat little chef holding up the specials list and crying a hundred rain tears.

Behind her Chelsea sat on the floor, both legs out straight, pushing the big red button on her playcentre.

'Chels' . . .' not speaking above a murmur, 'will you stop doing that and practise your flute,' pressing her foot gently on the pedal. Blue cloth slipped. The lights were on for this overcast afternoon, they left glowing magnolia patches on her bedroom's walls.

She'd painted this place with her mum and dad. Nothing was fragile in here. It was all childproof in here. The three of them had worked through days, Bethan pregnant enough by then that she'd got the treatment wherever she went. 'Out of the way, lady with a baby coming through.' So many chairs held out for her, it might've been worth spending the rest of her life with a cushion up her jumper.

Her dad had made a nursery in what was meant to be the spare room, painted that magnolia too – she hadn't wanted to know if it was a girl or a boy, better surprise for everyone that way. He'd made a cot. When they'd almost finished, her parents had come round with a camera. They'd drunk sparkling white wine and taken pictures, pictures of them sitting on the floor, pictures of her by the cot, pictures of her holding soft toys. She'd stood still while the bulb flashed and said, 'And here's Bethan and her stomach in the nursery. And here's Bethan and her stomach by the window. Oh look, here's Bethan's stomach on holiday in Greece.'

When they'd finished the wine, her mum had opened the window to let the smoke out and they'd pushed the mobile hanging over the cot back and forth and listened to the noise it made.

Her mum had said, 'This'll be the baby's first room. To the baby,' she'd said, 'all this will be new.' She'd been drunk. A little while before that she'd been crying and she'd still had the handkerchief in her hand. It had been spring then, it must have been spring.

'Wait till he gets to fifteen,' Bethan had said, 'and he wants to put pictures of naked women on the walls. Won't be so cute then.'

But her mum had only said, 'Might be a girl.'

After they'd left Bethan had tidied up; had told them she wanted to do it herself. She'd closed the windows, picked up the bottles and the ashtray and taken them into the kitchen, the only room they hadn't decorated. She'd been putting them in a low cupboard when she'd seen the mark on its inside wall. She'd had to crouch by then, hadn't been able to bend properly. Near to the ground there'd been two long crayon marks. Yellow. She'd looked at them for a while, standing with the ashtray still held in her hand, and had started crying.

Now Bethan sewed. Rain hit the fat little chef's face and dribbled down his specials' board. Patterns were laid across her bed, off-cuts across her floor, and Chelsea played and played. There were memories. Standing in the Lion with Tom, not so long ago, a Friday night maybe.

'What you do today then?' he'd asked her, though he'd seen – he'd been working and she'd been not. He'd given her that smile though. He had ones saved up for all kinds of different days.

'Today,' she'd said, 'I won a hundred grand on a scratch card. Right in front of your mum, so you can ask her. I was standing there, scratching it off quick so I could get at my Crunchie – I'd just bought a Crunchie – and there it was. You've won a hundred thousand pounds, it said. Obviously,' she'd smiled, 'obviously, it's not going to make much difference to me. You know, since I got that modelling contract last week, I've got pretty much all the money I can spend. Only the other day, I was down at the dealership in Aber. "Not another fucking Mercedes," I was saying. You know, "Not enough leather," I was saying. I want a car they had to slaughter a whole herd of buffalo to upholster the inside. I want a car that goes so fucking fast, you put your foot down on the pedal and you're left standing on the street.'

Tom had picked up his glass but hadn't drunk, only smiled. 'I rode an elephant today.'

'I rode a rhinoceros.'

'I rode a fucking penguin. There.'

She'd said, 'Well. I'm moving tomorrow.'

'Oh yeah?'

'Yeah, as a matter of fact. Bought the house already, all that money, like, you've got to have something to spend it on. Tomorrow, you'll never see me again. I'm off. Newfuckingfoundland.'

'Newfoundland.' He'd laughed. 'You don't know anything about Newfoundland.'

'Yeah well, go with it, like. It's got dogs.' She had raised her hand and pressed it flat against the air, as though she could steady herself on nothing. 'Dogs and . . . beaches.'

'It has not got beaches.'

'Look, it's a piece of land by a piece of water, isn't it? Everywhere's got beaches. If I want it to have beaches then it's got them, all right?'

'Fine with me,' he'd said.

'And not beaches like here either. Fucking sand-covered beaches, beautiful white sand and water that's hot as a bath. Coconut trees. In fact, it's a fucking Bounty advert and it's got the Bounties too. It's got Russell Crowe, right, in a loincloth. Only really, he's much nicer than he looks on camera. Really, the rough's just in his stubble and underneath, he's soft as candyfloss and he's so fucking in love with me, it hurts him just to see my face.'

Yeah, Tom had smiled, and told her to go on. He had a smile for every day.

Now Bethan raised the sewing-machine needle in the window's greyness and turned towards Chelsea. The lamps were bright all around them. She held what she had made up against herself.

'Come on then,' she said, 'it's the Winter Collection, what d'you think?' She looked at the girl's face. 'Come on then. Well?' As she felt the velvet move against her own clothes.

'Business grants.' Ruth's smile was a trapped second; a storm in a photograph. 'For the shops, they're hanging on by the skin of their teeth. We've got all those empty places. No one starting up in them because they've got no capital, even if they had capital, the businesses wouldn't last because the town can't support them. But if everything *else* was changing, if the *whole street* was changing and we could get them through the first few months. There could be an entire town . . .'

'Subsidies.' Through all the gifts Charlotte spoke of, there was no gift in her voice.

'There aren't enough people now, but people have left, they've been leaving for years. There's as many empty flats as there are empty shops. Houses with For Sale signs out front. If people can leave,' she said, 'then people can come. A place is just a blank piece of paper. If you were able, you could make it into somewhere else.'

You looked at Ruth and you couldn't help but be carried by her voice. Charlotte remembered the noiseless street that she'd walked that first day. The people here, she had thought, didn't own the landscape.

Coming here to change herself, not to change, or even touch the place. You looked at Ruth – she didn't seem to know how to hold in what she felt. And Charlotte wondered how she'd seem if angry, or truly happy, without this edge that kept her moving always, always talking. A crest she swam on, as if eventually it must carry her to where she wanted to be.

'A place is only a reflection of the people living there. If you're able, you can make it whatever you want. We're able,' she said. 'You're able.'

And in silence, Charlotte nodded. Smoke drifted away from them, rising to pass over the roof of her house. The seventh home that she had lived in as if it was not her own.

Tom had stood and watched the fat spit all day. Pat had shut up shop and the rain wasn't leaving. The rain had come to stay. It was almost November. Tonight was museum night, they'd synchronize watches.

'I want supplies,' Rhys'd said. 'I want torches, batteries, I want one of those gas light things, like. I want a fucking compass and I want your sister.'

'You can have her, like. If you can put up with that new fucking accent of hers then you're a better man than me.'

'I don't think she'll be talking much.'

'Fuck's sake. You know what, Rhys? You make me sicker than this chip fat I'm looking at right here. Green it is, I swear, starting to go hard round the edges –'

'So you're not bringing your sister then.'

'One lesson, she's had. She paid for it herself, like, one lesson, I swear, she opens her mouth and "The Antiques Roadshow" comes out –'

'Tom?'

'Sick isn't even the word –'

'Tom.'

'What?'

'I don't care.'

'Good. Museum night then. I'll bring torches.'

'And beer.'

'Which goes without saying.'

'And paint,' Rhys added.

'Paint? I haven't got any paint, what the fuck d'you want paint for?'

'I'm taking watercolour classes.'

'That's lovely. I haven't got any paint.'

'All right,' a pause, 'have to be mine then. I've only got white but there you go.'

'What colour did you want then?'

'Red.'

Rhys hadn't mentioned the story he'd been promised. Tom hadn't mentioned it. That morning, when Gwen had come in to tell them how Dai was doing, he'd told her that he'd found the bracelet. He'd said he'd forgotten it – taken it home with him after finding it – that it would be here for her when she wanted. Tomorrow, whatever. He shouldn't have tried maybe to find out what her coldness meant, not like that, not at the funeral. Hadn't been able to stop himself, though. He cared. Seeing the shock-horror on her face as he'd tried to mouth the words, he didn't care any more.

He looked at Pat, saw her turn and smile, familiar as the rain that was running down the window. He was all right now.

She said, 'Well Beth's got her lights on. She'll be painting one of her Van Gogh's, or composing one of her symphonies right about now. She likes to do that after lunch. She makes dresses,' Patty said. 'D'you know that?' She gave a wise nod, squinting through the smoke, like she knew Bethan better than Bethan thought.

He was still all right, nodding back to her, saying 'Is that so?' The telephone was still a minute from ringing. Soon he'd be a long fucking way from all right. If all right was a country, it would be Thailand then. Newfuckingfoundland.

He said, 'Well I don't reckon there'll be anyone in to finish off that cheesecake.' He shook his head. 'All those strawberries . . . that cream.'

'You're a little bastard, that's what you are.'

He watched her get up. 'I'll empty the till.'

'That'll take you a long time.'

He sprang it, looked at what was inside. It was only because he was standing there that he picked up the phone.

'McDonald's,' he said.

He was about to cradle it in his neck when he heard Gwen Morgan's voice.

'Are you happy?'
Outside the café's windows, the rain hit the street like gravel.

Ruth said, 'If you walk out of your door every morning, out into a place where things are possible, you can be happy then . . . Nothing's been possible here, such a long time. Thirty-three million pounds, that's anything. That's the possibility of any change, like, every change. That's walking out of your door, into a different life.'

And really, wasn't this what they had needed all along? For as long as Ruth could remember. To cut away the dead wood? To polish, preserve the parts they loved? The memories they wished to keep. To make a place which held those things safe, and to discard the rest, let go of all the rest and see it rise, thin as this flame.

Above the houses' roofs, the sky was livid.

'Are you happy?' she said. Her voice was a whisper like the children's would soon be, reaching her through the closed office door. Quiet as a kept breath now. 'Are you happy? I hope you're happy, Tom.'

Outside she could see the workman in his van, sitting with a flask and newspaper. His job was done, he'd go home soon. Perhaps, through another pane of glass, Tom was looking out towards her. He would have seen this tarmac, distant in the rain, he would have seen the neatly painted lines and the newly clean, red bricks. Through the bright glass of the last little window, he would have seen her face. She was looking towards him, certainly.

'Did you get what you wanted?'

Bare-faced, he'd stood in front of her this morning, talked to her like he expected some response. Like he owned a little part of her. She thought of Siân's Humphries's home, the dim kitchen with everything stacked away, the calendar hung on the fridge.

Perhaps the boy had been like this always. Oh, Siân would smile at her and talk as if every word she said was God's honest truth, but behind those hard-lined eyes, Gwen wouldn't be at all surprised if there things were hiding. She'd always kept to herself had Siân. For all Gwen knew, those times when she'd asked about Tom – Tom in primary school, in high school, his exams – there might have been every kind of problem. Who knew how the boy might have behaved? She could see quite clearly what his true colours were now that he'd become a man.

Standing here and whispering into the phone like some criminal, she found her mouth was dry and had to wet her lips.

'You certainly looked happy this morning. A pig in muck, and I've never used the term quite so appropriately. I'm looking out at the van at this moment, that Emyr had to hire and pay for with this community's money, just to clean away the obscenities that your friend saw fit to write on the wall. And if that was the extent of the damage you'd both done then I could tell you I'd be happy too.' She moistened her lips again. There was silence. 'Is Pat there? I hope she is. I hope you're having to stand there and nod and smile in front of her in just the way that I had to. How dare you even speak to me? How dare you, after what you've done?'

She took a breath. In the dull and tidy office, she stood very close to the glass. Seen from outside, there would have been reflections of the sky across her face, the window was so clean. From the closed door beside her, she could hear the first shufflings of the class. Five minutes and they couldn't stay still. And she wondered how the parents expected them to cope with primary school when they weren't even disciplined enough to sit through five minutes alone. She opened her mouth to give him more of her words, all stored up they were and waiting to slip down the telephone line and into his ear.

Her voice was a whisper as she began to speak. But she heard Tom say then, 'Oh yes, oh yes? Well if you'll just wait a moment, I'll have a look in the kitchen for you.' She heard him say, out into the room where he must have been standing, 'It's my mum.' And into the phone again, 'I'll check the rota now. Hang on.'

Butter wouldn't melt. The boy was so practised at lying, he must've been doing it in his cradle. But she could hear the tone underneath just as clear as a bell. The boy was worried now.

'That's it,' she whispered. 'That's it, you get yourself where no one else can see you. Wouldn't want Pat to know what kind of person you are. You get yourself into the kitchen.'

'Gwen –' Whispering just as low as her. 'I don't know what you mean. You were in here this morning, you were smiling like that. But I've not done anything so don't talk to me like this! All right? I've not done anything to you! So fuck you,' he said.

'That's right, yes. That's the kind of language I'd expect from you. The real Tom Humphries coming out now, is he? You've not done anything . . .' She laughed, high-pitched. 'Did you have fun, you and that Rhys? Did you have fun laughing about me? Talking about me? Spitting over your lies about me? I'm sure you *loved* it.'

Tom was silent. Standing here, Gwen felt the weight of it. She had struck him, then.

He said, 'I never fucking laughed about you, like. I've got better things to talk about than you. I just tried to help you, that was all I did. That was all I did.'

'I wouldn't bother lying now, Tom. It's too late. After what your friend did, I think it's a little too late for everything, don't you? What you should be doing is counting yourself lucky that the kind of friends you keep trail such dirty reputations after them that a man like my husband wouldn't believe one word that came out of their mouths. Should be thanking your lucky stars. Or I think you'd have more trouble than you'd bargained for.'

Tom's voice was cold. 'I don't know what the fuck you're talking about, like.' He started to say something else, tried and failed to find his words. 'I didn't tell any lies about you –'

'Do you not *know*?' Gwen said. She laughed that laugh again. 'Well how about that? He finds his own lies running away from him! Well you must know what you told that friend of yours. Did he not mention what he did?'

'He didn't do anything.'

'While he was busy painting his obscenities across this wall, my husband found him. Caught him with his hands still dirty. Your friend wasn't happy. Your friend tried to defend himself in the only way he knew. With more obscenities. With your lies!'

'I didn't –'

'I wonder how your mother would react if she knew about those lies. I wonder how Pat would react. My God, they all think you're so honest, don't they? What a clever front you must have kept up. Tom would never do anyone harm. Tom wouldn't hurt a fly. Tom? Oh no, not *Tom*, he's been a hero since he was eight years old. Well you think back through all the lies you've told and remember! Did you laugh about it? Did you? Now, why don't you imagine those words coming out of that friend of yours' filthy mouth as he stood there and shouted it at my husband!' Her hard whisper had changed to something louder, she had to take a breath.

Tom was silent.

She could hear the children now. The children were talking and laughing, probably looking right at this closed door by her side. And Tom was silent. Oh he remembered now.

He broke into a few words. They must have scraped in his throat, the way he spoke them. And when she heard, Gwen was trapped in silence for a moment also.

'Rhys saw the bracelet.'

She opened her mouth but she didn't answer.

He said, 'He saw it, I didn't show it to him, like. I wouldn't do something like that. I don't give a fuck what you think, I wouldn't do something like that. He saw it, he knew it was yours. I told him I found it. Told him every fucking thing I could think of. I've got better things to do than lie about you, like! All right?'

Gwen recovered herself. Only a minor slip. She held the phone very tightly. 'He just saw it. You happened to leave it lying around? Explain to me, why don't you, how that could've happened? How was that?'

'You want to know how?' His whisper, rising, and whatever it was, anger or guilt or just hurt, he wasn't holding it in any more. 'I'll tell you what happened, like. I was wearing it, all right? I was wearing it! You happy now? *All right?*'

Like this, she was stopped. Between them the rain came down.

'What do you mean, you were wearing it?'

But it was too late by then. There was no answer from the phone in her hand. Gwen stood in the rising noise from the children next door. She looked out through the brightly polished glass and listened to the tone of a disconnected line.

Emyr drove back into town through the weather. The flag dancing violently, windscreen wipers shifting in front of him. He felt deadened by all the things he'd said throughout this morning, the times he'd smiled into people's faces and told them how well Gwen was today, how she couldn't be better today, how she was on top of the bloody world and looking right down at everyone else on this particular day.

This morning, she hadn't been in the bed when he had woken up. He had gone to the bathroom, heard her downstairs, and when he'd come back from the bathroom, he had found his clothes laid out on the bed for him, just the same as every other day that had ever gone before. He'd stood and looked at them. The clothes had been neatly ironed, laid out in the shape of a person with the shoes underneath the trouser cuffs, sitting at the foot of the bed. A lilac V-necked, pale yellow shirted, grey jacketed person. The house was working, it was a machine. It churned out clothes every day and put them on his bed, it made breakfast and then cleared the plates away. The house was working. His life was working. It was only he who had stopped.

He'd come downstairs with the clothes on him and, seeing her in the kitchen he'd said, 'I've got the county council today.' Dai had sat in the open living room. But then Dai didn't understand the shape of their silences. Gwen, it seemed, did not notice them.

'I know that, Emyr,' she'd said. 'I've lived with you for eighteen years, I can remember a thing like that, I think.'

'Is that why you picked these clothes out then? You always pick these ones out for the meetings.'

She'd shaken her head slowly. 'That's why I picked them out, yes.'

'What if it'd been cancelled?'

'Is it cancelled?'

'No,' he'd said.

'Well then.'

'What if I'd been ill?' he'd said. 'What if I'd woken up this morning and I was ill? What if I'd decided that I wouldn't go, that I'd be doing something else today? What then?'

'What do you think, "What then?" I'd have put them back in the cupboard. What is this, Emyr?' She'd turned to him then and he'd seen a brief glimpse of something that was underneath her smile. 'What is this? Are you going to have some breakfast?' she had said. She'd put tea bags in the teapot and done other things without looking at him.

He'd said, 'I don't want you picking my clothes any more. I can pick them myself, I'm not a schoolboy any more.'

'Oh,' she'd said, 'and did that change overnight?'

He'd watched her turn and make herself busy so that she wouldn't have to talk to him again. He'd thought, I spoke out of place. He had watched her fumble with the cups and the toast rack. He'd wanted to ask her if she had fumbled and made herself busy like that after the boy had kissed her. Or was that something she only needed with him? He would have liked to ask her if it had been out of place for the boy to hold her. If it had been out of place for her to go there, to be crying, to speak to him, need him. Because he didn't feel like he understood any more. This house and his life, they were working, regardless of him.

At the council meeting he'd looked at their smiling red faces, he'd shaken their red hands. 'Gwen's fine,' he said, 'and thank you for asking. She couldn't be better.'

He thought that really this was true.

All around his car the rain came down. He wasn't indicating but driving straight, he wasn't turning into the lane but parking on the gift shop's forecourt where the raindrops ran down the double doors and hid everything inside. He wasn't going home at all.

He remembered very clearly the day of their reception. The smile that had been on her face then. He remembered the smile that she had worn this morning as she'd told him she thought it might rain. He wondered how it was that she could smile in the same way after she'd let the boy put his mouth against hers.

It wasn't really the kiss. Anyone can kiss. A kiss can happen before you've even realized and then it's done. He seemed to remember some New Year's Eve night at a friend's house, when he'd got drunker than he should have and kissed the friend's wife. It wasn't the kiss. He would've liked to explain that to her but he wasn't sure she would listen to him. The last few days, he wasn't sure if she heard him when he spoke. She'd cried that night, that was what she'd said. She must have talked then, told the boy what was wrong. Emyr couldn't imagine this situation, but before that night and after it were both the same for her.

'It was a small thing,' she had said. And all he could think of was, a *boy*. Small, like a crack that he might look up and notice running through the sky. Small like that, like he could turn and point it out to a passer-by and the passer-by would say, 'Oh yes, that's been there for months.' It wasn't the kiss. It was the way she looked at him now, after, and smiled her usual smile.

Outside, on the gift shop's concrete forecourt, on the bonnet of the car, the rain was running fingers. Emyr left his hands on the steering wheel and he watched it. He didn't want to go home.

Upstairs, on the new wooden floorboards, surrounded by balloons and streamers, he remembered Gwen's father turning to him and pointing her out, pointing everything out and saying in a low voice, 'Look at this now. This is fucking perfect, this is.' He had been drunk and smiling and he'd only sworn while Gwen and her mother weren't there. 'This place,' the man had said. 'Today,' shaking his head like he couldn't quite take it all in. 'Fucking perfect.' He'd clapped Emyr on the back and told him, 'Well done.'

'She's something now, isn't she?' He'd watched her move through groups of people with her mother. 'I tell you what, always get this feeling when she smiles, like she knows more than she's telling.'

'Well, God,' he'd said, 'don't try to work it out. She and her mother, they're cut from the same cloth. And you know what? They *do* know more than they're telling. Lived with her mother twenty-five years now, and I've not found out yet.'

'Here's to not finding out then.'

They'd been drinking sparkling white wine.

She'd been happy that day. He'd never seen her plan for anything the way she'd planned for that. And all of it had come to fruition, the sale of the gift shop, the wedding. Then the promotions, the seat on the council, and finally the big gold necklace, like that boy Rhys had said. Nothing really but icing on the cake. And he'd ask her, 'Are you happy now, then?' smiling, and her giving her little smile back. Since then, the building of the house, the planning of it and the filling it, and the night when, some place away from him, she'd cried so hard that she'd let a strange boy touch her.

Of all the people in the world she smiled at, he was the one she lived with, he was the one she slept next to. He looked after her when she was ill, and he could kiss her, or sometimes, in the evenings, he would put on a Matt Monroe record, try to get her to dance a little with him, holding his drink in both hands with his arms round her back. Her smiling. She loved him. That was why she shared her life with him, even if she didn't share her thoughts.

The Spar, he saw, in his wing mirror. That was where they'd done their first shopping together, two weeks after the wedding and back from their honeymoon, they'd gone in and decided what they wanted to eat together for dinner. Past the seawall there, down on the beach on the other side, they'd walked Lucky and Baby together, when they'd been nothing but puppies, pulling at their leads. He could see the wall now, coloured with the rain. This whole street. He could pick out all the times they'd walked here, planning many things, him holding her arm. He could see extensions he'd approved, bent over the desk in his study, or in the house they'd had before that, working in the living room. He could remember each one.

Emyr took his hands from the steering wheel and slowly opened his door. He looked at the umbrella leaning against the passenger seat and then he looked away. He put his feet on to the wet concrete where raindrops hit his shoes, got out and stood in their fall, stared at this street where he could chart the changes with his own memories. Because he'd made them possible, every one. He saw the gift shop in front of him: a long, low building, rendered and painted a yellow that looked dirty under this sky. He felt how cold its glass was, cupping his hands around his eyes as he put his face to it.

Hair wet, fingers wet, Emyr saw what was inside. In grey light, as the wind lifted his jacket, he saw it all. Behind these dim reflections everything was broken. Everything was falling over and broken and lying on each other. The sunglasses rack, with pairs of glasses spilt out across the floor, paperback books lying open like birds, the windmills on their little sticks, tangled in each other. There was a free-standing set of shelves, leaning against the wall. Emyr saw it. He saw the shards and sprays of china on the floorboards; mugs with Ynys-morlan written on them, that had fallen and broken there. In the shadows, where there was no wind, he could almost see where the person had stood and pulled these things down with their hands.

Amid the movements of wind and rain, Emyr stared inside – where he couldn't stand because he owned keys no longer; because it had been years since then. He could only stay, his hands sheltering his eyes, and wonder about Dai's empty, placid face. As he wondered now at Gwen's daylight smile.

There were reflections. Just one step back, just the smallest distance, and they could not be seen through.

The garden was empty, black in the rain. The ground was black, uneven. The walls were stained in long marks reaching up the red brick walls.

'It's still warm,' Ruth said, and laughed. They could have held their hands out to the smouldering earth.

The rain came down. It would be striking her car, parked in the half-shelter of the trees. It would be running in streams on the lane's tarmac, down the hill and winding, back towards the town.

It would be full dark by the time that Lennie drove into Ynys-morlan, the flag that Emyr had passed just a white shape between the trees. Tom Humphries sat looking through long-forgotten cards, cross-legged on the floor of his old room. He opened each one again, hated himself for doing it, felt a fucking fool and did it anyway. After dinner he'd come upstairs, knowing already that he would. What was the difference? He'd been made a fool of once today, what did seconds and thirds matter?

He sorted through them, six Christmas cards, five birthday cards, the oldest ones growing yellow now. The writing on them didn't look personal any more. When they'd come in the post each year, he'd almost been able to see the way they must have passed it around the table, each of them writing their names. The cards had stopped coming a couple of years ago. They were too familiar to look real any more.

He put them one by one on the carpet beside him after reading, carefully, so they'd be undamaged the next time he took them out.

Christmas '93, he read. Becky wants a bike this year. She's passed her cycling proficiency test. Hope you have a lovely festive season! In another pen, underneath that, With every best wish for the New Year and every year after that, Merry Christmas! It read, Nicholas and Julia, and at the bottom, in wide-spaced and crawling letters, it said Becky. Tom put it down on the carpet beside him. He stared out at the wall.

His shelves remained in here, there were Blu-Tack marks on the wall where his posters had been. It was the same bed, pushed into the corner, where a little window looked over an unseen shore. From the kitchen, he heard his mum and Stacey talking. The hallway's light lay across the floor. This room was tidy, a million miles away from how it had looked when it had been his; all his mess pushed under the bed, one big sweep. A guest room now, though he was the only guest who came.

His mum had said over dinner, her face vigilant as if it was something they should all put behind them now, 'Gwen came in today. Said Dai was a lot better. From here on up, she said. Slow and hard, I'm sure. But from here on up.'

And Tom had said, not looking at her, 'Well Gwen Morgan's never been through it, has she.' He'd remembered the pitiless tone of the woman's voice today.

A moment of silence there'd been, and then his mother's knife and fork scraping again. He'd looked up to see Stacey staring at him, like that new accent of hers had made everything she said, and everything she didn't say, more wise. She could put on whatever expression she wanted. She'd not been here then. She'd been a fucking toddler then. She'd been the baby in the cot while his mum had sat on the sofa, staring at the television screen, crying.

Knife and fork working on the food, Siân had said, 'Lost her mother six years ago, and her father before that,' winter-voiced. In the featureless kitchen light, their faces had been grey.

'You should speak to him, like. He trusts you. Always going in to see you in Spar. He knows you,' Tom had said.

'Gwen's no fool,' she'd answered.

And he'd asked if it was a day off for her tomorrow, if she'd like to take the bus with him to Aber, but the house didn't clean itself just because she fancied a day out.

Now, with their voices muffled, he heard them talk, the Christmas cards laid out on the floor beside him. He pictured himself climbing through the museum's polythene and boards, and his friend's face, in torchlight, grinning up at him. And what would he say to Rhys?

He kept thinking of the times they'd sat on the seawall together. Eleven or twelve or something, with only a couple of Christmas cards stashed away on his shelf, between two books. They'd sat, looking out and doing pretty much nothing and never talked about why they were there. Rhys'd just asked him where he wanted to go each Saturday and he'd always said there. By the old lifeboat ramp, it had been, sitting on the wall with their legs almost reaching the stones on the beach. Every Saturday for a couple of years maybe, watching the kids with their hair in the wind, and Rhys had never once asked him why. Carving stuff in the worn concrete of the seawall.

Time went by and Tom didn't count it.

Birthday '91. Not his – an August day – but Becky's; 1992. At the top of each card they had written it, Happy Birthday Becky! The things that Becky had done each year, what she liked in school. He remembered that Becky had had blonde hair. He remembered it lying in wet strings in the crook of his arm. Blonde hair and skin so white, you could've painted a picture of it and no one would have believed. Goosebumps. Hard sand. He remembered not much more than this.

Them running up, Nicholas and Julia or whoever they'd been. He'd not seen their faces, he hadn't known them. He remembered them pulling her away from him, leaving him kneeling, nothing in his arms any more, just the cold weight of his clothes.

He'd seen the girl from a distance. All in one moment, it had seemed like. And he remembered thinking later, how much you could see in just a moment: a girl's face, up to the sky, and then only waves. Further down the beach, two people calling. Little silhouettes with arms raised up to see against the horizon, their voices distant but shouting. All in one moment: the long beach and those silhouettes, a white-flower face between the waves.

For Christmas in 1993, Becky's parents had bought her a doll's house. She'd joined the choir in school that year.

Tom looked at the guest room's shelves in this half-light, a model ship there that had fallen once and broken. If he had been sitting here in the morningtime, he would have been able to make out the crack, old touches of glue where it was mended.

Ruth sat in the living room, waiting. With her news. In the air, in the silence, in every bright lamp's circle; her news filled the world. She'd been there for three hours now. Another night, a long-gone night, hung in the shadows and everything she saw seemed like a keepsake from it. The television had been on like this. Had the room changed? It had not. She had sat in just this place and listened to the final sounds of the cab's engine die.

Nia was here with her, the only difference maybe. Little sounds of her shifting in the chair. The memory was thick as silence, Busby

Berkeley's girls moved across the screen. The words she waited with. Two differences. Vast as continents, she thought.

Tom crushed his cigarette out in the ashtray. His mother's face was empty as she watched the TV, judging. She seemed always to have that look, seemed always to be deciding whether or not the thing she saw was worthy of her looking.

'I'd better go.'

She nodded, placed her hands on her lap like she would stand and see him to the door but she remained there. 'Well, it's nice to see you anyway.'

Like he never came. He looked at her face, made younger by the shadows.

He wanted suddenly to ask her how it was that she and Stacey just talked so easily, just nattered on like there was nothing in the world to stop them, like a fucking bomb could go off and they'd just turn to each other, start talking again. He wanted to ask her just how that was.

He bent over to her and kissed her cheek, felt the hard line of her bone. He would've told her everything. He would've told her how Gwen had stood in his caravan, picking up the rubbish from the floor.

'You take care of yourself then,' she said.

He looked away and nodded. He put both his hands in his pockets. He walked out of the living room with the television's noise at his back and when he opened the front door, there was silence, the sight of her left behind. He remembered Bethan saying once how all the houses looked abandoned at night. Looked derelict.

Ruth heard the door open. She heard the footsteps, long, heavy, pausing as he looked into the kitchen.

'Ruth? You up?'

'I'm up,' she said. She watched the girls' coloured feather fans make patterns as they hid their faces. 'I'm in here,' she said. Her hands were still now, resting on the sofa. Nia slept. She should take her upstairs.

Her back was to the open doorway but she felt Lennie's tired shadow.

'What's she doing up now?'

'I've got news.'

There was a pause. He said, 'I don't want to hear any news right now. Only thing I want to hear now's the sound of my own snoring. She shouldn't be up this late, like, end up lying in bed half of to-morrow.' He stopped talking, he waited.

Ruth turned around and she looked at him. He filled the doorway up, standing there. 'It's the possibility,' she'd said to Charlotte. There was no possibility in him any more.

'What news?'

She wanted to tell him the figure, with all its digits.

'What is it then? Come on.'

She wanted to say, 'Everything.' She looked at him, three feet away. It didn't feel like there could be anyone else awake in the whole town and she thought that she would remember this moment a long time. This second night. She'd sat on the sofa here and she had told him, never raising her head. She'd spoken the words like they had nothing to do with her, saying things about the hospital, about how nice the nurses had been, things like that. She'd sat here, not once meeting his eyes. On the table in front of her now, lamplight snagged and gleamed in the brown glass bottle that she had scrubbed clean of earth and used for the last of the season's roses.

'Come and sit down, will you sit down by me?'

'I don't think I will, with that expression on your face.'

She was silent for a moment, watching him walk around to stand on the other side of the table, between her and the television screen.

'The expression on my face is wrong then. It's good news.'

'Oh yes.' He folded his arms, waiting, like nothing could surprise him now. And that look that had been there before: the only thing left to place the blame, whatever blame there was. He watched her.

'It's good news . . .' she laughed but it fell away into the soundless evening of this room. 'It's good, just that I've got to tell you something first, that's all. And you've got to promise not to be angry, like, hear me through to the end.'

'Oh yes. And how should I promise that now? If what you've got to say's going to make me angry. I'm not going to promise that, am I?'

He stared at her across the table. There was the vase between them, and a cup of tea on a saucer, half drunk. He looked ready. She thought of all the things she would tell him, all the possibilities. He didn't look capable of planning a future. She remembered the sound of his voice, bent over Dai in the still and sunlit graveyard.

She said, 'Hear me through to the end.'

Tom didn't need to listen for him. He stood outside the window and he could see the light inside. He hadn't waited. Tom'd known he wouldn't. He stood and looked at the broken boards. Torn polythene slapped in the wind. On each side of him, the black-skinned buildings stretched. And the museum's high, pale render was an atlas, the guttering far above him cracked.

He'd tried to organize his words, walking here; he'd thought of all the different ways and which would make Rhys see the clearest how he'd felt today. There wasn't any organization to them now. He felt the wind on this side of his face, his bare hands. Standing here, the light from inside was faint in the polythene. And he looked both ways down the street but he only saw the black road. He rubbed a hand across his mouth and pushed the plastic aside.

Rhys was sitting on the floor. Cross-legged like a little Buddha, arranging cans of beer and torches, the gas lamp, in a circle in front of him, he sat in the centre of the room. It was huge and high-ceilinged, the floor was thick with dust. He could see the footprints: where Rhys had stood, where he'd walked.

There were wooden frames, dark arms against the walls, panes of glass in the ones that still looked like display cases. The fractured render reached towards darkness.

Pictures had hung here, all around; their little plaques. Pictures from fifty years ago, a hundred, more. There was nothing hanging here now. Tom saw it all in the young light of the gas lamp. Saw Rhys raise his head: the shadow of stubble across his scalp. At his back, he could still feel the wind outside.

'I don't call that synchronized watches. If I didn't know you better,

I'd say you were a coward, Mr Bond. Leaving your co-workers with the dangerous jobs. As it is, like, I can only imagine you were . . . delayed.' He fiddled with the lamp, it flared and settled, blue-white. He looked up again. 'Come on then.'

Tom didn't move, he felt caught, wanting to open his mouth and say it all, wanting to go and sit down with him, leave it all in silence. He saw the can of paint on the floor.

Rhys held his arms out and showed him the room, 'Look at this place, just take a fucking look around.' He spoke slow and grand, 'All ours.' He turned the gas lamp up again, swelling its white throws across his features and singing, 'One night in heaven . . .' dancing while sitting down in the high and silent room.

'Rhys –'

'Are you going to come in or what?'

He saw just how it would be as well: go there, sit down next to him, take a beer.

He'd say, 'How was your week, Mr Bond?'

And Rhys'd tell him, 'Shit.' With a grin on his face like he could eat all that shit and more on top. And Tom could sit there, tell him, 'Yeah, well same here.' And it wouldn't matter. Gwen. None of it. They had the lamp and they had this place, it wouldn't matter.

'Rhys,' he said. The story streamed through his head – and the quiet that had filled all the moments when Rhys might've reminded him that tonight was fuck and tell night.

'What?' Rhys was looking, a hand near his can. And an expression, just the same, near to being on his face. 'What now?'

'I got a call from Gwen today.'

Tom watched. Something passive came to fill that half-formed look. He wanted to step forward, hold out his hands, do something. He didn't know what to do. Picturing Rhys and that man, crystal-clear pictures. Had there been a pause in the shouting before he'd opened his mouth and let it out? How long might it have been? He saw those moments playing back, playing over, as Rhys met his gaze.

'You fucking told him,' Tom said.

'What're you talking about?'

'Don't say that. You told him. You know what I'm talking about.'
He did step forward. There was the tread of his feet on the floor, the
only sound. Rhys leaned his head to one side. There was a place in
his eyes that was uninhabited, calm. A floodplain. 'You want to say
it's not true.'

'Didn't say anything at all now, did I?'

There was no guilt, Tom couldn't see guilt. 'Are you going to lie
about it then?'

'I'm not lying.' Grit in Rhys's voice. 'Got nothing to lie about. You
want to come and sit down or what?'

'I don't want to sit down – fuck's sake, like! Fuck's sake!' He turned
away, rounded on him again. 'You told him.' He shook his head like
he couldn't believe it. He could though. Seeing Rhys's face, he could.

'You want to talk about this or what?' He moved things on the dark
floor in front of him. A little kid.

'Did you think I wouldn't hear about it?'

He stared down at the floor like he was waiting out Tom's words.
On either side of him, the blank walls ran. 'Fuck this,' he said softly.
'Two weeks, we spent organizing this. More. You want to come and
sit down and talk or what? Just don't fucking look at me like that, all
right? I didn't do anything wrong.'

He could've laughed. 'That's what matters then, like? You're
worried you won't get your fucking night? Look at my face, like!'

'I don't need to "look at your face".'

'Your big night . . . ? I tell you what, you live in your own world.'
He stared at him. Just by catching his eye, he'd make Rhys see how
he felt. Rhys wouldn't look back now though. 'Maybe tonight's not
the most important thing that's on my mind right now.'

'All right. So tell me.' Rhys raised his face. 'What's the most
important thing?'

Moving towards him on dusty, unsure ground, Tom just said, 'You
betrayed me.'

' "Betrayed you?" ' Rhys barked a laugh. 'Fuck's sake. What kind of
a word is that?' He laughed, embarrassed to hear it used. On his face
the fluttering shadows moved.

'It's the right fucking word, that's what it is. I told you something. And you went – you went and –'

'D'you want to hear what happened? Do you want to stand there and shout insults at me or d'you want to hear what happened?'

'I don't care what happened! Doesn't matter! You fucking betrayed me!'

'I didn't even tell him your name.'

Tom nodded slowly. 'Because she wouldn't be able to guess, would she? I told you something, and you went and fucking used it.'

'I didn't use it.'

'Used me.'

Rhys's movements were very slow, precise. 'D'you want to hear my side of it? Or not?'

Tom looked at him, mouth open.

'Do you want to know what that man said to me, like? Standing there like the king of Shit Hill. Do you want to know what he called me? Immoral.' Rhys laughed. Sitting on the dusty floor between the broken cases, he looked up at the ceiling and laughed like he didn't give a fuck. 'Immoral. Pathetic. Un-fucking-grateful. That was it.' He lowered his eyes. 'Man stood there and said it right to my face. Thick. That stupid bastard that only got to his big house because he paid his way there, because he licked his way up there.' Rhys reached and picked up a can of beer, held it in his hand before drinking. 'Thought it gave him the right – oh because he talks for everyone – gave him the right to say no one wants me here.' He nodded like Tom had already agreed. '"Not a part of this community,"' waggled his head back and forward, shades moving over his features. 'I'm so fucking immoral. While his wife walks round this town like she could grind everyone right under her heels. His wife, pointing her fingers, telling me how I should be acting and how I shouldn't. And all the time, all the time behind closed doors, like, what's she doing?' He laughed. There was nothing else now. 'She's bending over for you.'

Quiet washed in again. The sound of doubt. Rhys didn't listen to doubt, he raised the can and toasted it.

'I never had sex with her.' Tom swallowed, sick.

Rhys's eyes fell to him.

'I never fucking touched her.' His voice just trailed back to the stillness, everything he wanted to say pale as grit on the floor.

He looked at Tom in this stillness. 'Never touched her?'

He didn't say it again, didn't answer at all. And the expression on Rhys's face was not surprise.

Careful words now, which Rhys let fall between them as they faced each other across this slimmer space: 'Why the fuck were you wearing her gold round your wrist then?'

Dai had stood where they were now. He'd stood, moving gradually between the glass cases and looking down at the things, thinking about how you could see time as slow as one photograph laid on top of another. Through different cars and different clothes, but all the same houses.

Here, the picture of the stone-filled street had hung – in this dark spot in the corner, where there were screw holes still.

'Tell me,' Lennie said. He stood before her and the night lay outside.

There was no way to say it without this first, this was the thing that they had to climb over.

She said, 'I've been working in the garden with Charlotte.' With the woman, she had meant to say. And if she couldn't get this final thing right, how could she say the rest? She kept her eyes on the coffee table. 'Not a job, like I said before: it's not a job. Just that she needs the help and I wanted to go up there, take Nia up there . . .'

Lennie laughed. On the other side of the room, Nia slept

'Not a job, you just wanted to go up there. I see.' He was nodding. Already letting himself into it, she could hear. No pause, no shock. Ready. 'You just wanted to go up there, no matter what I said. No matter that we talked about this, that we had this out. Didn't we have this out? Because that's what I seem to remember, like. You and me, standing in the kitchen. And having this out.'

'It's not a job. She's a friend. I go to see a million friends and this is no different now –'

'No different? That so? You lie to me about all your friends, do you? Wait for me to get out of the house and when I'm driving off down the road, take her,' he gestured to Nia, 'and sneak off to them. No different,' he nodded. 'Well I might've seen it coming really. Stupid.' The bitterness cut off his laughter. 'Stupid not to see it, wouldn't you say that? Must've thought it.'

'I never thought that.'

'I don't know anything any more,' he said. Ruth looked at him and saw in his face it was true. He'd been ready, walking into the house. Since the funeral, he had been. Something was over for him. He looked caged, standing so still, trapped between their furniture. Beside them, she saw Nia stir.

'I have to tell you this so I can tell you the rest, the news.' And as soon as she'd said it, she knew it was wrong, could have cursed herself. She looked up at him.

'You had to tell me,' he said, nodding. Trapped, she thought again, by something even he couldn't see. 'What does that mean? That you wouldn't have? You wouldn't have otherwise. Just what exactly does that mean, Ruth?'

'Nothing. Nothing –'

'Well it must mean something or you wouldn't have said it! How many times did you go, then? She pay you for each time you sneaked out of the house? Another seventy quid was it? Each time?'

'I told you, she's a friend –'

'And I told you, I don't give a fuck! Doesn't even surprise me any more. You could turn round to me right now and tell me you'd been bedding some man and it wouldn't surprise me. There's no talking to you. How do you talk to someone that just lies? You can't reason with someone like that, someone that just goes behind your back.'

'Do you know how much money she's got?'

Standing still as glass in front of her, though, he was in his world.

'How much money she's got? *I don't give a fuck!*'

'Thirty-three million pounds,' Ruth said.

Her hands were on the cloth of the sofa. She was sitting forward.

She was leaning across the table towards him like he might hear her, really see her that way.

He did hear her, he stopped talking. She watched him swallow this new piece of news – swallow it down slow.

'Well maybe I should go and see her then. Maybe I should ask her for a job as well.'

She looked at him without words.

'Did you have fun up there, Ruth?' And when she didn't answer, he asked her again. 'Tell me. I want to know.'

She cleared her throat and looked at him. 'Yes,' she said simply.

He nodded. 'That's good. I'm glad it was worth it. When you waited for me to leave, smiled and lied and left this place empty, took Nia out of school – must've taken her out of school.'

'But it doesn't matter.'

'I know it doesn't! *I can see!* I've not seen anything else these last weeks! Look at this place . . . Look at us.' He held his hands out, palms up, showing her: all the things they'd bought together, all the things they'd kept and she'd arranged on shelves. He stood in the centre of it and he could not move.

Something had to give way; this place they'd made or he himself. Lennie broke the deadlock. His hand moved out, swept across the little table, caught the cup and saucer. They sailed with the arc of his arm, out and into the wall, and shattered there. Crashed there. Ruth listened to the pieces fall.

She saw his eyes, as bright as if he stood in sunlight.

'Doesn't matter,' he repeated.

He reached down for the only other thing in front of him, the bottle, and he held it in his hand as he looked at her. A rose fell to the tabletop.

'I'm sorry,' she said. The words came and were clearly not her own. Two differences but really it had been just the same. 'I'm sorry,' she said. 'I'm sorry!' She almost shouted. The bottle shook his hand. 'Break it then, break everything! Go on, break the house! I don't care! I'll fix it! *I can fix it all!*'

In the lamplight, the bottle glinted.

'I can fix everything.'

His hand didn't move. His gaze changed.

'I've got the answer,' Ruth told him.

The shade of something new in his expression. She saw it, uncom-prehending for a moment, because it wasn't hope. It was doubt that she read there.

'You didn't fuck her,' he said quietly. There was no silence in his eyes any more. 'Why were you wearing it?'

'Doesn't make any difference –'

'Really? Might not make a difference to you . . . Me, I'd like to know! What made you put that thing on? What do you mean, never even touched her? Come on!'

But Tom saw: he had never believed it. He turned away and back to Rhys, remembering her standing, looking at him like there was nothing between them. Not age, not fucking money, not the make-up she put on her face every day. And he'd fucking believed it. He'd tried to put his arms round her.

'You want to know what happened?' In the abandoned room, his voice echoed. 'You want to know? I kissed her.'

'You kissed her –'

'That's right, I kissed her! Found her on the beach and I took her back to my van and tried to kiss her! And when she'd left, when she'd run out the door quick as she could get out, I found her bracelet on the floor and I picked it up and I put it on!'

He remembered: the carrier bag in her hand, her wet face. Why had he done it? When he knew what she was really. One night out of all the days meant nothing. He'd thought he was seeing her as she really was, but it was the single night that had been a lie. He lived a lot of those nights, maybe they were all lies. Two years' worth now.

Rhys was silent as he looked at Tom. 'Why would you do that, like? You kissed her. She ran off from you. And you put it on, that thing.' He stared. His questions were blank seconds. 'Found it on the floor and wore it – for what? Fucking souvenir . . . ?'

'A souvenir. Yeah.'

Rhys blinked as though his own memories came in small waves, overlapping. Dull peaks as he opened his mouth. 'So why the fuck would you care what I told him?' He shook his head. 'What is this?'

'I don't –'

'Go on.'

But Tom had nothing to say.

'Go on and tell me then!' Rhys stood in the neglected room. 'That man looking into my fucking face and telling me I'm thick, fucking shouting it at me! You've not got a thing to hide . . . Just some fucking . . . some fucking *kiss*.' He looked at Tom and saw a stranger; could not imagine him putting his arms round that woman. 'When you've not even got a thing to hide why do you fucking care . . . ?'

'*It doesn't matter if it's true or not!*' His hands were held out. He didn't draw them back. 'People hear something like that, they don't care . . . They look at you in the street . . . *I don't want my mother hearing that!*'

Rhys slowly nodded.

They stood between the long glass counters, beer cans, torches, cigarettes, scattered on the floor between.

'Well I guess now I see what the important thing is, like.' In front of him, in the faint white light, Tom's face was as clear as these walls had been once. 'I guess I see.'

There had been maritime antiques and patchwork quilts, love spoons carved from single pieces of wood. Gwen had given a speech once, not so long ago. She had talked of Ynys-morlan. 'As rich in history,' she'd said, 'as it is full of life today.'

Looking at Ruth carefully, Lennie drew back the hand that was holding the bottle. And beside them now, watching them now, Nia sat up in the chair. They didn't glance at her, either of them, like they couldn't afford to break their gaze.

'You've got the solution.' Nodding, his eyes didn't leave her.

'I've got news, changes everything.'

'Everything. Well, you've got me stumped, I have to say.' He took a moment and she saw his tongue, running inside his cheek. And then, even more slowly, she watched him reach out and place the bottle, the roses, down. Halfway between them.

Loose as silence, Nia watched.

'You can't imagine.'

'No. I can't.'

Nia's gaze moved. And the room was so quiet, just the same as always. Paintings on the picture hooks that her mother had hung, softly shadowed. Ruth opened her mouth but the words didn't come to her.

Thirty-three million.

Neither of them saw Nia move. There was a dash, a motion in the corner of Ruth's vision and she was between them then. She was halfway across the coffee table and the bottle was in her hands before they even looked away from each other. She was throwing it.

It struck the wall, stonework three feet from the broken cup and saucer.

'My God!' Ruth reached for her, stretched out across the table and was crying already. She reached for Nia, dragged her in. She felt her moving, arms tight as wires under her hands. 'My God.' Half lifting Nia's weight, half pulling. Ruth hauled her on to her lap. Legs on the floor and drumming. She put her hand in Nia's hair, on her forehead, smoothing there. 'Nia,' she said. She raised her eyes and she looked at Lennie.

He stood still, as if there was a rift across this room.

'You want to know what the answer is?' she shouted to him. 'Shh, Nia, shush now –' But her leg kicked out at the table, struck wood. 'Shh now –' She stared at Lennie. 'You want to know? Money! That's the answer! And you wouldn't believe it! *Thirty-three million!* Shh, Nia . . .' Stroking her forehead. And Lennie only stared. 'Thirty-three million! For us! For the whole bloody town! Good news!' she said. 'Nia bach . . .' Her body twisted under Ruth's hands. *'Good news!'* She could feel it coming now, up her throat and in her eyes and spilling out. His face was full of dark blood. Ruth began to laugh as she cried. 'She wants to give it away! Can you imagine that? She wants to give it to us! *Laugh then!* Doesn't know a thing about us and she offered it to me . . .' They combined, crying and laughter, until she seemed to make both sounds at once. She lifted her face, this jagged mixture written there.

He didn't move. Felt his empty hand twitch.

'For the whole town. Just like you wanted! Smile, why don't you? Why don't you say something! Why don't you say something to me?'

He looked at her, tangled up with Nia. He felt the coffee table hit his shins as Nia kicked out again and it shifted. It fell back.

'Everything's going to be different. Perfect,' she said, looking out over Nia's hair. 'Perfect . . .'

'Ruth,' he said. 'What are you talking about now?'

But this laughter was the only answer he got.

'What are you talking about?'

He watched her move with his daughter, slowing gradually, watched the hand that was stroking her hair grow gentler. Nia gave one last weak kick, rocking together on the sofa in front of him.

'Ruth,' he wet his mouth.

She was worked up like it was true.

'Ruth!'

Never heard someone make a noise like that, never heard it. He said her name a lot of times. He just wanted her to be calm now. He just wanted her to shut up for a minute, to stop these sounds. He could have reached across the table and forced her. But standing here, watching her, he could not reach. There was something missing from him.

She was sobbing between the laughs, 'Thirty-three million pounds, thirty-three, my God.'

There was a lack in him, heavy as a weight. He couldn't touch her.

In the museum, Rhys was unconfined. He lunged for Tom, took hold.

'Don't want people looking at you like that . . . ?'

Tom was silent, he'd already given himself away.

'That man stood in front of me and he shouted those words in my face! That the sort of person you don't want looking at you? Huh? Talk to me! That the important thing?'

'You had no right, Rhys . . . No fucking right, you got that? *What did you expect him to say?*'

'You think he's right then? Well now it all comes out, doesn't it? Now it all fucking comes out!'

'Rhys –'

'"Rhys *what?*"' He shook him, hands in his collar now. On every side of them, the room was tar, and Rhys's feet, moving to get closer to him, caught the gas lamp and kicked it to its side. He held Tom tight.

'You were writing on the fucking walls,' Tom said, still unable to believe it. 'On the community centre! What the fuck d'you expect, doing that? You tell me, what did you want him to say? "Oh thanks for that, Rhys. That looks lovely there, Rhys." What d'you expect him to call you if not that?'

In the shifting light, Rhys pressed his face very close. 'If not what?'

'You know what!'

'Say it then! Go on! Spit the fucking words out! Go on! Right in my face. Right here!'

Tom tried to turn away, closed his mouth. Small streaks of light stretched across his face, he looked like no person Rhys had seen before.

There was silence.

'Look at me!'

In his coat, Rhys's fingers flexed open and closed, Tom's face turned from him like he couldn't even stand to look. And Rhys wanted it. He opened his mouth but there were no words to find. There were no fucking words. He took one hand out of Tom's coat. He drew it back behind him and he let it close and let it come down.

Tom jerked as he thumped him. Pushed away with the force, Rhys had to pull him back. Had to strain so he could bring his fist up again, seeing blood in the corner of Tom's mouth.

'Look at me!'

But he brought his fist down again, on to his face, his cheek. He was thinking, that's right. That's right. But the words coming from him were different.

'Look at me!' he shouted. 'Fuck you!'

And Lennie Lewis stared at his wife. He was shaking slightly, unable to move. She was repeating the figure, no other words but those now. And like he had sometimes imagined at night, he was trying to speak with nothing coming from him.

In the empty museum, Rhys hit his friend once more as the gas lamp rocked gently from side to side, shadows swaying with it over the walls where photographs had hung.

July 11th 1992

Dear Charlotte,

It's my 33rd birthday so I should be 41 today. I think
I'll spend it at Kensington Gardens. It's very
beautiful this morning, warm and clear and I remember
why I've kept on. Would never have seen this sun. It
was on the river this morning, took half an hour to cross
from the Albert Bridge to Battersea, I mean **so**
beautiful, and those moments like this morning, they're
everything. Other days and unhappiness only make them
more important. And you have to take hold, my God, every
second, every tiny passing instant, have to know you're
lucky. I remember, above everything, I'm not only living for
myself - that what I have is so precious because it's
stolen treasure.

Emyr got the phone call at half past seven that morning.

'I didn't wake you?' Ruth's voiced asked him. 'I know Gwen's an early bird . . .'

'Early bird catches the worm. And you know Gwen,' he said. 'Loves worms, she does.'

He heard Ruth's laughter, unsure.

She said then, 'Are you working today?'

'Wouldn't call it that. Got a meeting, planning council. Plant out by Clarech they can't wait to build . . .'

'Tell them you're ill, Emyr,' she said.

He stood in silence after putting the receiver down, the morning now a question. He turned to see Dai, standing fully dressed in the hallway, his coat over his arm.

'You all right, Dai?' he said.

'I'm all right now. Are you all right?'

'I'm fine. You look like you're off somewhere.'

'Yes I am.'

'Really? Good, well that's good. Where to?'

'Work,' he said. 'I've not swept the street for a week, so long, leaves'll be all over the place by now. All over. Won't they?' He talked like this, as if scared that no one could hear him properly, no one could quite understand.

'You know you don't have to worry about that if you don't want to. Do you want to work?'

And he made them talk like this back. He looked at Emyr. 'Got to work, like. We all have to work, don't we?'

Emyr wrote down the phone number of Lennie and Ruth Lewis's house. 'You can read that, Dai?' he said. He'd not written any words. 'That's where I'll be all morning.'

They both stood there, like foreigners to this house.

'You want a lift? Get the trolley and everything?' He held the piece of paper out.

'I don't want a lift. The trolley wouldn't fit in the car and it would be dirty anyway, and get on the car.'

'Dai . . . are you sure you want to work?'

He just took the paper, though, put it carefully into the pocket of his trousers, so that it didn't crumple there.

They put their coats on together and when they stood in the hall, looking back into the living room, there was no mess left at all. Departing, the room was perfect, the sofa, the chairs. It didn't look like it was waiting for anyone.

They left the house behind; closed the front door and stood for a moment on the step. The vines on his mum's home would have the only colour in the whole yard today, Dai realized. Together they looked up and saw November's sky.

July 11th '84

C,

25 years old. Or 33. So I should be making plans. A future. Give what I went through a meaning. I won't live in a world of psychobabble and self-doubt. There should be a better process. More certain each year that I don't want children tho' and isn't that the accepted way? 'I'll give them everything my parents didn't give me.' But isn't parenthood – any parenthood – the **most** selfish act? You form a little picture of the things that you believe about the world and then imprint it upon the voiceless, unidentified infant that you find in your arms. I see the children in Kensington. Brash because their parents smile on everything they do – and so smile on themselves.

I have no plans. I have no aims really. If I'm honest, I wonder whether it isn't better for me not to touch the world too much. I'd like to be responsible for something good, for success, but if I look into myself I'm not sure that what I find would translate into goodness. I'm angry often.

I remember tearing up work at school. I'll move through life like that if I'm not careful. Rubbing out my own footprints as I go.

Do you know what I'd like really? What sits in the place where my goals should? I'd like to make myself a channel, and do what you would want. I'd like to paint and watch you express yourself through it. Open my mouth and hear you talk.

Pulling his car up behind the bulk of Lennie's cab, Emyr glanced through the driver's side window – and he saw that Ruth was standing on the step there, waiting for him, and that Lennie was behind.

He sat for two hours in the Lewises' kitchen. When the phone rang, it rang into their silence.

'What do you think?' Lennie said.

Ruth stood for a moment but Emyr didn't answer – and when she'd picked up the phone she called his name.

She let him out into the street again and he stood with her, unspeaking.

'Looks different, doesn't it?' he heard her say.

It might have been a good few weeks since Emyr had really laughed. Standing in the museum, it felt that way. It was wrong, he saw the look that was stretched over Dai's face, but he stared at it all in front of him, took it in piece by wrecked piece, and couldn't help it.

Dai had shown him how the polythene was pinned back with nothing underneath, no wooden boards. 'Look there now,' he'd said. He'd kept turning to Emyr. He'd shown him how it flapped in the wind. 'This is where they got in.'

In here, the smell of cigarette smoke was thicker than mould and every shadow was grudging.

'Why are you laughing? There's nothing funny. Look at it.' Dai held both arms out to the broken mess. 'They're bastards! The people who did this . . . this is a museum,' he said. 'Bastards.'

Emyr shook his head and pressed his lips together over the sound, it echoed. Outside, the rain was beginning to fall again. On the wet pavement, Emyr pictured ten-pound notes.

They stood in the centre under a high ceiling, only the two of them in all the shattered piles. Emyr turned a slow circle, he looked at each shard of glass, each piece of cracked wood, and up to the paint that had been spread across the wall. His hands were light, and he thought of the way that Ruth had touched one, leaning out from her front door.

'Sometimes even when there's nothing funny, you've got to laugh, haven't you, Dai? I swear, sometimes.' He surveyed the room, the secret in his eyes bright enough to change its colours. 'People have to have an outlet, don't they? They laugh or break things.' He turned to Dai. 'You know what that's like,' he said, remembering the rain that had run helter-skelter across the gift shop's dark windows.

Dai's face became a mask. 'I don't know what you mean.'

Emyr didn't take his eyes from him, though. Every word had an echo. 'The last few weeks have been bad for you.'

Dai said nothing. He might have nodded, Emyr couldn't tell.

'You swept the street today. Did you clear up in the gift shop?'

'It's nothing like this,' Dai said, china-voiced. 'I didn't do this! This is a museum, I'd never break a museum, I didn't do this –'

'I know you didn't.' In the drear light, he held his hands out to quiet him. Behind, he could almost feel the words that were written on the wall. 'And everything in the gift shop, every single thing in there, yours. That's the difference. Did you clear it up?' Quiet rested over every sharp edge. 'Dai, it's all right.'

'I'm going to clear it up –' He stopped and started again, he put his hand out like he wanted to reach for Emyr's arm. 'You know you sat up with me, that night, and we waited for Gwen, you remember that?' His fingers flexed once and then his hand fell to his side. It was not that he couldn't understand Emyr, or any other person. It was the other way around. He baffled them. He tried to make his words clear now. 'I don't want the gift shop, Emyr. She never wanted me to work there. She was right. Look what I did. You see?'

Though they stood in a different room.

'She wanted you to be happy.' Emyr reached across then; the hand Ruth had touched as they'd stood on her doorstep. 'She wouldn't be angry with you,' he said, though he remembered Eirian – an arm around Dai like she could hold the whole world back – and truly did not know. 'You have to begin to think about what she said, Dai.' He put that hand on his shoulder. 'The property's yours, for whatever you want.' In the quiet town that he had driven through, on both sides of the street, Emyr had seen the ghosts of long-dead profit. 'I remember sitting up with you, yes,' he said. 'But you won't always be . . . confused like that.' An image came to Emyr, of the banners Gwen had strung across the gift shop for their wedding day: their names as large as the letters on this wall. He wondered if she was thinking of him now, if she ever did these days. And with his other hand, he drew a picture, a little sweep across this grey air. 'Ynys-morlan used to be beautiful,' he said quietly. 'Did you know that, Dai?'

July 11th 1981

Dear Charlotte,

Haven't done the candlelight trick since I was a kid but
can't resist it. I'm twenty-two today. It was hard to
shut out the light. It's blinds on the windows here - I
was hanging sweaters up. Locked the door. Stared into
the mirror - but it was never me I was looking for. It
was never the future. Just wanted to try and find
what was beyond my face, I'm starting to think. I was
looking for the girl I should've been . . .

What I want is a clear path, belief in myself. I make
decisions like I'm drowning, you know? Leaping from
stone to stone, but heading the wrong way, heading
right out further, I hate the things I've done before, the
ways I've been.

That night, Emyr thought about many things. He thought about the way that you can build a place, and put everything you have into it, and all the holes in you as well; the things that you still need.

He sat in bed with Gwen after Dai had gone to sleep in their living room downstairs. He told her what Ruth Lewis had said, as outside the trees were moved, the swathes of their autumn leaves, as though by deep water.

Gwen was happy. Gwen was over the moon.

He didn't talk about the museum, about Dai, or what they'd spoken of before they'd stepped outside and he had pinned the plastic back over the window's broken boards.

There was glass on the floor there now, strewn in shards and tiny fractions. The street lamps touched fingers in the polythene, in the beads of rain caught between its layers. Gold as the years' numbers, side by side, on the leather bindings of Charlotte Weyland's journals. That light was beautiful, reaching the old floorboards, the edges of buckled frames that had been glass display cases once.

In shadow above, the paint could hardly be seen.

YNYS-MORLAN IS FUCKING DEAD.
LONG LIVE YNYS-MORLAN

Winter

Charlotte heard the footsteps on the wooden floorboards behind but she didn't turn. It was the 12th of January. The day was sinking into night. It had begun, all of this, with the noise of breaking glass, unheard by Nia. There was silence now in the community centre, as hard as the white fluorescent light that lay in every seat.

She said, 'I don't know how they'll react.'

'It's half past five.' Ruth's voice echoed.

'How do you feel?'

Ruth Lewis saw shadows of this room submerged in each dark windowpane. It was frozen out there, winter winds. In here, the radiators leaked out warmth into the waiting quiet.

'I don't know . . . I don't know.'

She looked at Charlotte Weyland's back, the woman sculpture-still.

In Ynys-morlan's evenings, when the sun bled out across the sea's horizon, when the gulls left its rooftops to light on the wet sand and move there as silhouettes only, every window, facing out, reaching upwards, was caught with reflections of the light.

The evenings burned brief and cold before the nights came in. She'd gone to the shore with Charlotte and Nia, the last part of the day. The old concrete of the seawall ran behind the houses to frame little patios. Against it, grey stones were banked over each other, the wall almost buried by them now. She'd looked at the stones as if for the first time. Their slope reached from one end of this town to the other, and Nia had dawdled there, on their tumbled edge.

'We could use it all,' she'd said. 'We could use it to build.'

Strangely enough, she'd heard the noise of building. A hammer had echoed through the twilight, no more harsh than a ripple on the water. Ruth remembered how the echoes had fled. She had looked up from the stones and seen a beautiful town in the light coating each windowpane.

Charlotte had never built, created, anything. She had written, but the words had never been read, even by her. And she'd imagined all the pages of her journals – she could have torn them loose and walked the streets with them. Shaftesbury Avenue or Regent Street, crowded with faces. She could have passed, dropping one with every step she took until her hands were empty. People she had never known might have picked them up to read. It wouldn't have mattered. London was strong, she thought. You could leave your memories behind you there and not even be afraid.

Ynys-morlan was built from memories, laid over the land; strata of stone and cement. Here between the mountains and the sea, the past was set into every building like the only thing that kept them anchored to the ground. Small towns did not forgive decisions, as if the choices made were carved into the wood of each front door.

Charlotte thought of Ruth, still living in the house that her mother had kept and named. In the weeks that had led to this night, she had thought of Ruth all the time.

Looking out now over the table they had made – old school desks pushed end to end, long enough for many people to sit – her hands were laid flat on the covering cloth.

'Well, better afraid than eager,' she said quietly. 'I'm sure.' Still she didn't turn. She looked at the space between the final row of chairs and the door, room there for people to stand. And along that last wall another table was set. Crates of wine and two hundred little plastic cups, a point of light picked out on every rim.

She heard Ruth, 'It'll be all right. It'll go well. Think of what we're going to say. It'll be amazing.' She cleared her throat as Charlotte turned, tried to smile.

The fierceness she had seen in Charlotte as the garden had burned, it had withdrawn, consolidated its strength. A little pillar of salt in her.

Charlotte's hair was drawn back. Her clothes were dark, her face paler for them. Her eyes held still waterfalls.

Ruth would know their names; for each face a little history, and each knowing Ruth's in return.

'It's going to make them happy,' she watched Ruth say, and nodded for her.

Across the room, the office door opened. Emyr's shoes sounded rhythmically as he walked behind the chairs, his hair neatly combed, his beautiful suit brushed down, a ream of paper in his hands. He came and laid the three stacks out before them. Pink, yellow, green.

'You know where Dai's sitting?' she asked.

'I'll show him his place when he gets here.'

There was nothing left to do now. Three piles spaced along this table, they would look out over them. Printed at the top of each sheet, Ruth looked at the words.

'Application Form', they read.

'I have to tell you, Emyr,' Gwen had said, 'I think it's ridiculous. You should be asking for all the help you can get. I know where everything's kept in there. What are you going to do? Phone up every ten minutes and ask me where something is?'

'I'm sure we'll manage.' This morning it had been. 'Ruth wants to do it,' he'd said.

'This is your last opportunity to introduce Charlotte to a member of the community before she's swamped with introductions this evening. Weeks, I've been saying it now. Confronted with two hundred people, Emyr, more if we're lucky. Do you not think that it might go more smoothly if there was someone to bridge the gap?' She had looked at him, the keys in her hand. 'An intermediary,' she'd said.

'Gwen –' He'd tried to frame his words. More and more, though, these last few weeks, he'd found the things she said too serrated to fit his answers around. 'I've only met her twice myself, and briefly –'

'Well,' she'd looked away. 'I told you before, two meetings were easily enough for you to give her an invitation to dinner. If you'd listened to me when I told you that, we wouldn't now be faced with a situation where she has to meet everyone at once . . . To tell you the truth, Emyr, I'm surprised you'd let a situation like that come about.' She had shrugged without looking at him, like she could make a point, he thought, just by refusing him her gaze. He'd watched her. She must have made that gesture one thousand times before. He saw it more clearly now, though.

'Well,' she'd said, 'Obviously you know best.' She'd placed the keys in his hand as though they were fragile and he might break them, so clumsy and careless. She'd turned away, very busy.

Ruth hadn't told him that she wanted to set it up herself. It was the sort of thing she might have said, though. If she'd put her own wants above others'. In a way, he thought, it was almost a kindness to Ruth. Only a small lie. He'd never been a liar. Neither of them had. It was one of the things he'd always loved in Gwen. He remembered looking at her and thinking that, of all the people he'd ever met, she was the only one who knew the worth of honesty.

She had put her bag back on the coat rack without the keys.

In bed or in their living room with its soft light and reminiscences, he and Gwen had talked the nights thin over the last weeks: the changes, the money, Charlotte and Ruth. Some evenings it had felt almost like old times. This new project, best of all the projects they'd ever set out on together. It had felt real between them again and filled him with the past. The construction of the community centre, the gift shop, way back when.

He'd had to lie to Gwen this morning. It was important, in these last few hours, to keep her apart. Ruth could have mentioned Dai in front of her at any time. Everything would have stopped for Emyr then, movement, speech, and Gwen would have said in the silence, 'What does it matter where Dai sits?'

In here, the wooden floor shone. Curling against the windows, the crêpe-paper shapes must have cast their colours out across dark gravel.

There was nothing but the wind here through the winter months; moving round bare trees and bare homes, loud enough to cover the sound of the sea. The long road let it walk between each building and the slate roofs were black as the sky. No washing hung in the back yards, nothing left outside. Come winter, the houses drew everything in until all the life in Ynys-morlan was held inside them, only facing each other, yellow squinting through their curtains. The dragon weathervane that Charlotte had seen, walking into town for the first time, was moving now, a rusted shape underneath inkwash clouds. The street lamps gave out light at four each afternoon.

They'd weathered harder winters. The storms of '38, coming in on November gales, had dragged the waves higher than the chimneys. In '76, it had snowed heavily here. People had watched from their windows: snowdrifts on the coastline's stones.

At some point, some time in the past, Ruth thought, people had stood on these far mountains and looked across an empty plain. Tarmac now, cement and brick. Cars drove through the beating weather, their headlights thin as seaweed on the road. The posters had been stuck to every lamp-post.

Bethan Hughes looked out at them.

The smell of food was still hanging in here, mixed with Mr Muscle Kitchen Cleaner. The café was empty, her mum swept the floor and she could hear her dad's footsteps coming downstairs. 'Are we ready yet, ladies?'

'Just waiting for Siân and Tom now.'

'You talk to Gwen Morgan this morning?'

'I talked to her. Tight as a clam.'

Bethan could see her own window from here. She'd left the light on in Chelsea's room, paper patterns laid out in the dark across her own bed. It was the café that was really Chelsea's home, though, the place she'd been brought up. She was raising a girl who, when she finally blossomed into a woman, would always know where the chip shop was. She sat at this corner table here, with her mum or Siân or Gwen, depending on the time of day and some days all three round her. Not like mother hens at all, she thought, but more like cuckoos. She would see Tom's little sister in the street after the school bus had heaved out, done up like one of those Practise-Your-Make-up-On-My-Plastic-Face dolls. She'd hear them talking, all around her, and she'd wonder how it was that there had come to be this pane of glass between her and Stacey.

Her mother would say sometimes, hand on Bethan's knee and letting out a little smile, 'Bethan was a dreamer at school, you know . . .' She would shake her head. 'And before that even, dreaming before she could open her mouth and tell you about all the special things she could do that no one else could. Piano playing, it'd be one day. Ballet, pop star, film star . . .' And Patty would point up to the picture of Elizabeth Taylor that she herself had hung there. She loved to tell people this. Bethan couldn't fathom why. It was all right for her to say it now, though, because that time was gone.

Sometimes, through these days, she'd google into Chelsea's face and Chelsea'd google back. They could google at each other better than any two people in the world. She thought now, gazing out at the road, of the way her mum had sat in Chelsea's room and talked about how this would be the first place the baby saw. 'To the baby,' she'd said, 'all this will be new.' But she thought really, all this would be old as houses to the baby, because the baby had never known anything else.

She wasn't a dreamer. Never had been. She knew well enough that this place was her home. And she'd never shown her mum Chelsea's fingers and how long they were and how much she could do with them. She had never talked about music, or sewing, or holding a fucking crayon. Sometimes she looked at Chelsea's fingers herself, the girl gripped on to her hand, trying to stand, and she wondered if the most likely thing wasn't just for those fingers, when they were almost a woman's, to end up jerking some boy off. She'd never been a dreamer.

Patty had a dreaming girl's curly hair but she was a hard-boiled egg and salt kind of person under it. She had the walk and the smile of dreaming but she liked to know what was what and exactly where it was kept in the cupboard. And the funny thing was, the really funny thing, Bethan was more like her every week. It got easier to stay in this town, not harder.

She'd seen Rhys's face, the last times they'd talked to each other, she'd seen the look on him. She'd had this little table in the corner, even then. Rhys'd liked to offer her cigarettes every five minutes, he'd held the pack out to her and not looked at her stomach. She'd felt dirty with the place, soaked with it, like she was greying out to match the colour of the walls. And if she could have scraped the feel of Ynys-morlan off her, she would have done it then.

She had said to him, 'I saw this cutest kid in Aber today, little baby thing with his dungarees.' And she'd smiled. And she'd taken two cigarettes; one for later, for when he was gone.

She wouldn't scrape this place off her now. And Rhys looked like a stranger, more and more every day. Not just to her but to Ynys-morlan. He and Tom had had some thing. These last few weeks she'd seen them, passing by each other on separate sides of the street. She'd asked Tom about it but Tom had only shrugged, only looked away. Rhys was free-floating now, she thought. Like a chip wrapper about to take off from the ground.

She wondered sometimes how many children had been brought up inside these walls, when it had been a home, not a café at all. She saw Chelsea's lit window now, heard the wind walking outside. Chelsea had this pair of mittens, a string that went through the arms of her coat and frog faces on the backs.

Those shadowed posters chattered against the lamp-posts. The windows in the Lion glowed, but there was no one in there. She had seen Gwen doing her work, in here every morning before playschool, that secret little smile all over her face. She'd said it: 'I'm sworn to secrecy. I can't say a word.' But she'd told them to go, everyone.

Bethan now lifted coats from the back of her chair. She pulled out Chelsea's mittens and smiled down at her radioactive-pink cheeks. Above this door the bell rang quietly, and Siân and Tom stepped in with the cold as she said, 'Are you ready then?' looking down at Chelsea's face.

Some time before, they had scaled these mountains to see for the first time the waves, the rounding gulls that flew whether there was concrete or rugged grass under them, whether people walked or not. They'd seen this bay and thought to build homes here. Wood and stone, cement and render, like they could hold the ground steady. Until it wasn't a stretch of land any more, not a floodplain between two headlands – until it was a town. And those mountains, where they had been hit by a salt wind for the first time, those mountains were now the view from a bedroom window. They were pretty in winter sunlight. And it was nice, in the afternoons, to walk your dog along the shore. Ruth didn't know when it had changed but at some point, she thought, some person had woken in their bed, and the stone walls around them hadn't just been a safe arm against the world but had become the world instead.

It was good to paint those walls, to keep them unfaded, because they held your memories. It was nice to grow climbers up them and in the summer to sit and smile there. And when you stood in your garden, when you looked up, you could see yourself clearly in the choices you'd made. It was good to see that those things, though growing older, were solid. And if you woke up one morning, looked at those walls around you and felt that you couldn't leave – that you'd put so much into your home you couldn't tear yourself away – it was all right. They'd been built for that, to protect you from the world.

They came through the double doors in twos and threes and more. A few cars at first, and then the cars were waiting in the entrance, headlights thrown over each other and glistening, engines idling in the dark. Into the foyer – wrapped in coats and scarves, bundled in talk and laughter and relief from the cold. They spoke to each other as they walked inside, and then their talking slowed as they looked about themselves.

They saw chairs, waiting. They saw the table at their head, the noise of those behind still loud as their own footsteps came to a halt. Fanning out into the main hall, sluggish like a riverbed, Ynys-morlan's residents arrived.

The posters had read:

PUBLIC MEETING

For all of Ynys-morlan
An opportunity
January 12th

Queues for wine formed as the room began to fill with softly shambling sound. Charlotte watched them come. The seats were taken slowly. A shuffle between each row, children settling on laps.

Somewhere close to Ruth, Lennie's laughter coughed out. She looked but couldn't find him through these moving faces. Looking about her, she couldn't see Dai either, only this hubbub. Sinking now. She spotted Emyr, his eyes moving over the crowd as well, and then Ruth had to start walking herself because he was stepping forward, he was standing behind the central chair in front of everyone.

'Excuse me, sorry, sorry,' weaving between shoulders as she searched for Charlotte; for dark hair under these lights.

The woman stood at the other end of the table, as though she was waiting for nothing. She looked like she couldn't even hear the voices – or their spreading silence now.

Emyr stood still. Rested his hands on the back of the chair. And by the time that Ruth made it to her side of the table, she could hear her own feet scuffle the last few steps.

Emyr looked out, smiling, quiet.

Ruth heard the voice of a child. The mother hushing. She heard the breath Emyr took.

'Ladies and gentlemen,' he said.

He held out one hand, the other still resting.

'Ladies and gentlemen. Now, you're not going to mind if I take a seat? Not after all the running round I've done today, making sure you get that free wine you're drinking without so much as a thank-you.'

He looked so calm, Ruth thought. No one here but me and thee. And when he turned his eyes to her, every face in the room turned with him.

'You know Ruth Lewis here,' he said. 'Now, you don't know the woman on my left, or maybe she's had the misfortune to meet a few of you. This is Charlotte Weyland.' The eyes turned and then Charlotte felt their staring. A physical thing, like the lights stripped something from her. This was how she sat, bodiless, while Emyr began with his clear and rounded words.

He stared out over the audience as though it belonged to him and his eyes avoided Gwen. 'I want to tell you first, just how difficult the last few weeks have been for me.' Sitting in the centre, looking back at him, as though her gaze rested comfortably on every word he said. 'You know what I'm like. Don't enjoy keeping things to myself. I probably spend more time talking than you want to spend listening. Never been one for keeping secrets.' Face after face, he saw. Davey Thomas squinting. Sue Cadwallader with lipstick on; Swivel Jones with his big knees cramped and folded. Finally, past them all, he let his eyes touch his wife. 'Have to be forced into keeping any kind of secret at all.'

Hands on her bag, she smiled a little at the truth of that. He'd been like a boy, telling her about it on that first night, like he was pleading to tell her. Her smile flickered as his eyes didn't move from her, though.

'I'm not a great believer in secrets. A small town like this, we all depend on just the opposite in fact: honesty, togetherness . . . things that probably sound trite, antiquated even . . . but, a community like this, there's nothing more important.' He held his hands out to them. 'So, maybe in a few minutes you'll be able to imagine – how difficult it's been to not share this news with all of you. News of such magnitude . . . Well,' he said. 'I can tell you now. The kind of news that opens your mouth for you, so your jaw muscles needn't even do the work. That kind of news,' he said. 'That kind.'

Emyr paused for long moments. On his left-hand side, Charlotte's gaze rested politely on the plastic cup in her hands. Fluorescent light floated in the white wine. She didn't lift it to drink. Unsure of how her hands would react now, better to stay still now, better just to sit. She saw a tiny bubble rise.

In the silence that was laid over the hall, Emyr said, 'That's the reason that we've set this meeting up at the earliest possible opportunity. And if we're lacking in answers to some of the questions you might have, if we seem to be . . .' he smiled again, '. . . a little less than completely organized, that's *because* we wanted this meeting at the earliest opportunity. That's because we want to find answers to those questions *together*. And the little details we haven't organized . . . Well, maybe we can *all* sort them out. Tonight.'

He stared out at them. Garwyn and all the old boys. Towards the back, he caught sight of Rhys's parents, sitting side by side. Under these lights, they all looked the same; far away from him. And when he opened his mouth it was sadness he felt. Not togetherness. He thought of how their faces had looked, just like this, standing in a semicircle around Eirian's grave while Gwen's hands had held Dai down. Remembered Dai in the museum's fraction of light. An expression unlocked across his face as he'd told Emyr he didn't want the gift shop. It was sadness. He'd written these words down but he didn't need notes.

'The news I've had to keep quiet . . . is the most important piece I've ever had. For every person here. Each and every one.' He took one last breath. 'An opportunity, as the posters say.'

There was no lie in that. There was no promise.

'Ynys-morlan is a lovely town, even if I'm the one to say it. We have so much to offer to the people who come here, and so much to enjoy ourselves. Wonderful surroundings, a coastline which was given a clean bill of health while some others were not so unpolluted. Peace and tranquillity for families to enjoy their holidays, and which we ourselves treasure. A lovely town. And if I offer you a "but" here, it's only because of the glimpse I've been given, the *glimpse* of what Ynys-morlan could be.

'For the last five years, like so many other towns that rely, every season, on what they have to offer visitors, Ynys-morlan has suffered. And we all know. We've all been to Gulliver's Travels in Aber and seen the prices in the windows there. Cheaper all the time. There are many families too, that've come here season after season, who can't afford to come now. And not because they've chosen Tenerife instead, but just because they've found, like all of us, that they've a little less money left over this year for things like holidays. For whatever reasons, we all know well enough that the number of people who visit Ynys-morlan, it's been shrinking. Work that our profits would've paid for each year, well . . . that's been shrinking as well. Not just work on our businesses, not just work to maintain our industry . . . but work on our homes. Because, first and foremost, Ynys-morlan is our home. It isn't just a way to make ends meet each year, it's the place where most of us were born. It's the place we've chosen to raise our families in.' Emyr touched a hand over his mouth, let it fall. 'For the last five years, we've had to watch our town . . . lessen. I suppose that's the word. A lot of shops, too many shops, closing. A lot of people moving away . . . people who've had no choice.'

Emyr gazed out: Barry and Anna Jarman, Iohan Williams. He saw Dai's face and he thought of the keyring that the man carried in his pocket now. He spoke into these people's quiet, not even sure in truth what his words meant. 'We have set up this meeting tonight to tell you: those five years are over.'

The strip lights made their faces harsh.

'We have the money,' Emyr said. 'We have it now. The money to pay for work that should have been done, four, five years ago. The money to reverse every little bit of wear and tear that's gone untended these last years. Money to rejuvenate *every part of Ynys-morlan*.'

He paused.

Beside him, eyes down, fixed on the table, Ruth heard every word. Charlotte stared into the Sauvignon Blanc and listened. He was the only one to meet their eyes.

He said, 'But we have more than that. An opportunity, that was what it said on the posters, and that's exactly the truth. Not just to rejuvenate the things that we've had to watch fade. An opportunity to *build*. An opportunity to turn a lovely place . . . into a wholly beautiful one.'

He heard the rustle. He could see it moving through them like a breath. Heads turning slightly to each other, hands shifting in laps, whispered words. Outside, through the traces painted on every black window, he could hear the wind move.

'A beautiful town. With more to offer than we have ever had.' He said again, gently, 'We have the money. Only a few weeks ago, I had a phone call from Ruth Lewis here. You know what she said to me? Call in sick, she said. News, she said. And I'm not a man to take a day off without reason, I heard the way she was talking and I thought something was wrong. But I didn't believe what she told me when I saw her. I'm sure that you won't now. Maybe it'll take tonight to convince you. A "project", was the word she used. A "fund".'

Ruth didn't know what the words had been, couldn't remember now, couldn't think.

'Available to every one of us.'

Couldn't keep in mind what she had to say next or the tone she'd decided to use. She stared at the table as if it was the only thing still steady.

'A fund for our town.'

She swallowed, hearing the legs of his chair scrape as he stood up. Tried to feel what she should feel. This ought to be a moment for rejoicing. She had to stand now.

Emyr said, 'Maybe we can all give Ruth Lewis a little encouragement by putting our hands together.'

Emyr clapped. And she didn't hear his chair as he sat again, because then they were all clapping. Two hundred seated, more standing behind. She heard it start and build, and she heard how hesitant it was. Underneath the noise, they'd be turning to look at each other. They'd be speaking her name and she knew what tone of voice they'd have.

Gradually, she pushed her own chair back. She stood and every heartbeat hit her.

Her gaze moved up: from the tablecloth to the brightly lit wooden floorboards that lay between her and the first of them. Hands in laps. Faces. Men, women, old people, children. Families sitting together, friends, all dyed by the same unforgiving light.

Her voice echoed. Paper in her hand crackled.

'I'm sorry,' she said. And then she said, 'I'm scared. Feels like when the teacher used to drag you to the front of the class –' laughing into their hush. 'Emyr . . . can talk to you and make it sound . . . the way it ought to.' She looked at them, held out her hand and showed them the notes she'd made. 'I wrote a speech down, but I'd have to read it off the paper now . . . so I'll just tell you.' She looked away from them. 'I'll just tell you,' she said. Across the length of cloth-covered table, she met Charlotte's eyes. Charlotte was smiling, Ruth saw. Not pitying, not even encouraging. It was the sort of smile you gave when you couldn't hide the truth any more. Of all the people in this room, she was the only one who looked real.

Ruth said, 'Public Works Projects. A fund for improving Ynys-morlan doesn't just go to its businesses. But the street itself. Every bit of Ynys-morlan. Its undeveloped areas. I can be a bit of a gardening freak . . . so it's no surprise that I'd get, you know, all excited at the thought of public parks . . . but I'm talking now about the chance to beautify *every space in town*. That would make an improvement in all our lives. Just opening your front door. Seeing somewhere full of flowers, lawns . . .

'*Regeneration. Rehabilitation.* Not just parks but repaving – the length of the whole road. Renovating the seawall. There are a hundred possibilities and we're open to them. We are *waiting*, for any suggestions you have.

'Financial support for improving Ynys-morlan. Not just its public areas either . . .' She breathed. 'The houses – that's what people see when they drive in, that's what we all have to live with, day to day. Mine's the worst,' she said. 'My mother would turn in her grave, I'm sure, paint peeling, slates missing, hundred little things wrong with the place.' She looked down at the notes in her hand, damp. Without glancing up again, she said, 'There are extensions, entranceways, dormer windows have been added. Not more than twenty years old, some of them, and they look like they're already falling off. No one's got the money to have their house done up when they can't even pay the bills. Not me and Lennie anyway. But that's what this town's made up of.' And she raised her head again, 'That's what it is, as Emyr said, just your house and my house and the shops in between. They're not falling apart. Some of these buildings, they've been standing two hundred years, more. And they're just the same underneath still. Doesn't matter if the render's cracking, or if the paint's so old it's flaking off, doesn't matter. They're just the same under it. Beautiful, they are. And all the work that needs to be done on them, it's just surface work. Renovation,' she said.

They were muttering now, she could see them. And she didn't know if the things they were saying were good things or bad. Perhaps it didn't matter. She'd stood here. She had done this.

'Every one of our houses is a part of Ynys-morlan. If you would like yours to be a part of Ynys-morlan's project . . . it can be. You can take one of these forms that are lying in front of me. You can take one and fill it in.' She looked at them, from eye to eye, and she said, 'All renovation work will be free to you.'

And then the noise wasn't muttering. It was talking then. She heard their voices rise and she didn't know if what she saw was disapproval or just shock. There were voices lifted and she made out questions. Shoulders moving. People turning to the rows behind them. Ruth saw it all. She remembered standing with Charlotte in front of the garden's flames. She remembered laughing.

Lennie sat between them all. He didn't move. His eyes were on Ruth; staring out over their mutterings as if he heard none, the approval on his face wrought with hardened lines.

They were turning back towards her. Her hands felt empty.

'Ynys-morlan could be beautiful . . . I used to sit down, you know how, when you're little, you draw pictures of your house? How it's going to be? I used to draw this beautiful house, all perfect. And it would be in this . . . perfect, beautiful town.' Her voice left her for a moment. 'It could be wonderful. Every tiny little part.'

She would walk down this road and see a place she'd never seen. She would go home and open the door to a house that she'd never walked into before. Everyone in this room had that chance. She wondered if there had ever been a place, a time, when someone had been able to say this. All these things they wanted could be real.

'We've got the money. Any Ynys-morlan you can imagine . . . we can build.'

The expression on Lennie's face said that this was right. He believed in it. And through this expression his eyes stared out.

'We've seen a lot of businesses die in the last five years –'

A voice called out from the audience's low mutter, and Ruth turned, trying to find the face, 'You want to talk about businesses dying, you can talk about the rates.'

'It doesn't matter –' But she couldn't see who'd spoken and she heard another voice.

'You can talk about the lack of bloody customers, that's what you can talk about.'

There was laughter, murmuring agreement. Ruth saw him, a man in the second row, settled into his seat and staring at her. She knew his face. Selwyn Powell, the newsagent. Beside her, she heard Emyr shifting.

Ruth felt the notepaper crumple in her hand, not knowing what gesture she made. 'It doesn't matter what the reasons are. We could sit here all night and talk about that. This is *the answer*,' she said. 'The end of it. We can *subsidize* the businesses, we can *improve* them, create *new* ones. That's what we want to do! Listen –' She reached across to her left, in front of Emyr, held up three green pieces of paper. 'We've got application forms. All you have to do is apply. Do up your frontage, get more stock in, a million things, you see? We're just surviving at the moment. But we could be doing more. We could be *thriving*.'

They shifted, talking.

'It'll be funded. No borrowing. This is free.' Her hand fell slowly.

Too many voices to answer now. She looked from person to person and they seemed angry. A woman's rose, and the strip lights picked out hard-lined eyes. '"This money, this money." Council money? Government money? What? Grants?'

'I –' She heard a movement beside her.

And then Charlotte's voice came. Ruth closed her mouth. They were turning to her: a woman most of them had never seen, who'd sat before them silent as blank paper while Emyr talked and smiled.

Charlotte stared back. Ruth saw her wine through the opaque plastic, untouched. There was no restless motion now. They were as silent as she had been.

'It comes from me. It isn't government money.'

'If it was government money,' Ruth pattered into the quiet, 'she wouldn't be standing here. She'd be in a hall in Cardiff.' She heard her own voice echo.

'It's private money,' Charlotte said.

The woman who'd spoken stared at her, raw with scorn, voice bright as she leaned into the space that other people had made. 'It's *your* money?'

'Mine.' If it had been that, Charlotte thought, perhaps her life could also have been.

But she spoke over all her doubts now, over every word she'd ever written, she said,

'Yes.'

There was no sound.

A sudden laugh then, but Ruth heard the edge in it. Maybe in this silence others heard it too. Like the laugh that she'd given herself, standing in the garden's doorway. That sound was the beginning of belief.

She glanced at Charlotte Weyland. No clue to what the woman felt, but they were standing here together at least. Ruth was aware of the distance between herself and all those seats; people who said hello to her in this car park outside, every morning, bringing Nia for playschool. They asked how Lennie was. But she could feel the distance now, sudden and total, as if a tide moved in this hush.

'The money belongs to me,' Charlotte said. 'I made a decision, independently, to donate the capital at my disposal to charity. It was Ruth who came to me with this proposal.' She spoke into the wordless hall and her voice gave nothing. She asked for nothing back. 'I won't stand here and justify my decision. If you feel you need to know my reasons before picking up one of these forms, don't pick up the forms. Don't write down your name. If every one of you feels the same way, I'll carry on with my choice and give the money to charity. I'm making an offer. One that can be taken or left.'

The woman seated in the audience shut her mouth over laughter that was gone. She looked away as if in disgust. On the faces around her, though, were varying expressions. Charlotte's face was bare in this bright, staring hall.

'There are three different types of application form.'

'So far, three types. If there are other ways we can think of . . .' Emyr's voice came.

'There are forms to apply for restoration work on private property. For the inconvenience this work would cause, compensation money can be afforded to you. The figure is as yet undecided, but it would not vary depending on the property. A standard amount, for everyone.'

'Compensation money . . . ?' some voice spoke out.

'Here,' Ruth touched the stack of yellow paper. She continued, 'There are forms for people who want to sell their properties.' A muffled reaction came as she gestured towards the pink ream which lay before Emyr. 'Any homeowner in Ynys-morlan waiting for a buyer, your property would be purchased at its *original* asking price – that's your *hoping* price.' Cluttered words were drifting through the crowd but Ruth only spoke more quickly. 'There are forms to apply for capital to start, or subsidies to maintain, businesses.'

She moved her hand out to these green forms.

Reactions were being passed from seat to seat now. A woman, bent close to the man beside her, talking rapidly in a voice no one else could hear. A man with his arm on another, holding back whatever he was going to say until Ruth had finished. Sitting so close here, they could feel the radiator's heat and they were flushed, gloves and bags in laps. Lennie could feel that heat, all round him. The noise of them was thick.

Ruth couldn't hear the words, low as things moving unseen.

'All the ideas we couldn't put into practice . . .' she started. Low as the sound of stones, she thought, underwater. 'We now have the money for. We can make Ynys-morlan the most beautiful town in Wales.'

'I've got an idea.'

From the back of the room, she heard it: a girl's voice, and she saw a small struggle, someone trying to stand. Patricia Hughes's daughter. Ruth knew her.

'Ideas, you said.' Bethan nodded. 'If we had any.'

'Yes.' They looked at each other over the turning heads. Eighteen, nineteen maybe, Ruth thought.

'Well, I've got one. A restaurant.' And from beside her, below her, Bethan heard her mum say her name. But she carried on. 'What about that?'

Ruth only said, 'Yes.'

'Well, yes what?' Bethan shrugged, felt her mother's hand on her sleeve. 'We've got the café, right? Improvements, that's what you said. So. Our café into a restaurant. That's an improvement.'

'I think . . . yes, a restaurant.' Her hands moved, saying nothing. 'I think it's perfect. I was saying, the other day, I was saying . . . That'd be just what we need.'

'We could get funding for that. No loan.'

'Funding. Yes.'

Bethan was motionless, holding Chelsea. 'How much funding?' she said.

'Bethan –' Her mother's voice came to her, hushed in embarrassment, anger.

'No, because it costs a lot. I mean, that's not renovation. I don't know what you'd call it, like, an overhaul. So you tell me. How much funding then?'

Ruth opened her mouth, she held up her hands again like she was giving in.

Not far from her, Charlotte said, 'Enough.'

Bethan's gaze moved. She looked angry with her nerves, Charlotte thought, and knew that feeling well. More practised at it than this girl. She knew the way it settled, cold as stone, holding everything else in place.

She could have torn pages from her diaries and handed them out in this silence, she could have passed them from person to person until her hands were empty again.

'You'll pay.'

'Yes.'

'Do you know how much that'd cost?' Her last question was

laughter, it spilled across the floorboards between like broken glass. 'How much money is there then?'

Charlotte listened to it. She thought of the shards of bottle that had lain around Nia's feet, and Bethan's question faded away, like that glass might have melted in the sun. She saw how it would look, dissolving slowly, losing every jagged edge as the reflections on it changed. She wondered how Nia might have looked then, watching it soften like that on the ground.

Charlotte said, 'There are thirty-three million pounds.'

In the mounting noise of voices, she bent and took her bag from the floor. Opening it, raised her face. The girl saw what she had taken out. She couldn't look anywhere else.

'Thirty-three million pounds . . . ?'

Charlotte only made out the words on her lips. She held her cheque-book in one hand.

Emyr was saying, 'It's *something*, isn't it *something*?' hands out, a conductor. But no one was looking, even Ruth didn't see him, didn't see the small smile that edged his words as he raised his tone over everyone else's and said, 'That's not the last!' They didn't stop, no one stopped, though he didn't care. 'That's not the last.' His eyes were fixed on one point in the crowd as Bethan stood motionless, like some buoy in the sea, as Dai looked up around him from one to another. 'I know it's hard to believe, because I had trouble with it myself. I had trouble – But to show you, to make you see just how real it is, I want to tell you now –' Their clamour rose and fell, rough as tides. '– I want to tell you now, what our first project is going to be.'

He stood in the commotion. He sought out Dai.

The overhead lights shone on the gel in Dai's hair. There had been a kind of fear from the man, Emyr remembered, when he'd told him. 'It's a secret. I can trust you with it. It's between you and me.' A shocked disapproval – that Emyr could keep this from anyone – and it had seemed to add lines to Dai's face.

On his right, Ruth stood with a hand across her mouth. As though she would deal with this, all this noise here. Just a little later. To his left, Charlotte Weyland looked into Bethan Hughes's face with a small smile. On the tablecloth in front of her, her cheque-book was unopened.

Emyr said, 'I didn't want any of it to start without you. But I wanted to show you tonight, in actions not words, that this is real.' Under the strip lights, his glasses were blank. 'We've talked tonight, about all the empty shops up and down this street. A town like Ynys-morlan, it *is* the shops. It *is* what it can give its visitors. It is its looks.'

He saw them all, unsettled around Gwen, and she must have seen something in him because her gaze was stone steady.

'You know what we've got right now? Dai will tell you, he owns some. A load of empty, whitewashed shops, that's what. They're beautiful buildings! They're original! Two hundred years old, more. Fishermen's cottages they were once. And underneath all the white-wash, all the peeling paint and extensions, they're still the same.

'All those empty shops . . .' he said, 'and one great big one, full. Not an original building, and I should know. I helped put forward the plans. Now, I'm not saying that it hasn't served a purpose . . . I'm not saying it's ugly – wouldn't ever have let it go up if I thought that. But it was twenty years ago . . . Amazing, isn't it?' He tried to find the tone that he'd decided upon but couldn't get it now, couldn't seem to say it right as he looked at her. 'Twenty years ago. Ynys-morlan was thriving then. That's not what we're looking at now. We're looking at change. Not just a touch here, a touch there. But thirty-three million pounds. The kind of change I'm talking about, we can take this town and turn it into whatever we want.'

Everywhere around her it seemed that there was muted, soundless space.

'Change like that, takes strength. Takes resolve. For Dai Meredith,' he said, 'maybe more than any of us now.'

Dai stood slowly on the cue of his name, one hand moving to his hair.

'We can fill two, three,' Emyr continued, 'maybe four of those empty buildings with all the stock that's in the gift shop.'

'We can fill three,' Dai said. 'I've looked at it. Three it is.'

Emyr nodded before he raised his eyes to the crowd again.

'Dai has made the decision to use three of those vacant buildings instead. To convert them. I say "instead" because you have to get rid of the old as you bring in the new. Needn't be a bad thing. It needn't be sad,' he said.

In this light, very slow, Gwen's expression was slipping. As though emotions were slim things.

'Actions rather than words,' Emyr said. 'This week all the stock will be moved from the gift shop, stored, until the restoration of the new shops is complete. This week he's going to do it, and I'll be there to help him . . . After we have all the stock out,' he nodded, he finished, 'then the demolition work can start.'

In the wake of what he'd said, Charlotte spoke, but Emyr didn't hear.

Gwen sat in the centre. And he saw that all these people were turning their heads towards her, because it had been her wedding as well as his. Not speaking yet, not asking questions yet, but Gwen must have felt their looking, because he saw her try to put a smile on to her face.

Charlotte said, 'This is the first cheque.' She said, 'We've taken quotes. And if you would like quotes made on your own property, please take a form. I'll tell you, as I write it now, the figure we were given as the lowest quote for the work: eighteen thousand, six hundred pounds. Cambrian Construction is the name.'

In the quiet of the hall, total enough to hear the scratches of Charlotte's pen, Emyr saw his wife look out.

To his right, Ruth's voice was clear, 'This is the first cheque . . . this is the first night! Can we . . . Can we celebrate it? Please, I haven't had a chance to say a proper thank-you yet, to Charlotte. Will you help me thank her maybe? The first cheque!'

Ruth put her hands together, applauding. For a moment, the sound seemed to travel past their faces, blank. She heard the echoes return.

'The first of many . . . !' she said.

Emyr was watching as Gwen, her make-up perfect, slowly lifted her hands to applaud.

And he began to do the same. Somewhere else, the back of the room, Bethan stood again, Chelsea in her mum's lap, and clapped. She looked straight across their heads as, between the others, Gwen also stood. Two people only. Lennie slid Nia from his lap.

He clapped loud enough for many. Others began to rise around him, unsure, with threaded smiles, as Ruth saw his eyes on her.

They put their hands together, Charlotte placing the pen down.

She looked out and she saw them all. It wasn't long before the room was full with the sound of their applause. Growing like the noise of stones thrown on to the shore.

The car park was empty, black. Gwen saw it through her own barely drawn reflection. She sat, her body creased into the right shape, her ankles crossed, hands folded, and she heard the things he said.

He said, 'You remember when it was finished? We went to look at it, your father, us. Good piece of work, it was. You remember? It was raining, and we had sandwiches and a thermos and that. Sat on a blanket on the floor.'

Gwen made no answer.

'We had a toast. "First project together," that's what your father said.' Sitting in the driver's seat, Emyr raised an empty hand as though there was still a cup in it, and they were still sitting there, on the new wooden floorboards, looking out at the rain.

There was no rain. Wind moved through the dark in front of them, it moved around the car. She could hear the sound of old leaves dancing.

They had seen the people out. Standing, shaking hands and kissing friends, Gwen had found herself counting the number of people who'd attended, adding slowly in threes and fours as they'd walked out through the wide double doors, as though the arithmetic gave her some kind of frame to help hold the smile on her face.

Two hundred and fifty-six people. Above drawn collars their faces had been changed. Gwen had watched them. They'd left the community centre like the tattered edges of rain clouds, spent and dragged away. And next to her Emyr had smiled; it had looked like a lost thing, she'd thought, floating on his face. Every one of them with some comment, some slack exclamation as they held her hand.

'And you knew about this? Don't know how you kept it to yourself, Gwen. Must've been *bursting* to tell –'

'I can't believe it, do you know that? Thirty-three million pounds. For *God's* sake –'

They had looked back as they'd pushed open the double doors, seeing the table where Charlotte had stood, the place where Gwen herself had poured the wine. The overhead lights had still been dazzling on the empty mess: the uneven chairs, the cups left on the floor. And they'd walked out then, into the night, for the first time in two hours hearing their own footsteps again.

The car park had now been left vacant. Here, to her right, was the corner where Emyr had stood on a sunny day, a while ago, and seen a boy writing obscenities with spray-paint on the wall. The wind must have cut around that corner now.

For the longest time, she said nothing at all. Words came to her, but they were full of spittle and hate, and she would not say them to him. She would not give him anything. Instead she was silent as these stretches of black ground.

How carefully he must have planned it – while sitting with her each evening and talking about all the wonderful possibilities that a thing like this could bring. She unreeled the memories of those evenings now, and she saw, in retrospect, the moments of doubt he had had between his smiles. She remembered how he had reached out and touched her, telling her that first night. Perhaps he had been planning it even then. He must have imagined this moment many times, sitting with Dai, talking to him, calling demolition firms for quotes. Whatever response he'd imagined from her she wouldn't give to him.

'Do you remember?' he said.

'I remember, Emyr. They're very treasured memories to me. I think they must be clearer than yours. I remember him trusting you. It was your project really,' she said. 'Yours and his.'

Emyr looked out. He saw the streetlight fading into shadow where a fence would be, too black to see now, before the ground fell to dunes and ran down to the beach. It would have looked like this on the night she'd walked along that beach and come across the boy that didn't have any name. In the glass in front of him, Emyr could see the soft lines of his own face. He remembered her clapping

'What do you think? Do you think I'm trustworthy? What do you think?' he said. He had to stop talking then, look away, or he might have kept asking her. He stared at his hands, uncertain outlines, empty in his lap.

'I think that's a strange question to ask, after watching the culmination of a deceit . . . a deceit that must have taken you an awfully long time to plan.' He was silent and she said, looking out, 'Do you want me to answer it? Really? What would you like me to say?'

'Whatever you think . . . Just whatever you think, I don't know.'

Gwen took a quiet breath, she nodded very slowly. 'I think, during all that planning, you must have spent a long time . . . festering in your thoughts. I don't know what might have convinced you to do this, but you must have spent a very long time . . . *festering* over it. A long time persuading Dai to go along. I wonder what you said, to make him give up something that his mother spent a lifetime building. I remember all those years, Emyr. Do you? Eirian working in the shop, and Dai running around there, getting under her feet. Always there, he was. He used to love it.'

'I didn't persuade him of anything. Dai didn't want the place, he didn't know what to do with it. All he knew was the responsibility it put on him. All he knew was that he'd probably fail, and have to remember every day that his mother left the place in his care. I didn't convince him to do anything.'

Gwen looked at the touches of the light on the leather dashboard. 'But you seem to have convinced yourself of a few things.'

'I heard him, I listened to him. You wouldn't know, you never listened to him. You talked at him, that's all.'

'Well, Emyr. I'd say that it was a good thing, in all my failings, that you were there to look after him. How many times did you talk to him about it? Tell me. How many times did he ask you if it was the right thing to do? If you were sure? Did he ask you, maybe, whether you thought Eirian would have wanted this? And you must have told him yes. Yes, it's the right thing to do, Dai. Yes, Eirian would have wanted this.' In the closeness, she turned her face at him. She said in a bitter voice, 'Yes, and yes again.'

She let the words sink into the silent car. Outside, the white lines of the parking spaces rolled out. No one else here, not a single car. In other places, she thought, people would have their lights on now. They'd be sitting in their living rooms, talking, repeating over and over again the things that they had heard tonight. Somewhere else, Dai would be walking home. There would be no light on there. In the yard outside Eirian's house, the wind would move as freely as it did around this cold and quiet car.

Dai wasn't home, though. It took a long time to get home when you were walking, even longer when you were standing still. And, while Charlotte Weyland returned to the house where her diaries were preserved, thinking of the weight of a hundred thousand unspoken words, and of the merest few, on that cheque she'd held, the weight that pulled at Dai tonight spoke with his mother's voice. He had given the gift shop away. From the community centre, he had walked out past the car park, climbed over the fence that Rhys had looked at once, hearing the sound of Emyr's footsteps on tarmac. In this January dark, Dai went out to the beach.

It took a long time to walk home, even longer when you were walking in the opposite direction. His mother had asked him once if he didn't want to learn how to ride a push-bike. He had told her the answer to that one quick enough. Big things didn't balance on small ones, and he'd thought to himself maybe she'd like to stand on a matchstick, ride that into town. He'd often been full of thoughts like that. Lots of things she'd said to him, there'd been some nasty notion in him. He'd never meant to have them, they came to him. It wasn't his fault.

It had used to take him seventeen minutes to walk home. It'd used to be, when he'd been walking for fifteen and a half, he'd start to see its light through the trees.

One night, the first few days he'd been back home, he had left the lights on himself. He had walked back after work and seen them between the crooked-hand branches. It had filled his stomach with metal, he'd tasted metal in his mouth. It had been a lie to leave the lights on. She hadn't been inside.

They had been very bad those first few days. Every time he'd walked into a room, it had been empty. Every time he turned on a light, she wouldn't turn it off again. He remembered standing in the kitchen for a long time without doing anything. He had kept meaning to do things but the place around him had taken the actions from his hands. It had been twilight, he remembered. He'd looked at the gas cooker, blue in the light from the window. He remembered thinking that he could open its door, and he would smell all the things that had been cooked in there and all of them would be old and gone. That almost-light had touched the taps, the draining board, and every single thing in there had had no use. Like he could turn that tap on and no water would come. The kitchen was a lie. It wasn't real any more even though it looked the same.

He had lived in the house for three days without moving anything; not the sheets on his bed, he had slept on the sofa, eaten things brought home from the shops and had thrown the tins away outside, so there wouldn't be any change in the house. They would be lying out there somewhere now. He'd stood in his lifeless garden with the evening and thrown them far out. Somewhere in the grass they'd be. The grass was wet with winter rain. For three days, the only movement in his home had been the light of the television.

The clocks had not ticked. He'd stood in front of one of them and looked at the night of his mother's death. He did not know how to wind them. But he wouldn't have, not those first three days, even if he'd known. He hadn't cried. Like the clocks, he hadn't seemed to be able to move. He'd kept finding things of hers. He found a crossword, half the answers filled in, but he looked down at it and he couldn't cry, and he couldn't close the cover. He found her shawl on a chair by the sofa but he didn't put it round him. He sat and he looked at it. It pulled his eyes away from the screen.

On the fourth day, he had opened the door to his room. He had taken a clean shirt out of the wardrobe and he'd put it on, looking at the unmade bed. That was the first time he'd cried in the house, he'd sat and thought that there was no going back now. He'd changed part of their life.

That day he'd taken the key from the hook in the hallway and had unlocked the grandfather clock. Three hours to work out how it wound. He'd been afraid to touch it at first. Its long, old-man face hadn't broken under his hands, though. Its time had begun to move. He had pulled back, looked at it, stepping on its own. The pendulum swung to one side, the other, the seconds started up. And through the house, they must have moved. Echoed up through the ceiling and filled all the rooms. One, another, until a minute had passed and the clock was still ticking. He had done that. Put time back into the house.

All the clocks were working now. You could hear them, as you opened the front door and stopped, feet on the mat. Here and in the kitchen, upstairs on the landing, in everywhere. When you came inside now, although it was dark, you could hear them like a voice. He never locked the front door. If the wind pulled it open while he was away, it could come in, that was all right.

But Dai wasn't going home now. He walked on heavy unseen sand, caught his ankles on marram grass until he didn't want to move any more. And sat, looking out at the loud, shifting darkness that was the sea. Either side of him, the sharp grass reached up to his face, curved around his back like arms. It kept the wind from him, every part but his eyes.

Tonight the sky was empty and he could see the stars. There were different nights for stargazing, all kinds; nights when the constellations were set like pictures, and nights, like this night, when every star up there could be seen, when the sky was stirred with them like milk.

He shouldn't go home. The people at the meeting must've agreed. All of them with their cars, with their heaters and their radios and their little digital clocks that glowed, not one had offered a lift. He'd watched them leaving, out into the cold but not for long. They had run away from him like he'd got fleas tonight.

But he'd never done a thing like this before. Sitting, looking up at the stars, he knew that it was true, because he'd never felt like this. He had given the gift shop away. To be broken down into nothing, no hint left of the place where he'd spent so much time. Anything you want, his mother had said.

He remembered the dusty silence of its big room, that night when he'd stood in the midst of it and broken her things.

'That was well broken, Dai. Can you fix it as well as that now?'

Hands on her hips, she would've said it, she'd have raised her eyebrows at him. She was like that, knew a wrong thing for exactly what it was.

Anything you want. Of all the words in the world, there couldn't be any as huge, as hard to see. He'd never wanted this. Tried to keep telling himself that. He'd wanted her at home when he finished work. He'd wanted hot chocolate in the café at the same time every day. To talk to Bethan a bit and then go back to his mum. He hadn't wanted any of tonight.

'Getting a bit of the worry are you now, Dai? Feeling the pull? Well, you know what that pull is well enough. Should have learned a million times over. You know what "conscience" means, Dai.'

He did. Conscience sat in his mind now, low and heavy as the gift shop's slate roofs, dull as its glass in the sun. When the summer came, Mum had cleaned the windows every Saturday with vinegar in the water. Afterwards, her hands would smell of vinegar, when she touched his hair. In the Easter holidays, the gift shop was loud as a hundred people, and it brought the money in. She had used to say that, and he'd had the funniest picture. He'd thought of the gift shop, picking up its guttering like skirts, wading off down the road when no one could see, to bring the money in.

So there had been good thoughts too. Sometimes she had made him laugh. A lot of times, she had. But he thought now, of the gift shop bringing the money in, and he didn't know how it worked. People came in and they bought things, they put the money in the till. But what happened to the money then? How do you keep hold of the money? How did it get into accounts? He didn't know what you did with it after it had been brought in. And it was these thoughts, and the words 'anything you want', that always brought him back to the way he'd felt, standing there, in the dust-dark, before he'd started breaking things.

She would've said, 'I'd like to know, Dai, where you put your conscience in all that.'

Sitting in the heavy sand, he raised his wrist and he lit up his digital watch, he looked at the little numbers there. 9:39:56. They made a small patch of skin round his wrist go green. Even when he didn't have the little light on, those numbers moved. They made him want to cry, or they made him stop. Time was very strong and it did these things to him. It did them to everyone, he knew now, and they could run from him like he had fleas, they didn't know what it was like. They didn't know how time could make you feel things. He didn't want the gift shop any more.

'Anything you want, I said. And you want to break things, Dai.'

But it felt better to break things. When those things were full of questions that you didn't need, when they were full of memories that hurt you, even though they were no longer real.

Those people didn't know what it was like to need time; need it to show you the way. He had cried. Three months, he had. They'd been letting things go on, whether his Mum lived or not.

Dai knew now, he couldn't have the past any more. Time had shown him that.

'I'll miss seeing the place the cars were parked, you remember? We hired the cars for the airport? With ribbons. They were parked outside there. What'll you miss, Gwen?' He looked at her.

And when he said that, she couldn't help but turn, couldn't help but face him and say, 'I'll miss looking at my husband and seeing a trustworthy man.' In the quiet that fell after the words, she turned away from him. She rearranged her hands. 'I think that's what I'll miss the most.'

In the car now, chill was seeping in. The engine was dead, they sat like a pebble in this wind. She would not ask him why.

They'd been happy. In this silence after the meeting's noise, this sounded in her head. Over and over, isolated. They'd been happy. There'd been the incident, the incident with Rhys, but things had been better after that. Normal after that. Yet, searching back through those lamp-lit evenings, their home empty again without Dai, when they'd drunk tea together and talked it over like old times, there hadn't been any point when Emyr had changed. She couldn't remember any time when he'd come home and spoken to her with something new under his words. From the start then, she thought, he had planned it.

His expression was hidden from her. He stared out through the glass. 'You haven't even asked me why. Do you even care? You haven't even asked me, you know that?'

She remembered her own voice, speaking to Tom. 'I can't go home like this.' Quiet as the threat under Emyr's breath here.

'You stood up there and you clapped. Don't you think there'd be a reason? I love that place –' He had to stop. All the time, he had to. And she sat there in the passenger seat, saying nothing, giving nothing. He could have been a stranger, for everything he saw in her face. 'You must know,' he said, very slow, trying hard, 'that I would have a reason for doing it.'

'Was that part of the plan, then, for you to tell me why? If it was part of your plan, Emyr, you go ahead and tell me. You've spent long enough working this out, we must make it go right. Yes. Do tell me.'

He looked at her. He could have told her he hated her but even that wouldn't have been true. He turned back to the windscreen and it could have been their kitchen that he saw. Spread out here: not night but sunny afternoon, their kitchen table, with Gwen sitting opposite. Steam rising from bowls of soup.

She'd been sitting in this very same seat when she'd told him it was only a kiss, and that a kiss was a small thing.

'You don't even look angry. Aren't you angry? I hid it from you. We – we talked, you know? All those nights we sat up and talked about the proposals.'

'What do you want me to say, Emyr? That I believed you?' She shook her head lightly, shrugged. 'I didn't get any hint, no. You lied very well.'

'Do you care why?' he said.

She didn't answer, her expression staunched like a wound.

'What I might be trying . . . to do?'

In her profile he saw nothing. The memory of her applause as glances had been turned to her, it lay over her motionless face like a ghost.

'Say something, Gwen!'

But she did not.

He turned to see the vacant lot from which they'd watched every other car file out, leaving them here with just the street lamps.

Emyr said, 'The gift shop's still there. It's just down the road. We can go and drive and sit in front of it. What will you miss the most? The reception? Tell me. Or when we went that day with your father? Or, you remember this one, remember this: when we came back and Eirian'd filled it all up with stock, and we walked round. You remember? Which will you miss most, out of those? Tell me,' he said. 'Please.'

'All of them, Emyr. You know that.' In this empty place memories spoke: how she had thrown that bracelet to the floor.

'You know what I think you'll miss most? I could be wrong, I don't know you like I thought I did. You correct me if I am. I think the thing you'll miss the most will be other people remembering. You know? When Patty reminds you? When she points up at that photo and she says, "That was a lovely day. Beautiful wedding." I think that's what you'll miss, Gwen. Other people. The things they say.'

The sound of applause, remembered. As if it had been coming to her through thick cloth.

'What tools do they use for it, Emyr?' she said. 'To demolish a building. Do they . . . do they break it up piece by piece? Do they use a bulldozer? I don't know, I've never seen it done. Do you know what it looks like when it comes down?'

Emyr said, 'They use a bulldozer. They attach a steel rope to one end of the roof, inside. They knock a hole through one of the end walls, pull the rope out through that, attach the other end, drive the bulldozer away from it.'

Gwen looked out.

Behind them, the back seat was empty. There were stacks of paper there on the soft upholstery. Messed slightly, pink and yellow and green, their colours all shades of the same in this lean darkness. She'd stood and printed those, smiling at every possibility as she'd watched the words slide out over and over. 'Application Form.' Smiling, as she had done every evening. And he had looked at every one of those smiles and he had known.

'Well, that must be something to see.'

'Yes,' he said. 'Yes it is.' He spoke softly, 'Now's a good time for honesty. A lot's happened tonight. And they're talking about it now, all over town. Things are going to start changing. Very soon, huge changes. Now's a good time.'

In their house, they seemed now to be moving in two different countries. Nothing was changed for her. He didn't know how he could tell her: he looked at things like he'd never seen them before. The things that he picked up, they didn't look real. The flowers on the table, the saucepans hanging up. And he wondered, that all those things they'd bought and put in their home, all those things that they'd picked out together, they stayed on, unchanged, though she didn't seem to love him now.

There'd been many recent evenings when they had sat and talked. But there'd been others, and Emyr remembered them: spent in his office, with Gwen's movements through the rest of the house, indefinite with his door closed. He remembered sitting, looking at the telephone on his desk.

Dai had told him he didn't want the gift shop, his voice had cracked in the museum's resonating space. But that day, with the words 'thirty-three million pounds' buzzing like an open telephone line, Emyr had found it easy enough to talk about change, out with the old and in with the new. The plan had come to him, and had felt easy. He had looked at every building as he'd walked away, remembered each application he'd approved, and what he and Gwen had been doing in those times. He had seen the holes where those memories' roots should have lain.

Sitting in his office alone, the phone on his desk shining in the lamplight, it had not felt easy any more. The list of phone numbers in his hand had been those of foremen, demolition firms. Doubts had occupied the quiet spaces.

Eighteen years since their wedding. He had thought of how the gift shop would look with a hole gaping in its wall. His hand had moved out to call, and back into his lap. She didn't love it like he did; she had those same memories but she didn't cherish them. He had wondered if there was really anything she cherished. He would face her with a choice. He had been afraid, though, sitting there with only her foot-steps to hear, that he already knew what her answer would be.

A small thing, she'd said. A crack running along the flat surface of what he'd always believed to be sky. And he'd point it out to her, raise his hand and say 'Look at it! Look at it, can't you even see? It's a screen! It's a great dome! It's fake!' He'd shake her. 'None of this is real,' he'd say. And she would take herself very carefully away from his hands and answer him, 'For God's sake, Emyr. Really. It's always been like that.'

Perhaps it was right to tear up something that had no use any more. To break down walls that were built on lies. Now, staring out to the night in front of him, he had no questions left. There was nothing left but the choice.

'You didn't have to clap. You could have stood up and spoken. Said that you didn't agree.'

She nodded, like that would be just right, wouldn't it? 'In front of all the people,' she said. 'Two hundred and fifty-six people, I should have stood up then.'

'What would it have mattered? So what? People . . . ?'

'In all your planning, Emyr, all those nights that you must have spent wallowing in this, you can't really have imagined that I was going to just . . . what? Just let my objections ring out? Did you want them to see that you'd deceived me? That I had no clue what you were planning? I wonder what they'd have thought then.' She nodded. She knew.

'I don't care, Gwen,' he told her.

'You don't seem to care about very much these days.'

'I don't care what they think.'

But she didn't answer him.

Emyr looked at his hands, lying here. 'Now's a good time for honesty . . .' And so he said it, let the words come from him. 'You could have objected. You needn't have pretended.' He tried to steady his voice. 'You could still object.'

She laughed. He watched her.

'That's very kind of you.'

And silence then. It spun out.

This was how it felt to risk everything. Like stepping off a cliff, Ruth had said of the proposition that Charlotte Weyland had made that day. But the image that came to him now was not of his own falling. He thought of the books on their bookshelves, of the cut flowers she arranged, the furniture that she'd chosen with his cheque-book and the little china figurines that he bought her for each birthday, each year. He imagined them falling. He would stand at the top of the headland and there'd be a cardboard box filled with those things on the grass beside him. They wouldn't look so important then, not lying ready.

Gwen was calm. She looked out through the glass and said, 'I don't know why you've done this, Emyr. I don't know why you would lie to me, or why you would want a place ... that holds so many memories for both of us ... why you would want that destroyed. What's been in your mind these last weeks, I don't know. I'm sure you'd like me to beg now. But I won't beg you to do anything. You've chosen this.'

She loved him. She had told him that at the wedding, and ever since. And nothing had changed after she'd gone out on to the beach and let a strange boy hold her, see her cry. They were unaltered. 'Regardless of you,' he remembered.

And he said, 'You were prepared to stand there and clap, only because there were people watching you.'

Her figurines, tumbling as exquisitely as silence. Not one thing in their home looked the same. He'd seen through them all. He'd looked at them and had realized that they had never been put there for him.

When they walked through town together, they weren't walking alone. They were holding hands for every eye that might chance to turn on them. For all the windows that seemed blank as you passed.

Gwen turned to him. In the shadows and the streetlight, her eyes were open and asking him. But whatever he saw in there, she didn't let it touch the words that came from her lips. For all the difference between the two, she looked like she could have broken under her own strain. She said very carefully: 'Is that what you think? That because I applauded, I don't care?'

'You could have spoken tonight.'

'You think those memories aren't important to me.'

'I know they are,' he said.

And it was true, because he couldn't have made these plans if she hadn't cared. He was using that knowledge. In the way that she used his hand when she held it in the street.

He said, 'You can still speak now, object. There are a lot of by-laws I might not have checked, by-laws that might stand in the way of a demolition like this. There might be a hundred reasons that the work on the gift shop can't begin.' He looked at her shadowed features, he would have reached out and touched her hand as he said it, but he couldn't now. 'If you care that much about it, Gwen, you'll make your feelings known. You'll tell other people. Rather than let it carry on.'

It was just a choice really. Her own memories, or other people's. What she wanted, or what she wanted them to see. It was only a choice. He just needed her to show him what it was that she really loved.

Dai could have told Gwen but she didn't ask him. When she finally spoke to him, there were no questions coming from her. He would have told her that choices didn't matter, that choices, like brick and slate and stone, were works of will. Time was always stronger than them. It pulled you easily, like the hope in the words 'thirty-three million pounds'.

Bethan's father had unlocked the café's door for them and they had filed into the dark in here, speaking with no buoyancy in their voices. Pat had turned on the kitchen light only and they'd stood near the door for a moment, seeing the empty tables in here, as though the place had changed since they'd been gone.

At the meeting's end, Bethan had taken Tom to one side. 'Look at us all,' she'd said. 'Look like we've just been kissed by a bloody ghost.'

He'd not known what to think. Thirty-three million. The words had passed from person to person. Tom had looked away and said, 'Or like we just got fucked by one.'

In the car, squashed and silent with Chelsea on her lap, he'd kept wanting Bethan to glance up; wanting to see what he felt reflected on her face. She'd kept her fingers in Chelsea's hair. She hadn't glanced up because she hadn't wanted him to see. She'd thought of the Weyland woman's gaze, bitter, honest. The smile Bethan had felt inside had been an airless rift.

'Nice to be back in the warm.' Pat heard her own voice in the quiet of her own place.

'Nice to be out of the crowd, is what it is,' Siân said, and looked from table to bare table as if angry at being made to feel lost like this, in a place that she knew well. And, seeing Tom looking at her, she added, 'Well? Would you like to clear a table for us?'

Bethan's own table by the corner, they eased themselves down around it. The ashtray was clean in shadow there. Around the table's edge, the plastic had been picked away. Bethan had stripped it in little pieces, day by day here.

She stood for a moment, Chelsea asleep against her shoulder, looking at the distances printed on all their faces, like little islands in the café's dimness. There was something in her. She could have shouted out, wanted to say the words again because it looked like none of them could have heard. Thirty-three million. They would've fallen into this quiet.

You could do anything with that number. It was a licence. You could build whatever you wanted to build, tear down what you didn't want to see. Just for a moment, she stood. She carried Chelsea upstairs, to where the curtained rooms were unchanged and the smell of the café's day still hung. Coming down to the doorway again, Tom sitting and staring at the table like you couldn't have dragged his eyes up from it, Siân and her parents talking in brief little breaths, she said into the pause, 'Did you see their expressions? Everyone – when they all went outside again, in the car park. I've never seen anything like it.'

'Well, they've never heard anything so shocking, have they? I don't believe there's ever been anything so shocking.' Siân shook her head, her eyes passing over each of them.

Bethan only stopped, her lips still parted. Until she could carry on again, slow but unchangeable, a tide moving around stones. Tom heard her. She didn't say the words 'thirty-three million' but they seemed to lie on the table between them all, as if she'd let them fall there, speaking with open hands.

'Did you see them all smiling? My God.'

'I saw a lot of people open-mouthed.' Siân stared at her for a moment, then leant forward, tapped her cigarette's ash. In this room they could hear every scratch of a chair leg. Tom didn't speak but he wiped a hand across his mouth like he could rub away this evening, this itching in all his muscles, this joke. That's what it was. A fucking joke.

He looked up at Bethan's face, he saw none of what he felt there.

It was the way she'd stood up in the meeting, looked over the heads of everyone else. Her and the woman Charlotte. She had an expression on her now like she hadn't quite sat down yet.

'Did you see the forms? At the end? There were hardly any left.'

'Well I don't think that means anything,' Siân said. 'Of course they're going to take the things, they're going to want to see what's written on them.'

Bethan looked at her. 'Did you take one then?'

'I didn't take one, no. I don't need to see them. To tell you the truth, I don't want to see. My house doesn't need any work done. I get done what's needed already –' She looked like she was going to say more then but she only turned away. She said to Pat, 'Did you take one then? Did you see what they said?'

'I didn't take one, no.' In the faint light, she shook her head. 'The forms for sale, those'll be the ones that went. Because that's what this town needs, isn't it? An added hand for those who want to leave it. How many will go, I wonder. How many?'

No one answered her.

'Thirty-three million pounds . . .' Bethan said finally. 'I can't believe it.' She tried to laugh. And for the smallest moment, hearing her, Tom's feelings fell away. There was shock in the sound of it, but no bitterness, nothing like the way she usually laughed.

Even way back, those nights out on the beach, she'd laughed bitter, as if a laugh could cover all the things she knew, and all the things she didn't. Really, though, she'd known more than all of them. He remembered his mum saying that about Rhys once, that Rhys'd lead him in all the wrong directions. But it had been Bethan really, doing that. His mum had said, 'He'll push you and push you, that boy. And you'll follow, I know it. I can see it now. You can't realize it, Tom? I'll tell you why: too weak to see the bad in people, that's your problem. He'll push, and you'll follow.'

He looked at his mother, smoking her cigarette hard in silence, her glances moving. Maybe she was looking for the bad in what was almost being said now. Her expression was shaded, her back to the counter and the kitchen, lit behind. Their silhouettes lay across the table.

He hadn't told her about Rhys. He'd opened his mouth once or twice to say something but, looking at her in those moments, she must have seen, must've known. There'd been too many Saturdays these last few weeks, when he'd come to the house, helped out. And she'd marked them, asking him if he had nothing better to be doing. Once or twice he'd been on the edge of handing it to her.

'Rhys'll push and push,' she'd used to say. But really, it'd always been Bethan. He saw Beth now. Shocked, and Bethan shocked was a sight to see.

She whistled the words, 'And Dai was already in on it. No wonder he hasn't been in here. Keeping it all to himself. Planning, that's what he's been doing. Sitting up there in that house . . . Have you talked to him?' She looked at her mum. Shocked or full of hope, Tom thought.

'Planning?' Patty said. She raised one eyebrow, held it all in a glance; everything Dai Meredith couldn't do, planning being the first.

Tom was silent under his mother's voice, 'He's not said a thing to me. And he's been in. Every other day, he's been in. Buying his soup and his Angel Delight. As mad for that stuff as you used to be.' Tom tried to smile. 'I've told him enough times, watching him buying it, same as I used to say to you: Angel Delight stomach, he'll get.' She shook her head, 'I'd like to know when it was all arranged with him. I'd like to know who went to him with the idea. Was that Emyr, I wonder? And when?' But what she said was empty now. Everything was, he thought, that didn't include that number. Her face was hard-lined and her short hair held the yellow light.

Behind the café's counter, touched by a slanting bar of shade, there was a photo on the wall. Tom saw it every day, and Bethan too, so many times that they didn't even notice it. Seventies, it must have been taken. The colours in the photo looked like that. It showed three women, all standing next to each other, all smiling. Gwen Morgan in the centre, and Patty on her left, Siân there on her other side. They were all done up, wearing blouses and jackets in springtime colours. They had hats with flowers round their brims. They looked happy in the photograph. They touched each other so easily they didn't notice the touches. Siân had her hand on Gwen's wrist.

Tom looked at her now, mouth closed. After the lights, after the noise and pushing shoulders in the community centre, there was too much quiet in his mum. Every other table was wiped clean, ketchup and salt and that, all arranged. And he thought: I did that. Only a few hours ago when the day had been fading away. Now shock seemed to drift in the dimness over those clean tables. They sat, cups of tea going cold in front of them, tea bags leaking juice in the saucers.

Bethan poked at the ashtray with a butt. Thirty-three million. She tried to think of any way to say the words, make them heard the way that she could hear them in her head. She found none. She listened to her mum and Siân, their voices bouncing like little echoes of each other. Thought of all the days that Siân'd come in here, asked if she wanted anything, sat with her. They'd laughed together sometimes, though she couldn't remember the jokes now; though she saw Siân's face now and couldn't remember how.

Bethan didn't glance up to see Tom watching her.

She'd always been the one, not Rhys. 'Right now,' she'd say, 'truth or dare?' She'd raise one eyebrow at them. Always one question further with that sarcastic smile, so far from how she looked now. He remembered her, lying back on the blanket, rolling over suddenly and watching them both. And all the light, orange, all the beach, orange. You got that kind of light in late summer, it looked like every place in the world was flooded with it.

'All right,' she'd said. 'Truth or dare?'

And Rhys had said truth, with a shade of her smile, as though he liked that about her. As though he was running the whole thing, or letting her run it, and he liked Tom to see. They'd had bottles of cider, stuck down in the sand, getting colder with the evening. Underneath the blanket, marram grass had made miniature mountains and he remembered her scraping at that sand, building something that just looked like a shape to them, glancing up every so often. That same smile, every time. And Tom had looked at their faces, one to the other, before hearing her say,

'Who've you fucked? While you've been with me.'

She'd been like that. She would push.

The cigarette butt in her hand now drew patterns in the ash.

'I've met the woman too,' his mum said. 'Charlotte whatever. I've met her.'

'When d'you meet her?' Patty looked at her. 'You never said that.'

'I'll tell you what I thought, and I'm not the sort to go and gossip. After tonight . . .' she took a drag, 'I'll tell you what I thought. Thought her picture could come in the dictionary: right under the word "rudeness", it'd be. Didn't say a word to me. Not a "hello", or a "nice morning". And she's hardly been racing to come down here, introduce herself, has she? Living on her own up there. I'll tell you what I think for nothing. I think she's got a nerve. Money or no money. Comes down here, Emyr on her arm just about. And Ruth Lewis? Well.' She looked over the table at Pat like it was all that she needed to say, the whites of her eyes were very clear, they spoke it all.

Bethan's fingers stopped moving but she didn't look up. 'She's not a bad person just because she doesn't come into town. Does that make her a criminal or something?'

'I didn't say that. Did I say that?'

'She didn't say that, Bethan,' Patty answered.

And Tom saw Bethan's face, unchanged, as her fingers moved again. But you could drown a place with that much money.

Bethan said, 'I don't see how it matters.' The light was pale on her features. 'If she's got the millions, I don't see how it matters. If she wants to give them to us, my God.'

Siân exhaled a long plume of smoke, not looking at her.

'For God's sake, Beth,' Patty said, 'you don't take a gift without knowing who it comes from.'

'She's not a stranger offering me sweets.'

'There's a million questions! As many as there are bloody pounds. Who decides what changes are to be made? Who approves them? Her? You want to hand our business over for her approval? Control is what it's about. I'd like to know what Gwen thinks of her. And all these proposals.'

'She was there. She was handing out the wine, for God's sake.'

'I haven't spoken to her. Have you then? I don't know I want someone else's money washing round my business. We've never needed it before. We don't need it now.'

Siân said, 'It's all very well to dream dreams, these are real things at stake. Your parents' business, my house, any other part of this town. This is a decision, Bethan,' his mother leaned forward with her cigarette for just the slightest moment, 'for the entire community. And I hope to God other people are taking that into consideration. Not just thinking of themselves.'

Bethan's father said quietly as he put his cup of tea down, 'I'm not going to rush to take some stranger's money.' The long light fell over him where he sat in the corner, it drew faint lines around his eyes. 'If no one applies now, they're still talking about building work. Parks. And no approval needed. It's all very well,' he said, 'to talk about beautification, but it's January now. April's close. There's been falling trade, but that doesn't mean we'd be happy to lose it all. I wonder who'll make sure that Ynys-morlan's not a building site when the season comes? Whatever anyone decides, "Public Works Projects" will start, apparently.'

Leaving what, Tom thought, if none of them did apply? Little isles in the middle of whatever the Weyland woman decided to make? He saw a crazy image, of parks run wild, bushes filling the gaps between each building and overrunning the street, right up to the doorsteps. Their homes – Siân's three grey, pebbledashed storeys – looking out from all that foliage like the stained faces of statues in some forgotten garden.

Bethan was looking at them all – seeing their matching expressions, Tom thought. Unseen in the photograph behind, three smiles could just be made out.

He could have reached to Bethan over the shadowed table, told her to say what was on her mind. He remembered the night Rhys had come to him, told him they were finished. He'd talked about the pregnancy and her attitude then. 'Gets some fucking thing in her head, wants everyone else in the world to run around after her, like she's fucking carnival queen every day of the year.' He'd walked back and forwards in Tom's bedroom.

She liked to raise the stakes with that bitter little smile. Like she already knew. One question further. And Tom hadn't understood – didn't understand now – what it was she was pushing for. He remembered, in the sunset light, how Rhys's smile had fallen away.

He hadn't told her about the museum either. He remembered once, a long time ago, how she'd said to him that he was nothing like Rhys. And he would've liked to have told her – how Rhys had held on to his collar and whispered, 'Thick, that's what Emyr Morgan said.'

He couldn't tell her. Not without mentioning Gwen Morgan's name. Thick. Immoral. He remembered. He'd said to Rhys, 'What do you expect?'

And Rhys hadn't been there tonight. Rhys was somewhere else, far away from here it felt like. Tom watched the patterns that her cigarette made in the ashtray, as though she painted a picture there. Thirty-three million pounds. He remembered her hands in the sand.

And when she raised her eyes, grey with the café's semi-dark, looked across at him and asked him, 'What do you think?' the small smile on her face was just a shade of all the others she'd shown to him. 'You've been quiet as a mouse all night. You tell me.'

All their choices, Ruth Lewis thought – she sat distant from them – everyone's would surely seem like fragile things without the others'. A community.

Bethan remembered her choice. Rhys had told her she wasn't fit but he hadn't known. She had, even then. Hearing his feet slamming on the stairs below her bedroom, she'd known it even as he'd left. And she had walked to the living room where her parents had been sitting. She had stood in the doorway and looked at them, watching TV. She remembered it very clearly, how they'd been holding hands on the sofa, how the lights had been on in there. 'Brookside' on the TV, 'Family Fortunes' over by then. Her mum'd had her feet up with a cushion under them. When they'd looked up at her, she had walked inside.

Across the empty café, the windows were black. Tom gazed back at her, remembered her saying how the town seemed derelict at night. And this chequered floor, in all their quiet, could have had weeds growing up between its tiles.

If he could have done it, he would have passed to her, across the table and under her hand, all the things he couldn't say. He would've told her she looked different, looked young right now.

He said, 'I think we're all right.' He saw her face but couldn't stop. 'I think . . . I think we're good right now. We don't need any money, any changes –'

He couldn't show her how he felt. She didn't know: how Rhys had hit him, or how he'd deserved to be hit. Thick. Immoral. And he'd told Rhys, 'What do you expect?' He hadn't wanted his mother to know.

'We have to think about the whole town, like . . . the community,' he said.

He could have told her, she'd been right. He was nothing like Rhys.

In the star-strewn darkness of the beach, Dai pushed himself up from the sand. He felt the wind catch him fully, blow his hair from his face as he slowly turned around. The dunes shifted. He stared out to Ynys-morlan, the sea's noise everywhere. Curved around the bay, its lights drew a long, scattered arc, in the January cold making out the way this unseen coastline stretched away from him.

Streetlight and houselight and black beach-wind, they could sit inside with all their little lamps on, backs turned to him and the sea. Emyr had told him on the night he'd come to Dai's house, some people couldn't realize. They could look at him with their faces full of cheap rules they wouldn't tell him. The gift shop seemed strong, built to defend itself against hard times, like their eyes, but no one knew what he was starting to understand. Time made your choices for you.

Emyr had said to him, 'You have to do what you feel is right. Never worry what people think.' He'd nodded over his whisky glass.

He'd come to Dai's house that night, to lay out plans, to talk about moving the stock into the empty shops, the way the law was on these things. A week or so after Dai had moved back to his house he'd come, when the gift shop had been a secret still. Not to be mentioned, even to Gwen. They'd sat in the living room, in the television screen's shifting light – all the bulbs in the lamps didn't work now. And when they'd finished, Emyr had leaned back from the papers spread in front of them and taken the bottle from his bag.

'You know what we need to do now, Dai?' His eyes had moved all the time to the room around them. 'We need to celebrate,' he'd said.

Dai looked at the curling arm of Ynys-morlan a long time before he took his first step. Between the distant buildings, like this sea's sound through their walls, it must be audible. Thirty-three. A million pounds, and another million, and thirty-one million more. Through the alleys, rustling in thistles and sea cress that grew up between paving stones. Touching the thin surface of rainwater puddles. Every house hard, remaining. Charlotte stood again inside her own, eyes on the viewless window for minutes, imagining unseen out there a landscape with no paths. Dai heard the sigh of time, although here in their pools of light, the houses still looked strong.

Dai had looked down at the papers as Emyr had sat beside him.

'You don't need to worry yourself too much over them, Dai.' He'd rested the bottle on his knee for a moment, quiet before looking back at him. 'All the property's yours, and empty or not they're all shops. There's no change of usage even. There's no applications. No approvals you have to wait for. There's only what you want. Come on,' he'd said. 'Celebrate.'

'Emyr . . . like . . .'

He'd known what he had to say but he'd been scared to. Emyr loved this project. Dai had seen him, the days when they'd met to talk about it. Sometimes when Emyr spoke, his words caught up on each other for wanting to get out. He'd rub his hand across his mouth, like it was the most important thing, just to talk about this right. In the television's cast, his skin had been pale. Behind his glasses, his eyes had watched.

'Emyr, like. We're moving all the stock into the other buildings, the other shops, I mean. And we're doing all the properties, the flats, Bethan's and that –'

'Your flat too, Dai. I mean, it's her home, she rents it. But she rents it from you.'

'I know.' He'd kept his eyes on the papers. 'The rent goes into the Eirian Meredith current account. Don't have to tell me things like this.'

'I'm sorry –' He'd looked like he was going to say more but only waved his hand then for Dai to carry on.

'We move all the stock and set it up in the old shops, maybe three or maybe four if there's too much of the stock. And then they'll be the gift shop. Emyr, though . . . I don't, like . . .' He'd moved his hands. Spit it out, his mother would've said, if you've got something that needs to be spat. 'I don't know how to bring the money in from those shops, any better than the gift shop, those shops aren't different from the gift shop. When they're running, like . . .' He'd looked up at Emyr, tried to say it all. 'I don't know how to do that.'

He'd watched to see how Emyr looked, not wanting him to lose all that energy, the passionate way he talked about this project. But Emyr had taken a long breath, nodded slowly. Around the whisky bottle's neck, his fingers had shifted, half seen. 'That's a long time away, Dai.' And Emyr had lost the energy, and he had wished that he'd said nothing then. 'Dai –' His words had been laboured like he didn't want to speak at all. 'What you're saying now, see, this is the reason you're not happy.' He'd shaken his head. 'You try and fix everything, all at once. I know it's only because you're worried and you've a right to be worried, big thing like this. You've every right. But you can't try and make everything work all at once, can't try and hold everything in your head at the same time . . . that way lies madness.' He'd laughed. With the television's sound turned down, his laughter had faded into silence. 'These things that you're doing at the moment, all these decisions you're making . . . you're going to change a lot in the next few months. You've changed already, Dai.'

'I haven't changed.' He'd looked at Emyr. 'Do you think I've changed?'

'Yes. And every one a good change. You're doing things for yourself now and that'll change anyone, quick smart.' On the bottle, his fingers fidgeted around the words. He looked up at Dai and his eyes were asking for something. 'When the time comes, after everything we'll have done, I don't think you'll find yourself so worried, not over the running of a shop. You're . . .' He seemed to find the right word, 'You're teaching yourself a lot. Right now, this evening. And by the time that you've moved the stock, and the shops need to run, I'll tell you something, Dai, you'll know how . . . And if not, there's lots of possibilities: hiring a manager being the most obvious.' In the moment's unanswered quiet, Emyr had looked like he wanted to reach out. 'There are no problems for you now, Dai. You see? This property, it's yours. These decisions are yours.' He'd nodded, finishing suddenly, 'but I'll always be here to help.' In the living room's moving shadows, he'd held the bottle out.

'Emyr –' Dai had said, though. 'I doubt.'

'What do you mean, you doubt? I don't . . .'

'I doubt. I think, it could go wrong.'

'Everyone doubts. Do you know, Dai, I don't believe a thing like this has ever been done before. To change a whole town. To turn a whole town around. This is a good thing.'

Now, scattering sand as he walked, Dai came back to town and saw the houses: lit from within. A light in the café, as he passed on the street's other side. He thought that he was going home but time wasn't moving his feet. Just a few figures, picked out. He looked at them, tried to hold in his face all the reasons why he knew this demolition was right. He saw Bethan lift up something with her hand. She must have been drinking. It must have been a cup of tea. Standing under a street lamp, Dai threw two shadows on the paving stones.

Emyr had shown him his bottle again. 'Let's get some glasses. There's something I wanted to tell you and it's not a million miles away from the doubts you're talking about.'

Dai had stood up to get them and he'd seen the way Emyr's eyes still rested on the carpet, he loved this project. Sometimes he talked about what they would make and it was in his eyes like some other place.

'It's late,' Dai had said. 'You don't have to stay. If you don't want to.' He'd stood in the living-room doorway and seen Emyr raising his head.

'Well. We can stay up if we want, I think. We're neither of us spring chickens now.'

They had toasted the gift shop.

'To changes,' Emyr had said. 'To the future, Dai.'

He'd passed the glass, watched Dai take a tentative sip. He had looked down into his own then, raised it to his mouth and swallowed. In the moment afterwards, a stillness had lain.

'I have to tell you, Dai, doubts are one of the reasons I came tonight. You talk about them . . .' He'd watched the carpet, trying to find his words. 'You won't be the only one to have them. You know that, don't you?'

But Dai had just been quiet, looking. He hadn't been sure what it was that he'd seen in Emyr's face.

'This project, it's still a secret now, and it'll be a secret for a while yet. But not for ever.' His empty glass had been static in his hand. 'There'll be the meeting, and then it won't be a secret any more. And then . . . if people have doubts, they won't stay silent on them, they'll come to you. I don't want that to make your own doubts worse. If things don't go smoothly –'

'Why wouldn't they go smoothly? You said we don't need any plans or any approval or anything. Because it's a demolition and you don't need approval for a demolition.'

'That's what I said and it's true but, when this isn't a secret any more, there's going to be people, Dai, who don't agree with what you want to do.'

Dai had looked at him, lips almost parted.

'Some people,' Emyr had said, 'don't like change. Their doubts'll be strong ones. Some of them, they might not hesitate in coming to you, to tell you what they think. I don't want you worrying.' In the darkened room around them, the sound of wind had rapped at windows. This house was full of small noises, the clink of his mother's china on the shelves, the creaking of wooden eaves. 'This is all I wanted to say: if anyone comes to you with their own opinions, you should remember that you have a lot of people here in town who'll want to help. If anyone comes to you, and tells you that what you're doing is wrong . . . I don't want you sitting up here and worrying away by yourself. Sometimes it helps, in a situation like that, to talk it out. You can come any time and talk to me . . . And other people too.' After a moment's quiet, he'd refilled his glass and raised it, showing that Dai should drink too. And Dai had watched Emyr, holding it in silence again after he'd swallowed, looking almost lost in that moment – like he had done some time before, sitting on a different sofa, watching a clock with him.

'I want you to promise me something.'

Dai had nodded, he'd thought about putting his hand on Emyr's shoulder. There'd been a space for it. You couldn't tell, though. People jumped. Emyr had raised his eyes but the shadow on his face had grown deeper. They'd been the same, sitting there. It'd only been the two of them, everyone else in their sleep.

'I want you to promise me that you won't just sit up here worrying. Not when you've got so many friends. Siân Humphries for instance. She said to me, she hasn't seen you for ages. She'd want to hear anything you had to say, she'd want to help. Would you let her help? Would you go and talk to her?'

'I . . .'

'If someone comes to you, Dai, it won't do you the least bit of good to sit and stew up here. I want you to promise me, if anyone starts filling your head with more doubts, you'll go to see her. She'll want to help.' He'd spoken without taking a sip and his talk had left him without breath for a moment. He'd wiped at his mouth, looking then like he'd wanted to reach out himself, put his own hand on Dai. In the rattling sounds of Eirian's home, her pictures looking down on them, Dai had seen how people confused themselves. People had their changing minds, faltering like this.

And he'd said, 'Emyr, I didn't want to do this, take the gift shop away. But I do want to. Because we think something but then we think something else, don't we? I'll talk to people, to friends. I promise.' The wan light had rested on both their hands, Emyr's around his glass, and Dai's raised like there was nothing either of them could do about who they were.

Standing on Ynys-morlan's winter road, he remembered that night – the smile that Emyr had given and the trouble in it. Thinking of all their silent faces at the meeting, he thought he understood that trouble now. These were doubts, confusions: to stand on a dark road, looking into the café's lit window, to watch the people inside, your friends, and be divided in what you felt. To want to talk to them, but to turn away instead.

There were no such things as choices. Time was too strong. It made you cry and then It let you stop. It moved you.

He looked at the oncoming buildings, could see their dark glass up ahead. The empty shop that had been Owain's Family Butcher's, the old launderette. If time made him want to, he could take a stone from the road and throw it through this glass. All their silent faces tonight, he didn't care, they could turn away from him. He didn't know if they agreed or if they were the kind of people that didn't like change. He didn't know what sort of people they were.

Dai came to a stop slowly, looking at one place only, then at its illuminated window up above. Long minutes absorbing that light as he realized that he wasn't going home.

A street of stone cut between each low building: Ynys-morlan. So people could walk and look up, to see how strong their decisions were. You couldn't change them, not when you stepped out of your door and saw they were just small parts of something older, larger.

Gwen loved it. She loved to walk between the houses, know whose homes they were. There was order to a place like this, it was nothing like a city. There was community in a place like this, and morals within that community, clear to see as the network of alleys that held every house in its place. There was the flag, raised at the entrance to Ynys-morlan; coming or going, there for all to see. You could walk past the café and see where Bethan Hughes sat, her parents, and Chelsea. She'd made a choice and set herself there, where people could come and sit with her, where the toys could be left at her table each night, to come back to every next day. You could see all the determination that Ruth Lewis had put into her home, with an edge of the will her mother had had. She had kept the garden. She'd built a family in the house that her father had once walked out of, and looked up at for a long time before turning, moving down the path and getting into his car.

It was good to be reminded that your community would hold you. If other people walked out of their doors, looked up at their homes the way that Ruth's father had done, and drove away from all the choices they'd made, what would Ynys-morlan be then? It wouldn't take long for the weeds to grow, between the cracks in the pavement, clinging to the stones and breaking down the seawall until the tide was free just to cover this place again. It wouldn't take long, there would be no town, only a ruined bay at the edge of this plain. Without others to hold them, your choices were insubstantial things.

'I know why you come here, Gwen, you come because you've got nothing else.'

Reinforcement. That was the word. That was what all those separate buildings were when you placed them side by side. It was good to have your decisions echoed in the face of every person you knew.

Eirian had said to her, 'When you walk past the gift shop, Gwen, I want you to ask yourself why you care about the place at all.'

But it wasn't Eirian here now, it was Emyr.

Just a choice, it was, another layer of stone set down. And, as Charlotte Weyland opened the study door and stood looking at her own works of will, aligned on the shelves, her memories bound up in leather, Gwen listened to the silence of the car park, the stretching beach, and heard nothing in it. No resonance, no echo of the wind that would have moved here, before walls and streets and footsteps, when this landscape had been untouched by memory.

And Dai Meredith, standing on the road, staring up at the radiance of Bethan's window, heard the jingle of keys against his waist, feeling safe in the movement of time.

Gwen was saying, in the darkness, 'You want me to object. Publicly. You want people to know . . . that we're divided on this. To see that you went ahead and did it. Without my knowing, with no choice of mine.'

In the empty car park, their Lexus was painted with the softest reflections, tawny light and shadow. It was parked very neatly between the white lines, and every space around it was vacant.

And in here, inside, it was just as still. There was the slight smell of air freshener and leather. The shore where she had stood without hearing Tom's footsteps seemed far away from her.

'I don't believe that it will do any good, for you or for me, or for this community, if we appear divided now,' she said. She heard her own words fall, flat as paper, on the floor at their feet. She heard them and she didn't speak again. For a long time, neither of them did.

'I'm sure you're right, Gwen.'

She didn't answer him. After one moment, she nodded.

Emyr said quietly, 'I thought it went well tonight. Ruth got over her nerves nicely, and signing the cheque worked well.'

She didn't answer. They sat like this, each of them looking out ahead through their own shadows.

He said, 'All went well . . . We'll just have to wait and see now, how many application forms come back. We'll have to give people a little time. They'll need to talk about it. I'm hopeful, though . . .' he said. 'And it was good probably that Charlotte spoke. I'm hopeful. Yes.'

In this dry-sand silence, he reached forward and turned the ignition key. He found, as he had when he'd pressed the digits on the telephone that night, that his fingers had no sensation.

Outside, in the car park, the noise of the sea was cut by their engine. He didn't look at her as he checked his rear-view mirror and put the car into gear.

She said beside him, 'I'm sure people will . . . get to know her better. An incredible gift that she's given tonight. I'm sure . . . I'm sure we'll be seeing a good deal more of her, round town.'

'I'm sure that's true.'

'I'd like to get to know her better.' Gwen's voice, estranged from him in the lightless car, seemed to find firmer ground. 'Living up there on her own, that big house . . .'

He turned their Lexus around. Spread like something unreal in the street lights, the single road of Ynys-morlan stretched out. Two rows of houses, a broken line on the tarmac and their headlights, pushing forwards, pushing home.

He said, 'You mustn't judge a book by its cover, though, Gwen. You can't tell what a person's like just by the way they live.'

In her lap, Gwen's hands touched each other. She raised her head and looked at the street. She said quietly, 'You can tell how a person wants to be seen by the world. And that's important.'

'Really?' Emyr changed up a gear, the way he always did on this particular stretch of road. He sometimes thought that he could drive it blind. And he didn't look at his wife, sitting in the passenger seat. 'Do you think so, Gwen?' he said.

It was almost midnight by the time that Bethan stood in front of the door to her home. Chelsea's sleepy weight on one hip, the keys in her other hand. Blank houses rose around her, blank windows, every garden dark as the next.

In the mornings, when she woke up, this side of the street would be brushed in sunlight sometimes. She would look down from the shade of her flat, see the old paint, the worn signs, the paving stones. You'd get the slow rhythm of the day starting up, the first few people would come with their dogs. She'd see her mum put the sign out in front of the café. Sometimes, in the mornings, Ynys-morlan's street was quiet enough for her to hear the café's doorbell ring, even from behind her own window. She looked at it now and she saw none of those familiar things. The street lamps made every colour the same.

Tom could talk about community but if she wasn't a part of it then she didn't know what it took to become one. She couldn't even remember feeling the change in herself. She couldn't remember any morning when she'd woken up and realized Ynys-morlan would always be home. Things like that, they came and went like thieves; you didn't even know what they'd taken away. She knew this building inside out. She knew its smell, its feel. And when she turned the key in the lock, here it was: a difference.

In the darkened hallway, streetlight touched the lino, the edge of the stairs. There was no sound. She looked at them, reaching up to her door. It was Rhys she thought of and did not know why.

The same close walls, the same shadows. The little table by the side, empty. Eirian had used to put mail there. She'd drop by for her little visits, pick it up from the step, which was exactly where Bethan liked to keep it, and put it on that table there. She'd make her point just by neatening the edges of the pile.

In the silent hallway now, Bethan's eyes moved down to the floor. She saw the letters, junk mail mostly, scattered on the mat. And then she saw the shadow there. Across three envelopes, it was. The kind that offer you a unique opportunity. She shifted Chelsea in her arms. She didn't need to bend down, though. A footprint, that was what it was.

She looked up at her own front door.

No marks there. It was blank and looked back at her from the top of the stairs. Bethan stepped further into the hall and it was Rhys she smelled. Her shoes scratched on the lino. He couldn't get in here. She had no reason to think it. Could just see it, though. He'd have some fucking smirk on his face, like this was the funniest thing he'd ever thought of. He'd probably stand here and sort through her mail.

She could imagine him opening her own door, switching the light on and seeing all the things she'd left round on the floor. He'd go into her kitchen and see the dirty plates in there. Go into her bedroom. Be sure to. Stand and look at her double bed, the way that she'd made it, just to climb into herself.

Bethan felt whatever motion, whatever need the meeting had left her with, drain away and leave her cold. She looked at the door. She remembered then, the things that she'd left out, draped over chairs in her room.

He would have spoken. That would've been like him. So he could leave the things he wanted to say, like stains on the things she owned.

She held Chelsea tightly, walking towards the stairs. She thought of Siân and her mother, passing the word 'community' back and forth across the table like it got more worthy every time they used it. And whatever it was that she'd felt then lay like sickness in her stomach now.

She had photographs of her parents, framed, on the window sill. She'd built these things up slowly, in the months after she'd had Chelsea. She'd been given them or she'd decided herself: a little china cupid that hung on a hook above her bed.

She carried Chelsea up, heard the creak of the fourth riser.

Maybe he would have gone up to the pattern laid out on her bed. He might've picked it up by its paper shoulders. Might've danced around the room.

Bethan put her key into the lock. In the hallway's faintness, everything was indefinite. She touched the lock's plate with her fingertips. He couldn't do it without leaving a mark. If he could do it at all, there'd be kicks all over the door.

She stood for a moment, fixed. She saw again what she hadn't noticed before: that darkness. In the café, she'd glanced out at her window, lit. The lamp on in Chelsea's room.

Nothing came through the gap under the door. And that wasn't how Rhys would have done it. No, Rhys would've left every fucking light on, just to show her how much he had seen. Bethan swallowed slowly. It wasn't sickness she felt now, or anger. Someone had come in through her front door then. They'd walked into her home, through each room maybe. And then, as they'd left, they'd turned her lights off again.

She reached forward and she used the key and she switched on the corridor light. She stood, looked at her home.

It was silent. Whoever had been here was gone. Bethan saw the portrait of Chelsea hanging opposite on the wall. In her arms, Chelsea turned her face into her mother's shoulder, sulking in the sudden brightness. Bethan stood without moving, though. She looked at all the things she kept.

Rhys'd always had a skill for timing. She'd told Angharad this once: always coming at the wrong time – and she'd discovered he left that way too. Rhys hadn't been at the meeting tonight. Would have been just like him to walk in here instead.

In the corner, against the wall, the pushchair was folded up. On the table beside the telephone, she had postcards stuck with Blu-Tack to the wall.

After a moment, she looked away from these things. She walked through to her own bedroom, her lips against Chelsea's forehead. She remembered her first few weeks in this place, when she'd get up – the deep centre of the night – fat and heavy, needing to piss. Not being able to find the light switch or the doorway or anything. When this had still been someone else's home, with crayon marks on the kitchen wall.

She'd asked her mum once, standing here when the place was finished, if she thought it was all right. Her mum had hugged her and told her, lovely. She'd said that she was just glad it was close to home.

Her home must be a pretty fragile fucking thing, to look so different, only thinking Rhys had seen it. Pretty fucking fragile; this portrait of Chelsea, the cot her dad had made.

The dress pattern was laid out here, though, just the way that she had left it. The velvet was draped over chairs and the front door untouched. Bethan wandered. Somewhere between thoughts of locks and keys, Bethan opened her mouth. It wasn't Rhys that she thought of. She looked at the hallway. 'Dai,' she voiced.

She sat for a long moment on the bed, trying to see the room without the tarnish of Rhys's eyes. Not him at all. She wondered where Dai might have stood. She looked at her CDs on the floor. She wondered what he would have touched.

She'd thought that the crush had worn off; life must've worn everything off him in the last months. She remembered talking to Angharad once, staring into her hot chocolate like what she had to say was gossip, high and splendid. She hadn't lifted her eyes, though she'd heard her own tone of voice.

And Angharad had said, 'That's nice, Beth. That's really nice. Dai Meredith choking the chicken over you every night. You should tell Andrea that, after lunch, like. Might help on her way down to eight stone.'

'He said I was beautiful.' She remembered the smirk that she'd put on her own face. Not so far from Rhys.

Tonight, after the announcement that he must have been waiting weeks for, he'd come here, alone. Under the bright hallway lights, her flat was midnight quiet.

After putting Chelsea slowly down, Bethan found herself walking back through the rooms, turning off the lights again. She stood for a while in the close black air. She knew where to walk these days. She could have traced the rooms of her home, in footsteps, on any wide open space.

'My mum's garden, like,' Dai had said, 'that's a beautiful thing, that is. She keeps it beautiful, you know? Goes out there every Saturday, one o'clock, she likes to go out there, after the shopping's done. She's like you, she always does things at the same times. That's what I like about here. You go to some places, people do things any time they please. Might as well have dinner in the morning and breakfast at night. My mum, she goes and does the garden. It's good to make stuff beautiful. Like sweeping the street?' He talked like this. He had said, 'You're like that. Beautiful.'

Bethan stood in the dark, total now. This was how her home smelled.

Of her, that was his first thought. Sometimes, in the café, she'd walk past you and you'd smell it. It would only be a float on the air then, you wouldn't be able to catch it properly. Here, the smell was everywhere. He moved his hand, just a fraction on the door. Babies, that was part of the smell. But there were others, perfume and food, all mixed up.

Invisible, Bethan moved one hand. Her mother had said, 'To the baby all this will be new.' Whether that was true or not though, it would never be new for her again. She'd never again stand here and ask her mother if it was all right.

But for Dai it would've been. Bethan felt plastic under her fingers. Here was the light switch and now he'd see.

He looked at the phone-number book on the table, he saw her handwriting inside. She'd made drawings of things on the edge; of flowers. You must leave a little bit of yourself, he thought, on everything you touch.

His mother would have said, 'You think she's something special? I'll tell you, there are a million girls in the world like her, and all of them are pregnant. Get themselves with babies like it proves something, like it proves they're right. They put themselves into a baby, Dai, so they can hold it out in front of them like the best photo they've got of themselves. Anyone can have a baby, Dai,' she would have said.

But his mother hadn't understood. You could see time in Bethan's growing stomach. And it was time that had made him want to come here.

She couldn't remember Rhys ever using the word. She'd look fucking gorgeous, or she'd look fit. He'd told her she looked great when she came. And she could have told him the same thing, and though she wouldn't have used the word, beautiful would've been what she'd meant.

The last time they'd fucked, she'd ridden him like a wave from the Old fucking Spice advert, not that she could surf. In fact sometimes she had problems standing up on dry land. What she really needed was some stabilizers, one attached to each hip. That day, though, that day she'd had some fucking *agility*.

She'd known really, it would be the last time. She'd seen it in his face, the way his hands were awkward round her. After she'd told him about the tests it'd been. He'd come back still, a couple of times. They would talk, but they wouldn't know what to say. They would fuck, and that would be all right. And then, getting near to when he was going home, then he'd mention it. He'd talk about clinics, that sort of thing. He'd say that he'd seen a programme on telly, on where you could get it done. That day, on top of him, she'd known it would be the last time.

He'd come quick. He'd opened his mouth but he hadn't made any sound. And afterwards, still over him, she'd watched the orgasm slip away from his face. His eyes had been closed then and he hadn't seen the expression in hers.

She'd wanted to put a hand on his cheek so she could hold him, eyes still closed, in those few moments, and look at what she'd done. He'd been all the way inside her. Her mouth had been empty. He'd looked vulnerable in those moments but he hadn't been hers any more.

She'd killed them with that fuck, driven it between them like a screwdriver. He'd looked beautiful in that moment, she'd thought. But he wasn't beautiful, it had only been that he was leaving.

This was what Dai would have seen: a photograph of a child, taken so close that you could see the tiny hairs, a photograph that she'd thought was beautiful enough to hang in this gold frame. He would have seen the softest trace of her footsteps in the carpet's thick pile; he could have come in and seen all these things and thought them beautiful.

*

Hanging over her bedroom door, almost down to the carpet: dark blue velvet.

Dai bent down, still standing on the mat by her door, and he unlaced his shoes. He set them together and looked at them there.

The lamps in Bethan's bedroom made soft fingerprints. They made little streams and rivers through the velvet that he touched. And he picked up the paper pattern, very gently, must not tear it. He looked at it. It had her shape. But Bethan didn't wear dresses. She wore jeans.

Anyone could be beautiful in moments. That's what her mum had been too dull to see maybe, those days when she'd come home with a new idea, ballet, piano playing, whatever. It was the idea that mattered, she wasn't any dreamer. The idea was beautiful. And really Chelsea was the first idea she'd had that had lived up to her expectations.

Her mum had bought her the sewing machine for her birthday, a few months ago. Her mum, who'd laughed when Bethan had talked about dressmaking, but had still gone out and looked for it. And it had hurt her, unwrapping it and seeing it there. She hadn't known how her mother could do both those things.

She'd been working on the dress very slowly. An hour here, an hour there. Had embroidered the hem before the neckline was finished. She was scared that, when it was made, she wouldn't want to try it on.

As Bethan stood looking at her sewing machine, seeing the little empty space beside it, where an off-cut of velvet had been only a few hours before, Ruth Lewis was lying awake and listening to Nia's silence through the wall, the half-light casting its still patterns across the yellow-painted stone behind her. Her head full of pictures; little cottages, spires, shaded doorways that stood open to a sunlit street.

There'd been a time, she remembered it so clearly now as Bethan crossed the room to touch the place where the piece of velvet had lain, there'd been months when Nia's crying had broken through the night. It had used to rise as Ruth had stepped out from the bedclothes, till it had sounded like there were many notes inside it, many torn and trailing layers. Like the sound of applause tonight. Nia had used to cry all the time.

Little cobbled alleyways and tiny shops, Ruth imagined, Lennie sleeping beside her. Gardens and flowering climbers that spilled over windows. The sound of the sea, both constant and peaceful.

In the centre of her own room now, Bethan was sitting on the floor. She was looking at the cloth and the thin paper pattern, and she reached into her back pocket. It was a strange thing, she was thinking, a small drop of magic to look at the things you owned and be able to see them as if you never had before. She took out the green paper that was folded in her jeans. Its printing hadn't come out quite right.

In the week after this meeting, the week before the bulldozers came to Ynys-morlan, to grind around the bend in the road and lumber into stillness on the gift shop's concrete forecourt, there would be no noise, no motion. Silence would lie as hard and vivid as it did now in Ruth Lewis's home.

She felt it happening, like the ground outside could tighten itself against what was coming, like the houses could draw themselves together, the pavements harden till no tool could scratch them.

So rigid, under their feet the tarmac would crack. No object would be able to move. The forms, pink and yellow and green, lying in kitchens, on shelves and window sills, wouldn't even lift in any breath of air.

In the home that she had lived in for only four months, in this study's lamplight, Charlotte stood before the shelves, the gold of her journals gleaming like promises. Thoughts of Nia Lewis rose to her, and that milk bottle she'd broken on the path. The silence the girl must have heard, before, and as the glass fell across the quartz, and afterwards. She thought about the difference between those silences; the difference between her journals, and that cheque she'd held three nights ago.

So many pages she could cover a landscape with them. This land-scape, these mountains, or Hedera. She could have lain them out like the softest touch; Ruth's hand on Nia's hair while the girl had kicked in silence. She could have made a meadow white with them, or she could stifle Ynys-morlan underneath them all, thick and silent as snow.

The money had left her. Only a fraction in that cheque, but she had opened her mouth and spoken the words. Thirty-three million pounds. The weight of them had moved from her, out across that brightly lit hall, to touch the open hands that had lain in every lap.

There had been an oath once, twelve years old perhaps. She'd rewritten it many times – that she would never take a thing from her mother, nothing that was offered in love. She felt empty. She had given it all away. She would never again write the imagined conver-sation that filled the pages in many of these volumes – in which she confessed. In which she told her mother what she'd found at eight years old. She would never draw pictures of it again. They were spaced between the entries, from the careful etchings of a child to the quick scattered sketches of an adult who knows the lines so well that they are only tracing them. She'd drawn the shadows, leaf shadows, the way she remembered them, falling across it. There had been a blue sky that day. There had been sunlight. She could open any one of those diaries in front of her, could open the very first and find a picture beneath the opening date. She'd been full of something that she didn't understand, making its lines that first day, something that was too large and too close to see its shape. Maybe in drawing, in writing, she had tried to see it. Perhaps every time she had taken a pen to these pages. But she felt empty of it now. She was scared. She'd never draw it again.

She'd been waiting for this. Had pictured it since she'd stood watching a stranger's funeral, crying as if this wasn't Wales at all, but Massachusetts, as if the sky wasn't sunlit but full of beating rain and there'd been no iron railings between her and the church's walls. She'd been waiting, but hadn't known that it would feel this way.

Now, with the money gone in a breath, she looked at all the hundreds of thousands of words that were kept here on the shelves, and she didn't know what voice she could ever use to say them. She would have liked to have been able to speak to Ruth openly that day when they had burned the garden. But she didn't know, after so many silent volumes, if she could begin again.

She looked at the first, standing at the left-hand side of the shelf. On the leather spine it read '1968'. On the first page of that book: very careful, with the Caran d'Ache coloured pencils that her father had given her for her eighth birthday. She had only used yellows, whites and greens. Very careful. And she could not remember sitting over that page now. She had written about the memory many times since. She had written over it. She didn't know any longer how she might have felt as she had bent; what expression might have been on her own face.

After so long, it hurt her to try and look back and not be able to see. The memory should have been hers. Her hands had been on the paper. She should have been able to recall, and maybe then would have looked back and felt empathy for herself.

They must be hard things, memories, to hurt so much and then to seem so precious when she had finally left them behind. For the first time she saw the edges of the missing thing which had occupied Hedera's every space. In there, memories had run beneath the floorboards, spread into the paintwork. And she'd grown up, in the years before she'd found the meadow, walking barefoot on those floors, putting her hands against those walls.

All the leather-bound volumes seemed like fragile things suddenly, but she didn't know how to live if not inside them. How her mother would have understood her now. That landscape through her new home's windows seemed barer, forsaken. She was afraid to give the money away. She was afraid to write the cheques which meant so much more than these volumes' words.

Lennie's arms were folded before the table, where their drinks and their notes lay half used by the evening. 'What's the aim?' he asked. 'Talking about public works. Renovation, like. This demolition. We want to think about what we're aiming at here. Too many people, heads full of their own notions, have been let loose, too many places. Fucking silver and glass you see, great office blocks when the places around them, the places people live, aren't any fucking better. We need to know right from the start, right from now, that Ynys-morlan's not going to be one of those towns. The goal,' he said. 'You tell me what you reckon that is.'

Charlotte had spoken to Ruth often. She'd heard the quiet in Ruth's voice and knew what it was. She was sitting in the study now, where she had been spending every evening. It was memory. Ruth had asked her yesterday if something was wrong, if something had happened. Her own voice must have been as quiet as Ruth's. She'd told her, yes. Something had happened. She had given the money away.

There was nothing left now except to sit by these shelves and open the diaries. So she picked a page, a random page, and let her eyes fall to a line.

The kitchen held their low voices. The curtains were drawn and the street could only be seen across the kitchen table's surface. Notes and lists and scribbled thoughts there, telephone numbers, population figures. It wasn't the same town, Ruth thought, as lay in darkness again outside.

June the fourteenth 1971

Dear Charlotte,

NannaNancy and I had a private talk today for a long time. I still like to call her NannaNancy and she still lets me, sometimes if Mommy's not around. We talked about that time when I was very destructive in the Nursery, even though it's years ago now, and how she was never mad at me for it even though she should have been but she said, although I mustn't act like that again and I am better now, she didn't put the blame on me. She even said she spoke to my Mom about it back then and when they talked Mommy agreed that she shouldn't be so hard on me about it! and I do remember Mommy being nicer to me a bit afterward. I've seen NannaNancy even talk back to her and get smart with her although if your older than someone its not called getting smart. She's been here forever. She says she's been here longer than the grass and the water in the lake. I like her voice.

Anyway she was remembering this to me because of how I went bad again last week even though I never meant to hit mommy just the table and I would never try to hurt her. NannaNancy let me sit on her knee. The first thing she said to me was that I was special. She said she's met a lot of children and out of them I'm still special. She doesn't know though so she can't understand. I didn't say she was wrong. She said to me it's always hard for children born to privilege. But she calls children youngans. But its especially hard for me she said because of how my Mom is sick all the time. She didn't mean sick. She meant sad but she's not allowed to talk about Mommy like that. She's still staff no matter how old she is. She asked me if I was happy then and if there was anything in my life that made me sad except for Mommy being sick. I wanted to tell her but I can't tell her. She says our talks are always In Confidence but maybe it wouldn't be. I imagine Mommy hearing from her, all how I went to the Northern pastures and the meadow back then, coming

*to tell me how she knows and I got terrified because I don't
want Mommy to tell me about it. I don't want to hear about it.
So I didn't say to NannaNancy but I just shook my head.*

*That was when she asked me if I'd ever thought about going
away. I said that children can't just go away on their own,
but I said youngans like she does and she smiled. She said some
schools aren't just schools at all, but homes, and that the
children who go there can stay until they're not children
anymore.*

'It's renovation,' Ruth started gradually. 'We're not talking about
making this town into some other place, are we? Rehabilitation.' She
gave him a smile, tentative as the daylight in these months, looking
at his face.

He had been driven. Every night he'd come home and asked for
each new idea to be laid down for him, each choice, any piece of news
from Emyr on the council's views. His hands would shift on this table,
leaning forward like these were very precious, frail things. He'd listen,
like this project would save him but still couldn't make him smile. He
needed to know it wouldn't fail him. Driven, and she'd been scared
to watch it, though there'd been no bad nights between them. The
drive kept him ahead of bad nights.

Ynys-morlan grew stonier. The gift shop stood back from the road,
winter settling around it. The space where its signs would have been
set, its racks of sunglasses and dinghies, empty now. She had watched
through the window today, Dai and Emyr beginning the removals,
bringing boxes through the double doors and out into the January air.
Dai would come out every so often with nothing in his hands. She'd
seen him stand and look at them all and, after long moments, bend
down to rearrange the ways they were piled.

She'd taken cups of tea out in the afternoon, talked with Emyr about
the demolition contract, how soon they would start, while Dai worked
behind the wide, shadowed windows. Emyr had said there were no
laws. If you owned a building, one that wasn't historic, you could break
it down any day. The crew was scheduled to come in ten days' time.

He'd said, 'I've spoken to Edward about it, Ed Pritchard, County Hall. Spends more time buying boardroom furniture than anything else, budget's gone up for it forty per cent since I left, if you'll believe it.' He'd looked at Ruth, holding the tea. 'Thinks it's the greatest joke he's ever heard, all of them down there do. He asked if he could come up and meet Charlotte, "Just to shake her hand, like," he said. But there'll be no problems. So long as it's in keeping. Been waiting to do me a favour since the day I cleared my desk. Just waiting for me to ask for one.' He'd looked away, he'd shrugged, Ynys-morlan around him, not any other town, not any city; the place he and Gwen had chosen to stay.

Their breath had lain suspended in the air. 'It's a good thing you're doing for Dai, you and Gwen.'

'Well, Gwen's always been the first,' he'd said, 'to put the good of the community before herself.'

He'd been unable to hide it, unpleasantness. And she had to wonder, repeating what she'd said but hearing her own words fall away as Dai walked through the glass doors, she had to wonder at these feelings; Emyr's face, and Lennie as she saw him now – no happiness. She had to hide her own emotions. She'd get elated, get terrified. There was guilt, when she couldn't sleep.

Half an hour ago the phone had rung and she'd listened to Emyr Morgan's voice again. Jovial she'd always thought. She'd told him once. A round-sounding word you didn't get to use often – like 'egg-nog' it sounded, like 'pomp'. And he'd laughed at it himself when she'd said it. There'd been no laughter in his voice tonight.

Lennie drank his Bell's now and moved his hand through the papers.

'Emyr told me he's had the first forms in,' she said.

He looked up. 'You didn't say that. Which places? Whose?'

'Jarmans'. The Davises' house. He said Gwen talked to Audrey Pryce today and she handed one to her.'

'Well fuck me, you didn't think that was worth mentioning?' He raised his hand, glass held, whisky sloshed.

'They're the pink forms, Len. They're applications for sale.'

He looked at her in silence, images of people leaving in his eyes, but no reaction in the rest of him. She reached out, touched his hand and smiled, drew back though. What lay in this room, in this house now, seemed thin as glass. You took for granted, she thought, that the things you looked at every day were there to stay.

Emyr had parked his car, watching the path's automatic light turn itself on. He had stood in the corridor for a moment without taking his coat or shoes off, hearing the sounds of the house.

'Evening, Gwen,' he'd said to her, where she moved in a different room.

He'd looked at the framed steam engine prints, the landscape paintings and the three unopened envelopes lying on the occasional table by the door.

August the second 1971

Charlotte,

Mommy wouldn't look at me. We all sat in the little dining room, even Daddy, even though it was only seven o clock at night and usually he doesn't sit with us until at least eight forty five at night. She said she'd spoken to Nancy Robinette, she calls her by her whole name all the time. She asked me if it was true. All the way through the whole time she didn't even look up at me once but she just moved her ring round on her finger and looked at that. Daddy was holding my hand. I didn't want to say yes. Because I do love them and I don't want to hurt them or miss them or not know where they are but I hate them too. I don't mean to but I hate them too and I just hurt them. It comes out of me and I can't stop myself because that's the sort of person I am. I don't want to hate them but I feel like I'm not with them anyway. Then – because Mommy wouldn't look up – Daddy had to ask the second time. And I said yes. I want to go. She started crying but she wasn't crying about me because I'm not the one she's going to miss. They didn't ask me if I was sure

323

or anything. They didn't tell me to change my mind. It was like we'd all been waiting. Like we'd all known all along. It made me see that it was right. I hadn't been sure before.

Evening had settled into night now. Seen from the outgoing road, the town's lights would flicker between the trees' bare branches until they seemed to fragment; tiny beads.

'We had to expect the pink ones in first. I mean, they made up their minds a long time ago, whenever they put their places on the market, you know? Been a sign outside the Davises' place for as long as I can remember.'

'It's the demolition.'

She looked away. He had listened in silence, two weeks before the meeting, as she'd told him about what Dai wanted and how they thought they could announce it.

'A fucking knock-down job,' he'd said. 'That's how we're going to start fixing this town up, is it?'

'So Dai can move into the shops at the top of the street. His shops, three of them. One empty since Owain moved out, you know, the others for God knows how long. Beautiful buildings underneath.'

He'd nodded, looking at her, and then he had got up from this table without another word. She'd followed him as far as the kitchen doorway, to see him in the hall, picking his coat up off the banister. But he'd come back, four hours later maybe, and he'd not mentioned the gift shop at all. In bed, he'd started talking again about other buildings, about owners he'd spoken to. He'd stepped over the thought of the demolition without looking down.

'We shouldn't have started with Dai Meredith.'

'But it's done now, though,' she said.

'What fucking impression it's sent out. "And here's our first customer . . ." I'm not one to speak ill of those less fortunate, Ruth. The man can't even dress himself properly. Yes, it's done now. And we've had our applications in for those who want to leave.'

'I don't think it will have changed people's ideas of the project . . .'

'Want to look me in the eye and say that?'

She did, lamplight and reflections of this room depicted there. They could hear the fresh, cold rain outside. In here, the dinner's clean dishes were dried and the curtains shut, to be opened tomorrow morning on the street they knew.

'Wouldn't have changed my idea of it,' she said. It was a lie, though, and one he saw.

'How did Emyr take it?'

'He said that's what we had to expect.' The roundness in his voice, she remembered, not jovial but almost arrogant.

'The Public Works Projects,' Lennie said finally, quietly. 'We want to talk about exactly what we're going to do. We want to start doing them.'

She took her glass of wine from between the papers before looking up at him again. How could it not have changed everything already? A chance like this. Really it was a miracle, really it was the sort of thing people dreamed of. Like one of the stories: a dark and stormy night, you'd be sitting alone in the kitchen, just like this, hearing a knock at the door. And you'd go to it and let it open. Standing on the front step there he'd be, the old and ugly man, a walking stick, she thought, the whole business.

And he'd say, 'I'm a stranger here.' He'd say something like that. 'I'm lost. I'm tired.' She could just imagine. The middle of one of these nights, Lennie sleeping upstairs. The house full of Nia's silence, unchecked. Or anyone's, she thought. Anyone's house – anybody's coats and pictures in the hall. This old man, he'd ask you, 'Could you find it in your heart, do you think you could offer me a place to sit down and maybe something to drink? It's so cold.'

He'd be sweet-looking, she thought, wouldn't have any harm in him at all. Creaking in on his old stick. He'd sit in your kitchen and make you feel calmer just for being there, when calmness was hard to come by. And when he'd wiped his face and set his cup back on the table, then he'd say, 'Thank you for your kindness.' Old-fashioned words like those. 'There's a lot of people who wouldn't let a stranger in, this late hour. To give you something in return,' he'd say, levelling his rheumy eyes on you, 'I would like to offer you three wishes.'

Anyone could imagine it. She'd be sitting at the table just here. Everyone had a list of what their three wishes would be. But it wouldn't come out anything like the way you fantasized it. Because if someone came to you, she thought, if they offered you that, you'd only look away from them.

'That's very kind,' you'd say, 'but I don't need any wishes.' And you'd nod, she thought, the way that Lennie so often did now. Getting some control, just by believing that you had it.

He could say to you, 'You're unhappy. I know you're unhappy.'

You'd tell him it wasn't true.

He could say to you, 'I know your past. I know all the things that still make you cry, even though they're over, even though they were a long time ago.'

'I'm fine,' you'd say to him. 'I'm not sad. Nothing makes me sad like that.'

He could tell you that he knew of all the things you wanted, things you didn't believe you should have.

'There aren't any things like that,' you'd say to him. And you'd hold out your hand and show him where you lived and tell him that this was what you wanted.

She sat with Lennie, these papers strewn between them, while outside, on the dunes and in this wind, the grass curled hands around the cold, dark sand.

'The Public Works Projects,' she said.

Ynys-morlan drew itself in.

Dai Meredith sat in his living room with no lamps lit. On the shelves around him, the Toby jugs looked down. He had taken them from the hooks in the hallway, from the kitchen's dresser, and placed them in little spots here and there. The half-light blinked in their eyes. He'd worked for eight hours and thirty-six minutes and now he was eating his Angel Delight. All through the house, he could hear the clocks tick out the end of today.

Tom sat in his van, thinking of his mum and Stacey, around the table by now, while in her flat Bethan Hughes cooked her own dinner.

Sausages and mash she was having, she'd bought them in the Spar this afternoon. Chelsea was having sludge. She'd not been into the café today. Tom knew, he'd been working there since nine that morning. She hadn't come through the door.

All these lights. Needlepoint white marks around the bay.

August the twentieth 1971

Charlotte I'm scared. I don't want to anymore. It's not just going away but I can see in my Mom's face that she's gone away from me and Daddy too. He's more sad but they didn't have dinner with me last night. NannaNancy and I sat and watched a little of the Television and when I asked if we could go and sit in the drawing room she said they'd come and say goodnight to me. I'm scared. I have to go. They don't want me. I'm not sure anymore though. I don't know anything about England and NannaNancy can't come with me and I'm just going to miss her so much. I sat on her knee and I tried to stop it but I did cry. She just held onto me but she said I've got a whole new fresh start, a whole new world she was calling it and an opportunity and everything but she's not going! She's not the one! I haven't got any friends there like her. I want to make friends but I'm not the sort of person that people like to make friends with. They see me and they know there's something wrong in me. I see it in their faces and I'm scared to be on my own. I'm scared.

I have to go. It will be alright. I promise. It could be a fresh start. I could be happy there.

In the kitchen, Ruth and Lennie faced each other across the table. The quiet here was a missing person.

'We can resurface the road, lay new pavements,' she said. 'Working around the construction that's going on.'

'We're not talking about construction. It's renovation.'

'But they'll be big jobs, some of the properties. There's refurbishing the businesses, re-slating the roofs, extensions, rebuilding windows and doors, anyone who applies . . . Emyr's talking about using the council crew. There's the public buildings.'

Lennie nodded, glass in hand, watching her.

'The toilets,' she said. 'The bus shelter, you know, the museum, that'll be started on. Don't need any approval for that. It's a lot of renovation work, the building's in a bad state. He's saying four weeks, five.'

The tiny sounds of the papers filled the spaces between her words.

'If we're talking about public works then there's the garden, the park. Charlotte was saying a landscaping crew.'

'Where are we talking about?'

She tried to give him the smile she'd felt when Charlotte had first spoken, the garden burning in front of them. 'Where do you fancy?'

'Somewhere near the head of town.'

'So people can see it as they drive in.'

'There'll be a sense that way, coming into somewhere special,' he said.

She found the sheet, passed it across the table to him with the smile. 'There's a couple of possibilities . . . You get to the development boundary pretty quick but there's, look, all this concrete . . .' She gestured a hand to the window, where the night lay behind their curtains. 'By the seawall, that's public ground. Also there's the gift shop's forecourt. Dai owns the land where it's standing now but not the bit in front. I don't know, I asked him but he's not said yet, what plans he's got for the space, but the forecourt is . . .' she looked down and read; faint photocopies given her by Emyr.

'That's sixty feet by thirty, that's a big enough area.'

'You'll be supervising that then? You should,' he said.

'And Emyr's calling a team in for quotes on the toilets. Next Tuesday.'

'Doing what there? And the bus shelter?'

'Tell me what you think,' she said.

He opened his mouth but after a moment only drank. 'Should give the impression, with the buildings we don't need applications for, the impression we want the whole place to have. Showcase it.'

'Go on.'

'Historic. That's what we want. People to see the history in this place. Buildings that look like they could've been here two hundred years ago. Museum should be a focus.'

'Old stone,' she said. 'It's got that anyway. But the toilets, the shelter. You know we could have them remade, Len? Just like you said. Focus the impression.'

'Rebuild them.' He wet his lips, looking at her. 'I want you to see the responsibility we have in this. It's not just an opportunity because an opportunity's something you jump at. We don't jump at this. We could rebuild, yes. But where d'you draw the line, Ruth? We don't rush headlong into rebuilding. We don't fuck this up because Ynys-morlan's been here longer than Charlotte Weyland, and longer than us.' He didn't touch her, though he could've given to her what he was trying to say, just by doing so. In this house that had seemed voiceless for two years, unchanged, Ruth dropped her eyes. He didn't touch her even now. And the quiet held those other soundless nights.

'It's a duty we're talking about,' he said.

August the twenty-fourth 1971

Dear Charlotte

It's my going away day. It's a day for flying across the world today. I have three books in my hand luggage including my Little Women. They've already packed the car downstairs. I have refused to go up to see mommy. It will be better now because I can really be me.

'Emyr's got eleven teams ready. Do you know what I think, if we want to get the ball rolling? We should roll it ourselves, Len. Eleven teams that can start work in the next two weeks. We could fill out our own form. When they walked past, people would see it all starting, see what it means.'

'Or they'd walk past and think that's what it's been for all along. Your house getting to be a more valuable asset. Like they'll think when they see work starting on the ones Charlotte's buying. I wonder what sort of profit she's looking at.'

'You don't think that's why she's doing this.'

'I don't know her, Ruth.'

He'd told her he wanted to be introduced to Charlotte three weeks before the town meeting. She had told him then, sitting here as they were now, that Charlotte was strange, that Charlotte was shy, and at that time they'd had no assurance that she'd follow through on her miracle gift. Those were the words he'd used for it then.

'You want it to start, don't you?' she said.

'That's no question. It's not about what we want. Something like this, there's a million things that could go wrong. Something like this, it's the *duty*, Ruth, we need to be remembering.'

'But it could be the right thing to do. I've been thinking about it. All day, I've been sitting here, you know, I've got the peace and quiet, not like I haven't got that – let's fill in the form now. It could look like a different place in two months.'

But he didn't look at her, his voice level as the beach. 'Self-interest is what people'll think. This is the most important thing we've ever done, you or me. Right, every step, is has to be.'

'I can't wait, Lennie,' she said. She looked at him but it was another day she saw. 'I can't wait, you know, I can't wait.' She thought of the stack of yellow forms, here in a box. She thought of tomorrow morning and the next. He didn't see the beginnings of the days, when sometimes she would wake, moving from sleep to sitting up in the bed in one movement. Sometimes she cried in the mornings. Sometimes, she would press a hand to her hair and stroke herself, like there was another person calming her.

Ruth had drawn houses when she was little. Her mother had said once, if they'd had a penny for each one, they'd have been able to buy a new one for themselves. She'd used to say, 'You don't spend time, Ruth, you fritter it away.' But she'd often stuck the pictures up on the cork board on their kitchen wall. When her mother had passed on and she and Lennie had brought his boxes to the house, she'd found a couple of those pictures, tucked away in the attic. She remembered the sounds from downstairs, Lennie moving but trying to be quiet around whatever Ruth might have felt. She remembered the occasional muffled curse when something had fallen, the way he had shushed himself after each one. Under the slate roof it had been cold. In an old box beneath the eaves she'd found them, and she'd sat, trying to hold the torch, balance herself. They'd been kept with blank sheets between. Her mother must have tried to protect them that way.

Such careful pictures. Every single line perfectly drawn. She'd had a half-size ruler in her school pencil case; remembered cleaning it before each new version. They had slowly developed. Of the two she found, one was far later than the other. New ideas added. Shutters she'd seen in photographs of houses in Holland. A crazy-paving path like Lennie's dad had laid down in front of three different houses that year. Her mum had called it the Crazy-paving Year, she'd got a taste for the words. Ruth had loved them, would've gone to watch Lloyd Lewis laying them, except for Lennie and his sticks. If it wasn't litter or nasty words, he'd sit on a wall with one in his hand, ten, twenty feet from where his dad worked. You'd have to cross the road to avoid him. She remembered Emyr saying once, one hand on his glasses in that studied way he'd had, that Lennie Lewis was a coward, because all bullies were really cowards underneath. He'd been able to say that though. He'd been thirteen, and Lennie only eight.

Sitting on the attic's dirty joists, Ruth had looked down at the drawing: the crazy-paving path in the torchlight, leading up to a little front door. The paving stones pink and blue. A stone chimney, just like theirs. Below, she'd heard a hammer knocking.

In the corner, where she'd always put it, her name and her age had been written out. Ruth had imagined her mother placing these two blank sheets of paper between them. Had wondered if she'd been putting them away to take out and look at sometime later, or if she'd only kept them because she didn't want to let them go.

Lennie spoke to her now, his voice falling quietly across the table; the many reasons why they mustn't apply first. He left silence again and she didn't answer. This project took the past away from them.

331

The room where they sat seemed stranded – she could see that he sensed it too.

Papers lay between; plans. It should have felt like the beginning for them again.

He remembered as he saw Ruth, the day that he'd come home, great box in his hands to unpack. And she'd been upstairs showering and, when he'd done it, he'd called to her to come down.

'What's your favourite food?' he'd said. 'Thing you couldn't live without.'

'Marmite . . .' She'd had a towel around her chest and jeans on. A half-smile – too many recent bad nights between them for it to shine.

'How much do you reckon you eat a week?'

'A pot at least. Spread it on so it tastes like a barium meal. Lennie . . . ?'

'Been waiting to do this all day,' he'd said. He'd opened the cupboard. They'd been lined up, label against label. Not one pot out of place. 'So that's a pot a week, four a month. Know what my mother used to crave when she was having me?' he'd asked. 'Marmite.' And gestured to them, 'Four by nine months makes thirty-six.'

She'd been laughing. The distance had almost fallen away from her. 'Lennie . . . I'm not pregnant,' she'd said.

'I love you.' Several times, he'd told her. 'You know what we've got? I look around, I don't see any people *in love*, not with our spark. We've got some fucking spark. We've got something special,' he'd said.

But when he had reached out to hold her, his hand had brushed that bruise, and she'd stiffened. The first time, despite his gift, that he'd not been able to touch a part of her.

Now he imagined this house, in two months' time, maybe three, all its old pebbledash stripped off to show the clean grey stone under it. He imagined it, in the last evening light of spring. There was a warmth to the sunset then, a beauty which had always brought back memories for him. Which seemed to make the future clearer. That stone would be rose-coloured. He would walk down the new path, put his key in a new front door, and look into the same overshadowed hall.

Winter

'This is a great thing, Ruth.' He moved his hands to show her, but what he described, it had no shape for him. 'We have to do it right,' he repeated, unable to find any other words, sitting in this beginning with her.

She was scared to touch him sometimes. Sometimes she was scared to touch Nia. She didn't answer now but only nodded, put away thoughts of the yellow forms as the late night passed outside, and tried to give a smile to him. She did reach out – her hand on his – and was left with no movements to make.

333

'Do you know what beauty is, I think?' she said to Charlotte that week, speaking on the telephone, as they did more often than they saw each other. 'It's all the best parts of people. It's all the goodness people want, made into something you can see and touch. People are full of goodness in their heads, and the world's still covered with ugliness, you know?'

Listening to her speak in the receiver, Charlotte tried to imagine the project and could only think of the money, gone. Something inside people stood between wanting goodness and creating it.

Ruth's voice became clearer each time she spoke of it, though. 'Not just one beautiful thing, a *whole town*. It's something worth *aspiring to* . . . It's not just renovation.'

Charlotte remembered the story she'd told: her husband climbing a flagpole, calling her name out – and really she'd thought Ruth weak, easily led, to be so naïve then and so unhappy now. But she must have laughed that night, Charlotte supposed; shared something with him. It must be better to take life wholeheartedly.

'I just want to start. I just want to get going. Can't wait, you know?'

The sound didn't carry. In Nia's quiet, in her mother's house, Ruth's laughter ran like paint from the walls.

September the fourth 1971

Dear Charlotte,

I like the corridors here and the rooms. There are the kind of sounds all the time, like low sounds, that you don't really hear, voices, footsteps, the girls doing Physical Training outside. I think that places have personalities just like people and sometimes more personality because when you're in a building it is on every side of you but you can walk off from a person. Here it's in every room like it can feel you, even if you walk without touching anything. I think this place wants to be empty. I think something has happened in every room and all those things sink into the walls. What each different person thought when they were lying in each different bed. Those thoughts all join together because they can't when they belong to people and they make the personality.

All the doors are very tall and the ceilings are high. You can hear the people walking. I've just been lying here and I've been listening to them. I don't know any names yet. I don't want to be the sort of person who's always on their own.

There was a need inside everyone for a home. A thirst for one, Ruth thought. People had to put their lives into something. Their homes were sculptures of themselves. It seemed desperate in some way. She wondered if that desperation was to see your life solid; make real your emotions so they could never be taken away. Or whether it was deeper, simpler than that: if it didn't matter what you made – a home, a drawing, a child – you just needed to take the things you felt out from inside you.

She'd wondered a lot of times, all the way through her life, how her father must have felt when he was leaving. Just imagining, she'd felt the edge of fear, though she'd used to tell herself that she would leave. All your possessions, all your memories and everything you'd wanted, she'd wondered how a person could drive away from those things without ever turning around.

It was the 22nd of January today. The demolition of the gift shop – and so the beginning of the project – was scheduled for the 28th.

On her left now, Ruth heard the cistern working. You couldn't hear the toilet flush with the bathroom door closed, but it would be flushing, and Nia would be coming out in a moment. It was morning-time again. Winter dimmed the street with freezing fog. And here Nia's bedroom light was on and Ruth stood looking at the wall, stopped in motion.

She held Eeyore in one hand, dangling, from where she'd picked him up. She had bent and then she had risen. And rising, she had seen the patches.

Behind her Nia's bed was still a mess. She needed to make that, needed to get her ready for playschool because playschool was in the mornings, Monday to Thursday, and she'd be out of the bathroom soon.

A discolouration it was. A little grey, a foot above the skirting boards. Darker here and there.

She had to take Nia down to playschool, and soon now, drive back here, get on with her day, though there was no project yet; there were no applications but those for sale.

Damp, she thought as she stared at it. But that wouldn't have been regular like this. It would have been brown as it was on the landing, not grey like this. Faint. It was hard to make all the marks out, anything but a kind of blur. So faint, you could walk in and out of this bedroom a thousand times, never see them.

Outside this low day was raising its head. This room was full of drawings, arranged by Ruth, toys placed in one corner, crayons set side by side on the little desk, and yesterday's clothes were here waiting by her feet. The quiet in the house was another country.

What she saw ran all along this wall. Hardly there at all in some places. And in others the patches were clustered.

Ruth knelt here on the carpet, looking at the way that the stains resolved themselves into pairs – and after a moment touching her mouth. Over and over, as though she was stained as well.

Ruth filled in the form quickly, desperately, wrote about the problems in her home, though it looked perfect around her. The missing slates, the cracks in the pebbledash, the damp. But the application was just a formality to her. When she called Emyr's mobile phone number, the sound of distortion was louder than the tone of her words. He told her she'd see the man in no more than forty-eight hours.

Ruth would sit with her husband that evening and talk passionately about the future, never mentioning the events of her own day. Charlotte's project had made distant things clearer.

But when the foreman came and she heard Lennie, who should have been two hundred miles away and driving further, pull up at the kerb outside, she wouldn't feel any shock that he'd seen through what she'd thought she'd hidden.

Maybe it was just that, unspoken between them, their feelings had grown together. Though they talked and ate and sat in silence, never passed a word that expressed it, he had reached the same point as she had. He couldn't go on. Ynys-morlan drew itself tighter, the street, their home, until it felt like it must crack under the weight of the money that no one would reach out for.

September the sixth 1971

Dear Charlotte,

Thursday and my third day here. It's seven o clock now and we can do what we want at seven o clock until nine. Some girls read in the Study Room, or write letters. When you have written a letter here you give it to the House Mistress, you're not allowed your own envelopes and I think that's probably right because otherwise any person could write anything and send it out and the teachers wouldn't know. Some of the other girls have pen friends, they are part of a whole society of pen friends that goes all the way around the world, though they have never met their pen friends and don't know them. I think all these letters, all being posted from place to place are like little birds, all migrating with different routes to go, all of them heading for a person who's never been seen. I can imagine all those people's faces when they get up in the morning to have breakfast and they go to the door, and there is the letter with its little postmark sitting on the mat. I think it's a good thing for the world to have a society like this because it brings people together that would never meet or even know each other existed. I would like to be part of this society and I'll ask other girls if I can. You could have a friend that you could tell everything to but they'd never even have seen you. You wouldn't have to send them a photograph.

In the first year here, no one has their own rooms. We have our own beds and a shelf and a cupboard, we have our desks in the Study Room. All the girls talk about getting their own rooms and what they'll put in them. I'm glad I don't have one.

I was going to say that but they just wouldn't even agree with me or see my point of view. I have a space that is the same size as my bed and even if I just put my foot out then the place I'm in isn't mine anymore.

I saw the girl again today and I found out her name. And it wasn't just my imagination either. Sometimes you can just see what you want to see. But she does look like me. She has hair that's straight and brown like mine, her eyes are the same as mine but green not blue. Her name is Anne and she is in the second year. I won't tell her and I won't tell anyone else because they'll only think I want to be her friend. But it's not vain or narcissism to think someone looks like me. I bet we could count the differences between us on one hand.

I heard of a trick that you can do in front of a mirror. You take a candle and you move it in a circle around your face, as you bring it down under your chin it's like growing old in a few seconds. I would like to do it with her to see if we would look the same at fifty years old!

I might talk to her the next time I see her in the Hall. I don't know her last name but I was looking in the mirror and if you didn't know me and you saw my face, you could believe my name was Anne.

The 23rd of January dawned low and biting.

Gwen's peach curtains draped across the daylight and thawed it. She fastened her coat from the lowest button upwards. On either side of her, the carpet ran to clean walls. She looked at the painting, hung centrally, opposite: a woodland evening, long-shadowed. She had found it in a gallery in Aberystwyth – often bought there. She believed in supporting local artists.

She looked at all the other coats on their stand, each for a different kind of weather, remembering people they'd had to dinner here, her standing in the doorway, hand held out, offering to take them as she'd smiled. The stillness here seemed to hum. The wind that had hidden it was gone. Emyr was gone.

She had said to him tightly, 'How has Dai been? Emptying the shop?' Still calling it this, when there was no stock, no customers, no manager or future. 'It must be very hard for him.'

He'd told her, 'Dai's fine. Kind of you to ask.' His voice had been light, like these curtains across a view that the bulldozers would tear up in a few days' time. They moved slightly, she saw now, in the warm air that rose from the heaters.

The lane led past their garden gates, tarmac curving between the naked trees until she couldn't follow it any more. The important thing now was to be in control of her confusion. To be in control, she thought, of her unhappiness.

How was it for Emyr now? This man she'd thought she knew, emptying the place too on the days when the project could spare him. She wondered if he might see the street through its double doors, or just a space of empty floor, and be filled with doubt for what he'd done. Crippling doubt. Regret, she would have liked to believe.

She'd say in the mornings, 'You'll be at the shop today?'

'Back for dinner, though, always nice to be back for dinner.' He had begun to replace each part of their life with a little façade. This was her punishment.

He would be gone all day, she in the house alone, many afternoons, tidying, doing things that needed to be done. She'd vacuum the carpets and she'd dust the shelves. The energy she had still wouldn't leave her. And this silence lay like cold water behind. It had been there with the end of every task. Until she'd had to leave the house, and you should never *want* to leave your home, it was the place that you waited to go back to. Kept everything that was best about your life. This was what he'd done. Pushed her to this. With his schemes and his hatefulness and self-pity. With the smiles he used instead of honesty now.

Gwen secured her last button, she saw the cold outside. The lane would die as it led into Dai Meredith's yard, where no car had driven for months.

*

'Organized person, isn't she, Ms Weyland?' Emyr had said to Ruth the day before, eyebrows raised; a kind of sarcasm that seemed to come easily now.

Taking him cups of tea where he'd been working on the gift shop's forecourt, Ruth had asked him questions, hedging awkwardly around what she wondered now: if it was the beginning of these changes, the gift shop first and hardest, that was raising this cynicism like silt.

'And we should thank God for it,' she'd said then, a smile she hadn't felt. She'd thought of Charlotte's face, seen through the church's iron railings. 'Don't even want to imagine how this place'd look in three months' time if my brain was meant to do the organizing. Houses with one window and three roofs . . .' She'd wanted suddenly, crossly, to say to him that Charlotte was very different on her own, and perhaps he didn't know how organized she was or wasn't, or anything much else about her. She'd said nothing, but whether out of a wish not to have any conflict with Emyr – even the smallest, seeing that something was wrong for him – or whether out of some sense of loyalty to Miss Weyland, to her privacy, she hadn't known. But she'd felt closer to Charlotte, far up the lane and silent in her own home, than she had to her cousin, standing there.

She'd looked back at Emyr as she had walked towards her gate: pale amid the boxes on the dark grey concrete, muffled in coats. As though his mother had dressed him for a winter day thirty years ago, left him standing in that spot. As though he'd stayed that way since, she thought, his face the only thing changing.

She'd been struck by something then, unsettling as the feel of some cold surface: they were so untested, all of them. Herself and Lennie, people who she saw in the street every day but knew only by names, Emyr here; they were close, they'd always been, she'd tell anyone who asked her. But she had walked away without asking him his troubles. She'd been afraid to. There was a wall in her, behind which lay everything that couldn't be said with a smile. So untested, all of them.

She had seen Charlotte speak to Emyr and to the people at the meeting and there had seemed to be no doubt in the woman then, nothing with as much emotion, but she wasn't like that when they were alone.

It seemed to Ruth then that they were like empty rooms, all of them, rooms in the dark for all the ways they knew each other. The only things that gave them shape were the walls, the barriers.

Today, the gift shop's glass was muted beneath the low eaves. The slim daylight would lie in stretches across the first of its floorboards, brush the wall where local pictures had hung for sale, the paint darker in their shapes. Where Eirian had stood, day after day, summer coming in through the open doors, there'd be nothing but dusty glass and Formica. It was waiting. As was Ruth, for the foreman to come to her home and give her the project's first renovation quote.

We stood and watched the garden burn, she thought. We set up two hundred and fifty chairs and handed out home-made forms.

The Morgans had lain in bed last night, hearing the wind and rain run around them, loud enough to cover any sound they might have made. Gwen had heard the compost bin outside fall, overturning, and had felt him next to her. Awake.

'Listen,' he'd said after a long time.

The first occasion since the meeting that Gwen had heard reality in his voice. It was a low sound, defenceless.

'So stormy,' he'd said.

She had not answered in the darkness.

He'd spoken with some kind of tenderness. 'Even the dogs are barking.'

Now Gwen took them into their little room and stroked their heads and shushed them, closing them away before she went to open the front door. Nasty January air touched her.

It had been hope, embodied in the gift shop. One wrongful kiss couldn't tear it down. One kiss proved nothing; it couldn't make their life a lie. You had to win against your confusion; find the satisfaction in overcoming it. She would not allow her husband's sudden, unfounded insecurity to draw doubt from herself.

Siân had asked once, in the months after the wedding, whether it had been everything she'd wanted. The question had brought a sense of fear. You had to defend your choices against fear all the time. This was the strength that Emyr had mistaken for lack of care. It wasn't falseness, to want others' belief in the life you had. The love. She knew this, though she remembered Siân's attitude, asking that all those years ago. Not that she would ever criticize her for it. You couldn't criticize a person for seeing the world from the place where they'd been put. Of course, Siân had wished Gwen the best, would never have done otherwise.

Now she locked her home and walked away.

Eirian Meredith's house was winter-dry. The ivy was brown. By the front door that Gwen had left hanging open in the night, a long time ago it seemed, a terracotta pot had fallen and broken. The wind's last drags moved dirt across the yard and the slates hung heavy over the highest windows. Dai had told her he didn't want any help, many times throughout the last two months.

Gwen remembered hearing herself, in the noise of music, in the din of people, saying to Siân, 'I love him.'

How suddenly the words had come, she now recalled. This questioning was what he had brought her to. This constant raking over of things gone by. When she had no answers to search for. There was nothing in her life to reassess.

She had seen Patty yesterday. Patty, who had been so bright in those days before the wedding, always with a hand on Gwen's arm, always smiling into her face, as if those better feelings might rub off. She had walked into the café and Pat hadn't been behind the counter. She'd heard her voice from another room upstairs. There for a moment she'd waited on her own, looking up at the photograph against that vague grey wallpaper. Really seeing it, for the first time in years. Faded now. The three of them. All standing with their hats and the kind of hard sunlight that only comes early in the season. All three smiling.

From the other room, Pat's voice had been soft. Tom didn't work on Wednesdays.

After having to leave her house, she had found herself standing in that same silence still. In her own face, in the photograph – she wasn't sure what it was. It did look like happiness. She didn't seem to recognize the woman there.

When Pat had come through they had talked about the proposals, Pat mentioning who she thought was applying. 'I tell you, she's going for it. Wouldn't be surprised if that form is in the envelope now. Sitting here, swearing blind to me what a bad idea the whole thing is . . . she'll be applying. There's no doubt in my mind.'

Gwen had said, 'I'm sure she'd be honest about it. I don't see why anyone would lie about such a thing.'

'Well don't pretend, you know well enough why she'd lie. Who'd want to be the first? Look like a money-grabber . . . Siân's up in arms at the thought of anyone applying, I'll tell you that, reckons they might as well register Ynys-morlan as a national charity . . .' Gwen had seen her look down at her cigarette, tap the ash after a moment, and she'd wondered what Pat was thinking. Looking across the table, she'd wanted to ask her but hadn't known how to start on the words.

Patty had spoken after a while. Had stubbed her cigarette out and asked in some final decision, looking up, 'What do you think, Gwen? Really? What do you think of it all?'

And Gwen had answered her, 'I think it's a wonderful opportunity for us all.'

Everyone needed respect from the people they lived with, from the people who were their friends. One kiss. One night, and she could not even remember how the waves had sounded on the beach.

She saw how the house had been corroded by winter. She stood at the gates of the Meredith property for a long time, looking without entering. The ground-floor windows were lustreless. The kitchen here and the living room next to it. This was where she had come, all through the summer, with bags full of food, with messages from people in town, and each visit the plants in the flower beds had swayed, more sickly, the earth drier. The beds were littered with debris now: old leaves, couch grass. In clear spaces, Gwen saw puddles of rainwater, grey like those windows, with the same sky.

'Why do you come here, Gwen?'

She could see no sign of Dai.

She had come, full of efficiency and daylight, as though she could have brought any brightness to a place that was dying like this, every spare afternoon, every Saturday morning. 'I would have thought that was obvious, Eirian. I come here to help you.'

Walking towards the house, control seemed to lie in her hands only, thin as a coating on her skin. She grasped it but even this small steadiness was underwritten with doubt – she didn't know why it would feel like winning to take control of herself.

Ynys-morlan was distant. You could hear every gull call. You could stand and hear the sea move, half a mile away. Eirian Meredith's door wasn't on the latch. It swung open under Gwen's hand as it must have done that night, when the undertakers had come after her leaving.

'Dai?'

In front of her, the hallway showed itself.

'Dai? Are you in?'

Here they were. She saw them. Eirian's things. Still stacked up on the chairs that lined this hallway, soft with dust and nebulous with winter dimness. Spaces, she saw, where Toby jugs were missing.

'Dai –'

And a scuffling, two doors down.

'What? Who is it? What do you want?'

'It's me,' she said. She heard her own voice in Eirian's hallway, crisp and clear. 'Gwen Morgan,' she said. She could remember the first time she'd used that name, she'd spoken it aloud herself. Standing in front of her dressing-table mirror, she had repeated it and smiled at her reflection. She must have been very young then, it seemed like the sort of thing that only a girl could do.

She saw Dai's movement in the hallway. He came through.

His face was shadowed, his hair a mad woman's breakfast. At the end of the corridor, he stood and looked at her, where she must have been silhouetted against the small overcast light of the doorway. Her first thought, seeing him, was of how old he looked.

'Good morning, Dai. Hope I didn't wake you –' She cleared her throat. This gloomy place, her voice wouldn't sound the way she meant it.

'I was awake already. I've been awake for hours.' He didn't move, though, looking at her. There was nothing friendly in his stance. 'I've been busy.'

'Really? That's good. It's always nice to be busy. Doing what?'

He stood still as bricks between her and the living-room doorway. Through there, at an angle which Gwen could not see, his mother's living room was piled with things. They spread in a half-circle around the sofa; sandwich packets on the floor, clothes and blankets, all the things he needed, facing the TV. And on the little table, which Gwen would see with just a few more steps, beside the now empty whisky bottle, a piece of blue velvet caught the uncertain light.

He was not a liar by nature; remembered a time when even the littlest lie would come out wrong from his mouth. These last few weeks, though, hiding the plan of the gift shop until the meeting had come at last, and hiding other, smaller things too, lies came easier. It was not a good thing. Made him see people in a different kind of way. You couldn't trust others when you were lying to them. But he looked at Gwen's dark shape against the open door and he wouldn't have her seeing the cloth.

Every day he counted down, time made him less sure. Until last night, when he'd looked at the bottle Emyr had brought him and known what it did, and it had seemed like a better thing than just to sit and think about how the gift shop would look as it fell down. He remembered crying after drinking it. He'd sat and remembered how he and his mum had drunk glasses of sherry when they were celebrating something. He had heard the clocks counting out his ten minutes.

Before him now, Gwen didn't take a step forward. She could feel the house, above them, around them, heavy.

He said, 'Busy doing lots, I've got lots of things to organize.'

'Well, next week's going to be a big week for all of us, but for you most of all, I'm sure.' She looked at him, lost now in what she needed to say, cold with the open door and the open road beyond it, leading back to her home. 'Are you excited? Are you looking forward to it?'

'Yes.'

'I know everyone will be there anyway. You know Emyr's planned to string a ribbon up round it? He told me that.'

He had been sitting in the living room when it had come, unprompted. 'It ought to encourage everyone, you know – celebratory,' he'd said.

'I find it hard to think of celebration now.'

'Really?' he'd said. 'I spoke to Emma Jarman this morning. She said you'd been talking about what an incredible opportunity this was for everyone.'

He hadn't told her since the night of the meeting that there was still time to protest. She supposed that there wasn't now. That time was gone; she had walked through it towards the right decision.

Though now she stood here. She looked at Dai's face and she could have cracked and shouted, for all the strain of trying to filter what she felt through these few words. 'It must be a difficult time for you too, though, as well as exciting.' She would not crack. 'I came because I wondered . . . I thought you might want to talk about it.'

'I don't have anything to talk about.'

'It's natural to have mixed feelings about something like this, Dai –' She took a step forwards, saw him straighten, block her way again. 'Dai . . . I'd be worried if you didn't have mixed feelings.'

'There's no feelings to mix.'

'You know what I'm talking about. The gift shop, a decision like that, it must have been hard to make . . . It's the sort of thing one couldn't help but have second thoughts about.' She reached out a hand through the cold air, as though to show him that it was all right. Above her, the old ornaments glinted in hueless shade. She saw the door that had led to Eirian's room. 'Dai, it can be hard to talk about second thoughts, but it can be good to talk about them. I don't want you worrying on your own up here . . .'

He didn't answer but heard the repetition of Emyr's words; let them slowly sink into him so he could consider it.

'Why don't we sit down? You can't be too busy to have a cup of tea, surely. You'd like to?'

'No . . .'

Gwen stopped. Her mouth was open, silent for a moment. 'No?' she said. 'Well then, you must be very busy indeed, if you can't take five minutes from your day.' In his quiet her words came more quickly than she wanted them and she found herself saying, 'But you don't look busy to me, whatever you say. Worried is how you look.'

It seemed that he wouldn't respond but then he began, 'I told you –'

'You must be thinking about the new shops. A lot of things to keep track of, I'm sure. Forms to sign and plans to make. A lot of questions.'

'I haven't got any questions.' In the hallway between them, his voice was loud with the lack of being comprehended.

'Well that's hiding, Dai, because there are questions. If you're not asking them then maybe you should be.' Her hand fluttered and fell to her side.

'Don't tell me what I should be thinking about.'

Gwen's mouth closed. And though he looked away from her, regretting it, it was too late to take back what he had said, and he didn't. If this house could have made a sound, it would have been satisfaction. The shadows gathered at his back.

Gwen remembered, 'So it's for Dai, is it, that you're so worried then? What a caring person you are.' She hadn't since been able to summon up the memory of running that night, of what had been in her mind. These recent weeks she'd felt like she was falling but she had been pushed. Imagining the gift shop demolished stole something from inside her. Of course she stood here. Of course she'd come.

She heard Dai's voice and it was thickened by distrust. 'I'd like it if you went away for today, if that's all right. What are you doing here anyway?'

'Do you know, Dai, I wish I knew the answer to that. Of all the things . . . I could be doing, I wish it wasn't this.' She put one word in front of the other as if they were the only things now keeping her out of the water. 'I came here to talk to you, just like I said. About next week, the shop. All the pros and cons, if someone's put all the pros and cons to you –'

'I don't need any pros and cons put to me –' He raised his hand and shook his finger at her, closer to a woman's gesture than a man's. 'Why can't you just say, "Do what you want"? Why can't you just say that? Because you're *meddling* . . . You don't think I'm bright enough to choose. But I can do "whatever I want"!'

'I'm not meddling! In case you hadn't noticed, Dai, that gift shop affects a lot of people in this town. Ynys-morlan's dependent on that business. Other people's livelihoods. Don't you say that. Don't you say "meddle" to me!'

'I knew you'd be round here.'

'Is that so?'

'Mum *told* me you would be.' And Emyr's face crossed his thoughts again, obscure, as it had been in the darkness of the living room that night. 'And you know what else she said?' Emyr had talked and talked and made him promise, but Dai had never thought it would be *Gwen*. 'She said *that it was mine*. Anything I wanted. That I mustn't *let* anyone meddle. Things happen for a reason, you know that? The gift shop's supposed to be mine!'

'Your mother wouldn't listen to anyone's opinion but her own! You gave her advice and she'd call it meddling! You came round to help her and she'd call it meddling. Let me tell you something, Dai – your mother never had a good word to say about anyone.'

'That's not true!'

'Don't be the same . . . don't have her faults! I'm trying to help you, Dai! My God, can't you see?'

'You don't know anything because she did have good words.'

'I tell you, Dai, maybe you know what you want right now. But in a month? A year? There's no going back on a demolition, you know. In case you hadn't realized, a demolition leaves you with nothing but rubble in the street!'

'*I know that! I know it's rubble! Stop it now!*'

'I'm trying to help all of us!' She saw the place, a hole through its brickwork, falling. 'You think I want to be having this conversation with you? I did everything I could to stop it coming to this! Told your mother right from the beginning –' she stopped. What had she been about to say?

This was what Emyr had pushed her to – she didn't even know what was coming out from her own mouth.

'There are other people who care about that shop, Dai! It's not just meaningful to you! Your mother spent *ten years* building the business up! Emyr and I had our wedding reception there! *That gift shop was the only thing my father ever built!* I *made* that place, do you know that, Dai? Think about making things, you're so fast to break them down. I took my father, a man with an *idea*, a *vision*, I put him together with someone who could make it possible. I worked it, *eased it* through and that business – that business was the heart of Ynys-morlan's trade for more seasons than you can remember!' Did he remember? A fourteen-year-old boy moving in between the stock boxes in the back room every Saturday. Not knowing really. Not really understanding. And now doing this: destroying. Did he look back and see himself as someone who'd never made a choice before? 'You can't see the value of that work? Try to imagine, Dai, years of worry, hard graft, years of gambling your income on the weather. The weather! Something so insubstantial –' Her hands reached out and grasped the air like she could pull from it the heart of what she felt. 'You don't know what it's like to look back on your life and see it in the things you've made! I think you should take a minute to see that place, ask yourself what it means to you!' She heard the echo in her own words. '*Your mother wouldn't have wanted this!* She'd never have left it to you if she'd known you were going to tear it down!'

'*Well she's dead!* It's *my* place! How would you know what she wanted? You don't know! *She doesn't want anything any more!*' He walked towards her, dusty spaces on the shelves around him where the Tobies had been. The only things he'd changed that she could see. There were cupboards in this house he'd never opened. The memories he kept, Gwen saw, they were just outlines to all the details that lay in drawers here, untouched. They were just dim shapes. You had to have something definite, you had to make choices to understand the world. He walked to stand over her, his face unable to choose its expression. 'You just meddle! *You only come here because you've got nothing else!'*

She raised her palm, when the words weren't his. She saw his eyes, blinking once, in a moment, before her hand descended. She was slapping his face in the half-lit corridor. Her gaze broke away as, before her, her own blow fell. And making a sound, holding her wrist to her thin chest, Gwen Morgan turned away from Dai and fled the Meredith house again.

The foreman's name was Garvey, Michael Garvey. Those faceless clouds slipped by over Dai's sagging roof, over the hillside and the town, as smooth as oil.

Ruth told Mr Garvey, 'I want to make it beautiful. That's what we're going to do. That's the job. OK? Make the house beautiful.' She laughed with him and asked what it would cost.

He was a tall man, careful. White hair very bright above his red face. Slow as a tree; to speak and to smile, but still warm, holding his notepad by his side. Not wanting it to be intrusive. She could've told him to tear the pages from it and push them at her.

'It was my mother's house,' she said. She turned, moved her cold hands to show him the walls, and they were grey in this light. Even the pink pebbledash, as if the daylight leached man-made colour out of the world. Hugging herself, seeing her own breath in the air, she asked him, 'Do you know what we're doing here?'

'Emyr gave me a brief talk. Privately funded restoration. Throughout the town.' He touched the side of his hair with the back of the hand that held the notepad. 'It's a new one on me, yes.' He gave one soft laugh.

'The whole place,' she said.

Up the lane, eroded by his own crying, Dai was pulling his coat on wrongly and cursing it, throwing it to the floor before grabbing it again, no one to share these rooms and see his shamed face.

'Do you smell that?' Michael Garvey said as they stepped inside Ruth's own house. 'Like dampness? That musty smell? I don't know if you've got used to it, haven't recognized it because it's been around so long . . . I think you may have a deeper problem here,' he shook his head, standing in front of her. 'Have you had a lot of damp? Drips inside? You've had damp problems for a long time?' His brown eyes were passive.

'Damp,' she said. 'It's a cottage. It's always damp.'

He began to talk, pointing carefully every now and then with the hand that held his notepad. And Ruth wondered what his home was like, if he'd had children, if they had left his house now, for college or a lover or a husband. Looking at him, she couldn't imagine the rooms.

'You've a crack in the gutter outside.' He pointed back upwards to her roof, where stains had leaked down on the pebbledash, shadowed and ugly between her bedroom windows. 'You might find that there's some kind of blockage, water collecting, and you reach this time of year – that water will freeze, expand . . . Even steel will crack with just a few raindrops and dead leaves.'

He talked about how that rain must have run through the missing slates' holes. Lain in dampness on the attic rafters. Did it patch on her ceiling, discolour the paint? Hearing it spoken in his voice, she found there came a kind of gratitude. It was stupid maybe, when she didn't know this man, if he had children, a wife, what his own house might look like when he walked into his kitchen and sat down to feel that he was home. She couldn't prevent it, though.

The roofing may have caused larger problems inside. Damp spots.

In the corners of her kitchen ceiling and on the bathroom wall. 'I've painted over them,' she said. 'Or Lennie has.'

He described the way that the bits she'd painted had bubbled out after she'd finished them. He described the small peelings that she would dust from Nia's rug.

'It's not damp really any more,' he said, and grimaced himself over the news. 'That's the smell of dry rot.' He shook his head again, 'That's dry rot. Strong as anything.'

She heard him and gratitude spiralled to nothing. After everything that had happened here, she didn't hate the place, she still felt heartache.

Thursday September the seventeenth 1971

Dear Charlotte,

When I feel bad all I want to do is write. I was very lonely and unhappy yesterday. I wrote four pages. But when I feel good I don't know what to put down. It's not fair that it should be like that because I want to tell you good things as well. I don't want to only write the bad things, I would be a terrible pen friend, I would send all my letters like little black birds. Like crows. I'm going to tell you something good every time I open a page.

Here is my good thing for today. I talked to Anne. I sat in the Dining Hall and I spoke to her for three quarters of an hour. A lot of the girls here wouldn't think it's a very important thing but then I would never ask them for their opinion or anything they think. It is important. I feel scared as well as feeling excited. Maybe I'm an unhappy person naturally. Maybe that is the only reason why I want this to be important.

In reality when you see her closely she doesn't look exactly like me but that doesn't matter. Even some twins aren't exactly the same. It's when she smiles that she doesn't look like me. I am not like Anne, Anne is a very confident person. I told her my name. I opened my mouth and I wanted to say 'Anne' and I had to stop myself. I don't want to be but I am the sort of person that lying comes naturally to. She told me how much she missed her family. Her family's house is in Berkshire, there are fifteen bedrooms but no one ever spends time anywhere except the kitchen. They have proper fireplaces and a stables, all just the same, isn't it? Her horse is a palomino called Lucy.

Berkshire is all meadows, she said to me, but there are no

mountains. Her mother looks like her. Anne showed me a photograph. She keeps it in her pencil case. She asked me about my family. I've had no news from my Mom or Daddy but letters can take up to three weeks to cross the Atlantic Ocean.

I told Anne about the trick with the candle and she said she did want to do it with me. Anne is like all the good sides of me.

There was a stretch of dual carriageway, a lay-by. He had pulled in there and looked in his rear-view mirror, at how the road led back.

There were cities that he knew by nothing but their thoroughfares. Like there was nothing to them but that. Their buildings only blank, windstruck, solid. There were service stations, bypasses, unbroken white lines.

There was this wide passing place.

He had driven back, one hundred and forty-three miles until he passed Ynys-morlan's flagpole again. He'd got out of his cab and looked from the pavement at his house. The sense of fear that had begun days ago, or years ago, he couldn't seem to tell – it struck him as he stood here, with everything it had. Behind, in the street, winter life ground on in its quiet, half-lived way.

Down the lane and into town, Dai came to the Spar, standing by the noticeboard for a minute and looking through the gaps in the window's red lettering, seeing the racks of bread inside. The road was painted in reflection there, how it walked away behind him, and many different days it seemed, laid out, when there'd been no guilt and time had only been a cock's face or the hurry in other people's expressions. It was eleven o'clock now.

It was half past eleven when he left the Spar again, fluorescent light trailing out in his wet eyes as he stepped back on to the street. Bethan Hughes saw him from a distance, over Greta Pugh's shoulder as the woman told her spaniel that cold days like these would be over soon, that he wouldn't have to wear his dogjacket then. For a moment Bethan wanted to tell Dai, run the pushchair right up to him and tell him what she'd come out to do this morning. She watched him walk away, the heavy day stretched across the shoulders of his coat. And when she went to the postbox after seeing him gone – though the Lewises' letter box was twenty yards away – she went alone, a little bird in her head, a little cuckoo, asking her why she wanted reassurance from a man who didn't quite know the difference between real life and fairy tale.

She went into the Spar and Siân wasn't behind the counter but standing by the crisps, zipping up her coat. She only raised her eyebrows, seeing Bethan.

'Well that's timing. I was just about to walk down and see your mother. Thought she might like to hear what I've just heard, though I doubt she'd have liked to see it. Dai Meredith in tears is not a sight to cheer anyone's day . . .'

For as long as Bethan could remember, Siân and Gwen had been there, coming in and out, sitting in the early evenings while her mum took in the signs. Talking like words were about to go up in price, laying each comment down on top of the last, like slates, till no light could get in. A lot of her earliest memories were these. Two years ago, she'd come back to them, though she'd never gone away.

Patty would say, when they'd all been girls, they'd been inseparable. When they had been girls, she'd say, nothing could have pulled them apart. The problem between Gwen and Siân, her mother told her later, hadn't started until John Humphries had died.

Siân had been the first to marry, though it was the photos from Gwen's reception that still hung on the walls. Nice and quiet, Pat had always said, as though there was some other kind of respect that you gave to that. Her mum had been the first to have a kid of course, but Siân had been the first to the altar. Tom and then Stacey shoving their ways out a few years later on. John Humphries had been a builder and he'd had red hair. He'd died in a car accident outside Llanidloes. Pat had told her once that the crash had been on the news.

Gwen had stayed with Siân then. Emyr had been working at the planning office and, on his nights off, he'd been organizing the building of their new home. Most of her days and a lot of evenings, Gwen had stayed with her. Tom a toddler – a terrible two at five years old, Patty said – Stacey not even crawling.

Pat remembered the argument. This was what she said to Bethan, later on: 'I was there, Siân asked me to go round.' She said it as if she'd had misgivings from the start. But then all three of them, Bethan thought, had always been good at early misgivings later on. 'I went round, Siân was in a state already but you know how Siân gets in a state, won't be upset. Angry, is all she'll be. The first thing she said when I walked in: "Pat, I thought maybe you'd like to tell Gwen whose house this is. And maybe whose children these are, I thought maybe you'd like to let her know." And you could see it in the room. Her kitchen. You know her little kitchen? Half of it still a mess – the other half Gwen had started on. I swear, it was funny really. Looking back. Like they were just about to pull their gloves on, ring the bell. And Gwen was telling her, "Don't be ridiculous. If you don't want me doing this now, I won't do it now. I know whose house this is." Like that, but you know Gwen's way. She doesn't mean to but she'll work you up all the more. Just seen too much of each other, that was all it was. They're both stubborn.' Saying this, Pat was quiet for a moment. 'Just seen too much of each other and neither would let it drop. Siân going on about how she's not some cripple. And, course, Gwen won't accept the slightest thing. "If you want to be angry, Siân, just go ahead, and maybe I'll come back later." Like she's got nothing to do with it, you know . . . very understanding. Should never get in a fight with Gwen. Like Superwoman she is in a fight. The Woman That Shows No Anger, you can't rile her. Believe me, Siân tried that day. And I'm trying to break it up, I'm standing between them. I'm not the sort of person that likes confrontation, you know that. I'm doing a terrible job . . .' She showed Bethan; she was animated. The moments when Patty was quiet seemed like some other truth. 'And Gwen keeps saying, "Well obviously now's a bad time. I came to help not argue." And Siân says, "Oh yes, you like everything nice and quiet, and no one getting in the way of your doing things. You like it all just so, and God forbid that someone disagrees with you. How dare I?" she says then. "Isn't that right, Gwen? How dare I, in my own house?" Siân just got angrier. No one could blame her. Not really. Twenty-four, she was when John died. Gwen wouldn't give her an ill word that day – and she was right not to, I'm sure. Then it was only Siân, though. And just shouting and shouting. Tom crying in the other room. Screaming is more like it really.' Pat paused, gave a breath out, as though she might as well tell it all. 'If it'd been me, I would've been more worried than Gwen was. You can't tell what a person's going to do when they've been through so much, when you keep pushing them.'

Her mother looked away, telling Bethan, 'They made up of course. Took them a while, Siân *refusing* to let go. Couple of months, six months maybe, I don't know. Had me running like a blue-arsed fly, with messages between them. I wouldn't have ever thought either of them was the type to hold grudges, though.'

Bethan walked back with Siân to the café that day, past the empty concrete in front of the gift shop, the first few houses, the Lewises' little path, with only the sound of their footsteps and the gentle run of the pushchair's wheels. Ruth's windows were polished and Bethan saw through the glass – her curtains, her kitchen.

She heard the quiet in the street; the morning. Sometimes, in the days when the stillness seemed to lie over every roof and drape on to the road, you could hear the sea, even if the tide had taken it far away.

She didn't know when she was going to tell her mother about the form. She didn't know how she could start, or how Patty's expression might change as she realized just what Bethan was saying. Feeling the cold, she glanced at Siân. And her eyes in return: blunt as a swinging stick.

Garvey told Ruth, looking round her hallway, his voice delicate, 'If I can smell it so clearly it must be extensive by now. Some of the woodwork may need to be replaced. Other parts just stripped down maybe. It might be a lot of work, all in all. The roof most of it,' he said. He waited, looking at her to see her response. 'But I'd make sure that it was done well,' he said. 'I'd make sure the problems weren't just patched over, I'd do it thoroughly –' He stood, with her front door behind him, framed by the brown twists of the sweet pea around it. He kept his arms behind his back. 'I'd make sure that even the littlest things were done well, and done completely. I wouldn't leave a nail,' he said, 'sticking out half an inch too far.'

Nothing different, in this room or through these doors. The third board creaked as always as he walked across the landing. She would hear it, early in dark mornings as Lennie went downstairs to leave. He'd never wake her, climbing out of their bed. The first thing she heard was that creak, coming softly to her, so that she was always awake to listen to the front door close.

Garvey stood at the top of their stairs and looked up at the beams in the ceiling.

'It's a fungus,' he said. 'It feeds off the nutrients in timber, in a house's structure.' He pointed to the oak that must have been black in shadow, every time that Lennie left.

Once upon a time, she'd used to imagine the house upside down. You'd walk round on the ceiling, look up at the floor, sit down for a rest on one of those beams.

He said, 'You see – you see these little crosswise cracks on them, see all the little fissures? It will have been feeding off everything it can get to. It sends out trailers,' Ruth saw him curl his index finger, 'over stone or plaster, until it gets to more timber. Mycelia,' he said. 'They'll spread behind internal walls.'

He showed her internal walls.

He took the penknife from his pocket and she watched him walk from her bedroom door, to Nia's, watched him push the blade slowly into the timber around every door frame. It sunk in easily, she saw.

'It's at an advanced stage. The damp's definitely come down from the missing slates. And the rot's started where the masonry's clammy. Judging by the door frames here, I mean I'm going to have to . . . right-hand side doesn't seem as bad . . . but it's obviously progressed a lot . . . I'm amazed that there aren't any bodies here.'

She had never felt so much a part of the house, never felt its stone and wood more clearly. She looked at him now and saw the easy ten steps it would take him to walk away. She could not walk away.

'The fruiting bodies,' he said. 'Like a mushroom.'

Ruth thought of Nia slowly descending these stairs, early morning, her face a blank and sleep-ridden moon. They might be the fruits, the two of them; the fruiting bodies. She thought of grey marks, spaced out in pairs, undeniable.

As he prised up a floorboard on her landing, Ruth was bound by memories of her dad. From the landing, Michael Garvey spoke to her and she heard a sound outside, similar to Lennie's cab. These fruiting bodies, he said, they were structured with tiny holes.

'It's like cancer,' she responded.

In the attic upstairs they might be growing over rafters. They could be white or pink or red. She'd not been up inside there since her mother had died. This thing could hide behind the paint, though you might clean the walls.

She heard the engine out there die.

Her dad had driven away, glancing back at a house that was spick and span, pastel-coloured, and that he'd never see again. Maybe somewhere behind the windows he'd glimpsed, this rot had already begun. Very small then, growing out its first seeking cords. Years passing, Ruth at six and nine and twelve. She had sat on her bed in the room that belonged to Nia now, imagining a great growth of vine that would cover it all, while white mycelium had spread.

Now Ruth looked up and saw Lennie standing in the doorway. For one moment, she stared at him as if he were a stranger. For all the recognition she felt, it might have been her father who'd just walked in.

The bell above the café's door left them standing in other people's talk. Patty looked up from the tea urn.

Bethan stood beside Siân Humphries. She thought of Dai in her bedroom: reaching out to pick up that bit of cloth. He had a look sometimes, when he talked to you. He saw you from way across the water.

'Have you seen Dai?' Siân said. 'Has he been in here?'

'Not for days . . . Why? Is he all right?'

'Well I'm not surprised, didn't look fit for anything but home. No, he's not all right. He's the opposite of all right, I just stood and listened to him cry for half an hour.'

Bethan touched the hair of Chelsea's head, smoothed it out of her face. She thought of the framed portrait that hung on her wall, the first thing that he must have seen as he'd opened her door.

'Cry? Only natural, poor lamb. Having doubts?'

Bethan lifted Chelsea free. She'd always hated how her mother said that, 'lamb'. False as a bubble. She looked over the heads of the regulars as her mum finished serving and came to sit, chin in hand, carefully piled hair still as plastic.

Siân folded herself down opposite, looking at one point on the tabletop as she said, 'There was nothing natural about it. Doubts aren't his problem. Or not his own, though I'm sure it struck a nerve. No, he was crying because he'd just been slapped! That's why! Because he'd just had to listen to someone shouting at him!' She looked up at Pat and then reached into the pocket in her green Spar smock, took out cigarettes, but for a moment didn't light one. 'Gwen went round to him at eight this morning.'

Bethan stopped, Chelsea in her arms, halfway across the room. 'Gwen Morgan?'

Siân turned to her but said nothing as Patty asked, stunned, 'Slapping him? You've only heard his side of the story. She'd never.'

Bethan listened as Siân let out the words, narrow as smoke.

Gwen Morgan, who never had a thought in her mind that wasn't first inspected and approved. But not so shocking, Bethan thought. Hard to believe she *would* – not so hard to believe that she could. Not underneath that lovely lipstick.

'I don't believe it,' Pat said finally. 'Why would Gwen even want him to change his mind? I mean, Dai's emptying the place out with Emyr . . .'

'Well, there's something going on. She can't feel the same as Emyr, or she wouldn't be going to Dai's house, eight o'clock in the morning, talking till she ends up lashing out!' Siân looked down at the floor, like she would throw this whole business down there if she could, to get dirty, just where it belonged. 'While she's going round, day after day, asking for forms, telling everyone what a *wonderful* thing this is. Do you know what she said to him, Pat? That Eirian would've never have left it to him if she'd known. Believe what you want. You didn't have to look at him.'

'I won't believe it, Siân. You can't think it's true?'

Bethan said, 'Dai Meredith doesn't have a lying bone in his body.'

Their glances trailed back to each other's faces. 'After taking him in, two months,' Siân said, 'cooking for him every day, coming down here to tell us how he's doing. Makes you wonder how she was with him then, doesn't it?'

Pat shook her head. 'She stood at the meeting. She was clapping.'

'Well what does that tell you? She wants people to think she's in favour. *Obviously* she doesn't think it's so wonderful. Obviously, she doesn't want people *knowing* what she thinks. And that includes me. Includes you.'

'Gwen's not a deceitful person. For God's sake.'

'Do you want to go and find him? You don't believe me?' She stared at Patty, who was wordless as she looked back. 'To pretend . . . Pretend and all the while be working underhand. To take it out on Dai . . .'

'We've not heard what she's got to say.'

'No, and if she walked in here now and we asked her how she felt about this "project"? I've heard her the whole last week. I know what she'd say, Pat, I've seen it a hundred times over! "Behind it one hundred per cent."'

Pat was quiet, surmising, ascertaining. 'I'd like to ask her.'

'This Weyland woman comes with her ideas and her money. Grant system. Everyone can have a piece! Free for all, dig in up to your elbows!' Bethan saw her run a tongue inside her mouth. 'Why not? And there's Gwen, never still for a moment with all the nodding and agreeing. And then at Dai's house, eight o clock in the morning.' Siân put a hand across her mouth. 'She slapped him, Pat. *Hit* him. His cheek was red, you could make it out.'

Bethan saw her mum's face. Couldn't help but wonder, though her thoughts went out to Dai, what that quiet shock meant for the news she'd have to give.

'I'll go and speak to her. Not today. I'll give it a little time, if she's . . . if she's upset,' Patty determined, by inches.

Looking out through the broad glass beside them, the street was fallow. Cold lay in heavy currents. Quiescent. A feeling like the town had no reason to be here until the summer came again. Five days until this dormancy was cut with the noise of engines.

Bethan turned to see her mother's expression again, but it wasn't Patty who caught her eye. It was Tom. Standing behind the counter with nothing in his hands. He was looking at their table through the low flux of voices. Looking at Siân.

Bethan heard her mum say, 'It can't be true.'

'You go and speak to her if you want. I won't.' Siân pointed the words with her still-dry cigarette. 'I'll wait and see. How she is outside the gift shop.' She gave herself a nod. 'Demolition day – how she is then.'

Lennie Lewis had come home to a man in his house. A man with white hair and his coat off. Lennie'd stood for long moments and looked from this man to Ruth. He had been right. The fear had been. He stood lost.

'What are you doing here?' The town seemed like an island to him: sunk in the ocean a little deeper every time he came home. 'I don't know you. What are you doing?'

He saw the notepad in the man's other hand. He saw, around his feet, the carpet was pulled back.

'Michael Garvey,' the man said. He walked down Lennie's stairs and into his hall, and he held out his hand then. 'Your wife called me in for an estimate on this work.'

Ruth looked at him. 'Our house has got dry rot,' she said.

In the lull of their two voices, his own voice echoed like he was the stranger. 'Lennie Lewis,' he said.

October the third 1971

Dear Charlotte,

Today I showed Anne the trick with the mirror. I showed myself really because I'd never done it before. We did it in her dorm with a candle that a girl lent to her. She said that she would be the sort of woman who looks old when they are only twenty five. I don't think that's true. I drew the candle down around my face and you can see the shadows change. It looks like you're fifty years older by the time you hold it near your chin. I saw myself old. I looked like someone I didn't even know.

Michael Garvey left them in their house. He'd talked about treatment and rebuilding. And as he went, Ruth just stood, not an inch from where she'd been when Lennie had come in, her hand as light as rain on the banister. The hallway seemed to close around them and leave Garvey in the last space of daylight that filtered through the glass of their front door.

Turning back, unable to see his wife's eyes, it felt like safety to speak. Some listing, buoyant safety above this house's silence.

'Are you happy then . . . ? Did you get what you wanted . . . ? *Disobeyed* me, fucking did exactly what I told you not to.' He wiped his mouth as though what he felt might be spilling out to show on his face, but she wasn't looking at him. 'Is this how you think of me then? *Is this it?* Someone you have to get out of the way before you can do what you want to.'

She stared at the slates by her feet. The guest had whispered away.

'I don't believe you, Ruth. Don't believe how much you're fucking . . . *changing*. Becoming a selfish, lying, fucking deceitful woman! Got a bit of power and suddenly you reckon you can ruin . . . you can just . . .'

He stepped off their welcome mat and on to the slate floor, walking towards her with a look of confusion, misgivings as dark as the walls.

He was huge when he got angry and his expressive face would cave in upon itself. In their hall he seemed to drag up and wrap around himself all the slate and stone dark; tangled in it. He walked past the little phone table, the vase of dried flowers. Set perfectly in the centre of the stairs that rose behind her, she seemed like something from a painting to him. Sweet and small and dark. Full of hidden lies. He hadn't known what he'd been afraid of, all these gathering days, hadn't known. But it had been right to feel it. There was no trust between them any more. He reached her where she stood, the faint day only a hue on her, raising her face up to him. She didn't flinch or even look at his hand. He hit her with pain, with dismay.

She let go of the oak banister. She stepped back – and so up – and redness spread across her cheek. She could feel it here, this rot. She moved away from him, ducked down and from the staircase. He followed her effortlessly though; he came through the doorway into their living room and stared at her, voiceless. He stood in front of the bookcase, framed photos of the two of them and Nia set in little groups. The man in the photographs stood with his head up. Smiling or serious, that face would inspire feelings; handsome features that couldn't show anything but coal and confidence, eyes that were beautiful and didn't hide their intensity, or the need underneath them.

She couldn't look up at him now, where he stood in front of them, remembering the excitement that he'd had, that they'd both had, when he'd first moved in here. He had used to say he loved the house, rub the arm of the sofa that was at her back now, touch the wall as though these things were lucky, and it had meant something to her. She'd used to think of him as some wayward boy who'd never had a home before.

She'd been stupid. She'd been in love. She'd walked through the rooms in this house and made good things of all the memories. Believed in only good things for their future. She'd talked about how they'd get through any hard times, but the word 'hard' had sounded gentle. The meaning of it hadn't even touched her. People said that love was blind, they didn't say how it blinded you, by making the colours brighter when you looked out of your window. It was blind because it made everything beautiful. She remembered sitting on a bench in the street and seeing Ynys-morlan as a perfect place, the first and only time in her life. Nothing needed, no work, no change.

She stood with her back to the sofa now. Things like that could fall away.

'I come in here,' he said slowly, 'at two o'clock in the afternoon, and you don't even ask why I'm not working. You don't ask why it is that I might've decided to stop in the middle of a haul and pull into a fucking lay-by and turn around and start driving home. I find you in here with a man I don't know from Adam, like, pricing up a job that I've already told you we *mustn't start yet*! How would you feel, Ruth, if you came home and found me doing that same thing?'

The carpet, a pale soft pink, was shaded where it met the slate. 'I'd feel lost.'

'Angry!' he shouted. 'Angry is how you'd fucking feel!'

'I don't know,' she said. 'I don't get angry, do I?'

'No! Keep all your anger locked up in there, don't you?' He reached from the doorway towards the sofa, stabbed at her temple with his index finger. 'Take all your anger and store it up like poison, so you can spit it all behind my back, so you can act for just your own – your own selfish fucking interests!' He jabbed her temple again and Ruth tried to move her head away. In the subtle daylight of their living room, his words seeming to slide from the reflections on each polished surface, she could try to dodge or run from him, she could put her arms over her face so that he couldn't hurt her as much, she could go to the corner of the room, between the armchair and the fireplace, wedge herself in there where he could hardly reach her – she would feel the armchair drawn away. He'd hit her. And later she would come back down from their bedroom and put the sofa's wheels back into their little indentations on the carpet. She would drag up this crocheted shawl from the floor and arrange it again on the sofa's back.

He was saying to her that she took all her anger and stored it up to give back in lies. He wasn't making sense. Sometimes she thought it was confusion, all this anger. That he was scared because he was confused.

'D'you think just because you've got some rich woman prepared to let you in on her grand gesture, suddenly you needn't *listen* to your stupid husband, you can just wait till your stupid husband's out of the way and then get on with what you want! You've got some fucking ego on you now, Ruth! You don't care, do you? Like it's the first grand idea the world ever had, just because it's the first one to you! You don't care!'

'I had a grand idea,' she said. 'It was us.'

He took her by both shoulders and shook her, knocking her into the sofa's back. He pushed her but his hands were like wood, joined to this house. He kept shouting but his own voice was dull to him. He shoved her and he could almost hear her asking him to stop, though she wasn't asking him this time.

'You've not got the slightest fucking clue how important this is for me, have you?' He thrust her back again. 'This is everything! We're going to make sure *every single person applies*! When someone hears from fucking whatshername next door – a *thought*, a piece of news, the *tiniest fucking thing* – we've got to make sure it tips the balance the right way! You know what a fucking fine edge it is? Between applying and not applying? Between making this town something that matters and making a great fucking madness of it? Every night I'm lying in bed, wondering what could go wrong with this. Trying to think how we could stop it going wrong! Anticipating! *Trying to think of the million fucking tiny things that could end up ruining this for us!*'

'That's all you've seen, from the start.'

He stared at her, disabled: those pretty, pale eyes turned down toward the floor as she refused to look at him. It wasn't the things that she'd hidden behind her face which dragged up this fear and hate in him. It wasn't any secret that she'd kept. Because he looked at her now and she seemed more beautiful with this secret than she'd looked to him every night, standing in the hall, waiting for him as he'd opened the door.

When he hit her, pain showed on his face.

'Maybe you don't remember how it used to be, maybe it doesn't sicken you to watch this place shrink! Nothing but a dying dump!' He slapped her face, when he didn't know why. He saw around them, their little fireplace, their sofas and chairs. His hands felt numb. 'Maybe you never saw it – maybe you never saw yourself part of anything more than that in the fucking first place –' He drew his hand back and she saw the hesitation, but he looked as if he needed – and would have to – feel something as he brought it down. She bent, tried to move away, the sofa rocked behind her. He heard it thump against the coffee table, magazines sliding off the glass to lie boneless on the carpet. 'You've got no idea!' he said, but there was a rupturing in him, he felt it. 'No fucking clue what this thing means to me! I've been waiting . . . *I've been waiting!* You never wanted anything! *You've never wanted anything in your whole fucking life!'*

He watched her stumble away, her hand on the back of the armchair, her eyes woeful and cutting him. Saw her say, 'I wanted to have kids with you. That's what I wanted, have kids and live here and that was going to be amazing. Do you remember how amazing you said it would be?'

He wanted to raise his fist and hit her again, until his words voiced something. *'I'm not the one fucking lying and ruining it! I'm not the one!'*

He saw her put her hands up to her face and hold the places that he'd hurt her. Sometimes he wanted to punish her just for being who she was. He closed his eyes, as if the sounds in this house echoed back his own shouts. As if the echoes were as full of rot as this room's pretty cottage beams.

'What were you going to do if I hadn't come home? Just keep right on smiling, standing in the hall? Tell me what we were going to have for dinner, and bring me in, and sit me down. Ask me how my fucking day's been just the same as every other night! Then we can go to bed at ten o'clock and lie there next to each other, not touch each other just lie there till the fucking morning! What were you going to do? *I'm not the one who's ruined how amazing we could've been!'*

He came across to where she stood and he raised his voice and he raised his face over her but the violence in him was hollow. Like everything around them now, these fucking painted walls, these furnishings that shifted slightly as he pushed her. In their picturesque living room, both of them were worn through. They'd had their meaning stolen away from them. He could punch her. In this house, after three years, it would mean little. She raised her face. Lennie looked like he was grieving. There were cracks across his features.

And Ruth watched something pass through him. She felt it; something shared. A loss that they could not communicate. She looked in his eyes and felt it in her own.

Their house was filled by the sounds they made, each vacant room. There'd been a time when he'd come back to her and given her apologies and promises. He'd had to beg her to trust him again. It had used to take weeks, she remembered, before she'd even let him kiss her.

Tuesday

Charlotte, all my thoughts have all been robbed away from me
and ripped up just into pieces. Anne read my diaries. All
myself has been dug into and spoiled, just ruined. I came
upstairs because I forgot my Draftbook. I could hear someone in
the dorm before I knocked but I thought I was wrong. I thought
it was outside because I heard the relays starting down in the
quadrangle and most of my dorm have all got PT on a Wednesday.
But when I opened the door she was there. She was reading
them. She had them all out everywhere. How dare she how dare
she just take away everything that's mine like that and make it
hers. But the worst the worst was what she said. She said she
was trying to help me but she wasn't. She said she only read
them because she cared about me. How can I believe her though?
She was so horrible! They do love me. I'm not nothing to them.
It wasn't wrong of them. She doesn't know. She doesn't. I will
never speak to her I will never be her friend. She knew when
I'd be away. I feel so angry and I feel sad as well because I
don't know anyone here. I don't know anything about England or
London outside Haberdashers' even what the places are called or
what they look like. I could be nowhere. I'm so scared. They
haven't written. It's not true what she said. They did deserve
me.

On the 26th of January, two days before the bulldozers arrived, Patty Hughes went to the Morgans' house. She came to park next to Gwen's car, switched off the engine. No birds were talking in the frozen sky. She closed the car door firmly and left her coat inside there, waiting for the warmth of the house.

A lovely place. New brick but tasteful. Big but not too big. The flower beds were bare now but spring hadn't come yet. They were bare everywhere.

Her knuckle left three clean taps on the door. She ignored the bell beside it. And when Gwen came, and opened the hallway up, and stood between her and its white-with-a-hint-of-peach security, Patty found her hand falling again and wished she had brought her coat, or a bag, or something to hold.

Gwen's face was pale and closed. It didn't seem to know her.

She'd planned to be straight; the world was pointless if you couldn't be straight with the people you cared for. But there wasn't any way, seeing that expression, to use the words that she'd prepared.

'Are you all right?' was all she said.

'All right? Yes. I'm all right,' Gwen answered.

'Just came to check in on you. Haven't seen you. Wondered if you . . . if there's anything wrong.'

Gwen didn't seem touched, or surprised, or curious. Her face was a fading day.

'That's kind of you,' she said. Like Pat was trying to sell her the fourth layer of glazing for these windows.

They spoke of nothing. Really they didn't speak. Just exchanged hellos and goodbyes and Patty left, shocked, without having spoken Dai's name. Full of wonder, as Gwen waved from the doorstep and faded back into that lovely new-brick home of hers.

Wednesday December the first

Mommy's letter came today. It says I have betrayed her by leaving. I don't want to write.

That evening, the demolition approaching, just the day after to-morrow and everything in Ynys-morlan's sodium-glazed dark still unchanged, each front step frozen silent, Ruth stood before her kitchen sink, and the window, the house around her uncharted without light; full of Lennie's sleep. She looked out at the road and listened to the running water.

In the living room, the television played with the colours and shapes of Busby Berkeley's long-feathered fans. She'd let Nia fall asleep there, having taken her out of her bed once Lennie had gone to theirs. She had looked at Nia's face every minute or so, making certain that she slept, all cuddled up between the cushions and the shawl on the sofa's back. Yes here it was in one picture: embroidery and shadow, cosiness, childhood. Ruth had watched her, one hand across her mouth, and had cried.

The hallway was full of silhouettes, gentle glints from the glass that covered the wildflower pictures, a flicker on the mirror's brown oval as Ruth now slowly climbed the stairs. She carried the bowl full of washing-up liquid bubbles and they made a tiny tide there, they washed in and they washed out, from one hand to her other. The house seemed to hold them in its perfect picture as she pushed open the door to Nia's room.

By the 27th of January, the gift shop's site fully prepared and Emyr's team scheduled to set up site at nine the next day, there was a list of six properties for Charlotte Weyland to view for purchase. The first, called Ty Heulog, stood halfway down the stretch of Ynys-morlan's street.

On the telephone, the woman spoke slowly. Charlotte stood beside the small table in her hallway and listened. Audrey Pryce had lived here since her parents had brought her as a girl, fifty-seven years ago.

'When you look at Ynys-morlan now,' Mrs Pryce said, 'all the houses back on to the beach. See, no one mentions it, and all the tourists come here in the summer and they see the place and they think, well that's funny, because you get in most seaside towns, a line of houses and they all look out over the beach. Or a promenade. Silly to build a clutch of houses by the sea, all of them with their backs to it. They'll think that, the tourists, but what they don't know is that those houses weren't built by the shore at all. In the middle of a stretch of land, they used to be, with almost an acre between them and the coast. And the sea, it encroached.'

She said that she could remember when her back garden had looked out on meadowland. They had used to cut hay there, she told Charlotte. Her neighbours had used to rear pigs and she'd stood with a broom and shouted at them when they'd broken through, like her father had. She said she'd always been her father's girl.

The meadows had run in a series behind the houses. From their fenced edges, the grass had dropped suddenly away into a loose scree of rock which had met the highest tides every March and had fallen, for the rest of the year, to only the smallest stony beach, fifteen or twenty yards below. The boys, she said, had used to race each other down. All of them sitting in a line along those fences and pushing themselves free at the same time. Her memories were of the summer. Men cutting out there by hand and other things that sound now, she said, a sight more idyllic than they'd been for her father then. Everything sounds like it's idyllic when you look back, she said. And

Charlotte answered that she believed some people remembered only summertimes.

When the first fence had fallen, Audrey Pryce said, and left them with only a grassy cliff edge, they'd re-fenced it. September it had been, but over the years they had re-fenced it many times.

When the woman ran to the end of a memory, Charlotte asked questions which might encourage more. About the woman's own house, about her parents' background. She thought of this town, full of its residents and its history, full of its friendships and families, its colloquialisms, the accents she heard around her when she stood in the small shops and couldn't soften her own voice to blend with. When Ruth spoke of the project the way she loved her home was obvious; external. She threw everything she had into her vision of its ending. When Charlotte searched something that brought up feelings like this, though, it was the mountains that she found.

She would see them past the distance of the floodplain, the trees at their base blended to a brown line, the mountains themselves rising multicoloured. Rust and rose and the dim green of land never used. The furthest ridges would seem almost blue.

The sense that they brought swelled in the place of something empty. Curves and barren ridges, great sweeping cavities. The deepest beauty, as if the lines of people's bodies and faces were only brief reflections. Empty of people, she loved them.

She wanted to feel something for Ynys-morlan. For the project. The next time that she was with Ruth, watching her spill her ideas with that enthusiasm, almost thoughtless, she wanted to see Ruth's face and know she was capable of reaching out like that too. So distant as Charlotte stared out, the mountains seemed to give back love. She wasn't writing in her journals now, but reading them. At nights, she didn't cry but she lay sometimes, arms around herself, as if something threatened to escape.

Ty Heulog stood three doors down from the public house. A small building, huddled windows. Seeing it from the path, you might imagine twisting stairs and tiny corridors. She stood there early; nine o'clock in the morning as Mrs Pryce had requested. Rain-misted cobwebs over her umbrella as she stood, dressed as carefully as she'd been on her very first day in this town; the past seemed to draw closer, rather than diminish.

'This is Jo,' Mrs Pryce said, pointing to the toddler on her own lap in a photograph.

'And that's Claire there.' Claire was a girl of maybe eight or nine, wearing jodhpurs and standing in a field, holding her riding hat in both hands. 'You should see her rosettes. Three firsts she's had.'

'I used to ride. As a child,' Charlotte said.

She hadn't telephoned Ruth to ask for company. It might have been easier, better. Showing Charlotte the rooms, the woman seemed full of disappointment. She'd tidied and polished and cleaned, though of course there was no question of the house not being bought.

The photographs were framed in silver, set in little groupings on the mantelpiece and on top of the television. In the house behind her, Charlotte kept one photograph only. It was laid between the pages of her first volume.

Audrey Pryce showed her every window's view.

'This is the best in the morning,' she said. 'Light comes in here about nine o'clock and you'll get it then till one. This is a good spot for reading, by this window. I often read here.'

She turned to lead her through the next room.

'We could build a seat there perhaps,' Charlotte said. 'Into the window, for reading.'

Mrs Pryce turned in the doorway, nodded slightly. Her hair, curled and pale, shifted as if it might have been a wig. 'You could do that,' she said, her face unchanging. She glanced a moment at the window, the sea moving at low tide, more than a mile out it seemed. 'You'll want the backrest on the right-hand side if you do that. Light comes in,' she showed Charlotte with her hand. 'It'll catch you in the eyes . . . You can see the edge of the bay that way too.'

And then she led Charlotte upstairs to the bedrooms.

'This is the guest room.'

It was decorated like a palace for a child, lace and soft toys laid on the bed, a gilt oval mirror on one wall. Mrs Pryce shut the door on it.

'This is my room now,' she said, leading Charlotte through. The television was placed at the end of the bed, many books on the side table. Romances and cookery, Charlotte saw. The patchwork quilt was handmade and this window looked out on the sea too. The photographs were everywhere, set in careful patterns, a family gathering. She watched Mrs Pryce walk towards the television and wipe the dust clear with her sleeve.

She showed Charlotte where the catches on the bedroom window were broken, how they didn't close properly any more. She pushed it back and forwards, raised her hands like there was nothing you could say to a piece of plastic that wouldn't even do its job, and then she turned away from the window.

'There's nothing else really.'

'Well, there doesn't need to be anything else. It's a beautiful house.' She turned her eyes down to the floor. She heard, soft as the sound of the sea inside a conch shell, the stream of chatter that would have come from Ruth now.

'My daughter's down in Newport, works in Cardiff. She doesn't want a place by the sea. Couldn't have one even if she wanted it, because of the job, you know,' she took a breath and tightened her mouth, looking up at Charlotte Weyland. 'You like it then?'

'If it was my house,' as it would be soon, she thought without wanting to, 'I don't think I'd like to leave it.'

'Well. It's only a house. You get to my age, if you don't see what's important by then and what isn't . . . It's only a house.' She didn't look around, at the walls or at anything in the room. She seemed like the face of it all, standing there, though, an expression as bare as every private thing that lined her bedroom's shelves.

'You moved here about three months ago, isn't it?' She turned to sit on the edge of her bed, her palms resting on the patchwork, leaving Charlotte standing on her own.

'Three months ago, that's right. In mid-October.' She found herself unable to raise her stare from her hands, an awkwardness that was moulded into crisp politeness. But she felt the woman's eyes, unmoving on her.

'You've no family here, though.'

'No. My family was in the US.'

'Been down here before you moved in then?'

'No, no I hadn't. I'd never been to Wales until I came to look for property here. I wanted to find somewhere quiet.' So now the questions would come.

'Well it's certainly that. Or has been up till now.'

Charlotte lifted her eyes but didn't answer. There was no answer she could give.

'I only ask,' the woman said, 'because I'll be moving to a new place now in a few weeks. Mind you, I've got family where I'm going. And I'm still nervous of it.' Her eyes, though, pallid as if from the wear of watching everything at a distance, showed no nerves as she looked at Charlotte. 'Must be a sight more anxious-making when you don't. And when you don't know the place.'

'Well . . . it's always difficult. They say that moving home is the second most stressful thing in life, don't they.' She cleared her throat.

'After divorce, is that?' Mrs Pryce laughed.

'I don't know.'

And as always, the woman's laughter fell away and left Charlotte in silence. Standing then, her hands holding each other as she observed the view – the only place where her eye didn't seem invasive – Charlotte saw herself, the position in which she had put herself, with a clarity that cut. To come here, to buy and renovate houses which she couldn't even fix a gaze on once inside; she didn't know what she was doing. She looked from the grey seaview, soft and blending into the sky, to the woman on the bed. She thought of the day that she had watched the garden burn with Ruth, full of defiance then, and she felt punctured now.

'You've not asked many questions about the house,' Audrey Pryce told her quietly.

'Well, as I said, it's lovely. Obviously there's no doubt about the sale . . .' And her mouth filled with that politeness; privacy which had no place here. Perhaps her place was in her study, signing the cheques, fulfilling the goal she had set with this project; the only reason she'd begun it.

'About the structure,' the woman said, 'or anything like that, any problems it's got. You haven't asked.'

'Well . . . is there something I should know?'

'Well I don't know. There must be a hundred things.'

'Obviously the surveyors will deal with any details.'

'There's nothing that you want to know then. For yourself.'

'There's nothing I can think of.'

Her eyes didn't move over the room either. 'Mrs Weyland,' she said.

'Miss.' She shifted her hands.

'Miss Weyland, I'm sure you're going to think I'm rude in asking, being as we haven't met before. But then we're probably not going to meet again, and I'm sure standing up in front of us all and giving speeches counts as some kind of meeting. Think me rude if you want to anyway, but I'm going to ask.' She smiled a little. 'You know everyone in town thinks you're doing this as a business venture.'

'I don't know what everyone thinks.'

'Well there you go, I've just told you then. Personally I think that's the stupidest idea I ever heard. If you really do have your thirty-three million pounds, I'm sure there must be an awful lot of business ventures you could make more money on than this. Ones that wouldn't mean having to go into people's homes. You're obviously not comfortable with it.'

'That's not the case.'

'Well there's no need to worry about it. I wouldn't be comfortable with it either, not in this situation.' She shifted her hands on the patchwork quilt and Charlotte looked at her, for a moment without self-consciousness as the woman asked, 'It's not a business venture to you. Is it really, Miss Weyland?'

'I wanted it to be just the opposite.'

'Well, I'll ask you my rude question then.' Audrey Pryce's eyes were clouded. 'Why would you want to put your mark on a place you've got no connection to?'

Charlotte stood in silence. Mrs Pryce's eyes were old, on this girlish bed with pretty furniture all around.

'I don't want to "put my mark" on anything.'

'That can't be true. I don't believe that. You don't start something up like this unless you want to put your thumbprint on it, surely.'

Remembering all the words in her journals, all the hundreds of thousands of detailed, documented thoughts, Charlotte stood here now empty-handed.

Mrs Pryce said quietly. 'I'm sorry, if I put it badly. You're buying this house, though, I want to know.'

'I haven't considered it as putting my mark on anything. The project, the conception of the project, was Ruth Lewis's.'

'But you've come in here. What are you going to do to the place?' she said suddenly. 'The house, the town. All of it. What does it look like in your mind, when you see it finished?'

Charlotte had nothing to say. The words washed and broke against something hard inside her. She'd once termed it 'privacy' but it wasn't privacy to feel embarrassment, to feel disgust, for the things that came from her own mouth. It wasn't privacy to always be afraid.

'The project is only what the residents here choose to make it. If they want to apply for renovations, or to sell their homes, they're able to.'

'Of course, and people here are going to make everything of it that they can. They need some money, they're sick of returns that go down every year. They want to see the place built into something important. That's what comes with tourism. It was never like that. People have to rely now . . . on what a stranger might think when they drive round the bend and into town. What did *you* think then? The first day you came here, what did you think?'

'I thought . . . I believe I thought that the town looked temporary.' There was some admission in her voice.

'Are you looking to make it more permanent then?' the woman said with a small smile.

'No, that isn't what I meant –' Charlotte stopped; a breath. 'I want to give . . . to give the people here the chance to make the town into what they would like.'

She remembered Ruth's dawning, stumbling smile as they'd watched the flames.

'You don't know what mark you want to make,' Mrs Pryce said. She looked at Charlotte's face and seemed to see easily, clearly, past the expensive clothes, the faint lines around her eyes and touches of grey in her hair. She looked at Charlotte and seemed to see a girl. To show her with one silence the spreadeagled canvas that Ynys-morlan was now for whatever she might choose. 'Well,' she said, 'that seems more dangerous to me than if the project was a business venture.'

There was a quiet then, it seemed to bring the future to this woman's home, and the emptiness that would hang here.

'I don't want to put any stamp of my own here,' Charlotte said again; the first time she spoke to the woman with no distance in her voice. And Mrs Pryce nodded, but her eyes were as grey as the seaview from her bedroom window, where reaches of grass had once grown.

'Maybe not,' she said, 'but everyone who lives here does. And you want to give them the chance.'

She turned her face away from Charlotte. She seemed already to be a woman leaving.

The first form that was not an application for sale was returned to them that morning. Pushed through the letter box in the Lewises' front door, it fell on the welcome mat Ruth had bought from a catalogue two years before – just like the one her mum had once come home with. Something new every Saturday. As if to show guests how small the things were that she could buy.

'Twenty pence for that, I could have said to them: if that's all they think it's worth then I won't be the one to argue.'

It lay across the lettering, face upward. And Ruth, standing upstairs in a room that was as empty as Charlotte's childhood home must have been when she'd finally shut the doors and walked away, heard even the soft fall of the envelope. She had almost finished clearing. It was eleven o'clock. Tomorrow the bulldozers and in a few days, no more, Michael Garvey's team. Ruth was preparing.

The dry rot's growth was soundlessness. It had spread inside the walls. She turned away from the room, towards this single little sound. Outside, the postman turned and closed the garden gate behind him. She stood on her own in their hollow bedroom. She wondered if this was how Charlotte had felt last year.

Yesterday morning, she'd sat in bed and watched Lennie get dressed for work while the streetlight was still touching their curtains and the bedside lamp was on beside her. She had asked him how many forms he thought they needed to have in before they let the work start in this house. She hadn't been able to prevent herself.

He'd turned, shirt hanging loose against his chest, a pullover in his hand. He'd said, 'You do it whenever you see fit, Ruth. Do it whenever Charlotte Weyland sees fit. Just be sure to tell me the date so I'll be able to expect it when I'm driving home.'

'It's not like that, Lennie –'

'Stand where I'm standing if you want to see what it's like. You're sitting in bed there. I wonder what little decisions you'll make today, like. Wonder what fun ideas you and Mrs Weyland'll have today, and call up Emyr Morgan to tell him about. Let me tell you something, Ruth,' he'd said. 'I haven't seen this town in the daylight since last Sunday. It's funny that. You get to winter and you leave in the dark and you come back home in the dark. Gets to be so it's only places that you don't care about that you're ever seeing while they're awake. You could've started building six days ago, Ruth, I wouldn't have known any different.

'You know the funniest thing?' he'd said. 'Seems like every time I get off a motorway, they're building. Can't drive five miles out of town without seeing scaffolding. Doesn't matter where you go, they're building more of it. More to go round the edges, more to fill up the last little spaces, homes and shops and when you're finished with the shops they've got new cafés where you can sit, look at the other people shopping.' He'd nodded, gestured. 'They're building walkways between the shops then, they're building great big glass domes –' he raised his hands, the pullover shifting, roll-necked and thick for the cab's first morning cold, 'great glass domes,' he'd said, 'with so much chrome you'd think the things would fall down by the weight of themselves and end up as nothing but great big smashed-up piles of their own fucking shininess. You know why they're building them?' And she had shaken her head. 'Costing millions of pounds,' he'd said, 'and all because, when you put a great big glass dome over the top, the shops look nice in the light.'

She saw him clearly, every day more starkly, against these rooms.

'So maybe it doesn't matter whatever you do, like,' he'd told her. 'Whenever you do it. Maybe Ynys-morlan's not such a grand fucking project after all. Just a tiny little project that seems big to us, because we don't know the difference. Just the straggling tail of what's happening everywhere else. And you and me and everyone in Ynys-morlan can't even fucking see it.'

'It's important for us, though. It's something for us.' To her own ears, the dry rot's silence had stolen something from her voice. Truth maybe.

And, carrying his pullover still, shirt half-tucked in to the back of his trousers, he'd left the bedroom and, sitting, not looking after him, she'd heard his feet tread regularly across the landing, where two floorboards leaned against the wall, untouched since Garvey had pulled them up. Between the little velvet ottoman and the foot of their bed then, he came back to stand and hold out the address book that they kept on the phone table. His look, determinism as he stared down at her, seemed to rise and fall with his breathing.

'Phone him today, why don't you? Phone him today, tell him to come and start the ripping down just as soon as he can get here. Tell him to bring a sign, like, so he can stick it up in the garden just in case there's no scaffolding and people mightn't know that he's working on our place already. Tell him to bring a fucking sign.'

He had turned away and finished dressing, his back to her.

And she'd said to him quietly, 'Why can't you just be happy with it? It's all happening. The gift shop and our own house now and we've had in the For Sale forms, it's all happening.' Beneath them and around them the rot moved, a still wave of growth that spread like water. 'I can look out through the windows, you know? And I can imagine it, I can see how it's going to be . . . Why can't you be happy?

You said to me, you've been waiting. This is meant –' but she looked down at the address book, bent in her lap and cast away from him, and she didn't say what it was meant to be.

Lennie had turned around before he'd left and said, 'You look lovely. Really lovely at the moment, do you know that? Really fucking beautiful.'

He'd averted his face from her. In that moment she'd wanted to tell him that he looked beautiful as well, that he still looked beautiful to her. His profile and his eyes were dark, a curl of hair falling across his forehead like he was still twenty-two years old.

She'd said nothing, scared of him. Scared these days, that everything would hurt him. She'd only watched him leave, listened to his footsteps and the soft click of the front door, and lay there looking at their pretty room. Even this home, she'd thought, even now, still looked beautiful to her, and she'd wondered what beauty was, that you could see it in something that made you feel so sad.

When the first form fell into their home, Ruth had finished emptying the bedroom. She had finished Nia's room and constructed two new makeshift bedrooms downstairs. Working hard, without breaks, lifting, packing, hauling, she'd picked up Nia's desk and had not looked down at the clean wall, as if this house reflected the part inside her which could not be cleaned.

She took everything in the bedrooms that she could carry out through the doorways, and she thought all the time of her mother, like she could render over any thoughts with the working; just the same way that her mother had.

The envelope on her welcome mat read 'To Ruth Lewis'. Letters that were round and clear like bubbles. In the daylight that reached from the door, Ruth could see the colour of the form. It was green.

She walked to it and looked down without touching it. She read the words again.

By half past twelve, when Gwen Morgan stepped out of her house to drive to the playschool for its Friday afternoon class, Nia's bedroom and Ruth's own were vacant rooms. And Ruth was driving herself, dropping Nia in among the other children who stood around the community centre's door, driving herself, back down the road and into town again and through it, towards Charlotte Weyland's house, the unopened envelope lying in her lap.

White windows and stone, seen across a yellowed lawn. Ruth wondered how this would have felt if there'd been no dry rot in her own home. It walked and talked in her, grew in her. She'd told Charlotte about it. Charlotte had said that it didn't matter because the money was not there to be retained. Ruth had felt guilt. She'd thanked her – perhaps too much, perhaps too brightly.

She held the envelope in both hands, the car locked behind her. Charlotte didn't open the door when she knocked, instead Ruth heard her on the other side of its blank wood, asking quietly who was there.

'Charlotte? It's me. I should've called, I'm sorry.'

But she opened the door with a small smile, her face fainter, more bare. She must have been wearing a very little make-up on every occasion Ruth had seen her. Dressed to see no one, Charlotte's hair was drawn back in only a loose pony-tail. A long skirt, shoes that were worn. She seemed less like a woman with money and, seeming that way, more obviously a woman on her own. As if richer women were happier alone.

She held out the envelope and the green form showed through.

'I just got in the car and came,' she said, and laughed a little. 'Is that all right?'

'Of course. Of course it is. You know that.' She bent to kiss Ruth politely on both cheeks. Ruth said nothing, feeling her cold skin for only a moment, and then she was looking at her, standing in the doorway once again. 'It arrived just now?'

'Just now.'

'A proposal or an existing business?'

'Don't know, don't have the faintest.' She passed the envelope to her. 'We could have wine. Should be toasting this really, shouldn't we?'

'We could have wine.' Charlotte smiled. Behind, the leaden garden, the lines of cold, bare trees seemed to have no more motion than the expression on Ruth's face. 'First one.'

Charlotte nodded. 'I suppose that must mean it's actually happening.'

'Means everyone else believes it.'

'But you don't look happy.'

'Don't I?' The question was genuine, it turned like wood that's lain a long time in the ground; still dry, new-seeming on the surface. 'How do I look then?'

'Anxious,' she said.

'Good thing for us that no one else has noticed.' Ruth looked back at her. 'You don't seem very happy. You know how you look to me? You look anxious.' And she gave another smile.

The hallway was still and dim.

'What date will the work begin at your house?'

'ASAP now. Next Monday, Tuesday. I emptied the two rooms out today.'

She'd begun while there was still no light outside, unable to lie in their bed after he'd left when the first light wouldn't come till hours later. She kept a wicker chair beside the window, books resting next to it. Though she felt it, it seemed to the eye like there couldn't be dry rot.

'Took everything out, even got the bed out. Not the base, you know, but the mattress. Trying to get it downstairs. Shouting at the thing while I stood there, you know? "Why won't you move? Why are you such a stupid bastard mattress?" Only time I ever get angry, inanimate objects.'

She'd set it out in the living room. Moved all the furniture again and again, rearranging it in different circles, like this room was meant for a bedroom. She had put their bedside table next to their mattress on the floor, put their lamp on top of it, surrounded by all the real furniture. Hating herself for not being able to let go and just dump the stuff down there as someone younger would have done. Have fun with it, as someone else would have. Instead there'd been a sudden sense of the lack. Just of the small things, the arrangements, the normality of any place that looked like home. She had seen the bed and the clutter all around it; felt lost in her own living room. Stability gone.

'You'd think empty rooms would be the saddest thing to see.' She tried to smile a bit at Charlotte. 'It's the rooms that are full of too much stuff that are the saddest. Makes it all look meaningless, to put too much of it together . . . Saw a bit, how it must have been for you, emptying your mother's house. Massachusetts, New England, wherever. Saw a bit how it must have been for you . . .' In the quiet, she found herself giving the smallest breath of a laugh and regretting it even though it was so small.

Charlotte said, 'You start to see . . . lots of things differently, emptying a place. Things that were familiar.'

She looked as though she would finish there. 'In what way?' Ruth asked. 'I mean, it's true, what you say.'

'You start to see how much you painted on to it yourself, I think. It's a way to . . . to see yourself more clearly maybe . . . It's a sad feeling.'

'Yes, you start wondering what the little things really mean. You get this thing or that; something you picked off the beach on such-and-such a walk. Take them out of the places where they're meant to go, just put them all in a pile, makes you think you were lying to yourself when you believed they had . . . a meaning. You know? Some jigsaw puzzle you got at a car boot sale, or the books that you haven't ever read. They don't even look like a life any more, do they? All those things in their places, they look like a life then. All the books you've never read on your shelves by the fireplace, that looks like a life.'

Charlotte held the envelope and did not ask more, a look on her face that might have been compassion. But it hadn't been her own possessions that she'd emptied from Hedera. 'There's no difference,' she said, 'except in your mind.'

'But maybe what's in your mind is everything. Being happy, that's in your mind, you know? Being in love. Being lonely . . . Want to look at it that way, there isn't anything except what's in your mind.'

Charlotte looked at her, thought of Mrs Pryce's face as she'd said that the people here would take hold of any chance to make their own mark. But she wondered if Ruth didn't have a right. It seemed a great chance, to be able to take those things that were in your mind and make them, in the place around you. Even if you felt the need to change your home, beautify it, because your life was less than beautiful. She remembered how Ruth had held out her hand over the pieces of broken glass.

'We'll have a chance,' she said, raising the envelope in her hand, 'everyone here will have a chance, I hope, to *realize* the things which are in their minds.'

Ruth looked at her without a smile, taken aback like she'd been before by Charlotte. You could miss the generosity in what she said, hearing just the bareness in her voice.

'Thank you.'

But Charlotte didn't have an answer.

'Have the sales gone through? Audrey's house, the Jarmans'? There's seven now, yes?'

'Four are in process. I went to see them. I wish you'd come . . . I felt like the stranger I am.'

'I would have, you should've asked.'

'I know . . .'

'You're not a stranger. And I've missed you anyway . . .' she said.

'I've missed you too.' No pause.

'I've been lonely,' Ruth said, maybe by way of explanation.

'When you're lonely, come . . .'

Behind her, on the garden's high walls, the ivy was thinner, brown where it had been green and full of soft rustling. She had gone out and stood in the winter there, every other day at least. Rain had washed all soot from the brickwork and the burnt ground, black, was hardened as it would be now till spring.

'Do you want to open it?' she held it out, slightly towards Ruth.

'I think you should be the one really.'

'You could read it aloud.'

'Read it to me, yes?' Ruth asked her.

Charlotte looked at the envelope. Ruth's pale eyes were clear as she listened, and saw other places in the window's soft light.

'Title of business,' Charlotte read quietly, seeing herself the long and unused street, the settling of the birds she'd watched one evening, on rooftops, like years unchanged had made Ynys-morlan safe. 'Title of business: the Shoreline Café.'

At the head of the town, on the shore's side, the first three shops stood without signs above their doors, though they were now full inside. Cardboard boxes stacked badly, Emyr Morgan's handwriting on the sides. And all the houses clutched the cold to their low slates and to their dark, void windows.

Outside his house, where those gulls made small circles, tiny black points against the sky, Dai Meredith sat with his back to the stone, on a little bench where Eirian had used to rest between her bits of gardening. What he was doing, it was brave, Emyr had said, but he was scared of being brave. Bravery was something for yourself, and it was time, not him, that had made this demolition necessary.

He remembered Siân's face as he'd told her. And he'd known, even looking at Spar's open doorway before he'd gone in, what it would mean for Gwen Morgan. Of course. But time had a plan. People's parts made up the whole. No one could help that.

And in the community centre, desks all set out in the neatest rows, Gwen oversaw the children as they copied the few words she'd written on the blackboard. She watched as they stared up at her stiff letters, *The quick brown fox jumped over the lazy dog*, and screwed their eyes up at their own. All apart from Nia Lewis. She must have been sitting, Gwen thought, in almost the same spot as her mother had when she'd looked out over two hundred and fifty residents, shuffling her papers.

A wonderful opportunity. And it was. An incredible thing, full of hope. She'd hardly spoken to her husband, perhaps one week now. At night and in silence she cried, thinking of Dai, and then the mornings came, to leach the life and last days from the gift shop. She could never have reached as far, not in the eighteen years of her work for this town, not as far as an opportunity like this.

In this room, echoing, wooden-floored, everything was silent. Everything apart from Nia Lewis. Gwen hadn't been sure a minute ago; the sound had been so quiet that at first she hadn't even been certain it was real. But it was. Little tapping sound. Nia was staring down at her desk and from here, from this angle, Gwen couldn't see her hands.

'The café,' Ruth said quietly. 'That's the best we could've hoped for.'

'I don't know it. You think so?'

'The woman's daughter stood up at the meeting. Remember her?'

Charlotte nodded. Ruth watched her face as she read slowly. Her voice seemed to conjure pictures in the dust-soft quiet between them.

'Type of business: café. Proposed type of business. . . high-class restaurant with a country-like but also elegant-style atmosphere at affordable prices.' Charlotte gave a small smile, looking down at the folded form, with no cynicism. 'As if she wanted to sell *us* the idea. "Please estimate the level of the work needed, on a scale of one to five, one being minor exterior renovations and five being complete internal and external refurbishment." She's written three and three quarters.' She smiled again.

Ruth watched her continue. She saw, for the first time all day, instead of the disorder of her own house a picture of the Shoreline Café. It had a sign, set out in front every day, a little chef. Charlotte spoke and Ruth listened.

Bethan had knelt on the carpet, the street outside dark and well known.

'"Although the front of the building would need renovating very thoroughly, the bit that would need the most work would be the interior, as more space would need to be made to allow a greater dining area and, in an ideal situation, the first floor – a bedroom, an extra bathroom and a room we use for storage – would be knocked through to create an upper-level dining area."'

As she'd written, streetlight had fallen on the café's doorstep, on the Lion across the road. It had been her strutting ground in there, Fridays and Saturdays, getting ready in her old bedroom with Angharad. They'd used to go in, she'd make sure every person turned and looked when she got her first drink. She found herself still doing it now. She'd leave Chelsea with her mum and come back here to get ready. Standing outside the Lion's door, it would feel like she must've been a different person then.

'"As well as taking out the interior, we would need to refurbish with tables and chairs and equipment. We would need at least two new cookers, a freezer, so that the menu could be wider. There would probably be a great deal of new equipment needed to provide the kind of quality that you would need for a restaurant like this."'

Kneeling there, she should've laughed at all the pictures in her head: candlelight and the little clinks of cutlery, piano music. Like some little tender-lit bubble, something from a different world. She'd looked down at the paper and the cynicism she'd felt had had no substance. It had talked with Rhys's voice.

'"I think the style of the restaurant should be quite subtle so the décor inside would not be flashy but it would be gorgeous."'

She had thought of Rhys – standing by the cloakrooms in school; had remembered it suddenly, vividly. Checking the double doors were open on to the alley, taking his lighter out of his pocket and holding it under his report. It had been the Zippo she'd got him, she'd had an *R* engraved on it, everything, and she remembered him smiling and saying that he was quitting after the fifth year anyway so he could start on the burglary full time. Remembered his expression as he'd watched the flame, holding it longer and longer when the thing must've burnt him. And she'd wondered, bland and quick like the future really came, if what he said might not turn out to be true.

'"It would be with class but it would make you feel a bit of a thrill just to walk into."'

What the fuck, she'd kept thinking. What the fuck. It was the only thing that'd got her through. Who cares? What does it matter? What the fuck. Like she'd push herself, with every thought, further from the shore.

'"I believe that this project is the most important thing, the very best thing that could have happened in Ynys-morlan and we would be very proud to be a part of it, and we would be very proud to be a part of it right from the beginning."'

Now, in the silence that rested as Charlotte finished reading, its small image was full and bright.

'I think they wrote that together,' Ruth said. 'Patricia and the girl. You don't realize how little you know people, do you?'

Charlotte nodded and they looked at each other, some intimacy from the words she had read, like a far-off sound, seeming to highlight more clearly the distance between them and the town. Quiet was left now. Her voice, as Ruth had listened, had seemed to fall soft as cloth to the floor.

She had been asked if she remembered how childhood felt. As if your second one was a gift. But Gwen walked under their lowered stares now, each footfall clear as she moved between the first desks, and thought of the ways that that woman had really been like a child: selfish, caring only for what she wanted, not for who she hurt. That was what it *was* to be a child: to have no control over your wants, or what you'd do to fulfil them. She'd never planned to have them herself, the thought had always seemed in some way to impinge, a tight kind of apprehension.

Dai's reed-choked eyes in her mind, she thought now about a world full of children, a town of them; attention and need, no control at all over their own happiness.

She had always known what would make her happy, and she'd achieved it. Emyr only had to stand in their house, to look at the life they'd made. There had been no need for any of this. She couldn't understand him. There had come an opportunity, a pot of gold, yes the rainbow had ended in Ynys-morlan. And he had done this. What had he wanted her to prove?

No, she did not remember what it was like to be a child. Walking between the desks, she looked ahead at Nia Lewis's lowered face. Tap tap, the sound went. Tap tap. Insufferable. And she could almost feel the other children turn to watch her as she passed. In this wide hall, the overhead fluorescents showed on their faces like sallowness.

Nia was bent over her paper as though concentrating, as if that tap tap tap was just the most interesting thing in the world. And though the children's heads turned like cogs as they watched her go by, the girl's was low to the desk.

Tap tap. Tap tap. And when she moved to stand next to her, Gwen put her fingernails against the desk and made just that same sound.

They sat in the quiet for long moments and didn't look away from each other, the walls of the grey and quiet room fading around them to let in touches, colours from other places.

'You see?' Ruth said, 'you laughed at me but I told you, everyone wants to live somewhere beautiful. It's not just the look of a beautiful thing.'

'You think that it's the beauty that matters to people, honestly? Not the success?'

'I think it's aiming for something, reaching for something. Doesn't matter really what.'

She'd taken the alarm clock, the photographs and the books from their bedside tables, down to the living room. There had been some feeling, muted, some current. As though far above her waves had tumbled and reeled. She'd placed the books that she'd never read by the head of their camp bed on the floor. She'd seen herself suddenly, as she would have done if she'd come to stand behind, silent in the doorway: seen herself bent over, again and again rearranging possessions which she'd once believed would become precious family things.

'It must be a good feeling, to be giving that to people,' she said.

'If it's going to make them happy,' Charlotte nodded again, faintly.

This had been the place, Ruth had thought, as she'd seen the quiet mess, where she'd sat with Lennie, told him about cochlear echo tests, new implants. She had said that Nia had been good all the way through, hadn't thrown a fit once when she probably would have done herself. She'd told him all these things, her eyes watching the carpet. The way she'd talked had been calm but she hadn't been able to look up and meet his eyes.

'So we know anyway,' she'd said. 'We know anyway, no more worrying then. No more not knowing –' and she'd wanted to go on and list the things that maybe there'd be no more of: imagining Nia's first proper words, teaching her to read and write and sing songs. No more picturing the sorts of conversations they'd have when Nia was grown up herself – as Ruth had often sat alone and done when Nia had first been born. She'd used to think about a daughter, an adult – and they'd sit and talk about the men in their lives or just their lives, and she'd tell her daughter how she felt, heart to heart, things she'd never told anyone else, because that was the kind of bond they'd have. Maybe these things were over already, when they'd only ever lived as daydreams anyway. With her gaze unmoving on the floor, she'd said to Lennie, 'I bought two books on sign language, *Introduction To*, and *Early Learners*. Bought them on the way home . . .' And though her voice had stayed calm, she'd been crying by then, because she hadn't been able to remember a time when she'd felt so isolated. From Nia, from her husband, from everything she'd ever wanted. And she'd thought then, wasn't that how a deaf person must feel? She'd taken the books out of her bag and she'd put them on the coffee table and still her gaze hadn't touched him. 'I don't . . . I don't know if you want to look at them or anything –' And she had got up from the sofa then and all she could remember was leaving, going, needing to be far away. She would have left herself, if she could have then, abandoned in that room. She would have stranded that part of herself there, and the rest of her would have escaped.

Sitting and looking at their makeshift bed, so desperately, perfectly arranged, it had seemed to Ruth suddenly that the rest of her had escaped that day, and was living now far away in another town.

Seeing into Charlotte's eyes, she said, 'It's a wonderful thing, that you've given me.'

But Charlotte didn't answer, only spoke to that expression she saw, 'Maybe, Ruth, you have to look back. Take stock. Or moving forward wouldn't be real.'

'Yes. You're right. And when we've done this, and we can just stand and see it –' as though there'd be no one but them, 'if we know we didn't dash into it, that it's built from the ground right up, it'll mean more. Maybe you've got to look back, you're right. Reassess.'

She remembered that night, running out, leaving the books. She'd gone upstairs and taken Nia out of her big bed and she'd told her it would be all right, eventually it would all be all right, over and over again. You had a kid, she thought, and it was a part of yourself: it was the part you wanted to nurse and look after. It was the part you wanted to heal.

She said nothing as she met Charlotte's eyes. There was no way to say thank you for thirty-three million pounds.

She cleaned and tidied when she felt these memories get close. Picked up the pieces of the night before and put them back into their places. Sometimes she'd end up on the doorstep outside, just the same as her mother had. There was a soft indent from where people had walked, it collected soapy water and made her think of the rain. The little circles raindrops made when they came down on puddles, what it might be like if soapy water rained from the sky. Water that washed away colour, and she'd look up at the houses around her, imagine their outsides running, seaside pastels dripping down their walls. Bright streams to the road and the drains.

The world would be a better place maybe if more people got upset and cleaned. Twenty-year-old lads outside the pub come half eleven, she imagined, jeering insults at each other and then snatching at their back pockets, dragging out their dusters and dropping to their knees next to each other to rub the pavement down.

She had looked at her living room this morning. Every cluttered thing. A quiet rain had put shadows on them all and, outside, had washed the paint from the houses on the street to run in colours along the kerb.

'When this is finished, it'll be beautiful. In a way it never could've been, if we'd done no looking back,' she said, waiting for Charlotte's response.

And Charlotte, whose words had run without end, without her ever looking back, said yes, as if Ruth could pass her these unspoken memories. Pass her everything that she felt.

Gwen remembered opening the playschool, training four days each week, channelling their applications until, through sheer effort of will, she had found the notice of approval for funding, lying at ease in their postbox. She had called it the Notice of Defeat and talked about having it framed to hang above her desk here.

Those months seemed full of good memories to her. And full had been the right word; evenings of discussion, poring over any new information, any leads. Months when she and Emyr must have bored all their company with details of their plan. And that last morning: sitting, drinking coffee together in the kitchen, the Notice of Defeat propped up between them against the sugar bowl. Full, that was the word. She had walked in here for her first day of work on the 16th of September. There had been eight children waiting in the foyer. Mothers holding a lunch box or a younger child, with expressions, Gwen had thought, of quiet victory. Eight children. There were seventeen now, between the ages of three and five, and she couldn't remember any more how it had felt to see those women on that day.

Nia Lewis had registered some months ago. In situations like this one, any form of communication seemed impossible. In situations like this, short of lifting Nia's chin with her own hand, she could not even get the girl to raise her head. Nia sat in her own little world, under the curtain of her hair. And outside it, her arms made a wall. Tap tap tap. Over and over. Bending her knees very slowly, Gwen's face came level with that hair. Behind her, scratching pencils had stopped.

She couldn't speak Nia's name. She could not talk to Nia. This was the situation, and it was not new: the girl was doing something, the girl needed to stop it. Gwen could not communicate this fact to her.

She took her fingers from the desk. She reached towards Nia's hair. Soft as soundless air, it brushed against her nails, and Nia's face snapped up.

It was the shock of her motion, the suddenness with which the girl did every single thing that shook her, and Gwen had to hold herself still under Nia's stare.

'Nia . . .' she said. Always, even knowing, always she couldn't stop herself. And Nia's arms tightened around what she'd been doing. She held her eyes on Gwen: tiny, vicious, stubborn. The tapping sound was gone.

That's good, she wanted to say. Silence, Nia. That's good. But the girl knew nothing about silence or noise. And she would not stand here and gesture like an idiot, Nia's eyes on her like she could have scratched just with that stare. She would not stand here like some miming fool under the gaze of sixteen others.

Show me the piece of paper, she wanted to say. But what would come from her would be mute. This was the frustration when she was faced with Emyr's new smile. His blankness, and everything she said then fell, useless. She spoke to Emyr and his smiles and his platitudes stopped every word inside her throat and made her bloated.

Gwen held out an open hand, showing Nia what relinquishment looked like. But Nia only sat and glared, as though blind as well to every gesture Gwen could make.

She reached across the desk, over the circle of Nia's arms and put her fingers down. The girl didn't flinch. What control could you have in a situation where you were robbed of your voice? She had looked into Dai's face, helpless, stubborn, selfish Dai Meredith and he had looked back at her holding on to nothing but an empty choice. No reasons, no thought. He'd stolen her voice that way.

She would never have told anyone – who could she tell? Patty? – nights came and Emyr slept and she lay and held the hand that she had struck him with, unable to find forgiveness.

Gwen's fingers now tightened on the paper, trying to draw it towards her. And Nia's clutch tightened. In the anaemic winter light that fell across this plastic desk, her paper was hidden by her arms.

It was some kind of joke. Like some fool's idea of humour – Emyr's new idea of it. She was a tolerant teacher. On the day of her last birthday, eight of the children had signed her card. This was how her husband had left her. Doubting and confused and paralysed. She hadn't wanted to say those things to Dai. If she'd had control, she would never have.

'Nia –'

But the girl couldn't hear her.

'Give me the paper, Nia.'

You couldn't help the words coming.

Gwen pressed her fingertips as hard as she could to the desk and she dragged at the sheet that Nia's arms held down. The girl's face was hard as a pebble. Wilful. But there was no room in this situation for any will but the teacher's. Gwen endured Nia's gaze. If the girl wanted, she could stare all she liked. She could stare herself stupid, stare herself truly blind for all the good it would do her now.

Gwen would not play this game any more. The girl wasn't four years old yet. She would take the paper now. In front of Nia's face, she would hold it.

She felt the hardness of the desk underneath. She gripped, and she pulled.

In the quiet of seventeen children, Gwen heard it tear. And Nia's face, caught up with hair, flashing from the work she held on to, up to Gwen's eyes, seemed to erupt. In the moment before the girl moved, Gwen saw it. Like a wave it was.

Nia's chair legs scratched across the floorboards and she was moving, grabbing hold of the desk, twisted into a tantrum. One hand on the torn paper, she was lurching forwards and Gwen recoiled. The sounds dropped like wooden pieces in this silence. Halfway across the desk, her feet on the shifting chair, Nia brought her half-closed hand up and struck Gwen's face.

Gwen rocked back, away, noiselessly. She gaped at Nia Lewis.

'How dare you . . .' As quiet in this room as if deafness had touched every other child. 'How dare you!' Their onlooking eyes must have deadened sound.

She looked at the girl, like some little animal crawling over this table, hate scrawled on her face as clearly as in Rhys's spray-paint. A creature uncaring of anything but what she felt, letting out what she felt. Attacking Gwen with it.

This was how it was to be a child. And if she could have, she would have shown Eirian: this was a person without walls.

'How dare you slap me,' she said, in this silence that had no echoes.

She said, 'How dare you move across this table and slap me.'

She said, 'Have you got no discipline? Have you never even heard the word discipline? My God.'

Nia's face was fracturing slowly. She saw the hatred fail and something else blooming, gradual as water on paper. The tantrum blew away.

It seemed as though everything ebbed from Gwen. She could feel it wash from her and leave her dry. Everything Emyr had done. The things she had told Dai.

'What did you want me to do?' she said. 'I had to take it away from you.'

She saw a vision of that man, in his home, in the shadow-steeped corridor, retaliating.

'Do you think you can just do what you like?' she said.

She would have been knocked down. Dai wasn't a child any more.

'I'm a tolerant teacher. I'm a reasonable person.'

Nia was beginning to cry.

'I'm trying to do a good thing.'

In this quiet, there was nothing but her own voice, though. Ruth Lewis's daughter sat, deaf, mute, untouchable – but crying. And in the moments that Nia's voice, anyone's, should have filled, there were only echoes. The girl was no mirror. Unresponsive, she was no barrier, and the words that came from Gwen seemed to move further away. Without that barrier, seemed to leave her on her own.

'I'm a good person!'

But she looked at Ruth Lewis's daughter and there was no response. She wasn't saying it for the girl.

After playschool Nia came, small and drifting in the overflow of children from the community centre's double doors: a pretty little girl, three years old, who never came to the car herself. She waited for Ruth to go and pick her up. Her eyes, as blank as the houses Ruth had passed, held sounds behind, which were not formed as words.

She was stock-still in the back seat as they drove home. She had not smiled as Ruth had lifted her, coat and lunch box and all. Seen in moments in the rear-view mirror, she stared at the seat in front of her and didn't glance out at the view.

'How are you doing, Ni? Did you have a good day? How are you doing?'

From the end of their garden path where she stood with Nia, her mother's house looked just the same, between them and a view of the mountains. There was no dry rot on its face, no sign of the empty rooms behind.

Ruth put Nia slowly down on the path and watched as she walked between the quartz stones. Cold air, both Nia's breathing and her own were remaining in small mists.

The hallway was normal, a little cottage corridor with slate on the floor and carpet on the risers of the stairs. Always hoovered, always warm. Ruth watched Nia move inside and stand as she always did, waiting for her coat to be taken off her. Only waiting. Ruth turned her around as she took it from her arms and then rose, to see Nia notice that the bedroom doors were shut.

There was no expression. She looked at the landing. Her thumb went to her mouth.

'I had to change things round, had to do a lot of changing round.' She made gestures of change with her hands. Nia's eyes gazed above her fisted fingers. 'I had to rearrange the furniture.' She thought of Charlotte, the hour they had spent, and tried to take some strength from it. Still holding Nia's coat and lunch box, she walked with her, incapacitated now because she could not hide the vacant space behind these doors. Nia moved on to the stairs towards her bedroom.

'I had to change your room, Ni.' She touched her shoulder, made her turn round to look into her face but Nia only turned back to the door.

The memories seemed to come to Ruth in flashes between the soft sounds of Nia's feet: running up these stairs, leaving Lennie in the living room behind her with books spread out in the table's lamplight.

'I moved all the stuff downstairs into your room.'

Walking to stand at the corridor's end, she remembered, looking into her father's study, open for the first time. Nothing there but dust motes in the air.

'Your room's empty, Ni,' she said. She touched both of Nia's shoulders.

Crouching beside the skirting board – the memory that would

never leave her, not ever again – hearing the sounds of her own movements as she'd watched the grey smudges resolve themselves into little pairs.

Nia's feet fell gently, without apprehension or curiosity, up to a closed door that she'd never seen shut before. Not from this side.

Standing beside her, bundled up with all of Nia's things, Ruth reached down and tried to take hold of Nia's hand.

The room was a space shaped only by four walls. The clean carpet stretched from their feet to that skirting board and made a blank square like the ceiling. Her furniture was gone and the shelves, only their screw holes showing in the paint now. In the centre was the base of Nia's bed, and the uncurtained window looked out on the street. Ruth felt Nia's hand pull faintly away from her own. Not knowing what else to do, letting her arm fall, Ruth watched her walk into the room.

Nia went slowly across the carpet, unconstrained, touching nothing. She walked to the place where her desk had been and turned around. She wandered to stand next to her bare bed. Ruth's heart went out to her.

No movement in Nia's face, but Ruth seemed to see deep motion. Machinery whose noise would be tumultuous, just a flicker in her eyes. She looked at Ruth as if it was only expected now that Ruth would make it right for her.

Picking her up, letting her coat and lunch box drop with dull thumps round their feet, Ruth hugged her tightly, moving, quick footsteps. Banging through the quiet down the stairs. A sense of being lost in this house now, just as much as Nia was. Ruth turned towards Lennie's room. It seemed as if the skin of secrets, touched by Charlotte, was breaking now. She freed her hand from Nia to turn the doorknob. She pushed it open, carrying her through to show her the new room she'd tried to make.

– and it was empty. No desks or shelves or boxes. In the long-gone August air, dust floated, turned in the bars of sunlight that came through the blinds and made memories so perfect, so motionless, that they wouldn't ever leave this house –

No the room was crammed with things. To give the place the shape of Nia's bedroom, she'd hung cloth across Lennie's shelves and the long desk that stood against one wall. Old curtains, a patchwork throw that had once covered the sofa, anything she'd been able to find which was big enough, she'd drawing-pinned on to the walls. It had started slowly, the idea of recreating, and she had stepped back and checked what she was doing many times to see that it was right. It had started slowly but it had grown. She'd gone into the attic to find more cloth. She'd pinned it up without stepping back to look. Recreate their home. Even in this smaller space. It was a tiny, hotchpotch place. Between the pieces of material she'd pinned, the single window looked out on to trees and the flagpole. Ruth had put Nia's desk against the cloth that covered this room's corresponding wall. She'd stuck with Sellotape on to the collage cloth the pictures which had been pinned to Nia's cork board.

The effect was of a bedroom cast in the imagination of a child. Nia sat in her arms, recognizing maybe each of her things in its place.

'Like a Wendy house,' Ruth said in a quiet voice, her hand never resting on Nia's hair. 'See?' she said. 'It's just the same.'

Tight like this, Nia's legs began to fidget. Ruth felt it, stroking her still, thinking for just a moment with a kind of deaf hope that Nia wanted to climb down and explore. Ruth felt her legs contracting slowly, drawing up towards herself, felt her extend them again, just as slowly, just as taut. Daylight lay on all the little pairs of shoes that were set against the facing, pretend wall. She felt Nia shift again, out and in, reflexive, hard.

'It's just the same, Ni.'

Nia's cheek moved against her shoulder; what felt at first like nuzzling or would have seemed that to a stranger. Ruth knew it well, there was no search for comfort in it. Her head moved very slightly and very constantly and Ruth did not stop stroking it. Arms and legs, tightened, released.

'Ni fach, it's OK.'

First one cheek and then the other until it couldn't seem like nuzzling even to a stranger. Her hands rubbed against Ruth's coat.

'Baby –'

But Nia froze against her body. For that one moment, standing in the doorway, it seemed that they were locked together.

'No –'

Every part of Nia let out. A batter of a movement. She struck Ruth a hundred times, a hundred places, on her face, her throat, her chest. Ruth stumbled back into the hall.

'No, Nia – Nia, please –'

She thumped tiny hands at her, slapped her across the cheeks and nose, her head turning side to side in rejection. She twisted in her spine, in her legs and arms; reeled against Ruth's own. In the silent hallway, stepping back and back until she touched the cupboard under the stairs with her shoulders, Ruth was pushed by her.

' – please, Nia, please, Nia, please –'

But Nia's face was snarled up with red emotion. Twisting in anger, as Lennie's would. In the quiet that had always filled this house, though Nia's mouth was stretched as if to scream, the only sounds that she made as she struggled were the thumps and the patters of her limbs. Immobilized, Ruth saw her in the moments that her eyes were open, the moments between her hands falling, and felt her own strength drain away. Her arms, holding Nia, ceased to be strong.

Seeing her in this quiet as Nia pummelled her, Ruth's efforts failing into stillness, she wondered that Charlotte could have looked at them together, that any person could have looked at them together without making out in every saccharine cuddle she gave Nia, in every awkward silence covered by her desperate talk or in Nia's eyes and in her own, never meeting even when Ruth held her, a secret whose every edge was bare to see.

Nia's nail bit her cheek, the little fist struck her throat. Ruth felt the blows fall like snow on the sea, her back slipping gradually against the cupboard door.

The skies cleared in the west through an early evening. They left clouds gathered like a distant world behind the mountains, and in the last, cold light, painted Ynys-morlan's street with watery brightness.

Only half past four. Shadows from the shoreside, of washing lines and chimneys, reached over the tarmac. There were the sounds of footsteps, dogs being walked.

It must have looked very thin this town, seen from where the gulls wheeled and strayed. Stretched like a losing grip along the shoreline, these two long terraces. From above, you could have seen the lie of the land: the soft slopes of the mountains, their dead bracken in the sunset flowing down to this rough floodplain. There was a silence in the winter here that seemed to rise from the ground and lie settled in the bay that these two headlands formed. In the winter, the sea could be still as fabric. A gaunt place, Ynys-morlan: two opposing lines of brick and stone.

It didn't look or feel this way, though, to stand on the street. Even if the paving was cracked underfoot, even if the signs were gone or fading above the windows of the empty shops. To a stranger maybe, it might have looked like a failing town. In January though, there weren't any strangers here. They left like beads of water in the autumn, until the town was dry. In January, the people that walked their dogs in twilight had done so for years. And you could sit in the Lion, and you could ask someone, Edward Evans or Garwyn Davies, very still on their stools, and they'd tell you that they could remember when this stretch of beach hadn't been sand or rocks at all but land. Now the gardens backed up to the seawall, rocks piled against its other side. In the winter here, across the stones, the tide would leave dead oak leaves in curving lines.

It looked old of course, to any person who'd grown up here, between buildings which showed each other clean windows and doors. When the storms started in February, they glimpsed each other's curtained light, like a dialogue, strong and old and set.

From where Dai Meredith sat now, inside the gift shop's drawing shadows, he could see the little shops across the road. His mum's shops. His now. They threw their silhouettes on the tarmac and their windows were crevice-dark. And the gift shop here, it must have looked the same through their views. Dai sat on chill floorboards, hearing the gulls' evening sounds.

These opposing rows must have been talking to each other hundreds of years now. While day came, rose in an arc over Ynys-morlan's road and sank behind the buildings, the sea. Over and over, as though shadows were always moving in circles. The buildings looked at each other. It was twilight now and tomorrow, in the faint, late, winter morning, the bulldozers would arrive.

Sitting here, it seemed like the gift shop was dying. He could feel it under his legs. He told himself that he hadn't wanted this. He told himself, you could have any thoughts that you liked. You could lay thoughts down like stone walls in your mind. But underneath them, time always moved. Dai didn't even know which was better; which made you do the right thing.

He hadn't wanted this; to hurt the place his mum had looked after. But he couldn't be happy, couldn't ever be happy till it was gone from the town, he knew. He hadn't wanted to pull down all these memories of his mother. It was time that had made him need this.

Gwen Morgan sat on her sofa that night, looking at the blank television screen and at her ornaments, set on doilies on the top. There was no smell of cooking from the kitchen. Radio 3 was not playing in there. This room where she was seated was the only room with lights now. She liked to have all the lamps on usually. Even with the electricity bills, she liked to be able to walk from place to place and have all her house warmly lit.

There was a little sculpture of Thursday's child: a boy standing, dressed to walk, looking on and upwards a little. She had found it at an auction house in Lampeter, and she had brought it home to show Emyr, to tell him what a coincidence it was, because she had been born on a Thursday.

There was a ceramic Carltonware bowl up there, filled with seashells that she'd collected one day, a while ago, and laid out on newspaper on the kitchen table to sort, to pick out the best.

She sat without moving very much, only looking at her things. She remembered preparing for the reception in the gift shop, a long time ago, stringing banners from the corners of the ceiling and shaking out tablecloths to lie spread, clean and lovely; a sound like some bird's wings. And the boards had still smelled of varnish, everywhere in there had smelled of varnish. She remembered thinking that as she'd walked upstairs and looked at the new unfilled room.

Ruth couldn't talk to Lennie that night. He came home and he was angry, disillusioned, he said he didn't want to drive up and down roads any more, just to make money to pay the council tax with. She didn't know what to say to him. She felt like there wasn't anything left in her to say. She lay in bed with him that night and she didn't know if he was awake or asleep. She looked at his back and she reached out and put a hand on his side.

'Lennie . . . ?' she said.

Asleep or not, she couldn't tell. He didn't answer her.

'Lennie,' she said. She moved her hand on him, his hip and his waist, where he had thrown the covers off. She didn't know how to put everything she felt into words. She felt afraid, and on her own. 'Lennie,' she said. She wanted him to roll over and touch her then, hold on to her. 'Lennie, do you love me?' she said.

Charlotte spoke into the silent, sun-frosted air, 'What do you see? What do you imagine, Ruth?'

Looking out, for a long time she didn't answer.

It was beautiful, the morning that the bulldozers came. Standing on her garden path with her coat round her shoulders, she might've smiled to see the way it had begun; winter sunlight that trailed down to touch her face and throat above her overcoat, take all the colour from her skin. Ruth stood with the shadow of her house at her back and Charlotte saw in her expression a conflict that was obvious for the first time.

'I'll tell you what I see,' she said.

She looked out at Ynys-morlan; little houses divided only by low walls. Net curtains like cataracts. The winter morning's cold froze every sound, all echoes trapped into stillness. She saw the gift shop, the curving road that led past it, and the beauty that she imagined seemed full of feeling, blank of thought, like all the colours combine to make only white.

So quiet here now, the gulls and brittle footsteps. It was the 28th and here they stood, waiting for the bulldozer's sound.

'I'll tell you,' Ruth said, 'what I want to make.'

As the dawn had come slowly over Ynys-morlan's street and touched the sky and the pavement with grey silence, Emyr had come to the gift shop, to see his own likeness in the long glass doors as he walked with empty footsteps towards it. It was a hollow building, gulls motionless on the edge of its roof, as if on a derelict site. He had come to stand and remember, and to feel those memories hollowed too, so his last image of it would be this, some kind of final word. Through the reflections of the houses opposite and through that washed sky, Emyr walked, to find inside a man who had been sitting for hours already.

Dai Meredith was gazing off to one side when Emyr put his hand to the cold glass. His eyes lay on something in the veiled room that might have been there before. Though the sounds of Emyr's shoes had struck in an untouched street, Dai turned only with the shadow that fell across him. He looked up and for a moment could not see. There was a calmness in his appearance, and an intensity, which faded as he lifted his gaze and saw a dim face. Saw Emyr.

Emyr pushed the door open. As there'd been in the salt-touched air outside, there was silence in this unused room.

He stood there for the first moment that he should have spoken, and for the second, and Dai, gazing up at him from the floor with his arms around his knees, didn't begin for him. It seemed like many of the things that Emyr could have said did come from him, just to lose momentum in the stillness of the air.

He finally said, 'You've been here all night.'

'I've been here, like . . .' He moved his hand as though to say, only a few hours, but didn't finish. 'Haven't been counting,' and he nodded with a smile, because he knew what that meant about himself.

Emyr walked in as the door closed smoothly behind him, and only stood there. He looked from one end of the long, darkened room to the place where Dai was sitting, their few words small against the quiet – soft and low as a forest bed. Emyr listened to it and something gave inside him.

In the time that he had come to spend remembering past happiness, seeing how it looked in the morning light of demolition day, he found himself instead next to Dai's unmoving shape, wordless here. Without the strength to hold the past separate from the day that he watched rising outside.

Dai Meredith looked out at the long concrete forecourt and at the sunlight's first connections, across the chimneys of the houses opposite, like some other country.

'It finally came, Emyr,' he said. In this room, though, his features were dark with last night.

Emyr watched with Dai. That failed part inside him seemed to want to reach out, and not be able to. 'Have you been all right here?'

He nodded.

'I'll sit with you for a while,' Emyr said, as though he'd walked down here from his sleeping house for some other reason.

While the day had opened, there they'd been.

It had crept into the street until the shadow of the gift shop was laid before them, over the concrete and the deserted road. As gold as summer out there.

'People will be about soon . . .' Emyr said at one point.

'Not for maybe another thirty minutes, thirty-five,' he answered, unhesitant.

And Emyr fell silent, thinking of the many mornings when Dai must've walked the street out there, and of Gwen, sleeping maybe still in their bed, oblivious for a last hour to the day that she'd watched drawing closer for a fortnight now. It seemed to Emyr then that she lived in weeks and mornings that were made by no one but herself, while the sun rose and set and didn't hinder her.

'It's a good job you've had, seeing this time of day, every day,' he said.

'This here –' Dai raised his hand from his knees and waved it out towards the road. 'This here is how you know . . . time's a good thing. You see it come like this, every day. Even when it's raining, like, you'll get a clear bit at sunrise. Rare that it just rains right through, that's rare. Doesn't matter what happens the night before, anything, it comes back like this every day.'

Emyr said nothing, but the edge of a smile came to him that in these fading shadows looked like sadness.

'Time comes in circles,' Dai said.

Over the peeling paint of those highest windows, this sunlight – and down across the pebbledash, stained and cracked at their corners like crow's feet.

'Perhaps we should all have your job, Dai, see this . . . see the circle. You need that maybe.'

Dai didn't look at him, only out. From the peak of the rooftops to their right, a gull rose and moved away to some part of the sky where they couldn't see him.

'Time's got its circles . . . and it's got its reasons,' Dai said. He turned to Emyr sagely, and that calmness was pale and bright in the centres of his eyes. 'Look at today. What we're doing today. We don't know all the reasons. But just because we don't know them doesn't mean they're not here. People get up every morning and see it raining, and they think the morning's been grey all through. We don't know,' he said, 'we just don't know.'

That vividness in his gaze, Emyr saw, was belief. Dai looked haggard from the last grieving months, whose reasons he had not yet found. It left Emyr empty, that look of hope. The morning was beautiful but it couldn't make him believe in reasons.

Dai's arms around his knees were tight. 'Don't you think?'

He imagined Gwen waking. 'I don't know, Dai.'

'You must see it this morning, though – it's starting, Emyr. It's starting here.' With one hand, he touched the dirty boards on which they sat. 'This is time changing. This is one of the circles, you know, this morning. Right here. Today, Ynys-morlan's somewhere new.'

Emyr didn't want the feeling that came; they moved further from each other, with only the two of them in this silent town awake. The faith in Dai's eyes pushed him away, though he would have gone with it if he could.

'It's us who's doing this, Dai.'

'I know that, I'm not dull, I know that. But . . . but . . .' some pain crossed his face and passed as he found a meaning, as he tried to give it to Emyr. 'Spring doesn't come without the hawthorn leafing up. But spring isn't *leaves*. We all move in it, don't you reckon?' he said. 'Don't you reckon?'

He seemed shocked at Emyr's silence, for the first time seemed separated from that daylight growing outside.

Emyr raised his hands. 'I don't know.'

'I know,' Dai said. '*I* know,' and moved to face him, his body stiff from the hours on this floor, ragged tiredness drew his features more clearly then. 'Thirty-three million pounds! Things like this don't start without reasons. Doesn't mean we know them. We're not *time*.' He laughed at the thought. 'We're just, we're just like the leaves. The leaves don't know what spring means. They don't know why it comes. But they bring it, like.' He looked at Emyr's face, for some recognition, for agreement. 'Ynys-morlan'll never be the same again. This is the last morning,' he said. 'Don't you see? People'll look back, in some part of the future that we won't even see, and *remember* this day. When the gift shop came down.'

Emyr saw his face, in his late thirties, in his forties maybe, age sharper on him than it was on other people. He wondered if Dai remembered the day when the shop had first been opened. He remembered it. In this silver-edged sunrise, the memory was clearer than it had ever been.

'Our own reasons . . .' Dai said, struggling and vehement, 'are nothing.' He reached out and gestured to the empty room, to its echoes. 'Just look at what's happened . . . to make this start. What we've gone through. Time's going to make a *new era* in Ynys-morlan. Don't you see that?'

Even as he saw – a pain, a dimness rising in Dai's eyes – Emyr couldn't find faith in himself to answer with. He wondered which television programme it was that Dai had watched; in what context 'eras' had been mentioned.

'We're just lucky enough,' Dai said into the soundless minutes of the gift shop's space, 'to be the people time's using.' His hands were flat against the cold boards.

Emyr was quiet, heard the words again. Lucky enough. Heard them in the tone of his wife's voice. And it seemed to open other years – when he had worked with Gwen on some project, some small part of Ynys-morlan that could lead, in a future they might not ever see, to a better, more beautiful town. Lucky enough to be the people in that position. He remembered her pointed faith, and his own belief: in her.

He watched Dai, carried away by his dedication. Looking forwards without wanting to know the future, letting go of the past like he'd been baptized. The light of the dawn was as beautiful as happiness in the man's eyes.

As today touched the paving stones and the morning became full, Emyr remembered how he and Gwen had believed; their dedication shared, or so it had seemed. Dai had left pain behind him, on some other shoreline, on the sand. It was emptiness that must lie under every faith. Emptiness that came to the edge of Emyr's memories.

'I love this building,' Dai said.

Emyr's mouth moved slightly and for a moment the words would not come. 'I know you do.'

'I love it.'

'Dai, I know.'

And Dai said, 'Gwen came to my house.'

Fear approached Emyr, softly then.

'You said people would. I didn't think . . . I could just tell someone how I'm right. Do you know how Gwen came to my house?' he asked.

'No,' Emyr answered hoarsely, 'I didn't know.'

More doubt came to Dai's face. 'She was crying,' he said, 'she was angry.' Doubt that covered him as he went on, 'She hit me, and I . . . I wanted to hit her back. I didn't do it but I wanted to, I shouldn't have wanted to . . .' He remembered Siân's listening gaze and he said, 'Emyr, though – awful sad things have to happen . . . It's like winter, for spring.'

Emyr heard, and seemed to see her again, sitting stiff beside him in darkness. Staring out through glass and with her cold words, letting go of any chance she'd had.

'She came to your house to try and save it,' he restated. He didn't move his hand to signal this building round them.

'But I did like you said . . .'

In the heavy air, Emyr saw how her hand must have fallen. Saw how she must have been to do this. Crying, he imagined Gwen, and angry. Desperate – for what this place meant to her. And he remembered how she'd been in the last month: delicately chilled silence laid over every word she could have said to him. He had thought she'd made up her mind.

'I did it,' Dai carried on, his face brushed by uncertainties he didn't have names for. 'I told Siân. I was scared, if I was doing the wrong thing and if what Gwen said was right . . . maybe Mum wouldn't want this . . . I told Siân. You said I ought to do that.'

And it was true. He had thought of it only as a safeguard, though.

'– I shouldn't have told her but I didn't know what to do –'

And though Emyr felt for him, hurting there, in confusion, there was little in his heart at that moment that wasn't deadened with his own pain. He had done this to Dai, with his careful words, yet there was little for Dai still.

Gwen had been frantic for the place then. But what it held for her was not their shared memories. She had gone to Dai, crying. He'd not seen a tear from her. There'd been a thousand times when she could have stopped this. Just one moment in the café or in the street. 'I don't want it demolished.' All she had needed to say. All she had needed to do, to suffer others seeing the rift between them. Because there was a rift. Though she held on to normality as if it were her child.

She should have come to him. He'd been waiting with his by-laws, ready. Regardless of Dai.

Somewhere distant from him, in their sunlit bed Gwen was waking, to look at the windows and their bright, netted view. She was waking, a vacant place inside her, to see the day when this building would be lost, along with everything it meant to her.

She would open the curtains, look down at Ynys-morlan. The words of Dai's story settled in Emyr like dead leaves to form new earth. She'd see the town to which she'd given eighteen years. It wasn't memories of him, or of them both together, that she would see lost in that sunlit view. Whatever she grieved, it had been hers only.

'It's finally come,' Dai said. 'Time.' He stared at Emyr. 'A new circle. I've done all the right things . . . to help it come. I *had* to do them. Ynys-morlan's going to be beautiful – because I have. Isn't that so?' His last question had seemed to escape.

It sounded to Emyr like moments, silent moments, that he remembered of his own. Lying in bed with Gwen, touching her hand while she slept. Emyr pictured a woman who had lived for her own belief. And with his in tow – in love.

It wasn't caring or goodness that brought the words from him ultimately. 'That's so, Dai . . .' The day was innocent, and Dai's devotion helpless. 'Yes, that's so.'

Ruth said. 'I don't want Ynys-morlan to look like any other town in the world.' She laughed but it was an easily broken sound. 'There isn't anywhere perfect enough.'

In front of them, people were beginning to move through their daily lives. Three men stood on the pavement in the cold air, talking, glancing up through the clear sky at this drop of sun.

Across the road, a front door opened on a gravel and paving-stone garden, a woman walked out with full hands to bag her rubbish there; Ann Griffiths, whose son was in his second year of the army now, who sent photographs back to her that he'd taken himself, very good pictures. She said herself that he should've gone into that, though his father was an officer.

'You can't live somewhere,' Ruth said, 'without putting your life into it.'

She looked at Ann, pretty, getting older. Her son had been pretty, she remembered, when he'd been five or six. She'd used to dress him up in smart little outfits. As the sun crested the houses behind them, Ruth stood on the quartz-bordered path and spoke in a voice that was fused with passion, pale. 'I don't want one single ugly thing marring this street. Not a cracked paving-stone. Not a piece of ground without a planting. Not a pockmark in this road. You can't live somewhere . . . without it expressing the way you feel. But people express things without thinking,' she said. 'They feel things . . . and they just let them out, just let them right out. They're scared to speak, so everything round them gets filled with it.'

Charlotte watched her eyes fixing and moving on every house, looking at the street as if she could scratch the beauty in her mind on to it, tarmac peeling up like wax. And, seeing her, she would have given Ruth the knife. But the beauty she described as she continued, it departed from anything that Charlotte recognized.

Behind them the front door was open. Charlotte saw the hallway, neat and cosy.

'You can chart people's lives in their houses. But people's lives can be full of . . . mistakes, mess, things they wish they'd never done.' She turned to her. 'People's lives aren't always – whole. But you can take experiences, feelings . . . that aren't beautiful, and you can use them to make beauty.'

Ruth turned back to the road, determination in her eyes – and it moved Charlotte, though the words which she said then struck every discord.

'They look like scars all over the place, all these extensions, these bits added. They're not beautiful,' she said. Her voice was a little torn – and it hurt Charlotte to hear it. 'I want people to look down this street and see a whole. Rows of beautiful homes, do you know what I mean? Do you know what I mean?' she said.

'I know,' Charlotte answered. She saw Ruth's white profile.

Ruth looked at all the people, separated by cold tarmac and quiet, going about their business: Andrea Thomas, as thin and as blonde as a yellow iris, walking slowly with the Alsatian that she'd bought, rumour had it, after Edward had taken their terrier along with the suitcases she'd handed him – and then had it put out of its mourning. She saw two mothers with prams.

'I want colours, none that look faded, none that look uncared-for. I want the people here to be surrounded with buildings that look the way they were meant to: old stone. They were built from it, why can't we see it on every house? Small-paned windows. Windows that invite you in. Or when you look out of them, they don't show you everything in this big, bare picture. Gardens,' she said. 'Not paved over, used to dump timber in. Gardens that make you feel good just to walk past, like the people here love their homes.'

She saw the old men on the pavement outside the empty museum: Owain Mills, Ted Evans, cigarette smoke hanging in the air with their breath. Owain, with his back to her and to the road, turned round in moments with a slowness that spoke of no purpose, but looked past her towards the gift shop's blank concrete. A soft hat shaded the lines round his pallid eyes. Ruth wondered when the last time had been that he'd cried. She wondered what things might cause him to. If he'd ever tell Ted Evans or Garwyn Davies of it; he spent every day with them, drank with them every evening. She wondered what he saw when he walked home from the Lion afterwards, what he looked at when he opened his bedroom door.

She watched Andrea Thomas tying her dog lead loosely outside Spar. She wondered if she had made love in the six months since her front door had closed quietly on her husband, standing in the garden. She wondered if she had made love and whether it had been a sad thing for her to do, or if she'd felt good.

And she saw outside, two men leaning on their four-by-fours, and wondered when the last time had been that they'd struck out at something, in anger or in love; if they'd joked about it to each other afterwards, afraid of the feelings it had given them, afraid of going home. She looked around her and in that moment it seemed as though every person must be full of feelings that they could only take back to their houses and sleep with every night.

'I want people to be able to walk out of the homes in Ynys-morlan and see something . . . that they've created – with their hopes, you know? Something that's made out of everything they've felt. Used those feelings.' She stared at Charlotte and Charlotte saw under every passion, the years in her eyes, of which no use had been made. 'Homes that people love, not because they feel safe when all the world's shut out. Not . . . just because they never saw any other place. Not somewhere they care about because of memories, because they ought to – I want a town full of homes that people will love . . . because they're the *culmination* of everything they've gone through . . . because that culmination's beautiful.

'You have to let out what you feel. You can't live with it, you can't keep it silent,' she said, her voice snagging on the words. 'But any feeling can be used to make something better . . . Any feeling can be let out through beauty.'

Ruth looked at the town as if she could force the distance closed between herself and the people who lived around her. As if she could force the distance closed between what she felt and what she wanted to believe.

In Ynys-morlan's wide road, just an edge to the silence, she raised her eyes as the first sound of an engine came.

Gwen heard that faint noise. She sat for a long time in front of her dressing-table mirror before she left the house. A pretty thing: a triptych with a gold, scrolled frame, set behind her cosmetics.

She had applied her foundation this morning, blended carefully over her jawline with a natural sponge, concealer for under her eyes. Loose powder with the excess tapped off to fix the foundation in place. She'd applied brown eyeliner along her top lashes and light beige shadow along her brow bone. Mascara, top and bottom lashes. She had a small gold pot of cotton buds on her dressing table for wiping away any mistakes. Coral-coloured lipliner and lipstick, gently blotted. Always coral colours, they suited her complexion. She was forty now. She might look older than that, it was hard to tell when you were seeing yourself.

She remembered Emyr telling her once that she was beautiful, inside and outside. Early on that must have been, because she remembered that they had been in bed, but it was a different bed in her recollections; not the place where they slept now.

She had told him he already knew what she thought: that beauty *only* came from the inside, that a person could be a model and on the catwalks every day, but if they were ugly inside, there could be nothing attractive about them.

He had said, she remembered, 'I'll remind you of that one morning when you're putting your make-up on.'

She had tried to explain to him that she did not sit down in front of the mirror to make herself beautiful. 'Presentable', was the word she'd used. To make herself 'presentable'.

She looked presentable now. If there was any beauty in what she saw, it was in the make-up only. She had always told herself that she wasn't scared of getting older. Her eyes looked back. If you didn't focus on the lines around them, they were the same as they'd been when she was seventeen: a pretty, light green.

She looked at her tweed suit, the lacy collar of her blouse, the silk scarf tied neatly under it. Everything ironed, everything perfect. She saw the bedroom behind her in the mirror's glass. The pink curtains with yellow trim, and the sunlight shining through to lie over the carpet in lovely shadows. This was her house. This was her best daytime outfit. Her eyes stared back at her: the eyes of a woman who'd shouted at a grieving man, that he'd betrayed his mother's memory.

She would have to leave soon. Should have left already. She would drive down and park and Emyr would come up to the window and when she rolled it down would lean in to kiss her. People would be there by then.

Gwen remembered Nia Lewis staring up at her, and the sound of her own voice. She reached up to take a fragment of mascara from her cheek.

In this lucid sun, the gift shop looked too strong to tear down. Its doors were open to the keen, breathless air. Long and low, in brick and slate, with its skin taken from it – every object and souvenir and sign – it was abandoned; representative of nothing, only something they had built in a time before.

Emyr stood watching, motionless as Dai stepped out and looked to the curving road. Opposite them, the Spar's door opened and Siân Humphries stood under its arch, her eyes directed towards the sound, her expression cold as memories. In a street that had been salted with quiet morning life, normality slowly turned and was silent.

The bulldozer's noise churned up the quiet. On caterpillar wheels, daffodil-yellow, its rusty plough was raised up. They saw the clean sweeps of the wipers across its grimy windscreen, and the man behind that glass. He was glancing back over his shoulder. Behind him they made out sparkles of metal between the branches of the bare trees.

The machine came into Ynys-morlan under a perfect sky, and the vans that followed, and the flatbed truck with the yellow skip on its back. Bright glints on each as they drew nearer.

Siân watched Emyr raise his arms, walking backwards across the concrete, beckoning them in towards him. She glimpsed Dai in the gift shop's doorway, his face ill-defined, as if he'd seen this moment played out a lot of times. The man behind the wheel of the van opening his window to call the flatbed truck on with one hand.

Standing in this rigorous cold, Siân remembered how the music had sounded, so much louder than this. It had reached halfway through the whole town, and the street would have been empty here, all of them dancing upstairs, just the wedding cars parked at the pavement. John had been drunk as a fart that afternoon and he'd kept on at Emyr until he'd got him up to dance. She would've smiled at the memory if not for the look on Dai Meredith's face now. Emyr had pushed his glasses up his nose, looking down at his own messy feet. And John shouting, 'Look at him go! Just look at that man go!' Holding his hands out like he'd just given Pinocchio life. Siân remembered the confetti that had scattered across the ground there. It would've stuck to these caterpillar tracks, raised up over and over again.

It was utterly quiet today, the street becalmed, and the bulldozer's noise touched everything. The air, unstirred, was suspended over Ynys-morlan; over the beach's stone and sand. It carried the slightest vibration.

In her kitchen, dressed and ready, Gwen opened the window and heard that engine; the tiniest hum. A clock was ticking on the wall behind her but in her garden, the edge of that tone was drifting on the air.

When the engines died, one by one as they watched, the people standing there could have heard a leaf fall.

Ruth looked towards the vehicles without a movement. In this new silence she didn't glance at Charlotte but only said, 'Tell me what you see.'

The bulldozer's shadow was sharp on the concrete. Charlotte remembered the cheque that she'd signed in the inarticulate hush of more than two hundred people.

'It's hard for me to imagine a perfect place.'

Waking this morning, in a failing moment, she had doubted. She had lain in her bed as sleep had left her, imagining the rest of this day. A community, like anything that evolves, must be interdependent; its balance must be spun like glass. And she had remembered Nia looking down at something that had shattered without sound for her. These doubts had lain over her in her bed, airless and shifting like pages.

'I've never loved anywhere really, before.'

She watched the door of the flatbed truck open, and a man step out to stand in the broad light. He saw the people scrutinizing him.

In the days before, when she'd felt these doubts, she had called Ruth. Saying nothing of what she felt. How could she tell if this project was right or not? She'd never been part of a community; understood Ynys-morlan's no more than any other. She couldn't know what it meant to change a place, or to change even one person's life. She had never taken any canvas, lover or family or friend. No, because she had seen that from the other side.

In these moments, she'd felt no connection to anything and had raged against herself. It was isolation she felt. Not silent as Nia's was, or as her own had been once, but a clamouring and frantic isolation. She'd ask Ruth questions and listen to the answers, to the sound of her voice.

At the head of Ynys-morlan's single street, men got out of the vehicles, unloaded tools on to the concrete with small, ringing reports. They glanced up every now and then at the faces that watched them. People were gathering, moving to stand in groups.

'When you talk about what you want,' Charlotte said, 'your feelings . . . are natural. But there's nothing natural in the vision you describe.'

Ruth's gaze was ragged as she stared out at the bulldozer. 'It's wrong, just to let things out naturally. You leave emotions to be natural, you make ugly things as often as you make beautiful ones. You get the boys who scrawl their names on walls. You get the men, getting drunk, getting angry . . . People get angry all the time,' she said. 'There's no conscience in nature. There's no goodness in it.'

There was no goodness, though, Charlotte thought – but did not say as she saw Ruth's face – in transforming an urge towards expression into something so uniform that no feeling could break through its beautiful symmetry. 'I don't want,' she heard Ruth say. 'I don't want.' As if she would take everything from this town, piece by piece. As if that was what beauty was: some kind of emptiness that could be reached when everything else was gone, some kind of purity.

She thought of her diaries, all their beautiful bindings. She thought of the words scrawled inside, full of hatred and sadness and loneliness, which she'd so desperately needed to say; which she had said, and then closed the covers on. Looking at Ruth, she wondered how it was that they could twist their needs into these fulfilments, which covered up, denied the needs themselves.

A perfect town. The mountains here seemed perfect. She had finally dressed this morning, long awake in her bed, and she'd gone to the window, looked out at the day's first frozen hour and seen the last of the mist. It had lain in curls, heavy as water. You seemed to feel the mountains rather than see them. Great arcs. Lines. When the sun or the shadow of a cloud passed across them, it moved her in a way that seemed deep, seemed old. But the movement wasn't towards other people. She would watch the shadows passing over and away.

She didn't want to create anything that was beautiful like this. It was something full of expression that she wanted to make. Full of feeling – full of identity. Real beauty could transcend a person. Not by rendering their life smaller, as the mountains seemed to, but by embodying it. The heart of them. In something that could be seen and heard and touched. She had woken today, tried to push doubts from her.

'I want to make something beautiful . . . that comes from inside,' she said.

Ruth gave a nod of recognition, frayed but definite, and looked at Charlotte as the men in the distance crossed the forecourt towards the gift shop's doors.

'Do you think,' she said, 'to make something beautiful, do you think that's a good enough thing . . . that it doesn't matter why you do it?'

The men unhooked the truck's back-plate and began to drag out gratings. The street's stillness was cluttered gradually with the voices of a crowd. They erected a barrier at the edge of the forecourt while the noise of hammers began upstairs. With interlinking metal fences they segregated the building from the street and, as if the barrier changed its demolition to a spectacle, groups of people moved towards it. Set back from the road by twenty yards of safety, the gift shop, low and solid, cast its shadow over ground that no longer seemed a part of the town. Indiscernible currents of this January air moved through its open doors, no little plastic windmills chattering their summertime words.

Standing beside Emyr, Siân Humphries spoke quietly, without glancing at him, 'What are they doing now – I see they're working up there.' She asked questions with no question marks. It would've been easy to say that there wasn't a soft spot in Siân. Had there been gentleness in her voice, speaking to Dai after he'd gone to her? Had she sounded surprised?

'They drill into the joists. They set up clips. They take out the window there.' He pointed to the gable-end wall and its windowpane. Through the glass, she saw a shadow. There was the skip van, parked directly below. 'They run steel ropes then, from the clips out through the window hole. They attach the ropes to the bulldozer, take the roof down.'

On the concrete, inside the barriers now, Dai stood with his shadow sliced across the ground as the men rolled from the van, bumping into the sunlight, a huge reel of cable that shone bright enough to hurt the eyes.

Siân thought of Gwen, of the many collections, the many fundraisers. Gwen's own personal brand of charity – made, as she'd discovered once, years past, more for the giver than the receiver. She remembered that day even now.

This crowd was building. Out there, walking towards her, she saw Patty, Bethan, Chelsea in her pushchair, eyes not on her yet. Patty was done up to the tens, looking towards the gift shop with a bright disinterest. Tom was walking behind them, staring at the houses they passed. Siân wiped her hands against her pinny and any fluttering stilled. She felt something she'd not expected. A sense of loneliness. It came over her without warning.

Gwen saw the thin shadows of the trees' bare branches give way as she drove into town. She felt the daylight fall across her face and it was warm through this glass, whatever month lay outside. Not a stir of wind in here.

They'd held on to their hats, throwing that confetti and it had blown back in their faces and hair. She'd thought then that they would all be picking it out, sitting at home when the night came and she and Emyr had gone.

Dai looked at his wristwatch, every thirty seconds, every minute, but he didn't know what moment he was counting towards. Afterwards, he would know, would be able to look back and remember that the gift shop had fallen at ten thirty-seven, at ten forty-nine, at eleven-o-one. Not knowing was the hardness in Time. And afterwards, when you *could* look back, nothing could be changed.

Moments passed, he watched them go.

In groups that had drawn together with quiet raised hands, with low-called names, people congregated around the barrier. They stood next to street lamps, by garden walls, around every solid thing in the street. As the tinny noise of a radio reached them, they talked without glancing at each other.

'Your Ellen not about today then?'

'Gone down to Radnor for the next few days, see her sister. Off to the land of one headlight.'

'She a fan of all this then?'

'Oh I'll tell you. Left the form stuck up on the fridge, right next to the shopping list.'

Radio 2 played a love song, thin as this atmosphere, through the sounds of people moving and the words passed from hand to hand.

'Going to be a hellish lot of noise today.'

Gwen parked next to Spar. On double yellow lines, no less. Open windows. Open doors, she saw. The gift shop was bare. She touched her skirt, her jacket. She stared out through the glass as Emyr walked towards her.

And now she had to wind the window down. She raised her hand to Siân and Pat, Bethan there as well, and Tom. She saw him. She wound the window, fully, and Emyr bent, shade over his face, his back turned to the gift shop behind. He was wearing his best suit too.

There was nothing on his face but she saw him swallow, bending.

'Hello there, love,' he said. He reached his head in through the window towards her, and he kissed her on her mouth. She felt it, just a touch against the lipstick there.

'Hello, Emyr.'

'Not long now. Come out,' he said. And then, sun in her eyes like this, he opened the car door for her. 'Everyone's here.'

Ruth pushed her garden gate for Charlotte and Nia, remembering her mother with guests. How she'd never just show them to the front door but right down the path, as if to say that this patch of land was hers as well, all the way to the street it was hers.

She latched it behind them.

'I can't remember ever seeing so many people outside. Not residents. At carnival maybe.' She laughed slimly. 'Well it's a demolition derby we've got today.'

'It's going to be all right,' Charlotte said. There was the narrowest layer of resolve on her face, over so many feelings, as she walked to watch the first part of this project she'd paid for. With money owed to a name and nothing more.

'Gwen,' Siân said. She held an arm out.

Gwen stood in the centre of their group, Tom just three feet from her, but she didn't let her gaze touch him, any of them, but only rest on the gift shop. Its grey space spread out before them.

She remembered dimly the way Tom had walked beside her, looking at her in moments like he wanted to help and didn't know if he should. So shocked that she should act like that. That Gwen Morgan could.

Two men were working on the window. The sounds of banging now, drilling and then drilling again, sent echoes down the street. The men took out the frame, she saw it.

They finished unscrewing the hinges and they lifted it out from the wall as if it wasn't a window at all, had never been a window but only a hole. She saw them hold it, saw them look down to where the truck was parked, the skip on its back. They were squinting in the light as they held the window free.

She could have said to Patty, 'Do you remember?' Her hair had been curled up and falling loose. It had got in her drink and she'd laughed, standing next to that window.

And now the white-painted frame fell. It tumbled over. In Ynys-morlan's inertia and hush, with only the thin sound of a van radio, it shattered across the skip's floor.

And the men, Gwen saw, withdrew their heads through the empty space.

Underneath the bitter sunlight, Siân saw her: the outfit, that silk scarf. Gwen stared out. She was wondering how many bricks were in those walls. She wondered how many times, in eighteen years, some-one could tell you they loved you. They would fall across this clean concrete, break on each other in dust. She was remembering their honeymoon, a week into it, maybe a little more, when Emyr had come into the hotel room and found her crying. He'd asked her what was wrong, and she'd told him that she was homesick. That had been how she'd felt. She hadn't been able to put it any better than that.

The men began to park the vehicles further down the road, and all the area to the right of the gift shop was clear. Its concrete was pockmarked.

She remembered sitting with Emyr in the hotel room that day, sun that was too hot for her coming in through the balcony's windows. She remembered saying, 'Ridiculous, to be homesick after only a week.' But when he'd asked her what she missed, she hadn't been able to tell him. She hadn't known herself. And she never cried, even back then. 'We're going to do a lot of good for our town,' she'd said. She remembered. He'd told her he loved her then.

Beside her, Emyr took a roll of ribbon from his pocket. It sparkled. And from the empty frame where the window had been, a man's head came now and he called out, 'All clear down there?'

Behind her, the slow voice of the crowd that had accumulated fell into a kind of stagnancy. From that window, into this winter serenity, the edge of a steel rope showed, and shone. The man paid it out through his hands, down, along the brickwork, as the bulldozer's engine came to life.

There might have been a hundred people in the road by the time the glistening cable touched the ground. They stood in a loose circle around the Spar. They clustered at the edges of the houses, in their shadows, though it was colder there. Ruth and Charlotte stood with Nia between them, nothing to do now but watch these men whose names they didn't know. And no talking clouded the air. The people's sounds were quiet as heartbeats. The street was filled with a hundred tiny movements, and the sound of the bulldozer's engine seemed to fill the spaces between every cheek and every shoulder.

Siân watched Dai step slowly away. Gwen had told her once: to be a good person was the most important thing in the world. More important than money, she had said, or achievements, more important than happiness even. Sitting in the house that she'd chosen with John, Siân had cried without knowing it. For weeks, all the time, tears had come out of her. While she washed up, when she was waking up every morning. Her face had hurt, she remembered, from their brine.

So slow, the bulldozer moved. Manoeuvring into a turn: yellow paint and rust that ground towards the space where the steel rope sagged, suspended.

She had said to Gwen, one of those days, those many days that had been full of the noise of Tom screaming while she'd cried without making a sound, that there'd been a lot of things that she'd wanted to do, before she'd fallen in love. She'd been full of aspirations before she'd met him. She'd asked Gwen if she remembered and Gwen had said yes. She'd asked Gwen to recall them to her.

She couldn't quiet Tom, ever. He didn't even seem to want for anything. Stacey not more than eight weeks old. And she should've held them to her. In anyone's imagination, in anyone's eyes, it should've been that way. Because they were all of John that she had left. But she'd sat away from them.

Siân looked at her now, her make-up in the sunlight, her eyes fixed on the slow-moving wheels. Gwen hadn't needed any make-up back then. She'd worn it, always, but she'd been full and flush anyway.

That was how people looked when they first got married: full and flush.

One of those dark days – because, though Gwen had opened the curtains every time she came round, they were always closed when she came back – Siân had tried to explain. She couldn't carry on with the things she and John had wanted together, nor go back to what she'd hoped for before him. He'd left her. One way or the other, he'd left her really. Like this, in this house. There had been things, she'd said to Gwen, that she had wanted to achieve.

Gwen had said gently to her, 'Your responsibilities, they're the most important thing now.' How easy it had been for her to say. She'd told her, 'You'll do the right thing. You'll look after Tom and Stacey. Whatever it takes to look after them, you'll do it. Because you're a strong person,' she'd said. 'Because you're a good person.' And the authority she'd had, saying that. The way she'd put her hand on hers.

Siân turned to look at her now. She wondered how much authority there'd been in her voice when she'd told Dai he was betraying his mother's memory.

It was so loud, the noise of that engine. So loud, Gwen thought now. The kind of sound that filled your heart and mouth, that placed vibrations into your hands even when you tried to hold them still.

'We'll do a lot of things together, won't we?' she'd said to Emyr, sitting on the hotel bed. And she had had this vision, of their life, and it had been true.

In the empty space beside the gift shop's wall, the bulldozer came to a halt. She saw the men move up to stand behind it. She saw them heft that metal cord.

As she spoke now, Siân's voice lay in abeyance. 'I think it's a good thing you're doing, Gwen. I have to say. Must be hard, I know it must. But Dai wants it, and after Eirian going . . . It'll do him good when this is over.'

Gwen turned her head very slightly. She looked at Siân and she nodded.

Siân witnessed her expression, and then she added, 'Life's full of baggage, you told me that once and I remember. It's good to get rid of a little. I wouldn't be surprised if we see him blossom after this is all done.'

'Thank you, Siân,' she said. She tasted her lipstick, carefully blotted. 'It isn't easy,' she said. The words came from her stomach. 'It isn't easy, no.'

The past was close to the surface, Siân thought. First time in all those years that a hole had shown in Gwen's kindness. First time that what was right and what made Gwen happy hadn't run together hand in hand. How Gwen had told her, she remembered, that it wouldn't matter what she had in life, what she achieved, if she did the wrong thing to get it.

'To be a good person, to make the right choices, that's always the most important,' she had confirmed, slim hand on Siân's knee.

And they'd looked at each other, the wrong thing unspoken between them, in air that was filled with Tom's crying.

Now, underneath this unmarred sky, the bulldozer's engine died.

Beside Gwen, Emyr said, 'Well this is it now.'

And he stepped away from her, out of the crowd, the ribbon held in both of his hands. There was no noise as he made his way across the forecourt, only silence in Ynys-morlan.

He took one end of the ribbon and he let it snake out to the ground. Walking then, he paid it out through his hands, watching it fall and lie still on the concrete. He'd never expected to stand here. Above his desk there were books, great dusty old tomes, with red cloth bookmarks showing passages, the three by-laws, that might have made this demolition unlawful. He didn't know what he would have said to Eirian's son.

Across the distance Dai watched him, by his side one hand opening, though he'd never held the ribbon himself.

It slipped and fell to Emyr's feet.

He had expected Gwen to look at him that night after the meeting, into his eyes, and see in them what their life had been like since she'd found a stranger-boy and cried to him: Emyr no longer believed in her love. He'd expected her to see that. And her own façade. How she acknowledged no change. How she seemed to feel none.

He had looked at their home, peeked behind the pictures on their walls and seen that there was no paintwork underneath. He'd pulled up the edge of their fitted carpet and found no floor, but only the ground and grass trying to grow there.

When Emyr walked around the building's corner, the crowd was gone from him for a moment. The crowd was gone, and he could hear his own footsteps. When he glanced up, with the gift shop now at his back, he could see instead the fence before him, and the marshland that stretched out. Four miles of flat, rough plain before the hills.

He remembered her looking into his eyes that night, but she hadn't seen. After the last of all those tears, out on the beach somewhere, her sight had hardened up. And what she'd looked at hadn't touched her any more.

Had he been able to reach Gwen, had she taken the other choice, perhaps sitting with Dai in Eirian's house he would have brought out those books and read Dai those passages. Slices of history they were. Perhaps, though he could have felt no pride at it, he would have told Dai that time was directing them to let the gift shop stand.

There was no motion here, no echo. He might have been alone. Twenty years it must have been, since Ynys-morlan had been open to this view.

Gwen Morgan watched her husband come from the other side of the building. He picked up the first end of the ribbon from the ground, slowly gathered the slack until he had to walk closer towards the glass doors – drawing in, and finally tying there, a loose little bow.

In the sunshine, he turned around and looked at the people. A hundred and fifty. Two hundred. He didn't know. Their faces were red in the cold but they were standing here anyway.

He couldn't believe how quickly he'd fallen. Like his values had been led by her. Amidst the throng he saw her small face now. Yes, he looked inside himself and the hurt he found made right and wrong seem useless. Emyr spoke into the silence as the man behind him came forwards to open the steel clip on the end of the cable and fasten it to the bulldozer's bar.

'Change isn't only celebration,' he said.

He didn't seem to see a face he recognized.

'I know what most of you think of the planning council.' Their quiet was a wall, just here, before his face. 'But a good planner,' he said, 'a good planner, he sees the place that he's responsible for . . . feels a duty to do right by it.' He'd written no notes for this; did not need any. 'I can see . . . I can see this street. I tell you, I've got some memory for every change that's happened in twenty years. Littlest things . . .' he said. 'I can remember going through them all, watching them built. A good planner, he looks out at his area and that place is his life.' He raised a hand in the silence, where muttered words fell to pool in the long shadows at the crowd's feet. He marked out places with his fingers; not these places it seemed, but patches on some stretch of land that was woven small in the air before him. 'Your memories – they're in all the buildings. Dotted here and there.' Where his hands imagined them, they were distant from each other. 'This change for me,' Emyr said, 'should be the one to put my words to test then. Change isn't always celebration. Sometimes it's more important than that.'

Emyr took a pair of small silver scissors from the breast pocket of his suit jacket. At the crowd's edge, Charlotte shifted. Ruth looked at her and her skin was white as the sea.

'Sometimes change truly means moving on, letting go of what went before. Sometimes it means losing things,' he said. 'But I'm looking out now, I look at Ynys-morlan, and it's not the past I see.' The hand that had painted tiny cottages on a patchwork land, it fell to hang by his side. 'We can build anything,' he said. 'Anything we want.'

Gwen watched him through the shoulders of the thronging people. She would have felt pride. The lack of it inside her showed a hundred miles of distance.

'People are worried to apply,' he admitted quietly. There were no murmurs as Ruth's mouth opened. 'You're worried about what it'll mean for our town, worried about the figure itself. It's a monster of a number. You're worried what others will think of you. Well the time's come to stop caring what other people think. There's no other town here. Do you see another? No. Ynys-morlan's always stood on its own. The time's come for Ynys-morlan's *community* to stand alone as well. To make a future,' he said, his voice needing no volume. For no person walked, the bulldozer stood in sleep. 'The time has come to declare what we want. To tell the rest of the world that *we don't care* what any of them see. Change isn't always celebration, ladies and gentlemen. Sometimes it's rebirth. *Reformation.*' He and Gwen would have walked forwards into this future. 'Sometimes it's redemption,' Emyr said.

She saw the sun raised above that building now, where the shining sky stared down and made her eyes smart with its clarity. She remembered Dai crying, his many nights downstairs.

As Emyr turned and held the scissors out, Charlotte Weyland stepping from the body of strangers that had surrounded her, Dai Meredith was smiling, though. He was looking at this day, such a beautiful morning, and feeling it fade those nights away. He was waiting for the moment. Ten fifty-four, eleven-o-one. He'd take hold of it when it came, when he knew which moment it was. Doubts would expire. He'd treasure it.

Charlotte's footsteps were audible on the concrete. She walked into their stares, her heart hammering, dry. She took the scissors from Emyr Morgan's hand and turned. And here was the town, before her.

Everywhere she had ever been, she thought, she'd seen as temporary. Staunch and only lived in for a time. In her mind now she saw these houses' interiors. Mrs Pryce's guest room, a little palace for a girl. All these buildings – for a moment she seemed to walk through them. Passed before bookcases. Looked out at someone else's view. Stood motionless before a mantelpiece, hands by her sides as she saw the things that were not hers, just as she'd stood in Hedera.

'I'm a stranger here really,' Charlotte said.

She had lived that way all her life. Pale houses, colourless walls. She saw Ynys-morlan, the mess of people's lives, garden furniture and rubbish bags, children's toys, spare-part wrecks and working cars, satellite dishes, laundry – saw it all now as it would be if transparent. In greys and whites.

'I've moved here . . . and this has started. I would like to take the opportunity to say now that I didn't come to put my stamp on Ynys-morlan. We're using the money. A regeneration project. But I would have given it away.'

As though seen through thin paper, every piece of this town without a hue.

'I didn't come to make my mark, but just because I wanted a life here . . .'

She spoke against her own self-doubt, suffocating. She could have bent to touch the grass and each blade would be covered, colourless, the whitest wax.

'I don't want anyone to feel isolated because of this, not in the place that's their home. If the project's for anything, it's not for me to put my mark, it's so you can.'

She took hold of the ribbon with one hand. The entire town was latent, any whisper would have strayed upwards. She saw the blanched sky, as clear as over Hedera's meadows. Against it, the trees were smooth and Charlotte seemed to see wax covering them, grey as cloud over their reaching tips. Lawns pale as if with snow.

'I want everyone in Ynys-morlan . . . to have a chance to *make* their home themselves. No one to live here – without having played a part in creating it,' she said. They looked back at her and she couldn't tell if her words reached them. She could smell the sea, she realized. She could hear the birds and feel the passing of the seasons through this open town. 'I don't want anyone to live in Ynys-morlan without having made it their own . . . Take the money. Use it,' she told them. 'Make it into something good.'

And turning away from the mosaic of the crowd, from their home, she looked down to discover the ribbon in her hand still.

It was easily cut, Gwen saw.

It fell as Dai's wristwatch showed the numbers 11:11 and it met the ground without the slightest noise.

She took a step away from the building. Through this quiet, the engine's first noise came. Men had switched off the building's electricity supply and they'd cut the line. They had turned off the water and so, a shadow of itself, the gift shop was dry. This congregation of residents formed a semicircle, looking out from between the houses.

The machine moved forward. And, slow as ice, the rope was drawn taut. It gleamed blindly, a vein between the bulldozer and the shell of Eirian's shop. For a moment, watching it pull without motion, time might have been stilled.

Dai's face was painted with the sun.

Charlotte heard the first crack as she turned; the sound startled in her chest, desperate as birds taking flight. With her back against the railings, at the edge of these people, she reached out and seemed to touch this place, in tenderness, with the love she felt, and the building in front of her was smitten.

Each of those slates that felt the sun, they seemed to move, some heat mirage. It couldn't be possible that the building changed. It had stood for so long. Gwen thought – an unconfined moment – that it must be her sight.

The sound of it washed against Dai's expression, filled the air before all their faces and between their open hands, thrumming.

Ruth saw the long roof move. Held in her arms, Nia was still when the first slate fell. Real and harsh, unmuted. Ruth's expression broke. She watched the upper storey of this souvenir shop, which people might have walked in and out of, pull away from its windows and doors.

It slipped in the clear air, impossible. It moved aside as the rest of its slates fell.

Charlotte watched them, raindrops that broke. Saw them descending as if she pulled them down herself. If anyone applauded, if Gwen's hands moved, the sound of it was lost. Above the gift shop's wide windows and the shadow of its gutter, it tore away. Sunk over its own end wall as if years of neglect passed in the switching seconds on Dai's wristwatch. Into the concrete space between the shop and the first trees, its roof came down.

The gulls must have scattered up there, Emyr thought. At the head of Ynys-morlan's two long rows of buildings – small, canted angles in the daylight, seen from above – a cloud of dust began to rise. He looked up and it diluted the sky.

Their faces, one by one, were upturned and for a little while stayed that way, like flowers looking for the sun – as the trees' branches, clean and dark and open to the air, were swept into the dust's warmer storm.

June 1st '77

Dear Charlotte,

One by one they sank. Lower, gone. Fourteen of them
because it's been so long since last time. Felt a lot of
guilt then but not today. It's the timing.
Haberdashers' is over and it'll be King's now. Not very
young any more. I don't have to feel vulnerable. If I
choose not to read her letters, it's for me. Not a
reaction, not a backlash anymore. I feel stronger.
There's nothing wrong with that, I deserve some
strength. If I'm to be alone, I won't be alone and weak
and full of uncertainties. I took them out to the
Embankment. Walked along the river there for as long a
stretch as you're able. On the way I picked out my
fourteen stones. Several reddish, though there's no red
stone in the area, that I've seen. Sealed them up in new
envelopes. All her desperate begging letters with their pink
paper and their scent, all the hateful ones - the typed
ones and the others that came through solicitors. Felt
good. It wasn't raining then.

I don't know what people thought - if they saw me.
What should it matter though? they'll just forget. A
mention to the person they go home to maybe. 'It's funny
- know what I saw today?' But that'll be it, and it'll
pass out of their heads. I watched them, one by one
dropped them in, watched them sink and I tried to feel
some empathy for her. Really it's not so hard. No one's
evil. I mean, when's a person born to hurt others?
That's not how it works. People don't live their lives to
cause harm. It comes from pain, that's all, surely.
desperation. Inside me, the feelings aren't the kind
that create. I understand her. But I couldn't want
children. I wouldn't do that.

But I think in truth it's not what she did to me. It's what she tried to do. the orchestration. My wandering through this world – and I remember, I **do** remember – how it felt to realize. It **is** my memory. Playing my part in this life, this home, this childhood, which didn't belong to me, although it was the only one I had. Yes what frightens me is how happy they would have been, had I continued in that life unknowing.

I will change, I think. As I was watching the letters get darker, get heavier, found myself making promises again. I will heal, I think. I have a fresh start now. The fact that I've had other fresh starts doesn't mean that it's false hope. I won't let the wrong in me affect the world.

The evening that the gift shop was broken, the sky faded above Ynys-morlan to a high and star-pointed chill. The sea came quietly against the shore at the houses' backs, a shard of moon rising over the twilight water. Curtained light from kitchens and lounges reached into the gardens and left the main road dark. In this freezing air, the street lamps misted.

You could feel the calm of a place that's been left behind by the visitors. Passing by the houses, there was no sense that anything could change here. But at the town's entrance, you could see the gift shop's shattered ruin.

Three of its walls were still standing under the deepening sky, in the midst of their own rubble. Where dinghies had been tied in windy, sunny days, brickwork sloped. Burst heaps, dust and lumps, holding the last of the light. They'd collapsed around the trunks of the first trees. They were ploughed through by the workmen into clear, dark stretches here and there.

Above these walls, no roof. The lower windows twisted, empty frames – all but one. Towards the end, a pane had been left, miraculous, intact, and now the streetlight was cloistered in it.

Dai Meredith sat on the shop's upper floor, where his mother had stacked boxes, heaving and huffing, or had bent at a desk by the window over messes of books and papers. He was cross-legged under the freezing constellations.

He'd stumbled up over the bricks, feeling them slip under his boots, fall behind him – each cold and rough under his hands. They'd left his palms sore with grit, clambering over a broken rafter to step on to wooden floor.

This was the place where you had to bend your head under the A frame – or it would get you a good one, add another little notch to its count. And after bending under it, you could look out of the window at the people passing by; see them in the summer with the wind right in their faces, holding on to picnic carriers and towels. He looked at the window and saw a twisted piece of wood, hanging from the shattered edge of silhouetted brickwork. Above it, there was nothing but the air.

With all the empty cardboard boxes from the jelly shoes stacked up round her, filled with papers and files, his mum's face would be grey, frowning down at numbers and words and numbers. And he'd stood behind her sometimes, looking at what she was doing, asking if he could help. She'd start by smiling up at him. She'd turn and pat him on the arm, ask him to go to Spar, buy her a cream slice or just a bun, if there were none of those left. The books she had had were drawn with columns already. She'd go down the page, filling something into each.

Those days before he'd got the job from Emyr, time had never seemed like a good thing. There would be too much of it and he'd be waiting, always. He'd look at everyone else and they'd be moving at a different speed to him. He'd seen how strong time was then, how important. His mum's pen would scratch. He remembered the shape of her big back as she'd leant over, remembered the curve of her neck and the curls of hair.

'Mum?' he'd say. 'I've got a question for you. You know, when you don't have an idea, like, you're trying to think of what to do one day and you don't know, you can't think of anything, and then you sit and think and then suddenly you've got one. An idea.'

'Uh-huh?' She'd say. She wouldn't look up.

'Where does that come from? The idea, I mean. If it wasn't in your head before and then it is, what is that?'

Her pen wouldn't stop scratching.

Getting the job from Emyr, that was when he'd started to understand time. He'd get up and be sweeping before most other people were awake. In the mornings, it felt almost like people didn't matter. People thought they knew about time, they had their days and their nights. They were busy. They were sure. In the mornings, you saw the sky get lighter and you'd realize that people had nothing to do with it. You'd see the empty street, as though a place was stronger and more *there* when the people weren't around. He'd clean the town for the town's sake. He'd had a feeling that it liked to be clean in the mornings; it liked the before to be washed away. The gulls would land in the middle of the road like it was just a part of the ground. This was the sort of thing people didn't know.

Dai looked at the wooden floorboards, could hardly see them now in the day's last faintness. They were deformed, cracked. At the end of the room where she'd bent over her papers, all the floor was torn away; fallen through the hole or tumbled round it, a ruin. Not one inch of it was clean when he ran his hand over it now. He thought of all the times that he had swept the street outside. He wondered what it meant to clean a place over and over, to love doing it, and then to stop and turn around one day and to decide to make this pile of ugliness. People left disgusting things. Day after day, he'd picked them up. He leaned forwards now, he looked down over the warped piece of sill where the window should have been, and he saw what he'd done.

Dai reached out to put his hand where the wall had been and the feel of nothing scared him. He could put his hand outside, draw it back, no feeling at all. Just air. How could you not be frightened by something missing like that?

This was where the drapes of sunlight lay in the afternoons, over boxes of stock. But he looked to every side and all around him, through the vapour of his breath, he saw the town's lights. Like this was the first time all the things that he believed, all his questions, were laid out in the world. And his hands were still, now tentative, resting lightly on the wreckage that had brought him here.

The bus's headlights washed over the skip first of all. Rhys moved closer to the glass, seeing it, feeling the window's chill near his face. In the trundle of the curve, he heard other people moving. Glancing round, Ieuan Davies, John Griffiths were holding on to the backs of the seats, leaning down to peer out into the streetlight. He heard the scuffle of somebody else, shifting up to get nearer the view. Rhys saw the skip; the dirty lettering all along its side. He heard Ieuan give some kind of a laugh. 'Well look at that, will you look at that now.'

Griffiths gave some answer back, voice buried in the bus's noise.

Passing slowly by under the high lamps, the gift shop was banked inside the remains of its own walls. Rhys's eyes followed it around the road's slow curve, saw the dark piles of its refuse on the forecourt, the windows of the ground floor punctured and that one pane, dusty, blind. It looked like it had always been ruined.

Behind him, Ieuan was raising his tone over the rumble of the engine. 'I was telling David about it, up at head office. "What did we have to do to get the grant?" And what was it for? What's the ceiling on it? "So ours is the place to move to, then."'

'Well it's all starting. Look at it.'

Rhys turned in his seat as the bus drove on down the empty road. Shrinking away, it sprawled out across its concrete like some kind of fucking wound. The place to move to. The road was hard to make out in front of him.

Last night he'd come in from watching the TV and found his parents at the kitchen table. They'd had the form there, between them, his mother had had a pen in her hand.

'What're you doing?' He'd stood for a moment, just looking at them, before his mother had said,

'Well you can see what we're doing.'

It had taken them less than two weeks to work their way around to this choice. They'd stepped their way so carefully through each part of the decision that they'd managed not to hit one single obstacle. He'd talked to them on their own. On their own, they had doubts. He'd looked at them last night, sitting there together. He'd nodded, turned away under his mother's eyes, taken things out from the cupboard.

'Going to apply?'

'No,' his father had said, 'your mother's showing me joined-up writing again.'

Rhys had put tea bags in cups, still nodding like that, like some idiot in the quiet he'd just made. Eventually, his back to them, he'd said, 'What've you put down for then?'

'Bits and bobs. Bit of new roofing. Stripping the pebbledash off the front. They want to take all the buildings down to the original stone. Give that little porch a bit of a going over, that's not been touched since Lloyd built it. Come see,' he'd said then. 'Put something down if you want. They can only say no.'

'Thanks.' He'd picked his tea up to go. 'I think I can do without their yeses and nos.'

'Oh come on,' his mother had said suddenly. And he'd turned to her then, ready. 'It's not like that, Rhys, for God's sake.'

'Well,' he'd shrugged. He'd looked away. Standing there by the doorway, them sitting at the table where they'd set themselves out, he'd been too close to leaving to turn back. 'It's your house,' he'd told them.

'I know whose house it is,' she'd said. She'd had that pen in her hand, she'd liked the feel.

'Come on.' Always these days, his old man's voice was soft as padding. 'It's everyone's house, all of us.' But he'd been looking away by then.

And this was how it always seemed to go now: crossed words, shouted or quiet, this was how it seemed to go. He remembered Tom saying once, moving his stuff down into the caravan it had been – that it didn't have anything to do with how well you got on, or if there was lots of money or no money, you just got to an age where you couldn't live with your family any more, or they couldn't live with you.

They had taken his boxes of stuff down the road to the site, long and dusty, with Ynys-morlan straggling out around them. They'd had them piled in a wheelbarrow Guthrie Powell had lent them, and he'd said to them, 'Squeaks like a bastard.' And it had done, every turn of the wheel, every trip. They'd made three. 'I don't know,' Tom had said. 'You can like doing all the same stuff, I reckon. Could be the kind of person that really gets on with their family . . . Bethan and Pat, like . . . and you can still feel like it won't work any more. It's just that. You know you get the lions in the pride, like –'

And Rhys'd said to him, 'Lions. Right, that's what it's like. Not like gerbils. Chickens.'

'No not like fucking chickens. Like lions, all right? You get the young male lion and he's just a little kitten, a cub and everything. And the mother lion's bringing him up, but then it gets to a point where they're, like, fighting over food and the young lion's picking more fights with the older males . . .'

'You been watching a programme about lions by any chance?'

'Listen, right. It's like a natural thing. Doesn't matter if you try and fit in with it, you get to a point where you're not meant to be living at home any more. And you can feel it,' he'd said. 'It's not like you want to leave. Just feel like you should.'

Seeing him, he remembered, he'd kept smiling at Tom till Tom'd had to say something.

'All right. Fucking "Wildlife on One" . . .'

He'd looked out along the road, the ground roughening up around them then, little dunes and sharp grass.

'So I can have you over for, like, a dinner party now,' he'd said.

'Darling, I simply must come for tea.'

'We'll lay out a table, sixteen places, like. Have three courses. And soup.'

'A starter and a fish course and silver service. We'll all sit round and toast.' Taking one hand off and letting the barrow sink, Rhys had raised a glass to the long road.

'That'd be good,' Tom had said. 'That'd be a laugh.'

Rhys felt the judders of the bus move through him now. He looked out through the dark glass, thinking of Tom's caravan. Standing in the kitchen last night, he'd stared down at his cup of tea; all of them staring down, like they'd all failed at something.

He'd said, 'I'd have thought if you wanted renovations done, you would've got them done yourself.'

And she had told him it wasn't about that. If it had been about that, they would have. 'If there's going to be a drive to improve the place, if we can do our bit, I'm hardly going to say no then, am I? There's things that need doing on our place, there's things that could be done. Am I meant to say no?'

'God knows the council's not going to do it, Rhys. Town's falling apart and they won't send a man round to fix the pavements.'

'If this whole place is going to be done up,' his mother had qualified, 'I'm not going to be the only house left just out of pride. If this woman wants to pay, let her pay. It isn't any skin off my nose.'

'Obviously not, like.'

'If the council won't do it –'

'Then maybe it doesn't need to be done, like.' And then he'd said, 'Christ's sake.' He'd turned away. 'What difference is it going to make changing the buildings? There isn't any money here, still. There's no jobs. One pub and one church, I'd like to know what difference they think they're going to make, doing the houses up nicely.'

'It'll bring people in, Rhys,' his dad had said, like he was disappointed Rhys would ask when he must have known the answer already.

'For God's sake, Rhys.' His mother had shaken her head. 'Look at Cornwall,' she'd said.

But he'd stared at them and he hadn't been able to say what he felt. Knock the gift shop down, he'd thought, change all the fucking buildings.

He'd only said, 'I don't want to live in Cornwall.'

'Really? Well after all the things you've said about it, it didn't sound like you wanted to live in Ynys-morlan either.'

'I don't.'

'Then what difference does it make to you, Rhys?' She'd turned away from him then. 'I can't reason with you.'

'I'll tell you the difference it makes,' he'd said suddenly. He'd turned on them both like they had started this whole project, tea slopping over his hand. 'I just hate it, that's what. I hate all this . . . wandering round telling each other how wonderful it's going to be. "What Ynys-morlan's got to offer that it's never had a chance to show . . ." You go into the bloody Spar, it doesn't matter who's in there, that's all they're talking about. Go into the Lion and that's all they're talking about. What an *opportunity* this is, like everyone here's just been waiting for success, like, and all they needed was for the town to look nicer. Yeah, that's been the problem all along.' He'd looked at their sad faces. '. . . If people thought renovations were so fucking important, why didn't they spend their own money on them?'

'Don't swear at me, Rhys. Not in my own house.'

Rhys had turned away from her. 'Yeah,' he said. 'Well that'd be right.' He'd put the tea down on the counter and it had spilled there too, and he'd just looked at it. He couldn't get it out, couldn't find the words to tell them. And he'd wanted to tell them, not push them away.

'I hate it. Everyone suddenly walking round, chests puffed so far out it's a wonder they don't push each other off the bloody street. Looks like that's what they're trying to do. *Agreeing* with each other. Can't open your ears without hearing people *agreeing* these days. Oh the town's so important. Oh the community's so fucking important –'

'Rhys –'

'Well?' He'd looked at them. What he'd said, it was true. 'They don't care about any bloody community. They keep on talking about it. They feel good talking about it. But they don't care. They just like that it makes them feel . . . *significant* that's all it is. That's all.' In his memories, he'd seen Emyr in the sunlit car park, shouting every insult that didn't stain his own mouth. There wasn't any good in these people. They liked to talk about morals, right and wrong. There wasn't any goodness in them. Any right to judge.

Rhys'd turned away from his parents, seeing that look come out on his father's face, like Rhys was moving away from them. Like every time he said something, he moved further off and there wasn't anything they could do to stop it. It wasn't their faults.

Rhys had said, 'It doesn't matter to me what you do, like. Take the money. Why not?' He'd stood there with neither of them speaking to him. This was how it was, always. 'Go and watch the gift shop knocked down.' And saying it then, it had felt like the first time he'd really known it was happening. One day away, and then it'd be gone. It didn't seem like it took much, much time or change or anything, for a place to be suddenly different. He wondered how long it would take to change the houses and how long for the Lion and the Spar.

Bethan had stood up at the meeting. They'd told him. Typical Bethan Hughes, his mother had said. She'd stood up, holding the baby and everything, and asked the woman flat out how much money there was. And the woman had told her. Thirty-three million pounds.

He remembered one time on the beach, Tom and Bethan there, truth or dare. She'd looked up at him and asked who he'd been with while he'd been going out with her. He remembered the expression on her face then – she'd had it all the time really, all the time they'd been together – like she couldn't have put any more distance between them than she had just with her eyes. And he'd seen her, lying that way on the sand. He remembered thinking that he fucking loved her. He didn't know what it had been in her expression. She would have looked that way, he thought though, standing up in front of everyone at their fucking meeting.

In the kitchen, them not saying a word, he'd picked his tea up, wet off the counter. 'Take the money,' he'd said. 'Everyone could do with it. You could do with it. Take it.' His mum hadn't touched the form as it had lain between them. 'Go on,' he'd said. No anger in his voice. 'Go on, sign it. What the fuck.'

'Rhys.'

'What the hell,' he'd said. 'What the hell then.' He'd moved across to them, the closest that he'd got since walking in here. He'd picked up the form and pushed it gently at her. 'Go on, sign it,' he'd said. 'Doesn't make any difference.'

He'd watched her take it from him and he hadn't said anything else then. Letting it out of his hand, he'd left the room.

Now Rhys stared at the people round him, the street moving past them, dull yellow outside. He had left this morning on this same bus and the gift shop had been there. It had been standing just like it had always done, empty in the mornings.

He saw the old woman, Mary something who came in every other day on this bus, always sleeping along the way home. Her head would sink down on to her chest and shift like a buoy on the water. She had thin shoulders, this narrow back. He looked at the baby strands of white hair and wondered how it would seem to her when she walked past that place tomorrow. She'd lived here all her life. She'd probably been a kid here, when they were still fishing, harvesting, whatever. He wondered how ugly it would be to her, to see that building broken down, if it looked so ugly to him and he'd only been here eighteen years. Or maybe she wouldn't care, he thought. He watched her head go up and down, the wrinkled skin on the back of her neck looking soft under the bus's yellow strip lights. Maybe she'd only shrug. She must have seen a lot of change here in her life. He wondered at what she must have seen.

The Lion was busy with heads lowered close to each other in corners. The sound of slow pool balls filled the spaces between every voice. Through the little windows, the night was solid darkness, white-painted stone walls very bright in here, smoke moving through the air.

Jo Griffiths with a cigarette, sitting over a plate of half-finished food. Edward Evans, watching the final yellow go down, a pint of Guinness untouched on the scratched table beside him.

A lot of silences in here, patched over by others' talk. Sally Pritchard, speaking with Bill over the bar; her glass in one hand while the other moved, to show him little details of the room he lived in every night.

'I know,' he told her. 'I know, I know.' Because he'd run dry now of everything else he could say, and there was only the decision. In this room, the lights showed spaces where antique tools and fishing nets would have hung.

People had sat here drinking for a hundred years, more, when they'd still been real fishermen. They'd stooped over the bar and it must have looked just the same. Dark windows showing the deep cold outside, but so warm in here, full of comfort and voices in here, drinking through the night before they had to board and leave.

Siân Humphries's house was three storeys high, narrow between the other buildings. At its back, where the beach washed up in the gales, November, March sometimes, a low, grey block extension looked out; their kitchen, cemented against the original house. The garden was paved, broken in places. Summer lawn furniture leaned on one side of the porch, dirty from the rain. There were net curtains hanging behind every window. On the pavement, past the front of the building you could walk, and see your reflection caught in the space between the glass and cloth. Not a beautiful house. Tall like this, it seemed to hold its lack of beauty up for every other home to see.

Tom's bedroom window had looked over the water. Away from

the road, the town, you could stare out of it and believe this was the only house for miles. He'd never owned a lot of things. When he'd moved out there'd still been posters on the wall from when he'd been fourteen. The set of encyclopedias his grandfather had given him, a couple of Tom Clancy books, read so much all the pages had been loose, he'd had his stereo and CDs, a technical drawing set, but not much else on the shelves. He remembered looking at them, standing with empty cardboard boxes round his feet, and wondering how you could live in one place for so long without gathering more things.

Standing in the café that night, Tom watched his mum. He held the damp cloth in his hand but he stood without moving, in front of him the mess was wiped into piles. He listened to her voice as though through water.

'. . . clapping, I couldn't believe it. I mean, you saw her, Pat, she couldn't have put more effort into it if she'd tried. It was an outright *lie*. Like some martyr, she was: oh, wanting to give so much *support*, what a hard thing it was for her to see, oh, the *memories* in the place. You know what I said to her, did you hear what I said? I told her what a good thing she was doing for Dai. See how she'd react to that. And I saw.' Siân nodded, vicious, she raised her eyebrows. 'Oh, the *modesty* in it. "It's not an easy thing," she goes. "It's not easy, no . . ." No,' Siân said. 'I imagine it wasn't. Not as easy as going to Dai, shouting everything she could think of to get what she wanted when he was crying right in front of her.' Tom saw her look away from the table. 'Not as easy as slapping him, I'd think.' She put every accent on her face, as large as she could for Pat and Bethan. But her fingers were shifting on her bag, angry, and when she looked up at Pat, he saw something in her face that he'd hardly ever seen. It was pain, and he didn't understand it, didn't understand the sound of her voice.

She moved all the time, shifted in her chair. She turned away from the table like she was disgusted, turned back like she couldn't help herself. He remembered the day that Gwen had called him here, to hiss at him, insults and questions: was he happy at the damage he and Rhys had caused? And he'd realized then what had led to what: that he'd lied to Rhys, the worst kind of lie, not even wanting to do it. And that Rhys had fucked him, wanting to believe that lie just so he could use it. Shout it into Emyr Morgan's face. And he'd put the phone down on Gwen, told her he'd been wearing that bracelet, handing his pride to her like a head on a plate.

He'd been so full of blame, that night in the museum it had rushed in quick as the sea to fill the gap that pride had left. So full of blame, telling Rhys he didn't want his mother to know.

He watched her talk and hated what was in her face. She looked cruel. And Gwen Morgan today, what she'd done to Dai, the gift shop coming down with Emyr's help – he wondered. He remembered sitting with his mum on the sofa before going to the museum, looking at her as she'd stared at the TV screen. And he'd thought then that he didn't even know Gwen. Hardly knew the first thing about her.

What Rhys had done, it had been a shit thing. But what he'd done to Rhys had been worse. It'd been right and it had been worse. He was the one who'd started the lie, standing on the beach underneath that gaping sky.

When he looked back and saw Gwen standing in his caravan, he didn't understand himself what he'd tried to do. All those days around it seemed clouded, infuckingcomprehensible. Some light had gone on, seeing her standing there and crying, but looking back, it must've been false. He had seen a good person.

It seemed like he'd left Rhys, and he felt lost without knowing what he was moving towards. Of that whole time, the only part that seemed clear now was that memory of his mother, sitting on the sofa, looking different to him, looking far away to him, when she hadn't changed at all.

'On and on, she goes, her fund for this and her collection for that, all the committees she likes to be on. Her values and her morals. Like she's got the bloody patent, you'd think.'

They'd set bollards up around the demolition, outside the metal barrier. Tomorrow, the town would be filled with the noise of breaking as they started taking down the walls. The bollards had looked very small like there was no way to hem in what had started. A part of this town was already gone.

'I spoke to her,' Patty said quietly.

Siân raised an eyebrow. Tom saw it – something stuttered.

'I spoke to her. She didn't want to see me. Wouldn't answer, I asked if she was OK. Wouldn't answer at all.'

Bethan watched over Chelsea's grabbing hands.

'What do we need to ask her? We saw her today: "It isn't easy, no."' Siân looked away from Pat, and Tom saw her say, 'It's us she's made fools out of. You and me. It's us she's lied to. Don't think I want to help her any more.'

'Siân, she's not a bad person . . .'

'I'm saying she's not as good as she pretends to be! You know what I don't like? The time this has come at. What's made this happen.'

'I don't know what you mean.'

'Suddenly there's a big meeting, there's *private grants* and everyone in town has got the chance to have their houses done up, and their businesses done up and subsidies on top of that. And we find Gwen, clapping through all the meetings – and doing everything she can to stop it when she's behind closed doors.'

'Only the gift shop. Their reception was there.'

'I was at it too if you remember. There's no fault in my memories,' she said coldly. 'They might as well have had red carpet laid down.'

In her lap, his mother's hands were still. She looked old under these strip lights. A thin woman, hair cut short and dyed blonde like she'd given up on it a long time ago. She was the sort of woman who ends up with every bad thing that's happened weighing in the lines on her face. Tom remembered how she'd been, such a long time ago, when he'd rescued that girl on the beach. And the photographer had come round to take pictures, she'd stood next to him and straightened his clothes. She'd looked into his face like she could give him everything he needed without having to use words.

Old and tired and everything else, she was always strong though. She'd never let anything come between her and what she had to do. But it wasn't strength that he saw in her face now. It was hate.

She said, 'There's nothing wrong with wanting the best for yourself, everybody wants that. A nice house, the clothes. It's only wrong when you lord it over everyone else. You know what my views are. I don't believe that money's the most important thing, though that's what you're meant to believe these days. Having *worked* for it is the most important, looking back and being able to say that it's yours. However Gwen lives, I've always agreed with what she says: morals are the most important thing. Well I can see now how much morals are worth to her. And I hope she sees it too. I hope she can't ignore it. That she looks back and realizes what it's all been about. *Success*. Because I can see it, and so can everyone else.'

You could get to know the status quo so well, you thought it was for ever. You could know a man, a town, a way of life so completely, it seemed that there could never have been another way. But this was a lie, Gwen saw. Stability was a lie, in all its forms. Just a narrowing of the eyes.

Emyr Morgan and Llew, Gwen's father, had used to finish each other's sentences. She remembered smiling and pointing it out to her mother with one finger. How her mother, saying nothing, had smiled back. It had seemed to her then like the future must be broad as a landscape, like it must stretch out in every direction, whichever way she might turn.

She remembered the building work on the gift shop, the grind and slap of the cement mixer, she remembered the radios and all the men climbing over that space, putting up walls brick by brick. It was an amazing thing to see, something that had only been an idea, new and sudden and of a scope that had made them laugh when her father had first come home with it, to see it actually built, in a place where you'd never conceived of anything being before. It filled you up with possibilities. And then it had been finished, and it had stood at the head of town, new and shining and fresh-painted. And they had sold it. And celebrated it.

She'd said to Emyr once that developers and planners must always see the possibility in places; walking around, must see only the spaces. It would look like an entirely different world to them.

She couldn't remember the point when the possibility had faded out of the gift shop. There must have been a time when seeing it had stopped filling her with ideas of what could be, and it had just become another building. She didn't know how you could lose something like that and not see it happening. It seemed to Gwen now that she'd spent a lot of time searching for other projects which would make her feel the same.

Today, though, she'd seen the other side of possibility. This way she was, the home she had, the life, it wasn't *meant* to be. Yes, it seemed to her now that people lived their lives in a chaos of possibility. No wonder that they wanted to narrow their sight. No surprise they kept photograph albums to look through and remind themselves how they'd got to this place; this living room. People said, 'We met at college, most romantic story . . .' People said, 'Our birthdays are the same, isn't that incredible?'

The roof of the gift shop had shimmered like it was summer and the slates were hot. It had been torn from its rafters and dragged free to smash on the concrete. Now the bollards around its high barrier neatened it, just a slight diversion from the path you usually took.

Gwen hadn't gone home that afternoon, or when the afternoon sank into its evening. She'd got in her car and driven through town, and out, where the road passed the community centre and drifted into sand. She'd sat in her car and had seen the sun go down on the beach, doing nothing but watching for those hours. It occurred to her how rare this was: to sit without any activity for such a length of time. No one ever did this. She wondered how much you could know about yourself when you were always moving, always caught in the flow of doing. Nothing, it seemed.

It was a very beautiful sunset. All the air gathered into winter: a dim, blushed sky which was empty but for three lines of cloud above the sea. And they were so bright. They were golden. For a little while, all the still water was golden. The gulls stood in groups on the shore. You only had sunsets like this in the winter, where you could see the first stars even through the light. It must have been that the air was clearer then, that the coldness made it so. Sitting without doing for such a long time, only looking out there, she'd found herself wanting to cry.

She hadn't been able to. Stranded, nothing had been over. Emyr was at home, he was calling round building crews this evening, a little stack of application forms lying on the desk in front of him.

Gwen had thought of the small Carltonware bowl on top of the television, filled with seashells. Her home had ended, and she had stared out at the sunset before her, unable to touch any beginning.

'Well are you defending her then?' Siân leaned forwards, opened her hands like Pat must be able to see, spread right on her palms, that there was no way to defend it.

'I'm not going to take sides.'

'Sides? Is that what you think this is about? I'll tell you what it's about, Pat. I'm sick of seeing her walk round this town, hanging with gold jewellery that cost God knows how much, sitting in *church* with it on for God's sake, acting like she's the moral standard for this whole town. Tell you the truth, I've never liked the arrogance of it. But I damn well won't put up with it when I know where her morals *really* lie. In the bloody bank is where they are.'

'Nobody's perfect, Siân!'

'I know nobody's perfect! I don't know how you can sit here all innocent like I'm overreacting! Tell me you don't get sick of seeing it. I don't know how you can be so blind – specially not so wide-eyed as you're looking now.'

Pat turned away, drew herself back across the table, and Bethan's gaze was on Siân.

Siân didn't speak. She sat with her face turned away from them, held her eyes on nothing like she could see, right in front of her, the words that she'd just said.

She recalled. Sitting in her living room, she'd seen how smartly Gwen was dressed. Just to come down and help her out. Her jewellery, her hair curled, like she couldn't do without it by then. She must have sat in front of the mirror for an hour. And she'd looked at Gwen and wondered just how easy it must be, to balance morality up against personal gain, when you had both right in your hands. How she'd liked to talk about them. And only luck that they had run in tandem for her for so long.

Siân had said to her that afternoon, sitting beside Gwen, 'How many people is it that you go round to with reports about me? Tell me, Gwen,' she'd asked, 'when was it that I stopped being your friend and started being your charity case?'

After a long time, unmoving, Siân opened her mouth again. 'You can think what you want, Pat. And I'll just do the same.' And then she looked back at them, both staring at her.

Like she was the one doing wrong here, Tom thought. His eyes moved over their faces and he didn't even know what he was looking at any more. He'd been so full of blame in the museum, he'd been so sure of what was right and what was wrong. He hated to see her like this, angry, upset like this. He wanted to go over to her. Just sit down at the table, that would be enough. He thought of the way she'd look at him if he did that. She'd never needed anybody's support. He thought sometimes that she liked to be on her own under everyone else's eyes. She was used to fighting battles this way.

He would've gone to stand behind her but he wondered suddenly if it was support that he wanted to give, or if he only wanted to put his hand on her back so she wouldn't talk like this any more.

He looked through the doorway, across the empty café, her bag so tight in her hands, drawn up against Bethan and Pat. He loved her. He stood in the kitchen and didn't move any nearer to where they sat.

'You can think what you like,' she said again quietly. 'But I'll tell you one thing. I'll be getting myself one of those forms and I'll be sending it in. We've all worked long and hard enough to deserve the nice house.'

His mouth opened.

Later, trying to remember, he couldn't think of what it was that he'd been going to say. In the caravan that night, finally moving towards sleep, he had no idea. It seemed like there'd been a lot and he'd wanted to release it all at once. It seemed like he'd been full of memories, sudden and hard, and had wanted to throw them. Looking back, he couldn't remember one. Lying in his bed, seeing the curve of Gwen's shoulder, those hard things would seem lost to him.

His mother's house, strong and definite and old, the paint peeling round the window frames outside. His bedroom and all his old stuff on the shelves. The photos Siân set on the mantelpieces, only perfect ones, like examples of how the world should try and be every day.

He thought now of Gwen's face, as the gift shop had come down.

He heard Pat ask, 'Really . . . ? You're going to apply . . . ?'

And Bethan adding, 'For the renovations?'

He looked away from them, dropped his eyes to his hands, and closed his mouth over anything he might have said.

Around the time when Siân had started to talk about him moving out, he'd thought of travelling. Other people went off without anywhere to stay. You listened to them and they were going to India or Thailand, and they had their sleeping bags, big backpack-tortoises. Not caring where their beds were or if they had any of their things around them. You'd always be moving. You could get sick of a place, and you could just leave it behind, up and out, away.

He'd thought about these countries but he hadn't known how it would be if he went there. What if you got to a place like that and you didn't feel good? What if you got to India or Thailand, wherever, Newfoundland, and you still felt like you were on your own, even more than before? You'd just be lost then. Just the same as in the place where you'd grown up, only far away from the things you recognized.

He watched his mother talk. He tried to make out in her eyes some new kind of place, some country – to see if she was looking for happiness there.

Bethan had stood behind Ruth Lewis today. Under the noise of the bulldozer as it had ploughed the roof of the gift shop into heaps, she'd made her way through the crowds of people. Slow as running in dreams, seeing faces that she knew, all turned towards what was left of Eirian's shop as if their eyes were lit with something. She'd seen no smiles. In that noise, you couldn't have smiled. She'd seen them shout to each other with hardly any sound, not tearing their eyes away.

And a fucking incredible thing to see. Just there on the pavements, you could feel the vibrations. Like it was running under every thought. That's where we used to stand and get an ice cream after the bus in summer. She'd felt the vibrations in her stomach, her hands, tapping Ruth on the shoulder.

After a moment of looking at her, Ruth had led Bethan away. She had touched the woman next to her on the arm and when she'd turned around, Bethan had seen that it was Charlotte. Above the collar of her black coat, the woman's expression had been vulnerable, far removed from what Bethan remembered of her. There was nothing to be recognized in Miss Weyland's face.

With the sound of crashing and engines falling behind them as they walked, she'd followed Ruth back down the street to the shadow of the Lewis house.

'I thought you'd be here, and Patricia. I was going to give it to her but . . .'

'Well, better not be a rejection after dragging me all the way down here, like.' She had laughed, pushed her hair from one shoulder, then said, 'Now you're meant to tell me it's not.'

'It's not.'

Bethan had smiled. The woman had been looking at her oddly, though, still for a moment, saying nothing. She'd never really spoken to Ruth, just one of the people whose kid's name you knew, and husband's and mother's, and nothing else about them. She looked pretty, Bethan'd thought. In that way that women round here looked pretty; dressed up to be forty-five when they hadn't hit thirty yet. Bethan had thought these days she herself probably looked just the same.

And she'd said, 'Is that a "but" I can see?'

'No buts. I said at the meeting, I think it's perfect. A restaurant.'

'Good, well . . .'

The woman had gone into her house, leaving her front door open for a moment that showed a staircase, dried flowers, and when she'd come back she'd held the envelope in both hands like she hadn't known what to do with it.

'I went through it with Charlotte, I mean it all seems good. We'll have to come and view the place with the foreman.' She hadn't handed Bethan the envelope, though. Behind, softened by distance and cold air, they had heard a crash over the engine's noise.

'It's all happening,' Bethan had said. She'd laughed again, some stupid little sound. And an image had come to her, random, without warning: her little table in the café, her name scratched on it, and the pile of Chelsea's toys that she left on her chair every overnight. Standing there, all the noise of the breaking had been muted.

Ruth had looked at Bethan as if seeing for the first time that there was some distance between them, just by the fact of the envelope she held. And she'd said, 'You filled it out, didn't you? Not Patricia, I mean.'

'Slave labour. I'm trapped behind that table all day, can't get these thighs out. She doesn't bring me food, like, unless I do her jobs.' But her eyes moved to the envelope and back to Ruth's face and she hadn't been able to find another word to say. Behind them, the bulldozer had rumbled, moved and the noise had seemed to run through the ground, to where they stood; a distant earthquake. Bethan had repeated, 'No rejection. No but.'

And Ruth had said, 'The money's not mine, you know,' and then had fallen silent. She'd finally put the envelope into her hand.

Bethan must've looked very young to her. All her long blonde hair, her tight jumper, and her arms empty of Chelsea.

There'd been the faraway sound of destruction, and Ruth's expression had flickered, seeing the outline of what Bethan felt.

Familiarity made things unreal. In the Shoreline Café, empty now but for the three of them – her father rattling round somewhere upstairs – Bethan saw the tables and the bottles of ketchup, the salt, vinegar, all pushed up to the ends. Surfaces wiped clean.

If you moved house, she imagined, and you looked at the road outside and the houses opposite for the first time, you'd see them then exactly how they were. Familiarity took the surface from things like varnish. Not definable any more, just a part of your life.

This was the table where her mum always took her lunch break and never more than a sandwich. Bethan had seen her sandwiches, they were six inches thick. She'd sit with both her elbows resting on the table, looking out through the window glass. But she mustn't ever see what was really there, just the tiny differences each day: the weather or the passers-by. It was a kind of lie, Bethan had come to realize. Beautiful things or ugly things would fade out just the same way.

Now, Siân and Tom were gone and, where her mum stood, light stretched from the doorway. The chequered floor by Bethan's feet was made yellow by the lamp outside. Patty's shadow came almost to her shoes. And she thought then, for an unclear reason, of how she'd used to come back from school every day, walk in here, her bag on her shoulder. It came to her how the school bus outside, leaving, would sound.

Her mum was bagging up pound coins. In the shadows, she was shaking her head, Bethan saw.

'Dad cooking?'

She nodded without looking up. She sealed a bag while Bethan watched. She said, 'I can't believe it. Sat here and listened to it – I can't believe it. Gwen saying all that to Dai . . . making him cry for God's sake. Siân –' and she just raised her arms a little, helplessly, not knowing how to describe Siân's behaviour, so unfamiliar.

'Dai couldn't lie about his favourite colour.'

Movie prints looked down on these changes from the walls: Bogart and Marilyn and James Dean, smoky glamour between the plastic ivy plants.

'Well one way or another, I'm dumbfounded. Dumbfounded by Siân . . .'

'That she's applying?'

'Yes, after everything she's said! Dumbfounded by how this has made her.'

'It's the shop,' Bethan said. 'It's today.'

'So angry . . .' was Pat's only response.

'It affects people. Seeing something like that. It affected me . . .'

'It's a demolition. We've had building work in town before, you know. It's not the first time Ynys-morlan's seen a JCB for God's sake.' Bethan watched her stack the bags of coins on top of each other, adjusting them. She drew her hands away.

'I know that.' Bethan closed her mouth over anything else. She didn't want to be angry, didn't know why she should be. She said quietly, 'It affected me. I don't know, you were here before the place. I've never seen it, that bit of town, without it being there. Can't imagine anyone seeing all that demolition and not being affected by it.' Upstairs, softened like the noise of the damage had been by distance today, she heard Chelsea start to cry.

'Your dad'll take care of it. Are you all right?'

It wasn't the form. She knew why she'd sent the form in, she remembered standing in her flat and thinking of the way that Rhys would have smiled if he'd seen it.

It was how Ruth had looked at her today. She'd seemed to feel things falling away from her, leaving her standing bare. She saw her mum now and there was so much in her mind, she couldn't start. She wouldn't be able to explain it right, she knew just how it would sound, how it'd be answered, so instead she pressed her lips together and she reached into her back pocket.

She put the envelope gently on the counter and in the dimness watched her mother pick it up and slowly open it, Chelsea crying upstairs like the world was ending.

Tom was full of memories, tumbling.

That evening on the beach, him and Rhys and Bethan, and she had looked up, sitting like a little girl, hair moving in the wind as she'd asked. And Rhys had come back at her. Taken a drag of his cigarette, raising his eyes from the sand, and said, 'Angharad.'

She'd laughed, Tom remembered. She'd blown smoke at the sky and he had watched them like a fucking table-tennis game, waiting for a question to come at him. Looking out from the patch of dunes where they'd been sitting, he remembered, and seeing the rest of the coastline in the evening light, they'd been remote from the town.

He thought of the gift shop now, its booming, rolling roof. He didn't know if what his mum had said about Gwen was true or not. He pictured her profile on the shore: sloe-dark. And thought of her cold turn, ever since he'd been fool enough.

Horrible, he had seen his mum.

He didn't know if anything was true any more. He felt like something was being taken from him.

He remembered telling Rhys he'd never been with Gwen, that he hardly knew her. All he'd done was reach in to kiss her and watch as she'd jerked away.

The town thinned. The dunes came on. There was a little lock in the caravan door but he never used it, only pushed it open. You'd have to come all the way out here if you wanted to do the place over. You'd have to walk all these lanes and try every single door on every dark, permanent van.

She couldn't go back to Emyr, she wasn't able to go to a friend. In this state, it was the night with Tom that she remembered. It felt like fate, to go back now. It wasn't fate. There was no such thing. But even knowing that, hurting inside because she saw it plainly now, still she wanted to feel like she was returning to something. Like there was some pattern in this.

There was no evening left in the air as she drove the caravan site's tiny lanes. Her headlights moved over caravan after caravan, all of them bleached like bone as she passed.

She remembered the route, all these lanes laid out in a network. She'd always had a good memory for routes. Even when she'd been a child in her parents' car, had always known the way. In the silence here at night, Gwen turned the car engine off and looked at Tom's home.

Thirty feet from her, its window was lit, orange behind the curtains. The only one in the place. She must have been parked for four hours on the beach, though that seemed impossible, four hours with no doing at all. All afternoon she had thought of that building tumbling. It had seemed to fall over and over in her mind. It robbed her of everything. Her anger was gone. She couldn't seem to feel her sadness.

It felt like fate to sit here and see this place again. But it wasn't fate. She could drive away now, she could stay here.

There was the little door she'd opened. There was the rusty stepping stool that she'd almost stumbled over as she'd left again. Her face had been covered with make-up and her eyes had been bare. Just a kiss, she'd said, but she'd run down this path.

Couldn't run from anything now. Her hands had been tender for an hour after her applause today, there was nothing left in them.

Stranded, Gwen got out of the car. She shut the door with one hand and looked up at the caravan as the light broadened on the unseen ground between them: Tom standing, silhouetted there.

The letter rustled in Patty Hughes's hands. She kept resetting herself, finding her place again in the words. In the least light, she pressed her lips together. She swallowed and raised her head.

Bethan didn't look away.

'Well, there's another thing I can't believe,' Patty said quietly. 'Thank you for this.' She raised the letter again and read, '*We are delighted to inform you of the approval of your application for a Business Renovation Grant.* I have to say, I'm delighted to be informed.'

Bethan sat still.

'May I ask what reaction you expected to this?'

'I thought I'd deal with it when it came.'

'Well, you must've had some expectations. Must've been thinking it over quite a lot. So, you can tell me what you anticipated, and then I can give it you. I'll know I've played my part in your new business plan.'

Bethan's gaze didn't move.

'Well?' Patty said. 'Well?'

'I expected this reaction.'

'Then far be it from me to disappoint you. Lovely, Bethan. This is just absolutely wonderful. When will the work be starting? Have you decided on a date?'

'Well, I thought I'd do you the decency of asking what date'd be convenient.'

'Thoughtful. How does Sunday sound? Good? I'll just get all the furnishings cleared out of this old place and they can bring the bulldozers right in then.'

'Yes, that's right, they use bulldozers to refurbish. Wrecking balls to replace windows.' Her mother looked more frozen to her than in the photograph framed behind the counter. 'No half measures. None of that.'

'Well you were never one for half measures.'

In the dusk, the long-gone smells of food, Patty stared at her. Hair curled at the side of her face, as in that photo. She was pretty, still pretty. She'd used to say that if she'd had the straight hair she'd always wanted, she would have looked just like Bethan did.

The streetlight from outside reached hands over the floor, and it seemed like the town out there was a place that neither of them knew.

'I didn't ask you,' Bethan said, 'because I knew you'd say no. I thought, if I didn't ask you . . . we'd get at least to this point.'

'And what "we" would you be talking about there? The royal "we" is that? Would that be your father and myself, and you? Or would that be you and Miss Weyland and Mrs Lewis?'

'All of us.'

Her mother's hand was still against the glass counter, like she could steady this building by herself. Her voice fell, though. 'Well, you're not talking about all of us. If anyone's "got to this point".' And then she looked away and, shifting the papers, Bethan saw her for the first time disconnected from this place. Her mother said, 'So Miss Weyland and Ruth Lewis and whoever else is running this thing, if anyone's running it, they all believe we're applying. In fact,' the letter twitched at her side, 'believe we've already been approved.' She looked at Bethan, and speaking again with that clear-cut voice, her eyes were wide and seemed in disarray. 'Did you have a plan maybe, for who was going to explain it all to them? For who'd "disapprove" us? Did you think me maybe? That I'd be the one to do that?'

In the warm plastic quiet, Bethan said, 'Have you read it all?'

'Yes, I've read it all!'

'But not thought about it –'

'You can't be more than a child if you really believe I haven't been thinking about it for weeks! . . . If you believe I'd make my mind up without *thinking* about it. Bloody gift shop got torn down today!'

The things she said were chased by silence and she turned her eyes away. Her daughter sitting there stiff, Patty felt useless suddenly. It fell through her like rubble. And she thought of Siân's face tonight, of Gwen staring out as the gift shop's roof had crumbled. Under her hand she felt cold glass and it didn't seem solid.

Mrs Weyland had given her little speech and this room had been in her mind, on her list. Under her belt, Patty thought. When she knew nothing – had not a single memory of it. Not putting newspaper down on the floor here, to mop up the footprints when it rained. Not the fourth birthday party they'd put on for Martin Pritchard last year with hats next to all the condiment racks. She looked at the streetlight across these tables, her Hollywood prints watching over them with black and white know-it-all eyes, and it seemed to her that the echo of the demolition struck her now, that she'd been deaf to it all day.

Holding her hands over her ears, she thought.

She looked back at Bethan. Even her own voice fell away, this quiet newer. The little chef sign leant against the door. Tom, she called him. 'Just putting you out on the pavement,' she'd say. On the counter here, the till was open and empty. Some napkins that Bethan had folded, in their old ice cream tub.

Beside her real figure, depicted up in that photograph, she was laughing and moving. With the letter in her hand, something had been lost.

'Tell me the reasons you don't want to –' Bethan said.

'I don't need to talk about it! You had no right. You *have* done it. You can fix it. You can go to the Lewis place in the morning.'

Bethan looked at her mother, her curled hair, her make-up in the streetlight. 'Then you can at least tell me why.'

'It should be obvious to you.'

Bethan sat, all her daytime things packed up here, and it seemed to her like this place was already torn. 'The reasons why I do . . . they should be obvious to you.'

Pat moved towards her daughter, heels forming clean little sounds in the weak dark, she sat opposite and put the letter, like a thing she didn't want to care about, beside the ashtray and the toys.

'We don't need this. Do you think people walk past these doors and see a family who are struggling? No they don't. And when they see the scaffolding go up? D'you think they'll walk past then and say, "Oh that's nice. That's good to see. The Hugheses are finally getting what they've worked for." We've *already* got what we've worked for! This is it.' She pushed her hands out and she showed Bethan the place that she had seen already, so many times. '"Looking for a little bit more," is what they'll say! I tell you, this is the only business in Ynys-morlan that hasn't seen returns drop the last year. And you know why? Because my café's here for the people that actually *live* in this bloody town, that's why! I told them years ago, I told them, that's what we need! How's it going to look when I decide in fact – that's not enough for me? In fact, I'd like a bit more on top of that. In fact, I'd like to charge twenty pounds a head and serve the salt and pepper in organic handmade old-fashioned natural salt and pepper shakers! We don't need this! We're not struggling . . . Look around you. Does this look like struggling? *For God's sake open your eyes and take a look at what we've got . . .*'

On the surface of the table, Bethan's hands opened. 'I haven't got those things.'

Patty started to speak then said nothing. Behind them, Ynys-morlan's road began with a ruin now. This was a place already changed.

'I haven't got those things,' Bethan showed her dimly, 'none of them are mine. Look at what I've got.' These chalked shadows laid across it, the place where they sat was empty, Chelsea upstairs, quieting slowly. 'There . . . there isn't anything. I want this. I really want this.'

Her mother's hand shifted on the letter. Still she didn't find any way to respond. After a moment, she only stood and she moved towards Bethan, she pulled at her hand to make her rise. Standing like that, they were awkward as Patty drew her in.

She tried to answer her. Bethan was tall, standing close against her, and Patty felt her hair against her cheek. She held her for a long time before Bethan's arms came round her. 'I love you,' she said. 'I love you . . .'

'I'm sorry.'

She clasped Bethan tight, as if she could hold the things they wanted together. She heard Chelsea still, though faintly, up in the room that had once been Bethan's. Hugging her, Patty stared out of the window and it felt like the houses changed even as she saw them. The world was full, it seemed. It was always full and it was always spilling over.

The street gathered shadows like rags. Pulled them close against the wind and each house was its own little secret. At the town's edge, flying like the only life let loose, the flag slapped against its pole. It rippled out, loud and blind in the dark.

Lennie had never kept much of his stuff in the cab because the cab was not his home. A couple of those little ornaments. The hula girl. The keyring thing that hung down from the roof to tell him it wasn't Friday yet, ever. A couple of photos of Ruth and Nia. He liked to look at them when he wasn't at home. He'd feel sad, like he could see them more clearly when he was further away.

When people at the depot asked him, he'd show the photos, call them 'the girls'. He would feel bad because of the lie in it, and do it again the next time. Wanting it to make him feel bad maybe.

In this one photo Ruth stood by the cooker, looking into a pan, and Nia was up on a chair next to her, staring in just the same. Neither of them knowing he was coming up, ready to take a photograph. The light was bad in it, the skin of Ruth's face was like sand. Just one lamp on in the corner.

More than ever, the picture was a lie now. And calling them 'the girls', more than ever. He'd found he was doing it more often, though. There was no hardness in loving someone when their faces were always faint, looking down somewhere else, and they were never going to turn around.

In the street lights, the ruin of the gift shop was jaundiced. The bollards cast three shadows each on the ground. And if he looked, he could see the flagpole behind. It wasn't the flagpole at all, though, really. That was just the part you could see, put your hand out to touch.

Like sunflowers, he remembered his father saying – the way they'd looked to Lennie, his eyes watering from the wind, clinging to the top of that pole and looking out.

The lights looked nothing like that now; across this street, down this road. The low walls round every garden were solid as forearms. It had felt last night, in their make-believe bedroom, in the middle of the living-room floor, like the silence round them must have been make-believe as well. Transplanted, it wasn't strong. It was brittle.

He had looked at their clothes, hanging on a rail in the same order that they'd been in the wardrobe. Others folded in piles, a pretend chest of drawers.

'My ears are always ringing with it, the engine. They're ringing now,' he'd said.

She'd seen him, his neck cradled in the pillow, the carpet beside his cheek slanted with his silhouette, and it had seemed as if the part of him that stared out from his eyes every time he raised his voice to her, every time he raised his hands, had risen suddenly in silence, to lie beneath his stock-still face. Something released deep underwater.

'We should keep a radio on,' he'd said. 'We should keep the car running out there to fill up all the quiet.' And then he'd said, 'This is the quietest house in town.'

'All day,' she'd answered.

'Not for long. Your ears'll be ringing like mine soon. Every night, you'll be hearing it.'

He'd sat up in their bed and looked at the crocheted shawl over the back of the sofa, at the indiscernible line on the floor in front of it, where their new bedroom began.

'I get these flashes, you know that?' he'd said. 'Right when I'm falling asleep. I get these flashes, think I'm still driving. I can see everything. See the road and the verges, see the traffic coming on. There's no sound of anything. Like it must be, going deaf . . . Just a second, because I'm falling asleep. Can feel myself. It's just an instant. I think I'm falling asleep at the wheel. I wake myself up, like. Have to.' Looking at Ruth, he had told her, 'There's no sound and it feels . . . sad, like. I can see the grass, I can see the road.'

For a moment she'd said nothing, her answers had trailed far behind.

'Do you think,' he'd said, 'when Nia dreams, there's sound for her?'

Staring in his eyes, something in her had broken and scattered. 'Muted noises maybe. Maybe like what she . . .' and then she'd finished talking, and she hadn't started again.

Things had been hanging in the room's silence that might have started crying she couldn't stop.

He had looked at this bedroom, at the small stack of books on gardening that were set next to the bedside lamp. She'd arranged that light so the living room seemed to fade whenever she switched it on. She had set on the fireplace's tiles beside him the same photograph that had stood at his real bedside.

Twenty feet from Lennie now as he stood in this switching wind, the house crouched between its neighbours. And he thought of his father, bent over a mix and shovelling. In the image Lennie had, those sunflowers of light streamed down on him from above. He'd had this picture, clear as any memory, for years. Clearer than some – his father's funeral, his mother's domino death a year later. Clearer even than memories of his old man at home, when he himself had been nothing but a kid. This picture; he could hear the scrape of the shovel in the town's night quiet, and the heavy, wet slap of concrete laid into a hole. He could see his father's face.

He'd killed the boy for love, for Lennie's mother and a future with her, for a family. In a way, Lennie thought, he'd laid a foundation that night. Set it there to soak into the earth till every building was supported by it. And his own house, his family, set in that same piece of land.

He felt a loss well up as he saw the house, and leave him, though it didn't leave him free. A great loss. It ran from him and covered the dark grass, over the yellow quartz stones that lined this path, it washed and grew thinner, unable to reach the lit doorstep.

Behind him, the road was empty. His cab wasn't parked outside the gate. He had, in a carrier bag, the few things from it. The plastic rattled in the cold over the last sound of a taxi's fading engine. And of course the hall was quiet when he opened their front door.

She turned, sitting at the kitchen table, and she didn't smile, and she didn't speak as she saw him there. There were papers spread all over.

She'd gained something from all this, gained a lot, you only had to look at her. Still had that nervous way about her, trapped in every movement she made, it seemed like, but there was some purpose in the movements now: fast-flowing water, almost channelled.

He stayed in the doorway for a moment like this, not touching the walls. All the house was dark around her, he could feel that it had been filled with the sounds of her scratching pen for several hours.

'What you got there now?' he said.

She looked at him, smiled slowly, so pretty in this low light.

'Quotes,' she said. 'Emyr's been collecting them up. And the application forms. Quotes.' She held a piece of letterheaded paper up. 'Ten thousand, three hundred,' she said. She held up another, laughing, like even sitting in this house alone for hours with them, she still felt softened by the shock. 'Thirteen thousand, eight hundred. There's one here for the Davises, twenty-four something . . . Makes you want to add it all up. I've not shown them to Charlotte yet.'

'How many forms in now?'

'Total?' She smiled again. She was pleased at his asking, as he'd known she would be, and it seemed to put a barrier between them. Dismayed him for some reason that he couldn't touch. He looked away as she answered, 'Thirteen. Lucky for some.'

'There'll be more. Wouldn't be surprised, next couple of days . . . you'll see it picking up. There's a lot of people talking now, you hear them in the Lion. Lot of people,' he said, he wiped his hand across his mouth, 'more caught up in it now.'

'Really? What are they saying then? D'you talk to anyone about it?' She moved a chair for him but he didn't go to sit down.

'Just get a feeling of it, that's all.'

'Well, money coming from someone they don't even know,' she looked down at the top of the table. 'And she's got that accent and everything . . . I keep telling people, she's been in Britain since she was twelve and they're not even hearing. "What part of America is she from?" And "I've always wanted to go to the States," or some holiday they went on when they were six and they've got a photo of the Statue of Liberty somewhere and they'll get it out to show me tomorrow. Anna Jarman told me about her sister going off to live in Philadelphia. You know she had a sister in Philadelphia? Never mentioned it to me. Went out to live there years ago apparently. Anna said she's thinking about going to visit her . . .'

'They're selling, the Jarmans.'

'Sixty-eight thousand, and that's the asking price from eighteen months ago. You wouldn't think a house could go for so little.'

'Sixty-eight thousand, ten thousand, twelve thousand . . .'

'I know,' she said. 'I know.'

He watched her laugh nervously and it was leached away by his quiet. She gathered up the applications and quotes as if their memories lay on the paper surfaces. He turned away, stared into the unlit hall. 'Nia in bed?'

'Went down hours ago.' And then, when he said nothing else, 'You missed a crowd today. Hundred and fifty people, must have been.'

'That's good. That's more than you thought.'

'I thought, maybe fifty. Seventy at most.'

'There you go. And you got a hundred and fifty.'

'Amazing thing it was to watch.'

'I've seen the result.' He looked up to the shade of Nia's door and when he spoke then it was careful, stepping stones through the beer he'd drunk tonight. 'I've got some news,' he said. 'Doesn't seem fair that you're the one always bringing back the news these days, had to go out and get myself some.'

'Good news or bad?'

He didn't respond. He thought of the flag's white cloth blustering.

'Lennie . . . Good news or bad?' Her hands weren't moving now.

He remembered John's face in the warehouse, fat and grey with the cold, turning to him like he hadn't heard right. 'Well you can look at it either way, like. It's one of those bits of news, sort you can see any way you want.' She was delicate and dark-eyed in the lustrous shadows here. 'Gave John my notice today,' he said.

'What . . . ? What do you mean?'

'You know what I mean. Not a huge amount of ways you can mean that, is there? I just told you what I mean.'

'You quit,' disconcertion spreading across her face like oil.

'That's right, I quit. See what I mean? It's one of those bits of news – you can take it any way you like.' He watched the reaction swell through her. Didn't take his eyes away from it.

'Why? I don't – Why do that?'

'Well, like: there's not a huge amount of reasons *why* either. Is there, Ruth? Because I didn't want to work there any more.' He remembered John raising his eyebrows, rubbing his forehead softly as if he'd make his own conclusions rather than ask. None of that bullshit on Ruth's face now, though. Because she didn't have to hide anything. Mouth open with confusion. Wordless with worry. 'So go on, tell me. What do you reckon, Ruth? Good news or bad?'

'I –'

'Yeah, more like just news, isn't it?' He saw her turn again to the papers all over the table like she'd find some answer there. She must not have, though, returning her gaze to him.

'You could have told me . . . I would've thought you'd tell me, Lennie, I mean –'

'I am telling you. What's this, if it's not telling you?'

'Before! I would've thought you'd have told me before. I mean, it's not just *you*, it's Nia and it's me and . . .'

'Yes, but then I'm the one that goes in there to work every day. That's not Nia or you, is it? I don't ask you what I should eat for lunch, do I? Because it's not Nia or you that eats it. I don't remember signing any kind of paper where I had to check the things I want to do with you first –' he had to stop himself. He looked at the floor like it was calm there, at his feet, it was nothing but calmness down there.

'I didn't know you were unhappy with the driving.'

He said nothing.

'I mean, you've not been happy there, I know, but –'

'So there you go, just said it yourself. You knew.'

She turned away, tangled in her own quiet. 'You know I'd never want you to do anything that was making you miserable, and it's hard work, I know it is, and so many hours. Maybe if you cut down on the hours.'

'Well that's exactly what I've done. Glad you agree.'

She took a breath, he saw. 'I just – we could have talked about it. I would have listened, we could've made some . . . provision. Why didn't you tell me? Len, if you're unhappy you can tell me, I want you to. Then we could talk –' But she looked down at all those papers again, like all her strength was in them, everything she needed was in them. And he could've walked across and taken them from her at that moment. His hands closed at his sides as she said, 'I wouldn't have tried to make you change you mind, you know that? If you'd come to me, and said how you felt, I could have given you support . . .'

'I didn't need that.'

'I know.'

He was silent, looking at her bowed head. So hurt all the time or so distant from him. This was all she ever showed. This – or her fucking laughter at everything that wasn't funny – the only way he ever touched her now it seemed, the only way he got through this glass: the times he hurt her. He thought of the white flag moving over ruins now. Ruth would only keep her eyes away, like she couldn't expect anything but this from him any more.

'You never needed support.'

'Don't look like that.'

'Like what? I'm not looking like anything –'

'That hurt, disapproving fucking . . . I didn't need any *approval* from you.'

She turned her face up to him and in the twist of her expression he saw something he had never seen before. It stopped his words.

'I know you didn't! I wish you *did* need my support! I wish you needed something from me! I'm trying to give you . . . *Why do you think I'm doing this?*' Her hands pushed into the papers, made them fly and fall, as useless as every other movement she could make. 'I'm trying to give you something . . .'

'You want to give me something?' And he was walking towards her. 'You can give me something.' He put his own hand down, very close to the edges of the pages, scattered now. 'I tell you what. You can give me a job. Go on, you can do that. Can't you?'

'I can't give you a job! How can I do that, Lennie? I don't – why are you doing this? *Why?*'

Both of them shouting. Six inches from each other, he thought, and shouting just to be heard. Two years of deafness filled this house.

'You can me give me a job, Ruth! Well don't be so modest! How many crews you got coming in here? Ten? More? You can tell them, can't you? You can say to them, they don't get the contract without it! No need to be fucking modest, I mean, let's face it here, you can do pretty much whatever you like. So you tell them! Go on! Tell them you want a job for your husband!'

'It's labouring, Lennie, it's half the money you're on now, it's –'

'I know what it is! Think I can't hear the words coming from my own fucking mouth? I just *told* you what it is!'

She looked up at him then and he saw what was new in her face. He took it in as he stared at her, felt it sink into his heart and he held it there. It was disappointment in him.

'– it'd be unskilled –'

'*I know what it'd be, Ruth!* I know what my own fucking skills are!'

Disappointment. And really, wasn't that why he'd done it like this? Wasn't that what he'd wanted from her tonight? To see it finally exposed.

She held her eyes on him. 'Is that what you've decided? Unskilled labour, Lennie? For God's sake . . . *It's four pounds fifty an hour. . .'*

'*I KNOW!*'

In the tiny kitchen, from the pit of his gut where her disappointment seemed to fill him with everything he'd been searching for, his voice pushed out; pushed this house and everything in it away from him.

Her expression was splintered, her eyes on him.

Her house was full of absences, it seemed to her. No stain to be seen in any of the rooms. No sound made here had ever left a mark. She didn't know what it was in the sense of home, that she could still care for this place after everything that had happened here. It should have been poisoned, but she had scoured it every day. And it seemed stupid, seemed so cruel, to still be able to feel love for it. It seemed to take away the meaning that she'd once believed love should have.

She saw herself then clearly, Lennie looking at her; herself and this place around her. Sweet, pretty, fragile, false. The things she saw, she hated. She wished they weren't hers and still she needed them. Once upon a time, she hadn't loved this place. It was a slow tipping of the balance, the growth of a love like this. You stayed and you stayed, until one day you asked yourself what it was you wanted, and could only find answers in the things you already knew.

The project had begun. Regeneration. Rehabilitation. Ruth looked at her husband.

'If that's what you want . . . I'll do my best. I'll do whatever I can . . .'

Lennie couldn't take his eyes from her. It was weakness that he let her see.

Tom Humphries had opened his door to the noise of an engine. It had been his mother he'd expected to see there. On the unmarked tarmac where in the summertime, the kids would ride their bikes in posses, shouting past the vans' open windows, when this road would be the same lilac grey as the evening sky, now Gwen Morgan was parked. In January darkness. There was graveyard quiet here.

Tom's hand dropped to his side. Her headlights, splitting the black ground, faded and fell to nothing. She got out slowly and closed the car door. This battalion of vans surrounded them, each in its apportioned silence. Gwen stood silent too.

'What're you doing here?' His words did not move out to her.

She only stared at him, slim and tight, her handbag held in front of her, as though she had no answer herself, and had hoped he would know.

'What're you doing here? Come on.' Her make-up was pale, her tweed suit exact, but the way she didn't speak hollowed her image, her shadow thrown by the caravan's electric bulb behind him, unfocused on the ground. 'Don't know why you drove all the way out here! You want to insult me again, like?' Though she didn't speak. 'Don't really fancy spending my night being insulted. Or I'd have called you.'

Her voice was marooned in the quiet. 'I didn't drive all the way out here, as you put it. I was at the beach.' Her hand fell from the car door. 'And I didn't come to insult you. I thought we could talk . . .'

'Shouldn't you be somewhere else? Like with your husband.'

'I don't know.'

The woman standing on the tarmac in front of him looked like she was leaving home. Like she didn't own anything but these good shoes, this good bag. Her eyes were dim in the frail light. Tom turned away from her, he didn't know what to say.

And she saw him walk back into the van then, the door left open behind.

Gwen took the step up slowly, steadying herself. She remembered how dark it had been as she'd stumbled here, how she hadn't known which way to go, disorientated between all these long lanes.

She found Tom sitting on his bed, staring at the wall, two feet in

front of his eyes. A storm in a teacup. All his clothes hanging free of
it in front of the window at the caravan's other end. She stood in the
tiny kitchen area. He didn't turn his head, a beer in one hand.

'Are you all right?' she asked.

Amid the rubbish, the duvet that was lumped up behind him, the
chip shop wrappers and dirty plates with their cigarette butts, he
turned his face to her and said, 'No.' He raised his hand but she didn't
know if he was trying to show her this place or just himself. And then
he snorted. 'You all right?'

The linoleum ended before her shoes. She thought of her own
kitchen and how she'd opened the window this morning on to her
sunlit garden, hearing the sound that had hung there. 'I'm not – no
I'm not all right,' she said.

'But then you wouldn't have come if you were, like.'

'. . . Probably not . . .'

'It's funny, seeing you round,' he said suddenly. 'I hear everybody
talking about you. Funny.' He drank. 'You know what they're all
saying? Know what my mum's saying, like? That you went round to
Dai Meredith and did him in. Shouting at him . . . Funny, seeing you
clapping today.'

Gwen stood for a long moment without answering. Remembering
Siân's face today. She felt some dead weight falling. 'It's a good thing
you're doing for Dai.'

'Well then . . . I might as well . . . It's true.'

'That he was crying.' He turned to her, unable to hold the accusations in. 'That you slapped him. Funny, after hearing you tell me I've
got no morals. I see you round and I remember – you standing there
and crying – and I hear this stuff about you. They're all sitting there
talking about what a moral fucking person you're meant to be . . .'

Empty, she felt. Connected to nothing. In her mind, she saw the
gift shop's roof shimmer like a summer haze. 'Everything she's saying.'
She thought of Dai's crying. Nia Lewis's face. 'All true.'

'So go on then. Tell me about morals! How about you sit down
and you can tell me, like, how I should be behaving maybe. Give me
some advice. How about that?' He stared at her, in desperation, in

anger, and she stood open-mouthed, seeing for the first time these feelings. Seeing that he felt no better than her.

Gwen walked a few steps and sat down on the bare bed next to him. Feet together, bag held in both hands, she looked at the wall as he was doing and started to speak. She remembered the slates toppling, the bricks, and all the things she'd thought were hers.

In a slow voice, Gwen told him about the night of the meeting, the choices Emyr had given her. And which she'd taken. Some time ago, if she'd told herself this story, she wouldn't have been able to believe.

She described to Tom how Emyr had slowly cut himself from her, because of the night when she'd come here.

Now she told him about Dai.

'I've always believed in being a good person.' She retraced, 'I stood in front of my wardrobe this morning and I picked out my best suit and everything.' She spoke with breaths as if to take control. 'I went down and I watched Emyr giving his speech and when the ribbon was cut, I applauded.' She spoke as though all these things had been expected of her. 'And I watched –'

'Looked like you couldn't get enough of it.'

She saw it again, falling before her eyes.

'So everyone'd think, like, what a hard thing you were doing, how good it was of you –'

Gwen swallowed gently.

'After everything you did to Dai!'

'Yes,' she said quietly. 'After that.'

She didn't seem to finish speaking, just ran to nothing, staring at the caravan's wall.

She began again, 'I don't think it was even the kiss. It was . . . me coming out here at all. It was afterwards . . . not acknowledging, he wanted me to acknowledge . . . Because he couldn't believe that the person he knew ever *would*. And I kept being the person he knew. I could see it in his face. Talking to him, could see it happening. The person he knew must be . . . some kind of lie. And he wanted me to prove it wasn't – I wasn't. But I couldn't.'

She looked at Tom's profile. She remembered her honeymoon and crying, telling him she was homesick, not knowing really what she was sick for.

'Couldn't. I wanted to, I would have liked to prove it. There was nothing there . . .' She gestured to herself, her chest, where the heart of her should have been. In this silence, she looked at magazines and shoes and CD cases.

He said, 'I remember like, when I came up to you and I saw you on the beach. Saw who you were . . . Fucking shocked, I was. Never think, Gwen Morgan crying. You're not crying now.'

'What would you think?' She stared out in front of her. 'What would you think, to look at me?'

'Just what you try and *make* everyone think . . .' He tried to get the anger out. 'Good like, upstanding woman, "pillar of our community".' He tried to get the bitterness out. 'You must *know* how you look! Why do you think my mum feels so –' but he shook the words away.

'What does she feel?'

He didn't look at Gwen, remembering how he'd stood with Rhys and hissed Emyr's words into his face.

'Lied to,' he said. Tonight of all nights, she'd come here, when he didn't feel like he knew anything. 'You know she's signing up for the grants?' He turned to her, sitting so prim and fucking proper still, looking like she was going to a fucking polo match still. This wasn't any summertime, she was sitting in his shithole of a van, she was telling him how her marriage was collapsing, holding her bag in both hands like that, all her manicured nails. 'How does she feel? Lied to! Fucking *betrayed!* How do you reckon she'd feel? How do you think . . . ? These fucking grants coming up every place. You're standing there clapping in front of the shop. How do you think she'd feel?' He kept speaking but the anger didn't leave him. These words didn't touch it. He remembered Rhys's face, his fist pulled back. 'Maybe she doesn't know what to believe, like! Maybe she sees you walking round, talking about your values and then she finds out what a pile of shit it all is and *doesn't know what to believe!* I don't know!' And he was shouting again, not even wanting to. He saw Gwen's face, and she looked numb under all that make-up. '*I don't know what she thinks!*

I don't know what she fucking feels . . . You're meant to be friends, you ask her . . . I don't know . . .'

'Lied to,' Gwen saw a sunset on the wall. She thought of how young he sounded.

Tom didn't look at her. 'A liar's what you are. Everything you do . . . fucking clothes you wear.'

Staring like she could see the whole sky there, vacant, cherry-coloured, Gwen said, 'You never mean to be any of these things, do you?'

'No one's forcing you, like, walking round like Queen Turd of Shit Hill . . .'

Gwen opened her mouth to defend herself, stopped. 'No one's forcing me. No one's ever forced me to do anything.' But she remembered the will it had taken her, just to get out of the car this morning, just to let Emyr lean in to kiss her. 'No one's forcing you to be the way you are,' she said. She looked at his clothes where they hung free from the mess, in dry-cleaning bags and over hangers. On the floor underneath them, she saw a bunch of screwed-up tissues, they were lying on a plate with some kind of dried red sauce, baked beans maybe. Even now, feeling like this, it horrified her to see someone living this way. It was care that she felt for him, seeing it, but it was a kind of fear as well. 'I couldn't live like this, like you do.' But saying it, she wondered. A person could live any way. 'I love all the things in my house,' she said. 'Every single little thing there. I love . . .' she swallowed, 'having it all tidy, and getting up in the morning . . . and I'll have an early breakfast in the kitchen, when it's all nice in there. How can you love tidiness? My God, how can you feel love for a thing like that? I like to . . . get up, choose my clothes. I have my plate and my cup for breakfast . . .' She turned away for a second.

He found himself watching her and she looked desolate, but there was nothing weak about her. No need coming from her at all. She was staring at the wall like she saw herself laid out, unravelled there. No pity in her face.

'It doesn't give me anything,' she said, 'the organization . . . I've always loved the mornings. Best part of any day. Used to get up, five thirty, six, always. And you feel good about everything ahead. Whatever might come. You feel ready . . . And I get up at the same time now, do these things every morning, set a clock by me you could . . .'

'You don't have to be like you are. You lord it over people.' He turned to her. 'The way you walk, your . . . accent. How do you *reckon* people are going to react, finding out it's bullshit? You're no more moral than . . . anyone. No more moral than fucking Rhys.'

Gwen looked at his home.

'You know what Eirian Meredith said to me? She had a way of putting things so that you couldn't forget them. I wasn't any good person, she said.' Gwen laughed. 'That I was only pretending.' Nia's eyes on her, she remembered, glassy as a doll's. 'Helps if everyone else believes –' She stopped herself. She had to take a breath. 'If everyone goes on pretending to like you.'

'No one's doing that now.'

Gwen said carefully, 'That might be true. But then I stopped pretending, didn't I? I stopped being able to.'

Even seeing the barrenness in her face, he was full of the things that would hurt her. He held his hands tight together. He wasn't a hurtful person. But his mother's voice had been biting in the café's husky shadows, and the ease of it, turning round, saying she was taking the money. Applying for the fucking grant, the *ease* of it.

'What did you say to Dai?' Tom asked her.

'I told him he was selfish.' She took a breath.

'Go on then,' he said. Staring at her clear-cut profile now, 'Go on.'

'I told him he was ruining . . . everything his mother had worked for. I said that he was blind. I might as well have used the word "dull", I might as well have used the word "retarded". I said to him . . . thank God Eirian wasn't still here to see what he was doing to her . . . her place.' Gwen's hand closed, fitfully, desperately, but she'd already lost hold of what mattered. 'I said to you, didn't I? I'm no moral person! I said already!'

'Well I wanted to hear again, all right? I wanted to see you say it!

I'm sorry! I'm sorry –' He shook himself away like she was trying to
touch him, but she hadn't reached out. 'I'm sorry.' He could hear his
own voice, this tiny place seemed to fill with it, he sounded like his
mother had. 'You fooled me. That's all. Fooled my mother.' But he'd
put that bracelet round his wrist. He'd remembered the expression
that had been on Gwen's face as she'd picked up his mess to fill a
plastic bag – and he had put it on. Now, all the anger he had was
knotted. Wouldn't reach out, even to her.

The first changes were here. His mother was bringing them on,
just the same as every other person. What was coming was a storm
of rubble, he seemed to be the only one who knew it. It could never
be anything else. It was made by them.

It seemed to Tom like this tide was approaching and Gwen looked
back at him as if this was the only dry place left.

'You shouldn't have come here.'

'I needed – I felt . . .'

'Yeah, you needed! You felt! You come back, two months after
everything . . . Did you think about how I'd feel? You wonder about
that at all? No, you fucking "felt"! So you came.'

'What do you feel then?' she said. 'How old are you? Eighteen?
Nineteen –'

'What's *that* mean? What's that got to do with anything?'

'Nothing,' she said. 'I just meant – Tell me. What do you feel
then?'

'I told you! Lied to! Everyone believed in you!' He thought of his
mum, sitting in the watery light of the TV. Through the recollection
debris now fell, as if around her, in that dim-remembered room.
'There's no fucking community in this town,' he said. Wherever he
turned, there was nothing he recognized any more. 'I was trying!' he
said, hoarse and sad. 'I was trying all the fucking time, like, every day.
Working . . . Don't even know what I was trying for any more.' He
looked at Gwen like he wanted her to believe it. He didn't care what
she thought, but he could feel himself doing it. 'I was trying to do the
right thing,' he said, 'all the time.'

Gwen felt this messed bed around them. Eighteen, she thought.

'You make these choices, it seems like,' she said. 'They don't even feel important at the time, don't even feel like choices. You meet someone. Make this friend or lose one. Go to college or you don't, take this job . . . Not realizing, you're going to look back . . . and that will have been your life.' She snorted a small laugh. 'You think, "This bit right now isn't my life. My life's in front of me." Twenty-six, twenty-nine. You make these . . . choices, they're so little. And they're so hard to change.'

'I haven't made any choices,' he said.

'You make choices every day, you change a bit . . . And then the next day comes and it's easier to keep on going that same way. Suddenly you've got so far to go back, you can't even. You can't go back.'

'I haven't made any choices, why d'you think I'm living in here? Think I like it?' He sat motionless on the bed. 'I don't want to,' he said. 'Don't want to – have to go back on them. Move back here, like.'

'But that's a choice,' she said. 'I imagine . . . a year ago, it didn't seem so hard to move away.'

'It's not *hard*. I don't want to go. I want this place to be all right! What's wrong with that? Ynys-morlan doesn't need any changes, for fuck's sake! I don't want to go off round the fucking world, I just want it to be all right here.'

'You make them,' she said, 'they don't even seem like choices. I never set out to be this person. Of course it's a choice to stay . . . You don't think it's a choice to meet someone, spend time with them. You know it's a choice to get married but you don't see . . . you let yourself . . . How can you go back by then? A day at a time, your life gets . . . set. You don't even see.'

'Why did you marry him then?' Faces came to mind, Rhys's and Bethan's, his mum's – all of them two miles distant from him now. 'If you didn't want to, why?'

'I did want to. You can want something, you can love something –' she thought of that honeymoon suite, filled with foreign light, 'you can need something, that's all . . . doesn't mean it's right. There are hundreds of reasons why you can love a person. I wanted to do good,

I wanted to make a difference. I met Emyr . . . I didn't know what would make me happy – ' Turned to him, her expression was unsteady. 'It's frightening not to know that. I met Emyr, he wanted all the same things, we'd talk about it. We'd tell each other all the time . . . Tom, you don't see it happening. You look in the mirror one day, see your face, you find yourself remembering when . . . when all these things, your life, your home . . . when they were all just ideas.'

She looked at him, shaking his head slowly, his eyes on hers. She wanted to reach out to him and tell him again that he was only eighteen.

'You remember having other ideas,' she said. 'When your whole world was nothing but.'

They sat together in this little place she had never thought she'd come back to. Gwen gazed at him and images of her own home came to her, its spaces and its lines, its pale colours, its pale memories.

In this unsure light, Tom saw that she was crying, though there'd been no sound of it in her voice. He didn't know what he wanted any more. It seemed like it had been easy before, he'd known what was the right way to go, he'd been working towards it. He'd been believing. 'All I want,' he said, 'is for everything here to stay . . . all right.'

'Is that all you want, really, just all right? Because I've had it all right. And all I can see is how useless those days were . . . All I'm left with . . . is just the same feeling of being scared . . . and there are no possibilities any more.' She wanted to move her hand, cover her mouth.

He watched the person he'd known all his life dislocate, drift apart on her face and leave her bare. She looked just as she had that night. Like a lonely person. A good person.

And there was this flood now, he saw it, this project, rushing in. Moving here, it had felt like he was clever: he'd put all the choices off, he'd beaten them. He saw in Gwen's eyes now, it was so late for her to change. So late to feel scared.

Tom remembered swimming back with the little girl dragging behind him, kicking, hauling in the water. He remembered feeling the sand under him and looking up to see the beach, its houses, believing that the safety he'd brought her back to was complete, that it was simple.

In the dogged yellow light, he looked at Gwen and he reached out. He put his arm round her for the second time.

He felt her shake. Her whole body it seemed, moving with the sadness she felt. And she came in close to him, to put her face against his neck. Like that they lay down. On the sheet, like spoons. They stayed that way for a long time, dressed in their different clothes. Gwen had her eyes shut. He held her in the mess and he felt her cry.

Ruth sat at the table in their kitchen and Lennie stood beside her. She put her hand on his. She wanted to tell him again, so he would hear how much it meant: she was doing all this for him.

She tried to remember now, how he'd looked that day of Eirian's funeral when he'd told her what he felt about Ynys-morlan. How it was to have to watch it decline. She couldn't find those memories now. She remembered saying to Charlotte that though they weren't doing this for noise and rubble, she wouldn't be looking away when the gift shop's roof fell to the ground.

Lennie looked at the hand she'd touched him with. He crouched down to the same level as Ruth and once he was there, there was nothing left except to kiss her. The skin of her cheek felt cold to him, soft and like no one he knew.

He leant in to her suddenly, put his arms tight around her, his lips pressed against her cheek. And he held her that way, their faces touching, their hair, as the chair rocked and settled in the quiet.

'Well that's all right then,' he said. 'That's all right then, that's decided.' He put his hand up and stroked at her hair, like it was she who needed comfort from him. And when he drew back to kiss her mouth, she saw the emptiness that had come to rest on his face, over that weakness. He knew what he was showing her, he couldn't stop himself.

This was the place where he'd stood, she thought, holding seven ten-pound notes in her face, telling her she was damn right she wouldn't be going back to Charlotte's garden. He had held them so close, they'd touched her mouth, she remembered, the place where he was leaning in and kissing her now.

'I want you,' he said. It must have been a whisper but it sounded loud to her, so close to her. 'I want you.'

In the moment before he kissed her again she could have told him, she opened her mouth to say it: that was what she needed too, that was what she'd always needed, for him to want her.

Standing right here on the cold slate floor, he had spoken as softly as he kissed her now, 'Don't lie to me, Ruth. I can always tell.'

She let him kiss her and his lips were wet. She let her mouth open, because you couldn't stop your body from responding, if you needed someone and they kissed you, you couldn't stop yourself opening up to let it happen. She felt Lennie's tongue touch her own.

With the money in one of his hands, he'd held her shoulder with his other, and he was telling her now, 'You're beautiful, Ruth, you know that? You're beautiful.' He said it a lot of times, as if he had to believe it.

She remembered him saying, 'You look so ugly when you lie,' holding her shoulder that way. But it had been him who'd looked ugly, his face mixed up between anger and some attempt at forgiveness, like he was trying to give her a chance she didn't deserve. It had been him looking ugly.

She hadn't known then, never knew in those times when he was full of rage, how she had let a man who could be like that kiss her. In those times when he was shouting, she always asked herself. The question would fade, though. That was the thing that no one could understand, she didn't understand herself how. Things would get better, a day later, a week later, and she would stop asking. Sitting at the kitchen table, she felt him kissing her now. He undid the first button of her blouse.

He took it away from her, looking at her in the slate shadows of their kitchen, seeing her pale skin and her nipples through the white brassiere. He wanted very badly, very suddenly to touch her. He put his hand on her skin and felt like a stranger to her.

He kept saying, 'I want you, I want you,' pulling her up from the chair, frozen and soft, and every time he said it, it didn't let out what he felt. He had to tell Ruth again.

He had held her here, in just this same place, in daylight that had faded months ago. He'd shouted into her face, 'I won't be lied to by my own fucking wife.'

Ruth watched him take his shirt off and stand in front of her. But in some way, she thought, he was always standing here, he was telling her that he wouldn't be lied to. In her memory, he was always climbing the flagpole, ridiculous and making her feel wonderful. This was the thing that hurt her, this was the thing that made the question fade: in some way he was always there, shouting her name down in the night. He was always telling her he wanted her, as if these moments were captured, forever hanging in her, unresolved.

'I love you,' he said.

In her memory, he was holding the money into her face. None of these moments ever ended. She was living in every one of them. None were over.

He took his own clothes off and took hers off, until they were both standing in only their underwear and his breathing was heavy, needing her. His eyes were so dark, you couldn't see if it was love in them or if he was only blind. But she seemed to see it all clearly, and when he started touching her, she felt every brush of his fingers, so sheer they almost hurt. Where he touched, on her breast above the line of her bra, there had been bruises on that part of her skin. They'd been black and they'd faded to yellow, they had disappeared into her again. They'd sunk and left no trace. On her stomach, there'd been bruises there. They seemed always to be staining her and fading, her skin endlessly clear and endlessly marked. In the cold shadows now, Lennie moved up to her, pressed himself near, put his arms around her back.

In the daylight he'd shouted, 'Don't turn away from me!'

'I love you, Ruth,' he said. 'I love you,' like it all came down to that, everything he ever did or said, when you got to the bottom, it was him loving her.

She'd tried to turn her face away from the money. 'Please,' she had said.

Lennie reached and turned the light out over the cooker and she lay down with him, both of them awkward on the floor. If she was still standing there, still asking him please, she was standing in darkness now.

She felt everything, every slightest touch, lying still and letting him take her underwear off in little movements that were gentle, getting quicker. She could feel the need in him. And she remembered the tiny drifts of the notes falling to the floor. They must have lain on the slates here, where her shoulder blades were pressing now.

'I love you, Ruth,' he said. Like she wouldn't ever understand what the words meant, he would keep trying to push them into her so she could. 'I love you, Ruth. I love you, I love you.' Like he didn't understand them himself. He had told her the same thing, letting the ten-pound notes fall. The daylight had been in his eyes, so bright you couldn't tell if it was anger in them or if he was only in pain. And there was a look that passed over him, like he knew he wouldn't feel what he wanted to feel, but he was drawing his hand back anyway.

Ruth lay under him on the dark kitchen floor, hearing how much he wanted her in the way he breathed, and she'd wanted this so much, to hear this. She'd wanted him to touch her like this. He put his hands on her breast and cupped it, felt the whole shape of it and touched her nipple with his thumb. Breathing hard, breathing quick.

'I love you, Ruth.'

She wanted to hear him say it. She made no sound as he moved her knees gently apart. She wanted to hear him as clearly as she could. It hurt her to, some pain that sank from her mouth with all the words she'd never said to him and came to rest inside her. Still she wanted to hear.

He'd drawn his hand back and brought it down on her face. There'd been pain in her ear, and on her cheek, but the ear had been the worst. It had hurt to swallow, bending her head down. And her eyes had closed, not because she'd wanted to close them, she should have raised her face up to see him, but your body reacted like that, when somebody hit you. It tried to protect you, even when you should look up and say the things that might stop you from being hurt again.

In the blurred dark, Lennie leaned over her like he wanted to hide himself in the curve of her neck. She felt the edge of him, on her thigh and moving further, and she was dry but he needed her, right now he needed her, he pushed. She lay without any movement, letting him.

In the autumn afternoon, in their little kitchen full of stone and warm wood, he curled his fingers in to protect them from her and, with his eyes on her so desperately that he couldn't even seem to find her, he drew his arm back to hit her again. In her stomach. No breath then. No air, and you buckled over when someone hit you in the stomach, your body tried to curl itself over, whatever you wanted, whatever you needed to try to do. She'd held herself, and though she'd wanted to tell him to stop, ask him why, say that she cared for him, she'd held her stomach like it was herself that she cared for.

Lennie made love to her in the darkness, and she lay there, allowing him. She lay there, feeling his love. In the bright afternoon, for none of these moments ended, she held on to herself, feeling it.

'I love you, I love you,' he'd told her. 'I love you, Ruth –'

And he told her now, having his orgasm inside her.

She felt the pain inside her now, like he would always be hurting her, like he would always be walking out of the kitchen and leaving her, his feet moving away up the stairs. Really, a part of her must be always saying to him that she wasn't lying. It must make her very weak, to have a part of her always doing that, always holding her arm up.

As though this house was full of ghosts; herself, standing by the cooker here; herself, in the hallway, looking down at the phone, afraid of calling Charlotte again. As though all the ghosts in this house would move through each other, touch each other without knowing. Walking up and down the staircase, silent always. Pale as the shapes of tiny handprints on a wall. It must make her weak to be so divided. So many ghosts, never seeing each other.

Lying on the dark floor, Lennie lifted his weight and moved himself away from her. In a different day, in the quiet that was left of some afternoon, he took his hand away from her and what she felt was relief. Lying awkward on the slate floor, she felt it as pure as water, relief. Just to have him move away. Just to have her husband not touching her. What kind of a love was it, that felt like that?

Spring

The room was yellow. Across its smooth and even wall, pale daylight was a dye. In the centre, where the painting had hung, there was only a tiny hole now. There was no landscape. There was no hook. Just that hole, and below it, the carpet was gone. Floorboards, marked and dirty, reached to the place where she stood. She stood watching. Her hands, behind her back, held each other. They were touched by the slow illumination of the window, against which she was silhouetted now; against which, even grey outside and washed with rainwater that ran down the window's glass in fingers, her face was dim. Her eyes were tender in shadow, as if she was waiting for pain. She was free-standing in this room, in this house, as a stranger would have been, but she watched the man in front of her lift a chisel to the wall, and fear was in her mouth.

There were no roots that tied you to a place. Any person could walk away from their home. From Ynys-morlan more than many; a faded town it had seemed to her, in the years when she had spent her Saturdays imagining, in a derelict garden one mile away. The shadows of leaves falling to the pavement, the slow cracks of a road left too long; a street of sunlit, wind-driven footsteps, at the edge of this floodplain to the sea. Ynys-morlan more than any. There were no bonds that tied you to a place. Even naming it home, still the leaves would fall, and come down to rest on the paving stones in someone else's memory.

Yet Ruth stood here and looked at the wall and, in her mind, these rooms filled the spaces where the edges of her body should have been. It felt like the furthest parts of herself were this pale yellow, that had looked, when the room was full, like the summertime.

She wasn't ready. In this, the third week of February, she looked at the man as he raised a hammer, and she was not ready, even now. She had moved the furniture from here. It was a fortnight since this room or this house had been set out in the way she had maintained for so long. She would have told Charlotte, but she had been afraid of Charlotte's answer: perhaps she might never have been ready.

Rainwater, on the glass behind her, scattered, fled.

The man in front of Ruth struck the chisel with his hammer, and the silence that had lain against the walls, in paintings she had chosen, in the reflections of polished things and the clean glass of photographs, it was broken. It struck the floor in a rain of paint and plaster. Like milk-bottle glass, it had been fragile.

Behind Ruth, from Ynys-morlan's street, there came the sound of the wind.

It fluttered grass that was dark green, new and trampled, in the mud around the concrete that formed the flagpole's base. It moved through bare, wet branches, through the highest, finest twigs, and breached the edges of the trees at Ynys-morlan's beginning. It rose, towards a grey and broken February sky, and it carried the sounds of turning tyres.

It was like this: the pale yellow paint and plaster cracked, a little spider's web across the wall, fine and clear as the memory of something lost. Ruth watched him slip the chisel's blade into the crevice, then she watched him twist his wrist, and it fell free.

A deep and hollow pain rose inside her. She knew its shape. As the rainwater beat against the window, bare of curtains, Ruth stood and looked at the light across the wall and remembered deciding to stay here. Remembered clearing this house, holding objects that had had no meaning while her mum had still been here in this room. They'd found new meaning, little misplaced things. And she'd had a vision: of a good ending here, of a home, of a family's many cluttered belongings.

She watched as the man now brought the chisel up again.

'Be careful –' She raised her hand, but she faltered and the words she said didn't come clearly. The noises from Ynys-morlan's street seemed to rise like water with them.

The wind rattled planks in the scaffolding around the Spar, raised on the 15th of February, Ieuan Griffiths hired from down near Newport after Emyr's list of contractors ran dry. The owner of the building, a Mrs Tajifel from Birmingham, had taken a week of his constant calling only to be convinced to come. Emyr had met her finally, and stood with her beside the doorstep where puddles were gathering now. He had looked with her, from the building's eaves, down this street, and had asked if she believed him now.

Under the wind, these rooftops were dirty with the sounds of work. The sirens of trucks in reverse, with their thin, turning, orange lights. In doorways open to the small front gardens, there were men smoking cigarettes and staring at the rain; drills sounded, muted behind them. There was the sound of debris falling. In moments between the noise, it smashed down on the floors of wet and dirty yellow skips. Hammers rang, and carried on this wind. It was raining in Ynys-morlan, and the street was caught in echoes of the breaking.

Ruth Lewis watched the man in front of her chip the plaster away until she saw the rot underneath the wall. It was red.

No tears were on her face, and no sound came from her as she saw the house that she'd cleaned every day, as though reflections were peace, break apart, but she cried nonetheless. She saw the lath that was screwed to the stones, bending and breaking and falling too. She remembered those many mornings cleaning. She remembered the way that she'd arranged this room, the pillows on the bed in a semicircle, as though to cup the people who'd lie down there. A wicker chair had stood beside this window, and she'd kept a book on the carpet next to it, and swapped it for another sometimes. The chair had been filled with sunlight in the afternoons, and had looked beautiful, waiting for the peaceful reader. She remembered. The vision she had had, it had died in clean quiet and polished wood. It had lain in memory in empty, sunlit chairs.

Ruth watched the paint and plaster drop on to the floorboards. She stood in grief, for a home she'd used to tell herself she'd never keep. It wasn't a need for perfection that had tainted her vision, but perfection had been all that was left when the morning had come again into these rooms. Beneath these summertime walls the knowledge had hidden, of what Lennie had done to her here.

Ruth watched the workman fracture them. Behind her, the sound of the project took wing and she seized it.

Beside the seawall, where aerials and chimneys, satellite dishes jutted from the roofs, in the first row of six small houses, scaffolding was raised around five. There'd been fifty-four applications for private renovation grants. These scaffolds clung to the faces of the buildings until those still clean of it looked small. They framed the rooftops with staggered lines and water dripped, from board to board, down to the road.

On the 10th of February, work had started on the properties owned by Dai Meredith; the three shops opposite Ruth's house, the two beside the Lion, where the plaster cast over the door looked out from shadow now on a town that was struggling under change. The foreman's name was Gavin, the contractor's Pryce and Rose.

That first day, after leaving his dim house where the clocks counted seconds in muted chorus now, where the chimes rang together, Dai had gone to meet him. To see those three buildings, the gift shop's demolition site at his back, with barriers obscuring it. Before him, their three doorways had been dark.

After talking, Gavin taking him through a rough schedule, Dai had gathered his hands and thoughts showily. He had nodded, looking out. Quiet in the noise, he'd tried to sound matter-of-fact, 'Bet you've never seen anything like this.'

'I was thinking that: have I?' the man said, turning to glance back up the road. 'Only one I could think of was Portmeirion. Not that I was there, like. Don't know when that was. Fifties maybe.'

Moving his gaze from the shops' shadowed front steps, the date caught at Dai. 'How long did it take them?'

'Well, it was only one. He came over here from Italy, that's what my brother said. Wanted to bring a bit of it back with him and, course, 'cause he was rolling in it, a picture didn't occur to him. Built this whole place that's supposed to look like Italy, stuck on the Welsh coast. Used it for "The Prisoner". You ever see that, did you . . . ? Patrick McGoohan . . . ?'

'How big?' Dai had said, looking at him.

'Like a village. Smaller than this, it is.'

'Fifty years ago.'

Gavin had shrugged.

'And people live there?'

'No . . .' He'd looked at Dai, that short look: You simple?

But Dai had just stared back, any care he might've had moving round and past him, not inside. People had always been this way. He wasn't simple, though.

'It's a tourist attraction. It's empty but for shops.'

For the first time it had come to Dai, that there were more thoughts in his head than this Gavin's. And he'd said, 'Empty, but it's still there. Whatever the man meant by building it, it's still there. Even if he's gone.' He'd turned back to the three shops in front of them. Time wasn't like men, or women. It didn't make mistakes.

He'd looked at their slates, wet from the rain that'd come and would again. Our ideas of what was meant and what wasn't couldn't touch the way that time would pass.

Inside those shops, there was clearance work now; in the place that had been Owain's family butcher's, men set crowbars between the walls and what was left of the counters. They carried out the debris, the glass and the melamine, to the two skips on the edge of the road. Emyr had arranged for all disposal to be carried out by the same company, as for the scaffolding and for almost all materials, and had taken quotes from contractors for the work only. For purple Welsh slate, rare to find now, he had tracked down a supplier in Newport. He had arranged a discount of twenty-five per cent on timber from Travis Perkins, for ready-made frames that would come, he said, on lorry beds, in the shape of gable roofs.

On the many tipped porches and extensions, the many tarred dormer windows, rain fell and was blown away and cast again. There were the shouts, over engines, of men unloading, bent in the grey day as they dragged things free and set them on to the road.

Mrs Tajifel had looked at Emyr, he'd told Ruth, looked up at him for she was small, and the only thing she'd asked him, in the cold air and cacophony, was where the money was coming from.

On the 12th of February, work had begun on ten of the private renovation grants, those that were contracted under Hughes and Sons. The two foremen overseeing those ten sites were named Charlie and Wyn, and under Wyn, on the 13th of February, Lennie had begun a new job. That morning he had left the house with darkness rising as always, but there'd been no silence, and in the road where his cab had used to stand he'd seen the headlights of vehicles, queuing to park.

With tarpaulins now tied to the scaffolding, the roofs of their dormer windows were pried loose, the tar ripped free from them to show the chipboard underneath. In those gardens, rubbish was cleared, as the tarpaulins smacked and shook in the wind above. The house that had been the Jarmans' and was Charlotte Weyland's now. Mrs Pryce's house, where Charlotte had stood like an intruder. Siân Humphries's house, where the block extension that faced the sea was framed by scaffold now as well; iron poles set against the walls that Lennie's father had put together once, a long time ago, with John mixing up in the yard beside him.

There were men on the roof of the extension, kneeling with their weight on the rafters while the wind struck at their faces. They overlooked the beach, the surf and sea and weather, where a JCB moved now, churning on the strip of sand, as stones fell and were lifted in its scoop. Its noise merged with the waves. Its tracks led back along the beach at a slow angle until they met the seawall, and a gap there: a slope that had once served a lifeboat crew. Wet sand was left in breaking clumps beside the pile of stones the JCB had made. Next to the public toilet they were heaped to five feet already, dark and slick, and more sand slipped over them. From this point the stones could be taken by labourers, by men like Lennie, but with no past here, to the houses on which they would be used.

The JCB drove in the path Ruth had imagined, walking there with Charlotte and Nia when January had still been thin in the air. Ruth, now in her bedroom, thought of Charlotte with a gratitude, a tenderness, that sang like glass.

On the 14th of February, on St Valentine's Day, work had begun on the Lion. The name of the contractor on it was Evan Thomas, and he worked both as foreman and carpenter. He would build a bar, he'd said, that people would be leaning against when photographs of this town as today's residents had known it were hanging in frames behind it.

Ruth thought she would have a plaque made, with Charlotte's name on it, that she would pay for it herself and have it set in the public garden. Have it made in bronze.

The wall came away easily, and the rot's mycelium stretched like muscle across the grey stone from which her parents' home was built.

Her home, where her constant voice had sounded and been heard in empty rooms, where Nia had wandered in a wordless shroud. A man set a chisel to the wall here now, and the skin of both speech and silence was broken.

Many words that Ruth had never said seemed to rise in the pain that she felt. Coarse and ugly words for which a mouth should be washed clean. They were disgusting to her, they came and left her in silence. She would never voice such things but they came from inside her. They described herself. They described this house, and its prettiness, and its perfection, which she had worked each morning to preserve. With desperation, with obligation, with faultless care, these walls had been untouchable to her. You can do that, touch a thing so many times that it can't reach you through your moving hands.

The paint of other years fell, and under it the rot was red like the colour seen behind closed eyes. The sense of their home fell, and she mourned for it. She needed it. She turned her face away.

Sometimes he'd lain and held her closely here. Sometimes, the door closed, her voice only just escaping, he'd held her down and hit her over and over again. She'd allowed both these things.

In Ynys-morlan, through the window behind her, it was raining; the work was begun. And in the moment that her eyes passed it, she didn't see the diesel smoke, the rubble, or hear the churning noise, but instead saw a beautiful place. A perfect place, where the buildings were arranged in patterns so pretty that they called to the heart. Yes, she understood. So pretty that they looked like happiness.

Her mouth was open, her hand across it, as she swam slowly from this room. There were men in the hallway. Passing them, down the stairs, she saw the open front door but couldn't feel the cold, couldn't feel anything but the many chiselled cracks, the many pieces shattered and lying, of the house which she had kept and held. She walked into the kitchen and she shut the door behind her. Couldn't feel anything but the rot which had grown inside it. Inside herself.

And in the kitchen, she birthed the words which she had not said and, coming from her stomach, they formed a noise which was dirty, whole, which was as ugly to hear as the first sound would be if ever her daughter were to speak.

Holding on to to the kitchen counter, it came from her. She looked out of the window at this project. At desperate, driving beautification. And her voice lifted, as if to fall again; some new depth below it. It was an act of goodness, to take feelings that were ugly and put them into making something radiant. It was an act from the heart. It was not escape.

Her voice lifted, and when it fell she found Lennie's name. It was an act of love to create beauty. It was not escape, not any more.

In a street that was sluiced with the noise of construction, Lennie stood and saw his own reflection in the glass of a porch door, reed-thin, looking back. In the cold air, his hands felt like metal, no difference could be told between the reddened skin and the bolster held loosely in his palm. His dad had built this door, and its timber frame, peeling now with blue paint and rainwater. He heard the alarms of the backing trucks. He heard the shouts of men, with their accents from Radnor and from Bangor, from the Valleys, from the South. They'd come from every part to work on Ynys-morlan, and he wondered now how many miles they'd travelled, all combined. He wondered if it could match the number he'd seen roll beneath him to bring him back to this street. Four years spent on the roads between places that seemed like no one's home. When the project began, when the scaffolding was raised and the first vehicles came, to idle in the dark road in the mornings, Lennie Lewis came back too, and stood here, in the wind and rain, with only duty left.

Iron poles framed the small porch in front of him and he saw the shelves, dusty with the patterns of the things that had stood there on the other side of the glass. There was a noise of wrenching above, a tear and crack, as the first of the old work was split away from the bedroom's dormer windows.

The porch was six feet, six inches high. It had last been painted this toy-truck blue, but Lennie saw white underneath. It was timber-framed, it had four courses of blocks, and then these windows, through which he saw the shelves and the coat pegs – empty now – and the quarry-tile floor. It had a small glass roof and the sun would come in during the late mornings, through the dust, would warm it.

Lennie lifted the bolster. He set it carefully to the edge of the pine beading, dark now in the rain, and his reflection moved towards him.

There were men in the garden next door, he heard them talking without hearing their words. There was a man above him, and Wyn walked with brisk, cold footsteps back and forwards through the gate behind. The sound of skip lorries was constant, two in the town now at any time, Ruth had said, on one of the many evenings this week when she had talked and he had listened. She didn't seem to need responses any more for when she spoke to him, she did it without her eyes touching any part of him. In this grim February daylight, the lorries dragged the street constantly, unloading new skips, driving full ones away past the flagpole, on the road that led to Aberystwyth. Echoes were cast upwards, across the slate roofs, to the sky. The footsteps of people could no longer be heard on the street in Ynys-morlan.

At home now, Ruth would be talking and talking into the telephone, standing in the kitchen. In the one room that still looked like theirs, she would be rifling through papers given her by Emyr, or by Charlotte.

She'd be liaising. She had laughed as she had used the word.

'People liaise with me now, you know that, Len? Don't know what you want for tea, we'll have to liaise and discuss it. It's funny, isn't it? It's funny.'

She had laughed. Her glance had passed over him and he'd watched the way her voice had trailed into the movements of her hands. Behind each laugh and conversation, there was hatred. In the catching of her eyes on him, there was desperation, as if a skin was falling from them and the person she had been, in jokes and in conversation, had always been full of this hateful aversion, hidden. As if she herself had never realized it.

The project had begun. On all sides of him it stretched, like the white noise that rose in Ruth's eyes. He stood here, a labourer; a stranger at four pounds fifty an hour. In this, his hometown, a great work had begun. He looked at the porch his dad had built. He'd come back from the roads to do this. It made him cold.

No love for himself, Lennie stood with just this duty in his hands. He remembered the many nights, lying in their cornfield-yellow room, staring up towards the ceiling. Full of anger for this project, that had grown as Ruth had slept. Holding her knees, her own body, beside him. And in the hush her slow and constant breathing had come to him; it had come as a feeling of fear. He'd looked at the streetlight, he remembered, where it had reached across that darkened ceiling, with no vividness.

Lennie pried the beading free, so carefully, so carefully, with rain on his hands. He'd take it from this edge and the others and move to stand inside the porch then, where the light would have come if this had been a better day. He'd push the glass gently on to his palm and carry it away.

He came here to restore the work his dad had done. He'd told Ruth once that no one could be happy looking out from their windows to see a dying town. So he came here, to restore, to revive, one of two hundred and seventy-six men hired in the greatest project that had ever come to his hometown.

He had wished for greatness once. He remembered that. He remembered how the wish had lain like sand in his body, staring up towards the ceiling at light that was dim to him.

He remembered, and his hands moved dully. He saw his own reflection tremble as the glass moved. Rainwater ran over the shadows of his cheeks.

When Wyn passed him, Lennie barely heard the words he said. Holding the glass in two fragile hands, he had to turn, he had to ask him to speak again.

'Get the blocks out next, I said. There's a sledge somewhere in the back of Wrighty's Ford.'

Lennie looked at him. The glass was still beneath his palms.

'We're keeping the blocks.'

'We're not keeping the blocks. Why're we keeping them?'

'Keeping the frame,' Lennie said. He looked at the man's face, younger than him by five years. 'Keeping the frame, the blocks, the glass. We're here to restore them,' he said. 'We're not here to replace them.'

'Well I don't know what you reckon you're going to be restoring, like. Got six pieces of two-by-four and twenty blocks. What you going to do? Clean them and put them in again?' He laughed. In the grey rain, Lennie watched him. There was a moment and the man, Wyn, must've seen what was in his face; he said, 'Look, I've got a spec for stonework to four feet, windows – ones that open, like –' a smirk, '– slates on the pitch. Don't know what you reckon we're going to be restoring, less you want to take the blocks, chisel them down till they look like stones. We could paint the glass up. *Pretend* it's slates –'

In Lennie's gut, some sureness overturned and its hidden side was rotten.

'Call my wife,' he said quietly. He felt the rain dapple his skin. 'Call my wife.' His only recourse in this town, which held every memory he had ever claimed as his own. He looked at the boy in front of him, he might've laughed, that this was all he could say.

★

The phone call from Wyn came at half past one. In papers that were spread without method across the oilcloth, Ruth's moving hands died and were still.

Plaster fell above her like the spring rain in her garden. She listened to him and stared at the wiped, shining counter, grey light across its surface, at the vase of flowers there. In her mind as she heard his muffled voice, it fell.

He asked a question.

In her mind, it touched this slate floor and erupted in thousands of small pieces. Scoops and shards of broken glass, and she hurried to pick them up; to gather them in her hands.

Before her was this hoary, windswept view, and what came to her felt like strength. She might have been running, but still it did. Surely it couldn't be wrong to take hold of what gave you that.

'Not restoration, no,' she said. She saw the rain fall on a town where she'd never been happy. 'Not restoration, take them down.'

On the morning that Ruth Lewis saw the dry rot exposed beneath the walls of her bedroom, Emyr Morgan woke in his own, beside his wife, with a weight across his chest in the dry air.

He opened his eyes and felt her beside him, as they'd lain every morning for eighteen years. His voice was quiet.

'Gwen? Are you awake?'

She didn't answer him.

He sat up and he looked slowly at the window.

'I wake up like this every morning,' he said.

She lay silent for a long time. It seemed like she'd moved from sleeping to waking without a change.

'I know,' she said.

'What are you thinking?'

The ceiling was white above her and, in a brief tatter of sunlight through the February cloud, patterns were cast there like leaves.

Emyr felt the softness of the covers shift around him. He saw the breathless cloth of the curtains and he said, 'They're building our project down there.'

'It isn't ours.'

'You can't look at it, without seeing it. I don't believe you can. I wake up like this every morning.' With the air seeming to hold no sound, as if you'd speak into it and the words you said would seep into the cushions, the carpet, the bedlinen, to leave nothing. 'I feel so sad,' he said.

She couldn't answer him.

'That's our project down there, our vision. It's what we always looked towards. Didn't even say it to each other maybe but . . . I keep remembering the day, when you were trying to get the nursery, and the letter came. I was in the garden, you know? . . . You can't work towards something like this. But I tell you what, this is what was in our minds. Nonetheless,' he said. 'Nonetheless.' He turned his face from the window to her and there was something lost in it, pliant without his glasses. She only lay in the place where she'd woken, unspeaking as on the seconds that passed between them, the sound of the project came to rest.

He had taken everything from her. He had taken away any ability she'd had to blame him. In her mind, all the anger she had rained down – and struck Dai Meredith. In her mind, she was shouting, and every word left a hole in her.

She looked at Emyr. She held the same memories as him, of projects and long nights talking; they reached her like this passing sunlight, but there was nothing she could say to him any more.

'You can't tell me,' he said, 'that you don't look at it every day, and see our vision. It must be the hardest thing, not to have a part in it.'

Vehicle doors were opening in Ynys-morlan's street, the voices of men who didn't live here. Gwen lay, isolated from that town, even from this breach of sun outside and the bitter grey that chased it. From everything, it seemed to her, but the coral-coloured bedcovers. Isolated from the man who shared them.

In one hour she would drive through Ynys-morlan, its images would pass her by. No coherence, men working and scaffolding poles, wind and litter. It felt to her as though, even if she were to stop her car, to open its windows and look out at her home, she would find some barrier between. The sounds and smells and sense of it would be cut away from her.

'Eighteen years of working for this town,' Emyr said. 'Working against the tide as well, with Watson up on the council. Though I always thought,' he gave a tiny smile, of memories, and after them his eyes were lessened, 'that maybe you liked it better that way, to work against something. Always had more energy then.' He turned back to the window, where that infirm light waned on another rush of wind. They heard it even through the double-glazing. It would blow through grass that was not yet grown, down the uneven slopes of this headland to the edge of the town. 'A long time, eighteen years . . .' There were the barriers with peeling logos stuck across them. On the gift shop's site, *Cambrian Demolition*.

She looked at the back of his head, the smooth grey hair.

'To see the gift shop come down, as the first part of this – what would have been our ambition . . . hardest thing.'

'You knew it would be.'

'I knew it would be.' He looked down into his lap, where his hands lay motionless in the folds of the covers. 'For different reasons, though. I thought.' As she lay beside him then, he spoke without looking at her face. The work continued, far away from them, and changed this room with the remote touches of its echoes. 'I spoke to Dai. On the morning the demo started.'

Hearing the name without answering him, things seemed to blur to Gwen's eyes. These holes inside her widened.

'He was strong. Don't think any of us could have believed how he'd come through this . . .' But he remembered the faith in Dai's gaze, the fibrous hooks of that faith, and what he said came harder. 'He was sitting in the gift shop. He'd been sitting there all night, hadn't slept by the look of him. Still sure with what he'd decided. In spite . . . of what you said to him.'

Her vision distorted, as though she was crying. Her eyes were watertight, though. Her body was, like this house.

'You didn't come to me,' Emyr said. For a moment it seemed like he would lose the slight control he still had over his voice. 'You didn't come to me and tell me . . . to save the place. You wouldn't be honest and let people know what you felt about the demolition. Let them see – and it's nothing, really – to be divided, just to let them see that we . . . we can be divided. It's nothing, if the rest of those eighteen years has been us . . . united.

'That's what that building meant. That's what it meant,' he said, 'to me. But you didn't try to save those memories. What I did, Gwen, it was a hard thing to do. It was a nasty thing . . .' His heart broke in the moment's silence he had to take. It broke, to let water run down into the palms of his hands on this dry bed. 'But you must've seen, that it wasn't . . . just done in hatred. I was . . . you must've seen I was . . . hurting. You must've seen how I was scared,' he swallowed. 'I didn't know if you loved me,' he said. 'I didn't know if you . . . had ever loved me. To be just the same – when it's years since I saw you cry, but you did. I didn't think you had reason to . . .

'You could've come to me,' Emyr said, 'whatever you felt that night.'

She remembered confusion, unfounded fear. Homesickness maybe. Though as she'd stared out over the black sea, the shore on which she'd stood had been Ynys-morlan's.

'Just like, with the gift shop, you could've come to me,' he continued. 'There were a hundred ways, and you knew it, but you didn't ask. A hundred ways to postpone . . . cancel. I wanted to cancel it.' He was left in a voiceless moment, finally said, 'But what you were scared of losing . . . had nothing to do with me.'

Gwen watched him. She didn't want to speak, afraid of her own voice. She didn't know herself.

'Horrible things, that was what Dai said. I don't know what that means. You hit him, that's what he told me.' He shook his head. He tried to imagine but could not.

She herself did not know how. It seemed that there were things inside her that she'd never realized were there.

'You can imagine . . .' he said softly, 'you can imagine my surprise.'

She remembered Dai's red eyes. She looked at her husband now, and hated him, and hated her own actions more. He sat with the morning light across his face; the light of every morning on which they'd ever woken here.

'I know how hard it must've been, for you to hit Dai. I've been with you, all the way through,' he said, as if his presence had never been reciprocated. 'I know what sort of person you are, and I can't imagine . . . maybe I can imagine . . . what state you must've been in.'

'You must have imagined it,' she found words but she didn't believe in them. 'Many times, planning it all out.'

'I planned for you to come to me!' He turned his face to her and in this uncertain shade, it was ravaged. 'I thought . . . when you looked at what you were losing, it would be us you saw . . .' He swallowed bitterly and lowered his eyes to his hands again. 'I thought,' he said, 'you'd come to me, and try and prove that.'

There were words, answers, but they came in silence. They'd both pretended normality; that the other was all right. There were words of caring, which she might have said to him long before.

Emyr didn't look up from the bedclothes as he asked her, 'What was it that you were trying to save?'

Remembering the pain she'd felt, Gwen didn't even know; recalling her fear that the building would be gone.

He said when she didn't answer, 'Not our work, just your own. That's what you were scared of losing, wasn't it?'

He looked at her across the bed. She seemed to be hurting but he knew it wasn't sadness for them both; for them together.

'It's always, every project's . . . been yours. You went to Dai, scared of losing the one that started it. Never saw a partnership.'

She opened her mouth but the memory that came to her, of the long walk to Dai's house, rang quietly with the resonance of what he said.

'It's all right, Gwen. It's all right.'

She met his eyes and something seemed to fall away from her. Testing the thought, imagining their past projects as only hers, nothing seemed changed to her. This air lay still. And the look on his face was no different than it had ever been.

'It's been a long bloody road for you, Gwen, to get to this spring, like, and look out of the window, and see this project now. Be separated from it. How does that feel?' he said. He watched her, lying without a movement beside him.

Gwen only said, 'Imagine. Just imagine.' She hated the coldness of her own tone, though it was justified. She hated herself now. That was how it felt.

'This is what I want to know,' he said. He raised his hand to show her the day, the light outside, which fell now on Ynys-morlan, on the sea, on every scaffold-covered rooftop below them. 'I see . . . I see what the past must have been for you. All those projects. How precious. I've loved that in you. Do you know that? It's one of the things . . .' he said, 'I loved in you most. I could never have cared for someone who didn't have that . . . drive, to do good.' He drew what he had left into his voice. 'What I want to know is . . . why you've spent eighteen years doing good, if you could go to Dai after that, and hit him, hit him just to save it. How could it have been good?'

She lay, open-mouthed and stalled. Couldn't move to tell him it wasn't true. The words wouldn't come from her but widened like a rift instead, filled her it seemed.

'I want to know,' Emyr said, 'how it could ever have been for the community.' In his eyes as he looked at her there was nothing solid. 'Or if it was all for you.'

Gwen closed her mouth, but what she felt seemed to escape anyway. In her bed, with noise coming to her through the wind-torn distance, she couldn't find an answer for him.

Bright sun touched those barriers with their flapping, fretting signs that showed the demolition firm's name.

'Nothing's ever come to this town, that could do more good,' he said. Hammers and men's voices shouting, the tread of tyres across dry concrete. 'For every person here. Except you.' And then he began, almost inaudibly, 'I've been thinking . . . I've been thinking, I'll take you through it. The whole project, bit by bit. Because you should be glad to see it – despite everything. If you've been working all these years for people's good, then you'll be glad for them.'

Under this struggling sky, the three and a half tons of beach stones that had already been moved lay with dim surfaces, wet shadows crouched between them. Beside them the bulldozer coughed heavy, brutal noise. There was the remote and tiny sound of the new skips coming.

Dai Meredith walked down from the lane and into Ynys-morlan. He stepped over the development boundary, visible now for the first time where, for seventy-five years, on plans and maps it had been drawn. Now the clean edge of this disorder. He saw the people in the street. The fingers of scaffold. What drove in him drove like these engines.

In the three shops opposite the gift shop's remains, stud walling was being demolished. Soon they'd begin to lay the wooden floors. In a herringbone pattern, Ruth and the foreman Gavin had said. They agreed that a herringbone pattern was the prettiest. It wasn't the 'same-old, same-old'. He had nodded.

The same-old was gone, he thought. The new-different was coming.

Time had taken his mother's town, a place of memories, and was moulding it into another shape. He'd been pushed here, to a place at the crest of it all, walking again from his mother's house to see a town bedraggled with the work. He looked out at the trucks and waiting cars, the open doorways and the men who moved through them, carrying, hurrying, delegating. He looked above the walls to the rooftops, the figures perched there between the highest frames against a cinder-dark sky.

All through the years that the gift shop had stood, drifting around upstairs, Dai had gazed out and seen people on the street. And they worked or they went about their business, they were caught up in the worlds of their own lives. They owned their time. Didn't want anything to be bigger than themselves; had no need of anything like that.

But time had turned here now, and had risen up over their thoughts.

He'd been crying. On Emyr and Gwen Morgan's sofa, he'd looked up at their lovely carriage clock with realization flooding him like pale light: the times he cried and the times he didn't, they came in patterns.

He'd always wanted to love time. The way it changed, the fading afternoons. The summer would come and its memories would seem older than you, as if of somewhere you'd never been. How the numbers on a digital watch spilled over each other, never-ending. Even if the watch were to stop, never-ending. We couldn't see time, but only measure it. Little, changing numbers were all we understood. How *could* we see it? Something that held everything, everything in the world, and moved it all towards what was destined. Something massive, milling, pounding like this street, and unheard by us. Everyone of us was deaf to it.

'Their vision,' Emyr had said.

Gwen remembered many sunlit days, with goals in her mind even brighter, walking into Ynys-morlan, past the place where the stones were piled now.

They would be set against the seawall's chipped concrete, built against the public toilets' pebbledash and every modern structure within the boundary, extensions made from breeze block, brick. They would form new skins around the windows people viewed the world through now. Kitchens and studies and lounges, looking out from these lovely rounded stones then; looking out from history.

On the road which Dai was crossing, the visitors would walk in groups, the tourists, they would wander in happy little droves and make soft sounds of marvel.

Maybe this had been the place that had been in Gwen's mind, walking on those sunlit mornings. She didn't know. Whatever place she'd been reaching towards, it had been unclear to her really. Stepping on to the path of each house, papers in hand and words in mouth, it was only the walking she remembered.

As Dai stepped on to the pavement's other side, he had one small thought held in his mind. Cupped in his hands, he imagined, softly protected there from time. He saw the double steel gates to the demolition site, open, through which the lorries that he heard now could reverse with their new skips, ready to carry more away. Men moving there in the grey wind, their jackets and their hair blown by it. And as he followed the dirty barrier's curve, the sound of his footsteps submerged in the clamour, towards the place where the gift shop's wreck would come in a moment into his sight, Dai fixed his eyes on a pair of full skips. Hard yellow in the winter air, and overflowing.

Timber jutted from them, plasterboard that let its dust fall white to stain and fade the concrete. Things too broken, he saw, to hold any memory of what they'd been. Dai heard the fall of sledgehammers, their reverberations in his jaw, and the weight of a JCB's engine, flogging the ground beneath it all.

This was the thought in his mind: to keep a little. Just one skip of rubble, maybe two. And he knew what the foreman would say, but he held this thought carefully enough now, after many hours deciding, to tell him, not ask. They would keep it.

He walked with his back to the three shops inside which the gift shop's stock was now piled. Every night he went through town on the same route that he'd used to take home from work, and the memories of those old evenings seemed less distinct. Men now swept from the edge of each site the dust and mess he would have cleared: from the paths and the pavements and away. Ynys-morlan had become self-cleaning. Ynys-morlan had become a great machine. It was hard to call to mind the former quiet. The revving of all the cold cars that were ready to head out of town, their brake lights in the dusky air, the closing of their doors seemed to fall on the memory of his footsteps on a silent pavement. This must be part of its purpose.

Comforted by the agreement Emyr had given as they'd sat together on the gift shop's floor, he'd left behind the thought of Siân Humphries: words that maybe he shouldn't have allowed. He'd left behind guilt he might have had once for the shop. It had been the part of him which hadn't wanted to believe.

But the goodness of time's movement was everywhere and open to be seen. You only needed to look at his mum's garden. In flower beds that he'd thought were empty and dead, plants were shooting first new fingers. Bulbs had come to life. Time was loving, it was apparent everywhere: how it always moved towards beauty.

Gwen dressed and drove towards the town, watched the buildings draw closer through the thinning trees. She saw, between the sites and machinery and men, the little projects that had been so bright on their opening days. The seating area of five benches beside the seawall. The access ramp for the disabled and the interspersed dog mess rubbish bins.

Today was the day scheduled for the glazier company to come for measurements, for both the private renovation grants and the public. Emyr had streamlined, she had seen in the papers that were scattered across his desk, the fitting of the glass, for every building, to one company. And as with the slate, she had read, her hands slow in the many pages, as with the structural frames and the ornamentation – cornices and barge boards and soffits – he had lowered the supplier's prices by twenty-five per cent at the very least.

Houses were obscured by plastic sheeting, clouded as the sky. She saw the Spar and thought of Siân, the expression which must have touched her face as Dai had told her.

There was a tearing sound there. Even through the car's glass, she heard it, an angle grinder set against something inside. In her rear-view mirror, she saw the sparks' thin, orange wheel.

Gwen remembered her starting work in there, she was 'blessed with a clear memory', she'd always said it. She had walked Siân to work that first morning and her friend had looked at her from the doorstep, given a smile. 'Well . . . this is it, from here on . . .' Siân had said. Gwen had told her not to be ridiculous – but she'd had a busy day in front of her, busy and bright, she'd had to leave. And what Siân had said had been true.

Past the concrete space where the stones' pile grew, past the six small houses in the first row, five stretched with that rippling plastic. She wondered what it must be like to stand in those rooms now and hear its sound. She wondered if they were excited, Bill and Ceridwen, Clare, Thomas; if that excitement filled them with confidence and gave them a reason to get up in the mornings.

Gwen drove past Ruth Lewis's house. Men moved through the open doorway. Past the Lion, the café opposite, the museum. And, perceiving it all, her gaze wandering over the dredge and grope of grand construction, Gwen found she felt more tender towards Ynys-morlan than she remembered feeling for years; more than she had with every hour committed to it. It wasn't a feeling of closeness, striving to make a place better. It didn't put you in the bosom of that place, give you any comfort. If it was dark and you couldn't sleep and you felt sadness for no reason, it didn't give you love back, for all the years that you'd put in.

She drove that morning to the community centre, stiff in her seat. Her life working in this town had been good. It had been for this community's sake.

Ynys-morlan fell behind her and only the diminishing road was ahead, the sea, as she turned into the car park. And the three miles of her journey dissipated, to dead calm; left her sitting in an airless car. All her thoughts – every belief – fell only to this blurred ending: her hand on Dai Meredith's face. The final part of the stumbling descent which had started on the shore as she'd looked up to see Siân's son.

Siân Humphries had delivered her application on the 17th of February, with many details included in the space left for owner's ideas. Tom had seen it once, just briefly; her handwriting had been a cramped little scrawl, both on and in between the fifteen lines provided.

Her house was tall against the oblique sky. He was visiting as she'd asked him to each day while she still worked. The last pay cheque he'd had, a hundred and twenty, had gone down to a few folded notes. A month at least, Bethan had said, before the café would be open again. In a different town then.

It had come to Tom that he hadn't looked back, stepping out through its glass doors. He remembered walking the long road out with Rhys and a wheelbarrow. He'd looked back that day. But whether Ynys-morlan was a different town or not, the caravan site was a mile from its boundary.

On the 20th of February, the notice of approval had come through this letter box apparently. It was a joke, 'approval', he thought. He walked around the crowded, overcast rooms. He glanced out through the window in the stairwell where all the junk now had been cleared away, the old papers and dusty things that seemed to have no use, but that his mum had kept anyway. In town now, he'd counted seven houses that weren't strapped with scaffolding. He didn't know how many of them were in the process of approval.

Here, every window was being replaced. In the flat-roofed extension that had been the kitchen as long as he could remember, the window frames were already removed. Polythene was stretched across them, to leave the room unusable, in shadow and cold. Not that he ate here or cooked here, but there'd be no dinners now at all. In one week's time, the foreman had said, whenever they got the first clear day, work on the extension's roof would start. Wyn, his name was. Tom had listened to him for as long as he would talk.

This kitchen would have a little gable roof. The flat tar would be ripped off, and on to the timber wall plates that were hidden in here by white paint, the new A frames would be set. They came ready-made. They would lift the kitchen's ceiling by five feet. He'd walked on this roof once, feet on the rafters, breaking out of his bedroom at night.

Outside, the extension would look like it was built of beach stone. The skin wall with which they were covering the blocks would rise at six courses a day. Six courses was the maximum, Wyn told him, that could hold its weight in wet cement. The new windows that the team set in would be deeper and so, Wyn said, more homely. Across every other face of the house, the pebbledash would be broken away, the render under it, and then, at the end of all this work, at the end of all the work on all the buildings in Ynys-morlan, a sandblasting company would come, the man described, to clean the length and breadth of it.

Standing here and looking at it all on the days he came to check for her, seeing the blokes with their papers and fags in the yard, bitter thoughts came. His mum would have the home she'd never shown the barest interest in having, and the eight thousand pounds compensation money she'd always wanted.

He picked up mess in the living room. The house was out of order, it had gathered here. Stacey's socks, cups and plates, newspapers. In four days, the Spar would close for its 'major structural work', and its 'interior refurbishment' and he wouldn't need to come by here to check in then. He could come by of course, for dinner every night, she wasn't going to turn him away. But he wouldn't come. In these rooms, or looking out through these windows, it all made him feel the same. It was greed he saw. Greed and falseness – in Emyr's descriptions of the town's future, in his mother's cramped handwriting on that form, on either side of the road, for its every stretch.

This house that they were building around him, or camouflaging to look like they had built, it wasn't Siân's. Reflected nothing about her. And he wondered what sort of life she'd live inside it once the builders were gone and Spar was open again, 'interior-ally refurbished'. Wondered what she'd spend her eight grand on, and how she'd feel when it was gone. He imagined her stepping out of the front door, looking up at it all – not paid for by her, not worked on, or thought of, or designed by her.

Gwen drove down the ashen road, saw her little town changing in ways she'd always hoped for. But belief was no longer easy and obvious in the validity of her own hopes.

And Tom looked at his mother's kitchen, where the shadows were lost across dirty surfaces. He wasn't Rhys. Rhys believed in doing what you wanted, regardless of right or wrong. Tom believed in looking for the best way to be. He believed that this town had been all right; that there'd been a community here, whatever Rhys had thought, who'd all been looking for the right way to live. When you were on your own and didn't know where you were headed, searching for that gave you a sense of somewhere ahead.

They'd lain in his bed together, just hugged. He kept remembering. He stared out of this window at a town that was propelled by work, straining forwards with it, and he wondered what its destination was.

Ruth Lewis and her daughter Nia had stood on a garden path that was just the same as this, frozen like the days of Charlotte's past. Ruth kneeling, Nia beside her, broken glass around their feet while still-green leaves had fallen. Only the birches in the treeline yellow against that deepwater sky. Charlotte remembered. They'd had the same eyes, though the girl's had been dark and the mother's light. Even in silence, there'd been a bond, cloudless as the light that day.

Charlotte looked down into a garden now, of the same shape and size, and with the same path. She thought of how the bond that had been so clear in stillness had never been as clear again. Not after the first moment that Ruth had spoken.

Below her, two men carried an old melamine cupboard, broken away from these walls. Men had once carried the walnut bureau, the marble washstands, the Richard Dadd in its great leather wrapping, through Hedera's double doors like this. The ground beneath their feet was sodden, she saw, and the sound of diesel engines on the wet road carried to her. Echoes came to her through open wooden doors.

She thought of the way that Ruth had looked out at this town on the morning that the demolition had begun, of what she'd said then. Any emotion could be put into the creation of something beautiful. The garden Charlotte saw was her own, and the cold room where she stood, empty. The day outside was beaten with rain, and rain was cast in her memories.

The owners of thirteen houses had applied to her for sale. Twelve of the buildings were now Charlotte Weyland's. One family, only one, had changed their minds, to stay in Ynys-morlan through the work, for the future. Twelve, one for each year of her life at Hedera.

These were the only residential properties on which internal work would be done, apart from Ruth's, where the dry rot had necessitated it. Boards obscured half the lawn below. She heard the movements of a man, to her right, outside the window. He was nailing clear plastic across this scaffolding, which cost three thousand two hundred pounds each month – only this house. It was fifty pounds at least for every labourer per day. It was eight pounds an hour for every skilled worker; for the stonelayers, for the carpenters, the glaziers, the foremen, electricians and plumbers. Hedera left her, moment by moment. She had watched the fire rise with Ruth's face beside her, open and beautiful in the rain, and she had thought only of endings. Not of rooms, dim and unoccupied like this, which felt to her like a homecoming.

> Anniversary Day
> August 16th

Dear Charlotte,

Even before that day when I found it, the house was bereft. I remember. Like love had just been mislaid – slipped down between the floorboards. She used to cry. I remember how. It's a day for remembering after all. And of course there were always echoes, a house like that, and I swear, in every one I used to be able to hear it – what was missing.

I would have become that shape if I could have, moulded myself into it. Wouldn't any child? I mean they do. They see their parents' aspirations and their values – grow to fill them. I would have. Really I tried. I remember Mother's outbursts.

Oh I was so perfect, I was so loved, and then I didn't fit the picture. I was not the truth.

You learn where the walls are, don't you? You're born into a maze and you can't even see it – but you learn where the walls are every time you meet one. Till you walk with your hands out in front or give up, curl up, never try to move. Even before I found out, the house had this kind of deprivation.

So much rage in her. But that's the by-product, isn't it? Self-delusion can't be good enough, not ever,

513

not really. every telltale edge of reality when you're not drunk or buffered by anger.

I've read the fucking Post's descriptions of my father's refusal to leave her as a mark of his greatness, refusal to ever publicly admit error. But I remember him at home. Something in him had given up on the belief in his right to leave.

the days. He must have had a fair lot of guilt, seeing her with me. any incorrectness. Dislike the foods you're meant to like, or the stories or the toys or games, look wrong, sing wrongly, speak out of place and suffer the goddamn world caving in. Because for her it really felt that way I suppose. can she even imagine how it's taken me years — to reassess just **the food** I eat. In view of my own body. I had to dissect the person she made me.

And when I realized, when I saw the top of that fucking field, what did it give me? Knowledge of the fact that I had no entitlement to my life. That every feeling of mine was an appropriation. Every experience theft.

I remember, before I left Hedera, thinking or writing that I should take my life. And you know what's stopped me?

Learned it from her. Sheer bloody-minded strength.

How she hated everyone, I remember. The staff, even her friends eventually. I imagine her seeing the judgement on their faces. My God, I hope they judged. They saw me, they saw my unhappiness, **they saw the wrong in it** — I imagine her slowly losing every friend, I imagine her being unable to bear the recollections she couldn't remove from their eyes, the baldness of truth in them. I hope.

She created herself a vision, a perfect fallacy. Then she beat and cajoled and enticed and screamed me into

the missing part. No thought in her for healing, any
positive action. No, she saw how she'd been divested of
joy and had no qualms in taking it from others. She
could have changed her grief into something better. Put
it into my life. With the strength that thirty years of
fighting for it has brought, I'm able to say it now. She
could have loved me.

Lennie walked on to their garden path that night and saw the scaffolding against the carbon sky. The windows lit between, its framework wracked the building. Each black plank cast a shadow down the wall and each black pole cinched the shadows in. A platform over the doorway. On his left, the curtains were open, the window cradled between rusty arms, and the kitchen table clearly visible inside, the oilcloth. As if the house should always have looked this way; it had found itself. He didn't want to recognize it.

As it had done so many times before, Ruth cooking in the sweet and perfect kitchen, Nia drawing or watching the muted TV or only playing with toys on the floor of her open bedroom, the front door swung to show him voiceless rooms.

It might seem peaceful. He might've come in and looked at Ruth now, where she sat on the staircase, and seen only a woman in an empty hall; seen his wife only, in his empty house, waiting for him to come home.

In the doorway, bare-lit by the bulb above them, he stopped.

She'd waited for him as the vehicles queued and left outside, hearing them over that tiny fraction of a noise, high-pitched and so familiar, of Nia's favourite programmes. Behind one of the doors here, she was cuddled in a chair. Where Ruth had sat, everything had been sunk in quietude, each slight change of her feet on the floor easily heard.

She saw him with the clarity of a stranger. He was a big man, a man with some kind of nobility in him, that had seemed full of passion to her once. There was only a grimness in it now, the edge of something barren, like this countryside.

'Welcome home,' she said. She lifted her hands, to show him the room; the many things that weren't here. 'Welcome home,' and a laugh trickled from her, uncontrollable as tears.

He didn't answer or move to take his coat off. He didn't walk from the doorway, but he watched her. The rooms, vacant or overflowing with clutter, were undifferentiated now, no reason really to stand in any other place.

'You've been waiting,' he said.

'I've been waiting, yes. Just sitting here. Just been waiting. How was it?' she asked quietly.

He stood with aching hands, dark from the work today, from the years he'd taken down. He looked at Ruth on the staircase, and felt a hatred that would not reach her. Like every feeling of his that fell on her – could only touch her and turn to sadness. Snowflakes on spring ground.

'I spent the day taking down the work my father put up.' He spoke without emotion. Dark hair, wan eyes and the gap between her teeth that showed if she smiled, or if she spoke, or if she cried out.

'Spent six hours on a porch he built, must've been twenty years ago. Don't know how long it took him. Took me an hour and a half to knock it down.'

She wanted to stand but she did not. The ring of the television was constant to her, constant. And the house in which she'd sat, an hour now in stillness, its quiet seemed to intensify.

She said, 'It only took them an hour to knock most of the plaster off of the bedroom wall. Not very long at all, is it? Scares you really, how quick. I was just thinking how much work it takes . . . to keep something, maintain it. Makes . . . it makes it seem like a sham, doesn't it? You know, like everything you've been trying to hold together was . . . very thin, all the time. Like all you were maintaining was . . . belief.' She saw him. 'Isn't that how it made you feel?'

'You've no idea how it made me feel.'

'This house was my mother's.'

She didn't move from the wooden steps. She was scared to stand without touching something, the banister here, the unadorned wall, any part of the house she'd looked after for two years while she hadn't – no, she had let him use her – hadn't looked after herself. It was using someone, wasn't it, to be angry at them, to hurt them, because you hated the life you'd once imagined would make you happy?

He'd used to have this wild smile. He'd come in just like this, the first six or eight months maybe, and say he wanted to go out on the dunes, say he wanted to make love out there.

'I remember when it was Mum's house,' she said, 'still my dad's really maybe, in all the spaces, you know . . . And I used to tell myself – somewhere like that – be the last place I'd end up living. Never mind,' she gestured again, 'never mind the same walls. But it's funny because you can't control things like that, just can't. Maybe nobody can really control themselves, you know?'

On the floor between them, her words spilled out to run like beads. And on the bare walls, on the closed wooden doors, shadows lay. Memories exposed. From the cracked, renderless hole in the yellow wall of their bedroom, they seeped out.

Lennie moved into the room. He stood a few feet from her and he saw a face she'd been hiding, two years maybe. Only the last few weeks he'd seen its glimpses. He looked at himself, like he had done in that glass today; the actions that had led him step by step downwards till he'd come from his last day on the roads and asked her to find him a new place in the new town she was making. He saw them both. It was only him who deserved hatred.

'You got what you wanted, Ruth. I spent six hours taking it down, really careful, you know? Took the beading off from round the windowpanes and got them out.' He held up his stained hands to show her how he'd gently caught them. 'I took the door off. Unscrewed one of the hinges, like, had to prise off the other one with a claw hammer, twenty years' worth of sinking in. Really careful.' He looked at her, at what was only just contained in her eyes, just brimming over her silence. 'Really careful.' Loss fell through him and left him, under her stare, as bare as this floor. 'Knew they'd be going in the skip, knew it'd be me putting them there. Careful anyway I was. The amount of work he did in this town . . . sheer fucking number of houses he did. I've been standing there all day . . . didn't have the right, it felt like, to be anything but extra fucking shaking-hand careful.' He wanted to look away from her but he wouldn't do that. 'You got what you wanted.'

Ruth rose from the uncarpeted stairs, for a moment her hand rested on the rail. She felt its oak underneath her palm, felt its warmth. Like she was free-falling as she took herself away and stood alone on the slabs.

'Do you know . . . this house . . .' she showed him, one rising hand, the places where the wildflower paintings should hang, the spot in the hall here where there should have stood the little table, the dried flowers, over an endlessly clean carpet which had led to such clean rooms, 'you can't stop yourself, doing things you least want to. You hate yourself . . . you know what it's like, to hate what you do? And not be able to stop yourself?'

She was tiny, pale. He said slowly, 'I know, yes.'

She moved and then they were standing close.

'All the arrangements, you know the photos on the bedside table, you know the chest of drawers I had here?' Her movements were unrestrained, as if the air in this room was thinner than it should have been. 'All the arrangements, you must've seen them. You must have, every day. Always the same. I mean, you must've seen how nothing ever changed, putting it all back – You lived here every day.' And in her voice there was a plea. She herself heard it. 'I hate myself for the way I am,' she said. 'How I've had to live, I hate it . . .'

At her back, the landing lay in gloom, and the doors to the bedrooms, shut. She had been through the house, he saw, and closed each one before she'd started waiting.

'Do you know what, though?' she said. 'After everything that's happened here, two years of this horrible . . . more, living like this, after everything you've done to me – because you have, you've done things to me, you have – I watched today, this man put a hammer, chisel, on the wall. I've been waiting here, to try and tell you . . . It hurt me, Lennie. Because I need this place. Need it to be nice and to be cosy, look all right, look pretty, and stay . . . stay the same. Because after three years . . . you've made me need that.'

Lennie saw her and she was crying without knowing. He felt the hole that she had watched being made today, inside himself, as she raised her eyes again. And all the hours that he'd spent with the grey sky over him, ocean-washed with the past, those hours hadn't left him. As though he'd always been this man, and the years that had gone by before, when he'd laughed or shouted or thought himself in love, they had been a veneer.

His mouth was closed, though it seemed like for the first time in such a long time, he had words to say to her. Words with real meaning. His mouth was closed. This empty house was the home he'd made.

Ruth looked slim and precious to him.

'The man called,' she said. 'Wyn. One o'clock. He said to me, was he meant to be keeping the frames, and I told him no. I could just tell him. I said no restoration. You know . . . you know, because I wanted to . . . make you feel it.'

His hand lifted as if to gesture, speak, but it only fell again. Placing that glass in the skips, he'd imagined his father, at a distance, seeing what was happening. He would have shouted, called out, what was going on? In overalls and work jacket, Lennie would've turned towards him and from far off, his dad would have made out who was breaking it down.

'Did it make you feel bad? Because I stood here, I felt so bad, like this wasn't my place, you know? But Mum's. And I'd ruined it. Like it was my fault, but I never hit anyone, I never did that. You were the one that ruined it. I told him, no restoration. Said I wanted you in charge of taking them down.'

His palm came up, came up to her shoulder height and it was so quick, so natural to him. She looked into these eyes that she knew well.

'No. Hit me, Lennie – don't stop, hit me, go on.'

He was captured by her loveliness; the lines of her face. Snared by her.

'Hit me, go on . . .'

He raised his hand and he did it. He raised his hand, brought it down across the face of the woman he'd married.

A bald-handed slap, no more, but she took it and didn't look away. Only a slap, but it was the fear that came before it which she stood with open eyes and bore. It had never really been the pain. She saw what was left of his nobility. Saw hatred that was only for himself. He tried to speak again but had no words.

'Hit me, Lennie, don't talk to me because I don't want you to talk, you just hit me, that's what you do, go on –'

He brought his hand up again and shut his fist. He struck her, across her face, where her skin was flushing already from his palm. He punched her there, where he'd hardly dared to put a mark before.

He felt the connection between his knuckles and her in the moment before she fell away from him. In the starkly vacant hallway, she cried out and the sound was bare as stone beneath a sunlight-coloured wall. He heard it. It was an awful sound, muffled and ugly and it seemed he'd never heard it before, though she'd cried out in this house so many times. His own blood had been rushing then.

Ruth lay on the dark floor. She'd caught herself on one arm, her hair in her face. And Lennie stood inert, letting in the sight of her. Her long skirt was in disarray above her knees. He saw a line of pale skin between her waistband and the bottom of her blouse.

It seemed to him that he fell, like she did. It seemed like he fell, to lie next to her on the floor. And that, lying there, he held her.

Ruth turned to look at him, unable to see clearly, water in her eyes. But he saw her, blinking, rising, his vision unclouded.

She spoke, voice thin as wire. 'Hit me. Come on, come and stand . . . come and stand close. Come and be close to me, hold me. Come and hold the collar, like this . . .' She pulled her blouse out in her hand for him to take. 'Hold it like this, you know, come on.' She dragged herself up to a sitting position and beckoned him on.

He came. Like she told him to, like he'd done so many times, he took her collar so he could hurt her. So that he could do it over and over without her being able to move away. He looked into her sky-white face.

'Hit me.'

He drew his hand back and slapped her loosely again.

'Hit me, Lennie!'

He saw her crying and he made a fist. Her blouse was soft cotton and it slipped in his fingers. He saw the curve of her neck, where he might touch her, where he might put his hand to comfort her.

'I want you to!' Ruth said. The water in her eyes spilled and left them clear. 'Hit me, go on! *Hit me!*'

He felt something move inside his chest, numb and fluttering, trying to rise. But this was his wife on the floor in front of him, and this was how he gave himself to her.

'Hit me,' she said.

Words in his throat, he didn't speak. He raised his fist to punch her but it slackened and only fell as another bare palm across her cheek.

'Don't you want to? Hit me, Lennie! *Go on! It makes you feel better! Doesn't it? Doesn't it . . . ?*'

He slapped her, holding her collar. His hand fell again and again on her face, weaker, open. Kneeling over her on the floor, the blows struggled like a bird's wings.

Ruth Lewis. Ruth Morgan. He remembered lying in bed with her when, for the first time, he'd been her husband and she'd had his name. And as his movements died and his aching palm lay against her cheek, touching her, he looked into her face.

Her eyes were open, they were lucid, light blue. He felt her skin, he moved as if to speak. Moved as if to tell her he was sorry; to begin to tell her, and never stop.

But Ruth stared up to him, crying and wretched with other years.

'You hurt me,' she said, 'go on – go on – hurt me –'

He didn't have the right to tell her he was sorry any more. To hold her or imagine any future together; to imagine anything that was not true to him.

She went in to Nia after he'd left them; opening the door to a draped and tiny make-believe world, and seeing her seated on the floor. There was only the light of the TV and her body was small, silhouetted. Ruth went towards her slowly, sat down behind and put her arms around Nia before she could turn and look.

She tried to shift but Ruth only hugged her as Nia's gaze trailed back towards the film. Ruth sat in shadow and put her face in Nia's hair.

'I love you,' she said. Like she never had before. Like she could only make up for it by repeating. 'I love you . . .' she said as she held Nia, feeling it.

In a night that was driven by a turning wind under black and breaking clouds, Ynys-morlan's houses stood, their rooftops framed by scaffolding, their slates wet with the throws of rain that clung like tears to each iron pole in the streetlight. The road itself, as yet untouched by the work that hung from these houses' faces, still gathered its puddles in potholes, wind-roughened and in moments mirroring the brief, cold points of the sky.

The door below the plaster-cast lion was opened and closed for the last time that night. Rhys stood on the pavement, cold, pissed, unsettled, and looked at Lennie Lewis. He was staring at the buildings opposite, his face unchanging: grimness that was open to this road and to the weather, like he could soak up everything he saw. Like it bled down to the palms of his hands.

'You want to take a walk with me, Rhys?' But he didn't glance behind.

And Rhys was silent as he stood under the scaffolding. He wanted to answer no. There'd been no laughter tonight, set and quiet, almost no talk at all. Lennie had hardly looked at him. Now the man stared at this street that was filled by redevelopment, in stillness, and Rhys was scared that he knew what weighed on him. Could only be what surrounded them. He watched Lennie turn towards the head of town; the broken line that was yellow-stained by night-time. There was this distance in Lennie's eyes.

'Where you walking to?'

'I'm walking this way.' The houses lumbered dark towards the stand of trees where this road curved off; towards the rest of the world. 'Come,' he said. Not a question, not quite.

When he turned back, Rhys with no reply, there was some moment on his face that for the first time tonight held recognition: fragments of other evenings. Rhys saw him. Questions came up to him that really should stay quiet.

Lennie's face was changed by shadows, and they were shame. 'Come with me, like.'

He went.

They walked in this silence that Rhys had listened to all night, felt through every pint as the memories of all the other nights they'd spent together there had slowly turned amber in the beer. The wind caught whatever litter was left of the day and scattered it in the alleyways between the houses; gusts that turned washing lines and rattled boards against yard walls, all the way down those dark stones to an open beach.

In this street, people slept. Bethan slept and her kid, in a cot or in her own room, Rhys didn't know. Didn't know how a child of any age slept. Some board of photos above her that Rhys had never seen – all kept behind the windows of the flat above the empty launderette.

Throughout the Lewises' house quiet was now composed and in the soft-lit kitchen, Ruth sat before the telephone. She spoke sometimes, though the place was unoccupied but for her daughter. Her hands moved and were still against the oilcloth. Not words for Nia now; words empty of the pretence that her daughter heard.

When she dialled Charlotte's number and Charlotte answered, Ruth's voice still held the tone with which she'd spoken to herself. She didn't tell Charlotte that anything was wrong. Waiting after she had hung up the phone, Ruth couldn't remember really what she'd said. But there must have been something, for in another silent house one mile away from her, Charlotte was preparing to come. She was placing the receiver down, taking her overcoat, her mouth closed over anxiety and the memory of Ruth's broken voice.

Not far from here, her husband looked towards this window.

'What d'you think of it all, Rhys?'

Rhys didn't answer, not sure now of what Lennie might say back. There were angry thoughts in his head, seeing the man, but deeper, formless things lay underneath them.

'Your folks've applied, like, I saw the form. Come in late. What do you reckon?' He held his hands out to the houses on either side of the road.

Rhys's footsteps sounded in the wind. 'What's to think, like? You're building.' Hands hard in his pockets, eyes hard on the end of the street, he said, 'It's still the same place.'

'Still want to leave?'

'If I go, it won't be till it's finished.'

'You want to see it finished.' He didn't glance at Rhys as the wind struck him.

'I want to see what I'll be leaving.' On the tarmac, his shadow was cast in many vague directions.

'Your home's what you'll be leaving,' Lennie said. It didn't sound like judgement, though. 'However it looks, that's what. Know what my old man told me, like? Told everyone, I heard him. "There are three important things in life."' He looked past these windows, lit or dark, he looked past them. '"Your home," he said, "your family and yourself." Heard him say it to Garwyn once. In the Lion, that was. Had a lounge bar in there then, used to have the darts. 'Part from working or being at home, like, used to spend his whole life in there. I heard Garwyn say to him, "What about your friends, like?"' He smiled a little with broken, long-ago memories. '"Fuck your friends," he said.' He turned his face to Rhys, his hair blown across it, and in his eyes, Rhys saw, there were tears. 'What d'you reckon to that, like?' he was asking.

Streetlight moved over Lennie's face.

With a bare nod, Rhys only turned back to the road; saw where it led out of Ynys-morlan. 'Reckon you're asking the wrong person.' And he said nothing else, even through what he felt.

He'd not seen Lennie in the last fortnight but had thought of him often, sitting in his room at night watching videos – watching other places on the screen. They'd been the only thoughts of this project that Rhys had let in; all the others closed outside the door till the 3rd of March, when his parents' work was due. In this whole fucking project, it was only Lennie that might bring some honesty. Rhys'd thought there'd be one person left after he had gone who gave a fuck – and held sway.

It was in the set of Lennie's shoulders, though, every movement of his body, it was in his words as he cast them to lie on the rain-slick road, walking onwards. Hatred, Rhys saw, and some kind of penitence, interlaid. They passed darkened gardens, the shapes of tools under tarps, polythene-covered scaffolds – some houses wholly obscured by them – where the water made streams and pools and pearls before the wind shook it free. And the empty launderette. And Lennie's house they passed – without glancing. So Rhys's anger grew, when he hadn't thought he *could* feel further from this town.

'You know why I reckon the home's important, Rhys? We're not here for very long, like. Fifty-three my father was when he first got cancer, and he never made it to sixty. Start rotting as soon as we stop growing. Not very fucking long. You know what a home gives you? Fucking sense of who you are in that. You spend those sixty years just driving motorways, what are you then? You're nothing then. But you have a home . . .' he nodded, 'and you put yourself into it, then you'll leave something behind you.' He watched the last part of the road run out beneath his feet. 'It'll remember you,' he said. And when he spoke again then, raising his face to look at Rhys, he must have seen a young man, or just a man now, Rhys realized, who'd been leaving for two years. 'What do you think Ynys-morlan'll remember of you? If you go?'

He opened his mouth to answer but nothing came. Lennie watched him with no pity, and no pity rose in him in return. The answer was nothing.

Lennie began to walk again as Rhys only looked. This fucking wind hit him. Sadness came and took him. 'History's not in the fucking place,' he said, 'a place isn't nothing more than the fucking people. And I'm sure they won't remember much, like, and I won't remember much of them.' But Lennie just stared out again towards the beginning of this town, and Rhys wanted, all he wanted then, was for the man to turn and see what was in his eyes. 'History's nothing but what people choose to fucking write down, and I'm sure they'll write nothing at all, like . . . And this? This is just a bit of building work.'

Lennie blinked as he listened, one moment before he said, 'It should be in the stones, history. Feels like it is, right down in them.' And now ahead, he saw the white shape move between still-bare trees. Almost forty years ago Lloyd had raised it. Not long by the stones or by anything solid. Long to him, though. Forty years.

Between their bleak branches, it fluttered and was played by the wind that had always spoken here, maybe even when there'd been no town. He saw it now and his footsteps died, he only stood: its milky outline flying.

'You know what I did tonight, Rhys?' he said. His mouth seemed to tighten around words that he didn't want to speak. And Rhys would've told him then, he didn't want to hear them; would've told him just to go home, to let them both go home, leave this changing street to the rain. Lennie's eyes were hard. He seemed to be crying, but they were hard. And his voice was quiet. He said, 'I hit Ruth in the face.' It flew there, bright, unreachable. 'That's what I did, like.'

Rhys stared at Lennie. The weather hit them.

'Home and family, the most important things in life,' Lennie said. He nodded as he began to walk again.

He passed from the roadside to where the flag sailed; lost the sound of his feet as he stepped on to the grass. And Rhys stood and saw all the branches' shadows fall across his shoulders, Lennie's head bent low as he moved under them.

He thought of Bethan. In the February night, on the outgoing road, Rhys remembered standing over her – she'd been lying on her bed, when her bed had still been in her parents' house – laughing as she'd told him what two blue lines meant.

He remembered feeling violence. In the memory, she seemed far from him. And he didn't know, slowly following Lennie Lewis, with a fear that thinned deep strengths, foundations, if he was moving back towards that long-ago memory, or finally leaving it behind.

*

Charlotte Weyland came when called, to stand on Ruth Lewis's doorstep ten minutes after they'd passed by. Beneath its dripping planks, there was rain in her hair and no make-up on her face. She held her overcoat closed, saw the front door's glass, yellow with light from the Lewises' hallway. In the telephone line, Ruth's voice had shaken.

The emptiness of the many houses she'd been through today, so much like Hedera's, seemed to fill her, until she stood here an empty place herself.

'Tell me what's happened,' she'd said.

'Nothing. Nothing.' Just that word, then laughter or tears.

She knocked and the sound fell to nothing, waiting.

She stood, as though to be still was to be ready.

Lennie looked up at the flag, not speaking till the feelings left his voice. Somewhere in its floundering white, there were pictures. Disordered. Ruth falling. Her hands held up.

Ynys-morlan, gnawed by work that was motionless now, stretched out behind – as if it had taken this, every still piece of machinery, a scaffold on each darkened house and Ruth's ruined voice, to bring him here.

He remembered nights a long time ago, when he had taken off her clothes, when they had made love, as if her body was something to revere. He didn't glance at the boy as he spoke.

'Did you think that you loved her, Rhys?'

The wind struck Rhys's face.

Answers seemed to come to him and leave him, with as many questions, backlashes, on their tails. Standing behind him in the streetlight's edge, he didn't respond. Far back down the road, there was scaffolding around the café now. He didn't know what they were building inside.

'It was two years ago. What does it matter now?' He could glimpse it: Lennie hitting her. His chest was empty, open. He remembered Bethan, tests in her hand. 'I thought I did . . .' he said. 'Back then.'

Still the man didn't turn to him.

This last fortnight, Rhys hadn't paused to look through into the café. He remembered seeing her once, months after they'd stopped speaking, standing behind its windows. The first time he'd seen the kid. Wrapped up it had been, and she'd stared out through the glass. What he saw in Lennie came to knot up with every change in Ynys-morlan, like the project could separate him even from things he'd already lost.

'You know what I thought,' Lennie said, 'when I asked her to marry me? When she said yes. Thought no one in the whole world, in all the towns and the fucking cities everywhere, thought no one'd ever felt so much in love . . .' The flag flew, luminous and trapped. 'My old man,' he amended, with no feeling in his voice. 'It's the two things, like. It's the both of them together, home and family. It's being here,' he said. He remembered how the street lamps had shone that night, how they'd shone like blossoms as he'd shouted down her name. As if the word would fall and sink into the ground here; have meaning. 'It's the two together that make it so strong. It's your place. It's your life. You can believe . . . because you've got the past all round you. Got the future right in front.'

In the star-thrown stretch of Ynys-morlan against the coastline, he remembered the outlines of these same trees, that looked no older now. His name was carved, kid's writing, in one of these trunks.

'Knew soon as I met her, she was the one I'd marry. Sound corny, like? Sound like bullshit? She was the one. I could see . . . how we'd get old together. She had this look. She was beautiful . . . she is beautiful.'

The things Rhys might have said were wedged inside him. He remembered seeing Bethan putting on weight slowly; the odd day he'd chanced across her, chanced across the street away from her.

'She'd never been with anyone else. Could see it just in the way that she smiled, like. It meant something to me.'

Bethan had lied to him. She'd told him afterwards, lying in her bed, when it had been too late. Trapped, the feelings in him, behind images of Lennie standing over his wife. On the floor, Rhys saw her.

'They have a lot of those phrases, corny phrases. And I said, did you think you loved her? Because you know, like.' He gave one brief smile. 'Because all those phrases, they came up with them for a reason. You realize. I was *out of this world*, when she told me yes. *Turned me upside down.* Know what I mean?' He blinked for a moment and he looked down from the flag to the black grass. 'It's more than that, though. You fall in love, it's so fucking strange, I tell you . . . It feels like something from the past. Like, you never thought of her before but she's always been there. Like you thought of her right back when you were young.'

Rhys listened. His feelings were paid out inch by inch, right from his chest, into cold air they'd never touched before.

Lennie closed his eyes to the pole's concrete base, where rainwater ran and shone darkly over old pockmarks. Behind his eyes, there was the picture: light like halos. Not really his own memory. Though climbing up this flagpole once he'd almost made it his own.

'Would've killed for her,' he said, 'would've killed anyone for her, without a second thought. That's how strong I felt about us.'

Rhys's voice was empty. 'I believe you.'

Lennie turned to the boy and seemed to ask if that was true.

With no confirmation from Rhys, he stared back down at the concrete, though, a bitter smile at the corner of his mouth. After a moment, he nodded and raised his face again in the wind.

'You know the truth, like?' he said. 'The truth. I would've liked that chance. Loved it.' As he said it, there was no kind of judgement in his voice. An old and hollow joke – and even that fell from him. 'You know how many times I've hit her, Rhys?' And the boy saw dimness come to take the place of every other expression. 'You know how many times . . . ? I can't count.'

Ruth opened the door to her and in the warm light of the hallway – bare behind – was silhouetted. She stood unmoving, did not speak. Charlotte stared, her eyes adjusting. Ruth's outline was clear against the dismantled room as she met Charlotte's gaze; the shadowed rise of a swelling changing the right-hand side of her face.

Charlotte went to speak. She found no words.

Ruth's small laugh was saltwater. 'How does it look then?' The quiet after left her naked. 'How does it look?'

And she took her hand from the door, she held it to her right cheek and with a clean space between, seemed to cup it. Cup the air around it. Her face was full of hate, like a kind of light.

'Bad then? Bad.'

Charlotte couldn't answer. 'He hit you,' she finally uttered; words like pieces of broken glass.

'You wouldn't think you could do that to the woman you love.'

Rhys remembered Bethan on her bed. The laughter she'd given had been pretence – and he hadn't known how she could do that. Why.

'The woman you thought you'd spend the rest of your life with,' Lennie continued. 'I can't count them, Rhys. So many times.' Behind the planes of his face, feelings lay like cold ground. 'You wouldn't think you could.'

'I wouldn't. You're right, I wouldn't,' Rhys's words grating in his mouth; nights he'd spent with Lennie brought to his mind, nights laughing and quiet. He could scour up no other answer.

'I don't believe,' Lennie began again, softly, 'that any man in the world would have done for their wife what I would have for Ruth. Would have died for her. My old man –' he moved his hand, a gesture. 'What he said was true.' And the hollowness in his eyes, it was failure, Rhys saw. 'Home and family. The two most important things . . . *grandest* things a man can have in life.'

'I don't believe that.' This town, in its first wrenching days of spring, it was behind him, Rhys told himself. He kept no memories here. 'Three things, you said. *Yourself*. That's the most important. Maybe what your old man never said to you . . . sometimes you've got to choose between.' He was leaving; didn't need to see this finished place. He looked at Lennie now and what the man had told him surely robbed away any last strand of any reason to stay.

Lennie said, 'I thought I had them all, together.' He stared to where the road arched out of sight and marked the end of his home. He didn't know how feelings like those could change. Just belief, that couldn't have felt so strong surely. Just belief – it could never have felt so whole. 'When we got married, she didn't want to stay in Ynys-morlan . . . She had her mother's house. You know what it meant to her? Nothing more than the place where they'd been left. But she stayed,' he said. 'Stayed here anyway, *in* that house. D'you know why?' He nodded slowly to himself. 'So she could put a good ending on it.'

Where she stood in their hall, the uncovered bulb's light across her face, there was a silence that echoed with her own voice. Shouting, crying. Unheard by Charlotte. But Ruth heard it.

'So she could lay some roots, like, that hadn't ever been here for her. A good ending. That's the sort of person she was. I loved it in her – fucking determined – I wanted it.' It sounded very simple to him now, for a feeling that had seemed to come up from the earth, that had seemed to fill his soul. 'It was beautiful.' His face was barren. 'Not beautiful like Ynys-morlan'll be soon. That's not beauty to me, like. Prettiness is all it is, the way she's dreamt it up. Decoration's all it is. That *emotion* was beautiful . . .' his eyes held a past that his face would not show, 'like nothing we can put up. Nothing we can even put in pictures in our heads. It was grandness. It was greatness, I think . . . That's what it was,' He looked at Rhys, a moment. For agreement maybe, Rhys didn't know. 'Real beauty,' Lennie said, 'the kind that stirs you up – there's ugliness in it as well.'

It was leaving that brought Rhys that feeling. In his imagining, it had both: ugliness, beauty. He didn't know even where he would go.

'Feels like greatness. Not many things in life that'll give you that feeling,' Lennie said.

This concrete – gleaming beneath the branches, trampled new grass at its edge – it was nearly half a century old. No time at all, even by the buildings they could raise. Long enough to create a history for him, though. He wanted to say to the boy, but the remorse he felt stopped him – that life had few things in it, had few moments that rose above it and were meaningful. They were the times you should hold inside. There were no words that could tell how they felt.

There were actions, Lennie thought, that touched it. He looked at the flagpole's base. He had wanted that chance.

His voice was quiet now, but what was rising he couldn't stop. 'She didn't believe me. She was like that house, she was empty and full of fucking ghosts. I'd tell her how much I loved her. Said I'd do anything for her in the fucking world. She had this laugh, moments like that . . . She'd look away. Do you know what she thought?' In the cold air, he laughed himself. 'She thought . . . that being in love so strongly wasn't really being in love at all.' Rain fell against his face, felt indistinctly. He looked down at the stone like he didn't know himself any more. 'Do you know what it is, to say you'd die for someone and mean it? It's everything. She thought, like, to say those things only proved . . . I was dreaming it. It hurts,' he said. 'It hurts then it numbs off . . . Like it does to get a beating.' He turned away from where his voice ended.

Patterns of shadow and streetlight were running across his profile. Rhys didn't speak. He saw hate, deep under Lennie's eyes, and he wanted to say something and he wanted to leave the man. Just as much.

On this blank stone there was the memory of love, of sunflowers. Of a boy's body, falling.

'Your wife doesn't believe you love her . . .' Lennie said, 'there's nowhere for the love to go. It fills you, fills you right the fuck up, can't get it out . . .' He turned to Rhys, 'You know what it's like then? It's ugly and it's beautiful . . . and you think . . . It must be a great love, to hurt you both so much. It's a kind of greatness.' Ynys-morlan lay behind Lennie. It was the most selfish thing that he told Rhys, and the place he loved was emptier for it. But it was something made from being unfulfilled. And you couldn't help how it formed. What Rhys knew of it was twisted up as he stood here at the end of his hometown.

'You hit the woman you love for the first time,' Lennie said, 'there's nothing worse you could've done. You've lost her.' He saw the boy and hate left his face. It left him, void, and he was only broken then. 'But the day after that first time . . . you've never felt so much in love.' Round them, the trees were left still for a moment by the ebb of the wind.

'That's why feelings mean nothing,' Rhys said. 'She thought it was just belief? I tell you what, like. Fucking feelings mean nothing, you can't ever trust them. Belief's stronger.'

Lennie's stare gave way to the ground. Like the ground itself would do if this rain didn't stop; if the seasons failed to change into each other. He stood still on the wet soil in which his father had once buried a man for love. With the last of the control he had, his voice was hard to hear.

'We made love, the first day after I . . . hit her. And I told her all the things I felt, like. How much I needed her. Could never do without her. I'd never meant them so much in my life. To her, must never have sounded more like . . . belief. We lay in bed. I was holding her. She's so fucking small.' Lennie's face seemed to splinter. 'I couldn't tell her I loved her so that she'd believe me . . . I would've killed for her. Would've died for her. But just living . . .'

At the foot of the wooden staircase she'd fallen down so many times, Ruth spoke and her voice was shaking.

'. . . I've beaten her,' he said, 'I've fucking beaten her, I have told her, while I've hit her . . . how much I love her. And I've convinced myself,' his words faded to touch this stone and maybe they were blown away, 'it must be a great love . . . to hurt this way.'

He looked through the trees, to nothing: just the night before the builders would drive again into his home.

'It fades, though, that feeling,' he said. 'Full of greatness, like. It fades . . . That's how you know the difference,' he nodded to Rhys, 'between real feeling and . . . just belief.'

She said. 'I've not seen in a mirror yet.'

The front door was shut behind Charlotte. Her throat was dry.

'Must be pretty bad, because you've never looked at me with that expression on your face.' There was nothing in this room but the shut doors. Charlotte saw the anger in her eyes. Intense as escape. 'Tell me.'

'What do you want me to say, Ruth? It's terrible.'

'That doesn't tell me anything, does it?' In the air beside her face, her locked fingers trembled. 'I want to know how it looks.'

Charlotte stood where the welcome mat had lain. She was motionless.

'Well?'

'Look into a mirror . . .' Charlotte said to her.

It wasn't the bruise. It was the way that she spoke. She saw the expressions she had known all these months, but made a parody, a savage pantomime. She saw Ruth try to throw herself, like an insult, into her face.

'He did this to you tonight . . . ?'

'Well you're just not answering me now.'

'Tell me what happened.'

'Tell me how I look.' She saw Charlotte's expression like ice. 'Tell me!' A tear overran, unnoticed.

'Ruth, you've got to be calm now.'

That prettiness, which had once brought some slight distaste – her pretty jokes while she would cry, coy as a child when she was a child no longer – it was gone from Ruth. She seemed to hold it up in the light; a mask. And Charlotte couldn't help but turn away.

'Bad enough that you don't want to look at me.'

'He did this just now . . .'

'Don't talk, look at me! You can't do that even? I thought you were my friend!'

Charlotte raised her eyes, wet as the beach where two thousand miles of sea washed up. In the silence they saw each other. Ruth crying too, but without knowing it.

'You look . . . like he must have struck you very hard. Your entire left cheek is swollen . . .' It wasn't that she'd been a cold person, it had never been that. It was only that she was afraid. And feelings which she could not control rose now to show on her face. Afraid of them. 'Your eye's half-closed . . . your skin's discoloured on that side of your face . . . Your lip . . .' she tried to clear her throat, '. . . it's broken. I'm looking at you, Ruth. I'm looking at you. I can see.'

In the bare light, Ruth said, 'This is me.'

'This is you? This is you after you've been struck across the face by the man you're married to.'

She saw Ruth cross the floor as if it were water.

'You don't . . . you've no idea. How long have we known each other . . . ?' Ruth asked her.

Stillness filled the room with her first doubt. She remembered days, many of them, when she might have looked closer. 'Longer than I've known anyone else. Even if it's not long. This isn't you. It's . . . it's degrading yourself to say that, Ruth.' Those early days when Ruth had cried, she remembered, and she'd watched and then, being noticed, she'd turned away. 'This isn't you.'

'This is me.' These rooms were naked for the first time, and Ruth looked at her from the heart of them. To Charlotte, she saw, they were vacant. On every side of her own vision – though they seemed to hold each other's gazes – memories rushed in to Ruth. This, if it was hatred, was all she had. Couldn't let it go. Any more than she could the project.

She would not let that project be an escape – a beauty that silenced, like she had kept in these rooms. It would spill over with all the words she'd never said, and with those she'd called out when only Lennie had heard. It would flow with everything she'd felt in these last three years, until they were gone from her; until she could step out of this house and see something that those feelings had made – that was beautiful. Something beautiful just to see as you opened your front door. Only to stand and to look out at.

She couldn't hold back now. If she wanted this, she could not hide.

'Come upstairs, come up with me,' she said, 'I'll show you how I look.'

'My wife gave birth to our daughter on July the fourteenth. She couldn't smile at me. I came into the room, the little room, she was holding her. She couldn't look at me. I blamed her when it faded,' Lennie said.

Rhys was still. The tangle of what he felt, though, it reached out. He was sorry for the man. He was disgusted by him. He was scared to recognize.

'Driving home, there'd be this road, coming round the corner. Seeing Ynys-morlan. I'd look at it, the potholes, like, empty shops. Knew it was the end. Knew the difference then between belief and what's truly . . . great.' He remembered the twilight in the street, turning off the cab's engine and looking down this street to where it faded into sand and shore. 'I lost the feeling. I'd go down the path, go in,' he recalled their hallway, full, as it had been before the project. 'See her in the kitchen . . . I wouldn't feel anything for her. Real love . . . holds your whole fucking body till cancer takes it away. That's the difference. I lost it. I didn't deserve it anyway.'

He remembered the way she'd stood by the stove, not turning for a moment as he'd come to the doorway. A lack in the place where his love had been. He remembered the clean and perfect rooms.

'I'd look out of the windows, see the town . . . How could I have any of that feeling left? Seeing what I'd done to my wife, my great fucking love. Seeing what I'd done to her here.'

The pain on Lennie's face rose and fell in tides. 'The house got emptier. It got . . . just silent. She started bringing her mother's stuff back down from the attic, like. A year maybe, getting worse. We'd look at Nia, wouldn't talk about her . . . Then Ruth took her for the tests and they came positive.'

She'd waited on the sofa for him. She'd laughed, helpless and shattered. It had been over before that for him maybe, but that had been the night when it had ended for her.

'You can hit someone, over and over, not even feeling angry. You can hit someone, just to punish them for the lack of feeling.' He remembered holding the collar of her shirt, remembered its softness.

Rhys spoke quietly, some memory of his own colouring what he said, 'That lack is what you get when you know what you've done . . . is fucking wrong.'

In the cold air before Lennie, there were memories of an autumn day, when he'd sat with his hands still shaking from holding Dai Meredith in the graveyard. 'I know that,' he said. He heard again, Ruth's quiet voice that day. 'She asked me what was wrong,' he said. Their bedroom window's view, he saw: the street, its scattered litter. Leaves had run along it as though always in the wake of someone's passing. 'She asked me what it was that was wrong in my life, to make me be the man I was. You know what I told her? Do you know?

'"How could anyone be happy," I said, "looking out of their window and seeing their hometown fall apart."'

The words were empty of feeling. He couldn't fit into them what they deserved. He had looked out of the window and he'd seen this street, and he had blamed it. He hadn't known any other way to voice the failure that he'd felt.

Now he surveyed his old man's work, on the ground in front of him. 'Home and family, most important things in life. I beat her . . . till I lost that family, then I blamed my home.'

He took a breath for the last.

'She started this project for me.' Behind them this wind moved, not through trees, but through the poles and rivets of the scaffolding strapped in dark outlines to every house. Lennie's smile was bitter and mournful. 'She came home one night with thirty-three million pounds.'

The stairs creaked as she climbed them. The second step, the fifth, like always.

Charlotte didn't want to see. In her coldest moments, she'd felt no respect for Ruth's childlike manner. In the moments when her own coldness was the only thing she felt no respect for, it had called to her. The way Ruth overran, laughing or crying.

'They took the skin off this wall today.'

Ruth reached the balcony and she opened the bedroom door, put her hand to the place where she knew the switch lay. Standing at her back, Charlotte saw her talk, and tried to find one final word that would take them away from the door. Had written hundreds of thousands, full of compassion, full of loneliness. And Ruth was lonely, totally. Searching for only one to say aloud, there were none inside her.

From darkness to light, under another bare bulb, the yellow room was empty.

'Hammer and chisel, they took it off,' Ruth said.

Charlotte glanced, she saw. The paint and plaster ended with roughened edges around the stone they'd revealed. Covered with rot, white and rust red, creeping over it like fingerless hands. Charlotte was stiff inside the doorway.

She watched Ruth signal to the wall, uncontrolled. The bruise on her face seemed less brutal as she stood beside it. Like her coquettishness had seemed less of a sham perhaps, when these rooms had still been picturesque around her.

'I was watching him do it – and I'd moved all the furniture out already, it wasn't anything like our home. Really, nothing even changed today. It's all been empty here, weeks, you know? But it was like . . . you can always move furniture back. I mean, you can arrange it again. You know how I've kept this place? Like . . . a museum.'

Charlotte didn't speak. Though pictures occurred to her, she would not have described them.

'I had all my things . . . you know me, you know me. It was lovely this room. Sun in here in the afternoons.'

'You've been living,' Charlotte chose her words like footsteps in the empty space, 'you've been living in a house where you haven't been happy.'

'You could have told me that months ago. Couldn't you? I wouldn't have listened, but . . . watched him take the plaster off today, just started crying, you know, couldn't stop, couldn't stop.' She gave her smile.

'Ruth, what you've been through here . . .' It should have sounded like comfort but in the austere light there was only a feeling of fear. Charlotte reached out a hand towards her but it fell short. 'This is a time of change for you . . .'

'You must be glad to see it.'

'I'll be glad to see any change that's for the better, Ruth –' She saw the bruise that covered one cheek, dark under the eye, she wanted to say something, to keep Ruth talking, but her own words were ensnared in this fear.

'You must be very glad.' Standing on the exposed floorboards, Ruth held her hands out to show Charlotte who she was. Rigid, a hatred flowed from her with the tiniest motion. 'I've seen you, and I'm not blaming you because, you know, I would've looked at myself in the same way, if I'd met me.'

'In what way, in what way have I looked at you?' Things moved inside her, painful, with no shape.

'Contempt, you know.'

'No, I've never looked at you with . . . I've never felt it so I never could have.'

'I don't think really that's true, is it now?'

'Ruth, you're not . . . rational . . . You need to be calmer. Please . . .'

'I don't blame you . . . You know me. I know me, little jokes, pretending everything's just fine. Pretending to be . . . someone . . . I don't blame you.' As if Ruth thought her a cold enough person to favour this self-loathing over the sweetness she held out in her brightly lit palms for condemnation now. 'You have looked at me with contempt, like I would have done. Always trying to please, that's it. That's what it really is, isn't it? You must've thought that.'

'I've never judged you –'

'That's just not true. Admit it, why not?'

Charlotte saw her face, its left side lovely. 'You've always chosen to show what you feel . . . you've always chosen . . . to be open. I don't feel contempt for it. If I could – I'd do the same sometimes . . .' her voice fell from her. She looked at Ruth with nothing left. 'You've always chosen to reach towards something . . . That's all I've thought of you.'

'It's just a lie, to act like that, when really you're running away.'

Ruth looked so bitter, but tears fell. Charlotte stood, not moving towards her. Afraid to – her mother's tear-dirty, uncontrolled face drifting like a ghost below the expression she saw. 'It's not running away to take something bad – and use it to make something better.'

'You only say that . . . because you want to do the same and you can't! You don't think the project's making my life into something better. You think I'm running away from my life –'

Charlotte's only answer this outstretched hand, far from Ruth, she didn't speak.

'Let me show you,' Ruth said. 'I want to show you.'

Charlotte shook her head, cold, desperate words in her mind, and nothing but silence in her throat. She was afraid to see what lay underneath. She was afraid, just to see the pale skin.

Like the fall of harsh light on these boards, years seemed to lie around Ruth. Months. Mornings alone. Charlotte saw her raise her hands.

She undid the first button of her blouse. A white blouse, and her hands were shaking. She glanced up at Charlotte for the barest moment. She pulled at the next. Charlotte could only watch. She took it from herself and let it fall like hope down to the bedroom floor. There was no bed now, no lamps with their little gold tassled shades, no photographs.

Charlotte had never seen this room full. She stood here for the first time with only the uncovered walls and Ruth's figure. In her long skirt, in a white brassiere. And the pain she'd feared as she'd climbed the stairs to stand here filled her now. It left her with no sound.

Across Ruth's stomach and around the arc of her hip, the bruises were brown, they were yellow as the walls. On her ribs, below the curves of her breasts, bruises. There was further discolouration over her collar bones. Across her abdomen, they seemed to continue below the waistline of her skirt. Dark, although they looked as if they'd healed for months already. The contusion on her stomach, the largest, included small red lines where the capillaries had broken.

Autumn filled the room: three months when she had known Ruth, and watched her cry. And her own remoteness, just as Ruth said, had been the wall between them. She spoke the woman's name. She moved her hand but there was distance in between.

'You know how I pick my clothes?' Ruth didn't look down at herself, and the loathing for what she wouldn't set her eyes on seemed to move out to Charlotte instead. 'Apart from – by their long sleeves, you know, long hemlines? I pick them when they look like the sort of thing . . . that a young mother would wear. You know what I mean? The sort who'd live in a little cottage by the sea. Who'd have a husband who'd grown up in the same town . . . someone she'd known as a boy. I pick them . . . to look like a homebody. I find the sort of clothes she'd wear.'

Charlotte's gaze travelled over every bruise. 'How long?' It came from her finally to fall on to the bare floor. She saw a woman who flowed over with laughter and sadness and chatter as if they were all the same. She saw a woman who had been beaten so many times that the parts of her skin which were still pale seemed almost small between the marks. 'How long?'

'Since a year after we got married.' Her voice was as bright as sunlight through these windows. She stared out to Charlotte like she couldn't escape the house. 'I hate myself.'

'There's nothing to hate in you –' She moved towards her but didn't cross the floor, scared to reach her, scared to touch. 'My God,' she said. 'Ruth, it's not you that you should hate . . . Hate *him* . . .' She moved forwards but still she didn't go to her. She saw a woman who didn't know what she wanted, only that she wanted escape. She thought of this project. She thought of everything they'd begun and, as she looked at Ruth, so close, she realized: Ruth wasn't aiming for a goal. She was running. And what she ran towards, it didn't matter, Charlotte saw.

'Do you love this town, Rhys?'

Rhys's heart and mouth were cold. He didn't know if it was anger he felt, or only loss. He looked at Lennie and remembered all the nights, when he'd talked, and Lennie had never judged him. He'd thought in some way that this man held a history that wasn't Ynysmorlan's any more.

'No,' he said. 'I don't love it.'

Lennie's words came thickly. 'Do you not feel, like, after twenty years here, don't you feel some fucking duty to love it?'

'I've not seen anything here to love. Apart from you, liars is what this town is full of. Apart from you . . . it's all about the face you show, whatever fucking face. You know what this town's problem is?' His voice rose, he felt trapped by Lennie's expression, and by the truth. 'Been around too fucking long, that's its problem. People decided wrong and right, should and shouldn't . . . decided on the three important things in life.' He thought of her, sleeping in the streetlight, in some silent room he'd never seen. 'They set up this tiny little way of living and it gets to be around so long, they forget how fucking small it is.' He shook his head. 'They forget their wrongs and rights were just . . . someone's fucking choices. Think God laid them down. Think he built the fucking hills out of them . . . There's no life here! There's nothing great here – Lennie, there's no fucking love! . . . Duty's *all* there is. Duty and how well you can walk between their fucking walls – well *fuck duty!* You want to know what I think? *Fuck duty!*'

He stood straight as Rhys talked, looked at the flagpole.

'They don't know what's wrong or right,' Rhys finished gutturally. 'Kind of people who live here . . . they think greatness looks like a pretty town.'

'And what do you think?' The wind cut into him. 'What do you think it looks like, Rhys?'

'I wouldn't know.' The words fell to lie between his feet with Lennie's story. 'How would I know? But I've never fucking . . . had the gall to tell other people. Never tried to tell other people . . . any fucking thing . . .'

Lennie turned to him. 'Don't you feel . . . something lacking inside, not loving it?'

Rhys raised his eyes but his acid face was silent.

'I'm asking you,' Lennie said, 'so you can tell me the answer.'

The trees moved here, each branch dancing, leafless, but Rhys's gaze held a deserted place. 'Of course I fucking feel it . . .'

There was compassion in Lennie's face before he turned it away, closing his eyes. When he looked back at the flag above them though, once again there was only that distant revulsion. 'I know why, like, I can see how you'd look at this town now, and not have any love for it.'

'You'd die for the place,' Rhys said. But the cynicism in his voice was just the brink.

'I haven't died. And just living . . . this is what I've done.'

He watched Lennie for a long moment, alone himself. 'There's no one else here who could say it, though. Ynys-morlan's not worth it, but knowing you would . . . is something on its own.'

Lennie turned and as the shadows of the trees' hands crossed his face with a sudden wind, he said with savagery, 'It's nothing on its own.'

'I –'

'I'd die to defend it. What does that mean?' He laughed, and in that laughter, Rhys saw how much it had once meant. 'There's no war. Where's the war, like? There's nothing to defend! I'd have *loved* to die for it.' His voice fell, slick. 'Just living . . . do you know what gives you that feeling? Like giving up your life for something? Being in love,' he said, 'being full of pain. Hurting her because she doesn't see it's real. The great fucking ache in you. That gives you it.'

Rhys looked at Lennie Lewis. He had thought he knew him. Seeing him now, he was scared he knew him still. And this wind moved viciously from winter into spring.

'How many times have I told you home's the greatest thing in life? . . . There's nothing greater than thirty-three million. And I'd waited . . . watched Ynys-morlan get smaller, every fucking day. And something great did come here . . . Build this town up like it's never been before. Restore everything my old man made so . . . a lot of people across the country have heard of this place . . . You know what I felt?' He raised his dusky face. 'Thirty-three million pounds,' he said. 'I felt scared.'

Above them, amidst the sounds of these trees, the flag shook, unchanging. He looked at Lennie, the town this dark confusion behind, and it seemed clear to Rhys in that moment how feelings of grandeur could pale to nothing. Their home had lessened – from the past to the present day. Ynys-morlan wasn't somewhere where greatness had a place any more, and the emotions that reached up out of life, transcended it, were too strong to be valid. You couldn't stay in that. You couldn't hold on to what mattered.

'This is grand if it's nothing else,' Lennie said, his hand held out to the project.

'This isn't grand,' Rhys's voice was a shell.

'What is it then, if not the greatest thing that ever came here?'

'It's greed, that's all it is! And you didn't want it . . .' He looked at the man that he'd thought was driving it. Between Charlotte Weyland and his wife, the only person who could want it for the right reasons. Some last tie falling from him, Rhys said, 'You never wanted it.'

Pain crossed his face, a current through his features. 'Rebuilding? Restoring. Putting the importance back here? Of course I did!' He turned to Rhys and in his voice was confusion. 'Heard Ruth talking about it that night, like . . . all I felt, looking at her, thinking of it . . . all I felt was fucking *scared* . . .'

Rhys stared out to him; had never felt so cut away from Ynys-morlan. Lennie seemed like the only part of it that he could still reach out to.

'How could I not want it?' the man was saying. 'The greatest thing.'

'Is that what you think? *Is that what you really think?*'

'Of course I do.'

'Why'd you feel like that then, if it's such a good fucking thing? It's the *project* – it's the fucking project that's wrong! It's the people in this fucking town! What the town's become!' His words only sifted down, though, seeing Lennie's face. Nothing he said could touch the years there.

Lennie looked at Rhys with their history painted plainly on his face: belief, its loss, its memory.

He'd gone to work here in the last five days, to restore his father's buildings. To use his hands, where his life had failed; where his love had. Maybe he'd thought in some way of punishment, and forgiveness. Today he'd found that his father's work was not to be restored. She'd taken that from him, in the first act of strength that he had seen from her since she'd become his wife.

'I know it's a great thing. Because I was scared.'

You walked on the ground of your home and the feelings it gave you seemed noble. Full of emotions and memories more deeply rooted than any man's could be. They could surpass a man it felt like.

He wasn't a great one or a good one, and maybe the wants of a man who'd done what he had done were meaningless. He couldn't have lived without searching for feelings of greatness, though. And the absence that he'd found could not have been prevented.

'I was scared,' he slowly articulated, 'to see thirty-three million pounds put here.' His eyes, though they rested on Rhys, saw a perfect town. The nights they'd spent together talking were gone and in this moment, the boy was hardly here. Lennie saw only daylight, as it would lie, unshadowed, over new paving stones. 'I was scared to see it finished,' he said. Their pale grey was on his own skin. 'Scared to see it . . . and still feel what I've always felt. Since my old man died. A lack. Looking at this town . . . and seeing what it really is.'

In the Lewises' house, behind a locked front door, his wife stood undressed.

'Ruth – things are *changing*. Look now, you're standing here, you're showing me.' And she gestured to the town outside. 'Look what you're moving towards . . .'

'Things are changing.' The way she nodded, brisk, brutal, held words which lit her eyes like metal. 'Look at the expression on your face,' she said.

Charlotte's hands opened for understanding. 'The expression, my expression, Ruth – it's shock, nothing more.' But through this fear, it was distance too. In the unadorned houses through which she'd walked today, she'd been dry with Hedera's memory – with the memory of being nothing more than needed. Images of the nursery had come to her and left her worthless, its faint walls and the things bought, not for her, but only for a daughter, any girl.

This project spread outside now, she saw Ruth, a woman running with no destination, only pictures of a beautiful place. Not looking for a friend, but for anyone who could give her what she needed.

'The expression on my face, it's sadness, Ruth.' Through tears Ruth was looking at her. 'You should have told me,' she said.

'For what?'

'So that I could try and help you –'

'You wouldn't have. "Leave him," is all you'd have said. You wouldn't have had any sympathy for me. Not if you'd known.'

'That's not true!'

As though afraid of being touched, as Charlotte moved, Ruth's voice rose, 'A lot of cold words, you'd have had! Would have looked at me and seen – I'm weak. *Pathetic* is what I am.'

She shook her head. 'No . . .'

'A lot of cold bloody words!' She pounced on anything that would make her feel hate for herself, Charlotte saw. 'More even than I get from you already!' As her self-disgust rose, aimed towards Charlotte, the tears fell more freely, though. There might have been another woman caged behind the face that Charlotte saw. Someone desperate to change.

'If that's true . . . Ruth, if they've only been cold words . . . it's because I care for you.'

Charlotte stepped towards her, the harsh light bright in Ruth's eyes. Someone who wanted to heal, she saw. And if this could be Ruth's healing, then their project, their feelings – what had grown between them – was real.

To her own ears, her voice sounded empty. The past seemed to return, she thought. It was never over. She moved her hand, to try and touch her.

'You've had no respect for me,' Ruth said. 'You've never had any.'

'I've had respect for you. *I've had respect . . .*'

She held on to the words Ruth had spoken at the start of this project. It was an act of love, to take the pain you felt and put it into something good. She didn't know any more if Ruth had said it only in desperation. But it had meant something to her. In a way had meant everything.

She reached out through this autumn space to touch Ruth's unclothed arm. And their skin met. There had been a barrier: fear. It left Charlotte without warning. She looked at Ruth and felt it, naked on her face.

Around them the colour seemed to fall from the room. It dissipated and was gone, to leave them standing bare in a moment of no season.

Close to her white brassiere, she was touching her.

The realization rose slowly from her hand to their faces. In Ruth's eyes, fixed on her own, the hatred stuttered. Just a touch. Only Charlotte's palm on her skin. It formed a hole, though. They saw each other. Fear rose in Charlotte, totally. Into this hole fell every wall she had. Every coldness. And what had lain beneath, it was exposed. For the first time, they saw it; both of them.

In that clear moment, there was a flicker in Ruth's gaze. Reciprocation. Like the first movement of a single bird's wings, it rose. A tiny reflection.

It was fear that killed it. Charlotte saw it in her eyes. As a flock it rose behind the stillness. Into the beautiful sky of some place Ruth had never seen, drowning that first glimmer in commotion, it took wing, desperate, brutal.

Ruth moved. From stillness, she jerked suddenly.

She took hold of the collar of Charlotte's blouse as Lennie had taken hold of her own. Petrified like this, exposed like this, Charlotte couldn't step away. Ruth pulled her into that hatred, through tears. She dragged Charlotte's face down for what she had seen there to be ruined: she kissed her.

Pressed her wet and bitter mouth to Charlotte's. Paralysed, Charlotte felt the press of it. Ruth shoved her tongue against her open lips, between them, to hurt her in the worst way. To scrape away every caring Ruth had seen on her face. Any feeling of love.

In the empty yellow room, she pulled away to leave Charlotte standing, shaking in vacant air. She didn't move as the hands were drawn from her. Tears fell and ran over Ruth's face.

'Is that what you wanted? *Is that what you wanted?*' She sobbed. In the colourless room, they fell like heartbeats.

Charlotte stood immobile. Hands seemed to come from her, hands of glass, that reached out to Ruth, unable to touch her.

'I don't want . . .' she said, 'I don't want anything from you . . .'

From the fear she felt, though, she did move. From every dread she had ever had; of being nothing. Needed, used, unseen. Faltering, Charlotte reached. She took a step. She heard her own feet on this floor. Everything paused to tumble: the revulsion for herself that had always covered Charlotte, and the hope that had been hidden throughout those years, beneath it. She didn't know if Ruth even saw the person who was reaching.

She tried to hold her gaze as she put her hand on Ruth again. Memories of Hedera washed over her, where she'd loved before and had been nothing to that person but an escape.

Ruth's skin was cold in silence – crying as Charlotte moved closer, leaned towards her. Through this soundless air, Charlotte lowered her face and tried to touch Ruth's mouth with her own.

She held her hands on Ruth's. She kissed her.

There was no going back. Their lips were still against each other. Ruth did not move. Hate was stifled under that awkward, gentle kiss. Ruth saw the fear in her eyes.

Charlotte moved her hands, the barest hold. She put her fingers to the collar of her own blouse, numb there.

In this naked space that had been a bedroom, Charlotte couldn't break her eyes away; bare feelings written across her face. She saw Ruth's blackness, saw it there restrained and verging. Her fingers sightlessly found the first button below her own throat – and unfastened it. She looked at Ruth, the fear that she could feel on her face seemed the only thing that held Ruth still.

In this spartan yellow light, Charlotte released the second, and her hands moved down to the third and the last beneath it. Her eyes not leaving Ruth's, she slipped it from her shoulders. She stood uncovered in front of her.

A small woman in a white silk slip. A thin woman. The tiny curves of her breasts showed through it. The unshaded light cast softly in its folds.

Ruth was stock-still. She watched Charlotte hold the blouse out to her, and her own hand wavered, rising. There were hateful words in her mind, but they weren't her own words. Ruth took the blouse as she held it out, as she only stood before her.

Love lay like a stone in Charlotte's mouth. And she reached behind her back, touched the zip and found it, its sound was quiet. She opened it, clumsily. Let the skirt slide down over her hips to lie around her feet on the floor.

The caring she saw on Charlotte's face brought a deeper panic than anger would have done. Charlotte came closer and took Ruth's other hand from where it hung, and she felt pain as Charlotte placed it against her thin hip. Ruth would have given herself, to be hurt or to be made dirty, but she was afraid of the tenderness she saw.

The days they'd spent together unravelled between them, fell to lie with their clothes. The months, of friendship or distance, were lost in stillness as they stood there. They might have been strangers. In this silence, Charlotte didn't know what they could be.

She took Ruth's hand and put it to her own hair, still wet from the rain outside.

They made love in that room, though they only kissed. Though they only touched each other through the clothes they still had on, they made love. Because love was not sex. Love was the frozen moment between two people that held all other feelings down.

In this house that Ruth had held as though it were her self, she felt herself touched. Abhorrence and fear, that she had only ever turned inward, for the first time seemed to move out. It lashed at this place. As it had never done when she'd lain prone on the bed that had been here, it reached out to cause these walls pain.

They made love. Charlotte looked into her eyes and saw a chance. She didn't know if it was healing, or only flight. On this, all her own past seemed thinly balanced.

She saw that perfect place. It might have been a mirage. Only somewhere for Ruth to run towards. She didn't know, as she gave herself to it. It might have been a haven, somewhere beautiful, where Ruth could find a home.

The Shoreline Café was three storeys high, built in 1902 from local stone that was covered now by render and limewash. The windows of her parents' bedroom were high enough for them to see across the rooftops opposite and out on to the sea. It was a pretty building, adapted, neglected, its lower storey nothing but steel frames and wide glass.

On the day that Lennie Lewis stood carefully dismantling the porch that his father had built, men could be seen crouching on the floor in the café. Ruth watched cracked plaster falling. Here, they were unbolting tables. They began near the door and moved inwards towards the place where the counter was being torn away. On the chequered floor, scuffed and marked in the spots where customers' feet had rested, there was sawdust, and the holes from which the first tables had been unscrewed were dark and filled with dust between remaining tiles.

They worked their way towards the table where Bethan always sat. The bag of things that she left here every night was lying now on the floor of the living room upstairs.

Bethan stood on the staircase and watched as they carried out the pale green toilet with the wooden lid that had sat in the little bathroom next to her room.

This was what her mother had said to Ruth Lewis:

'In a business of this kind, you have to take into account your regular customers. You know as well as I do who our customers will be come mid-December. Edward Evans is not going to want duck *à l'orange* for breakfast. So tell me what you think. It's as important to have a café as it is to have a restaurant, more. And I know what was talked about on the form, but consider this, because we've got the space, the second storey, consider this: down in *this* room,' she'd held her hands out to a cafeteria that was empty, its 'Closed' sign hanging on the door, 'down in this room, still a café. Refurbished, just as discussed. And upstairs, *upstairs*, a restaurant.' She had held her hands upwards, and her long pink fingernails had unfurled, as though after they'd finished their arc Ruth Lewis would know there was no other way. 'I know what it'll mean for the costs.' Bethan had seen Mrs Lewis look down at the black and white tiles, uncomfortable at the mention of money. And she'd wondered then for a moment at the woman's part in all this; to stand here with a spec on a clipboard and drop her eyes when costs were mentioned.

Her mum hadn't looked at her after Ruth Lewis left, packing cutlery into a box that she'd set in the place where the till had been. 'There you go,' she'd said. Just that.

And so today, a Thursday, Bethan watched not only the table where she'd sat for the last two years, working on her motherhood and chips project, ripped free and carried out of the café, but also the interior of the room that had once been hers.

A single bed, a guest bed that she slept on when she couldn't be bothered to go home. The wardrobe that had been hers, which they'd never moved out. It was an old thing, dark wood and a little metal handle with a curling pattern that wouldn't turn properly any more.

There'd been some laughter in her – couldn't have expected it, or hadn't – at the course of three short years that had led from high school through a delightful sixteen-hour labour to a restaurant of her own. She'd stood in the corridor, moved out of the way of the men carrying things past her.

The wall of her bedroom was being torn away. A man called Davy with blue eyes and bad skin was putting a sledgehammer through the hole he'd already made. Plaster fell on to the carpet where she'd used to lie, talking on the phone. It didn't matter, the carpet was going to be taken up and carried out to that same skip. They were going to lay a new floor here. What kind she didn't know.

There would come a point when she'd have to know. In a room that would stretch across this whole storey, lit by windows that would reach along one entire side, she would stand, and want to laugh. Design, she'd tell herself. Create.

The rain had come in from the sea. As Dai stood in front of the site manager and explained that he wasn't asking but telling, he felt the strike of it, cold and clean. It wouldn't stop until the night was over, but for Dai the world would change before that, while the town was dark and it still fell.

He got drunk in the Lion that night. He sat in the corner of a bare room. He ordered beer three times. The decoration had been taken from the bar, only the stools left beside it, and sawdust was swept into a corner where the furniture had been. They'd torn it off the walls with a crowbar. And above the bar, over Bill's head as he sat and spoke with Garwyn, the ceiling had been ripped away to expose beams that were marked, still unvarnished yet.

Dai held his drinks carefully and thought of his empty house, back down the road and full of shadows. Looking across the people who were here, every time his glass was empty he still wasn't going home. There were people in here who did this all the time. Geraint Pryce bent at the bar. It seemed as if there'd been a lot of before Dai had never seen. The men had a history just in the way they sat; looked like the last parts of this place that hadn't been broken free and carried out. They didn't even need to talk to each other. The past seemed a bigger thing, and him smaller in it, as he looked at this room. They must've noticed how naked it was. It must have been full of a past to them, that he didn't know, couldn't see.

He listened to the rain that was thrown outside.

Tom heard it, sharp against the caravan windows' toughened plastic. He was slowly drinking a beer as the radio faded in and out.

Gwen left her house before Emyr returned to it from his meeting with the council. Placing her keys into her purse and turning off each light in each room, it seemed like there was confusion everywhere, and she could only keep it from the tiny space around herself.

Bethan closed the café's empty rooms behind her and looked up at the wet night. The wind was freezing but she stood there for a moment, watching the way all the droplets were caught in wide circles of illumination around the street lamps. She gathered her coat and collar, crossed the street.

Bethan put Chelsea into bed, half asleep already, pattering at her face with soft hands, and went to sit in her own room, the edge of her bed. She put music on, looking out at the street through the glass and telling herself, every five or so minutes, to get up and stop feeling like this.

On the back of her open wardrobe door, the dress that she was still making hung in shadow, its hem fixed with pins.

Tom stood and moved in the little clear space beside the bed, looking through his CDs, dropping them to the seat beside him. And as Dai felt himself get drunker, and looked about him at those who didn't come over to talk, Gwen closed the door and sat in her cold car, as if she was the only person lost in this town.

The rain beat against the plastic stretched over the many scaffold poles to cover holes that should have been windows; in Siân's kitchen, where the light bulbs still worked, and were the only thing that did in the dust and mess. Stacey was staying at a friend's house, rehearsing the play they'd do for their mocks. *Top Girls*. Siân had seen the book lying in her room.

Rain chattered over every surface of the bulldozers, parked yellow-black. Those droplets in the street lights were motionless sparks. It spattered gardens where the beds were only mud now and the grass beside them mud too, shadowed, broken. And at the base of the slipping stonebank which led down from the seawall to the sand, the ocean was loud, a thousand smaller sounds congregating.

'I haven't seen you in town very often.' The caravan was ramshackle and the wind was shaking it easily.

He said, 'I've been in every morning, checking on Mum's house.' He nodded.

'I've been busy anyway,' she said – speaking of the playschool, the only work she had left now. She stalled rather than say what was in her thoughts. A blast of that wind rattled the curtained window beside her and she looked at his quiet, hardened face.

He remembered holding her. They sat now for a long second, as if an embrace could push you further apart.

'How do you feel about it all now?' In her mind, she drove through a town that was estranged from her. He didn't lift his eyes to her often. And she sat in silence, the words she'd hoped for seeming to dry between them in this air that smelled of ash, of a young man's bed. She looked out from her make-up, took a slim breath and said quietly, 'Tell me, Tom?'

'Tell you what?' For the first time, he looked directly at her and she was taken aback by the anger that had been in his eyes; that slowly weakened.

'How you feel about it.'

He didn't answer.

'I can see, I saw before . . . that you feel a lot. That's all.'

There was no going back. Stiff-backed, dressed in a pale blue skirt-suit, she kept her bag in one hand. As if it rested on the movements she would have to make, leaving here; on the life she had outside this caravan. But the gesture was a lie, and maybe he saw it. It was lost to her, that life, in all but these token movements.

'You want to know what I think? That's why you came?' he said, turning to her.

'I suppose so.' The answer came and left her, below her gaze. It was only that she didn't know whether the person she'd seen in moments was real. Tom looked back in the thin silence and did not know himself.

'I think it's wrong,' he said.

'Why?' Her eyes were sea-green.

'Because . . . that's just what it makes me feel. They're like vultures . . . all of them,' his voice ran out. She saw the edge, so clearly, of someone that she recognized. 'And what they're doing to Mum's place . . . and all over town they're doing it, with stones. Like they're fucking ashamed of reality! Covering everything up. I think it's bullshit.'

She barely heard the language he used. 'Why?'

'It's a lie. It's not real. She'll end up living somewhere . . . it's got nothing to do with who she is, like. Nothing to do with who any of us are. All it's about . . . is who everyone fucking . . . wants to be. No one's happy with their lot, not in the whole world. That's the way it is, heard her say it a million times too. You shouldn't, just because you're not happy with yourself, you shouldn't put on a fucking mask.'

Gwen looked out at him, from these clothes she'd chosen so carefully this morning.

He took a shallow breath. 'What you are's important in life. Staying true to it is important. No one's given the slightest thought to that. It's not the changes,' he said. 'The changes are . . . it makes me sad to see them. But it's not them.' He looked at her as if trying to prove it. 'It's how everyone's just rushed into them. Two weeks, like. All of them saying, "Not me, oh no, not me." But now it is them . . . You can see what matters to people by how they take something like this. Without thinking if it's right or wrong.' He looked at her and though the words he said seemed small, their worth was on his face as clear as day in this dimness. 'I reckon there are two kinds of people. There are people . . . who care about doing the right thing. There are people who look at life and need to find what matters. I thought Ynys-morlan . . . was full of people like that. I thought like, a small place like this . . . people here could keep what's important . . . in their minds.'

Gwen's hand slipped from her bag and she said, 'Emyr used to tell me that, two kinds of people. Those who care and those who don't, he said. It's a good belief to have in life, Tom.' Her voice was quiet with what turned inside her. Many memories, like a lot of last year's leaves. 'It doesn't necessarily bring you happiness. But I believe, I've always believed . . . there's more to search for in life than happiness. It's a selfish thing, that, to set as your only sight.'

He was silent as he saw Gwen. Things seemed to fall through his hands and without them he was lacking. Years with Rhys. And with his mother. His life; familiarity. Everything seemed transitory, when it had never done before.

'Do you believe it's a good thing?' he asked her.

There seemed to be this pale air between them, as if of her own coral bedroom. 'Yes, I think it's good,' she said. 'I think it's good. I believe it's right.'

'How can you?'

'Because it's giving people chances . . . Because it's giving Ynysmorlan a chance it's never had before.'

'A chance to be what?' His voice sounded harshly in the confines of the caravan – which only a moment ago had seemed less like his home.

'I think . . . that that remains to be seen. You can't blame people,' she said, 'for wanting more. For striving.' She thought of her house, and of the many pretty things which had never brought her the feelings that they should have. 'But, Tom, what you've got, they're good beliefs. The way you think – it's a good way. The project's not important in the end. You won't always live here.'

He looked at her, his anger failing across his face, and seemed to see her then through a distance he couldn't breach. He felt alone and homesick, looking into her eyes. There were misgivings, a reflection of what he'd seen when she'd come back crying, that first night. All the feelings that lay behind and couldn't be expressed. Something that was good, he saw, and was hidden.

'You believe that? It's a . . . a good thing.'

'I think it's like anything. There's goodness in it, and there are other motives. You can't tear them apart.'

He didn't say anything, staring out to her, where she sat in his mess.

'It matters,' she said quietly, 'that you want to.'

She looked back at him. She saw the edge of the person she had been.

'Tom –' but it wouldn't come through what she felt. His expression was unbarred for the first time and he looked young. There was guilt in her chest, that had seeped over things she'd once believed without doubt. But while she was with him, she could almost believe in them again. Believe again in her past. Like anything, there was goodness and there were other motives in the words she'd given him.

She drew her hands back into her lap. Rose-coloured nails. Lines of age that, as she looked down at them, seemed to leave her far away, both from him and from her town, which would be so new.

'You know, like,' there were traces in his voice of the sarcasm he'd picked up from Rhys a long time ago and never been able to let go, 'you know, of everyone in town, like, you're the only one who's even looked at this and just thought about . . . what it means.'

Her face was shadowed, she didn't raise it. The only one who didn't stand to gain.

Tom remembered the tiny overcrowded sentences on his mother's form. Clambering her way to that decision, everything in the past just a foothold. 'There's no one else, like,' he said. He couldn't hide what was in his voice. He could talk about belief, but he was lonely.

Gwen was still, as if she'd said everything she had. As if there was no goodness in her but words. 'Tom . . . you're a good person. Do you know that?'

He sat just a foot away from her, a twist of bedcovers in the drear light between them. Her hand shifted as if to touch him. But a lot of time seemed to lie in that light.

'So are you, like. I think you are.'

She felt herself, her own made-up face, her tight body, acutely. Whatever reached between them, she hadn't come here for it. Whatever was in his face.

'I don't know if there's any such thing,' he said, 'but I think you are.' And he asked her then, 'Do you believe there is?' She saw a pain in his face. 'Right and wrong?'

And although she didn't know any more, without hesitation she said, 'Yes.'

He looked at her: scared, he saw. And he was himself. He didn't know what he was doing really, what it would mean, but he reached forwards as he had done once before here. He touched her arm.

Feeling it, she didn't withdraw; looking into tentative eyes. The touch was awkward, there was nothing of seduction in it. Yet she found that under it she couldn't move. The fear she felt, it seemed to break away from her past – had nothing to do with right and wrong then, but was only of Tom, of his hand on her.

'I don't – I don't want anything,' he said.

She saw him almost turn away.

His own fears made him hate himself. It broke something in Gwen, and she came closer, to sit right beside him, where his hand fell from her and lay. She put her own on it.

'It's all right,' she was telling him.

Tom brought both his hands up, touched her upper arms through the jacket. In his eyes, there was only unhappiness, and hope, and seeing them she didn't pull back. Not even as he drew her, very gently, to lie down.

Turned to stone, she lay. Staring down at her, though, he just touched her hair.

'I don't want anything,' he said. 'I don't want to do anything.' He looked at the gold around her eyes. 'I just want . . . it sounds stupid . . . I want to take your make-up off,' he said to her. 'Can I do that? That's all I want.'

His face was softly shadowed. She felt the sheets under her back, uneven, and she opened her mouth to speak but after a moment, nothing came, her silence clumsy.

'Can I do that?'

'My make-up?'

'Yes.'

Gwen didn't answer, her mouth still open as if she had a thousand words. She had nothing. And because she didn't tell him no, he put his hand to the pocket of her jacket. From where it lay open, scant inches from her breast, he took the handkerchief she had folded neatly that morning and arranged there. Personalized it was, one of a set that she'd first had when she was twenty-two; G for Gwendolyn embroidered in green on their corners.

She looked up, into him. He was as scared as she was.

Her head half resting on his pillow, she lay still while he put the handkerchief to her cheek and wiped slowly at the skin; passive as a child. Her hand on the bed beside her shifted involuntarily. In the quiet and the sound of his caught breathing, she only lay there as sadness came. It flowed over her and took the fear away. She felt tears, rising without warning.

Gazing up at him, she was remembering his picture in the papers, a boy of eight, a hero. And she was crying, as if all the water that he had once dragged that child out of was inside her, and could not be held back.

The bed was unmade behind Bethan.

She'd made her choice two years and two months ago. They'd ripped up the café's chairs, and what did it matter? Those two years didn't rest in the slope of that fucking chair. Objects couldn't hold your past, any more than your own hands could.

She remembered talking to Rhys on the telephone, sitting on that carpet. With her back hard against the door, with a smile on her face that wouldn't leave her, a tart smile, that had seemed to reach roots down inside her.

'You want to end up doing nothing but fucking getting stuck here?'

'Yeah, that's right, Rhys. That's what I want.'

'I'm not doing that! I'm not doing that, like, fucking . . .'

'Did I ask you to? Don't remember asking. Don't remember mentioning your name.'

'*What is this?*'

'It's a small collection of cells of an as yet undetermined gender, that we call, round here, a pregnancy.'

'What are you doing?'

And silence, she remembered. Her own silence, staring across the room at the single bed where the damage had been done. Some resolution, she remembered. Like gravity it had seemed to hold her steady.

'This is a decision, Rhys.'

'A decision! Out of the fucking blue! A different decision than every fucking one you've ever talked about, like!' What she'd heard was fear. Loss maybe, she might've heard that too. 'You're a fucking idiot if this is your decision,' he'd said.

Her own quiet like a weight in her chest as she'd stared at the room where they'd made love, if you could call it that. Where she had sat on her own with every thought she couldn't tell to another person, not even him. Thoughts of the future, before this small stick with its little blue bands had come to fuck her more royally than Rhys had ever done. Till she'd had a thought. She'd thought of a baby. The thing about a baby was, it was innocent. It had never made mistakes.

He had said to her in a quiet voice, 'Three weeks ago, you were saying Cardiff. You were saying London before that.'

'Two years ago,' she'd answered, just as quiet, 'you were telling me you were going to be a DJ.' She'd hung up the telephone. She remembered hearing him talking still as she'd put it down, remembered hearing her name.

The road outside was as dark as it had been then. Bethan sat with her hands in her lap and heard music rising, falling behind her. She thought of the café and of all the prints on the walls – that had hung there as long as she could remember. Marilyn, Elizabeth Taylor, Rita Hayworth. Bogart and Bette Davis with her big aged eyes. She thought of the work that lay in rest, rough and shadowed behind those windows now. But objects didn't hold the past. Only memories of it, and they were invisible to anyone but you.

Gwen drove back through Ynys-morlan to her home and turned the car's ignition off, before its lit windows, at twenty-five past ten. She sat for long minutes with only its ticking engine, knowing that he'd heard. Looking at the living room's curtained windows, in the darkness, her face was naked.

She reached for her bag on the passenger seat and opened it to take out her make-up. Placing the pieces down on the dashboard one by one in a dim line, she opened bottles and compacts, and she looked at herself in the blueness. Pallid, her skin soft or seeming that way, her eyes undefined. She heard her own faint and uneven breath like a memory of control.

From the cold garden path she opened the front door, her bag held low beside her and her gaze held high, as that door closed behind to leave her in their brightly lit hall. The peace of evening lay throughout; on the cream carpet, across the glass surfaces of Emyr's steam engine prints and in every lamp's glow. Rooms beautifully ordered. Ornaments in their own clear spaces, many lovely things. Gold brocade cushions across the settee, crystal in the cabinet. Above the unused fireplace, her commemorative plate collection had gathered a thin layer of dust and the synthetic flowers were a spray of false summer in their basket on the fireplace's slab floor. Through the open doorways and the empty rooms, she heard the rustling of papers. There was no sound of his voice but her footsteps were clear as she passed through the kitchen towards his study.

He sat before the desk's walnut surface, his back to her.

Gwen looked through the wide-open door and saw the litter of papers. He did not turn as she came to a stop behind. He didn't move, as the rustle of her footsteps ceased, but there seemed to be no tension in the way that he sat. His shoulders were a low slope, his shirt collar loose, and she saw the reflection of his face, a white smudge in the black windowpane.

'Where have you been?' he said.

In that reflection, his features were hard to make out. And the rooms behind with all their clean things arranged seemed to her as she met his mirrored gaze, a network of memories. Returning of her own free will, to this test, Gwen stood and looked at her husband.

She lied. Because a lie was a small wrong, and she would prove to him that there were many greater, right things in her. That the most important, the deepest part of her was right: the drive which had impelled her through eighteen years, to get to the place where she stood now.

'I've been with Siân,' she said.

Emyr turned, the chair creaking. 'I have all the paperwork out,' he said. He moved his hand to show her the disordered papers. 'I'll take you through it all,' he said, 'I'll take you through it and . . . I'm sure you'll be happy for everyone.'

Dai left the Lion drunkenly, out of its smoke and quiet, with thoughts of time's great breadth. The project was sleeping as he turned left and rambled, his eyes on the houses, trying to keep a straight line.

Tiny in time's passing. While it changed the world, he only wandered through.

For an hour maybe, he didn't know, he walked and thought of the two full skips behind him. Turning, halting steps on this blank road where the street lamps ran to nothing.

As Gwen Morgan went to sit with her husband in the leather chair next to his desk, to talk slow and difficult words around the past, try to find answers for it in this project, which had swept the future clean, Dai stood alone.

The future and the past, to him, two stretching arms, holding them all as a mother would. Tenderness sometimes. Sometimes just control, but always for good. Held inside it, you couldn't see, that was all. Time flowed through him and on. There was no struggle. Just those two skips. They were the only things he'd keep.

As Gwen stared at the plans on paper, she remembered the struggle she'd always felt, impelling her forwards. Emyr asked her questions now. And they both saw her responses. What had that drive been towards?

Dai looked at the dark rise of hills that ended the bay, with no goal as he walked on. It was one lit window that ended his footsteps. He stopped walking to look up. It was one small glance. On the cold tarmac, the sound of his shoes shuffled into nothing, silence and wind. A dapple of rain came against his face as he raised it.

Above the empty launderette, Bethan Hughes stood in her bedroom, where two years ago the smell of clean washing had always been in the air. When she'd moved in, she'd smoked as much as she'd liked and had still dragged her giant stomach out of bed each morning without any guilty smell left. Now the net curtains were drawn back forgotten and, from the road, she could be clearly seen against the soft light from her bedside anglepoise. Where she stood it was warm and there was music, but the double-glazing and the noise of the wind cut the sound away from Dai.

Beside the kerb, he stood and stared up at her, and his hands hung without moving at his sides. In the rain that struck his cheeks, his fingers were cold, his lips parted in astonishment.

She stood in front of the bed. He couldn't see the bed but he saw her looking down at herself. She turned slightly to one side and then the other, her hair falling in strands across her face. Long. Blonde. He remembered, in the café, with his crossword, his hot chocolate, seeing her sit down on it once. He remembered – the afternoon light, a walk home in front of him. In that moment it came to him with a clarity he'd lost. He could hear Patty's voice through an old day. The way the gulls had cried when there'd been no other sound. It hurt him suddenly.

He looked up at Bethan. She was moving slowly. He would've walked away, pushed his eyes down. But he felt these memories. Clear as flowers in him, they were. Time had brought him here.

She stood in front of the bed, wearing the dress she'd made for the first time. Beside his own bed at home, its little cousin lay, blue and still interlaced with an unravelling seam of thread.

A cigarette behind her, which Dai could not see, was going smoky in the ashtray. Her shoes were pulled off and thrown to one side as she looked down at the unfinished hemline.

Eight months it had taken her, on and off. A night here and an afternoon there. Eight months since she'd seen the pattern on the front of a magazine meant solely for bored mothers with no sex lives. She'd ripped it out and pocketed it; left her ideal monthly unpurchased on the shelf behind. In the street, she'd looked at it fully.

It was a long dress. It was ankle-length, but the adjustments had been minor to make it hang right down to the floor. Long-sleeved and not even low-cut, not even so sexy. The sexiness was in the way it fell. Fitted around the waist. Hanging down over the hips, cut on the bias so it would swish. The sexiness was in the neckline. On the pattern, it was made out of cotton with a flower print. In the picture, the woman was thirty-five and all she wanted to do was go on picnics. Bethan had found the velvet a fortnight later maybe. Twelve pounds a bloody metre.

She held the skirt out with both hands but the pins along the hemline stopped it from falling the way it ought to. And she turned from side to side, breathing just as slowly, as if she was tired after only ten minutes, bored and worn out to the point where only a lovely picnic might revitalize her spirits. She held on to the velvet and turned to look down at herself. She was fat and felt disgusted by herself.

The dress was beautiful. It was a hard bloody pattern but she'd made it, and altered it, and after those eight months – just beautiful. Better than on the packet. Unfinished at the cuffs, she felt them dangle around her fingers as she moved her feet to try and stop herself from treading on it.

There wasn't a mirror in the whole place bigger than the one in the bathroom, and she'd have to straddle the toilet to see the hemline in that. So she stood before the window, holding the skirts out and craning her neck to look. Her body seemed a separate thing. She stared down at it.

In the low light, Bethan held the skirts then let them fall heavy to her sides. Should have felt good. After everything that was happening, standing today and watching the men break down her old bedroom wall to make a room that she'd design, a *restaurant* that she would fucking design, she should have felt full of the future.

Like a fourteen-year-old she stood, saw her reflection in the window and felt ugly. A stone lighter than she'd been for months, and still. A fourteen-year-old's body, lumpen, wrong – and a voice in her head too old to be pre-menopause.

Bethan stepped back on to the bed. She stood, balancing between the duvet and the pincushion, the paper pattern crumpled in the soft light, and she stared at the darkened glass, where the houses opposite were shapeless.

The reflection of her face was cast against the rooftops, mirrored over dark front gardens. And, squinting, bending slightly to find that hemline, she looked through – to the pavement, and saw Dai.

Saw Dai standing, looking back at her.

She stopped moving. His eyes were fixed. His figure indefinite, she saw the way his face was lifted. The way he was turned to her. He'd been watching a long time.

For a drawn moment, only the music reaching out like the final part of her hour alone, no reaction came. She met his gaze and was empty, as if you could catch the tide between its ebb and next flow. Every thought fell through her hands and the velvet she was holding. She stood before the window in her blue dress, with nothing but its reflection between her and empty, rain-swept air.

The wind struck against Dai's face. He didn't notice, looking up. He had seen the patterns. He'd seen the cloth of course. But the dress, on her, he had not seen that. Something was stopped in him.

He'd seen her a million days. She wore jeans. She always wore jeans. She looked to him, as he stood there in the cold rain, as if she was going to some amazing kind of ball. Some amazing party. He could imagine just what that party would look like. Full of people, and they'd be wearing feathers, tiny gold shining jewelleries everywhere. There would be music and when they danced, they'd dance properly, holding each other. He could just imagine as he saw her. They'd close their eyes when they danced. In the silent street, he looked up at her. She never wore dresses. She wore jeans.

Bethan didn't take a breath. She saw his face. There was nothing lecherous, though, nothing sexual. Her hands were little weights at her sides. It was an expression of wanting that she saw.

He watched her stop. He saw her focusing suddenly, looking down, and with a fear and a guilt that came without warning to wash up on the wet pavement where he stood, he realized. She saw him. Peeping at her. Spying on her.

Thirty feet between.

But Bethan didn't look away. Did not shout. Moments elapsed as he watched and she did nothing. And Dai was sure then, he knew inside: what stopped was time.

In the silence that came as the song behind her ended on the CD player, they moved, her hands, in the fall of cloth that hung down. It slipped a little through them; cut on the bias so it would do just that.

Bethan moved on the bed. Between her fingers, she held the velvet, as she had done when looking at herself and her eyes were on his face as she turned, very slightly.

Thirty feet away, his lips open in the rain, he saw the tiny movement.

And Bethan stared out at him, the stereo's silence settling through the room like this heavy cloth. As she had done when staring down at herself, she raised the skirts a little. She made the same bare half-turn. Little motions on the mattress underneath her feet.

He saw her small shifts, her eyes fixed on him too, and something in him turned. The spring rain around him turned. What was outside and what was inside moved together.

Very gently, Bethan lifted the dress, a few inches. Very slow, she made a proper turn. In the tender light, she felt herself straighten, the cloth hanging in the right way. It was how his face didn't change, not into embarrassment or anything else, it was how he stood there seized – he couldn't judge her – that let her stay as well.

Through the glass, through the distance, time suspended, he knew their eyes were touching. He knew. What turned in him, it was everything. Every second and minute and hour that had gone before. He stood in the dark street surrounded by the work that time was doing, so huge it seemed incomprehensible, and in that moment understood it. Saw its whole. Before the window up above, Bethan was turning for him.

She heard herself.

She had once sat with Angharad in the café, talking to Dai Meredith, taking the piss out of him. Once; a lot of times. Telling him, she remembered, what breast-feeding Chelsea was like. He'd stared at them with this dim openness, while Angharad had laughed the laugh of someone who wouldn't be there in the morning. Bethan herself hadn't even known what she'd been trying to pass to him. Something so personal only her own voice could make it bitter. Now the words came back.

Shadowed and yellow, caught looking up at her like a kid, it was love she saw in his face.

Who she was hung as a reflection, just that. In the velvet, her hands faltered. In this fucking dress. She saw her own face. Modelling for Dai Meredith, while he looked up at her and it was love, plain as that fucking afternoon had been, it was love, all over him.

A current of sickness for herself, just swimming through her. But what she saw on his face, it kept her too, before the window it kept her still, like you could be two different people.

There was only this hushed room between them, this changing building, where the scaffolding put bars through the streetlight, to frame the window like a birdcage when seen from outside.

Dai gazed up at her. She looked as precious as something already lost.

Emyr Morgan stared into his wife's face, hesitant to speak. What they had been was lost, though. In Gwen's expression he saw the same passion and control that he remembered. Though what they had been was surely a lie.

'It's everything you would have done, I think. I don't think I've left anything out. It's made me realize how much you've got in you, how much it takes . . .' He touched the papers gently. 'Just the organization. Just the phone calls. It makes me see, you know, how much drive you've had. I mean, I've always seen it but I've never realized . . . the intricacies.' His voice wavered and he stared at the sheets in front of him, clearing his throat. 'Must be a huge determination to have kept you . . . fired up every day.'

He couldn't remember a single morning when she had lacked the will, the motivation to work on. And it seemed to her as she watched him speak that the mornings which had passed in this last month came again; the unclearness as she'd opened her eyes, unclearness in herself, and clarity everywhere around her. Everything she saw.

'But I think,' she said slowly, not lowering her own eyes, 'that you see things more clearly when you're . . . not applying yourself to them. You see the world more clearly. It's a cruel thing really.'

'What've you seen?'

'Just all of it. Just looking out of the windows every day.'

'The project?'

'Everything.' On houses she'd thought of in some way as her own, these scaffolds were raised. Waiting for the fitting of new glass, new slates, beautiful gardens that she would have given them if she could. Gwen looked at Emyr, pale in the lamplight, and she said, 'Take me through the plans for the next two weeks then.'

Emyr put his eyes on the columns and dates that were listed in front of him, and with a quiet voice he began to describe the project that should have been the culmination of their working lives.

'It's clearance work at the moment . . .' he started. 'There are twenty-three business premises within the development boundary, currently we have twelve contractors on them. The Spar's a single site. We've got internal removals going on in all of them right now. Total refurbishment in Spar, the Lion, the Shoreline Café, the newsagent's. We have . . . we have refurbishment of a lower key in the other premises . . .' He cleared his throat again. 'Three shops owned by Dai Meredith. The two smaller gift shops . . . Ian's . . . the internal work'll be minor. The place that was Owain's, minor. In the launderette, obviously we'll need more of an overhaul. There's some stud work that needs taking down in there to open out the stockroom as well. Fish and chip shop . . . minor. Cladding the counters in there rather than replace them. The chemist, the same. Today's the . . .' He looked down at his watch and his voice was too bright, 'The last day of February. There you go.'

The sound of his hands shifting papers on the desk came very softly between them. And they sat, he speaking slowly, she listening, with a resolve in her chest and every other part of her full of the weightless past. The carriage clock in the lounge that Dai had once peeked up at, tears stopping, could be gently heard. Gwen didn't move as she listened to the project's details. She held the memories back from that single place in her chest where some self-belief could still be felt.

'The glazier's men are measuring up at the moment. The estimate for the preparatory glasswork is three days. After that the construction, off-site, a fortnight. And they'll be coming up from Newport then. Internal structural work . . . one week, major structural work, i.e. the construction of all the pitched roofs . . . they're waiting for the weather and then they estimate . . .' He ran his fingers from page to page. 'For the fitting, a week. For the re-slating, another, two at most. I told you . . . did I tell you? The slate's coming up from the same place in Gwent that we got . . . that we got these from.' He gestured towards the ceiling without looking. 'Measurements for the frames have reached . . . maybe halfway so far. They've just done Siân's I believe.' He raised his face and it was open as he watched her, with a sadness which slowly he'd adjusted to, months now. 'She must be excited,' he said.

Gwen's hands were still in her lap. 'You know Siân. She's excited in her own way.'

'Did you talk to her about the work?'

Gwen thought of her, in her bedroom by now maybe. She remembered the expression on her face as she had looked at Gwen, the day of the gift shop's demolition: coldness there and nothing else. 'We talked a bit.'

'She won't have had the compensation money yet. Miss Weyland has organized it for a single date. Does she know what she's going to do with it?'

'Not yet.'

'You didn't ask?' He was searching for jealousy or sadness but she only sat stiff, her eyes set on him as well.

'Only a little. She was talking mostly about the house. About John, you know.'

Emyr looked at her for a long second then turned away and, as he seemed to find his place in the papers, said, 'Are you happy for her?'

'This is what she's needed for a long time. As I said at the beginning, when I was at the meeting, this is a fantastic opportunity for everyone. For Siân more than most. It's not as if she hasn't waited.'

'Are you happy for her?'

Gwen looked at him and some pain filled her. She was. And she said, 'What do you think of me, Emyr?'

'I don't know you . . .'

'Eighteen years – that isn't true. I'm not a different person. There's nothing,' she said, 'that I've been hiding from you. There's never been anything underneath.'

'I don't believe that.' He didn't raise his eyes. 'And you can't look at what you've done, from that first night, from that . . . kiss, you can't look at how you've acted and believe it. Or you'd be lying to yourself. Were you happy for her? Can you tell me,' a tiny injury came to his face and he tried to smooth it away, 'can you tell me you sat and listened to her and that . . . all you felt was happy to see all this?' His hands moved too roughly through the sheets. 'Can you tell me everything you've done here hasn't been for your own sake?'

She sat in front of him and seemed to feel the lie across her skin; the touch of Tom's hands still on her face. But she believed it. She believed it.

'It's been for this community.' Her hands opened as if to show him but they only gestured to this house and its many possessions: this beautiful study and the crystal in the lounge's cabinet, the layers of paint in different colours that had covered these walls with each change of her mind. She opened her palms but they only gestured to herself: a woman dressed in the smartest clothes that she could find, with touches of gold at her wrists, her neck, with make-up newly applied. 'I was happy for her,' Gwen lied. 'I was happy to listen to her, talking about it.'

He stared back. The hardness across his face gave out.

'Why did you hit him?' he said. 'Did *she* ask you?'

'Because . . . what you've put me through for the last two months has had the desired effect! Because I was upset, Emyr. Is it so *hard* to believe, just that I would be upset?'

He didn't answer, but was only static as he saw her, envisaging Dai's tears. From the woman he'd known, it was impossible. After a long moment, his hand still on the paper and his voice falling as he spoke, Emyr said, 'I loved . . . the way you were always full of so much energy. I loved your drive, Gwen. I loved your . . . ambition. Did you know that?'

She didn't move her eyes. 'Yes,' she said. What she had felt inside herself, for as long as she could remember, she didn't know if it could be shared. She wasn't sure any more, so isolated, if any feeling could be. Maybe there was no such thing as an emotion that could be passed from one person to another. She thought of Tom and of his thin, single bed. Maybe there was no such thing as communication, but only the description of what you felt, and the recognition of it by someone else. Maybe we were all that isolated.

'Do you remember the night we were talking, at your parents' house? The first night. You were telling me what you wanted to do, in the future. The gift shop was under construction. You know, you've got this glow that comes . . . when you get excited to do something. You looked brighter that night than when we planned the wedding. Do you know that?'

The word came dully from her, 'Yes.'

He could only ask, 'Why?'

'I don't know.'

'You must know what you feel yourself.'

But maybe there was no such thing as a feeling which could be passed from one part of yourself to another. From the heart to the mind. 'No,' she said. 'I don't know why.'

Emyr dropped his gaze to the figures under his hands; Excel spreadsheets that he'd printed out one late weeknight. He spoke with a catch in his voice that might have been anger, or only difficulty, she didn't know. She saw him bowed over them and the sadness she felt for him hurt her. Below everything he'd done in these last months, she saw the man that she'd married – brighter with her own future than with their wedding.

Emyr said quietly, 'We've had fifteen applications for new business grants so far. A delicatessen –'

'Who's applied to run that?'

'That's Madryn,' he said. He didn't look up from the papers. 'We've singled out the second premises down from the Lion. We'll pass that,' he said, his voice quiet, stiff. 'An application for a . . . for an antique emporium. That looks fairly firm.'

'John Thomas,' she said.

'John Thomas. The other definites are a book shop . . .' He had to find his place again. 'And a crafts gallery that Jo Evans has been talking about, though she's not applied in writing yet . . .'

'A crafts gallery. Put Jackie's landscapes in there. Has Jo talked to her?'

He didn't look up, palms on the desk, flat.

'Jackie would be over the moon. The landscapes are good.'

'Those are the definite ones,' he said. His face was frail. 'The subsidies will be sixty per cent in the first year.'

It was an incredible thing. Thirty-three million pounds. She looked at Emyr, hearing this harsh spring night moving outside their home.

'Thirty per cent in the second,' he said.

'Jo must be . . . ecstatic. I know how long she's been waiting . . .'

The lamplight cast shadows beneath his eyes, so that he seemed older than he was. He had given up trying to hold his gaze away from her. With only that expression he saw to prompt him, a stillness in her face, a sadness, he asked Gwen, 'What do you remember?'

'I remember dreaming, fantasizing things like this, with you.'

'I was there.'

Gwen remembered nights clearly, when this house had still been incomplete. In their bedroom, when the ceiling had been bare plasterboard. 'We shared them.'

'You remember that? Can you tell me that? You tell me, it wasn't just you . . . ?' He looked wretched.

'It wasn't . . .' she couldn't explain to him, 'it wasn't for success, my own accomplishments . . .' She had thought he knew her. 'It was . . . for my peace of mind.' She remembered those mornings: the energy he'd loved, like something dry inside her.

Emyr watched her lower her eyes. In the quiet of their house, he looked at the woman whose drives had barely touched on him, and who he had loved through eighteen years anyway. He stared into his wife's face and the question in his mind, in his open mouth, was not for her motivations, but for the thing inside himself, which had let him stay.

Bethan Hughes sat on her bed, velvet spread all around, as Dai walked away from her down a yellow-lit road. She looked at the room she had seen a million times before and shock was unlocked in her.

The girl who'd tell someone with half a brain, if it was that, what breast-feeding felt like – a friend beside her who'd left her long behind but for the holidays. For whose benefit had she done it? To prove what? That she had no ties here that'd make her care what others thought, any more than Angharad with her new home?

She had ties here. And for whose benefit? Did it matter? It was the sort of thing Beth Hughes had always done. The sort of thing really, she thought, that only a person who was tied here would.

She stared at the wall in front, a hole opening in her. He'd gazed up at her like she was beautiful. And whatever she'd felt while his eyes had been on her, it seemed like Dai still had hold of it, for it got thinner as he walked away, and left her emptier. Like something lifted out of life, he'd looked up at her. She remembered life now. It came back.

Whatever she'd felt, Dai still had hold of it. As he walked down the last of the street, it came from him, between these rows of building sites, in the rain. Whatever had been in her eyes as she'd looked back at him, he was wrapped in it. It touched all these houses he'd seen a million times before, it went past them and out, like understanding. He'd believed. It had been hard but he'd believed, through the worries, through guilt as his mum's shop had fallen to leave the rubble he passed now – finding no less confusion after its demolition than he had in its empty rooms – he'd *believed*, but he'd had no understanding of what these changes might be leading to.

Time's changes. A great dark mass of them, spilling through the street behind him, in utter silence now, with grinding motion in the daytimes. A great wet tide of them that had started with death and a dim house left empty but for him; a tide that had to take you somewhere. He saw this changing street every day. A better place.

In the rain that fell on his face, his hands, what he had held on to, it bloomed in him.

The velvet had fallen like water, if water were to stop.

They could look at him like he knew nothing. They could think his belief was just dimness – and they would, he knew, they would. But through life and all the things you lost in it, through confusion, there were feelings that reached beyond. If there were feelings, and when you looked up at the sky that made sense, then there must be purpose to the world. Dai saw the wet road home and he thought of Bethan's face. When that purpose came to you, it came with more beauty than you'd ever seen. To take away your doubts. To give the grief you'd felt a reason. He looked back at the town. He saw Time in the lie of its lights against the shore.

And on her bed, in her mess and memories, Bethan looked at who she was.

She thought of the restaurant, some place no doubt where ball gowns would fit right in. She could've laughed. But whatever Dai held did not let go. Catching the street lights' shine bright and clear. Spun glass, it must have been.

The night would pass outside, February would pass into March as a colourless dawn came. In the last dark hour the sounds of vehicles would begin, headlamps leaking out as they queued.

Through the first windswept hour, tools would be unpacked, unlocked, men would climb scaffolding past drawn curtains, their faces as grey as the buildings and the sky.

'Getting rid of the render, that process will take place bit by bit,' Emyr said to Gwen. 'The sites with the porches undergoing replacement, teams'll want to take it down as soon as they're gone, so they've got an edge to work from. The others – probably in a fortnight. I've given the sandblasters an estimated date of the thirtieth; a Friday.'

In vans parked on the pavements, men would open flasks and look up at the houses where people would be waking. By seven thirty, the work would begin in earnest and there'd be no sleeping then, those curtains opening one by one as the street was filled with noise and purpose.

'By Friday the measurements for all the A frames should be taken and they should be delivered within two weeks, by which point the stonelaying ought to have reached completion. They'll wait for the frames, finish the courses under them. Then slating.

'Ruth'll be designing the public gardens. She asked me – like she needed to. She's to have the specs in, the nineteenth. The landscapers will come then. Newton's.'

As the morning rose, the bulldozer beside the seawall would cough into life again. It would churn slowly down on to the shorefront and take another bite. In the street then, the flatbed truck they'd hired would carry stones down to the sites; the same journey every fifteen minutes, to a different house.

There would be footprints visible around the flagpole, of Lennie's boots and Rhys's trainers, throughout the stand of elm trees and all across the rough ground that led to the gift shop's forecourt. This was where a garden would be made.

A park, to open the town to any person who drove around this arcing road. Flowers and soft stone, benches, hand-cast street lamps which would stand beside the trees and emit new light when the summer evenings came.

Emyr had said to Gwen, his hand resting on the close-printed papers, 'By the beginning of April it could be finished.'

He would walk into Ynys-morlan today instead of driving, to see laid out before him their vision. It had seemed to Dai as he'd stared at it last night – an intricate stretch of lights that made each space blacker – like understanding; unity. Emyr had less hope in him than that, these days a lot less. The wind striking his face this morning, it looked to him like a eulogy. As the first day of March broadened, ashen, bitter, and all those curtains opened, the residents of Ynys-morlan gazed out at a town that was mired in work; in this drive towards the summertime.

Friday augest eigth
nineteen sixty nine

Mom is crying again. I can hear her in The Music room. This morning
she took Laverne in with her and you could here her all screaming and
shouting because Laverne put evrything in the wrong place when she
cleaned up in The Nursery. I said to mommy how Laverene would
NEVER be able to do things like claudy did but she didnt listen to
me. And Daddy says to me "You know how mommy is and you have to
forgive her." But that isnt a reason. Beaceuse if I cry or shout or
somthing its because somone has made me sad and usualy mommy or if
nannanancy isnt happy with me or bacuse of how I'm bad inside me.
But mommy isnt bad inside because she isnt wrong for who she is. its
like there is no reason. but I know why really. Mommy never goes
round the gardens anymore she is just in the house. Even I can hear
all the sadness and the quieit so it must be just TERRIBLE for
her. like when I stop writing this. Now I can here it. It should be
that beacuse of me our house doesnt sound like this. Thats why I
was born but I'm not making it allright for her. I need to try
harder and remember what she likes better but if I get it wrong I
feel so bad and Im horrible. I say I hate you or something or hit
her. Then she cries more. She runs away from me sometimes. I wish I
was more like I should be.

Charlotte and Ruth awoke in different rooms on the day after they'd
first made love; a spring morning. Daylight permeated the curtains in
Ruth's crowded, cardboard box-littered living room and she looked
towards the window for long moments.

Her first thought, panicked, dreamlike, had been of her daughter,
and the opaque sky she saw through the drapes seemed to leach it
slowly from her gaze. She heard the traffic moving on the road
outside; many vehicles. Her second thought was of the project.

Opening her eyes in a grey stone bedroom where no one else had
slept, Charlotte saw the room where she was lying and remembered.

Ruth heard the footsteps and the distant sound, clanging, of something falling. Her face swollen and sore from crying, she listened, and some tie seemed to loosen in her chest; to unravel and spill from her with no warning.

In the night's final cold, far from Ynys-morlan, Charlotte remembered walking back into this bedroom and how the silence had lain.

And sitting up slowly in her improvised bed, the third thought that came to Ruth, an image, was of Charlotte Weyland's face. For a long time she did not stand, what she felt overturning with each memory of last night. She looked around the room; the clutter of a family's things packed up and waiting, as if their lives would be taken out of the boxes soon and set on the shelves again.

She remembered Charlotte's pale skin.

And rising finally, walking across the room where Lennie was not lying, Ruth peeped out through the curtains from her window alone, and she saw the project that they were making. Under a new grim day, it was in motion.

It was a town of tarpaulins, walls that turned into rubble as your eyes ran up them. It was a road full of weather-faced strangers in their work clothes, full of polythene-covered equipment. Stonemasonry rose like a beautiful dress from the ground, timbers jutted to the sky.

There must be a line. A line between your thoughts and the world. There must be, but Ruth couldn't feel it.

Ynys-morlan, around her, evolved. In this room. In this house. Through its always-open doorway and out into a road filled by a spring rain, always falling. In this street. This bay.

Ruth looked out, unable to feel any boundary. She didn't know what she was making. Every house on this road was in metamorphosis and she stood, wrapped in blankets, naked under them, touched by Charlotte.

She'd wanted to build somewhere where the goodness inside people could be free to live; a place that was empty of the past. She had wanted to let out the feelings of her last three years by making something full of beauty. Like atonement.

They took up the beach and laid it against the houses. Stones that had spent a life in the sea. And they would keep their gentleness through any weather the land could throw at them. They were soft as skin. Curved like a body. Beautiful. Over ugly Sixties' extensions that had still been modern when she'd walked home from school each night, they laid them. Back then, with their angles, small windows, with their shadows and the paint that had still been new, they had made her feel hollow, as left-behind as they'd seemed. Now over them, the stones were set. Ruth watched them rise past the houses' knees. The windows above were removed, walls left open.

She'd needed somewhere when she'd been a child – a place where happiness would be easy, taken for granted, where it would grow like grass did – somewhere imagined. The new town rose up. She'd carried its picture like a little landscape inside a snowshaker, like she could have taken it out to show other kids. 'No, look. There *is* somewhere. Look.'

She'd been afraid yesterday that this project was no different than that; just the same imaginary home that she'd tried to keep with Lennie; carrying that toy, a little cottage maybe in the glitter-drifts, like the last part of being young. When she was young no longer, nor innocent, still holding on to it.

Now she remembered her resolution of the night before. It wouldn't be that way. Crying in front of Charlotte, she remembered, screaming at her ugly things. Desperate to expose the lie she had lived here, so that she couldn't live it now.

And what had happened after that. Standing there as the softness of sleep fell away from her, Ruth's memories disclosed themselves. Staring out from her window in the rain and noise, the dirt, this place was not a picture. It wasn't captured inside glass. Her feelings overran. It must be different to hide behind beauty than it was to express yourself through it. To speak with it. It could not be the same. She and Charlotte had made love.

The men completed the exposure of the second wall.

She checked on Nia first, before she'd dressed; before they had come. Pushing the door to Lennie's study open with a quick and nervous hand, she saw her sleeping in the makeshift bed beside the desk, voiceless dreams. Ruth just stood there; remembered telling her over and over that she loved her. Something shook in her as if to break.

She turned away as though involuntarily: picturesque rooms, she remembered.

In their bedroom, where Charlotte had undressed last night, he had made a bed on the floor, there were blankets scattered there. He'd come back then after she had unlocked the front door and let Charlotte out. Where they had kissed, he had slept, or had lain without sleeping.

Looking down at the blankets, envisaging him, the only new feeling that came to her was hatred, though she had said to Charlotte once that the place they created would be better; that it wouldn't be built from that.

He was working where she made him work.

The daylight was bright here – showed the scrapes and the marks on the timber frame in front of him. In the places where its surface had been hidden and was bare now, Lennie saw the lines that had been drawn. Little crosses, carefully scratched here on the day when the lengths had first been nailed together.

He wondered how it could be that a small mark a man made, just a little motion one long-gone afternoon, could last years beyond the man himself. He looked at them and what he felt was stripped and stark. The difference between him and the man who'd built this had never been so clear. And for the first time Lennie seemed to feel something fierce, something truly his. Sadness.

He heard the sounds of banging and wrenching above him, the dormer window being torn away. He heard the crash of a sledgehammer next door, and next door to that, and the sluggish noise of the vehicles that drove past behind, the many peals and echoes of every job that had begun throughout Ynys-morlan. He saw the little marks, made by a biro. He could remember his old man's hands. The cacophony of the project came to him in tides as he looked at them. And knew it now. He'd never loved this place.

He put the hammer's claw between the lengths and he pulled them slowly away from each other. He dragged the wood, with its little crosses his father had put, across the ground, to the skip beside the pavement. He put them down into it slowly.

Driving back along the curve of the road in the evening-times, or looking out of the window in his study, walking down this street with his head raised up like he had a thousand times, it had never been love. Not in any moment when he'd seen Ynys-morlan without belief.

It was a hopeless thing, that a place could seem so wholly different, just because of the memories you saw it through. He knew it, staring down at the broken bits of the timber, the sounds of the work around him so many and so loud it seemed like they must reach out to touch the grey sky, Ynys-morlan below a place of tangled echoes. The memories he'd looked through, they'd been full of radiance.

Lennie turned back to the house. This place was small. It was a tiny town. And all the nights that he'd driven back here seemed to return to him as he stood before this little, mauled cottage. They made the sky darker. He felt broken and ashamed.

It stood in this row, exposed under scaffolding, with the tar roofs taken from its attic windows, with the remains of this porch hanging on its face as if the weather had scoured everything away; left it skeletal.

He looked at the six courses that had formed the base of this little entranceway. From a garden wall where Martin had left it, Lennie took the sledgehammer. He rested it against the house's face while he took away the rest of the frame. Dragging till it came from the masonry.

The nails drew themselves slowly from the mortar, rusty and bent. The wind caught dust. Three great things in life. He thought of Ruth as she'd been when he'd looked in on her through the living-room door in the last part of the night. Sleeping there, he thought of her. The timber scraped across concrete. She'd lain on the furthest side of the mattress, beside the wall, with her face to it.

In his memories, love was a thing full of motion, full of moments that were luminous, that ached inside you. It was a thing that took life and transformed it. Between this belief and the sound of Ruth's voice as she'd asked him to hit her and hit her again, only his own actions lay.

He let the last of the frame tumble. And it seemed to him that in that moment, Ynys-morlan was quiet despite every sound. It seemed to him that all he heard was its fall. It was Ruth's bare skin he thought of, her arm lying across the sheets in sleep.

Lennie turned back to the house and he took up the sledgehammer, raised it over his head with both arms and brought it down on the brickwork. And as it cracked and the pieces fell down on to the path, he felt some rush of sorrow. It felt good. He didn't know how sadness could feel like a release.

Lennie stood in the spot where there would have been coats and boots and ornaments and air that smelled of sun, he stood in wind that smelled only of the springtime now, and from the inside of what was left, he broke down the porch's low walls. He saw them drop on to the ground, lifting the hammer and bringing it down again, and he was crying. Like an ending, that sadness felt. Ynys-morlan's past fragmented. But it had been heavy – he'd believed that he loved it, but it had borne down.

He could have told Ruth he was sorry a thousand times before last night. He could've told himself that the things he had believed had never been for Ynys-morlan. Could have admitted that he'd never felt like those beliefs were truly his.

He tore it down. Hefted the hammer, tore it down. The first course and the second, on the ground then. He ruined it, his shoulders aching, filth covering his boots as he raised it to strike again. With his eyes snared in an expression that was nothing but grief, acrid, wet, staring out from roughened skin, Lennie didn't stop.

And the noise that had seemed to flow away from him, leave him with only deafness as he'd dropped the last of that frame, it returned. As if on a wave of this work which filled the town, it flooded back, from the flagpole to the place where Lennie laboured: a groundswell and all he could hear was its great noise.

This was the project he'd been afraid to see. Made grand, made great, what could he have blamed for the lack in his heart when he saw Ynys-morlan? The dead place he'd filled with belief all these years, he couldn't have hidden it any more, not if it was beautiful and still left him empty. This was what he'd known, lying awake with Ruth throughout the winter nights as this new year had rolled closer.

They were struggling, building, breaking into it now. It had come.

He raised the hammer, swung it down. As if it came to him on the shift of the March wind that drove between both trees and rooftops, the noise of the project that reached him, it was huge. Deafening. He looked up with the sledgehammer falling to rest on the ground and he saw what was happening here. Saw it and only stared with unsheltered eyes for minutes – at the buildings, the whole – at what they made.

It was astonishing to witness. A mammoth thing, even in this little place, thirty-three million pounds and every home changed, shop rebuilt, stocked again after years. Two hundred and seventy-six men hired, how many buildings, he didn't even know. Every piece of concrete in the town to be covered and flowers grown there instead, chosen by Ruth. Curling with the coastline that lay behind these houses, he saw Ynys-morlan in its new year. And felt something as he took it in that he'd never felt before. Savage and beautiful, full of grief as he gazed out. His hands were raw from the demolition. What moved inside him, it moved without any barriers. It was greatness maybe. It was greatness.

We didn't know ourselves, not really. We were homebodies or we were explorers, we were extroverted or we preferred to be alone. Driven by goals. Drifters. Good people, bad. None of these things, she thought, were real. We knew each other so little but we were just the same.

Charlotte Weyland was a strong woman. You could see it only by looking at her, she wore her personality across her face like a warning to trespassers. Charlotte Weyland was a woman who'd left her past behind; she'd risen from a hundred thousand words, five hundred thousand, with only recollections like the ashes falling from her, to colour the person she was now.

None of these things were real. We knew each other, we knew ourselves, not at all. You could touch that person who had risen up, and she fragmented. The character, the face, the clothes she had chosen to wear, everything that she'd become. It broke apart. You needed only to touch her.

Five hundred thousand, and the words had meant nothing. She knew it now because they'd never reached inside her to make the change she had felt, lying still in her bed, eyes on the ceiling as she remembered the night before.

It was different, she could have told Ruth, it was different to express a thing than to eclipse it with expression.

She remembered Ruth's own expression, that first kiss: the self-loathing in her face. She remembered how it had petrified and fractured there as she had kissed Ruth back.

We didn't know ourselves. One misplaced hand on Ruth and emotions that had never been felt before were standing revealed. We were bitter people or warm, givers or takers, full of love or coldness. Like reflections on water, all of them. Like spills of handwriting that degraded through years while its emotions never changed, none of these things reached below the surface. Creativity, maybe, was the only thing that did. Creativity. Touch.

Opening her eyes, the churn of engines reaching her as the softest echo, Charlotte had felt desolation, worthlessness, seeing where she lay alone. She'd remained, without moving from the bed and had begun to cry, unable to hold it back. It had seemed as if many other places were strewn in the shattered glimpses of her room; places where she had never put down any personal thing. Houses she'd not allowed to become homes.

Ruth's mouth open, she remembered, a bare bulb's light in her eyes as she'd looked at Charlotte, and sometimes seemed to see her clearly, and sometimes seemed to be blind.

She didn't know if Ruth was healing or if this place that they were building was only somewhere for Ruth to bury her past. And she'd played that role before. In a different country, as a different person then, she had filled someone else's void.

As Charlotte had taken herself slowly from the bed, she had thought of the diaries in their bindings downstairs. She'd once believed they were expression; resolution, but they had given her neither of these things. She could not play another role. Seeing, as she'd wandered down and stood before the kitchen window, brick walls shielding the view of an untended garden, Charlotte had recalled those houses she'd lived in and left behind as if to fall in rubble, to be overgrown and lost with the turn of every spring. This was the last. She couldn't leave it. She remembered Ruth's bruises and pity overturned in her. She didn't know – after every place she'd moved through – if she'd come to find this final home, just to love someone again who couldn't love her in return.

Looking out at a dark, vernal morning washed with new rain, it seemed to Charlotte that she'd never left the continent where she was born. Had never crossed the water.

Ruth did not go upstairs to see the dry rot's exposure.

She dropped Nia off at the playschool. She came back to sit for two hours with all the business application forms and she read them with a memory of Charlotte behind each word. Three she marked for approval to be sent to Charlotte's house for her decision, the last for a patisserie; a cake shop. On the inner leaf of the envelope she wrote, 'Remember?'

Her memory, of a burning garden, was shadowed as she stared down at the envelope, by what had changed since that day.

The telephone rang five times during one hour. The tongue and groove they'd bought in for flooring the Spar was only tongue. She gave them Emyr's number. The delivery of cement could not come today, would have to be brought tomorrow afternoon. Ruth told him that tomorrow was fine. How many more skips would they need today than they had needed yesterday? She didn't know. They already had Emyr's number.

A woman rang and, for a moment, she didn't recognize her voice.

It was Beth Evans, Ty Nant cottage, by the museum. She called to ask if the same foreman would be coming today as on Tuesday, but when Ruth asked her what she wanted to discuss with him she said that there was nothing. She only wanted to know if it would be John again.

The last call was from Emyr himself. There was gravel in his voice as he talked about the skip company, and the demolition site, about her plans for the garden designs, the landscaping, Mrs Tajifel and her decision about Spar's windows. He left her to hang up the telephone receiver, with nothing personal, not a single question or comment to suggest that they were not only family but friends.

Hearing the noise around her still, she kept the kitchen door closed. She looked out of the window always, though, glances that drew into her the crowded, moving view until it seemed that she could feel it. She held the memory of Charlotte up, like a pattern clearer than the windowpane.

The telephone rang five times, but the doorbell only once. The last private renovation grant application was delivered to her door. Swiv' Jones stood on her garden path, and the men in her hallway moved around her as she saw him and the smile she'd put on fell away with the expression on his face. He held the form out to her without a word. He looked her in the eyes as cars moved behind, and when her hand closed on the form, he took his own from it and he turned his back to leave her in the crowded, open doorway, alone.

Ruth stood looking out at the half-built street. The nervousness under Beth Evans's clear voice, she thought of. And Emyr. She looked out at all the houses; people's homes. A better place.

At the kitchen table, she was lost in designs for the garden areas, or for the ornate finials and fascia boards that would adorn Ynys-morlan's rows. When they brought the plaster down in blue plastic sacks, she stood in the kitchen doorway watching them and tried to feel some resolution, which didn't come from anger, from hate.

Was it possible to put these last three years into something beautiful? A *good* place, that was the vision. Ruth tried to draw on the feelings brought by the night before, as if she could go back to other moments in time when she had needed it and be healed with the images she had now. As if, back in those moments, she was still crying.

A better place for the people who lived here. Doubt ate at her; the image of Swiv's face. A better place for Nia. Ruth fixed on this. The moments she and Charlotte had shared gave her hope. She didn't know if it was love or not to feel that. They seemed to offer her the shore.

There were changes, inside and outside, in Ynys-morlan now. There were rivers in the road. It didn't feel like answers mattered in a place like this. The town they were creating, it hadn't yet been seen. That was the only worthwhile thing now. They would each have a home in that unseen place, as they'd never had here. They would be happy, as they'd never been. Whatever her motives were, everything rested on the ending. On its goodness – or its beauty maybe, for she used that word.

'I want them to look . . . homely . . .' Charlotte said.

'Well that doesn't mean much to me. You can do that with the curtains, like. What do you want on the floors? What d'you want done with the walls? You want to leave the render? You want the stone exposed? You've got plaster on the three rooms in here, you've got the bedrooms in Ty Heulog. What d'you want done in the kitchens? I mean, you want to think about what kind of fitting you want done in there? Homely. You want the fireplaces opened up then? Got central heating in . . . what's it called? . . . Ivy Cottage and Croesty, the other one. Chimney breasts are there, might be blocked. I've not looked yet. What do you want done? See what I mean?'

Charlotte only stared at him. The things he talked about conjured pictures, but they faded. Empty houses she'd owned herself. Pale walls and bare carpets, the few pieces of furniture that she had moved from place to place. Behind these pictures lay Hedera.

'Fireplaces,' she said.

In the ballroom, the fireplace had arched over her head. She thought of Ruth and Nia on a rug, playing a game maybe, sitting there. She remembered Ruth's story of the house where she'd grown up, and of trying to put good endings to bad pasts. Pity came for that idea as it hadn't done before – that you could try to mend, with love, the loneliness that love had caused you.

'Real fires,' she said. 'Log not coal; not stoves.'

'Fireplaces, all right, we'll need to open up the chimney breasts. I'll get checking out the stacks this morning.'

And she added, 'I think flag floors perhaps, around them at least. It would be nice to have an area, a hearth. That would be cosy.'

'OK then.' He took his pad from his back pocket and wrote notes on everything that the money from Hedera's sale would buy. She watched him, and though her body was stiff and her expression remote as it had always been, each time she had ever seen it in a mirror, what moved inside was neither any more.

'So,' he said. 'Flooring in there then, if the flags'd only be a hearth. Still got them in Croesty. Lost them from this one a long time ago. Expensive stuff, slate, these days. Must've made a killing taking it up.'

'Maybe . . . four or five square feet around the hearths.' Charlotte thought of a rug and of them sitting together, Ruth and Nia alone.

'Right,' he said.

He left her.

In the broken kitchen where she stood, where the daylight grew brighter through the hole in the roof as it was widened with tearing sounds. He left her, to remember kissing the woman who'd been really her only friend.

Walking into Ynys-morlan that morning, Charlotte hadn't gone to her. Many different roles had chased each other in her mind, running through fast water: that she was an abuser, to have taken Ruth from pain to this, that she cared less for Ruth's needs than her own. Her emotions must have been shaped into reaching hands by the years she'd spent in Massachusetts. Abuser, uncaring user. Blind distraction for Ruth as she fled from a marriage she would erase from her heart if she could. Many roles, none were of lover.

But they'd made love. Everything she was could tumble into those words. She surveyed the work-laden rooms of this house and something had been pierced inside her. There was no coldness left. It was rent open as her diaries had been, to let out their voices in a torrent of these thousand sounds of building.

The rooms were dull or lit by bare bulbs. Charlotte had hollowed them; the only touch she seemed capable of. But she wanted now to make something which would embody the things Ruth had told her. You could put the pain that you felt into making something full of love. Charlotte wanted to, and learn herself that it was true.

And when Ruth felt lost, or full of hate as she had done last night, when she looked towards the place that they were making as some Utopia where the past did not exist, she might take Ruth to the homes that she'd made and show her, that it could be done: you could let go of suffering, express it. No escapism and no hatred. Perhaps that way the place they created would be somewhere that Ruth could stay.

In the shadow of this building, under its eaves and in the pale light of its windows, she saw Hedera. It seemed revealed. She thought of Nia too. In some way that she had not allowed herself to recognize before – that she could no longer be blind to – though the daughter was silent and her presence never clear, though Charlotte felt so many emotions for Ruth for so many reasons, the two, mother and daughter, had never truly been distinct from one another in her heart.

In the kitchen that evening, Ruth sat with Nia at the table, papers laid out, drawings and sketches, Nia's scribbles. As Lennie came in, Ruth raised her head. His daughter was hunched and intense over her own hands. His wife looked at him, the spot that had been a red mark when he'd last seen her now a bruise across her eye and left cheek. It made her ugly. He'd done that.

For a long time Ruth held his gaze without speaking, face tilted up towards him in lieu of anything she could say. She couldn't have left the house today, he saw. If the men had glimpsed her as they were coming and going, he didn't know.

'I haven't cooked for you,' she said, and finally dropped her gaze to her own hands. It wasn't fear that she hid there, Lennie saw, though. 'We've eaten already, me and Nia. I don't want to eat as a family.'

'All right.'

'There's food here if you want it.'

'I'm not hungry.'

'Then don't eat.'

He looked away from her, this room the only one which still had the sense of before: more boxes, a greater clutter, but it still felt like their home. He had hated everything, it seemed to him now, except himself.

'I'm sorry,' Lennie said simply, before he left the room.

She had shouted at him to hit her – to hurt him yes, but really so that she could own herself what he'd forced on her for years. It hung between them now in Nia's bent and bated silence, that he could not be apologizing for that.

Nia drew pictures of people, with large halos round their heads. She took great time choosing the colour for each one. She became frustrated at her inability to keep inside the lines and seemed to want to screw the picture up, though she did not. Anger and a calming process, she went through, all spoken within her own thoughts – and using words maybe, though they would have been words that no one else could understand.

She seemed to turn through cycles that Ruth knew – and knew alone like that. She watched Nia draw, as though to learn, her own work forgotten under her hands. She watched as the girl waited, staring downwards, for the emotions she felt to drain away.

'I've done a lot of thinking today.'

Ruth didn't reply.

'About us, like. About me.' He went on because, although she didn't look at him, he had set out to say this, to say something.

He believed he had the right to speak his thoughts to her. She didn't know – except in silence – how to answer that.

'It's been different today, just being here. Just seeing it all. Last night, this morning, done a lot of thinking . . . I reckon I saw for the first time what's going on here . . . think that's what it was.'

'You've been very blind then.' But she didn't want to say anything, any words at all; didn't know where they might take her.

'Yes,' he said. 'Blind, yes.'

She looked at him. Like he could make reparations with only that.

'Yes,' he repeated.

In the wordlessness that followed, it was a picture of Charlotte's face that she held on to. Soft cloth in naked light. Those emotions.

After she'd put Nia to bed in his study, stacked with every ornament from every other room, after she'd come back in here to sit with her plan for the garden that would be grown in the place of the gift shop's forecourt, Lennie had come down the stairs from the bedroom. She'd heard his footsteps. He'd made his camp up there, with his self-pity and stray blankets. She'd listened to his unhurried descent and sat, rubbing the skin of her crossed arms over and over – movements meant as control. And she sat now, her eyes on the sketches she'd made, of possible plantings, possible sculptures, places where benches might be set to see a view of this street and the sea.

She didn't want to reciprocate what he'd given to her. But she felt hate, seeing him. It ran circles in her. She stared into his eyes and couldn't face the images of what he'd done to her, not without wanting to hurt him, or hurt herself, or without having to turn away. Ruth looked out at him like he still held her down.

The chair creaked softly, he sat opposite her at the table with only bare wood between them. He didn't move to touch her or try to make her hold his gaze. Sadness moved as water would, inside him in tides. Overturning on to itself.

'There's nothing I can say –'

'Don't talk at all then, Lennie,' not one glance at him. 'Don't talk.' Charlotte's hand she thought of, moving to hold hers.

'I've hated my life,' he said.

Ruth held her eyes down. All the times when she had asked him how she could help – what she could do for him that would take away the ache he felt. Failure came over her, that he could have felt that way at all, but anger too. He'd blamed her. Holding her hair off her face, she remembered, with one flat hand on her forehead, so she would have to see, as clear as he could make her, all the rage that he had pushed into his face. This was the way he'd treated her. And then left her on her own, to keep this house and wait till the day came when she found herself forgiving him again.

He sat at the table. 'I've hated my life,' he told her, as if his honesty was a gift.

Ruth raised her face. She slowly digested the expression he chose for this statement. It was a vacuum. Waiting for judgement maybe. It was grim and dilapidated as though spring had ground him down. He looked old. He looked like, in the long night and day through which she hadn't seen him, he'd already judged himself.

'Ruth . . .' he said.

Twenty hours. Long enough, he must think.

'I want to tell you,' he said, 'I've been wrong. Not that it's going to mean any . . . fucking thing to you. But I want you to know, like, what I'm feeling.'

Her mouth was shut tight. Something had to come from her.

'I've been wrong in how I've seen things, Ruth, been lying to myself, in everything.' The ruined timber frame in the rain's old light, he saw. 'About the way that I feel,' he stumbled over the words. His voice, that had once run unimpeded, fell like this, fell apart like this, in an apology. 'The way I feel about myself . . . told myself I've been happy, like. That we have. That I loved you –' He stared at her like he could pull the right words from her returning gaze. 'Told myself . . .' bitterness came into his voice; self-disgust that she recognized. 'Told myself that I've believed in things that maybe I haven't believed in. Told myself . . . I loved this town. But I haven't loved it,' he said quietly. 'I've felt . . . a failure here. Like this whole place is a failure. What I said to you that day, like – you remember? You asked me . . . It was true, Ruth: this place falling apart, people leaving, places closing . . . But I want to tell you now . . . I know it's my fault.'

There was no asking for forgiveness. He spoke like he was alone.

'If I'd have loved this place,' he said, 'it would've made me sad to see it, and maybe I would've tried to stop it. But it was me, Ruth. It was me that didn't fucking live up to . . . what I wanted. My feelings.

I didn't have any fucking belief, but I told myself I did. So I'd be . . . part of something bigger.'

Slick with hate for himself Lennie's voice was, and she remembered shouting in front of Charlotte. Cutting herself with the look of pain that her hateful words put on Charlotte's face.

'I couldn't blame myself,' he said gradually; dragged the words out. 'Couldn't admit I'd never felt any . . . anything great here . . . couldn't feel it after we'd been married . . . a year, I don't know. And I blamed you, when the faith I'd had . . .' he opened his hands to show how it had faded away.

Ruth sat with no answer. It was disbelief maybe, to hear him say it so late. It was the edge of tears, and behind them there were things that she could not control.

He looked at his wife. Allowing himself nothing now, pity or forgiveness or the right to apologize, to tell her how he hated himself for what he'd done. He saw her face – and it seemed clear to him as it hadn't for years, as maybe it had never done. He loved her.

'I want you to know why I've been . . . why I've done what I have, Ruth. Want you to see . . . that *I* know.'

The rooms above were derelict. She felt that way. So much blame inside her, it could have run out to break this street. To wash the houses of all work. Leave them there, she imagined, unfinished, with their jutting wood and empty windows, for the stones to reclaim. Leave them all, with a feeling of justice at how they stained the world and made this coastline barren.

It seemed like there was no way to leave violence behind for something better. She stayed in silence. She stared at him.

'Say something to me . . .' he asked.

But she didn't speak.

'Say something to me . . .'

What a child love was, to come back with its arms open, every time. And she thought of Charlotte, and would not have tainted the time that they'd shared with that word. She thought of goodness. Not love but goodness. Seeing him, though, she couldn't find it.

'I'm sorry,' he said. 'It doesn't matter. I know it doesn't, but I feel it.'

The words came to rest before her on the table's surface. After everything she'd felt for the last three years, she had the right to answer him – hurt him. The right to make him see what it had meant.

'I've looked around today,' he said, 'at Ynys-morlan . . . It's looked better to me – it's looked like mine,' he said. 'Because I've felt like this. Can you understand?'

He had taken something from it then. From all of this, he'd given himself something. 'You should never have been with me,' he told her finally. 'You should have had a better man.'

But she had been with him. If she'd deserved a better man, she wouldn't have let it go on, wasn't that the truth? Ruth struggled, with no voice as she looked across the table at him.

Unable to hold himself back, so much remorse as Lennie saw what was on her face, he said, 'You should have left me . . . Two fucking years ago, you should've gone – I can't believe you stayed with me –'

'Yes, I stayed! Because I'm weak! *Because I was scared!* I stayed and I let you and I stayed, three years, I had a family, I had a home and I stayed. Because I'd wanted it for so long and I had this picture in my head! Because I'm a . . .' Her voice fell and she had no thoughts, her hands hard against the tabletop. 'Selfish and pathetic and full of fucking childish fantasies!' Dead, insufficient words, and behind her unsteady voice memories came to her, of his hands. She would punish herself if he didn't do it for her. 'There isn't any way to . . . to say how I feel about myself after what I let you do! Hate is . . . it can't hold it! Disgust . . . can't . . . means nothing! *Do you know that?*'

He watched her. Sadness suffused his features. She saw it.

'Sometimes I can't speak!' she cried out at him. 'Remembering . . . And all the time the fucking door was there and the car was outside and I stayed! Sometimes I can't move . . . I lie there and I can't move. I'll hurt myself. Can you even understand?'

Unspeaking, he shook his head.

'I let you,' she said.

He didn't answer. He deserved to hear it, every single word. In his guts and his hands and his heart, what he felt for Ruth then was as total as the love he'd once imagined.

'Everything you did to me . . .'

Revulsion for his own actions, Ruth saw as she stared at him, and misery, and she drew it all in. She wanted him to understand, in that moment more than anything. The project seemed to fall away from her, and Charlotte's words last night. She didn't care. She let them go.

'All the times you've said you hate me,' she told him, 'you couldn't have felt the edge of the feelings I've got for myself. Inside myself. Every day, Lennie, every day.'

His hand was out to her, shadows almost reaching each other across the table. Still he was trying to touch her.

He wanted it more now, maybe more than he ever had.

'Look what you're doing, Ruth –' he told her. 'Look outside! I saw it today. I've been fucking . . . I've been so blind! But you have to see it –'

'You don't even know what I'm doing. You couldn't understand what it means to me – not even the first part. What I'm doing –' but she lost her voice.

Was it creating something better to speak like this? If she could have held him down, she would have. If she could have beaten him, she would have left him unable to raise his own hand in defence. She would have beaten herself.

Unmoving, he sat in front of her, held himself here to be punished by what she said. And she said it all.

'I hope it hurt today . . .' she couldn't stop herself, and sobbed between the words, 'all the things your dad built, smashing them down. I hope you stood there and thought – that you can't make anything. *You can't make anything except unhappiness!* Tearing things down, Lennie, that's all you're good at!' She stared at him, her hands jumbling in these papers, diagrams and sketches; meaningless lies and nothing more if she could use them just to hurt someone. She looked for forgiveness inside herself and all she found was this hate.

He sat and watched her, and the wind today, he remembered. How it had moved, all through the town, all through him. He nodded at her, slow with resolution, as she told him the buildings he'd work on next and what he would tear down. It wasn't penance, though. It wasn't only that. He couldn't tell her – but there had been something today, something he'd looked for all his life.

She turned her eyes away from him, crying with every memory from this house moving in her, darker and more vivid than they had been to live. And she had to have something, to get away from them.

'Everything that's ever had any meaning to you, I'll break it down . . .' she said. In the dusk of their crowded kitchen, Ruth repeated herself over and over. 'You know that?' she turned her face away. 'Everything you've loved . . .' She couldn't release what she needed through the words – she felt mute and desperate, as she'd used to watch him feel. And, across the table, unable to look away, Lennie watched her cry.

The 6th of augest in 1968

there is something wrong with me. My love is a bad thing. My love is horrible and I am not her daghter. Im like a stranger who comes up to you on the street and says they love you and you dont know them and you just want them to LEAVE YOU ALONE because theyre horrible. My love is nasty and disgussting. She doesnt want it because I am the WRONG person. She doesnt know me but I am living in her house. My love is BAD.

Charlotte Weyland, a 39-year-old woman, who had never slept in a man's bed, who had shared only three kisses through the course of her life, held her place on the diary's page with a child's hand. She cried a child's tears. Because there was nothing wrong with the girl in the books, but the woman who read them had spent years alone and lost.

In the pages after these, the entries began to open 'Dear Charlotte'.

The love she had now felt the same. Had she wanted Ruth all along? Kept the desire hidden and nurtured while Ruth trusted her and spoke to her and she told herself that Ruth was weak and coy? Had she fed the feeling? And every time Ruth had looked at her, some uncontrolled part had reached out and held on, as silent as Ruth's daughter?

She had touched Ruth and it had spilled wet from her, too clear to disguise.

Had she felt this way and, undisclosed, Ruth had cared for her anyway?

She was a stranger to the woman she'd made love with. She could give these books to her to read. But Ruth was the victim. Ruth was desperate because for three years she had let a man treat her devotion like nothing. What would it be to give them to her but an attempt to ask for love? For understanding. When it was Ruth who needed that.

Against a coastline that seemed to thaw into the town, mist and rain suspended on the air, the houses that backed the sea and their low yard walls grew new clothing of rounded grey stone. The beach seemed more broken than the sea beside it, JCBs driving, lifting. They tore down debris, they dug out against the litter-line of yards. At quarter to three every afternoon, they left the shore via the tarmac beside the public toilets and parked there, empty windscreens watching the grey, incoming tide. The air was filled by salt and by exhaust fumes.

Block walls that they couldn't clad, they destroyed. JCBs using their scoops as strongarms against the rubble. Ruth called a company whose pamphlets came on embossed paper, Worcester Productions, and ordered wicker screens, eight feet high and twenty wide. Forty-three of them would replace all hand-built, miscellaneous windbreakers that cluttered the houses' backs and rattled in any storm. She sat with her designs, for the finials and fascia boards, scattered in front of her and saw again and again, like the blank half-light that fell through her kitchen window, the fact that Charlotte didn't come.

Doubt grew in her alongside the dry rot they exposed. It must have been clear on her face that night, though, that she was changing. When they looked in each other's eyes, Charlotte must have seen that Ruth wasn't blind. What they built was not the same as the dream she had kept inside this house.

She was desperate. At nights sometimes, she screamed at him. She threw things at the floor and broke them like he'd used to do. He'd listen to her or he'd shout himself, but only with self-hatred, and he never struck her now. Words pouring out into his face, in rooms that were cluttered with their things or with her plans, chaotic and with no feel of home, she'd see his expression. Open. The things she screamed, she hardly heard them, not knowing even what she was trying to draw from him.

It was an act from the heart, she had said, to make something beautiful. That might have been the first thing Charlotte had loved in her, those words. Though she'd seen Ruth's desperation even then, they might have been the first.

There were the hammers sounding everywhere. There was the grinding of cement mixers beside every building where skin walls were being set. They laid slabs for the open fires' hearths, setting them into screeds on the floors of Ty Heulog, Croesty, Seaview, others that now belonged to Charlotte Weyland. They cleared the chimneys, rebuilding two, in sea stone instead of the brick that had been used in the last fifty years to mend them. She didn't come to see the progress. In her own home, where the sounds were a border to the silence in which she had once talked with Ruth, Charlotte sat, the images tumbling, of what they'd done.

She thought of the bruises Ruth had shown her and she feared for her, and for Nia, in that little, scaffold-covered cottage at the beginning of the town. She thought of the curtains closed at night and light edging through, into a quiet street. She must have feared for herself more, though. She didn't go to Ruth, though she knew that during the days her husband would not be there.

Abhorrence for herself, memories that she'd closed in leather bindings now underlay each certainty that Ruth couldn't love her. Not now. Not as she was: bruised and desperate. Hedera lay behind – the place she was giving Ruth was nothing but fantasy.

Charlotte remembered the nursery; the toys and games stacked on shelves, untouched by her, parts of someone else's life. Dusty, they'd waited for that child to come home.

Each day now, Charlotte spoke to the foremen, checked the progress of her houses. It seemed like the words of all her journals must speak themselves there, at nights, when the workmen left the rooms vacant.

She called, she planned for them, she tried to think of ways to make them into homes. Though she didn't go to Ruth, she was waiting for the day when she could take her to them.

They waited for a spell without rain for the re-roofing to begin. It didn't come. The road crews were scheduled for the last week of the month: resurfacing, laying the pavements on either side. Most structural work would be complete then and the street, now crowded with cars, emptier.

There were vehicles on every wet stretch of it. The skip lorries caused standstills and the rain-shaken air would be filled by the noise of car horns through the queues. Tenuously lifting their loads on quivering chains, winches sounded, grinding wheels, the heave of the debris as it settled on their backs. Throughout, the flatbed truck made stops on both sides of the road; a weaving route between them to deliver the stones from the seawall. They took them from it, hauling them out on to tarpaulins or into barrows to be dragged to the places where the stonelayers worked.

The truck drew up outside Croesty, Ty Heulog, across the road for Cartref Bach. It moved on. A little blue cab, much smaller than Lennie's had been, and he looked as it drove by. It passed the Lion, the museum, its tarpaulin-covered window holes, and the Shoreline Café.

It was the 10th of March, it was twenty-five past eleven and nine days since he'd looked up from the road and seen Bethan in her window. Dai Meredith stood in front of the café's door.

All morning he'd tried to keep himself from it. Now he was scared, his hands empty and moving by his sides as though the energy of the hours he'd spent in town already, talking, walking, at the sites, wanting to come here, not letting himself come here, left him from his fingertips now. They were dirty from raking through the rubble of the two skips at the back of the gift shop's site. On the tips of them, plaster and brick dust showed his prints.

People moved behind him. His face was shaded under the café's scaffolding. Bethan wasn't in the main room. Through his own reflection, he saw that the tables were gone. Marks on the chequered floor, holes where they'd been bolted.

No counter and no till, no string curtain over the doorway that led to the kitchen, and no kitchen there. It wasn't a café any more. Where the counter had been, men worked on the last three tables. And Dai saw, in the corner there, the one that had been hers.

Upstairs, her hands lay on another piece of blank paper, bland like the others with the light from the window at her back – one of the three at which Dai now stared up, to see mirrored a cloud-thick sky.

It was the scale, Emyr thought, of ideas like Dai Meredith's. It was the outreaching they brought; their stretch so vast, they caught you up inside them. Nothing could be safer.

Beside his three new shops at the head of town, they'd talked together that morning. Emyr had been meeting with the public works crew, with Evan, looking at the bench beside the changing pile of sea stones on the tarmac. Stacked with tools under plastic, it looked out on the sea if you sat there. He remembered evenings.

Nothing could be safer than what filled Dai's eyes. They'd talked – Dai had talked – about time again. He'd found God, Emyr had thought, staring at his face with a bitter little wish.

Dai had been glancing past Emyr Morgan's shoulder. Looking at the street that led towards the café's door. The energy in him had still been ripping and tearing then. Rain had fallen in moments. A brief conversation over plans for the gift shop's space.

'The little parts don't matter,' Dai had said.

Emyr had looked at him, long, and from rather far away. 'What's going to be there? No, I think it matters, Dai.'

'Mrs Lewis is going to put a garden round there . . .'

'Round there. Not actually there.'

'When the time is right, you know, like they say, it'll come.' He had given nothing else but only stared like he knew something Emyr didn't.

'You've had no thoughts about it yet.'

His face was ragged and bright. 'They'll come. Look at everything.' There'd been a smile, full in the grey day like a burst of childhood. 'Just look at everything.' That rain had fallen. 'It'll come.'

Seeing that smile, Emyr had left the questions lying still. Behind, through the doorway of the first shop renovation there was noise, of the nail punch on new floorboards which would run throughout all three.

It was the scale of ideas such as Dai's. He thought of Gwen, of her drive, and its range, so precise, so different. It was the thoughts in Dai's soft eyes, he realized coldly, which he most knew.

And he'd said then, 'Where d'you think it's leading, Dai? Where d'you reckon . . . it's all going then?'

'How would I know where it's going? What the finish'll be, like . . . I wouldn't know.'

He'd been afraid to say what he thought, what he'd thought two hours before, walking down the hill in the morning's first part. He had been so sad for such a long time. The destination he had seen – he was scared to be wrong. It didn't make him a coward.

'Tell me what you think,' Emyr had said. 'I'd like to know.'

And the man had been sad as well, Dai had seen it in his face then. Through hope that came up to him in rushes when he thought of Bethan, through fear like these falls of rain, he'd looked at Emyr's sadness. The man was lost, he knew nothing about Time.

And he'd said it, scared like it was naked then.

'I think it's making somewhere perfect.'

'Somewhere perfect.'

'Somewhere where everything works right. For everyone. Somewhere . . . that's like the place we should be. The place where everyone should be . . .' he'd said quickly. 'I think it's making somewhere perfect. So there's somewhere, like, there's somewhere, in the world.'

Emyr had looked at him. The melancholy he felt had seemed to move out from him, but not to touch the things that Dai believed. After the longest moment, he had asked, 'Do you think we're owed that?'

Dai had been silent, dim days remembered. The way what you loved could be taken, he recalled, could just be carried away like a bag of things, when you'd never even done anything to deserve it.

'Maybe it doesn't matter . . .' he'd said finally, quietly. 'As long as there's somewhere in the world, like. Maybe it doesn't matter who Time gives it to.'

'Do you think time repays you, Dai?' Emyr had asked him. 'Do you think it gives you things, if you've earned them?'

'I think it always makes things better,' he had said, only that. He'd looked at Emyr Morgan's face.

After a second Emyr had turned away from him. Behind, their town had been laid out beneath a misty spring; cement had hardened, rubble had fallen, and he'd remembered many springtimes here.

Dai had left them behind. He envied the man. That was the truth.

'Do you think . . .' he'd asked, looking at Dai with waiting eyes, 'do you think . . . you could give your life to "time" . . . give yourself up to it, Dai . . . and still not be repaid?'

Bethan Hughes wasn't in the café's main room, there were only strangers there. Dai walked like a stranger himself through the dust and noise, between the kneeling men.

Since the night that he'd stood outside her window and seen her in the dress she never wore, everything had changed in him. At nights, he'd not been able to sleep. He had lain in the small room next door to his mother's, with the sea moving inside him. It came up with his breath, through his chest to his eyes where it caught everything he saw underwater. Yellow light swam around every object. He'd exhale but there'd be no release; too much to hold in him. Time's shape had drawn in to become the outline of her figure, caught between the scaffolding poles.

Dai found her there on the second storey, where he'd never been before, sitting with her back against the wall, the window's light, from above, falling on her hair and on her hands. For a moment, she didn't see him, and with the work's noise round her, didn't hear. Jeans and a jumper she was wearing.

There was a hole opposite the top of the stairs where a door had been before, and the shattered remains of an internal wall. A corridor had led by all these rooms. From the next, there were the sounds of men's voices between the crush and crumble of what had been here.

Balls of paper lay around Bethan. It seemed to Dai as he saw her sitting there, that the window's light cast silence.

After trying once and losing his nerve, he spoke her name.

Bethan raised her face and saw who'd come.

This morning, she'd drawn, screwed up the pages, drawn again.

She had scratched condemnation in capital letters over her sketches for a bar. She'd said in all the noise, not able to hear herself clearly, 'They can change from their swimming costumes into their ball gowns while they're in the bogs.'

Since the night that he'd stood outside her window, a sewage outlet had risen; it had come up from her guts to her eyes where it caught everything she saw under shit.

Dai took a step into the room.

'Is it all right?' he showed her with his hands how he was standing in her home. '. . . I don't know if you're too busy to see people, you look busy . . .'

Dai Meredith. Retarded or mad, or just enough of both, to walk round this town like it was some foreign country. Dai, who'd had adoration on his face that night.

And Bethan – now Beth Hughes was an eighteen-year-old nothing with a mouth on her as bitter and quick as a right-hand orgasm in the middle of a weeknight. Beth Hughes, with a girl who'd be two years old this spring and a fucking ball gown in the cupboard – crumpled up there now on the floor of it, where she'd dumped it in the grey light of a coming morning. Like a lot of memories, it had looked, lying there; like the memory of every year since she'd grown breasts.

Now Dai stood and stared at her. He opened his mouth but said nothing else. And she was forced to speak, or hurt him with rejection right then and there.

'Course. Course it was all right to come.' She stared down at the paper in front of her, saw nothing on it but some dark shadow of velvet fantasy. 'Oh yeah . . . busy as a bee I am.' But she didn't look up at him again. 'Isn't that what they say? Busy as a bee that flies its head into windows all day.'

There was silence, and then she had to bring her eyes up again. A nervous smile on his face and no words, he stood there, dark and ragged as some belonging left outside.

'Never been up here before,' he said.

'Well . . . it's not the same place it was.'

The room was pale around her. Its reaching floor was covered with plaster dust and the last, the smallest pieces of debris. Dirty, paint-splattered boards for its first part, up to the place where she sat, and peeling lino after that, faded in places, bright in others, where there'd been carpet until two days ago.

She took one glance around as he stared at it. Her palace. Her *restaurant*. Her little takeaway by the sea. She watched how his gaze coasted, her hands dead on the paper where they'd lain since she'd raised her head.

Here at the top of the stairwell, the windows' light grazed the boards before his feet – and seemed to him to fill this place, despite the noise, with a kind of placidity. Like a church's windows would. A church of old paint, in different colours. He remembered Llanfihangel Ynys-morlan indistinctly.

'How'd it look before?' he said.

'It was, like, a stuff room. Used to store everything here – there's my parents' living room upstairs see.' She went to push the paper away and then held on to it. Through this wall, there came the hammer's impact. 'That was a bathroom.' She raised her hand to the broken door through which dust began to waft, thick as cigarette smoke. 'They're taking all the fittings out, the toilet, the sink.' He nodded, and he never took his eyes off her. She couldn't recall ever seeing a crush so clear and, remembering, was saddened. Had it been for someone else – if he had come here to tell her about it as he'd used sometimes to tell her things, both of them sitting in the café's long, unstirred afternoons – she might've smiled to see it. He couldn't fall for someone without plummeting. It was sweet maybe, that kind of naïvety. 'Then my bedroom,' Bethan said, as she looked again towards the hole.

'Until you got your flat.'

'Till we started smashing it up, I was thinking.' But she was the one who'd stood in the darkness downstairs and handed her mother the grant's approval. She looked up at Dai and wanted to remember what kind of feelings she must've had.

He came into the room and, because she hadn't stood up, he sat down opposite her on the grimy floor. He glanced at her and then glanced away. He held the memory of her silhouette, she saw, as hard to hide as if that night was there in the reflections of his eyes.

'It makes you feel sad, like,' he said, 'all the demolition work.'

She realized he was trying to offer her wisdom.

'But it's not a bad sadness, you know?' he said, waiting for her to agree. 'You've got to feel sad because you're saying goodbye to things. My mum's shop . . . But it's good to say goodbye to things. With all this . . .' He held his hand up to the window behind her, where, in the hazy rain that had not stopped since that night, every building looked like this one. 'Moving to onwards and upwards, like. It's a good kind of sadness.' His smile was transparent.

She would have liked to agree. She remembered filling in the application form in the subdued hush of her home, after realizing it was he who'd been there. After looking at the room, seeing what he must have. Bethan couldn't seem to breach that gap now.

Moving onwards and upwards. Her designs were balled-up waste-paper. All velvet and lamps and low tables, colours that seemed vivid in her head. More than anything you saw in the real world – they had no memories attached to them at all, but only her imagination. But she put them down in her notepad and they lay there as her dress had on the cupboard floor. 'It's a good kind of sadness, yeah,' she agreed greyly.

She looked at Dai, passed him a weak smile that rose in fullness on his own face.

His home, back down this street, back down this lane and unchanged since his mum had died, was a tangible thing. The gift shop too, in ruins, and only two full skips of rubble left, which must have meaning. They were the only parts he'd saved. He stared at Bethan Hughes in her own place. Its purpose, all that Time passed, its *reason*, was the future.

Dai's voice was untried as he asked her if she wanted to show him other rooms, or, maybe, if she'd like to see the demolition site.

It gave you the strangest feelings, to see someone with that inno-cence. Made her sad; a sense of loss. With some good inside it, though.

Naïvety led nowhere but to world-weariness, Bethan knew. Give it just one moment, though – give it this instant that she saw in his face – and it seemed like it could wave goodbye to every old, familiar thing.

'We're opening up all the three rooms into one.'

They wandered round men whom neither of them knew. She had to shout sometimes and then a silence would descend around the ends of what she said.

'They reckon just another few days till all the partition walls are down.' She showed him the windows, one in each room and high, and how they'd form a line when this was a single space. The only building in the town which was tall enough to overlook the opposite houses, out to the dark line of the sea: undefined. Rain clouded the glass and in here, plaster powder floated on the air.

'They get the evening light,' she said. 'You know, in the summer it stays light till whenever, like.'

He nodded but he seemed caught up in the view, or what it might be one day soon.

'People'd be eating, like,' she said. 'Eight o'clock or nine o'clock. They'll get the sunset . . .' She wanted to ask him what he saw, staring out in that way, and how clear it must be to give him that expression. 'I was thinking about having stained glass in the windows,' she said. 'And it would shine all the colours through.'

Things were brighter in your imagination than they could be in life; there was no way maybe to create them. You set them into the real world and they were judged by everything round them, till you couldn't help but see what the truth was.

Llanfihangel Ynys-morlan had stood in autumn sunlight on that day, the sun too low to cast anything but shadows through its leaded windows and on to the cold floor. Too low to do more than blind you as you walked out through its doors on to the vibrant grass. He was nodding slowly at her oval face. 'What else?' he said.

'Haven't got anything else yet. I've made some plans . . . I can't decide. It's hard, you know.' Something cynical brushed her, and eroded; embarrassed by it as he looked back at her. 'You've got all these blank pieces of paper staring at you. Or worse, like, blank rooms.'

'I don't know what to do,' he said, 'in the new shops. They're knocking holes in the walls there so they'll be all one, like this. You understand? Like, because they're next to each other?'

'Sure.'

'It doesn't matter,' he said. 'It'll come to me. And you. What to put here, I mean.'

Maybe right from this morning he'd meant to tell her about Time.

Shaded, vaulted, with torn walls and stains, with puddles that had collected slowly in the many nights of rain, creeping down through holes in the slates to fall with echoes, the museum did just what it was meant for, Emyr thought. And he remembered Dai. It kept time still.

He'd spent all that morning with Evan, before seeing Dai and after. The public works crew would begin with the street renovations in three weeks' time maybe. There were another three to four days of stonelaying on the public toilets and a week then for the rebuilding of its roof. The A frames would be delivered in two days. After that, they would begin on the bus shelter.

The bus shelter, one hundred yards behind, where Rhys now sat and waited.

The public projects, Emyr thought, were the ones that would've been Gwen's babies. He looked into the museum's single room where the sound of two men's work above him fell, like cold air will, towards the floor. He'd waited weeks before coming here.

Pryce and Rose, who'd been contracted for most of Dai's business properties, had a small crew here as well, he didn't know the foreman. He'd not come to check on their progress, though. He had come to look through the mess of old exhibits that had been left behind when its doors had last shut. Only photographs, things unwanted in Aber, locked up in the little office that Rhys had broken into. He came to see those that the boy had not ruined.

Over him, strung on thin chains from the beams, was a platform where the men were working now. He spoke, just to hear the sound of the place.

'How you doing up there, boys?'

The small, pale shape of a face appeared, and recognized him maybe.

'How you doing down there?'

He smiled a little.

This town had shaped his life. And in small ways his aspirations for Ynys-morlan had shaped it in return. He thought of Gwen with Dai, so desperate to save the work she'd done. You had aspirations – not drives but *aspirations* – and you didn't have that need inside you, to cling to your own work. They weren't focused on yourself.

He gazed at the stain of graffiti Rhys had once drawn across this wall. So eager to destroy and make worthless. The boy had painted something that looked, after months though, like an exhibit itself. He read the words, long dry, the feelings it had given him still no weaker. *Ynys-morlan is fucking dead.* He read it over. *Long live Ynys-morlan.*

Internal renovations would begin in one week. Emyr looked around the room.

Rhys watched the bus on its slow trip towards him, every word that was written round him seen in shadow. Twenty minutes the bus could take sometimes, through the work and the traffic, just to get from one end of this road to the other.

He was thinking of her, couldn't sit here without doing so; thinking of all the changes behind the café's wide glass. Remembering. Couldn't sit here and not.

He looked at rain that wasn't falling; the street cowed by its hanging mist. These were the only moments he saw the project, waiting here. His hands rested on the edge of the shelter's seat, a roll-up, gone out, in one.

What he felt circled something untouched inside him like gulls would wheel around a landfill site.

In black, indelible ink at his left shoulder, the words read:

You r a fat cow and you always will b

They read:

Lick me out I fucking love it

In red, above him:

Sarah J is a fucking slag

Biro, almost obliterated:

Caned as fuck

In spray-paint across the glass that framed the 'Go Further!' poster:

GO AS FAR AS YOU FUCKING CAN!

The night with Lennie Lewis had taken things from him that he hadn't known he still possessed; filled him with disgust for the only man who'd seemed to own any kind of principles here. Disgust at his own pity. In the whole of Ynys-morlan, Lennie'd been the only one who hadn't slated him for not wanting to be some kid's dad at sixteen.

It was the town that had drained those principles from Lennie. Hearing his confession, the road out of this place didn't seem like a choice any more.

Rhys imagined sitting here with packed bags, for the last time. He imagined how that was going to feel, and it caught him up with anger, fucking frustration, sadness, that the image of leaving Ynys-morlan could seem like running even to him. Some connection to the place, that he hadn't known was in his hands, he'd lost it in Lennie's hollow story.

Perhaps there had been some time, like Lennie'd said, when this sea hadn't washed against concrete and souvenir shops and Ynys-morlan hadn't drained the life out of its people. Some time when it had lent them life instead. A feeling of home. Rhys could imagine that past. Before Lloyd Lewis maybe, perhaps even before the photographs that lay on the museum's filthy floor: some era when the people here had understood what fucking mattered. You only had to see the mountains – get out from these rows of houses that stared at nothing but each other – see the coast.

Ynys-morlan made no room for feelings like that any more. Every person here must be struggling like Lennie under that. Everyone must have this missing thing inside them. Be full of anger at Ynys-morlan, like Beth had once been. Be full of failure, and not know why.

Rhys looked down the long road and it seemed to him like all this work was the final false varnish. He remembered talking about leaving with her, sitting in this very spot and writing whatever they fucking wanted up on this wall; hating being here.

He didn't know how long the bus shelter would last now. A week? Of this whole town, it was one of the few structures that wasn't already drowned with work.

Claire takes it up the shitter

He saw:

I went 2 ynysmorlan n all I got was crabs

Everywhere, over every inch of wall:

Oh I do like 2 b beside the fuckin seaside

But it wasn't what the words around him said. It was the feelings they'd been written with. It seemed to Rhys as he watched Emyr Morgan, in the distance walking through that high, arched doorway, that there were a lot of memories in Ynys-morlan, unpretty memories, that were being left behind. That there was a museum, just one hundred yards behind his thin back, which was designated for demolition soon.

Bethan Hughes was to be seen wandering with Dai through town that day, out on the beach. In conversation as slow sometimes as if weights hung between the words, all the project and its moving vehicles round them. Dai pointing: the debris and the barrier where the gift shop had stood before, the three little buildings in reformation opposite, where the new shop would be made. Bethan following the line of sight from his rough hand. His hair streaming out like waterweed.

You could see words in Bethan's eyes that she didn't say. You could see how, without speaking them, they made the things she did say seem untrue. Watching Dai still, though, like she'd brazen them out, like she didn't care, you could see her.

In the three shops, they'd stripped the render from the interior walls already, leaving old stone to surround the wooden floor they had in process. They'd set the screed and built the framework, like some game that kids would play. Across the new concrete, they'd jump in and out of the two-by-four to which men were nailing the floorboards now. The team laid them around a double set of pillars where the wall between this shop and next door had stood before: cast iron. Lovely, old, Bethan thought.

'They told me about different ones they had, like, on the phone. Emyr came down to do it with me. I saw these.'

'They're the same, going through to the next building?' She couldn't walk inside the room to see. What they'd done already was shocking.

'They're the same, yes.'

No interest in his face. No connection to it maybe.

Bethan walked with him back through the doorway, out into the swill and wash of the street again, and past the Spar, the scaffolding like arms about its face. Across the concrete they went, past all the stacks of new materials under rain-dappled plastic and up, beside the seawall, to stand together and look out across the broken beach where the sea moved without walls. There, he told her about Time.

He described the way that he lived. He said that if you did anything that you felt the need to, then you were doing Time's work. It changed the things that you wanted, he said, and if he followed them then he would be playing his part. Watching the grey turn of the tide and its broken white horses, he remembered thinking this when he had gone to tell Siân about the things Gwen Morgan had screamed at him. He didn't mention that part to Bethan. He wasn't stupid. He felt the guilt, the doubt. But these were parts of Time's movement. Bethan saw a stretch of months behind the words he said, and a home where no one else lived that he could speak to.

While the work went on in the Shoreline Café behind her – in the lower rooms where her mother planned the overhaul, bitter and short-tempered, though she didn't want to be, faced with changes, as she stared out from its chaos through wide windows, that she'd never thought she'd see – while the men broke doors from their frames above her, Bethan's plans lay blank, and she walked through Ynys-morlan's crowded street with Dai, listening as he slowly let himself speak.

'Something like this,' he said, 'you can't be sad for what's gone. It's *momentous*.' His expression was more open each time he turned to Bethan. He'd come to her, after she had stood for him in the window. She hadn't told him to go. She couldn't ruin what was in his eyes. It was sweet and full of things he hadn't told her yet. 'You don't have to believe what I say, like.' His hair was blown like freshwater weeds. When he looked at her, he looked without judgement, and that was a kind thing to feel. 'You don't need them like I did . . . When my mum died, I thought for like, for ages, there wasn't a reason. But there's a reason for everything.'

She saw a past behind him – and how he wasn't bitter, surrounded by a project that he didn't understand. Very small and bitter indeed her own past seemed, though every place that had held those memories was changing now.

'You think this is the reason, Dai?'

Maybe she saw doubt, she couldn't be sure.

'I didn't have any friends when my mum died. Didn't want to come down to town or anything, like I didn't know anyone here . . . ? You understand? Like it wasn't home . . . ? But Time, the project, it's for everyone . . . I needed it,' he told her. In the wind and the sea's salt, looking at her, he admitted it easily. And she wondered how he could see that and still believe. What part of you was it, that could be taken away and leave you free from questions? He'd seen the cloud cross her face, though. 'Time's a healer, everyone says that, and they don't even know . . . Because they don't need it, like you don't. Time makes you understand. It makes you . . . matter.'

Fresh casts of March were thrown in tiny raindrops, against the pavement round their feet, across the backs of every builder, crouching, working in their coats. Hammers sang, their echoes falling to the metal discord that pounded this work into the road.

'You don't think that I need that,' she said, a small smile on her face.

'No you don't need it.' He seemed taken aback by the thought. 'Not *you*. I mean, you're . . . in the centre. You don't *need* to see time. You're part of – if something happens here – whatever happens here, *you're* part.'

Maybe he thought it was a compliment. Bethan's smile faded from her into the rain, and seemed to leave her unclothed there. In just the way she'd seen him look up at her from the street, he looked at her then. The sea's noise ran beneath every other sound. Differently, she seemed to hear it then, though. Seemed to realize, fully realize, she wasn't ever leaving it behind.

He'd looked at her like she was something lifted out of life. She saw his confusion now – saw how that look of clarity only came from his eyes with will, with faith. The whole of this community was something lifted out of life to him.

She couldn't seem to tell the difference between the JCBs' noise then, the noise of all this work, and the beach's waves. It seemed a cruel fucking world, when blind belief could give you everything you needed, and understanding couldn't.

Behind her, the café was waiting; her mother there, resentful of the differences every day now brought to the town that she'd never left behind.

It seemed to Bethan that what they were trying to make, or any creativity maybe, any change for the better, needed an innocence she didn't have. Chelsea was waiting at home. Time didn't seem to her like anything too large to understand.

She looked at him. 'They're lovely things, Dai, to believe. Everything you say, like. But don't . . . you shouldn't forget, thinking about fate or time or whatever, anything big . . . you shouldn't forget about yourself. You were the first to say yes. You were the one who applied.

All of it . . .' she raised her hand at the town behind her but she didn't look back, 'it started with you.'

And he was staring at her in the noise. As she ran out of words, there was a look on his face that she hadn't seen before.

If she'd been inside his house through the last months, she would have known that it had never touched him. But it had only been an hour or so that she'd spoken with him, only one afternoon, and Bethan didn't see the meaning of that look – or of the things she had told him, as she said goodbye and slowly left Dai, standing by the seawall, in the changing light of the early season.

There was a line, he knew it, between emotions and what passed in the world outside. Like love, he would think, as he left the dimly outlined peace of his mother's house each night that week, to walk down to the gift shop; its wreck-strewn site; the pieces of its rubble in those skips.

Like love, or grief, it felt sometimes like you couldn't get emotions out to be seen. And they'd turn on themselves that way, as the March weather did while he walked in the dark.

The rain came through its final nights, young and brutal as a child. Thrown by varying winds, it beat with Nia's temper against the windows, the tarmac, was torn to quiet under a distant moon before it came again. She slept in a home of silent rooms while it battered itself against the walls. Like love, Dai thought, it struck for moments in a greater cycle, though; one you couldn't even see.

The world turned so slowly that only the stars changed. Time was like this. You only saw the weather that marked the changing year. Could only sense Its evolution in the feelings that changed within you. Above the rain, it seemed to Dai, somewhere in stillness above everything, Time moved with the stars.

You had to understand this, so you weren't broken by that line; so you didn't lose all faith when it seemed as if the grief or the love that moved inside you would fade and leave the world without ever having touched it.

The street lamps laid threads across the skips' wet debris, cleaner every night as the rain fell on it and washed the dust down to lie in pools below. Boards, lengths of what had been window frames, even slates, he saw.

He did nothing through the nights that he spent there that week except search through them and lay the pieces out on the ground, or only stand, look around him at the wide, jackhammered space, puddles everywhere – those street lamps lighting his own skin.

He did nothing but think of Bethan and the things she'd said to him. The words had begun subtly to reform what he saw, in the same way that the daylight would come to change the gift shop's neglected site through the measured mornings which eventually sent Dai home.

He remembered planning with Emyr how they'd announce this demolition at the town meeting. Looking back, it seemed like he'd had the power to make a different choice.

Dai would stare at the last pieces of his mother's shop, spread out across the ground, as daybreak made the street lights turn themselves off in that quiet. It was the cruellest thing that Time had made, this line. Even grief wouldn't hurt you if in some way it could be let out. You couldn't break anything that Time had made so fundamental as the line must surely be. He didn't want to. He was only trying to think of ways – just to step across it, that was all.

On the 15th of March, the builders finished the demolition work in the Shoreline Café. They took the last of the studwork from the upper rooms, until the three were only one. On the roughened side that faced the street, the long line of windows which she'd shown Dai was revealed. Each cast its oblong over the floor.

She lived with her mother's whip-quick temper – and the sadness unspoken beneath. Decorations from the room that had been there before, or the 'previous furbishment', as Pat had taken to calling it, had been put in boxes and kept, Bethan saw, inside the closet on the top floor in her parents' hallway. The Hollywood prints in their frames, the things that had been stuck on the noticeboard. She'd watched her mum take them down in the first week, though, full of anger that wouldn't hide under fastidiousness. It was resentment that Bethan saw in her, like she'd packed softer feelings up and left them for some future time in the cardboard box she'd put inside that closet. Bethan wondered what Pat had felt, looking down at the pictures in her hands, off their hooks for the first time in years. But maybe she only needed to imagine her own future here.

Her mother had opened the café on the 5th of June, 1983. Though there had been no project then, Ynys-morlan had been busy. Patty had said many times – how the street had been so crowded with tourists some years that even before you'd walked down the path, while you were still standing on your doorstep, someone would've walked over and interrupted you to say what a 'great village' you lived in – so you had to turn round to them and tell them it was 'a town'.

It couldn't have felt so different, opening her new business to a road that was filled with sun and cars, decorating its rooms with those pictures of Lauren Bacall and the like, couldn't have felt very different at all, she thought, to standing and looking at the three great windows in this new, undecorated room. How old had her mother been? She could've worked it out. She'd been nineteen when she'd had Bethan, and how old had Bethan been when she'd opened up the place? When Bethan was small. She had half-recollections of pink streamers.

During the last week Patty had begun to tell her things about running the business, had talked about the books; keeping separates for the restaurant. And though, standing and looking, envisaging the way this room could be, Bethan still felt the desire that had pushed her to fill out the application – and the sudden rushes of self-doubt, self-contempt, that were its other side – it seemed like she began to understand both for the first time.

This was how all fantasies would make you feel when you realized that, even making them real, they'd fade eventually. Yes, it must have been just the same in 1983. They would fade, to leave you standing in the same town where you'd begun them; staring out and wondering whether, in some other place, they might never have seemed like fantasies at all.

It was an innocence, being able to create something. As if by crossing a line, what you imagined, created, could be greater than the sum of all your parts. It could be the things you couldn't. She remembered having thought the same before she'd given birth to Chelsea.

That innocence now, like any she'd had before, only tarnished to experience when set against the picture of this ever-changing and never-changing town. A blue dress on a girl seen through a window, that was an image full of innocence, until you knew the building where that window was set, and that town, and that girl's life there. There was a moment that came with creating things, vivid and bright as she must've looked to Dai, there was a moment when it felt like you could touch something, taste it, feel it with a greater radiance than anything the real world had ever shown you. That was innocence.

It crossed over the line into Ynys-morlan and was nothing beautiful any more.

It was the process of trying to erase that line which was begun and scrubbed out and torn up and begun again across her sheets of notepaper. She sat in the new room that week, beneath its central windowpane. She stood, stared out often at the unending drizzle and the lines of scaffolding. She tried to believe the town was changing; that this whole place would be a new one. It was not a belief she could hold on to, hearing her mother below.

When Dai Meredith walked to stand beneath Bethan's bedroom window again, and she was wearing the dress, as she had done three times since she'd taken it out of the bottom of the cupboard, she didn't freeze. Thoughts of who she was and of what she was doing, they gave way when she tried hard enough. To a moment. And, almost, it would seem like Ynys-morlan was nowhere at all.

She put her hands into the material and, standing there, turned for him.

The sea-stone cladding round each of the buildings too modern to be built from stone themselves was completed along the street that week, and they waited for the weather to break so the re-roofing could begin. Those walls that were covered by the cladding, in amidst the scaffolding and the tumult and the old pebbledash, they were a glimpse as you walked past, of the place that Ynys-morlan would become. The rain continued. Pointed and cleaned, they looked like cobbles, wet with drops which seeped between slick-dark planks. Waiting, an inch below the tarpaulin-covered flat roofs where tar and roofing felt had already been ripped free, until, under clear sky the new A frames could be set into place and the slating begun. This new wall that looked so old with its soft, grey curves and its touches of quartz, it came to an end and revealed stained pebbledash beneath. There it was if you looked for it: grey from years of this dripping water.

From the fronts of the homes, where the old porches had been broken away, to leave just an edge of the render disclosing how the stone underneath had once been buried, they began to remove the rest. Lennie saw it, on the houses he'd worked on: they started with a chisel and they went on from there. It cracked with long lines and came down, little pieces that broke on the slipping pavement. The old stone beneath was left lumpen with its remnants, crusts, as if many years of dilapidation had been waiting underneath the paint. Bit by bit, this process would begin along the street throughout the weeks of March, until all the render was gone, and all the pebbledash concealed.

*

Dai looked upwards to Bethan, turning for him, not knowing what struggles were up there for her. But he saw and recognized what she was trying to do. In her face, it was, in the way that she moved. It stirred in him. He knew it from the hours that he'd spent looking through the gift shop's litter, trying to find how to use the last year's hurt and memories in making something real. It didn't have a name maybe, that struggle. Slow circles, she turned.

In the house that had once belonged to Audrey Pryce, Charlotte ordered the aperture widened between the kitchen and its extension behind; a storage room when she had come to view for purchase. A greater kitchen they started to make then, with room for a table which Charlotte imagined with benches and which she called a designer on the New Kings Road to order. Eight feet long and made from unstained ash. Over years, ash would yellow, soften with every stain. At Hedera, the ash table had stretched from the great hob almost to the door. On some evenings, with the staff, more than twenty people had eaten there. She had sat, legs slow-swinging, fingers touching its edge. She had drawn pictures there, in four windows' long light.

Here, where she watched the doorway broken wide, the windows were a cottage's and could not match that light. There were touches of it in the living room at Tyn y Ffron, something in the way the shadows fell. She did not want to remake Hedera, but she searched for something that meant home inside herself, and it was there. Sadness came to her, each time she found that the images she conceived of were made with its pieces. And she held on to recollections of Ruth and Nia, for whom she looked to make these homes, as though the thought of them could put a future to this past.

In the last of March's wet weather, Ynys-morlan was a churned and shattered town. On its shore the diggers completed their work as the cladding of the modern houses came to an end and, in a fog of pending rain, blurring the beach and casting the shapes of the working men in vague pearl colours, the machines began to leave the sand again: a rutted, ruined surface, cut with the tracks of their weight, which the sea would smooth in one tide.

The stones that they'd taken from the beach and piled on the concrete to be hosed down could be seen behind the houses' backs now, encasing walls that had been block and limewash before. Edging each yard against the sea, they crowned the slope of stones like some makeshift castle, these soft, undulating cobbled walls.

Emyr called and he described it to Ruth. It had been five days since she had left the house. She was ill, she said to him, and to the foremen who called sometimes to ask for an inspection and decision of some kind; ill and overworked with the plans for the garden areas, amidst everything else, the landscaping of which must begin in a week at most. There'd been a pause and then he'd spoken, unlike the last time that they'd talked.

'Is there anything you need?'

Ruth had stood, holding the phone carefully away from her cheek. It had faded almost to a shadow now; would not be noticeable at all soon. 'There's nothing. But thanks. Except to know . . . how it's all looking.' She thought of Charlotte, who must have walked into town that week, and passed her door. 'I know where we're at with it all . . . but just to know how it's looking.'

And he'd told her about the wall at the houses' backs, the completion of the cladding on the extensions, little things, little spots that they both knew; his pictures wandered in a street that sounded empty of working men. He'd wanted very much to tell her, she heard it in the way he spoke, and wondered what lay behind that coldness before, and this hesitation, sadness now.

It was like something from another world, another time, that long wall, he said – though where hanging baskets and ivy should have overspilled, there were only tools and builders still pointing. Where slate roofs and spires and gable peaks should reach behind it, only fluttering pennants of plastic could be seen in the rain, advertising each scaffold company.

'It looks . . . like it's happening,' he had said. 'It's the first time you've been able to see it coming through, you know. Patches, here and there. And in the shapes. I mean – you can see a bit from your window there.' She'd nodded. 'Looking at it as you come in though, into town, you know? Been very foggy, the last few mornings. You look on down the street, the shape of it's changed. They're constructing the frames for a lot of the . . . you know, the porches now . . . You can see the way it's going to be . . .' Slowly the mornings had dissipated from his voice, though, and he had said, 'Too ill to go out? Really? Even if you wrap up?'

'Too ill to go anywhere that's more than fifteen feet from the toilet at the moment . . .' She'd given some laugh that was very close to the woman he'd known for the last three years. That bright little laugh. Laugh at me too, it said. Laugh and don't look too closely. Before the kitchen table, Ruth's eyes were glazed. What she saw, though, was very clear. Clearer every day: three years' worth of images. And they were not still, as she seemed, sitting there.

'Are you sure,' he'd said, 'that you don't need anything? Just some company maybe, I don't know . . .' He wasn't offering but appealing, she heard.

She couldn't say yes. Three years' silence, and it seemed sometimes now as though it might be a better thing to walk out of this door with her face bare, her arms maybe. Sometimes the urge to was strong, as if the memories might stay in the house behind her that way. Unable to pass the doorstep, as she herself had often been.

She couldn't. Not standing at the forefront of this project.

'Well, doesn't matter. You give me a call anyway, when you're feeling better.' And he'd hung up with a quiet goodbye.

The garden that had been her mother's was a ruin before Ruth's house now like every garden in the town. The roses pruned almost to the ground. She'd taken a few of the smaller shrubs, dug them up in the quick-falling dark as the crews were leaving, she had potted them. They were lined along the sill before the kitchen window now, still winter sleeping in what little light came from the March sky. They were waiting until Charlotte called, or until she came, when Ruth would ask her if she might like to plant them inside the brickwalled garden.

Before Ruth, it seemed that there might be an ending. In those plants, darkening the window's light there, she could make it out. In that long ridge, imagined, of gentle stone walling beside the sea. In every moment when she closed her eyes, trying to sleep. There were pictures, of beautiful things. But maybe they were plucked from all parts of life, from her beliefs about happiness, maybe really the end she reached for had no shape.

Bethan showed Dai how she looked in the dress, from each side. She had no smile. Soft anxiety was in her face. Not of fear, but of its opposite; the things you tried to move towards.

She held the skirt up a little.

She made a half-turn and the curve of her back was revealed.

And he loved her. She could see that. But it was nothing ugly, it wasn't exploitative. She didn't want to take anything from him. In some way, she thought, Dai was perfect – she could never have changed the blamelessness he had.

Standing by the seawall with him, damp hair blown from her face, this grey street had shown her its grip; the many windows, old or new, that were her home, had all looked down on them.

There was no innocence for her in Ynys-morlan. Maybe there were no moments that could stay. So, wearing her dress, she turned for Dai and she watched the expression in his face. Held that moment, as he must have done: something that was shapeless, like all their goals now, and yet, because of how it would vanish, was brighter.

Sometimes Ruth could almost reach it.

She had designed the finials that would top these houses' gable roofs and windows, a long night working on her own in the kitchen while Lennie slept in the bedroom upstairs, the wall above him stripped and all the dry rot showing. She'd turned each page of each catalogue, found nothing except empty prettiness, and she was scared to put anything like that into the project; scared of what it recalled.

The finial she designed – specifications to be sent to the workshop outside Bangor in the next week, where the sculpture would be rendered first and afterwards would have a mould made from it, to be reproduced over a hundred times, four-feet-high spires of ceramic that would rise up where the TV aerials had been, against a summer sky then – they were drawn thus: a woman's figure, vague, with her hands at her sides; her face a smooth, gentle curve. Raised up it was, but with what emotion, expressionless, you couldn't tell.

It was very saddening, that you could live for so long in the way she had done, and each day find yourself enough staring hope to carry on in the same home – to not cry, to not ever spend time alone, and to not leave – and yet, when that violence had finally ebbed away, you could sit down to draw a picture and not be able to stop yourself crying. It was, it had always been, that close to her.

It took your heart away, she'd thought as she had looked down at the paper, birds beginning to talk in the dark that was still outside. That staring hope, though it had felt strong, it had been blindness, for the grief she felt to come so easily now.

Did he believe that Bethan loved him back? It was hard for him to, looking up towards her. But it was hard not to. She moved so slowly. She moved for him. He had listened to her talk about his own part in this project.

Behind him, feelings grew clearer round each of the broken things inside the skips he had kept and, above him, she shifted her hands from the dress and held her arms, open and up, slow as a figure in a music box. Beautiful she was. Perhaps, if she didn't love him yet, then she was meant to.

The A frames, measured and constructed to perfect size, tagged with the numbers of the houses for which they were ordered, began to arrive: there would be fourteen lorryloads in total. Near the stock of sea stone, they formed towers.

Dai saw them there one early morning, and stood looking for a long time.

The spring sky was low. In plastic, he saw with wonder, they touched it.

*

Sometimes, it seemed to Ruth that she would never reach that ending, and the memories behind her pushed her away from hope. She needed Charlotte – but she needed Lennie, as March rolled with that spring, like she had never needed him.

She shouted at him, with no stream to her words, of the ways that he had made her feel at night, when alone and while he slept. He would scream back at her sometimes, behind the closed kitchen door, their voices echoing in every other empty room. But never in defence: 'I know!' he'd holler at her, and tell her of all the ways that he was a failure; love, life and self. Never in defence, unless that was one.

She saw how something had changed him, and she hated it. She saw how, in some way, he was freer. And he never hit her. Not once. Though she stood in front of him and she screamed words into his face, though she provoked him, he never hit her now.

One night, alone in the cluttered living room where she slept, and consumed by feelings she couldn't name, she sat and she hit herself. On her legs and her arms and on her own stomach, over and over, violently, until she lay in pain and breathing dryly, panicked on the floor – believing that to have done it made lies of every claim of healing. It seemed to make lies of the abuse she might have healed from. Hating herself, she lay there, wishing he would hit her, and for this hating herself again. The floorboards were dull and dry underneath, her whistling breath coming back to touch her face again. Alone, she put herself in this posture, hugging her knees, small as she could make herself. A victim's posture, as if it had always been this: she alone, and attacking herself.

twentyseventh of july

nineteen sixy eight

A cuckoo flew into the house. It came into the window in the morning
when the man and the woman were out. In its beak there was a
hankercheif and it was made of didnt white lace. There was a little
baby in the hankercheif that was wraped up well. The cuckoo said to
himself 'This is the right house. This man and woman need a little
baby and they will take good care of it until it is fully grown' and
so it put the baby down in the fireplace because it knew this was
where its friend the stork put babies. But when it put the baby down
its wing hit thefireplace and a fether fell out into the hankercheif
but the cuckoo didnt know. it said goodbye to the little baby and it
was happy because it had done its job well. It flew out into the
woods again and all across the meadows and in the fireplace the
little baby waited. Just like the stork had put it there but with a
black fether in its hair.

Ruth was drawing when the doorbell rang on the eleventh day and, hearing it finally, she rose to walk through the barren hallway and look out, to see Charlotte Weyland.

In a thick coat, with an umbrella held over her, standing between the ruined flower beds, Charlotte looked back. Her expression was waiting, unsure, like a quiet in the midst of all this din.

She didn't move as she stood there, expecting judgement on each of the days that had passed while she'd not come.

Rain reached in across the doorstep as Ruth saw her, and didn't speak, remembering dimly the autumn morning when she'd first stood here. It seemed as if everything that had passed since then moved around them, their gazes knotted, and they didn't speak.

'You came then,' Ruth started.

Charlotte just nodded.

'I was starting to think, you know, we'd got the plague.' The smile took time off her face, Ruth saw. It was lovely. Caring could do that. She took in this proof. It could give back to the world.

'I'm sorry.'

She tried to offer Charlotte the same smile and could not. 'I didn't know what to think, that's all . . .'

'I just wanted to give you some time –'

'I didn't need it.'

Looking into her face, Charlotte said nothing else.

She followed Ruth into the hallway, the fourth house in the first row that backed the floodplain along Ynys-morlan's gradually reforming street. The door closed behind her and she saw its rooms again.

Where the day's light was cut away by the rows of uprooted, potted shrubs that lined her window, all the lamps were lit to show the papers across the table. Spread out over the oilcloth there were pencils and pens, the telephone, lists of numbers. She saw catalogues and Ruth's own gardening books heaped on the many cardboard boxes that drew in the little room's walls closer still, application forms, suppliers' stocklists, and all the other things that Ruth had filled these last days with.

Nia's drawings, she saw, many of them on the walls. In the silence, Charlotte looked. She remembered Ruth's skin.

'You've been busy . . .'

'Of course,' Ruth answered.

'I wanted . . . I wanted to give myself time . . .'

She nodded. They both failed to silence. Ruth said, 'I've missed you.'

'I've missed you too.'

'I've needed you.'

'Ruth, I've needed you as well –'

She raised her hand to her cheek, as she'd done that night. Each of the men who worked here had their own special expression for that side of her face. Pity, she saw, and disgust. A sort of humour, the roots of which she couldn't guess at. Had they talked? She didn't know. 'I've been here,' she said. 'I couldn't go out. I've been here if you needed me.'

'I know . . .'

Charlotte looked at the expressions that passed over Ruth's face, trying to see where the woman was now. Was she desperate? Yes. And running. Of course she was.

'You've just been, the last week . . . you've been doubting me,' Ruth said with slow acknowledgement.

'I don't want to hurt you.'

'You think I'm so vulnerable?'

'. . . Yes.'

She nodded, acid-eyed. 'And you don't trust me.'

'I didn't mean that.'

'You don't believe the things I do . . . are real.' But, with all the doubts she felt herself and the hatred they brought, still she saw Charlotte's face and was waiting to be told it wasn't so. 'If you're not going to believe the things I say – or believe in the things I do then why did you come here? You . . . believe in me,' she told her. 'If you come here then you believe in me!'

'All right.' She was afraid to, though.

'You tell me you regret what happened.'

'I don't regret it –' and she saw the relief, but Ruth's voice didn't fall from its pitch, needing to hear it again.

'You tell me you regret it.'

She wanted to tell her, there were years behind the things she feared now. Years and thousands of words. There were a hundred decisions scrawled on those pages, that she wouldn't open herself to this again. She wanted to tell Ruth, she couldn't play some false role again. She didn't speak.

She was afraid that she had led herself back here, inevitably. That the lack of others' clear love was really a mar inside herself.

What she said in the quiet seemed empty, but it wasn't empty. Through those years she had never touched anyone like she had Ruth. It was hope and fear and desperation that stole any depth from her voice. 'I don't regret it, really.'

'Would you . . . if it ended, between us?'

In the stillness of the stone house a mile from this town, she'd found no answer to the question. She needed to answer now – as much for herself. And thought of those journals, every shelf of the little, locked study in her home, every home that lay behind it. She tried to say clearly, 'No. I wouldn't.'

She watched her. Beneath the wire of Ruth's expression, hope was lying. Hope for them to stay together, or just for some faith in herself, Charlotte didn't know. Perhaps hope born of nothing more than somebody else's belief in her.

'I wouldn't regret it,' she said again.

The work moved in the street, on the other side of this window.

'Are they ready to treat the dry rot?' she asked.

'I don't know. Yes. They're ready.'

'And you have to be out of the house.'

'Yes.'

Charlotte's words flickered but she didn't stop, 'Will you come and stay with me then?'

'Yes,' Ruth nodded. Told her again.

Charlotte looked in her eyes. She wanted to ask, would she leave him? But Ruth had no answer, she saw, for any of these questions in her now.

They didn't kiss that day, made no move to even touch each other's hands. At the table, as Ruth showed her the designs on which she'd worked, there was a space of air between them that their voices couldn't break.

She had planned a fountain, a central piece for the garden which would cover slopes and rises with flowers, palms maybe, or grasses. The concrete forecourt there was now being broken by drills. This fountain would be a low dish, a circle of ten feet, filled by sea stones through which the water rose.

There was a look in Ruth's eyes as she showed them to Charlotte; wanting her to see what she was trying to express. Perhaps alone she might have looked at the drawings and been moved by them. Perhaps they might have recalled emotions of her own. But in Ruth's kitchen, she saw nothing but a woman who had been through so much that her feelings overspilled into anything. Empty and clear as water. She held the paper in her hand.

Perhaps Hedera didn't live on in the houses she owned now. Other people, many people, had made homes in them. Maybe there was nothing evoked by fireplaces, hearths to sit on or tables at, by ash wood or by the certain light of windows. People brought their own memories to what they saw, maybe that was all. And even speaking, it might be so. You could talk about love. Was an emotion something you could give? Something passed between? It was a need on both sides maybe, nothing shared. If so, was this project worthless? Ynys-morlan would be a theme park then, a wonderland. A beautiful and rugged bay, covered by the pretty things those people thought were meaningful.

It was a precious gift, your feelings to the things you made. And how bitter, to realize then that no one else could see them. That what you created did not contain them and that line had not been crossed. Although maybe, she had thought in evenings, reading entries now long past, if to make something took away the hurt you felt, it didn't matter.

She looked at Ruth and she nodded, to show that she saw what Ruth wanted her to see. Maybe she did, maybe not. She didn't want to think, though, that that line couldn't be crossed. Creativity could give you a way across the water.

Ruth said that perhaps they could put the shrubs – they were small, they wouldn't be too damaged by the move – against the farthest of the garden's walls. She talked as if she might live there with Charlotte one day. She seemed to believe it.

These things would be built from pieces of themselves. Fountains full of sea stones or the curving, cobbled wall that held the shore back from the houses, places to sit beside open hearths, spires or finials that reached upwards. With the vast arching beams that would be exposed above the museum's single room, Emyr's memories would rise. Things were supposed to be released with the sky. For a long time, that had been its meaning. In the new timber frames too that Lennie slowly constructed in view of the foreman behind him, hammering them together length by length to replace the ones he'd taken down. What you made, you made with pieces of your heart. While the rain fell or only strung mists along the trough of this street, he remembered three years on the roads.

A place wasn't a place at all where no one set their feet. Somewhere seen through a windscreen had no resonance. It had no meaning. There was land under the roads, he thought. There was land underneath them still, but we were people, we looked out and only saw the people's work: the buildings, the tarmac, any town, if it was lying on a plain that stretched past vision, still. It was something momentous to see a shadow cross a mountain. It was something wonderful. We were people, though; we saw the AA signs and drove on through.

Our land was covered with these roads, he thought: every space between every home, like nothing small could matter and it was only the great patterns, the great spread of people across countries and continents that made us grand. We'd covered the country with these places that weren't places at all. He'd spent three years in a wasteland, to return to Ynys-morlan and stand with Rhys, let go everything he felt; to see that flag, and remember what had some meaning.

On the scaffold-covered pavement he slowly put the frame together, and what he felt moved into it, into the ground here where it would be set. These were only buildings – it was all they could make – but he touched the place underneath this town as he built them. The place reached out to him in return. For a long time, the ground had had this meaning. What we felt was not isolated from it.

The windows that Bethan Hughes designed, sitting late in her bedroom while Chelsea slept, were of stained glass; of different colours. Dark reds and summer blues, yellows like the beach could be. The patterns formed tributaries which paused for the spaces of blank wall between, to be continued in the next. In this way, the room, when it was a restaurant, would be filled with the gradual change. You might sit in the cast of one colour or another. White tablecloths, she decided on, to catch them.

She sat for two hours in the silence, her pencil scratching and her own breathing, only that. The world came in on you and touched you in a thousand ways that made you old; if you tried to be young, still it did. She drew hair that moved like waterweed. She left open the door of the cupboard where her dress hung. He might come again tonight: he might come and stand down there on the pavement, looking up at her, to give this war she felt a window frame. She looked down at what she had drawn for the restaurant and the way that he'd talked about time came back to her. Thoughts that could only be had without any knowledge of the world.

Just as it had done on the first night she'd seen Dai, rainwater veined the window, it left beads there that caught tiny points of this lamplight. When she looked up from her drawing, there were scaffolding poles, rusty, shadowed, in that light's final reach. The memory of their nights unfolding gradually around her as she drew, Bethan was thinking of him when the doorbell rang.

Tattered, ash-dark clouds had moved across the sky. With the nights and the slow fall to silence of the vehicles and the voices, the echoing tools, in this wind you could hear those tarpaulins trying to take flight. One car might drive on the wet road, its headlights spilled there, and you'd hear its wake fading for a mile.

Before Emyr could come back to their clean, quiet house, Gwen left it, looking towards the caravan site and the cold, blue floodlights that formed a field there, seen from the distance.

Dai came to town that night, not just to look for Bethan, but to go to the gift shop's site again. At the end of that week of nights, he'd felt an idea growing. Its shape was perfect.

He wanted to tell her but there'd be glass between them, and silence. Looking up, he thought, he would want to let her know that she'd inspired him with what she'd said about his part in this. She inspired him in all the ways a person could get inspiration; he wouldn't have used that word, but things were lovelier without names anyway.

The low lamps would glisten in her hair, he imagined.

Something could be made, this was his idea, this was what he wanted to say to her – something could be made, that showed the shape of Time. That *revealed* Time. Made It real.

'I think some people are driven, and it's not achievement that they're looking for. It was never . . . achievement. That makes you think of goals,' she said, 'of finding the energy in yourself to get to them.' As she spoke her voice was quiet, looking to see if it was recognition in his face. 'I think you find the goals to justify the . . . reaching.'

He had no goal. He remembered swimming back, cold, to the shoreline, with the girl's body dragging behind him. He remembered sitting on the seawall with Rhys later on, he didn't know how much later, but both of them old enough then to be drinking cider from the Spar – they'd used to get Gavin Pryce to buy it for them, a bottle extra on his daily list. Sitting there, he recalled, looking out across the summer people brazening out the wind. Waiting, in case anyone, any kid got in trouble. He missed the goal.

It'd been a small thing then, the missing, like the black spot that came on your vision, looking out for too long with the sun down low. He sat still as he looked at Gwen now and the rain was a whole world outside the caravan. Her car was parked in the last few footsteps of the light. That one black place had grown.

'It's about looking for something maybe,' she said. Her eyes were resting in her lap. 'You're hunting for something but it doesn't seem to have . . . any kind of . . . shape.' In her voice, there was bitterness, but it was only slight. 'So you find other things, other goals . . . to justify the hunting.'

'Or you don't find them,' he said.

She raised her head.

He'd opened the door to her tonight and taken her hand as she'd moved to step inside and, inside then, his hand had moved and he'd been holding her. Standing in the warm and tiny space, it had been awkward, wonderful in a way that had hurt her somehow. She couldn't remember ever embracing like that, with nothing said, no expressions even.

She seemed almost to say several things. After one moment, her eyes on the stiffness and the gentleness of his face, she only said, 'The world's full of goals. If that's what you want.'

'I want to find the thing,' he said, 'that doesn't have the . . . the shape.' He smiled but it was just a compensation over what he'd said. 'Went into the café yesterday, they're putting floorboards down in there. I was looking through the glass, you know . . . you know what it looked like to me? Watching this whole place now. Looks like everyone's hunting for that thing. They reckon they're going to find it in . . . some new fucking life.'

'Did you go home?' Gwen asked.

Sitting with Siân this evening, the colour of the sherry in the glass Gwen had held had looked like sunset, she had stared into it for so long. She remembered, watching Tom now.

He didn't answer her for a long time.

'Did you?' She remembered: the smallest quiet had lain like glass after the last weeks of silence between them, after the lie she'd given to Emyr.

'I went through,' was all Tom said.

They broke down the dormer windows and the porch of the house where Tom had lived and dragged it out to be disposed of. They took the roof off the kitchen extension and tarped it over, waiting for the peaked A frames. As with the houses on either side, as with every house in Ynys-morlan, men topped the scaffolds to build new gables where the dormers' little flat tar tops had been.

In the Humphries's yard, they set another six courses of stone against the kitchen's walls each day. And from the spot where they mixed and shovelled, you could look down the rows of backyards now, to see stonelayers kneeling outside every house. Standing out there, Tom had looked at them.

'Want to bring your moping face inside?' He'd heard her in the doorway, where polythene was hanging in a mess, the kitchen counters filthy with falling dust. 'Want to help a bit?'

She'd been angry with him, angry with his silence as she directed the men who were moving the last of her things from downstairs, and he'd helped and been unable to hide his expression. She'd asked him, do this or do that, short-cut tones. And he'd done it, and watched her, looking for something in her face that wasn't either anger or self-righteousness.

He no longer had a reason to come to town, the café closed, Spar closed and his mum here overseeing this work. He came anyway, every day, walking in from the caravan site. 'It's a selfish thing, your own happiness,' Gwen had said, 'to set as your only sight in life.' Tom had looked at Ynys-morlan as he'd wandered in that day, full of progress. More pieces missing from each house, garden, garage. People's greed eating away at their own homes, he'd thought. He couldn't call Gwen, couldn't ask her to come to him. Passing by the community centre on his way, he had looked through the windows and seen her there.

He'd always felt far from his mother. Not like this, though. When she'd turned to him in the unlit spare room that had been his bedroom, standing amidst the boxes that the men had brought up, their footsteps fading again down the stairs, when she'd asked him in that curt tone what exactly was wrong with him, he'd told her. The things you believed when you were on your own, they were lies unless you could say them too.

'You want to know what's wrong?' He'd looked down at his hands, like that was where he kept all his beliefs. In the smudged light that came through the window where he'd used to look out at the sea, there'd been the sound of men moving on the boards. 'You want to know?' He'd raised his eyes. 'I don't know how you can stand here in the middle of all this and ask me.'

Siân had watched his face for long moments, what he'd said draining down from the look in her eyes to rest lightly in her hands, it seemed. She raised them slightly to this room without looking away from him, and she said, 'You think this is wrong? You want to judge me, Thomas? You judge me. Go on and tell me the words that sit behind that expression.'

'You can see them. Don't need me to tell you anything. You must've been listening to them from your own head enough.'

Coldly, she'd said, 'You go on and tell me what you're thinking, unless you've lost so much respect for me that you don't even give me your judgements now.'

'Respect?'

The work had been a muted racket below them and for a moment he'd not been able to answer her, every word he'd stored up in these last two weeks dragged down by what she was doing; by her thin reasons. He'd felt dry in his mouth, and inside.

'Respect?' he'd said. 'Yeah I have. You must've lost it for yourself . . . By everything you've ever told me, you *should* have . . . I can't believe you,' was all he finished saying. 'I can't.'

'Perhaps you'd like to give me a reason for that.'

'This isn't you!'

Siân had looked at him: his face determined and ready. She had recognized the expression well.

'It's got nothing to do with who you are, this! Like, this is your house . . . You know it's not going to be when it's finished? You know you're going to end up sitting down here, not even feeling like it's your own home?'

'That's right.' She'd nodded again. 'The lack of a dripping ceiling'll give it away for a start. New coat of paint, the fact the kitchen's not full of draughts. You're right, won't feel anything like my house.'

'You won't like it when it's done.' But he looked at her and was scared as he said it, for the first time maybe, that it wasn't true. 'It's going to be finished . . . and you're not going to be able to go back on it, you know that? You'll regret it! Maybe . . . maybe other people won't, but you will!'

There'd been silence between them, and the dust of many things already moved.

'You know what they say in life, Tom? You only regret the things you don't do.'

'There's a lot of things you're not doing. By this, there's a lot of things.'

Something softened in her face as she watched him, a glaze of shadows cast across her features and making her gaunt, but she said, 'And what's that? What is it I'm not doing?'

He hadn't dropped his eyes. 'Not being the person you have been for the last twenty years.'

Siân had stood still. 'Have you thought maybe I'd rather that?' The motion around them had seemed distant from the dimness of that room. You could only see the sea from here, and that was the same as it had always been.

He hadn't answered her.

They'd always treated each other this way; as he'd got older it hadn't changed. Angry, each of them, at things the other hadn't said yet. There was nothing of John in him.

It was herself that Siân had seen. But she'd stood there and found that she couldn't let go of her anger, not even with the loss of seeing her own bitterness in him.

'Have you thought maybe – that I'd be glad of that change?'

'Why? Why would you be glad of it? What's wrong with how we've been?'

'What's wrong with how it's changing?' She'd countered quietly.

'You tell me! Tell me what was so bad! That you'd rather live in a house like you're a fucking guest now!'

'*Why* should I be like a guest in it?' Without hesitation, 'Because it's not falling apart? Because it's a *nice* house? Because it's *expensive*, is that why? Why should that have nothing to do with me, Tom? Go on and tell me why I should sit in a beautiful house and feel like a guest! Go on!'

His mouth was open, grasping for words. He saw injury in her face and her blue eyes, and all he wanted to tell her suddenly then was that he'd never meant what she'd twisted his words into. She shouldn't feel like a guest in a house like that.

'It's not the house . . . Not what it looks like. But you'd never have taken this money! A year ago, any time before. You'd *never* have taken it! You haven't earned this! What've you done to get this, like? You've got to earn it . . . you've said it yourself . . . How many times've you told me? You've got to earn it or it isn't yours! These are *your words!*'
He was shouting. He didn't want to shout at her.

Siân's hands had fallen to her sides and he'd just stood before her, stubble under his chin, hulking like he'd always been. He'd never wanted to be tall. In the mute air that had descended, she'd seen his face and something sad in her, something terribly sad had seemed to come and to leave her, as empty again as this wordless moment.

'You think I should turn down this chance, to keep . . . hold of what I've said.'

Tom looked at her but no response came to him. She only saw him stay silent.

'Do you think it's wrong not to?' she went on.

He'd put his tight lips together and looked down at the floor. Dirt tracked in footsteps there between the boxes they'd moved. It had seemed to him, his bedroom window behind and its clouded sea moving, like he gave her the house in that string of seconds through which no answer came – though he hadn't lived here, more than a year now.

When he'd spoken eventually, depleted, what he'd said was true. It had run against everything he felt, gritted like sand, but he'd seen her expression and known. 'It's not wrong.'

Siân's voice had carried the final strands of the tone she always used: that abraded self-belief that made everything a solution she already knew. In her eyes something had remained, though, something that had not been found. 'There's a difference between charity and taking something that's being offered to everyone. That'll make you happy.'

'I know,' he'd said, but two different coasts had seemed to stretch apart in him.

'Do you think I've changed? This isn't charity. It's not greed, Tom . . .' her mouth shut securely for a moment, as if she'd held words there she didn't like the taste of, she'd looked at him. Believing them still. 'There's a difference,' she'd said, 'between greed and taking something you need. You think it's better to do without, Tom?' she had asked, levelling her eyes and voice at him – and he'd felt, under both of them, like he was distant even from himself; a choice had to be made and he'd be far away, whichever one he took. 'You think,' she'd said, 'that it's better to hold on to what you used to believe, even if it doesn't make you happy any more?'

Where his mother slept, she slept in the cold. Where she slept the sound of the rain on the tarpaulin that now served as the kitchen's roof must have been a noise to rival the beating of it here, on the caravan's every side. Everything that house had been was her. Stiff with slate shadows, under-heated, under-decorated, and in those shadows, in the planes of its walls and the curve of its staircase upwards, there had been a thing, a thing without shape, he thought: the coldness in that house had made it a better place. That was what had lain beneath the walls. Some kind of triumph. Some goal.

'I thought my mother was full of beliefs,' he said. 'Right and wrong. Morality. That it wasn't about . . . what you got in life . . . but how you lived it. You've got to work. Life's work.' His features were static. In the caravan's half-light, Gwen thought of his mother and it seemed to her like Siân had brought an adult into the world – no previous childhood at all. 'You work . . . and you do the right thing, every chance you get, you do the right thing. Not because it's going to pay you back, it won't – but because of rightness,' he said.

'Do you know what I believe?' Gwen asked. 'I believe that . . . drive, that *search*, it exists in some people, because the world needs it.

That sounds arrogant maybe.' Her eyes fell to the floor. He had tried to tidy. The table was clear in the caravan's close corner. 'I've been arrogant,' she said. 'A lot of times in my life I've been that way. Arrogance is what breaches the gap, maybe, when it seems there's a gap between you and . . . other people your own age . . . I do believe it, though. Nature abhors a vacuum. Fills a space like water. Puts everything there that needs to be, and any community, the world . . . or a town, needs people with that drive. People looking for something they'll never find. Or that place can't ever improve.' She raised her eyes and saw him watching her. It didn't feel like a lie.

Her memory of the last hour before this night had set in, it lay behind her gaze. Siân's expression, her soft words to Gwen in a house that had been hushed with the end of the day's work. Bright now behind Gwen's eyes, on him. Still it didn't feel like a lie.

Gwen remembered Siân Humphries, when her face hadn't been hard and there'd been no lines around her eyes. That tone of voice, it'd always been full of questions but she hadn't had any answers then. She remembered Siân, when she had first been married. She remembered her when she'd given birth to Tom.

They'd shared a sense of the world; the way to live. Gwen remembered other girls pairing off, even Patty – Sy, her first boyfriend had been called – and she and Siân had talked, asking each other, saying it was right to wait.

Her son was now eighteen years old, and Gwen had lain on his bed with his hands on her face, afraid to feel them. She'd abandoned the belief that she was a good person.

Her life's work in Ynys-morlan, though, had always been more precious than feelings about herself. She did not believe that that work had been selfish. She couldn't believe it. In her mind, as she'd watched the town dismantled piece by piece through the final days of February, the work she'd done here had seemed more precious than anything else she'd experienced in life. She remembered her hand coming down on Dai's face; right and wrong were confusions to her, as they'd never been. She felt loneliness, sadness at the project that was in motion now, but it was the memory of her work that she most feared losing. Faith in the thought that it had been worthwhile.

After telling Emyr that she had been at Siân's house – that she'd been happy for her – the question had come, of course. They hadn't spoken for a long time now. She had remembered sitting with Siân in the weeks after John had died, her home full of rubbish, full of Tom and Stacey, and trying to hold Siân to the right thing. Her own home had been in progress then, up on the hill. They'd been building the double garage and the spare rooms. They'd been landscaping the garden. She remembered, in Siân's grief-stricken rooms, talking slowly over her silence. The right thing had been easy to see.

She had gone to Siân's today, late in the afternoon. Disassembled, now being rebuilt, the rooms where they had once sat together no longer existed. She had gone to prove the things she'd said to Emyr. To find some kind of clarity – to see a friend perhaps, perhaps just that, who'd known her when her ideals had still been bright and far ahead.

The men had been packing up as she'd parked her car at five o'clock, having worked late in the playschool alone. Gwen had driven into Ynys-morlan on to a road crammed with waiting cars. It had taken her more than ten minutes just from the edge of town, three hundred yards, to Siân Humphries's house.

The front door had still been open, the paved garden a mess of tools and footprints as she'd walked towards it. In the still-thick noise of engines, she'd heard movement inside, looking into the dusk-settled hall.

'Siân?'

For an instant it had crossed her mind that Tom might be there also, and when she'd stepped over the threshold, she'd tried to leave her fear behind. If he was there, she'd just say hello to Siân. She'd be friendly. Try and cross the gap that had come between them in these last months of change.

But he hadn't been there; when she'd called Siân's name again, the woman had come from the kitchen to stand in the doorway and see Gwen's face. They'd said nothing for a moment. Under Siân's eyes, she'd felt stiffness rise in her, that was years old.

'Well now. Hello.'

'Hello, Siân.'

They'd only stood there for unbroken seconds as the reasons they hadn't spoken passed between.

'What can I do for you?'

'How are you?' Gwen had asked her.

'I'm good. Very good, thank you.' Her hands had hung by her sides in the doorway, and thin blue light had permeated, from the kitchen behind, through the tarpaulin that now covered its broken roof.

'Well, are you not going to do me the courtesy of even asking how I am then?'

'How are you, Gwen?'

She'd stared at Siân, lost. Had remembered a time when there'd been no children, no Tom or Stacey, and it had seemed for an instant like the hour she'd spent in Tom's caravan had not passed at all; as if no time had passed since those early days. She felt open, vulnerable.

'Not good,' she'd said, and kept her eyes on Siân's face, despite her feelings. She'd seen the past cross there, and seen it banished. And all she'd said was, 'Can I come in? Sit down?'

They'd gone to the living room together, where the building work had left nothing more than a crowding of boxes and uncovered frames round the windowpanes. Gwen had seen that other things had been packed away too, photographs and ornaments that had stood in their places in the mess here, ten years. The pictures on the walls had been taken down. And she'd remembered: days when the work had been in her own home. It wasn't jealousy, though, but just sadness.

Siân had stood beside the cabinet and taken out the sherry decanter; hadn't offered tea. Gwen had watched her pour two glasses and, outside, the last of the working men had started their car engines and left the town in silence.

They'd sat in it. She'd sipped the drink, looked down into its colour. Hadn't know any more what she'd come to say.

'So. Is it all going well here?'

'It's all going well. Had the measurements for the windows yesterday. They probably will have finished the removals by tomorrow.

643

They've taken all the windows apart upstairs, got almost the whole roof off the kitchen. Should be bringing the frames in a few days.'

The memory of building, planning, executing plans with Emyr on their home, seemed to Gwen as she looked out of the window at the backyard and the sea beyond, like a time of difficulty rather than happiness. Seeing Siân's face, she didn't miss it. She didn't want it. She felt stirred as she held the glass: some little revelation.

'Would you like to see what's being done to the kitchen extension? Outside?' In the narrow western light that came in from the shoreline, she hadn't moved her eyes from Gwen's face, and Gwen felt the look, sharp as a gull's.

Siân had been thinking of Tom. The expression he'd had. It had seemed to lie inside her like cement, drag down at what she'd said then like some distant thing she couldn't let go of, seeing Gwen's lowered head.

'Why have you come here?' she said.

Gwen looked up into Eirian Meredith's eyes. The glass in her hand unfelt, what she had done to Eirian's son lay between them very clearly in the failing light. As Siân's unspoken choices had once hung here.

Evening sun had penetrated the coastline's overcast sky and, in here, crept from the window opposite to lie across the carpet and the sofa where they sat, to touch the sides of their faces.

'After more than twenty years, I hoped that you'd listen to my side of the story before judging me.'

Siân had taken her gaze away and stared silently, rigidly, at her own hands.

In the quiet, the memory of Eirian's words was inescapable. She'd looked at Siân, and the lack that she'd felt, not knowing what to say, what to ask, had left her; a small and simple defeat. 'Or maybe you judged me a long time ago.'

Siân didn't answer, but her stare was floodplain-even on Gwen's own again. 'I'm not a judgemental person.'

'That isn't true.' She'd looked at her sherry and in a moment then, drunk it all; in a moment, hadn't cared. Memories, of the friend she sat with and of every part of her past, they seemed to run away from her. Alcohol had touched her stomach. She'd remembered fleeing Eirian's house. Remembered crying, Tom's hand on her arm. In those few seconds – though they passed – there was nothing she wanted to hold on to. You couldn't change the person you were in one moment, though. You couldn't leave yourself behind. 'That isn't true. You've always been. And me,' she said.

'Don't place us together like that. Don't try and do that.'

'Did you not think that it was strange, Siân? Did you not think that when you heard? Twenty-five years . . . it didn't come to you that there must be a reason? For me to do something I never would have? I'd never have hurt him! Did you not ask yourself what might be wrong for me?' It was poverty that came into her voice. Emyr had asked her, lying in their bed, to prove the worth of what she'd aimed for. And she couldn't. Could only believe. She looked at Siân and remembered a time when they'd told each other that they were right. How safe they'd been in that. When she saw Siân now, the expression was still there, though it no longer included her. 'Did you not think about me at all?'

Siân remembered telling Patty she would apply.

'Dai came down to see me that same morning. He came straight from his house, where you'd left him. Still crying by the time he got to me, he was. And you know what he asked me? You know what the first thing he said was? Would Eirian not have wanted him to do it?'

Gwen was silent. Low tides moved in her and did not cease.

'He told me what you'd said. What you'd done. Didn't care about the fact that you'd hit him, only mentioned that right at the end. It was the thought you'd put in his mind, that was what he cared about. Would she have not wanted it? Know what I told him? Told him the truth, and hopefully I got that thought out of his head. Told him the only person who didn't want him going ahead was you. Only person who cared more about the gift shop than what he wanted, two months after she'd been put in the ground and left him on his own – that was you.'

She was silent under Siân's voice. In her mind, her hand came down, over and over, with no relief. And Emyr's words returned, the coldness in his words; her husband, who'd loved her once. 'What were you trying to save?' She couldn't tell, she couldn't put it into words, what the work in her life had meant to her.

Siân watched her, and some remorse came and she looked down at her drink. But she had seen Gwen today, dressed just the same, with her gold, with her faultless make-up, and she'd walked no differently into this house than she had done eighteen years ago. No differently, she pictured, than walking into Dai's. In this pause, though, she saw again the look that had been on her son's face today. Like doubt, his expression came back to her: his seeing someone he didn't recognize.

Siân looked up at her. It seemed in that quiet, there was only one difference between them and it wasn't what she'd done to Dai. It was the belief she'd lost. She saw Gwen in the waning light.

'What happened?' she asked quietly. 'You changed.'

Gwen lifted her eyes to Tom's mother and said slowly, 'I came to ask you.'

With the last sun fading to night in the west through the bare window opposite them, and with a new sherry curled in each of their hands, Gwen listened to a story told, of a girl who'd had only good intentions in her mind. A story of three friends.

Where they sat, there was a cold draught from the tarp-covered kitchen. Even under the door as Siân closed it, it came to brush them where they sat. Siân stared at her with feelings held down as she spoke. She told the story of a woman with ambition, with a need in her, a drive, even young. The girl she spoke of, with the sound of the incoming tide slowly reaching them, seemed distant to Gwen.

'It's not wrong to have ambition,' she said. 'There's a reason it's there, for God's sake, a good reason. The work you've done in this town has benefited everyone here. And you know that, Gwen. If no one had your drive, imagine where we'd be now. It's for the community that ambition exists. And God knows you put yours to that.

No,' Siân said, 'there's no problem with *ambitions*. When they're reached, that's when the problems start. You know what it was, Gwen? I saw it, even then. Not that you'd have listened to me, you'd got Emyr by then . . . Your problem was success.'

She heard a story of a girl who'd been full of striving, to do right and to live the right way. And with the sherry glass full between her hands, she listened to the way that her striving had been fulfilled, how ambition had changed into achievement, and how a good drive, a drive *towards* goodness, had become selfish. Self-righteous and alone. How it had led her to Dai Meredith's door.

Gwen had left her house in darkness, and Siân had watched her walk down the path. With an effort against the sight of her moving away, against the memory of Tom's expression, she held on to what she felt. She turned to look back at the grey, empty hallway of this house that hadn't changed since she had moved here with her husband.

'The world needs people, or just a town,' Gwen said, 'just a town . . . it needs people who are looking for something that's more important than . . . just happiness.' The gift shop, Gwen remembered, and the community centre and every fund-raising call she had ever made. Every petition. The days visiting, in hospitals, in people's homes, in Eirian Meredith's.

The need to strive that she had felt throughout her life, though it might have led her astray, become arrogance – it had been a drive towards good things. She still believed it.

'It's when – it's when that drive gets fulfilled,' she said, though doubt moved under her at the way Tom looked at her. Was it right to be here? 'It's only when that need to do right turns into . . . knowing you're right . . . If you want to think of Ynys-morlan,' she said, 'it's a selfless thing to let your own home be altered so much for the sake of the whole town growing. When you see the gains everyone will make . . . The personal gains, though, when you start seeing them, and the things you've been doing for other people start being for yourself . . . just for yourself, to make yourself happy, that's when they stop being right . . .' Sadness came to her. It was an answer with no compassion; for herself, or Tom's mother, or any person. Trapped as she'd been for these last weeks, though, it was the only answer she could find.

She saw that sadness on his face as well, and regretted having nothing else for him; no answer that would give him confidence. But she'd found none.

'She deserves it,' he said, his face bleak. 'My mum, she deserves it, that's the thing. Gone without it all her life. Still . . . taking it, she's changed.' Like it was a question, he said to her, 'She's lost what I respected.'

Gwen couldn't answer. She wondered what sort of person she was – and Tom too – to care more for some shapeless thing, some goal, than for happiness. You couldn't change what mattered to you. She might have, seeing him sitting before her now, far from everyone they knew. If she could have, she might have changed it for both of them.

But the works she'd done, their value, she couldn't let them go. He was stranded in the things his mother had once believed. He'd made them part of himself. It was precious, goodness. When you found it, it was worth more than anything. She stared at him, the sound of fresh rain all around them while they were dry. It fell on the phantom town she'd driven through.

He had taken the place where he'd been stranded, and grasped it. He held on to it now and every time he looked away from her, he looked to it for reassurance. Was it just to give self-belief then, she wondered? Morality, or searching for it. Was it only that, for her? It seemed the worst answer of all, that goodness was only another kind of coin in the payments which people gave themselves.

She'd not been rich, though, and she looked at him now and saw he wasn't. Her home was an empty one really, it had always been. Reaching out and putting her hand on his carefully, awkwardly, she knew she'd never looked for self-belief. She'd been lonely, and she'd needed it eventually as he needed it now, but that loneliness had only come from the search. It was the search. The shapeless thing.

'You reckon,' he said, and his face held small, bitter humour, 'you reckon doing good is only good when it doesn't make you happy?'

She didn't know how to answer him. She could have told him, many years had passed since she'd been eighteen, and she didn't know yet. 'If it makes you happy then it's for your own sake.'

It was not an answer at all, for it made what they spoke of meaningless. She only had to look into his face, though, to see that it was not. Or to look into her own memories. It wasn't an answer at all, yet it fitted this place where they sat now, two miles from Ynys-morlan. It fitted the way they sat – looking at each other – like the missing piece between them.

Where was she? Emyr did not know. He came back to find this house, redolent of her in every room, in every object she had chosen, but uninhabited. Her absence sat on the cream-coloured sofa and drifted between the ticking moments of the carriage clock. In the places where she'd once left him notes when going out, her absence lay.

It was not something that had come without warning. They made a ghost in this house. They were living the part of their marriage that had always seemed to lack: all the times in their silent bedroom as they'd lain reading side by side, and really had not been there, as they'd eaten wordlessly at dinner – in those vacancies they resided now. As if during those moments, this was where they'd been.

Two miles from the town, it seemed like somewhere out of time. All the shapes of their home were here and yet it wasn't home. Perhaps it was that Ynys-morlan was so changed and that no object had changed in here.

In these rooms, though, as if the space between them had given her the quiet in which to develop, Gwen had differed throughout the last two weeks. Emyr walked through rooms now as if entering the place she'd just left, following, always an open door behind. He had expected bitterness. From the woman to whom he had realized he must be married when he'd heard Dai's story, he'd expected hatefulness. He told her of the progress on each public building. There was no hatefulness. She sat in stillness in these ghost rooms.

From the woman he remembered, bright and hard-driven as a spring wind, so focused that working with her, you forgot yourself and didn't even see how she had forgotten you as well, he'd expected some slow kind of cracking, separated from the project: taut silence, unwarranted bursts of anger. That she would wear herself down till she was bare with her own selfishness. But, sitting by her side on the living-room sofa, as he described work that they might have shared, there was no defence in her eyes. Just an empty look, sad and beautiful, he thought. It brought him the same feelings as his vision of this project. A memorial, transparent, deserted. He had watched her for long minutes as he'd spoken, envisaging the town that might have united them and brought to woefulness by that reaction. Unexpected. She seemed to hold no expression at all in her eyes, as if goodness was the lack of yourself.

Where was she? She lay still as ice, transparent here, on the bed in Tom Humphries's caravan. He kissed her and she did not move her mouth; looking into her eyes, he saw she couldn't. He stroked the hair back from a face painted with thinner make-up than it had been. Cleaning it off, he remembered, though he didn't try to now. He was scared to touch her; scared of how much he wanted to. She wasn't a girl. The feelings she brought up in him weren't those feelings. Between his hand and her skin lay the silence of the house that Emyr walked through now.

Where was she? She was lost in some kind of memory and she was trying to be free from it. She was almost crying. She was almost touching him. Looking for goodness, this was the closest she'd found to it. This: his mouth, earnestness in his eyes, his hands. And this was wrong. He was eighteen years old and this feeling – of need, walled-away and locked up – it was love.

'No,' she said. 'No, no.'

And she moved away from him. She put space between.

'No . . .' she said.

She was right, he knew she was. She had a husband and home.

Where was she? She was underwater, it seemed. He'd been a boy hero once, rescuing a girl from that. He'd been given a moment of something pure, an act of goodness, as his hands had got to her in the water. He'd reached that formless goal. Just a moment, long enough to feel how wonderful it was. It absolved you of everything. It acquitted you with the world. It was a moment of loving yourself and, when you felt that, you'd lost it, for then it wasn't an act of goodness any more. At what point, he wondered? As he'd coughed up water, laid her down on the sand and raised his face? As he'd looked up at the row of houses that had wavered and almost seemed to fall, kneeling there at the edge of the sea? When had it been for his own happiness? What he tried to reach for, you couldn't hold on to it.

Where was Gwen? She was under the water's surface as he drew his hands away. He seemed to be beneath it too. But there must have been land between them somewhere, separated, seeing each other alone. There must have been dry land. As if all this water – such a distance – was really only one thin surface. Like it was really just a line.

Bethan looked up as the doorbell rang, her hands numb on the paper suddenly. The room was silent as it died away. On the bedside table, the clock read 11:42, and all the quiet of the last hours she had spent fell away. It must have sunk into her more deeply than she'd thought; it left her hollow without a warning, staring at her bedroom door.

She looked towards the dress. In the silence, she waited to hear if the bell would sound again. Over the papers her hands hovered, isolated in the air as she remembered the look of hope in Dai's face.

She knew what it made her, to stand and put the pencils aside, to think of going down – even with the window's glass between, what it had made her, to let him fall in love. And what would he come here for but to try and take that further? What did any man, stupid or full of brains, come to Bethan Hughes's home for in the middle of the night?

She waited but the quiet waited with her. She stood slowly, walking to the window.

If it hadn't been for the scaffolding that ran below it, and every other window in this town now, she would have seen him. But in the darkness there were only grimy planks, fingered by the lamplight, cut with the shadow of her.

Ynys-morlan's road was empty and wet with rain.

And this small room was held by the silence, as if it lay at the edge of some place she'd made herself, with her drawings, her silence, her thoughts. She could open the front door and the real world might wash over it.

Behind, where the door was softly shut, her daughter slept as Bethan walked out of her bedroom. Sweet sleep, Bethan thought, full of things never done; full of pictures that didn't even have names.

Outside the house, the rain came again. A squall that knocked against the building's face. In its wake came the sound of her bell.

It was done in a second: the door was open, the stairwell cold. The pictures his mum had once picked hung in darkness and Bethan's footsteps sounded loudly, even bare. With a pause she had to push down and out and away from her, she opened the front door to a black, freezing road.

He stood only a few inches away from her. In the streetlight, wet-skinned and dark-eyed, Rhys stared back into her face.

Looking back from this moment, a March night full of winter leaving, it seemed to Rhys, and to Dai Meredith also, that the years they'd spent had been full of confusion here.

Dai climbed the locked gates of the demolition site. He thought about all those years, sweeping the streets, in the gift shop with his mum, full of bewilderment, they'd been. He had seen this town, and he'd been full of beliefs that had never made sense against the world around him. His views had been right, though. He felt Time moving through Ynys-morlan like the stone-filled tide now, and all was clear to him for the first time. *It* had been dim; not *him*, but the *world*. Gazing down at many pieces of Time past, jumbled into the street-lit skip, it seemed to Dai Meredith that for the first time he understood it.

It was beautiful. It was so intricate. And every end touched another, came together to make a whole. A whole that made sense of love, made sense of everything: loneliness and confusion, even death.

And though it left him full of falling rain, Rhys had found the edges of a pattern too. Lennie Lewis's story had taken away the last of everything he had. What it had given him, though, seemed to balance the loss, as he looked at Bethan for the first time in months.

'Hello, Beth.'

She couldn't answer.

Maybe the world wasn't a place to be trusted; or maybe that was just herself. The boy who'd once given her a pregnancy, and fifty quid, had decided to come round and see her. The edge of the wet front step beneath her naked feet, the wind touching her throat, Rhys looked back into her face.

'Hello, I said.'

Her hand was loose on the door's edge, reached for the first time by the cold. 'What are you doing here, Rhys?'

The street lamp's light lay across his skin. 'Are you going to let me in?'

'No, I'm not going to let you in . . . What're you doing here . . . ?' A voice so faint, she couldn't seem to catch it herself. He looked younger than he had done, seen from a distance on any day, in any afternoon. His expression was open to show her two years and longer.

He stood in silence.

'What are you *doing here*, Rhys?'

Her hair was up, a bun tied badly. She wore loose clothes he didn't recognize. Standing in her own doorway, he watched emotions fall away from her which seemed to leave her homeless.

'You're going to come and ring my bell and stand here saying nothing? *What are you doing at my house?*'

'I'm seeing you.' He'd had a lot of words stocked up for this moment. Thought out, with weeks of nothing but a single room to make them perfect; a single room and a view of a street that didn't stay the same, one day to the next. Staring at her, those words left him like they'd never been his. He had to hold on to the memory of Lennie's face. In wind and silence as cold as this, the man had laid out his past, piece by piece. Rhys saw his own now – that he'd never come and seen before. It was no guilt to admit that. It had never been beatings, it had never been violence that he'd left behind him. 'Let me in,' he said. No question in it. He looked at her as if he'd never left.

Like what he asked for he was owed. '. . . Go away, Rhys . . .'

'Let me in.'

'You . . . How dare you . . . you come here and you wake me up. How dare you . . .' The dress hanging in her open cupboard upstairs and thoughts of Dai Meredith in the quiet of every room, her papers scattered, her designs. The cold air made her numb. She'd come down here to let Dai into her home. 'You thought I'd ask you in? You came here thinking that?' She laughed and let out the air inside her.

'You weren't asleep,' he said.

'We've got nothing to talk about, turn around. Turn your back, like. You know how.'

'We have, though.'

Mouth open, no laugh would come. She seemed to stand with every thought of Dai exposed, to be seen by this person whose slightest fucking expression had always robbed her of defence.

'I've got things to say to you. You must have things to say to me.'

'All the things I had to say . . . I lost a long time ago. They went away.'

'Try to remember. Maybe I want to hear them.'

'Maybe I don't want to say them any more!' Two years it had taken, for them to drain away. At night she'd used to lie in bed and compose the speeches: all the words that would best take him apart. 'You had no right to just come here . . .' Visions of her own figure came to her, wearing that dress in this window, and left her unable to control her voice. She thought of shutting the door, no other word, slamming it. Going back up these stairs. 'Do you know . . . that you've got no right even to ask to come in here . . . ?'

'Maybe.'

'*Maybe*? You stand here and say maybe? You arrogant prick. You came to stand here and insult me?'

He smiled at her, 'Who's calling who a prick?'

Full of his self-belief. Many things that she'd treasured seemed to turn to water, trickle from her, just seeing that smile of his. She recognized it.

And snared, she didn't see behind it what he risked, though it should have been plain on his face, it felt so clear to him.

'Don't speak to me,' she said, gesturing to the cold street laid out behind him.

'Maybe I've got no right to ask to come in. Maybe you want to hear what I've got to say anyway. You think I'd come here . . . you think it's easy for me to stand here, Beth, and ask it? That I'd do that for no reason?'

She turned her face away but couldn't close the door.

It was the image of herself, how she would be in her bedroom after, that kept her there. She looked without hope at Rhys's face, looked properly for the first time in two years. It was her vacant room she thought of. It was the dress on its hanger, it was her designs; the way they'd look as she went to sit again, leaving the echoes of her feet on the stairs behind her. She stared at him, hamstrung. The memory of what she had been finding with Dai Meredith would be a silence that spoke back to her in that room. It was this: the picture of what she'd be left with after she'd run away from Rhys.

'Thank you, Beth,' he said as he passed her.

On the 12th of March, she let him into the home that she'd taken after he had left her.

She went up before him and closed the door to the bedroom, turning to see something she'd sworn she never would allow.

His hair was almost shaved, the scar through his eyebrow white and bright under the electric lamp. He stood with his hands by his sides, like he wouldn't reach out to touch anything unless she let him. In this silence, that had made her feel like another person before the bell had rung, she looked at him and could have struck him, only for the care in his hands there at his sides.

'You got somewhere we can sit? Or you want to talk standing up?'

'You want a little tour?'

'Just somewhere we can sit, like.'

The light switch was cold under her hand.

A small living room, he saw: one two-seater sofa and a chair, purple throws over both of them. A television. Magazines. They were scattered across the room, just the same mess he remembered. Under this bright light, all the objects in her home came to rest in the places where there'd been questions.

'It's nice.'

'Thank you.'

'Cosy, like.'

'Welcoming?'

He looked at her in silence.

He stood on the carpet, the curtains drawn on windows that would have looked out to the sea. Her bare feet hardly made a sound, going to the sofa. She dragged across a cushion and held it in her lap, staring back at him. He saw her do this; he wondered who else might know her now like he still knew her. The light was pale on her lifted face. If maybe there was no one.

'Take a look,' she said. 'Take a good look round.'

He nodded, his eyes not moving from her. Rain fell inside him.

There were books on the shelves above her. He couldn't remember her ever reading. Stephen King, he saw. Fat books and thin ones and CDs in a pile at their end. On the walls there were posters and he saw a picture of the baby on top of the TV.

On a blue background, she was smiling with an expression she couldn't quite control. Little lacy outfit. Little hands. His gaze curved back to Bethan.

'It's nice, a good picture . . .'

The carpet was stained at his feet. 'How would you know?' she said.

They stared at each other as Rhys tried to pull together the words he'd had, two years suffocating the quiet between them.

'I've seen the work in the café,' he said. 'Upstairs, I've seen the work.'

She opened her mouth to answer.

'Hear me out, yeah? How about that? You've got stuff to say, but hear me out, like.'

She let replies escape in silence. Couldn't stop herself from thoughts of her bedroom, every naked thing behind the closed door. He stood here like all the late nights of the last two years brought in.

Slowly he sat down on the carpet beside the gas fire. Cross-legged there.

'I've seen the work. A restaurant upstairs, right? Was that Pat's idea?'

'Why would it matter to you?'

'It was yours.'

Her fingers tightened on the cushion and she sat forwards, but what she tried to keep couldn't be held in her hands. Only at his mention of the work, she seemed to lose it; only the contempt on his face.

'You wouldn't recognize it. The spare room, the bathroom, my room. It's a different place,' she said. 'They've taken out the walls.'

'Where is it, if it's not the same place?'

She met his muddy eyes. 'Fucking Timbuktu.'

'You're lying to yourself if you reckon it's going to be a different place.' Though she leaned forwards and words came out of her, he was talking over them. 'I came to tell you, like . . . you ought to know. You want to set up a restaurant. You want to take that money. It's your choice. I came to tell you, so you'd *have* the choice, what this project is all about –'

'And you'd know that, would you?' she said quietly. 'Sitting in your bedroom, you'd know.' But something was empty in her.

'– What this whole town is about,' he said. Since his night with Lennie, it had grown: wandering, directionless feelings finally settling to this resolution. 'You want to set up a little business here,' he didn't take his eyes away from her. 'One of the few times I came out of my bedroom, I saw Mr Lewis.'

'I don't want to hear what you reckon this project's about.'

'Must've sat and talked to him for three hours, or he talked.' What Rhys had felt that night, all those emotions with no fucking targets, they'd found themselves one finally. They'd broken knots now two years old. Sitting in the bus shelter, he'd remembered school-days with her – and the ways she'd hated, feared, ending up here. Just like him.

Until a plastic stick and a stream of piss had changed every thought in her head. Until that phone call. She'd laughed. Hung up on him. It hadn't been her. Not ever since.

'I don't want to hear it! You want to ignore me? Want to come into my home and *ignore* me when I say something? *I don't want to hear it, Rhys!*'

'Well this is what I came to say, so listen to it or I'll fucking leave. Three hours I sat, I heard him. Want to know what he was talking about, Bethan? Talking about his wife. Talking about how him and her are falling apart. Project's pushing them the final steps –'

'Yeah? Maybe she doesn't need him! You think I care what her personal life's about?' Two years. He would come, to try and ruin this.

'But it's not the project that's the problem for them, oh no. He was pretty down, like, he was fucked. He'd just spent the hour before hitting her in the face.'

'Shut up, Rhys.'

'That's what he said to me. You know, the one with all the plans? You know, there's two of them. One with the plans and one with the fucking money.' He couldn't keep the bad blood from his voice. 'Don't know why they'd be doing that, the middle of this amazing project. You'd think they'd be happy now, wouldn't you? Want to know why . . . ? Because it's what they've been doing for years.' He told her, eyes still, with the coldness of last things lost. 'Just what they've done since they got married and had their kid. And even building *all this place* up, putting all that money in, he can't stop. Punches her. Fucks her up. Makes you look at the thing a bit differently, doesn't it? You think it's going to be a some new place? That what you reckon?'

She sat in a reach of silence.

'You think that I care how they live? I don't care.'

But the words she found were purposeless. She thought of Ruth Lewis, dropping her face at her mother's talk of money. 'I don't care,' she said again. She looked at Rhys, the project spread outside this room, but some dimness seemed to come through her. Hitting his wife. She saw Ruth Lewis's face again, bruise-covered. For a moment she didn't speak.

A woman beaten since she'd got married. And now engineering this project. Thoughts of it couldn't help but dim.

'I'm sorry for her,' she said, her voice like concrete. She didn't take her eyes from Rhys. 'Maybe it's a chance for her, like.' Ruth at the meeting, she remembered, a white face under white lights. 'Maybe it's a chance for a lot of people, who've been through enough to be owed one. Maybe it's a fucking chance for her.'

'This project's built out of the same shit Ynys-morlan's always been made of.'

'You're a bitter fucking person, Rhys. A bitter little shit. That's what you came to say to me? Came here to try and fuck up the first thing I've started since Chelsea was born.'

'Came to tell you the truth of it.' There were more words, many of them, and his low voice was quick across every silence. 'I see you,' he said. 'In there, like, putting roots down. That's what you're doing. Setting up this business. Setting up a fucking life in this town. You know what Ruth Lewis's life got her? It's fucking falling apart on her! Got her a husband who hates it so much, he can't stop himself using her as a punching bag! You should've seen his fucking face, telling me. Lost everything, lost everything – that's what this project's all about. What this town's always been about. The same shit, Beth! That's what you're making your life in. Those are the roots you're putting down.'

'You've become . . . you've become a horrible fucking person, Rhys. Do you know it? You selfish, ugly little fucking child. Two years, you waited till you had something to bring here that you thought would ruin stuff that matters to me. That's a lot of bitter days. That's what you've been spending your time waiting for?'

His shout was sudden, uncontrolled. 'Waiting till I could show you, yes! Waiting till you'd fucking have to listen to me!'

'I don't have to listen to you.' And she stood up on the carpet.

'Waiting till I could make you see!' but shouting, he lost track of his words. 'You should've seen his face! *I saw it.* Know what it was? Years of hating everything he fucking had! Everything he did! That's what a life here gave him!'

She walked towards the living-room door. 'You fucking disgust me.'

'If you'd seen his face you wouldn't say that to me – *you'd understand why I didn't want a fucking life here!*'

He stared at her across the stillness, the trail of his words falling between.

'. . . You came . . .' she stared into his face, 'to tell me that . . . that you were right. To leave me, you were right.' Many expressions caught her features, of acidity, disbelief, humour. All fell down to sadness. He saw it twist her up. He looked at her and both of them were torn by the thing he'd chosen to do tonight. Outside, in Ynys-morlan's empty road, though, the memory of what Lennie had told him lay in the reflections of every dark windowpane; the café's; the changes there already a stalled vision behind all that shadowed glass. It was everywhere in this town, Lennie's story. You couldn't escape it, not staying.

He looked at Bethan through everything, through the hatred that he'd put on her face. Through his own, in this warmly lit room. He looked through the last two years to her, only hoping that she saw it in him. 'Been sitting at home thinking of this place all night, all last night, all the last three days, deciding about seeing you.' His hands lay empty. 'I came to ask you . . . to come with me.' Through every doubt and anger, he stared at her. 'I came to ask you to leave with me . . . Tonight.'

Dai spread the pieces of the gift shop out across the ground. He picked them up, each of them, put them together and moved them, rearranged them. In the darkness, their touches were rough. They made no shapes with any sense but he repositioned them anyway: broken plaster, bits of wall, the timber that had lain beneath them, half slates that had once held the shine of the sky in even, perfect lines. There was a debris of confusion behind him, a past he'd never understood. He stood in this cold night with its pieces held in his hands.

He slit open the bags of cement and sand set ready with his thumbnail.

The plan would come to him. It had to. Because this was his place in the project. He knew it now; Bethan's words had come to rest in him. Remember the part you've had in it, she'd said.

Time wanted to *show* itself, through him.

'You want a life, like,' Rhys said. 'I see you trying to put one together in the café. You want a life? You know what this project's about now. Only thing, *only* thing that offers you a fucking life is the road that gets you out of here.' He took a breath. 'And I want a life,' he said. He gestured to the door. 'No half-measures, like. No fucking half-measures.'

'. . . The road? There's no road . . . that offers me a fucking life with you –'

'You didn't use to say that.'

'You expect me to say yes . . . ?' Hollow voice on the hollowed air.

'Don't expect you to say anything. I don't know what you'll say. I came to ask.'

As if the conversation he'd imagined, and all his beliefs, were so real that they must be real life. He'd always looked at her that way. In bed. Laughing, he'd used to.

'Leave with you.'

'Yes, leave with me.' Everything seemed distant from her. The only thing she could see in that moment was the curving road. 'Maybe before I knew what kind of *person* you were. What kind of decisions you'd make . . .' He sat before her with a desolate stare and that road lay behind his eyes. It always had. 'Maybe before you showed your

true fucking colours!' But what he offered – it wasn't anger she was
left with. It was fear, disconnected as the image of that turning road.
And a fall of pictures then – herself in her dress, turning circles for
Dai. How it would've felt if Rhys had seen her. 'Tonight,' she said.
She nodded. 'And we'd be taking Chelsea with us. Or had you thought,
maybe we'd leave her behind?'

He swallowed. He stared at her. 'Taking her.'

'That's kind of you.'

'I'm giving you a choice . . . That's more than you ever gave me.
A lot more, like . . .'

'A choice to have you *and* have my kid. That's more than you ever
gave me either.' She didn't know really what she said, images seeming
to rise with no reason but fear, coming as she thought of that road:
how it would be if she lost Chelsea. How she would live without her:
a room, empty, where she would stay.

There was no prospect of going with him – this boy with fucking
belief in place of life – but still the silent little visions came.

'Are you happy here, Bethan? You're not fucking happy!'

'I'm happier than I've ever been in my life.' All the hard-won
things – this home and the restaurant behind, her designs – seemed
threatened by the memory of times when she'd thought of leaving.
'This is the place I want to be.'

'*Why* . . . ?' Memories tore suddenly. He heard them in his voice.
Nights when he had asked her that question, long-ago nights, when
the choice before her had still been an open one. 'Tell me *one fucking
reason* why you want to stay here!'

'Because it's my home.'

And she looked at him from it, from the lay of it, the things she'd
made. She looked at him as if Ynys-morlan was a long way behind him
already. It had never been behind; he'd gone with Lennie that night,
though everything in him had told him not to. He stared at her with the
knowledge bare in his eyes: he would have left already if he could have.

'It's my home. You wouldn't know how that feels.' She turned
away from that road. From all the places stretching after its curve.
Dark, as they must be now. Wet with rain, as they must be.

He saw that answer was her last: something settled over her, a soft and bitter look. He had nothing to persuade her with. 'You know what, Beth?' he said, and he stood, every plan he'd made in the nights since he'd seen Lennie falling against that pride on her face. Nothing could get through that, good memories, or blame. 'You know what? It used to be my home as well.'

Dai wandered along this empty road, where rain fell and ran in patterns like the sand beside the shore. He left the gift shop's site behind him, wanting to remember where all this was leading, what that past might rise up towards. He wanted inspiration. In the cold wind of the street, Dai looked up at the houses.

Even dark, he just wanted to see it. He'd remember every tiny second then, when the window had been lit, the way she'd seen him. Bethan Hughes, who'd been the one, of all of them, to look into his eyes when they'd talked, like there was something more than dullness in him. Of all of Ynys-morlan's people, all Time's strands, it was right. He knew it was. What bloomed in him, it felt like tears.

Dai looked towards her window.

'I never took your home away.' Her own voice seemed the distant thing, though it was him, it was him who moved away. 'You did that to yourself, Rhys.'

'You know what you did. You don't need me to tell you. Thank God there's nothing I fucking want here.'

'I know what I did. Spent every night thinking about it! I should do! Back in the days when I still had something to say to you. I know what I did: I lived with what you left me!' Further from her, her own words seemed to travel, and she couldn't grip them.

'But you're happy now, so it's all right. Sitting in the café with Gwen and Siân, like, your mum . . .'

'Fuck you.'

'No, Bethan, fuck you. Fuck *you*. What do they call me, like? Do they call me *him*? Use words like *ignorant*? *Immoral*?' He stared at her. 'Must've been a lot easier for you, hearing that. Easier to believe?'

Insidious, soft light lay over everything between them; things she owned, as if they'd always been shadows of what she'd pretended they were.

'You know what the mayor said to me?' he stared at her. 'Emyr Morgan? Told me I don't belong here. He was right. I don't. With people like them. Not with people like you spend your life with now. Your face is a fucking lie. Two years, it has been and you know it! Maybe they can't see it. They're ignorant! Don't sit here pretending like you can lie to me just the same.'

She was silent. Stone was held behind her eyes like the rubble Dai now walked away from.

Rhys kept a grip on his voice. 'Tell me, Beth, doesn't it prick at you? Doesn't it get you from inside, like when you're not with anyone, when you don't have anyone around to tell you what a fucking bastard I am? When you're lying in here and you can't sleep, does it get to you? Knowing what you did to me?'

'I didn't take anything away from you!'

'Is that what you tell yourself?'

'*Is that what you tell yourself, Rhys?* When you're lying there at night? Is it?'

'*You made the fucking choice!*'

'I didn't have any choice.'

'You made it. You fucking made it.' He couldn't hold on to his voice, his words, any fucking thing any more. He looked at Bethan. 'Change it, like,' he said. 'Change it . . .'

She stared at him with this silence in her throat. In the middle of the night, after two years and no words; he was still the boy she'd known, so full of himself that he spilt into her. 'I wouldn't go with you . . . I wouldn't go anywhere with you now.'

'You had a choice then! You've got one now! Fucking take it!'

'You bastard, Rhys . . .'

This place, Ynys-fucking-morlan, turned around him till he couldn't even stand here.

He raised his face to her and it was cracked. '*Bastard?* You used to know me! *You used to fucking know me!*' He shouted across this room to her. In the silence that fell then, what was left of this town was barren, and no one knew him here.

'I didn't have any choice, Rhys. You left me.'

There were shadows laid out here, of all the nights he'd walked past and had seen its windows from the road. Either dark or lit like this. There were shadows, and the room seemed fragile with them, so clear. All the things she called her own, she seemed to lose a grip on.

'I was *sixteen . . . bitch . . .*' he said.

'So was I.'

'I know that. *I fucking know that . . . Why did you do it to us?*'

'*I didn't have any choice!*' That black curl of the road, she saw. 'You've got no right to say it to me even. I was pregnant! I was *fucking pregnant*! You even know what that means? It's a fucking *baby*, Rhys! It's a child! It's your fucking *daughter*! How dare you say I had a choice!'

'You could have had an abortion.'

Everything in her, every memory sank down through the floor.

'You know . . . you know how you can stand here and say that?' her voice was a rasp. 'Because in the last year and a half that Chelsea's grown from a baby to a toddler, you've never even picked her up to see what her face is like. They're *people*. They're not fucking *mistakes!*'

He saw her beneath the new eyes, though, beneath everything she tried to hold up. There were conversations long past in this silence. When she had used a voice as cold as if he'd been a stranger. There had only been days between them then.

'You could've had one,' he said, 'the person you were then. You made a choice . . . it had nothing to do with the pregnancy.'

All the things he had ever meant to her were written clearly in the light of her new home. And it seemed like the last pieces of that home left her. 'Does this look like a choice?' She couldn't hold on to them. 'Does this look like a choice to you . . . ?' She put her hands out to show him the place where she'd lived for two years and slept with no one. '*You look around and you fucking tell me if it looks like a choice to you!'* And she was standing, everything slipping from her, she was moving to him on the carpet. In her mind, fists came down. She remembered Ruth Lewis, pale and delicate as this room now was around her. 'You want to take a tour?'

And when he didn't answer her, she moved forwards, took his collar in her hand. She pulled at him. She clutched at his jacket with her fingers and nails and she grabbed him up, wrenched him from her floor.

Caught in her eyes, in the hurt there, he moved where she pulled.

Out into the bare-lit hallway where her phone and her book of numbers lay together, so she could never use them with the greatest ease. Past the darkened door to Chelsea's bedroom, where maybe she still slept, or maybe lay and wondered at the sound of a voice she'd never heard. Through the bedroom door she pulled him.

The sketches that she'd drawn, of stained-glass windows, different patterns, different colours, they lay across her bed, still resting in the hours of quiet she had spent there. She looked into Rhys's face and what she lost welled up in her.

'Does this look like a choice to you?' she said. 'Does this place look like my fucking choice? Look! I've got a bed! I've got a stereo! *I've got some fucking clothes! You cunt!'* Her voice fell through the air, into quiet, to settle on each of those things like ash. 'You tell me what my choice was! Run off into the fucking sunset? Become a dancer? Oh yeah, go to London and find my fucking fortune! You know what my choice was? Have an abortion! Have an abortion so I could end up working in Kwik Save in some town where I wouldn't know anybody! *No!*

'You know what I did instead, Rhys? I fucking succeeded at something, I won at something because I had a little girl, because I've got a baby and *she's mine!* She's beautiful. She's *precious,* nothing's ever . . . nothing's ever even *touched* her! *You know why I never had a choice, Rhys? Because my fucking dreams weren't worth as much as she is!'*

'That's what you think . . . ?' Those nights came back, her voice on the phone. Cold as the place outside these rooms now, just as stranded from the past. 'Change it,' he said. 'Fucking change it . . .'

It was over for her, though. There was no struggle in the thought of staying any more.

'And if I said yes, Rhys, if I came with you, would that make it like you never left?'

He looked at her and the rain in him was awash.

'You left me, Bethan. What we wanted, both of us, like, both of us . . . was worth more than fucking anything! Just as much as I left you, you left me!'

'And you came so I'd say yes, and then you'd be forgiven.' What her words held, the place they came from, was not herself. But it wouldn't give out on her and leave her.

'Two years I've been here,' he said, 'seen the way they've looked at me. It's me who should be forgiving you.' But there was a weight in him.

She said for the last time, looking at him, 'I didn't have a choice.'

'An *abortion*! *Weeks* and it would've been over! You could've come with me! *There was a million fucking things we could've done!* You could've made it nothing but fucking weeks! *This wouldn't have been your life! . . . It wouldn't have been mine!*' What he admitted dropped from him, right down to the stone below them.

'You were scared, Rhys. You were just fucking scared, and you know what you were scared of losing? Nights out at the fucking pub. Hardly your higher education, was it? Fucking nights out, that's what you were scared of. D'you know how that looks to me, like? I'm a mother.'

'I didn't want to end up here! *You didn't want to fucking end up here! FUCK!* Go and see Lennie Lewis! *Then come and fucking tell me what I did was wrong!* Have a kid and stay, that was my fucking choice! Lose everything! *I was sixteen! You fucking bitch!*'

'Swear at me, Rhys. Swear at me. Did I not salve your conscience like you expected? Did I not make you feel better?' It seemed to hold years, the sound of her voice, when she wasn't that old. A thousand miles from the place where she had stood when Dai had been looking up at her. 'The only thing you came here for was to be let off!'

'*I don't feel any fucking guilt for you!*'

He moved towards her across this room that tried to push him out. He took her by the shoulders and held her and her face was close enough to put his mouth on hers, or his spit. Her hair touched his cheek.

'Keep telling yourself that,' she whispered. 'When you've gone, and you remember, you tell yourself that: I didn't come with you when you turned up in the middle of the night, when you turned up after two years not speaking, not looking at me when you passed in the street. You tell yourself, Rhys. I didn't come with you! You don't have any guilt to feel!'

It seemed like he was losing some part of himself, his hands still on her while a sea came between. His face was wet and close to hers, twisted up with the last of what he lost. She might have felt it. Some time before, she might have done.

'*I used to love you . . .*' he said, vicious and low. Every word touched her skin.

'No, Rhys. You used to think you did. Then you had to choose. Remember?'

He held her shoulders and his fingers dug into her like every word he'd said tonight could not. And all the hatred rose up in him. That sea took him from parts of himself.

It was Lennie Lewis who came to him as he held her. In himself, he felt the man.

He took his hands back from Bethan's shoulders. He stepped away from her and from everything that this town did to its people. Let the water wash between.

He saw Bethan there in the fraction of light. He told himself some memory was made in that image of her against the bedroom wall. As the rain came again across the windows that he'd looked up at, these two years, Rhys turned away from her and from the doorway, open one dark inch to the place where Chelsea slept.

He saw the brightly lit hallway. Wanted to leave something, some word, that would show he had been here. There was nothing to leave but memories, though.

Rhys closed the door behind him and he left her standing against that wall, breathing them like they could fill the darkened air.

On the 12th of March, Dai Meredith saw Rhys through Bethan's window. Saw him leave through her front door. He stood on the other side of the street with the mute shouts he'd watched pass between them filling his head, and full of sound there. He watched the boy turn without seeing him and walk away down the wind-struck road. Above, the window was dim.

Like the currents that crossed each other, far out from the shoreline, Dai's feelings tore at him. It seemed, as it had never done, all through the time since his mother had first been taken, that the place Time was moving towards was some harbour far away. Through the glass their figures had been blurred as they'd moved to hold each other's arms. Before his feet, rain washed towards the gutters. The thing that Dai might make lay in broken pieces across the demolition site behind him. In that half-blind room, as Rhys had held her, Bethan's face had been obscured, Dai hadn't been able to see her eyes. They were seeing each other, being together again, though.

He didn't know if he had lost Time's path to be given this. It seemed as though he'd never known that he was adrift before. It seemed he'd never known a lot of things. He thought of all those broken remnants, set together to rise up into the sky. A destination, an ending for all this. In the rain that fell round him like a stretch of miles, though, it came to Dai as it had never done before. Maybe Time meant for him to stay at sea.

Bethan picked the drawings up slowly, one by one. In the half-light, they made little sounds.

She remembered, hands stopping for a moment as the silence, that had seemed so soft before Rhys had spoken into it, seemed to touch her skin: standing at the meeting, she remembered, asking Miss Weyland, across the room and every person between them, how much money there was. As if there were two parts of herself, it felt like. The greatest part was desperate. Ruth Lewis beside the woman,

Bethan remembered: wan skin under a fluorescent light. Nerves like grass.

She held the sketches in her hand. One part of her desperate, the other was deadened by a sadness that wouldn't leave her; it felt as if those two parts were tearing her, looking down at the papers. She saw their patterns, sitting now in the memories Rhys had left behind him. She saw their different colours. She wanted them to tear with her. She did not know what would be left.

That night, Gwen Morgan walked into her home, placed her keys on the occasional table where they were always kept, and knew he heard her. Through the living room into the kitchen she moved slowly. Copper pots hung above the oven in their own quiet little gleaming worlds.

Down the kitchen's steps into the cellar she walked, and took from the darkened room, where the smell of wood and of dust was a closer thing to the spring outside than any part of the home above, three old cardboard boxes, unfolded. She climbed the stairs again with them.

From the closet in their bedroom, she took the black plastic bag of clothes that she'd set ready for Aberystwyth RNIB; things bought from catalogues, which hadn't fitted, that had made her feel ugly to an extent which, she'd known, staring into the mirror, could not be real.

She moved with grace out on to the surface of the water. In their living room, before the mantelpiece she stood, with the old clothes and the boxes beside her.

He came to the doorway. He looked at her back; the stiff and delicate curve of her neck. She made no motion, staring at the shelf above the unused fireplace. Porcelain figures in their little groups.

She remembered, the last time that she had driven back from Tom's caravan, looking into Emyr's face and lying, that she had been with Siân. She stood here now with that visit's real memory and no lie: just the answer it had given her.

'Do you remember, Emyr . . . do you remember me changing . . . ?

Did I change?' She only remembered a hollow feeling. It had grown with each achievement, not lessened. With each thing that she'd bought.

'No,' he said behind her. 'I don't remember you changing.'

Whatever selfishness had lain under the ideals, the motivations he had fallen in love with, it must have been there from the beginning, for he remembered no point when he had seen it and, seeing it, loved her less.

She didn't turn to look at him. Tom's face was in her mind. She held on to the beliefs that had always pushed her. She held on to them, though they might now be so obscured by doubts that they were meaningless. Though sadness swept through her, both for their obscurity, and for the things that she'd lost already, trying to keep them clear.

'When someone works for the sake of their community,' she said, 'it's natural . . . wouldn't you say that it's natural for others' better opinions of them to be part of their reason.'

She thought of the photograph on Patty Hughes's wall, the one which had hung there until the last few days. Three of them standing at a wedding, their hats on their heads and their hands on their hats in an April wind, years ago. Looking at the things on the mantelpiece, she remembered a great clarity in the years between, and a great unhappiness too, which had lain unseen beneath them.

'Maybe it's got to be like that,' he said quietly. 'People care what others think of them . . . or the world would be a chaotic place.'

He'd never seen her worry, never heard her talk of worrying that other people thought badly of her. Had that been the start of it then? Her own opinions of herself had always been harsher.

Such a sadness for the things she'd lost, and yet it was goodness still which mattered to her most. She saw the world and there seemed to be absences in it, deep absences that she might fill by doing good. Decorating this house, all these little things, she had felt that space. Just living, waking up in the morning, setting out her three breakfast plates, she had tried to fill it. As if there was a perfection to be found and she might achieve it if she could only align each part of her life.

She didn't remember changing, but these little, well-dusted ornaments had accumulated, and the clothes, every piece of jewellery,
each slowly becoming part of her reflection And she had lost her
friends. Working every day, holding her ideals, she had been alone.

'That's where it comes from, isn't it? Wanting to do the right thing.
Children learn . . . But have you thought, because I've been thinking,
doing good for the sake of others' opinions . . . it's not really doing
good at all.'

He was silent. He looked at the boxes beside her, the full black
plastic bag. 'Maybe – maybe wanting others to think well of them is
the only reason people ever do good, I don't know. I don't know.'

'You don't think . . .' she laughed. He heard it. 'You don't think
that just takes the goodness out of it?'

'No –' There was compassion in his voice that he himself hardly
made out, seeing her there, '. . . I don't think it does.'

Gwen turned to him, neat and beautiful and seeming somehow to
have drawn herself in, as if she might make mess by touching anything.
'It's when the things you've done start to give you a better opinion of
yourself. That's when it stops being right.'

'Maybe . . .'

'It's when you do them for your own self-satisfaction.'

'Yes.'

'So when . . . when trying to do the right thing in your life turns
into being . . . being happy with yourself because you have . . .' here
was Tom's bitter little smile, but her eyes were broken, 'then they're
not the right things any more.'

Emyr didn't answer, seeing her. He couldn't.

'And that's a very thin line. It's the thinnest of lines. It's a moment,'
she said.

He watched her turn away again, put her hand up to a figurine.

The shepherdess in a bonnet who, with curly hair, with blue eyes
and a green dress, was Spring. No rain in the seasons where she lived.

'What are you doing?'

'I'm doing . . . just what it looks like,' she said.

He saw her take from the black plastic bag a skirt, a floral skirt, and wrap the figurine in it. When she had folded the corners, made it as small a parcel as she could, she bent and put it inside the cardboard box.

'You're packing things up.'

She said nothing.

'What are you going to do with them?'

'I'm going to give them away.' She thought of Charlotte Weyland. Smaller gifts seemed better somehow, though.

'To charity.'

'To charity, I suppose.'

'Why? Why would you want to do that?'

'You said . . . you asked me . . . if what I'd worked for all these years was really the community. Or just myself. I want to know. Know where that line is. I'd like to understand how we're meant to live on one side of it. What doing the right thing is if you have to stop yourself from ever congratulating, ever feeling, ever feeling better.'

Wind struck the windows beside them and died. Emyr watched his wife.

He had expected anger. Resentment, and none had come. Some slow and sour implosion as she would have worked in this house, every clink and clatter from the kitchen growing tighter with the selfish drives that he'd prevented from touching the project. Standing in front of him, she seemed younger. Confused. As if she was losing the years she'd collected in these ornaments.

He watched her pack away everything on the mantelpiece except the carriage clock, which belonged to both of them, and the copper component engine he had made when he'd broken his ankle, six, maybe seven, years ago. He saw each movement.

How she allotted herself a space, how she turned and filled it, putting the next thing away. There was some kind of perfection to her – she grew emptier with the room. In other times, long-ago times he remembered reading of, they had considered justice to be a state where everything was acquitted with its opposite. A state of complete-ness, in which nothing exceeded its space to make its own imprint on the world. He saw the perfection in her. Where there had been ambition, there was none now. Where her own needs had been, there was this justice.

'You were right, Emyr,' she said quietly. 'All our projects . . . you were right . . . I never saw them as ours. Do you know why it was? I lost sight of the fact that they were for other people. Otherwise I would have remembered . . . us. Two can do more good than one.'

He stood in silence. Even if she had remembered him then, it would have been for the sake of her work.

'You know, if I'd kept sight of it, we could have done this even. Maybe we could have done all this.' She gestured towards the window and the hill, in darkness, to Ynys-morlan's scaffolding beyond. 'It wasn't selfishness. I know it wasn't. I just lost sight.'

But in selfishness she said these things and waited for his agreement. She had never been alone. He had been with her, every working night.

She turned to him, red-eyed and still. 'What is goodness exactly, if it disappears when you become happier?'

Mute, he only looked at her. He'd expected to see her deception fall away throughout these weeks. It must have been a deception, because he'd loved her.

'I don't know,' he said. 'I don't know what it is then.'

He saw how much she cared, whether that caring was goodness or not. She could give that lemon smile but here she was, a cardboard box next to her and a small pile of clothes from her wardrobe, packing everything away. There was a beauty in her – in each of her drives fulfilled, in the way another rose to take its place. A completeness. How could you not feel love for someone like that?

And as she saw him push away the emotions that were rising, she felt like she was cornered here, all exits gone. Because she hadn't spoken what she most feared. It might be that goodness was sacrifice and happiness just made it wink out. A distant light. Gone. But she had never been happy. This was the truth. She was afraid of it. The things she packed away now, they had never satisfied her. The absences had only grown.

She had driven back here, planning this, Siân's words in her mind.

She had stood in front of the shelves and something better had seemed to lie on the other side of giving away what she owned. She had gently wrapped Autumn, a woman in a russet dress, and Winter and Summertime, put them away. And she could feel it now. A harmony in the room that had never been here. She could feel it. A salve.

Sunlight came to the coast for the first time that spring, as the skies began to break, to reach through the open space where the gift shop's shadow had used to stretch in each morning, and touch, amongst the mud and rubble that lay there now, the first four feet of what Dai had made. The sand and cement lay open beside it, covered by him with a tarpaulin in the night's final grey hour. The shovel that he'd made the mix with leaned against them, where both sun and water were caught in the tarpaulin's crinkling, blue folds. A few frayed clouds, weighted with the last of March's rain, crossed an empty sky that looked down on the clutch of crowded movement that was this little town beside the sea; on its people and its busyness, already long begun, on the JCBs that moved inside the gift shop's barriers where the sound of pneumatic drills broke air and concrete and Dai's work, noted, laughed at and finally ignored by the men who moved here, in this new morning stretched its first height.

The demolition work neared its end; the jackhammered forecourt now a space of unevenly dissected concrete. The ground that they had already pulled the broken pieces from was dust and filth, now drying slowly in the sun. Only two or three days, the contractor told Emyr, until the work was done, and their tools and their barriers would be packed away; the first lorries to leave the town without returning. At the site's edge, hidden from the pavement, from each person who passed, what Dai was making cast its shadow against the barrier's inner face, crooked on sun-pale wood.

It had reached to the height of his stomach when he'd finally stood before it in the receding darkness – the first two feet completed before he'd gone to Bethan's window, and the last after he'd returned.

He'd dug a foundation hole of six feet, two nights ago. He'd filled it with concrete and into the concrete he'd set the metal girders which had once strengthened the shop. He'd been watching. All this work. He'd been learning. It had to have foundations in the ground. The deeper you reached down there, the higher you could reach up.

It began with timber. Laid one length on the next, set to form the face of the hardcore and cement with which he'd surrounded the inner girders. They made the rough shape of a cube against the ground. Like a jigsaw, he'd fitted them together slowly. When he had finished last night, all his feelings and his thoughts a damaged chaos of the belief he'd started with, he'd knelt on the ground and with a wire brush, scrubbed away the excess mess until the wooden lengths were clean. When it was completed, whole, he would varnish them, he'd thought. Staring at it, with the memory of Rhys and Bethan through that glass, the wood had looked guiltless; beautiful to him. The second part, the next two feet, he had stood then slowly to see.

It made a feeling clearer, to build something out of it. You saw what you'd made and felt a kind of love for it that you couldn't for yourself. You wanted to reach out so that you could give that thing compassion.

The second two feet were faced with pieces of broken glass, pressed into the concrete so their surfaces were dark with it and they could not be seen through. Underneath them, he'd set some of the small objects from the skips. A ring, he'd found. A curtain ring, he thought. A piece of window sill that he recognized from leaning, gazing days. Lots of small things, he'd put there. Somewhere inside, they crowded up against the glass, but they couldn't make themselves seen.

He didn't question Time. But this whole part of what he'd made was a question, with no words. He didn't question the place to which it led, or the many places, or its circle but he questioned his place in it. What it was to be lost in it, to believe and still be lost. These little things, they were just tiny pieces of what had been taken away from him. His mum had died so that Time might start these changes. And the destination to which it was moving, he might not have a place there.

He had made a question which held everything to him, so that it couldn't be said in words. And from its roughened top where the innards of cement and debris could be seen, the iron girders reached on up.

Another eight feet, waiting.

★

Emyr came into Ynys-morlan, the sun a white landscape across his glasses. With this breaking weather, he'd begun to make the next calls. If it held then tomorrow the re-roofing would begin. Every slate and frame had already been delivered. He saw their plastic tower in the distance. The walls that had been clad with sea stone were ready, every extension, every garage, their courses ending three inches below the wall-plate, to be finished once the roofs were new above.

Gwen had taken her pictures down from the living room and left only his steam train print beside the kitchen door. The two boxes she had filled were sitting there, as if waiting for work to start on this house as well, after the years it had taken her to perfect it. He had looked into her face this morning and seen the heart of something; the heart of the person she had always been.

This project had to have a heart.

There was no goodness in packing away your possessions but he'd watched – surely the way she was now, no bitterness but only that calm application, that control, surely something deep in it was good. He wanted this project to show the meaning of what he felt. He'd realized, seeing the shelves this morning, how few things he owned. Set between all of hers, he hadn't even been able to see how few they were.

Late at night now, when he sat in his study, deep into the evenings when she slept, he could admit to himself that it felt like communing, to work on this project. To express the love that she'd never given him back, through Ynys-morlan.

A memorial. With the road crews and the public crews, he would work in tandem: organizing so they could build, ordering so they could install. On the business and private renovation grants he would try to do what she would have, visiting people throughout the town and asking for their opinions, their hopes, to make some picture of a perfect place. And the heart he wanted for it – he saw the museum's roof, jutting, shining above the others – the heart of it would show how it mattered, how what he'd given her, though it had never been reciprocated, still had meaning. He would take the things she'd packed away and lay them under a museum's glass.

*

Bethan wasn't in that morning, across the street her curtains were closed, and Patty was alone when Emyr came.

'This is how it'll be,' he said to her, the sixth person he'd seen that morning, and his words were right by then. They were just so. 'This is how it'll be: alongside the older exhibition, the photographs, the artefacts, the fossils – they'll be reclaimed from Aber – we'll put together another. One with greater reference to the community as it stands now, or as it stood before the project. The museum will show . . . a continuum then. The changes that have taken place over the passage of the last century will be . . . represented in a fuller way. It's a sad thing, after all, to have a town museum with no connection for the people living there. And so . . .' He smiled and took his breath, as he had taken it at just this moment, during every other conversation he had given. 'I'm doing the rounds, asking what each member of Ynys-morlan's community might like to contribute to this exhibition. A photograph for instance, or something which might represent to you . . . the change. You know. How the town will be.'

Patty looked at him with the lack of expression that represented both to her. Around them, where they stood in the doorway, in sunlight that had not touched this town for months, the builders worked on in the room that had used to be her café.

'You're going to exhibit people's contributions. The things they give you.'

'I think the project's affected us all enough to justify a collection like that.'

'When did you come up with this?'

'You think it's a silly idea,' he said. He didn't drop his eyes, though. There was a place in him, an open place in which his ideas for the project stretched, white as this first clear day.

'I think people won't make contributions.'

'Will you?'

'You want to exhibit photographs, what? Objects?'

'Depends what people give. I couldn't guess.'

He'd had reactions of anger, incredulity. Like it was an offence to ask. Kate Lowe had left him standing on the garden path while she thumped upstairs and rummaged, to bring back a picture of her parents, standing on the doorstep from which she'd looked at him, though the place in the photograph was not the same.

'I think that's a very sad idea, Emyr,' Pat said finally. Her voice cut the ends off the words. 'That makes it seem very morbid. All of it. Don't you think? They'll sit in cases? You want something?' she said. 'I couldn't think of anything to give you that wouldn't seem morbid to me.'

'Why do you say that, Pat? Surely it should be . . . celebratory. You're not happy?'

'I'm not the one who wants to put the past in display cases.'

'I'm sorry you feel that way . . .'

'Emyr,' she said. 'Oh, I don't know . . .' and she sounded disgusted – felt disgusted – with herself then. 'Maybe people will think it's a *wonderful* idea. Maybe everyone here'll want to go and see a collection like that.' She looked at him but he couldn't understand, and she finished, 'Maybe it's a sweet idea. I don't know.'

'You have a think about it. There's no rush. I know what you're saying. I spoke to Bella just now. She was the same, no one wants to hand over personal things, do they? Gwen'll be putting something in anyway.'

'How's Gwen?' she asked. 'She's not been in. She's all right?'

'She's working, at the playschool, you know.'

Pat nodded, something softer replacing what had been on her face. 'It's been a difficult time for all of us, you know? You tell her, if she fancies a chat, she should come down here. She should come and talk to me. I've got no . . .' But then she only said, 'you tell her that.'

'I will.'

'You tell her to come by,' she called after him as he began to walk away, the sound of her voice fading as she moved back into the café's work-wrecked space, carrying the look of Emyr's empty face back in here with her it seemed, though she'd rather have left it at the door.

The small-paned, handmade windows were ordered. Tomorrow, or the next day, they might come. Thick spirals they had in some panes; the kind to be seen from outside in a winter's night, light coming through. That kind of window. Before her they were constructing the bar. The partition wall had been removed between this room and what had been their kitchen. Backing the building now, having grown up there two feet per day during this last fortnight, a new extension stood. Through the open doorways, Patty saw part of its roofless room. Block walls, utility white, twenty feet long and ten feet wide, stood to collect the rain which had not dried in puddles. Where there had been a backyard – Chelsea's old toys, a shed, a broken cooker and a doorless fridge – there was only this new kitchen now, and enough room for them to keep the rubbish bins. The outside of the new room was clad with sea stones, though there was little enough space to stand and look at it. Perhaps it could be seen from the distance, over the tops of the yard's walls, Patty didn't know. Grey sea stones, small ones, to cover every trace that it was made of blocks.

She looked up at the other doorway and the corridor behind it, that had used to lead through to their home – men re-plastered walls there, so the customers could walk through to the staircase and the restaurant without being offended by any traces that people lived here.

She didn't see Beth coming in through the doorway that Emyr had just left behind. In one arm, Chelsea was wriggling from the wait on the pavement. She had stood as people had passed, watching the conversation.

She listened to her mum describe it after Pat had turned and noticed her – brushing from her expression the moment's quiet which Bethan had walked in on. 'He wants to put people's own things in the museum. You have anything you want to give for that?'

'I can think of eight and a half million things.'

'Well, good. Good. I'm sure he can do without mine in that case.' And then, 'What would you give for that . . . ?'

'You could give the pictures that were up here,' Bethan said. 'You've got them in that box upstairs, I saw them. Maybe that's the sort of thing he means.'

Pat stared at her, the look of being snagged not longer than an instant and the anger in its wake very quick. 'What would *you* give, I asked. I keep those because they mean something to me,' she said, 'not because I want to look at them in a *museum*, all right?'

'Doesn't have to be a sad thing. It's only a sad thing if you think like that. What does it matter?' Bethan said, last night just a pair of grey bags under her eyes now, just a dimness in her face. 'Give it all away.'

On the 18th of March, Ynys-morlan's re-roofing began. On a street dried pale by the eastern wind that came with the first clear days, a thin stream of new traffic moved between the other vehicles. You could see it from the garden outside Emyr's house, where the project's noise was a tiny thing to be caught in fingertips. Seven clear days was the estimate for the re-roofing jobs; the removal of the old tiles, broken in places, worn and green as if the sea air carried more salt than its water; their disposal, their replacement. The towers of purple slate in thin misted plastic, laid out on the tarmac, rose up.

There had been a bench here. Every morning, Dai had been standing in just about the same place as it had done, two ripped-out holes where its little foundations had been set, just big enough to put his foot in and out of. Water had collected in little pools as he'd done it, showing his face when he looked down.

In her home across the street, Ruth Lewis designed new benches. Dai had been staring up at the stacks, the same time each day, exactly. To the minute. Now he came and didn't let his eyes move up to them till it was right to the second. He watched them flick past on his watch and even if someone had spoken to him, he would've ignored them. You had to be touching the pattern, running identical to it like hands pressed palm to palm. If you lived like this surely you couldn't lose Time's path.

Today, though, they began to be disassembled. Transported to the buildings. He stood in just the right spot at just the right time, but the tower was smaller. He didn't know what he was meant to do. He turned, looked about him like a view of the project would guide him, but the van that ferried those slates meandered into the street and was lost between three hundred other vehicles. Every scaffold-braced house looked down into an estuary of work.

Men climbed through the day's first part to stand on the rooftops, clear miniature silhouettes against the paler sky as they began the process. On every building – house, shop, toilet, café, B&B, pub, extension, porch, dormer window and garage – it began. Emyr saw it from the distance.

On the extensions, where old flat roofs had been, the new A frames began to be set in place. Hoisted up with slow, tipping movement, held there by four men on each roof, they were white; new wood in the sun. They were the first structures, the houses with the old extensions, to have walls that reached upwards that week and ended in nothing but bones. Every building: seven days of re-roofing. There would be a few days in the centre for each when their walls would rise up that way.

The gable ends of these extensions had been built upwards. Tarpaulins were taken from makeshift frames and what had been constructed under them could be seen. Where stonework had stopped for tar roofs before, it continued now, in high triangles, free-standing. Equidistant from the A frames that were being set into place, these thin walls stretched into the air, like they should fall, nothing but daylight on each side. The A frames mirrored them in lines between.

From this new peak to the corner of the original house's roof, a ridge beam would then be set: a slim plank running on the points of the A frames to complete a different building's skeleton. You would look at it, not a small, squat house that spilled its extra room into the backyard, but a delicate, L-shaped cottage then, with gable points, echoed in the new peaked frames of its dormer windows. The wind blew between the bare wood, out to the sea, and took away the shouting voices of the workmen.

On every original roof throughout Ynys-morlan, the old tiles' removal was begun. In the upper corner of every tarnished face, on the tops of the Spar's many roofs, in the rows of houses whose old stone chimneys huddled together in the first bare patches made, on the public toilets which stood swamped by stocks of materials, on the

Shoreline Café, Siân Humphries's house, Dai's newly adjoined shops and above the bedrooms of every person who lived in Ynys-morlan, the roofs were taken away.

From the highest points, it started; each old tile lying on the one below. With claw hammers, rusted nails were torn free. The plastic chutes clinging to the houses' faces, between the scaffolding, echoed with the breaking noise of each tile's fall. Three torn free and then the line below could be prised off. From each upper corner, an openness spread outwards as every tile revealed the next to go. Old felt was ripped free to drop soundless down, and land in the skips on top of Ynys-morlan's roofs.

That day, in his spare minutes, Emyr walked between the cars and men to doorsteps. Whether Patty Hughes thought it was morbid or whether she wanted to contribute a bucket full of things, there would be people who did. Or no one even thought that this project was important. Couldn't even see.

He gave his request. People looked at him and the past crossed their faces as if they'd thought they had left it behind. Every kind of memory there was. They said no but he imagined them, later at night when their partners slept and they still woke, looking gradually through their old things. Boxes, cases, however people kept them; from whatever time in their life they thought most of. Cardboard boxes maybe, like the ones in his living room.

Sara J is a fat fucking slag n always will b. I sucked JMs cock and I luv it **Fuck you.** U r a WHORE. *n we fuckin hate u leila* CUNT

All written over itself. So much, you could have unpicked it for years, like hair, Rhys thought, pulling each strand slowly. All the different pens. The words tried to eat each other.

Men unlocked the museum doors to begin work, switched on the floodlights hanging by their cables from old nails. Eyebrows were raised. That was the only reaction.

He'd begun it on a different wall to the one where he'd once written *Ynys-morlan is dead*, looking over his shoulder at its faded letters, thinking of Lennie's description of words that wouldn't hold what you meant by them. And, crouching, turning back to the blank, stained paint in front of him, he'd begun the copying.

Every five minutes, he'd had to go back out to the shelter to make sure he didn't mix them up. He'd tried to get all the handwriting the same. Some of it was round, bubbles instead of dots over the 'i's. Some of it was fat, done with paint. He'd tried to copy it.

About two feet, he'd covered. He'd come in through the ripped window hole at one in the morning, something near it, and it had been light when he'd walked into the road again to see the struggling homes under their scaffolds and the gulls, wheeling to set down on each steel pole.

Now they rebuilt the museum's door and window frames. In the evening, this first clear evening since winter had filled the air, Emyr stood and looked at the beautiful timber, reddened by the west's last light. He didn't go in; the foreman passed him by.

'I want these frames constructed.' He handed the plans over. 'The materials are listed, the cases to run in the four lines indicated. I want them all to be begun simultaneously so there's no chance of the deadline not being met. You understand?'

John Prydd-Jones didn't answer but wrote the word 'Prick' across his face instead.

Emyr didn't care. You couldn't understand his manner – how the way he spoke was justified – unless you had as your responsibility the job of bringing together two hundred and seventy different sites into one project. Chaos it was, unless you kept it clear in your mind. That responsibility was owned by no one but him.

The first real sunset caught in colours this work, indescribable, he thought. Reds and oranges, in the few windowpanes which still looked out from the buildings' faces.

He didn't see what Rhys had done. He only looked upwards when he stood inside the museum. What he felt just pulled his eyes that way. Like Dai looked up at the A frame's towers. Like people were drawn to see the sky when they felt happy, or when they needed to feel it – maybe all the unspoken things in you just drew your eyes that way. A lot of people had ceased to believe in heaven, but the needs hadn't gone away. In Ynys-morlan, the building continued.

Ruth had drawn a circle that sloped down towards its centre, where the fountain would stand; lawn which would be brought in, tied in rolls like carpet, in the back of a single truck. Around its circumference, ash trees, twenty years grown, would be interspersed with wrought-iron benches. The circumference itself would be of roses, the images of which would be cast in the benches' frames. These specifications had been faxed. The rose beds would hold the circle unbroken. You would sit then, looking at the fountain, its rising water, lit at night and spilling down in a curtain to be drawn up again, and all the roses would lie between you and the fountain with its smooth surrounding sward. She wanted to see it lit in the evening and not be able to walk down to it.

She drove through the reaching evening to Charlotte Weyland's white stone home, an unclear shape against the pallid western sky. Nia, next to her in the twilight, shifted her hands on the seat belt like little animals as she saw the gates approach, her eyes wide to the dusk and the house.

Ruth parked in silence outside it, seeing its doorway with memories of autumn mornings; thinking of her own home as they'd left it tonight, unoccupied, uninhabitable, its upper rooms doused with fungicide.

The treatment of the rot began. She'd held a paper mask over her mouth, walking slowly upstairs. In the room where Charlotte had kissed her, a stretching hole now ate away one corner of the ceiling, tarpaulin nailed to cover it, and when she'd gradually worked the nails free, Lennie's own claw hammer in her hand, there was a reach of blue, star-bitter sky in the place where her gaze had used to lie, looking up as she had lain in bed.

She didn't know what she had driven towards, sitting with Nia in the quiet car as the wind stalked through the evening outside, but whatever came now was her choice. The pale skin of Charlotte's arm as she'd moved to touch her own, Ruth remembered. She had asked herself what she wanted, hearing Nia's soft movements as they'd driven in the near-dark. She'd found no answer but the same rush of emotion that came to her now when she envisaged the town completed. No clear knowledge. But it was hope, that emotion; wanting. She looked out at the doorway and told herself that it wasn't wrong, just because she was unsure. That she deserved this. That she wouldn't hurt the woman who sat in silence behind these blue stone walls – listening as the half-heard car's engine died.

Their faces were vague when Charlotte opened the door to them. There was a silence. She said, 'You came,' and gave a smile.

The house was lit, as Ruth hadn't seen it before; bright in every corner with the lamps' glow, all its curtained windows dark. She walked with Nia's hand tight in her own, into rooms which were waiting for them. It was clear to see: they'd never been arranged like this before. On a table in the living room, beside the couch, fruit was set out and a bottle of wine.

She looked at Charlotte, a glimpse exchanged as Nia moved below them. And while they sat, the town very distant from this room's welcome, the girl pattered on the rug between them with fussing hands, picking things up and leaving them scattered, eyes everywhere but on the adults' faces – motions that Ruth knew too well as precursors to worse behaviour. Unspeaking, she sat though, casting glances at her daughter, unable to forestall Nia as in the quiet, she and Charlotte stood alone.

She had hardly been able to look at her daughter, driving here. Her eyes had slipped away from her as if from memories of the night she and Charlotte had already spent.

'They began the treatment then?'

'This morning. On schedule. Tomorrow afternoon, we can go back.'

Wine glasses in her hands, Charlotte saw them sitting here, wondering if Ruth meant herself and her daughter, or if her husband also was included in that 'we'. In the light of all these lamps which she'd switched on one by one as she had waited, the sight of them was a reflection of images she had thought of, planning the interiors of the houses in this last week.

'You came –' Charlotte saw Nia stirring on the floor, putting her palms on the glass table's surface and underneath, looking up through it, '– without any problems then.'

'No problems.' And Ruth herself stirred.

'I wasn't sure you would –'

'I said I would, though.'

Charlotte nodded slightly, she took in Ruth's gaze. The decision there had been made already and Ruth held it out to be seen. After a minute Charlotte took the glasses and sat on the couch, a few feet from Ruth as Nia fidgeted beside them.

'Where is he staying?'

'I don't know.' On the table, Nia's hands went up and down with bumpier sounds. 'I don't care.'

After a few seconds Charlotte turned away, the sound of the pouring wine was clear. 'He knows where you're staying?'

'There is only here.' Then Ruth finished, 'He knows. I told him.' Her hand moved out but could not reach Nia's hair to quiet her. Caught between the two, Ruth only sat.

Behind them, her home lay static, unlit, and she didn't know where he was. In twenty-four hours the treatment would be over; all the demolition and the scouring, and only the rebuilding would then be left.

'He's not going to come here.'

'You understand why I'd be concerned.'

'He'd never come up here.'

She gave silence, though she didn't want to, turning, handing Ruth a glass. It was not herself she was concerned for. Nia moved on the carpet next to them.

'Where do you think he'll go?'

'I don't care – said it because I mean it. Haven't thought about it. I don't care.'

Charlotte said nothing. This room seemed to be waiting still, though they'd come, though Ruth took the glass from her hand, and gave each response without hesitation.

'I told him I didn't.'

'That you didn't care?' Charlotte asked. 'He couldn't have taken that well.'

'I don't care how he takes anything.' Beside her, Nia shuffled and her hands counted the quiet with their growing patter-pat-pat. 'If I did, I wouldn't have come. Nia –' She reached out again but couldn't touch her without getting up. 'Nia!' She stood, put her hand on Nia's shoulder and the girl broke with the turn towards her, hand lashing out. She hit Ruth's arm, and for a moment then there was no other movement.

Charlotte saw the quick scatter of wine from Ruth's glass on to the floor. As if all the girl's motions hadn't been play at all but some little combat which she shared with her mother. Charlotte saw anger drain from Nia's face, down to obdurate resentment that, seen, Ruth moved away from; backing to sit on the couch again as if this was the spot her daughter designated for her.

The instant had come and had ended in three breaths and, as Nia moved across to her, sitting at Charlotte's feet, pulling her sleeve as if playing with something as inanimate as every other toy she had, Charlotte was left looking at Ruth's expression with the memory of that sudden hate like an echo in the silence.

As she might have done in the same way many times before, Ruth dropped her eyes, gathered herself. 'She's been worse recently . . .'

Charlotte looked at Nia. Hesitantly, she put her hand on to the girl's shoulder. Though Nia pretended to ignore everything – the touch – she was stiff. Ruth's voiceless moments filled the room. It seemed as though Charlotte caught a memory that years had separated from her. Nia didn't move under her fingertips. Somewhere in the past, where Hedera's rooms still lay arranged with the possessions she had now sold, where they still sounded with her footsteps, somewhere back there a girl was touched, as she moved her hand to Nia's hair. A girl was touched, who'd never been. Not without hate rising up in her, so scared she wasn't loved.

Nia moved her fingers in the rug.

'He won't come here,' Charlotte said.

'I hope you don't believe that I'd . . . that I'd put you in danger. I left the house before he got back. Last night I told him where I'd be. He's not the same person he was. There's no danger in him.'

Charlotte didn't know the recent days, whose shape touched that expression. She saw Ruth was telling what she thought was the truth. She saw the confusion, though, that she hadn't left behind in the dark as she'd left her empty house. She didn't know what future might be in Ruth's mind – or what kept that expression at war.

Sitting before her, Ruth held it there to be seen, as if she wanted to hide nothing, Nia moving away from her mother across the floor to sit instead by her friend. Or lover. In the silence, Charlotte looked into Ruth's face. Confusion, yes. But she hadn't come to hide.

'Go wherever you want,' she'd said. 'Do whatever you want.'

'Sleep on the ground,' she'd said. 'I don't care. Sleep on the beach.' Rain had still battered at the windows then. 'Take that fucking face,' she had been screaming, 'take that fucking voice and you stay out in the road for all I care. You understand? *Do you understand?*'

'Yes I understand!' He'd been screaming too, and there'd been pain in what he said, 'I don't blame you! I don't blame you! I'll sleep in the street! It's what I fucking deserve – I'll sleep there!'

'I hate you! *I fucking hate you!*'

'I know you do . . .'

His arms had been open. All the things she'd said, he'd brought them in. On her face, his eyes had been open and never blinking and never turning to an easier place. There had been passion in the way she'd looked at him. She'd truly seen him as she'd never done. These last nights, there had been no glass between them.

Sometimes she hit him now. When words failed her or she needed more than them; across his face with bitter palms, on his arms or body, ineffectual. Sometimes she took up his hands to try and make him hit her. He'd only hold himself away from her. What he gave back to her in these moments felt like love. It was unsealed like that. It had that weakness. Every other thing stolen by the sight of her.

Whether she was trying to punish him, or herself, he didn't know. She'd said to him she felt afraid of everything; that this was what he'd done to her. Afraid of shadows, sudden movements, afraid of herself in the dark. It was the worst part, this, she'd said: to lie in safety and still be afraid, like he owned some part of her she couldn't take out of herself. She tried to make him hit her. Maybe then she'd have a reason for the fear.

Ruth sat, letting Charlotte look into her eyes as though she had nothing concealed. And on his front step, in the cleanest of dark air, Lennie unscrewed a bottle and stared up at the back sky's map. Behind him as he drank and let the bottle sit, the fungicide in the upper rooms worked slowly, deadening that dry rot inch by inch. Tomorrow, they would come to clean the walls and there'd be no infection there; they would be ready to re-plaster, to repaint. Lennie looked over the street, and he seemed to see it as he'd never done.

'I remember this one time,' she had said, 'when you were doing the Stockport route. You hated it so much. Coming home, saying it was what you deserved, how you were never going to do any different work. I remember, see? All of it, everything you've ever said . . . Trying to make yourself feel worse.'

She pushed the things he'd done into his face. He was appalled and marvelled at the change in her. There was some kind of triumph in her face as she looked at him now. Maybe this woman had always been there, maybe he'd forced her out. He didn't know.

'"What do you want to be with me for?" you were saying, like. We were upstairs, you picked up this photo of us. You remember the one? The one with the silver frame, like in bluebells. You remember the one . . . "You want to stay with me?" you were going. You know what you were saying?' She'd shaken her head, and her hands had shaken. '"You must like it," you were saying. "Must be sick to keep with me. You must like it. You must like it."'

It was true. He remembered vaguely; images that had never been clear to him were spelled out by her words. It hurt to remember, like a kind of embrace. All the things she said he took in. There was this strength in her. Even hateful, it gave her a kind of beauty. Freedom from him, that was what it was.

'Every word you've ever said, I can hear them all. You did that: you got unhappy about who you were, you got . . . hating yourself, and you made things worse . . . pushed yourself out there! That's what you did! Further from me, further off from being happy! Why did you do that, Lennie? You tell me, why did you do that? You wanted to punish yourself? Because you hated yourself?' He'd seen a tearing on her face and thought it looked like empathy. 'Or is it . . . you think the farther you push yourself away, the more you ruin . . . if you just damage everything . . . it'll have to be me to pull you back?'

He had remembered that night: shoving her back, back until she struck the bedroom wall. Shoving her against it then. 'Both maybe.' Standing there she had shouted at him and, as her shouts had dried, as she'd begun to cry instead like she often did now, his hands had still been held out. 'Both,' he had said.

She was disconnected from this house now, and from him; that was the beauty in her. That was the violence as well, though, he thought. As if its rooms had held both down. She had kept herself between the painstakingly arrayed ornaments. Now they were gone and there was nothing left to hold her in. She looked at him with more reality in her eyes than she ever had. Knew him now. They were brutal and somehow liberated. Free-standing here, Ruth chose to stay.

The wind strayed between the buildings, washed his face and anaesthetized him. Tomorrow all the wrecking in their house would be over. He sat hearing every word of hers again. He sat looking out, at the last parts of the town he'd known.

These things had happened. In the dark of one night she'd gone up to the room where he slept and she had taken off her clothes. She had kissed him and hurt his cheek with her nails. Alone and with no warning, Ruth had made him want her. With no light, not letting him see her face, she had taken his cock in her hand and pushed it inside herself. Holding him down, she'd put her fingernails in the skin of his shoulders and had made him come. She'd pressed her hands over his mouth and nose, and when the contraction of his back had released and he'd lain there below her, empty, she had taken all of herself away from him. Every touch of every part of their bodies she'd taken, to leave even his skin needing her in the dark.

These things had happened. Charlotte stared into her face. Open-eyed, Ruth didn't look away. She wanted to hate him. It was nothing more than that. You could see, there was pain in every memory she had of this last week. She didn't need him.

Charlotte saw her, not dressed as usual in her neat, sweet clothes but in a shirt and jeans, as she'd been when she'd come here with her daughter to empty the garden that was black outside now.

Nia sat in silence below them and they found nothing to say, like she held their missing words.

'You have to leave him,' Charlotte started, almost inaudibly. 'You know that, don't you? Not for any other reason . . . than your own safety. Your own physical safety.'

Ruth's eyes were for an instant turned away. 'Of course I know.'

'You told him you didn't care where he slept, you're pushing him. You don't know what kind of reactions that might provoke. Do you understand?'

Ruth held the glass in her hand while this soft lamplight lay on everything around her as if too bright for her to look up into. 'Of course I understand. You don't need to tell me. I'm not in danger any more.'

'A week ago, I came to your house and your face was swollen to this – It's only now that you look anything like yourself. You're . . . in danger.'

And what was Ruth to tell her, her eyes on the floor? That she had asked him that night to hit her. She wanted to hurt him – but she didn't need him. She couldn't make Charlotte understand that. 'Have you lived in my house?' she said, her voice quiet. 'Do you know him?'

'Can anyone know a man who's capable of what he's done?'

Self-hatred was clear in the words, 'I know him.' Strands of hair hung round her face and her jaw was tight. Pale eyes caught the lamplight, Charlotte saw, and did not give it back.

'Ruth –' she struggled, 'for your own safety . . . your own sake . . .'
It might have been the truth.

Ruth looked up. She didn't love him. But she couldn't do without
the escape. There was shame, there was terrible guilt; a different
country lay on the other side of leaving him. Charlotte couldn't
understand. How she was afraid it had been her who'd caused the
violence. She needed him to prove it wasn't so.

'You have to leave him.'

Seeing Charlotte's conflict, for the first time since their night, Ruth
tried to touch her; moved forward and put her hand on hers.

It didn't seem like anything could be hidden in her eyes, Charlotte
thought; there was too much hurt in them.

'There's nothing he could do that would make me scared of him
now.'

But Charlotte couldn't believe her. And if she had, would it have
brought relief? Was it really for Ruth's sake she'd said it? 'What about
Nia? It can't be safe for a girl of her age, with a man like that. He gets
drunk . . . I've seen what he's capable of when he's sober – think of
Nia –'

'You don't believe I think of her?'

'No, I didn't say that.'

'You think I'd let her to stay somewhere she was in danger?'

On Charlotte's own, Ruth's hand was still then.

'But you can't judge the situation. No one can.'

'I can't believe,' her voice was low, 'I can't believe that you'd care
for someone who you think would put their own child in danger just
to – to what? – to not leave? Not face . . . being scared? Is that what
you think of me?'

'No . . .' Charlotte shook her head. She'd come back to this volun-
tarily. There might have been people in her life who she could have
loved, who would have returned it, simple, complete. She'd chosen
this.

'What kind of person does that make you?' Ruth was saying,
incredulity in her eyes, 'to care for me, if I'd do that . . . ?'

No answer, she only shook her head.

'If you think . . . I can't leave him when my daughter's in danger, how can you believe I'll *ever* leave him?'

'Because you're changing.'

'You can't believe that, obviously!'

'You've been changing since I met you . . .' Through thick silence her voice came, through her own doubt. 'You're a different person than you were then.' *Because you have me,* she wanted to say. But she couldn't look at the expression Ruth wore and believe they had each other.

'How do you know I'm different? You don't.'

'I see it in you . . . every day.'

'You haven't seen me with him! You think I'm a victim? Think I'll be safe when I'm free of him? A victim's not the sort of person who puts their own daughter in danger! And I'm the one who stayed. Three years. Does that make me a victim?' She took her hand from Charlotte's, shaking slightly in the soft light. 'Didn't leave him then.' Her voice quivered, she didn't know what she was trying to prove. She pushed herself further out as Lennie had once done. 'Makes me an accomplice, not a victim.' She thought of how she screamed at him, as she never had through the three years, shoving at him till she thought he had to lash out – and him, never lashing out. While he hit her, she must be innocent. 'And where would you suggest I go? Should I come here?'

Watching her, feeling Nia tighten under her other hand, Charlotte reached out, could say nothing.

'Is that what you suggest?'

'Anywhere where you're both safe . . .'

'You think you want me here? You don't even know who I am. You think . . . because you touched me, you know? Maybe he knows me then. A lot better, he's touched me far more . . .' She wasn't sure what she was saying. This room and all the things that Charlotte had laid out here for them seemed far away. Seen through glass now.

Not speaking, Charlotte only stared at her. The woman she'd first seen that night, bitter, unreachable, she was so close under the surface that she must be the truth.

'You want me?' she was asking, laughing. 'You don't want me here!'

Tight underneath Charlotte's hand, her daughter watched, arms round her knees, immobile.

'*Look at me!* You think you want this here? You don't even know me. Just because – just because you *touch* me? You think I'm a good person. Why, because I cry? Because he hurt me? Doesn't make me a good person! Believe me! *You don't want me here!* I'll hurt you,' she nodded, her words dropped, each a fall below the last. 'I'll hurt you. Look. You see? See the expression on your face? . . . That's what I am . . .' She turned her eyes away and left Charlotte, with no ability to answer – seeing the person she had fallen in love with.

'You see?' Ruth said, and then with no space between, 'I'm sorry.'

Captured, robbed, Charlotte looked back at her.

'I'm sorry, I'm sorry. You see? I'm sorry . . .' She saw Ruth put a hand over her face. The words punctuated the silence.

Charlotte remembered Ruth's story: a house left by a father in the morning, just as usual. And a room full of the boxes of his things, never locked but forbidden. She saw how Ruth had tried to change that house, and how she had only led herself back to silent, flawless rooms. Pretence.

'I'm sorry . . .' she heard her say.

But this could never have been easy. Ruth couldn't magically be happy. Surely you didn't always have to chase in these circles. Surely they could make somewhere else.

'*I'm sorry* . . .' Ruth faced her, moved across the space between and put her hand on Charlotte's own again. And Charlotte let it stay there.

Ruth said, 'I don't want to hurt you, I won't again. I love you.'

In the new and frailer quiet, here were the words.

'Do you . . . do you believe me? When I say that? I love you.'

She looked at Ruth and memories tumbled from her eyes that didn't leave her free.

The words were senseless, as they'd been in Hedera, but she'd waited since she'd left that place to hear them said again.

*

When Rhys went to Lennie Lewis and found him, a silhouette in the streetlight which lay across the doorstep, a shape there, with the bottle in his hand, looking out and over and staring on it seemed, the town around them was a different place than on the last night they'd walked through it. He'd hated it then, no confusion and no fucking doubt.

Round the unfinished buildings the wind walked its miles. The details, the words, he'd shouted at Bethan were half remembered. Only the feel of them was clear. Hating this place and hating how it had been taken from him. As if Lennie's story had been built of the thoughts that had first made him leave that girl, pregnant. To the life she chose. And leave himself without a home that he could believe in; leave him on this road, unable to stay.

It didn't matter who he talked or listened to. There wasn't any decision left in it: he would finish what he'd started on the wall in the museum and then he'd go. The last couple of weeks – whatever he was – fucking wifebeater if it was that – it couldn't matter that he wanted to see Lennie.

He stood outside the gate and Lennie saw him, the ruined garden path between them, with a smile on his face as he recognized Rhys, a grim one. He held the bottle out like an old joke.

Though Rhys had come to find him here, it took a moment to open the gate – to walk towards the lightless house and take the bottle from him. Mud was under his shoes. He looked at the shifting whisky for a second and then drank, as though there'd been no hesitation.

In the night quiet, Lennie said, 'They're treating the dry rot. Upstairs, it is. In all the rooms up there. Poisoning it.'

'Where's your wife?'

'My wife's somewhere else.'

'Your kid?'

'Is with her.' Lennie smiled as he looked up. Though they might be gone and this home empty, him drunk on its doorstep, there was something real in the smile. Rhys saw it, how it caught the shadows on his face into an expression that was something like liberty as he asked, 'Want to have a walk?'

As he'd known it would, that look made something whole out of the things Rhys felt.

It wasn't anything that fitted with the town where he'd grown up, or with the one that would stand here soon. Maybe it was only this half-built place that it matched, where the houses' walls didn't end in roofs but in timber, where the past seemed to lie exhumed, in the rattling window holes or the boxes of people's things set aside in corners, waiting for the future. Some time in the past when Ynys-morlan hadn't been the place Rhys hated.

She took Nia to bed, into the small room that Charlotte had made up for her; a duvet on the sofa in there, beneath the books that lined the walls. She kissed her once as she set her into it, stroked her hair. She was unable to look at her for long, unable to hold all the things that Nia meant to her, without deserting them. Closing the door.

She came back through the corridor to stand in the doorway where music now played. Charlotte held her glass. She felt Ruth come in but didn't look up. Ruth knew she felt it, but didn't speak.

'My wife's having all my old man's work taken down. Everything he built. No restoration.'

Rhys didn't answer, but remembered how much hate there'd been on Bethan's face as she'd laughed at him and chosen to stay this second time. Nothing they built could offer a way to keep hold of both yourself and this place. After some time, he said, 'His stuff wouldn't fit with what they're making here anyway. A place like they're fucking . . . so keen on living in, just make his stuff into fucking . . . memories, nothing more.'

'But it's never been more, has it? Not to me, like. And whatever they're building, whatever this place is in two months' time or ten years . . . it's more than just a memory to me right now. That's a fucking precious thing.' Rhys watched as Lennie pointed a finger out at the blackened street. There seemed to be no past here, no future but just a moment: frozen in the throes of building. 'Most fucking precious thing I ever had.'

'How's that then?' his voice was quiet.

'I begin to understand what that look was on my old man's face when he told me . . . how he put up that flag.'

The shapes of the buildings, the fingers of their frames under plastic and the half-built reaches of their roofs, they came up from the road and seemed to stretch on, to where the moon hung still despite this wind. Lennie had played rugby in the road here, when he'd been younger than Rhys, in front of these shops that were sites now.

Rhys watched his face, some discovery there.

'He took me down there in the van, like. We sat in the back, with it open . . . He was getting to look fucking old by then. Looking back . . . later on, you could see how he was ill. But he was telling me, pretty much like I told you, he was telling me. He . . . was remembering, and there was a . . . grimness to him. He knew what he'd done. I bet he remembered,' Lennie, in the blue light, had his own memories now, with Ruth's voice in his head. 'Every ugly fucking nasty moment of it, I bet he had them like crystal. There was a grimness, like. But there wasn't any fucking regret. He knew what he'd done, and he knew what he'd got out of doing it. Not just his wife. But the way he felt about her. The way he felt about the world, everything in it. Freedom, like. That's what it was. Fucking freedom. What he'd done was worth it.'

Rhys heard. There were things that should've filled the lack this town had given, and freedom was one, he imagined. There was no fucking resonance in Ynys-morlan now, but standing with Lennie Lewis, Rhys searched inside himself and couldn't keep lying any more – believing there was nothing to love in a sense of home.

They sat on the seawall with the wind against their backs, the moon's light scattered across the water and no horizon, as Lennie told him what he'd discovered through the last days. The town was a dark, reaching mess behind as he described breaking down his old man's work; just breaking down. Ruth had told him, he said, as if it was a weapon, that he didn't even know what this project meant. No creativity for him.

'Fucking bullshit, horseshit . . .' And shaking his head, he moved the bottle to show the fall of what Ruth had said, down to the truth. 'Creativity,' he said. 'Only touching something, that's all it is. You got inside like.' He looked at Rhys and put a hand to his own temple, meaning the sadness and the release that was in his face. 'And then there's outside.' He raised his arms and on the one side of him, Ynys-morlan lay, and on the other side, the tide. He heard its sound, wetting the cold stones of the beach below him as he said, 'You got the fucking line between, like. "Creativity", it's just crossing it, that's all.' His blue finger in the last thin reach of the moon's light pointed towards Rhys as he said, 'Can cross it by making things, I see that . . .' he said. The roofs rose, full of holes. 'But you can cross it by breaking just as easily. Just as . . . fully.' He turned and looked out at the water. 'Maybe . . . for some people, it's always breaking. Can only be.' His voice was dim as he remembered: his father's images. So clear they'd been, passed over to him, that he still lived in them. Pictures of breaking – all they were really. Though the lights had swelled to a size that had taken the breath and carried it up there with them, though they'd grown to look like flowers in the night, it was only breaking: to kill a man and put him in the ground. 'The last week . . .' he said, '. . . I gave up last time I saw you, boy, gave *it* up. The last week . . . it came back to me,' he finished softly. The water moved in patterns, rhythms that never left you here, and he could find no other way to put it. 'I *believed*. I believed in it before. This week, I had it,' he said.

He looked at Rhys, and Rhys saw him from the distance, full of his own sadness from this last week, but it was care in his eyes. It wasn't even what Lennie said maybe. A place was conjured by his voice. Hearing him long enough, it seemed it might even be this place, this shore where they sat now.

'You know what did that?' Lennie said.

'Admitting . . . this town, like, you said to me you never loved it. Admitting.'

He stared at the place before them: the stones gave way to sand, tranquil where the marks and runnels of caterpillar tyres had been.

'Hearing Ruth, like,' he answered over what Rhys had said. 'Things she's told me.' There was some feeling in the sight of what she did now – he couldn't explain it for it was mixed up with all the wrongs, but he'd looked for it all his life. 'Maybe,' he said, 'it's just that you need to break things to cross the line. To touch a place. To touch a person. Anything.'

Though she needed Lennie, it wasn't love between them.

She crossed the room towards Charlotte. She sat down on the couch beside her and they looked at each other, the past in Charlotte's eyes. Ruth leaned slowly in to her, and it seemed like she might touch it, so clear there. Its images might have spilled and shattered.

'Do you trust me?' Ruth said.

Though she didn't want to, she answered truthfully, 'No . . .'

'Do you love me then . . . ?'

'Yes,' she said. And she let Ruth come closer.

Ruth kissed her, so different to the way they'd kissed before, in an empty room cast with the shadows of other broken nights. This was a light and tremulous kiss; it might have been broken easily itself. Ruth's hand rested on her knee and Charlotte raised her own to Ruth's hair, not quite touching, a seam of air between. Their figures were turned to each other on the sofa, all the windows dark around them in a careful and uncluttered room. Her hair whispered when Charlotte touched it.

Ruth's breath came and in reciprocation – she couldn't stop it – the breath swelled in her too.

'Nothing . . . nothing you don't want. I promise,' Charlotte said. 'And nothing that I don't. Will you promise me?'

Ruth nodded.

These things meant nothing maybe, for a person can promise and still what they want – call it love, that wanting, or anything – it can break promises. But Charlotte needed them.

It wasn't love between her and her husband now, but it was something that had never been there before. It was desperate. If Charlotte had made her choose, she didn't know if she could have let it go. She couldn't face the thought of happiness. The things she'd allowed, they'd made her hate herself. It was only here, with Lennie in the town behind her waiting, that she was free enough to do this. To talk about love or try to create it. Though the things that Lennie spoke of as he sat beside Rhys – nights when she had hit him or when she'd fucked him – though they'd given him something that he'd wanted all his life, she didn't want them, they hurt her. She didn't want violence in her. Or for it to come out. It was ruining her, but she couldn't give it up.

'I begin to understand what that look was on his face. Maybe . . .' he said, 'there has to be a breaking to feel things like he felt.' He turned to Rhys. He nodded at his own words and what was dawning in his eyes wasn't faith any more, Rhys saw. 'Maybe there's got to be a . . . violence to it. Do you understand? Not . . . not what I've done to her, not that. Not fucking hitting someone because you know the things you want . . . aren't true. But real love, like? Great love. I look at her now, and I loved her. Never loved her before, not like I have . . . seeing her shout at me. She throws things . . . She looks at me, she's trying to give me something. And it's bad. Trying to give it back to me. But she sees me now, same as I see this place now. It hurts. Do you understand? But it feels . . .' he looked at Rhys like he was asking for acquittal, 'it feels freer,' he said.

Rhys didn't know how he could answer. What Lennie had done, it sickened him. But it was this fucking place . . . You saw the words scrawled all over the bus shelter – people who'd already given up on it. He didn't know how he could answer. Other people saw wrongs behind him too. And what Lennie said, it felt true.

'I can see a future,' he told Rhys. The sea sounded below them. 'For the first time, I think about a future here and it's not just . . . greyness . . . In this place, and with Ruth. I see a chance, for all of it. All of it together, after this. The three things. Remember?' he gave a cracked little smile. It fell from him, though, so that he couldn't disguise the hope under it. 'Maybe there has to be a passion, a breaking . . . violence,' he said.

In the darkness, Rhys saw a fuller man.

They finished the bottle on the seawall, where shadows dissipated the line of the coast before them. They stood and turned away from the bay, and this town was a no-man's-land.

Rhys had had no part in touching it. He hated the town. He hated having it taken from him. But it wasn't the Ynys-morlan of Emyr and Gwen Morgan, it wasn't the Ynys-morlan of Bethan's future that it hurt him so badly to lose – of little ways and backs turned, fucking hypocrisy, everything that Ynys-morlan had become – but a different place. Maybe one that had never been. Maybe it was a place you came to by crossing some line, he didn't know. Or if only Lennie could live there, and it wasn't real.

Somewhere that wouldn't force you to give yourself up, give up the things you wanted to believe in. In the dark, Rhys lied, 'I don't believe the things you say.'

He stayed on alone when Rhys had left him, in the burnished sodium and shadow of the street. Saw it all around. Like sunflowers, the street lamps were, and the houses broken walls. He spoke alone, to himself, and he didn't care. He laughed and in the road where he'd used to run – just for the feel of it and the sound of his own heart beating – just for a short time, he ran again.

They took their clothes off in the darkness, separated from each other by the slight air and by the sound of their breathing: Ruth's low and fast and barely kept, Charlotte's quiet, hardly heard. It was cold then and only the faintest light from the windows round the room brushed their outlines. They couldn't be seen.

With the knowledge of her daughter next door like a hand at the back of her mind, Ruth held Charlotte. In the darkness, the woman didn't move. She saw the shape of Ruth, so indistinct that she did not recognize it.

Ruth's hand brushed her waist.

'Do you care for me?' She couldn't stop herself from saying it. 'Not love me, Ruth – do you care for me? Do you care for me?' And she would have asked again if not for the sound of Ruth's voice, very close.

Very close. 'I care for you . . .'

'For me?' she said.

'I need you,' Ruth answered.

'Tell me that.'

'I need you . . .'

'And do you love me?'

'I love you.'

'I love you too,' Charlotte said. She felt her body. They touched: torso and waist and arms then, around them, the scent of skin. In the dark, they moved slowly to the floor. She felt Ruth's shape beside her, a hip, and the slip of her stomach as she lay back. She felt the fear but they were both afraid. So that it seemed like it belonged to neither of them. It must have lain in some other space of this room.

Ruth's hand reached her abdomen and stopped as though the touch was too clear.

'Nothing can hurt you . . . nothing can hurt you,' Charlotte said.

Tiny kisses, she put, all over her neck and the turn of her chin, her collar bone, kisses of gratitude that she didn't know how to stop. They flowed out of her as though in the blackness, each bruise unseen now might have changed, once kissed; might have coalesced and run from Ruth as water.

Through the night, they lay next to each other. They touched each other, slowly and with battles, quickly as if they seemed sometimes to win. When the thought of leaving Lennie came to Ruth, feeling Charlotte's hands, she wanted to strike out at them. They seemed to hurt her, though it was not this woman but her husband who'd done that. She would begin to breathe without control, her body would tighten and, hand on her hair, Charlotte would wait for her. It was a frightening thing to feel. Ruth alone, and tearing at herself. She said things to her, calming her in the dark, which later she wouldn't be able to remember. They lay talking. They couldn't see each other's faces and seemed to trust the words more easily this way.

Charlotte let herself be touched, actions never written of in her journals. They didn't say each other's names. It was some release, to lie in the dark and have no look and have no name, but to be given love by someone.

As the blue of a morning touched every window, as it touched the floor around them, she ran her fingers over the face of the woman beside her. The light rose gradually and Charlotte looked down at her for moments that did not pass. Her hand on her skin, on her arms, that had been hidden, she saw more and more clearly who she kissed.

There were feelings that did not have names, which came with the seasons. Finding a place and feeling, not that it was yours, but that you belonged to it. A home. Finding a person whose connection ran like water in you, like water through your veins. There were feelings of spring which did not have names. There were memories that lay behind and seemed for the first time a part of something complete. Autumn, she thought of, and Hedera.

Charlotte stood in the walled garden and she saw new hair-thin grass. The ground all around it was ugly, blackened still and cracked from when they'd burned it. She stood hugging herself in the cold wind and looking, with no expression of her own on her face, at the garden that had first brought her here. Can a love be different, or a life, or a place, just because you try and make it so? Memories in her mind of a meadow and its long-lost treasure, she looked out. They'd blended without barrier into the memory of her own drawing of it through the years, that first page of that first journal, for she had not gone back. After its discovery, she had never gone back. Her sketch and the image of it had merged together, as if she'd been falling since then and the world had blurred.

She thought of Ruth, of loving Ruth, of loving her daughter Nia. She remembered her own mother as she stared out. The second clear day to touch this coast. March's rains, which had assaulted Ynys-morlan and had held it close, were broken in ragged clouds across a sky that now left them – everyone here – left them for the distance. And Charlotte, seeing it all, seeming to feel seasons grow and die, standing there in that small, brick-walled garden.

On Charlotte Weyland's houses, the removal of the pebble-dash began. The new gable doorways were constructed against walls covered with the render's remains. Across their faces this spread: old stone revealed, dirty with remnants under the shade of the scaffold boards. That week she began plans for the upper floors. She stood and looked at the spaces that would be children's rooms.

The 25th was the day set for the distribution of the compensation cheques. The money would flow out, to leave a space as vacant as these rooms.

People waited, planned what they would buy, they talked about the project's end like it could make up for the chaos. In these houses it was hard to sleep, to cook, to find the kids' clean clothes, the car keys or the photos that you'd had on the walls and put away; to find the memory of what normal life was like. Every shop was shut. No person who worked in town was working now. You couldn't buy a loaf of bread. To make your way out through the stream of traffic that filled the road was a half-hour job. All post was left at the Spar, its back room open for collection. In the morning, you'd go there and find others, passing letters round and trying to pass on the bills; laughing, because there wasn't another way to take this. Clear weather continued and the project went unhindered. Charlotte Weyland prepared her accounts.

Bethan had to let Tom Humphries go from his job. He wasn't a chef and he wouldn't want to be a kitchen porter. She could have laughed, that she hadn't realized. Her mum couldn't keep him on, pay any separate staff for downstairs, so there was no deliberating to be done. She danced into her new career with a few well-disguised mule kicks to anyone in her way. Family? Friends? Fuck them.

In the daylight or when the early nights came in to fill this half-built space with shadows of what would be here, shadows of what had been before, standing here with Chelsea or while Chelsea slept, everything the project offered her seemed threatened by reality, contaminated with it, since the night that Rhys had come. She would see her restaurant, trying to hold on to the picture of what she wanted to make but, like her dress, like all fantasy, it seemed hollow against the real world; gaudy stage make-up, tarty rags.

'I used to love you,' Rhys had said. Hadn't loved her enough to give up what she'd had to, though. The thought of leaving here. Life was full of losses and innocence was the first to go. He hadn't loved her enough to accept that. And any chances for a little bit of that innocence again, people like her had to take them, every one. Because they knew they weren't real, they'd soon be gone. She wore that dress every fucking night. Like Ruth Lewis, she thought, must sit and look at this whole town.

Everything he'd done was half begun and unending. The bus shelter's words across this wall. Drawn over each other while the paint still dripped: filthy things, and what the girls had written the filthiest. Savage things that couldn't help but make you feel sadness. He'd copied them. Inch for inch as similar as he'd been able to make it to the wall they'd leant against so many days. Each name, each fuck and cunt and bitch and slag. How many years' worth, over each other? On the surface of the shelter's walls, the names of kids who had been maybe five or six when he'd still been going to school.

So much hate in them – standing back he had passed a marker pen from hand to hand in the darkened quiet, over and over as if just to fill it with some other motion than his own breathing – so much hate and they didn't even know why they hated. In that silence, every word that had sounded in his head as he'd written, bent and cramped against the wall, would fall back to the noise of his own heartbeat. The museum was empty but for him.

Everything he'd done twisted into some other thing. In these moments he'd be caught by another image, have to start it.

To the left of the graffiti, so carefully copied to look like scrawls – taking minutes when they'd taken moments in the shelter – a picture rose across the museum's stone. It was only an outline so far, only a few colours, but he'd tried to choose them just right, so they'd show the glass, the skin tone. He'd not put any details on, not when he'd started, and he hadn't gone back to it to add them, knowing he wouldn't be able to get them right. Her face. The baby's blanket. He had a clear picture in his head, but what was in your head meant nothing.

The Shoreline Café's name above, he painted, where it'd been visible until just a few weeks ago. The windows that had been there, their frames, which were gone now with polythene across the holes. The quiet. How could you draw quietness? It had lain between her and Ynys-morlan as she'd looked out.

He'd painted the colour of the blankets round the baby. He'd shaded the bottom line of the baby's shape, to show its softness, its weight. He didn't need to draw its face; he hadn't seen it as he'd walked by that day.

In the doorway of the café now, a flap of that same plastic hung in case of rain that didn't come. March moved towards its end with clear days. The door handle, and the edges of the old, bolted tables as you would've seen them through the windows – all the little details were gone now and he couldn't copy them. And the rooms above, the memories of which were years old anyway. The toilet where he remembered standing in silent moments in long nights, when it had seemed like the rest of Ynys-morlan, her parents above them, all the houses outside, might always stay asleep. It felt like the past grew clearer the further it lay from you. He didn't know what kind of changes those rooms had gone through.

They'd started chipping off the pebbledash walls that had made tiny shadows when the light went low in the evenings: every little bump casting one in the same direction as the sun went down.

On the café's exterior, as drills and hammers sounded through tarp-sheeting to reach outside, a thinner noise in daylight, the render beneath that pebbledash was cracked away. The pavement was a mess of its pieces, as it was in front of many houses now. And up on that second storey – pebbledashed and grey-white still where they hadn't reached yet – the windows were being removed.

★

She'd designed nooks for the room, alcoves, set along both end walls. Unable to knock holes in the walls themselves which were supporting stone, they built two new skins. Timbers were set there to form frames where plasterboard would be nailed. Horizontal two-by-two along the floor, covering the old skirting boards, vertical to create wide bars against the stone, they'd begun to build the alcoves' shapes. Like a skeleton, you saw them. She'd thought that when they were finished they could be tiled to match the stained-glass windows, multicoloured. She wanted them for when the sunset ended so the room would still have the different colours. Candles could light them up. She saw clearly how the room would be. White, the tablecloths, the chairs' upholstery, the mosaic that they'd have for the whole top of the bar. Dark reds, deep greens. The floorboards were polished black wood.

She had to let Tom go from his job. She told him in person. You couldn't do that over the phone. As the builders plasterboarded the skin walls' frames, they stood by the windows' naked holes. Perhaps he knew already; walking upstairs, looking round the room, the expression on his face seemed to tell her that he did. She pointed the bar out to him. She described mosaics there.

She began to compile the invoices for furniture and wares in the new accounts book, a black-bound thing that Patty gave her. At nights, they sat and her mum showed her what had to be recorded and how. She worked on completing the dress in any moment spare. Late hours, though Dai didn't come. Standing without a mirror, she had the same look in her eyes that Patty saw each evening, teaching her how her restaurant must be run. There was someone old in her face, waiting to kill her off. The memory of Dai standing down on the road was a perfect little image, caught inside a bubble. She wanted him to come again and hated herself for wanting it. If and when he ever did, she thought, that little picture wouldn't be held at all but would run out and into real life, and they'd see what it really was. It wouldn't be long before the designs for the restaurant were finished. Then the building work would end. The traffic would leave. She'd see that life.

'Looks amazing,' Tom said.

He had walked in through the shattered arch of the café's door, seen the carpenters kneeling, hammering. He'd walked on the joists of the frame that was set across the floor, ready for the parquet. The carpet that had started when you walked through the doorway from the café into their home hadn't been taken up, and had gone grey with bootsteps. There were extra bare bulbs hanging from nails in their wall-papered corridor. Men scowled at him for being in the way. It was a fucking joke. He climbed the stairs and looked at where their hallway had been. He knew before he saw her.

'Moves fast, doesn't it?' she said.

She described the candles on each table, tall vases put along the bar, the flowers she'd have in them, the chairs that she'd ordered and how there'd be no pictures here, just the alcoves she showed him. They were almost completed when he came, the men were plastering.

He nodded, gave her his smile. Glad for her, she saw.

'You can't recognize the place.'

He'd been upstairs here a few times, a lot of them really, when Rhys hadn't for years. They'd used the spare room, which wasn't here any more, for keeping extra equipment – cookware, cutlery, that sort of thing.

He'd left spaces; to the right there was a big one, at the top of the wall and beside the edge of the graffiti. He was starting to decide what should go there now the time he had to finish it was draining down. He'd left one for a picture of Tom.

Sitting on the grass, Rhys remembered him, the wheelbarrow there with all his things in it. The sun had come down on them; the first light that stuff had seen probably, after so long in his room with his red curtains. Maybe he'd been skinning up, Rhys couldn't remember now. The shadow falling across his face, he remembered that.

Halfway down the lane between Ynys-morlan and nowhere. Asked to move out, not wanting to get a flat in town. Been scared to, just as much as Rhys. But he hadn't wanted to leave this place either. Halfway down the road, and though Rhys never saw him, he was still living there now.

Like the sea, this town pulled you back and forwards – in to the shore and far out from it. Ynys-morlan tricked you. You looked out from here and you seemed to see nothing else but water.

'How long's the estimate now, till it's finished?' Tom asked her.

'Till it's ready to open, four weeks.'

'Wouldn't think they could do it all.'

'There's not so much left to do,' she said. 'Wouldn't think they could do it all so fast through the whole town. Would you?' There was silence, though there was never silence here now; she'd come to think of the work's noise as that. 'Paul told me that they'd never have so many men on a job. They've done it on all the sites. Twice as many to get it done on time. April the first, you know, or it's meant to be.'

'That's the date? That's fucking soon.'

'That's the date.' She watched him nod. 'Paul's the carpenter. He's downstairs. The chippie, they call a carpenter. They shout to each other, "Oi, chippie! Oi, sparkie!"'

He nodded again.

'How's the work on your mum's house?'

He smiled sourly but said nothing to her. They'd used to share smiles like that. She didn't know how to answer it now.

'You know, like, why I asked if you'd come in . . .'

'I can guess. I reckon I can guess.' He looked at her and Bethan saw behind his eyes evenings, days, out at the beach, blankets and cider and black. She saw how he let go of them, just opened his hands.

'It's very hard,' she said.

'Course it's hard.'

'We can't have separate staffs for the two. We can't afford that.'

'I knew it'd happen.' He hadn't, though, not until he'd seen this place.

'Going to have to hire someone with a lot of training . . .' she saw his gaze but didn't falter. She'd placed the words out for herself in lines. It would never have been easy. 'There isn't a post. If there was then you'd have it. You know that.'

'I know.' The same wry look. He'd not changed at all, she saw. It wasn't him moving away.

'You wouldn't want to be kitchen porter. Peeling spuds . . . If you tell me you want it, it's yours. The money's shit, though. You don't want it.'

'I don't want it, no.'

'Say if you do.'

'But I don't.'

'OK.'

'How's Chelsea?'

'You know what she did the other day? Walked halfway across the room.'

'Got any more words, like?'

'More than me.'

He smiled again but it was softer, maybe because Chelsea had nothing to do with the past. Or maybe that was just how she saw it. She remembered a lot of nights talking. Weeks after she and Rhys had stopped all contact – eye contact included – she'd ask him how Rhys was. Tom didn't know any more, though. He didn't know how any of them were these days. And they could look into the other's eyes, see the confusions there, but they weren't the same confusions any more.

'What d'you do today then?' he'd ask her.

'Quit the model agency,' she'd say. Something like that. They'd talk about desert island beaches and Russell Crowe. How she was sick of him and all his misunderstood soulful quests.

She hadn't been in to see the changes in the Lion where they'd sat those nights.

'I'm sorry, Tom,' she said.

'I know, yeah.' But he looked away.

She watched him, men passing them as the cold sunlight came against the plastic that covered the windows they stood beside, the wind rattling them, changing the patches of light that they cast across the floor. From downstairs, the bandsaw's noise, falling hammers; from outside, every kind of din. There weren't any other things she needed to say to him. These weeks of creating things, of ideas, they were passing.

'Tom, I'm sorry.'

He just nodded, though.

'You know, like, this has been the best thing for me. A restaurant, you know? Never thought I'd be doing that.'

'I thought you would.'

'Is that so?'

'Yeah,' he said, he looked up at her. 'Could've told you that years ago, that you'd do something big. You know, wherever you did it.'

'It won't be big.' Her voice was quiet as a well-known street. 'Just seems big now.' She couldn't stop the bitterness showing any better than her mother could.

'Wait for the tourist season.'

She didn't answer.

They saw each other, this hard thing between them, that neither of them knew how to remove. She wanted suddenly, in that moment, to tell him about Rhys, how he'd come to her flat and what he'd said to her. How, after two years, he'd come. Asked her to leave with him. And she could've said it and Tom would've known, just knowing the person Rhys was, he would've understood all the feelings tangled up in it for her.

At night-times, she stood in her dress. Waited for Dai Meredith to come. This project was drowning her in opportunity it seemed. Not even Tom would understand now.

'It's been the best fucking thing for me,' she said again. 'Planning this place, all the details. It's been fucking springtime to me, Tom. Never had anything like it . . .' And she said, though she'd said it before, 'I'm sorry . . .'

Whatever it was between them, she tried to hold it in her eyes so he'd see that she remembered.

'Do you – I'm a needy person, can do this, see? and still ask you. If you forgive me.'

He looked at her, this eighteen-year-old who'd been some boy hero and never, not once, matched it again. He'd never got up off the sand. 'Fuck's sake, course I forgive you, like. There's nothing to forgive.'

And now it seemed to him, like Gwen had talked about the last time: good actions were only that when they were fucking sacrifices. All these things, this restaurant, this new town, these things Bethan had taken and built herself a springtime out of – she deserved them. Just like his mother did. He remembered when Siân had sat in front of them all, said she was going to apply. Thought of Pat, who'd been so sure she didn't want this money. He watched them board and leave for the new world, all of them, and lying in his caravan at night, he told himself that what he cared about, doing the right thing, just trying to find it, mattered more.

'There's nothing to say sorry over,' he told her.

He couldn't believe in the goal any more, but remained here anyway, giving a good old adios wave from the fucking beach, watching Bethan and all the rest move away.

In the museum, by torchlight, it had been hard to see the photographs. Finding them here again, he'd remembered breaking the cases that had already been broken, and had looked at them, waterlogged, dried in great patches, and useless to Emyr Morgan or any other person. He'd thought of what Lennie had said. Breaking or making, for you to know a place. Rhys had gone through each photograph.

He remembered all the times he and Beth had talked, agreed, every fucking word, agreed. How they'd leave. Like the slowest kind of suicide, they'd said, to stay. Not hating Ynys-morlan so much as being scared of it. And it was a good enough way to describe what he'd been scared of – to say that you walked and walked here and you never touched the ground, so the place never knew you.

Making or breaking, Lennie'd said. He had broken these. There was something in the pictures – not in the days they'd caught and held but just in the past. Its whole reach. He went through them, remembered picking them up before, not knowing what they were of. Remembered tearing some. And over the yellow-stained paint of the museum wall, he was making now. There was something in the photos – he'd felt some kind of small wonder really – he'd seen a bit of what was missing from the town he'd always known. Wonder and the kind of sadness that leaves you distant, as though across a floodplain from the thing you're staring at. They'd made faint dry sounds.

He hadn't hated Ynys-morlan before he'd left her. Not truthfully. He'd been sixteen, and only hated it like a sixteen-year-old could. Rhys had begun to copy the first of the photos on to the wall. Smaller than Bethan's unfinished outline. Unfinished too. He'd begun all these different pictures, unable to keep them apart. In yellow and brown, he'd started this most recent one: all the figures in the picture and the stones they were clearing away.

It was during that week, half the town covered in his door-to-door request for contributions, that Emyr returned to the museum to check its progress and saw what had been begun across its wall. They hadn't told him. Perhaps, with the painting work still to come, they hadn't thought it important.

Eleven o'clock. The vaulted space reached up to a roof one quarter of which was still missing. He stood long minutes staring. The interior refurbishment would begin in one week. These doors would be locked and these windows boarded, Emyr decided, when that day came.

Paint was not adequate in the removal of graffiti, for most spray-paints were oil based and very rarely were such things written in pale hues; they liked their statements to be seen as clear as could be. They liked their statements to fill the eye. Their emotions were primary colours.

He stood – the longest minutes. Weightless recent nights, his home filled by Gwen's absence, their mantelpiece bare, seemed to amass in him as he studied what Rhys had done. The pictures he saw filled him with a kind of sickness, with dismay. They were of this town.

And as he stood, absorbed them in the echoing room, the memory of a sunlit day, cold tarmac, shaking hands, overtook him: that boy's face – raging and full of shame he couldn't hide – as he'd told Emyr lies.

On the 22nd of March, the gift shop's demolition crew finally completed the work and disassembled their site. Early night set in, lowering winds and diffuse shadows as the crew took their vans from the bare ground and left it. Behind the space that had been the forecourt, what Dai had built was left exposed.

The following morning, the landscaping team arrived to begin. Five vehicles, three trailers. Men climbed out into a clear day and saw the panorama of the project that they'd only heard described. Standing in the place where they'd create the garden which would welcome visitors to this town, they shaded their eyes from the hard spring sun and looked at Ynys-morlan's expanse.

On the Spar, the re-roofing was three days from its end. The laying of new slates was in progress everywhere; on the first rows of houses, the Lewises' among them, on the public toilets opposite and the row of shops in front; Dai's three, on the chemist's, the terrace after that, on almost every property between the flagpole and the development boundary on which the community centre stood. Over the course of the last seven days, changes which had been two months in the making in Ynys-morlan had come to be seen throughout the street. The Spar's pitched angles, half bare in brittle air that continued to dry the winter from the coast, were clad gradually: battening first, felt in dark rolls, hammers sounding, echoes bleeding away in the wind. On every building at varying stages, from a lower corner, upwards, outwards, the finished roofs spread in the same gradual way they'd been made bare. The windows had begun to be delivered and stored in the houses corresponding to their plastic-coated tags. The heap of stones beside the seawall, no longer replenished, would be used to complete the new-clad walls underneath their finished eaves. Those dormer windows rebuilt into gables were covered. Caught inside scaffolding, to be seen in every building and alleyway, a new town was emerging.

What Dai was building, also unfinished, was set back behind the broken space of the forecourt. It was eleven feet high, on land he owned. Turning, talking slowly, as they stood in the place where they'd been commissioned to build a sea-stone fountain, Dai's sculpture, seen finally, didn't even look out of place. From the town to his spire they switched their eyes, and laughed. To see it revealed and understand that it was out of place, you had to know the project, live the project, and its goals.

Emyr had watched the windows delivered and set ready for distribution on the concrete beside the seawall, he had taken the road crew's plan to the landscaping company's foreman, Watt, and checked their schedule against its forthcoming dates. He stood unmoving after the conversation had ended and Watt had been called away. His last thoughts trailed as he saw what Dai was building in the gift shop's empty space. Long minutes, he stood, after Watt had called from a distance, 'You commission that?'

And some other voice, 'Because I could've done it at half the price.'

'No,' he said, as they worked behind him. 'No, it wasn't commissioned by me.'

He heard the sounds, clearest in the project's mass of work, of tools unloaded on to dry ground. At home, far up the hill behind him, where there were no dinner parties or coffee mornings any more, the air-fresheners diffused their scents through naked rooms. Gwen had taken her books from the shelves and packed them into carrier bags. He'd looked through the piles last night. Beautiful picture books, wildlife, interior decoration, gardening. Biographies. Perhaps fifty lives, perhaps more, removed from the bookcases and ready to go on some new journey. Emyr's small collection on the industrial revolution and the copy of *What Shall I Do?* that he'd kept since he was seven now leaned there on their own, and fell over, without Gwen's to keep them in place. She had begun on their bedroom.

She was trying to rediscover herself, her values maybe. He looked into her face and, though something was broken, though she was afraid – beliefs she had cherished gone hollow – he saw that in some way she was succeeding. He saw the core of her. Rising up, right there in her eyes. She put each next thing away. As she had dealt with every obstacle, she now dealt with herself.

'All the work, the gift shop, the community centre, all the charities,' she said, 'I never did it for myself, Emyr.' She had sat with him, talking through the project's new details, two nights ago. 'I didn't do it to bolster myself or any other thing. I had to do it. You must know – what it's like, to be compelled to do things.'

He wasn't sure he had known. Gwen had been that holy grail of engineering, a perpetual motion machine. A motor that needed no fuel. It wasn't necessary to be compelled when you were with her, you only needed to extend your arm and her cogs fed you into your proper place in the machine. No, he wasn't sure that he had known, but he did now. Because the project was his. It was the only thing he had made in life that wasn't just plan, a speech. It was an expression.

A monument to them. To the love they hadn't shared. And Emyr imagined – a boy's wandering thoughts really, but all thoughts were free to wander where they pleased across this landscape now – Emmeline Pankhurst, Mother Teresa, Margaret Thatcher. There had been women throughout history, women dedicated, and there must have been men who had seen them, whose hearts had fallen towards their work. A love like that, perhaps it had to be a pale thing, but beautiful, because it couldn't be returned. In his mind, when he envisaged the project completed, the houses stood alone and empty in their loveliness, as their own did in the evenings now. As he imagined it, the day began, and curved over the street, and ended all in silence. The museum pushed its shining roof above the others and there inside, all Gwen's possessions lay under glass.

'I can see,' she said, and she gestured to the boxes that she had lined up in the hallway now, neat lists of their contents pinned to each, 'I can see it clearly. I look back. I never did it for self-satisfaction.'

He had loved her and she hadn't seen him. But goodness was a thing to love. She had said that maybe it had no meaning if happiness with yourself stopped it being good at all. She'd looked at him and he had remembered, over and over, the things she'd done in these last three seasons that had robbed the truth out of her values. He had tried to hold in his mind all her recent absences – the parched questions that came from them – and let them dry his feelings for her. But now she packed up everything she owned, and that wasn't a 'good' thing, not in itself no, but the *way* she did it. Surely there was purity in it. Separated from Ynys-morlan in the final phase of the greatest work that had ever come here. No hate in her at all. Surely there was a beauty, or why was there love in him?

'I feel better,' she said. 'Everything gone . . .' She had moved her hand and gestured towards the empty bookcase.

She had looked back at Emyr, Tom's name in her throat, his face unseen behind her eyes. It was true that she felt better; peace seemed to lie on these bare surfaces. But doubt under-ran it in strong, transparent currents. Once upon a time, she'd filled the rooms of this house with a thousand decorations in just the same way. It was only that full, they had never satisfied her.

What was goodness if it winked out once you were contented? What was it, if she could look at the eighteen-year-old son of her best friend and feel it in his hands? And this sense of accomplishment that she found as she removed from herself everything success had bought, it was even as the seabed under all its vast and quiet water. And she'd never felt it before.

Didn't that pierce through Siân's view of the past? Even her closest friend, her oldest friend, believed that her prosperity and her years of perfectionism had brought her just that feeling.

Emyr stood with the project around him. What Dai had made rose up above his head. He thought of the words the man used to describe time. He saw in a moment what it had taken Dai months to conceive of. A statue, depicting what he believed. And Dai's aspirations, as Emyr had seen them, were punctured and slowly deflating now. Seldom in his life had he seen such an ugly thing. Reality pierced through the pictures that Dai's faith conjured.

'Time is changing Ynys-morlan,' he'd said, sitting on the gift shop's floor. 'What's starting is time coming here.'

The steel girders around which he had made his column protruded another five feet above its rough end. Its lowest section was made of smooth wooden blocks. Emyr recognized them. They were the chocks that had held the skip lorry's wheels in place when it had parked on this uneven ground. Its second part was covered in a filthy jigsaw of glass, cement underneath, and shapes he couldn't make out. Its last part was made out of timber lengths, jutting out as far in every direction as those girders did above. Different angles, forming fingers, stiff and in the centre set by concrete.

Emyr looked at the rough timber lengths. He didn't put out a hand to touch them.

In the museum, where the window frames were covered only by plastic, it was currently impossible to keep the boy Rhys out. When he went door-to-door and asked for contributions, most reactions were blind, negative; full of themselves. Yesterday he'd been told by the slates supplier that, though the order seemed complete, it was in fact one quarter unfulfilled. What could he have done? Stood there and counted? They were out, they had said on the phone. Simple as that. Stocks gone. He'd asked Emyr if he should go out and mine. Emyr had not yet been able to find another source. The supply for the museum dwindled, stacked in its room below the unfinished roof. In the daytimes, sun spilled down through the holes to touch it. Tarpaulins covered the gaps at night, filling the empty space with sounds, louder even than a ship's sails. The business interiors were three days behind at least, still laying the bloody floors in some of the buildings. There were ten thousand holes that needed mending if he was to shape this town into the achievement, the tribute it should be.

What Dai was making rose above his head. Ten thousand and one. What Dai was making went like a stick through the heart of Emyr's empathy for him. It perforated his own vision for this place. And his vision was all that kept the chaos here under leash.

Yes, this was the sadness that lay underneath beliefs like Dai's. It was nothing but need that informed them. You held them, and it seemed as if the world couldn't touch you. Safety was the goal. Some kind of safety in your own smallness. This town had no room for it; some dogmatic crutch. The town had to embody more than that: *love*. It had to have *meaning*.

Emyr's face was set in a moue of distaste, regret. He walked away. Behind him, it rose against the view: timbers and broken debris, cement. In cold sunlight, the wood was dry and the reflections on its glass shards dimly turned.

Three days of digging and eight men to form the shape of the new garden. Ruth went to it daily, four times daily. She looked from its work, to Dai's behind, and her hands held each other.

The landscaping company set out pegs, roped off, to delineate the circles of bed and lawn. The foundation hole for the central fountain was dug by hand and its interior concreted, ready for the pump's installation. Around it, the land's contours were changed, downward-sloping. Kango drills had left the ground without a surface. Filthy and waterlogged at the subsoil from three weeks' solid rain, a team set shovels in as around them the re-roofing progressed.

She walked slowly back to her home. The road was a mudflow. Between the people, the badly parked cars, the scaffold poles, she made her way. When Charlotte had first come to Ynys-morlan, the street had been a tranquil place, this gate had stood open, and at the end of the path had stood a small pink house with a few missing slates. She saw the gate now. Men walked through it carrying bags of plaster. She saw the quartz stones, spaced every other; saw brown ground around them, where footsteps overlaid each other until there were a million paths. Round the doorway, scaffolding formed a mouth. It darkened the windows to either side and the pebbledash that they looked out of was now being cracked away. Men straddled the flower beds and they tried – she saw them – not to damage what was left. Upstairs Michael Garvey was on his second visit this week, and somewhere inside, she thought, between the builders climbing the stairs, or on the mattress in the living room, very faint because the world was so loud now, the ghosts Ruth had left in each room were sitting down, nothing left to do. They could see the paint tins in the hallway. Yellow. Garvey's men had matched it perfectly. And when she'd seen them, what could she have said to him? That she didn't want the walls to be that colour? That she didn't want them to be smooth with new plaster so she could lie in bed again beneath them? Standing in corners, washing the grey marks from Nia's walls, watching coloured outfits move on the television screen, these ghosts were waiting for the house to be silent again. They hadn't tried to leave before. Why would they now?

Ruth walked inside and closed the kitchen door behind her. She remembered with desperation the perfection that had filled this place. She thought of Dai Meredith's half-finished thing. The sound of the re-plastering going on above her, though, made her vision of this project's end, its finished image, more important than it had ever been.

The flagpole Lennie's father had once put up was taken down. On the 24th it happened. He knew the day and the time because Ruth told him. Go see it, she said. Go and see. She was crying, as she did more and more often now. The fights, coldness and shouting, they seemed to die to this. He thought she was reaching the end. Though he didn't try to touch her yet, he could see that soon she'd let him. He'd gone into the living room where she slept one night, an hour maybe after she had gone to bed. Opening the door, the room had been in darkness. He'd stood for a long time without speaking but he'd known she was awake. He knew her breathing.

'I just came to say, I want to tell you so you know, you don't have to say anything . . .' Her shape, in the doorway's light, had been motionless. 'I'll never hurt you again. That's what I wanted to tell you. That's all.'

A moment's silence had stretched and receded, like the light across the floor as he'd slowly left the room.

Go and see it he did. He watched it, lowered through the sunlight to battered green grass. He watched the flag itself taken off. After, when they had put it in the skip, he went to it and removed it and took it home. Feelings came from him, strong as pain, but they weren't pains. Making or breaking. You had to go through something like this to feel what he did now. He thought of his home with Ruth, being rebuilt, and it didn't matter to him that the pole was gone from the land. The breaking they had gone through seemed finally to have let him touch it.

'Did you watch it?'

'Yes, I watched,' he said.

'You know what that flag means to me?'

'I don't know.' From his seat on their bare bedroom floor, he looked up at her face. Tools and planks and slates on every side of them. Plastic and a heap of his clothes. The nods Ruth gave him were little walls to hold her words in.

'I remember him, your dad. Grim bloody man – grim, and to you just as much. Back when we were kids, I remember. And you used to trail round town after him, you know? Like he had your fingertips stuck to back of his shoes. Full of his own grimness. Loved himself. Know what I thought about you when you asked if you could take me out? That first time? You know what? How you had his shine, I thought, how you had his shine and none of that . . . that shit under it, nothing like that, all his best bits.'

She'd never used ugly words before, just like she'd never dressed in clothes without long sleeves and long hems and pretty colours. But she grasped them now, as if that meant she was breaking apart the person he had made her. Destroyed, she couldn't make that woman's mistakes.

'Did you watch it come down?'

'Like you said to.'

'Maybe it was me. Blind, like. Maybe desperate . . . Or maybe you changed. And lost the shine, and got . . . got that ugliness underneath. Maybe it was you. You know, I used to see that flag through the window in your room, go in there, put flowers in there . . . You faded into him. You ever realize that? That's what that flag meant to me.'

But she wouldn't believe, Lennie thought, that he had always had it. And that she had always seen it; the ugliness and the shine weren't separate. If he'd seemed to burn brighter once, he'd only been mimicking.

'Did you change? You tell me, the first time you hit me, you tell me if you remember changing then.'

He wanted to. He only said, 'People change just like . . . no different than a beach, is it? . . . you know it. They never stop changing. The last two months, like.'

'The first time! Tell me!' As if that single day had held the key to all those others. 'Did you feel different after, Lennie?' But the turning point she saw when she looked back did not belong to him. Had she felt herself change on the first night that they had slept together afterwards?

'Yes, I felt different. I felt worse.'

He wanted to, but couldn't tell her. It had been the fact that his shine was just belief – not only in his old man, the flag's story, but in that whole world they made – it had been the fact that it wasn't real that had made him blame her. Year by year he'd begun to realize, and had continued trying to pretend.

'It wasn't just mine, it was your own life you started ruining that day. Do you realize that, Lennie? You realize? You understand?'

'I know,' he said. Each barrier that had been between them broke, so they saw each other. Violence had allowed this: not blind with fading faith, but real and open. Not him striking her, but the violence that their last two months of metamorphosis had been. He couldn't tell her, for he saw a chance now.

Holding her own arms, shouting, sorry; he watched Ruth. He knew, when he saw her face now, that nothing would fade, not in fifty years if they were given it. Same as it had never faded between his old man and his mother.

'I sit and remember,' she said, 'I wonder if you even realized . . . you could've been a bright, special person. Could've done anything you wanted to do. Do you know that?'

'I know, Ruth. We could've had everything that we used to talk about . . . I know. You remember?' he said.

'*I remember! Of course I remember . . . !*' brutal, her voice.

They'd made love here. When he'd needed forgiveness and she had needed to forgive him, they'd seemed to pass the most precious things they owned to each other in those hours. Where the bed had stood, there lay blankets on the floor. Above them, fresh plasterboard was set as the ceiling. Around them lay mixing buckets and trowels, dirty plastic, left behind for the night. On every side new walls were clean, the delicate pink of plasterwork.

To put the bad parts of life into making something good; to express sadness through it, that had been the intention. The project's end was now just two weeks distant, and all questions had been shoved from her by designing, planning, creating, struggling to achieve this intention. At its height now, all the project's parts were madness around this attempt.

Unforeseen, one person's choice had come and thrown doubt on to everything. Maybe any small thing would have done it. She didn't know. What was Dai's object if not expressive? Behind the garden. Overlooking it. The first idea he'd put into any of this since applying for the grant to demolish the gift shop, the first since his mother had died. Putting grief into creativity. She stood and looked at it from the ruined ground where the garden would soon lie and it was wretched, it stole beauty out of what she'd hoped for here. It was so full of sadness.

But what was her vision for the town if she had it condemned? How *pretty* it would look, so uniform it could suffocate bad memories. How would it be any different from this house, where it was horror she had hidden?

The rebuilding in their home and Lennie's reactions to her now, acceptance that stopped anything she did from wounding him – her attempt to hurt him something in itself she'd said was wrong – and the way he looked at her, like it was hope all her hate gave him, these things pushed her with harder hands towards the need for perfection in Ynys-morlan.

Perfection, like before. She looked at her husband's face, frantic in the silence that returned each night now, for something that would break the deadlock. It was hope that she saw there, without question.

She thought of Charlotte. Of kissing her.

Sunday fourteenth July nineteen sixyeight

I don't want Mommy to do my hair anymore because she is always cross with me and she hates me when she does it and i don't want her to because its not mine. it shuold not even be yelow. I dont want it yelow I don't know how I look because all the pictures and in the mirror its pretty and fair but its dark at the bottom where it grows

This was the week for the distribution of the compensation cheques. Charlotte signed them in her study, like it gave some ending as she had first imagined. There was no ending. In the quiet, she would look up at her journals, she would think of Ruth. It wasn't necessary to open them now to know the feelings written there.

Each day of the project's continuation left her with a clearer image of Ynys-morlan as her home. But she had no knowledge of the choices Ruth would make. She planned for her houses and each plan was fulfilled. In any one of them, she pictured Ruth and Nia. The three of them made a circle in her heart. They made a whole.

One compensatory grant per private property. Eight thousand pounds per home. More than a million, which she'd never touched. The 25th of March, they were distributed.

In a way, it had been a vision of home that had led her mother to take Charlotte's identity away from her. The need of that vision, missing only one role. She thought of Ruth constantly, continuing to work through that week on the designs for her houses' interiors.

Dear Charlotte. Dear Charlotte. It was the greatest distance, to see your name written that way. On each cheque she saw 'Charlotte Weyland'. The greatest distance, more than two thousand miles, for though she remembered every detail of Hedera, clearer-eyed for each day she spent inside the new houses, she thought of playing a role for Ruth, and once again it didn't seem as if that name or any other should be hers.

From Emyr's lists, the cheques were written and deposited in Spar's back room. Siân oversaw their distribution as people queued outside, her own cheque, found in the first hour of that morning, sitting in her coat pocket. Smiles and laughter that bubbled a little hysterically, people opening them, comparing how the number '£8,000' looked on each piece of paper. Siân tried to smile as well. There were memories that should have been washed away. Through the street in small groups between the barely moving vans they went, while others still queued, their own giggles escalating, hands itching. It was an incredible thing. She watched Pete Thorpe and his kids, handing the slip of paper to one of them to carry, another on his shoulders. An incredible thing. She left the room. In the small stockroom in the basement, she locked the door.

Ruth had refused Charlotte's cheque of course; a minute's tangled quiet. Who would she be giving it to? Lennie? Yet she'd offered it as they'd stood in Ruth's jumbled kitchen. She'd wanted to offer her own study as well, where Ruth could take some of the project's folders and files, to work. She'd hadn't offered, though. She'd reached out, fumbling slightly, and they'd held each other's hands. Ruth was very pale.

'If you need time, I can look after Nia. You trust me with her?'

'I can look after her! Course I trust you – I can look after her, she's never too much for me. But thank you. She's uppity, but she's fine.' The girl had been at playschool then, and Charlotte had seen lies.

Some cheques were cashed immediately. Each morning, she called her accountants to hear how much more of Hedera's money was no longer owned by her. People came to her in the street sometimes, no longer talking about the project. About the weather, or the news, they'd talk instead. She began to learn their names, as well as the names of their homes.

Home, Siân went with her cheque, and beside her bed she put it in a drawer. She told Tom, after two nights without touching it, deciding, what she would spend the money on. She would have the house's interior decorated. After. Not until all the work was finished, but then, eight thousand would be enough to do all the rooms. Stacey she told first. Stacey asked if redecoration included a new television. If they bought a new television then the one she was watching – the one with its pictures spilled all across her face and moving there – she could have in her bedroom. Looking at her back, fourteen years old, Siân tried to imagine some time, three years from now, maybe four, when she'd ask her to start looking for work, looking for a place to live. It was an important process. There was a time when you had to make your own way. There were things that you had to prove, not to another person but to yourself. All this, Siân remembered clearly with Tom, but she couldn't imagine the conversation with Stacey. Sometime in the future. Though she was trying to hold on to them, thoughts she'd had, beliefs, grew weaker. She wondered how this house would be, empty. Some hard thing inside her was leaving. Really she didn't want it any more. Maybe it had hurt her more than she'd believed.

Tom came and walked between the builders, in through the doorway, to see their hall. The staircase, sawdust there beside its little window, the carpet risers removed, stored somewhere. Through into the kitchen, he looked, where the ceiling now reached up four feet higher than it had done: bare whalebones of the new rafters exposed. He saw boots, through its window, on the scaffolding. Three hammers' sounds. In the backyard he found her and they stood beside the low sea-stone wall, looking down along a great and matching row of low sea-stone walls. In this yard, all the stuff she'd kept was gone.

She took him through the changes, pointing, stiffness in her voice. She was expecting anger from him, he saw. Meeting his eyes steadily, as she'd always done anyone who seemed to judge her, she told him how she was intending to spend the compensation grant. He didn't judge her, though.

'I'm not going to be replacing anything, just redecorating. I'm not going to be buying a new refrigerator. Painting, I'm thinking of. Curtains. A couple of pieces of furniture. But changing the place. Seems ridiculous to walk into a new house with the inside just the same as it was before.' In her coat, despite everything in her voice, she seemed to have shrunk somehow, he thought, in just these last two months. She seemed to have overreached herself. She'd been grounded before.

'I lost my job,' he said.

She didn't answer him, her words withdrawing from her.

'I lost my job. Foregone conclusion, like. Should've fucking realized really. They need someone with experience. They need qualifications. Maybe even a name chef. Draw the people in.'

'I'm sorry . . .'

'Well there's no point in being sorry. You tell Pat to sack me, like? You tell Bethan? What've you got to be sorry for?'

'You'll get another. If there'll be a lot of anything here this summer, it's jobs. You'll get another.'

He wanted to look around at this place but he didn't. Beside them, the sea continued to move in and move out. 'You're going to use the money to redecorate? Don't know if you'll need it. You're not working . . . not having your wages paid while Spar's closed down, I wouldn't think.'

'That's not more than a few hundred pounds, if I have to use any of it.'

He nodded. 'Long as you're all right,' then he added, 'you could do a lot more with it than redecorate the house, you know that? Eight grand, it's not so much. But there are things you could do. Take six months off work, you could do that. You could go away somewhere . . .'

'Do *you* need money, Tom?'

'You think that's why I came here?' A moment's look at her face left him standing a step further away. 'Glad the compensation cheque's come, like. I came to say . . . I lost my job, so I won't be able to bring you my bit this month. That's what I came to say.' Understanding and condemnation. He couldn't tear them apart. 'I'm sorry about that,' he said.

'Tom, for God's sake. I don't need your money. Thank you.'

'I know you don't need it. I like to be able to give it.'

Walking away, she saw his back. Like her he was. Nothing like his father. Why should he have anything of John in him? Had never really known the man. It hurt her to see him, though, see him just the way she'd always been. She wanted to tell him she was sorry – wasn't sure even what she was sorry for. For everything, she wanted to say. But the guilt was her own, Tom hadn't given it to her. And it was false. She had nothing to be guilty over. The project had changed everyone.

The date that Emyr Morgan had proposed for the sandblasters' company seemed to be achievable. An eight-hour final sweep while the public works crew replaced the street lamps. The course of March's third week took the shape of Ynys-morlan away from the homes where its residents still lived.

Inside the Shoreline Café and Restaurant, the plastering of the walls was completed to leave blank rooms which waited for deliveries: furnishings, soft-furnishings. The decoration company, assigned by Emyr, arrived on the afternoon of the 23rd. From Bethan's flat, where inside rooms were shaded by the scaffolding and covered with messes of drawings, sewing, B&H, the render was taken in crumbling shards.

She had advertised the chef's position in nine different weeklies, leaving her own mobile number. 'With creative free rein possible across the menu,' she wrote. Patty looked them over as though there might even be spelling mistakes in the gaps between the words.

'Yes, they're fine.'

'I'm glad you think so.' Unable to help the shortness in her voice. In everything her mother did, she saw resentment, sharper every day. As though the work here got further and further from her control, when it wasn't so, Patty washed her hands of it all and came back to get them dirty again five minutes later. Unable even to sit in a different room.

She remembered them sitting together, the café dark, two years ago. 'I can only tell you how it's been for me. I'm glad, I've always been glad of what I did. I can only say how it's been for me . . . I wanted to stay.'

Now Pat would stand on the top floor, in the living room above the sound of every hammer and drill, every alteration she hadn't applied for, she'd watch the work in the road below like it was shrinking her. Her daughter had found her there.

What if you'd had a lot of dreams, Bethan thought, and they'd all been ridiculous, movie-print dreams. And when you'd been faced with a choice, the now or never kind, you'd given them up and made a business, a life, a family. Then one day all those dreams came rushing back in on you – a great fucking tide of them – and swept right through what you'd made. What would you feel then except bitterness?

In the afternoon, three days after it had been exposed, Bethan saw what Dai had made – though someone had described it to her already. It was uglier, a lot uglier, than she'd been told.

What did he mean to make? She couldn't tell. It was a crazy, confused, fucked-up thing. Did he think it was part of the project? 'When you want to do something,' he'd said, that day when they'd stood before the seafront, 'and you don't understand the reasons, that's Time working through you.' That was innocence. That was creativity. Rhys would've looked at this and turned to her; wouldn't have needed to say anything at all.

With all these changes heard and felt around her, the ideas of which were so vivid, so beautiful, it seemed the cruellest thing, to see the kind of freedom from the world that Dai had, opened up, with this beneath it in cold sunlight.

Dai made a routine. He tried to follow everything that the movement of Time made him want. If his body or his feelings told him to do something, there must be a reason for it. Maybe not all his wants, but among the things that you felt compelled towards, there must be the pattern that led to what you were meant to do. Dai made a routine. He followed all desires like instructions from inside his body. If Time meant for his place in all this to be nothing but building this statue, he couldn't change that. But maybe it meant for more. For seven days, he'd found that the fear was bigger than the wanting to go to Bethan's window. Time must not mean for him to go yet.

The statue itself was hardest, though. He spent the last parts of the nights, when there could be no one else around. He searched inside himself, holding all the different pieces from the demolition for so many minutes, not knowing which desire to trust. Trying to find the idea that came from Time. Not knowing how to tell them apart.

Surely it must be simple. Not any intricate pattern, but just to do what was meant. Follow where it led. Whatever Time planned for him, good or bad, he'd know that he'd done everything he could then. If he didn't – could he be punished for it? Could Time's intentions change like that?

*

There were quiet homes, tarpaulins shaking in the wind. Half past two in the morning and his work on the statue not yet started, Dai stood with the materials and borrowed tools around him.

There was the broken white line of the tarmac. The street lights almost illuminated it. The scaffolding hugged the houses' rows. Just looking down this street towards her the fear grew. And behind him confusion rose in wood and glass.

He'd bent a long stretch of tin guttering, set it against the pavement's edge and given it five corners. A rough, jagged spiral. On top of everything he'd built before, sitting in the fingers of the horizontal timbers, Dai had set it so its end spiked up and out. If Time controlled every thread, was there such a thing as the wrong choice? Or any choice? He had lost himself since the night he'd seen Rhys in her window. Lost himself in a pattern that grew more rigid, locked him tighter every night. Each addition to the statue was harder won, coming into being in the dark. How did Time want him to show its shape? Every part turned into a question. If there were no such things as choices, right or wrong, was it pointless to try to do what Time meant? What he felt was a spiral. He tried to create it. What he felt was a jagged tin spike.

Trapped inside it, he stared back down this road.

Parked cars with shadows scattered over their windscreens; owned by people who had no thought of Time. Were they following it better than him? Just by having minds clear? It looked to him like they were gaining. All these houses, Dai saw, becoming beautiful.

Did he fear it more or want it more, to go down there and see her? The sky was clear, only silence up there. Everything was clear but his thoughts. Dai tried to feel Time's will inside himself.

There was no window in her bedroom any more, though. Between the room and the outside air, two sheets of thick, transparent plastic had been nailed. They held the street light in a small cloud of condensation there. Her home was open to the road, but even if she'd looked out, she couldn't have seen him.

Dai walked between the cars, no movement but the scattering wind. Bethan's window was lit. Maybe he pushed himself farther out.

He climbed over the low wall to the Barries' front garden, fingers curled around the sea stones that clad it now, dust in the cracks that felt like sand. He took a handful of gravel from the path. If Time was a great net, a spread and glorious pattern, then surely no one could do wrong.

She sat, Chelsea asleep in the next room, her plans for the tables' layout all over the duvet.

She'd put on the dress four times that week. To finish the hem, to begin on the lining and then just to put it on. The last time it had been a tight race between getting it off and starting to cry. Hanging it up, she'd tasted the brine and felt disgust. She'd closed the wardrobe door and thought of Rhys like his face was painted on its shut wood. She wasn't a kid, she wasn't any girl. Innocent things were lies on her and maybe they were lies in every part of the world. Fooling herself to think Ynys-morlan would be any different place. Maybe innocence was never anything but fucking naïvety. Maybe ugliness, like Dai's handmade tower, always lay underneath.

She hadn't opened the wardrobe again. She'd thrown herself into the final designs for the restaurant like she still was trying to believe those beautiful colours she imagined could be made real, and those sketches lay in drifts around her now, as gravel hit the plastic across her window frame.

The shock that went through her shoved her up in one movement. She stood, she turned, staring.

Who's that knocking at the window? Was that the boy who would take her off into the sunset, via the abortion clinic? Or the Incredible Man With The Mind Of An Eight-Year-Old who thought she was the most beautiful thing to hit Ynys-morlan since the first Angel Delight delivery truck had swung in round the bend?

In the silence, the second cast of it rattled down on to the scaffolding's boards.

She didn't care about the cold. She told herself she'd sleep in Chelsea's room. She took her sewing scissors from beside the machine. The smile fell into a grimace and fell further, to the sadness that lay in the foundations of everything now. She seemed to be running away, she seemed to be running down every road there was. And here she was. Still here, in Ynys-morlan. She put the scissors through it and she tore the window open, to feel the air, to look out, and see who stood down there.

Silhouetted against the light, she wasn't wearing the dress, Dai saw. The last few bits of gravel dropped from his hand like a tiny stone-filled tide. Bethan heard it. The night was cold in front of her.

'Dai,' she said. Only twenty yards between them, her voice was clear.

Dai nodded as they saw each other. Emptiness in his face, not hope or sadness yet, as she stood on the road that Rhys had left bare. She didn't speak again, emptiness came to her too.

In town at night, she thought. To work on that thing, or maybe just to see her. He looked shocked. She wasn't wearing the dress. Two o'clock in the morning and she had her tracksuit bottoms and a T-shirt on. Shocked by real life.

'Dai . . .' She couldn't find anything else.

In the cold down there, he said, 'You want me to go. I can go. That's OK.'

Mouth open, what could come out? She didn't have anything in her but vacancy; a few memories, of nights when she'd stood here almost believing there was no such thing as reality at all.

'You want me to go,' he said.

Rhys stood between them, unspoken. She didn't know Dai had watched them – he didn't know what they'd said. But here Rhys stood anyway.

'It's OK,' he said, 'I'll see you tomorrow.'

As if what was here now would be there then.

'Fucking hell,' she said, under her breath, but with no footstep around them, no breath but the wind in this plastic's torn edges, he heard it, and the loss of hope that she saw on his face, she felt herself.

'Dai?' her voice low. 'Dai?' she said. 'Do you understand?'

'Yes.'

'I don't . . . I don't want to be anybody's girlfriend. Not anybody's . . . You believe me?' The most ridiculous thing, to stand in her fucking window and say this, down to him. The most ridiculous, to still want what she'd had – or what they had had maybe. And when Bethan spoke again, she didn't know what moved her. 'If you understand that . . .' She was a cruel fucking person. A disgusting person, must be. What he wanted her to be, though, she wanted to be it too. For the half an hour she could. A cruel person, but she wasn't a liar to do it – not like that – because if Dai loved it, whatever it was, her standing, him watching, if he loved it, she did too. So low, her voice, it touched the pavement; this road here by his feet. 'If you understand that, do you want to come up here?'

He didn't answer her. Her figure was black against the light.

They died as they left her, the words. But she wasn't trying to use him. It wouldn't be a lie for her, any more than for him.

'You can come up here . . .' she said, 'if you understand that. If you want to.'

'Yes,' he said. 'I want to come up.' It wasn't an answer. He didn't move.

In the street lamps' glow Bethan saw his features, upturned. Like a broken clock face.

For him, or for Time, he wanted to. Staring at her, he couldn't explain, though – how he was scared to love things, how nothing was secure. You could lock your house and bolt your precious things in boxes, what you really loved Time could whisper in and steal from you. It laughed at locks.

Nothing was clear to him now. He didn't want to go up there, was scared. He thought of her dress and wanted it again.

But if this was all that was designed for him, it was something. A little bit. And you couldn't say no. How could you do that when Time stared down and saw you, even in the dark, even in this bedlam town?

'Yes,' he said, 'I want to.'

'Wait . . . wait here then,' Bethan's voice faltered and she took hold of it again. 'A minute . . . wait.'

She left the frame of the window empty and he could've run away from it then. What would be in front of him, though, knowing he hadn't taken the one chance that Time had given him? Whose fault would it be then that he didn't have happiness?

He was moving under the shadow of the scaffolding that framed the doorway. He was standing, putting out his hand, just standing, holding it parallel to the door's face. Air between. Like it would make the choice for him. Long minutes. And it did.

She was standing there, not in pyjamas any more. And not in the world she knew, no of course, not any more – for the last time, because she'd told him there couldn't be another. He followed her, understanding that. So it couldn't be abuse.

Behind his back, she closed the door on outside.

He had been here before though he said nothing. She didn't mention it; didn't speak at all.

There'd been a great plan, it had drifted down to lie atop Ynys-morlan's coast like the thinnest of shining weaves, and capture them. In this plan, he'd had to use his keys to walk into Bethan's unlit home. He'd had to go to Siân, after Gwen had screamed at him – as he supposed Gwen had had to do. No decision had been theirs. He tried to hold on to the picture of that filmy web, floating down, floating right down from the stars.

The picture slipped through his fingers. There'd been a point when all these tearing feelings had been no more than whispered doubt. He could still remember how that had felt. This darkened staircase, he'd climbed it on his own.

Now Bethan moved up behind him. And the door was pale ahead.

Reaching past, pushing it open so that he could step through, Bethan looked over his shoulder at the rooms they were entering. There was one last hour in front of her. Of naïvety, she thought. Fantasy. She took hold of it, knowing what it really was, and so consigned herself to the daylight of each following tomorrow.

Chelsea's sleeping silence still reigned here.

The empty rooms watched them and saved judgements for later, when she'd be here alone and would listen. On the carpet, Dai's boots made no noise.

There were a million words she could've said – that she didn't want to hurt him – but they were excuses, for she was standing here, in the bedroom's low light. And anyway they were in her eyes. Here, Rhys had held her, up against the wall.

With parted space between them, she looked at Dai. He didn't know how to stand or make his face still, and she didn't either. Helplessness in both their expressions, like she'd never let a man touch her before. In the quiet, lies seemed true.

She reached out, picked his hand from by his side, and the blue velvet of the dress shifted. Eyes on each other, as memories seemed to fall and settle somewhere underneath them, the shoulder strap of her dress slipped down a little. She moved it the rest of the way, using his hand.

The skin of his fingers was rough; the skin of Bethan's shoulder, he felt, soft. He pulled his hand from hers, back towards him, where it couldn't feel anything new. She didn't reach for him again but only stood, isolated by the fear she saw in his eyes, separated from everything, it seemed, in a floor-length, blue velvet ball gown that she'd made herself.

'I don't know,' he said. 'I don't know about this.'

She didn't answer him. Her blonde hair hung back behind her shoulders as it had done since she'd been a kid, and her eyes were old. How old was he, she wondered. In his late thirties maybe. And she wondered how it was to reach that age never having had another person touch you. The idea was lovely. Lovely to her and just lonely to him. She put out a hand again; didn't take his with it but only suspended it between them and looked in his face, waiting to see if he'd hold it himself.

He moved slightly. Her skin, he saw, and the curves of her, the hair, the dress. With a faltering motion, he reached out and took her fingers. He followed her as she drew his hand in towards herself again. The second shoulder strap.

She was beautiful. There was crying starting up in her eyes as he gradually pushed the second strap down. He saw it. As sad as him, he realized.

Emotions were moving in his body, made real.

It slipped down a little under his fingers, the loosest thing. She stood in front of him and she was motionless. As sad as him that Time would only give them this. A part of the hurt left him, seeing it. His hand was in the air, near her face, and he touched her hair, he moved it and pushed it back from her neck, like it were a doll's.

'Come . . . come and kiss me?' she asked him.

He made one half-step towards her across her bedroom's blue carpet. In his eyes, there were shapes. Sad shapes, of the future. He seemed to lose them, though, the closer he got to her, and as he put his face no more than an inch from hers, the past fell from him too. Left him without memories.

As still as if she slept, Bethan felt his face come to touch against hers and his lips on her own. The smallest kiss. She could smell him: earth and rain. She didn't open her mouth but only stood. His touch seemed to make her a different person.

And he opened his, but didn't move. Bethan gently brushed the edge of his lip with her tongue. Small kisses, she put, on the shape of his unsealed mouth. His eyes were shut. She reached up and put one hand against his cheek and then his forehead; she put the tip of her finger, as gently as she could do it, on to the tracing surface of his closed eyes. All his face, she felt.

Into her hair and the smell of her his kiss went, into the feeling of her skin, and he put both hands around her back and held it, held her hair against it, and made her small enough to keep inside his arms. His kiss went into her mouth. And then he pushed the side of his own face against hers. They were breathing. Her body grew and lessened. He felt it in a rhythm.

She stood a little way from him, this room around her and all its history. She began to undress. She lifted her left arm and unfastened the blue button at the top of the dress.

He saw her put her fingers on the top of a little zip underneath that button. He saw all the dress shift as she turned herself. A few parts of hair dropped off her shoulder, made curtains down over her face. Finding the zip, she lifted her head up again and met his eyes, staring at her like she was a fairy tale.

He was aware: movements in his face. A twitch he didn't want her to see. The sounds of the zip made the silence thinner. There were tiny motions in her body and her arms.

He watched her put her fingers to the top of the dress and slowly shift it. It opened up around her. Two parts. It moved down over her and it left, first her torso, and then the rest of her body, nude, as she slipped it past her hips down to the floor. Dai looked at her breasts. Nothing under that dress. His eyes went down, and he looked at the curve of her tummy. Bethan stood unmoving with the dress soft round her feet. She let him look.

Pale skin. Very pale where a swimming costume had once been. He looked at the hair below her stomach: a triangle. He raised his face again and only gazed at her.

Bethan didn't speak. She filled up with things to say: what do you think now, Dai? What do you think now, with that lying on the floor? She said nothing. She took in his expression and the words wilted from her, as she'd hoped they would.

And, thoughts fleeing him as he saw how defenceless she was, it seemed to Dai like there was no Time, regardless of everything that had brought him here.

She went to him. With weighted hands, their eyes on each other, Bethan opened the first button of his shirt. Her fingers descended to the next. He felt himself get hard and couldn't stop it.

She took his shirt away from him and put it down on the floor beside the dress. He looked at it there, not really believing. Raising both his hands up over his head then, she slipped his T-shirt off and away from him, as his mother had stopped doing years ago. In his boots and trousers, he looked at her.

That unfilled expression. Afraid. Overjoyed.

He had dark hair on his chest and a scar above one nipple. Down at his stomach, that hair thickened and then was hidden by the waist of his jeans. She asked if she could, but maybe he wasn't capable of saying no.

In the quiet, she undressed him and pulled him gently towards the bed with her. Then she pressed him to sit, and then to lie, coming up to kneel next to him and seeing that he wanted her. She found she wanted him as well – felt it openly. Truly wanted him – inside her. All over her.

The cushions and the sheets were soft. They enveloped. Her blue eyes caught the light and she moved. She moved her leg over him and sat above him. He felt her thighs touch his waist. There was no precedent to lead him here. There was no context for the touch. It ran through him. He thought of, and clutched at, the nights that would come after, when he wouldn't know her any more. Even this couldn't stop it running through him.

'Bethan –' he said. He heard his own voice.

She moved then, though, whether to make something beautiful or only to make it end, she moved and she took him in her hand and she pressed him up into herself and she sank on to him. She held his fingers and looked in his eyes to see if it was love or blame or fear there.

But it was only shock.

Tender shock, that depleted, that became pleasure. She squeezed his hands in hers. He was lost, astray, but he looked up at her. Couldn't hide that pleasure from his face. How his features changed, how they moved. Lips open, he couldn't control it. Under her hips, he rose up to feel it all. Sounds with no edges came out of his mouth, to move over her body, it seemed. She saw his lips wet. Wanting, getting, changing his face into an open shape. Loving her. She was speaking without knowing it and he was moving, into her, into her. Stomach and back rising from the bed. She took everything he was and she pressed herself down to him. She was coming. Just looking at his face. The sensation rose up and over her. Split-mouthed, closed-eyed, he drove forwards. Everything in his head gone and only his body moving, only his features, as he let go and whole, unbroken noise slid from him.

He took hold of her hips. He held her. It went through him. The press of each finger was felt by her. The breath that came with those sounds. If she could have taken him – if she could have kept him for ever in that moment – she would have done.

Dai's face: the look before that joy slipped away from him, left his skin, before Time came again into the room. Crept into these soft sheets.

Here were the walls. Dark red. And the sound of breathing, here it was. The corner lamp's light that tipped the shadows of the things on her sewing table. Here on the floor lay her dress.

Bethan didn't speak.

Above them, the evening's constant sound now, when the day's noise left you free to hear it, the sea. A low voice that never left her.

In other places, places where she might have gone if life or 'Time' had given her some other ending, there would be silence instead of that. Some home she might have had without Chelsea. Nights unlike this, she might have listened and tried to remember the sound. In the same way that Dai's statue lay exposed beneath his faith, that daunting silence had lain below her thoughts of leaving here.

What would she have been in that? No crying from Chelsea in the night. Exposed, she thought. Exposed as she lay now.

'Bethan . . .'

She didn't answer him.

There was the need to draw these covers up, grey as Ynys-morlan's days.

'Bethan . . . ?'

She turned to look at him. What they'd done was gathering in his eyes, and he was waiting for her to tell him. To say what? That it wasn't over. That they had some kind of future.

'Do you think, Dai . . .' she said quietly, '. . . you think Time controls everything?'

He looked at her, remembering how he'd stood outside her window. It had seemed like he'd had a choice. Maybe Time wanted it to seem that way, though.

'Everything,' he said. 'Yes.'

If not everything then what did it leave to you?

The purposes of entire towns, Time controlled, whether people lived or died. It had to be everything. Or how could it join all its threads together? How could it make sure that the lives, the deaths, led where they were meant?

'Everything.'

'And if,' she said, her voice coming from a dimmer place, '. . . if this was the last time we talked, saw each other, like, that would be . . . what . . . ?'

'What Time meant to happen . . .' He couldn't tear his eyes from her.

'What it meant to happen. No choices, for you or me, anyone.'

'No choices,' he said, afraid.

No choices. If she'd never fallen pregnant, then those places with their silences or the sound of their unknown traffic, they would have waited for her, like that rubble-sculpture at the gateway of this town. 'What are you building, Dai?' she asked. 'Where the gift shop was.'

He gave no answer; didn't want to let his thoughts out into this room that he would have to leave. He spoke finally. Maybe it was hope that let him.

'I'm building . . . Time,' he said. 'I'm building something to let It be seen.'

'It's not a beautiful thing,' she said.

'It's made up of all the parts . . . all the parts . . .' scared of her judgements, he fumbled, 'that It told me to build.' He sounded like a kid in the quiet room, he thought. 'Doesn't matter if you think it's beautiful, or not – I don't mind.' A lie. He looked at her. What they'd done – she saw it in his gaze – it threatened to spill. Years formed on his face to keep it from doing that. 'I don't care – beautiful or not,' he said.

'But you think Time's making this project.'

'Yes, it's making it. A perfect place . . . I told you. So there is one in the world.'

'A beautiful town,' she said.

Naked, he drew himself in. She was sorry.

'I'm not dull –'

'I know you're not.'

She couldn't say it. That fucking thing he was building, it was them. Time was lovely in his head. His faith died to its cement reality. Like every hope Bethan had died back to the memory of deciding to stay here.

'You're building at the start of town, in the garden that's meant to welcome the tourists in. If Time's point is to make a beautiful place, Dai, it's going to ruin that.'

He looked back at her, about to answer, but his words hung crooked and unspoken. There was no answer.

'Do you understand?' she said.

None.

'Do you know what I'm saying?'

'I'm not dull! I can hear you, I know what you're saying –'

Of course he wasn't dull. And she was a princess. She was a debutante in her blue velvet. He wasn't dull and she wasn't an abuser.

'You can't carry on making it, Dai, not if you believe this place is meant to be perfect.'

'Why do you say that . . . ?'

'Because it's the truth.'

'Why d'you want to say that . . . ?'

This, the real world, was what lay waiting for them. After all the things that felt like innocence, here it was.

'You need to know it . . .' she said.

Because she was Bethan Hughes, carnival queen. She showed herself to him plainly, and what her vivid colours really were.

Into the road again, he left her, on the bed where they'd shared whatever it had been. Bethan might have cried for a long time there; might have lain like a little girl making noises – that wouldn't have touched the memories Rhys had left behind.

Dai was gone, and then she told him she was sorry. A lot of times, she told him. Before that leached out of her, to leave her in her home, the sea's voice replacing her own again.

That night, she picked the dress up off the floor and she said to Rhys, though Rhys was a long way from her, 'There you go. Just done in a couple of minutes, see? That's how I chose. Quick and simple. What are you going to do? Run off and get married?'

She tied the dress into a little parcel – small enough to hold in two hands. She wrote the address in letters not dissimilar to her mother's, and she glanced up at the window to the town where her mother had lived and where her own future was laid. She was lying to herself if she thought her imagination could come and touch the world and change it. Make it beautiful. Someone else was crying. Not her.

Out into the road where the cold air hit him, hands hanging by his sides. Past all these houses with their new shapes growing, under Time's unmoving, dark belt of a sky. This was the street that It wanted to make: these peaked houses, the soft-shadow bumps of these sea-stone walls. A perfect place.

Once, these ideas about Its work had been blurred guesses and he'd only loved Time. It had given meaning to things that hurt. Once, he'd snatched at that. But the love of It was more now. Its complexity, its higher, stiller shape – these things brought belief up in you like the earth was rising. Whether it took, whether it gave – and you'd cry, or you'd be happy – the knowledge of it was always there. Out into the road and far away from her window.

Minutes only, It gave. Beautiful minutes, and then robbed the beauty out of them.

Down the street towards his statue, Dai walked. Time's structure was greater than any feeling. Below his feet, the broken white line was paid out. He cried for lots of different losses. His mother. Bethan. Her cold voice. Cried for his work. For this ugly thing.

Shadowed, protruding shapes reached up to make a tower in the yellow light, because a tower was the shape that most matched Time's feelings. He stood, stared at it across the garden's pegged and broken space. How could this be against It?

But all the logic she'd talked with – winter sense – Dai knew it was true. A beautiful place, growing up on every side of him, and he hadn't been able to put any beauty into what he'd made. Only questions.

He stepped out into that space, a clear footfall in the silence. Time's cruellest part was Its distance. You could never see it. You might look up – and the universe showed you that there *was* some great map – but you couldn't ever find it in the world.

From the collection of tools that he'd brought here, hidden in a plastic sack under the bags of cement, Dai pulled a bolster and hammer as others spilled with ringing tones across the hard-packed ground.

He wanted to do right by Time. This was what it came to. After grief, and needing It, after hopes that It would lead to him to happiness, this was all it came to really. Dai saw a soundless town, his home, and felt Time's structure all around him, and wanted to do right by It. He wouldn't hurt Its plan. It could seem like the cruellest design, like it was meant to hurt you. But you couldn't understand. Time flew far above kindness or cruelty.

The first part he took from it was the gutter's spiral. Reaching up, pushing it over the girders where they stretched for him to continue building. He looked at it in his hands; not Time's work at all – only his own thoughts. He had believed the two were one.

He dropped it down to the ground. He put the bolster between the first timber length and the concrete that held it. And though he didn't raise his eyes again to see it, he felt the sky look down on him.

There were emotions that could have stopped his hand: there was anguish, the things he'd loved stolen away. There was hate – it was real and raw inside him – a new, bitter shoot, he wanted to reject Time. He might have looked at this sculpture and declared that he would leave it; that he could hurt Time too. If It took everything, then let this statue stand, to spike through all Its work. There were outcries in him.

But faith was stronger than them. He might have asked how that could be. Everyone would have given him a different answer, though, the truth was no one knew. Gwen Morgan, crying as Tom tried to touch her face, might have told Dai if she'd had the chance, that it was faith's patterns. It was a structure of living, from your first thought in the morning to the last you set yourself at night, that it could stop doubt and pain. Tom might have thought, reaching out, even as Gwen shied away, that it was just the possibility of the world making sense that caused faith to be so strong. The people around you making sense, and your place with them. Gwen's pattern really, but held up to see others through. Emyr was seated in his study as Dai raised up his hand, the hammer in it. Safety, he would have answered. He would have told the man that there was comfort in being smaller. Beauty in it. And Bethan, alone now, lay there telling him, innocence, which really just meant hope.

Belief wasn't anything maybe, not an object inside you with definitions and reasons, but instead like water. It ran to fill the spaces. Faith was what you lacked in your life. A picture of those losses. As empty spaces only, they couldn't have been seen.

You made a shape, an unbalanced, jutting shape with cement to fill the gaps. A shape to match those spaces as closely as you could, and then you stood and looked at it and saw that they were empty spaces no longer.

Dai had lost everything and this work, this work was the last thing that he loved. But he wouldn't ruin what Time was creating with his own wants. He lifted the hammer. He'd give himself up to Time: give this last thing. A gift like that, in itself it could make you believe. A gift like that couldn't be meaningless. To let go of the things you loved, even more than to hold on to them, filled you up with the knowledge you were right, and gave all the stars this look – in black up there, in splendour.

But Dai's hand didn't move.

He had the will to use it, but it didn't move. In the cold and the dark, no cars passing, this thought came into his mind: If what he built ruined Time's work, how could he have the power to make it?

He wasn't going to make it any more.

But the cement bags lay three feet from him. If what he made was ugly, and Time's work beautiful, how could it have the power to even stand?

It was the questions, not anger, but the questions.

The hammer was lowered slowly to his side, the bolster then, to hang in a silence as still as the sky.

Time had spoken to him; he had followed every want. How could it be that what he'd made rose against Its work? Perhaps his own path in Its plan had been nothing but building and destroying – but why? If he'd been wrong then he'd learned nothing that might set him right. If he'd sinned in some way then he knew nothing after building this that would help him keep from doing it again. Unless his sin had been to try and learn. Unless this sculpture had been his sin.

But how could learning threaten Time?

It was the questions. They dropped Dai's hammer from his hand. They moved him across the broken ground where the streetlight pooled in strangers' footsteps, to look down at that tin spiral again, and pick it up, and continue what he'd begun.

'And finally, we come to Dai.'

'We come to Dai,' Ruth echoed.

Emyr looked up across the kitchen table, neatening the paper in his hands. She saw resignation in his eyes, like a little piece of Gwen.

'The time's come. It has to be discussed.'

Behind him the morning's sunlight, seen through her window, struck the unfinished houses, render-dirty, windowless. They gleamed. She dropped her eyes from them and heard the soft noises of Nia playing, behind her on the floor.

TuSday 9 th july nineteen sixty eight

I am very sorry. today mommy got very mad with me and She was going no no but i didnt mean to do what I did. I broke evrything and it wasnt mine so I shouldnt break it. i ruined

Hand in that weak sunlight, Bethan pointed. 'Look.'

Pat, beside her, pulled her gaze from Siân's face, a little distant in the Spar's doorway where she'd just seen her, and followed the mark of Bethan's finger to the spot where Dai Meredith worked, standing on three cement bags to raise himself up.

You could see the garden's circle clearly now, figures dotted round it. You could see the slope and just the heads of the men working in the middle. Hair streaming out like waterweed, Bethan thought.

'Look,' her voice remote. In the open air, where the machine-gun rattle of jigsaws and the hammers' falls were carried to spread on the wind, this voice faded too. Twelve feet high now and growing still, the sight of him next to it was a stone in her.

Looking at it for the first time, Patty didn't speak. Dai's shoulders were hunched in sunlight as he built. Surrounded by building. Just part of everything that was going on here, she thought. Pity came up. Wood stuck out of it and metal. Concrete formed fat lumps to hold the pieces there.

'I see it,' she said.

Bethan's face was expressionless.

A way from them, Siân saw where they were looking.

He might never have gone up to Bethan's flat. If there were such things as choices – and there must be if he'd sinned; how could you, without being able to choose? – the minutes that she'd been gone from the window frame, he could have left the street and run. Last night might not have passed at all. And he would have gone on working, just like this.

'Have you talked to him?' Ruth asked.

'No, I haven't spoken to him about it, no.'

'Do you know why . . . why he'd have started it on his own like this? Didn't come to one of us and talk about . . . the idea for a sculpture?'

'Embarrassment maybe.'

'Well there wouldn't have been any reason to feel that, would there? None of us – no one would've been opposed to a sculpture. We could've discussed ideas . . .' She heard her own excuses, preparatory excuses, and was disgusted by them. She stared at Emyr but there was no answer in his face. There was nothing to discuss; she saw it written there. Just in the way he was shuffling the paper. 'We could have talked to him about it. Surely he knew that?'

'Maybe he knew that what he wanted to build would not be approved.'

She was silent. She saw no compassion even. Not the same man who'd once told her she should use her green fingers to dial Charlotte Weyland's number. There was only forced purpose in Emyr now, control, and the last glint she'd seen – or heard as on the telephone himself, he'd meandered through descriptions of the work she'd not been able to go out and view – it had extinguished itself, she saw.

'We can't decide without talking to him about it.'

He looked at her, pressed his lips together, raised his brows.

And was she any different? The sounds of rebuilding upstairs, the roof's completion, the plasterwork in Nia's room and in her own, left her mouth empty. She had seen that thing. Higher than ten feet, horrible.

'What is it?' she said. 'Do you know?'

'Maybe neither of us would be able to understand. I've listened to him many times, not about this subject in particular, but many times. His mind works in a way that's difficult to grasp.'

Memories of shouting at Lennie the night before echoed in her head. *Do you know what that flag means to me?* So desperate, as their house regained its shape around her, both for this project to be different, and for it to be perfect. Images of some beautiful place reached away from the feeling now constant underneath; guilt, clawing its way upwards.

'When you have spoken to him, what did he talk about?'

Siân turned and locked Spar's door slowly behind her, raising her eyes again to the street, brimming with watery sun, its colour now changing, warming from that winter white, and resonating with the noise of new slates hammered in, one by one.

Changes hard won and deserved. A different street when you narrowed your eyes; when the sun's reflections bleached details from the houses and only their new shapes could be seen. It had taken a long time. Was a turn away from the past, such a distant bloody past, a choice to feel guilty about? Memories of things she'd said herself back then brought it up, beliefs she'd made when she'd needed them – that kept on talking now. But she wasn't in their debt. She'd paid all debts, a grinding bloody instalment plan. Her eyes on Patty and Bethan, and on Dai Meredith, keys jingling, she stepped down from Spar's door. The skip truck, fresh-loaded and heading out of town, drove between them, tyres turning on the sun-dried road.

I went into the Nursery after she made me take off the blue dress and I didnt stop myself. I was lookeing at them all neat and nice. I know why they all have the names that there called and why I cant be allowed to change them and i couldnt help it.

'Dai!' Bethan called. There was sadness but everything, even that, seemed far behind her. Fantasies seemed far behind, and the belief that her imagination could open up real possibilities. What replaced it was an image of herself, turning for him in the window, like some fucking figurine.

'What're you going to say to him, Bethan? It's not our business, my God.'

'And if I decided I wanted the restaurant covered with pictures of people shagging?'

'God's sake! You want to get involved? You think there aren't people dealing with it? There's proper channels!'

'It's everyone's business,' she said. 'Everyone who's going to be living here.' And she was certainly one of those.

'Pictures of people . . . ? Just leave him *be*,' her mother whispered harshly.

'Look at it,' Bethan said. She didn't quiet her voice. 'You want to see that every day?' she asked. Because she would not be able to bear it.

He turned to see them both, figures against the others passing behind. And between, on the forecourt's barren, upturned earth, men bent and dug. It was a valley now; a wide circle falling to its centre of half-erected machinery.

Here he had looked out, sitting beside Emyr on the gift shop's wooden floorboards. With a view in front of them, though it hadn't been this view. Time's great movement, he'd talked about, with no confusion, only slow-shifting doubt, and even that allayed by Emyr.

I told Siân. Memories of Gwen shouting, his hazier denials. *Time's come here. It's going to be beautiful. I did everything right. Isn't that so?*

Before the demolition. And if there was such a thing as choice, he might never have decided to destroy it. Would Time have let the building stand? Did It have other endings? Many endings? There might be one in which his statue remained. Perhaps It intended that.

Maybe his hour with Bethan wasn't meant to make him break it down, but build it higher. He had worked the night and the morning that followed and found no answer – on the tail of every question mark another hung, as if Time's threads didn't join but knotted worse and worse, to make him think of his mum's shoelaces when she'd tried to tie them in those last months.

As the morning had grown and strained away the greyness around him, as it had left him standing here in the street's full view, he'd worked. And now he turned and on the pavement, he saw her, and questions left him alone. She shouted his name again.

The trowel he held, lumpen with dried concrete that he couldn't clean off any more, it didn't want to leave his hand. Standing under their gazes – she, and Patty too, and he saw Siân approach – he had nothing but these dirty tools and a mouth as vacant as the air above this street.

He saw her raise her arm and call to him. Her hair, he remembered. But memories like these he was holding far away from himself. Her cold voice, he remembered. He stayed across the distance. This land belonged to him, as if everywhere was wasteland but here.

Gwen had been coming here during her lunch hour, Tuesdays or Thursdays when the playschool's earlier days were over. Not to speak to anyone, only to sit on the seawall and look at Ynys-morlan. She could see the whole street from this place, toy houses and toy traffic in the distance. And she could see the cracked ground where the gift shop had stood. In the sunlight she would take her sandwiches out, refold the tin foil and put it back into her handbag.

Her unfilled home would lie behind her. The emptier rooms brought that sense of calm and pushed every sound of building farther from her. She would look out, at her own work gone, and the desperation and the separation she had felt before, she could control them with the sight of this project's achievement. Spanning the arc of this coast, she would see their hometown's progress.

However she'd struggled to stop the gift shop's demolition, this project had provided for everyone; that man owned properties that would give him a future under others' guiding hands. What Gwen felt, as new as the bare shelves where dust hadn't gathered yet, was a sublimating peace. Like vapour sinking, repressing her doubts, permeating them with Ambi-Pur Liquifresh Citrus.

The kind of calm that achievement ought to bring. She didn't know what the point in striving could have been if success ruined its goals. And if she'd managed to change, selflessness to self-regard, when she'd never even found contentment. The struggle must have been a worthless one, if sacrificing it could make her feel this armistice.

She'd seen Dai's statue on the first day it had been revealed. Remorseful memories of her own had joined with the realization of what would become of it. And had been assuaged, as almost all fears were assuaged now, by the fact that this project was devoted to the community. Her acquiescence left her empty of strain.

'Dai has come to believe,' Emyr said, dissatisfaction entering his voice, 'in God, I suppose. That's the only way I know how to put it, though it certainly isn't God that he's found . . .' There was no breeze to rustle the papers between them. This window was closed on the street. 'Since Eirian died, it's been. He needed something to help him through it. Well, it's obvious, isn't it? We all find spirituality in times of need . . . I couldn't put it to you in a way that would be fair, Ruth . . .' Faltering, she saw the person she knew come to the fore, as she hadn't seen properly in months. 'I wouldn't want to belittle what he thinks by describing it . . . without thinking it myself.'

'I won't see it as *belittled*. Like there hasn't been enough stress in the project to make us all find God.' The little laugh she gave, though it had been hers once, shouldn't have been any more. She wasn't hiding now, not under sweetness, not under lies, not at all. Though when that bruise had covered her face she hadn't left the house for a week.

'He believes in . . . "time". Fate, I suppose. Predestination, I don't know . . . He believes it's all happening for one grand purpose, Eirian's passing . . . then the decision over the gift shop, the whole project . . . He's very confused, Ruth . . . He's lost. He can see it all happening, and it's easier for him to believe there's a greater meaning in it than just . . . regeneration.' Nights at his desk were lucid in Emyr's mind. When Gwen was gone and he didn't know where to. When he thought of her taking her possessions from the shelves, and found he loved her again, and found justifications for feeling it.

He remembered the morning of the gift shop's demolition, long-lost now. *That's so, Dai. Yes, that's so.*

'And what meaning is that?' Ruth asked, looking at him.

'He knows Ynys-morlan will be better . . . He thinks God wants to make it so there's somewhere in the world, a kind of paragon – I don't know – a Utopia. He thinks when Ynys-morlan's finished, there'll be nothing to stop it short of being perfection. You understand . . . ?'

But Ruth was silent, looking back at him, while Nia played at breaking things behind.

I stood very still and held them out and there was elizabeth who has long hair and white dresses and then I just all broke her and there was cherry who only broke on her face because shes soft. I watched them and they went very quickly and there was all of them never be nice again. You will never see them and have them and I will never. I dropped the musical box four times because it broke more and it made its musiuc but it couldnt sound nice anymore   I have made it dead too

The sound of beautification was all around them. They had to make their voices loud.

'Hello,' Bethan said to him. 'How're you doing?'

Dai looked back at her face. 'I'm all right, like, I'm good, thanks for asking.'

She pretended not to have seen him, and the more they'd done than see.

'How're you?'

She nodded at him and nothing more. She wished she'd never, he saw. She was ashamed, he saw, in front of Patty and Siân. He hardly even saw them on her either side.

'You're good?' he said.

'I'm fine.'

They looked at each other and still their gazes didn't meet. This was the ending, in bland sun and a cold wind. All her blonde hair hung round a face that didn't know him. There was this deadness in her eyes – unmistakeable now, like it had been on the pillow.

He looked at Bethan and sunlight made everything dimmer, though it couldn't be so. That hair blew and waved and made pretty lines. 'Good . . .' he heard himself say. 'Glad you're fine.' Like the meaningless words he'd used to talk before Time. He glanced at Patty and at Siân Humphries. He saw their stares on his statue.

'I'd like to talk, you know,' he said, 'maybe I could come down to the café later, but I'm a bit busy at the moment, like.' And this was no lie.

'We were looking at what you're building –' Siân said.

Pat's gaze fell away. He saw that.

'– is it safe, Dai?' Siân asked.

'Yes it's safe.'

'Are you sure? It doesn't really look it.'

Bethan's still face had no colour. 'Have you had anyone check it?' she asked. In the sheets, she remembered, low light, he'd thrown his head back. She'd made him come. And that was all it was. The newest, most precious thing to him. But she'd seen it a lot of times before. 'It doesn't look it, Dai. People are going to walk past here.'

'It's very important,' Siân said. He only glanced at her. 'Someone could be hurt if it fell. Children are going to be playing here.'

Had Bethan told them that it was against Time? Last night's abandoned hatred rose up in him though this couldn't even be true. They didn't know about Time, wouldn't have understood what it meant for his work to be with or against It. His eyes turned from a face to another face.

'It's safe.' The only thing he found to say.

'Things get older, though,' Bethan told him.

'What do you mean? It's safe, I've *leaned* on it, like, all the different bits. They're all *strong*, they hold me up. It's safe. It's got its own foundations.' He looked at her and no other words came into his mind. Time didn't tell him what to say. There were too many feelings to make out: anger, regret. He'd given her every secret thing he had. There was only turmoil, and that couldn't be Time's.

The sun came down to drift around them. A little way from them, he saw Kate Lowe. Echoes of machinery ran from air as Siân Humphries spoke again. Memories behind her, far further than Bethan's were, she said softly, 'Do you have planning permission for it?'

It had to be said. For the project to end without some grotesque spike jutting from the first place you saw when you drove in, it had to be. She didn't want to be the one. No one would. But it was better from a friend.

'What do you mean . . . ?' His eyes switched from one to another of them.

'Do you have permission?'

He raised a hand to the town, all of it clanging, ringing. 'Permission?' All of it clamouring. But they gave no answer, and he said, 'I didn't have permission for the shop . . .' He remembered really, though – the ignorance was just a lie.

'Demolitions don't need it,' Pat said. Sadness, the reality of it, made an empty voice. 'It's got to be approved, the officials will tell you the same, Dai, the committee.'

In the wind, Siân said, 'A lot of this work,' and she also raised her hand, 'is nothing but exterior resurfacing. You don't need permission for that. Only for new things you make. Patty and Beth here were given permission for the new extension, for the café's kitchen.'

Seeing his face, gradually tearing, Bethan didn't speak.

You couldn't hold fantasies up as more important than the real world. It wasn't the real world that had made her what she was, this fucking user. No – it was her fantasies that had made her that.

'I don't need planning permission!' Dai's eyes were ragged-wide. Had Time brought them here? To tell him the statue was wrong, because he'd tried to continue? 'I don't need it!' He just used the same words. 'I don't . . .'

'Dai,' Siân said quietly. How many nights down here making this?

And now he was building in the daytime, in front of everyone. He had to be told, and not later, but now. 'Have the building regulations people seen it? If you keep on, they'll tell you eventually. They won't let you keep it, Dai. They haven't seen it, have they?'

He couldn't answer. No one proper had seen it. Twisted in silence, he saw their faces.

He'd learned nothing from it yet. It hadn't shown him Time. From person to person he turned. They didn't even believe in Time. They didn't look at what he'd made and see something that was ruining Time's intricate plan. How could they even care like this? To stand here and tell him he mustn't build it? What did they believe?

'It can't be allowed to stand, Ruth. You can see as well as I can what it does to the town. To the project, and what it should mean.'

'It – ' she was going to disagree but couldn't. What they were making was a better place, and what was in Dai's statue but misery? All the confusion, she thought, which Ynys-morlan should make sense of, once complete. 'We *shouldn't*, though. You must see that . . .'

'I don't know what that's supposed to mean.'

'He's got the right. Just as much as us.'

'Ruth! He doesn't even . . . doesn't even know what's beautiful and what's not!'

'Emyr – '

'*Well?* He doesn't know the difference between something that's meaningful and something that's just – just blind devotion! Empty, stupid faith in something . . .' Emyr turned away and pressed a hand over his mouth, staring at the sites across the street. Stone-clad walls under scaffolds, waiting to be revealed.

He was trying to stop himself from crying, Ruth saw with amazement. The last two months of strain she had seen in him were bare there suddenly. She watched him giving himself little, bitter reproachings behind his glasses, and crying anyway. She put a hand on him and he jerked away.

'What he's doing isn't any different . . .' she said. 'He's unhappy. He's trying to make something out of it.'

'Oh yes,' he said. He was muttering with the same voice he'd used to have but his gaze was tattered as he stared out. 'Yes I'm sure there's no difference and we're all just like him. Just as full of stupid faiths and silly, blind lying to ourselves. Just deceiving ourselves . . . What are we *doing* this for then?' He turned to her again, red-eyed, pale-faced, lifting his hands, he said, 'If we're all just the same as Dai Meredith, what are we saying with this? *Nothing?* I know we shouldn't knock it down!'

He covered his eyes up and as she moved her hand across the table to him again, he raised his shoulders, his head. She saw him exhale tears away.

'Emyr, what's wrong . . . ? Tell me . . .'

He held his gaze up. He would look at her, he thought, and let himself cry like this. He could feel it all backing up, saltwater. He'd let it fall right out of him. *I believed in her,* he'd say. *I loved her for twenty years.*

Opposite, across the dust-cast road, Gwen was standing. She was walking slowly past the sea stones' pile, between the vehicles, still or moving. To the edge of the pavement she came, where the voices could clearly be heard.

A man's voice: she saw Ieuan Davis, his glasses slipped a little down his nose as they were always slipped, standing five feet from the small group that had gathered around Dai Meredith's figure.

'No one likes it, but there's reasons why planning committees exist. We've all got to play by the rules. Don't have to smile about it, but, you know . . .'

'It's my land,' Dai said.

Gwen heard the tipple of laughter – false, she heard it – from Ieuan's mouth. And his thinning hair was laid carefully across his scalp. He brushed it, she saw, with a practised hand. 'Don't think they'd care much over that, you know, who's going to build on land they don't own? No, it's "in keeping" they care about.'

'This land was my mum's.'

Bethan looked at him, her reserve cracking as she saw his face. So would she live in a daydream then? Playing in a ball gown? Would she like to run away with him, round this curve in the road and out of town? 'I know it was,' she said. 'It's not fair –' she said, as though she had the right to even speak those words, ' – but you can't build it, not even if it is your land.'

'Not that.' Kate Lowe's reproachful voice, Gwen heard in the short distance, bluster compensating for the lack of sureness that had crippled her since she was young. 'It's got nothing to do with the project.'

And quiet then, if you could call it that amid the sounds of building which filled every room of every house in Ynys-morlan, that leaked out into its street between the traffic, and seemed, to all of them – even her and she was stranded from it – to give the project a meaning that must be great, tremendous, it was so loud.

Dai turned from each one to the next, and finally to the thaw of Bethan's face as the sun cast pallor over her. If Time gave choices then either they were meaningless and only led to the same end, or It had a thousand ends to give, and what was Its power then? What was Its pattern? As he stared from one to another – Bethan, Patty, Siân and Kate there, Ieuan, John Griffiths who he saw standing behind, and other faces, hanging back between the slow-moving passers-by, slowing more by the second – he looked at them all, and he had to see that choices were real.

Because he could agree. He'd always done that, back when he'd been lost. *I don't really know about that. Don't really know about anything.* And why had they thought him dull? Of course they had. But he didn't have to agree. He could speak, he saw now, and find out what Time's design brought for him then. What it brought for everyone else.

He raised up his hand again, pointed to it: higher than anybody's head. Cement-dirty timber spikes and the tin gutter's thin spiral, dusty in this sun that gave no favours. Into its cup he'd set cement. Into the cement, he'd set every object he could find in the gift shop's remains. As if from mud they stuck their edges out, small with the distance of the garden's site. Pieces of window sill, pieces of the slates, a door handle that he'd found. When he had used each broken thing small enough, he'd taken out his keys and had gone to the new shops opposite, where the old stock was stored in the upper rooms. Things from the sale racks that had stood outside, he'd wedged into the concrete. Objects as common as the summer here and all its memories.

He pointed. 'Do you even know why I'm building it?'

He heard their voices, how it didn't matter, how they were sure that there were lots of reasons, and the planning committee wouldn't care. Under the blue sky, they sounded no clearer than voices had in the days after his mum's funeral. He looked at Bethan. Fear and sadness, he saw. Maybe she'd needed to believe after all, and still never tried to, not in the things he'd told her. Not even when they'd been alone.

'You don't even know why I'm building it! I haven't ever seen a place as . . . as bad as this!' His words tried to hide from him, the logic he needed tried to hide. He'd never seen anywhere else. 'I can't imagine any place as bad, you know? Ti – the project's making town perfect, like nowhere else. And I'm making this . . . Town's not perfect!' Speaking was full of jagged edges, full of rocks. 'It can't be ever. Even beautiful, you know that?' From face to face and none with understanding. 'People are horrible here . . . People are meant to care about you but they don't, there's no caring . . . Gwen came to my house and she was bad. Saying . . . But I'm bad,' hard as a river bed, each piece breaking and flowing from him. 'I went to see you . . .' He looked at Siân, face closing up like a snapdragon as he did it. 'Told you and I knew it'd hurt her and that you'd think bad things. I'm bad.' Breaking into Bethan's home, he remembered. What Time made you want could be wrong, it could destroy things. 'People are bad and I'm the same.'

With his shouting, confused, their voices had died. What could you say to a man who stood in front of you, unable to put words together in ways that made sense? Shouting at you, when you weren't the one who'd brought planning committees into existence? What could you say to a man who understood nothing and stood raving that the world was not fair?

Nothing. You said nothing. You looked at him. You listened till he was quiet again. There was no way to build Dai up until he met the real world.

'This place is going to be perfect.' His arm waved from his own work out towards the road and all its houses, past their shut or lowered faces, past the vehicles, like all the homes could be touched in one gesture. 'I believe . . .' Dai said, 'I believe that . . .' falling words he tried to hold. 'But it can't be perfect. Mum's dead! She's just dead! How can it be perfect then? How? And we're all the same and Ti – the project – makes us all the same and keeps us all together? But look at me! Look at me! How can it be perfect? I've got nothing!' His home, behind him, all his mother's things in places covered with dirt now and the few objects he used day to day like shining, fresh stones in all that oldness. *'I've got nothing!'* Not Bethan, not even the dream of her. Here she was, after they'd been together in the most beautiful moment Time could make. Here she was: couldn't even look at him.

Panicked. Though he couldn't see it, desperate. Would she defend him? After starting this? No, she wouldn't. Would she rather live like he did? Believe in him? What did it matter? She couldn't. Dai's beauty was nothing more than a lack of understanding.

'I've got nothing,' he said, 'and all of you, you've all got everything you want . . . and that's why I'm building it.' Finally, it came out of him. Not only to make a statue of Time. 'Because it's going to be beautiful. But it can't be beautiful. Because I don't understand . . .' he said '. . . I'm building it because I don't understand . . .'

There was the wind, whispering between the traffic's noises. Pushing a strand of hair across Siân Humphries's eyes. There was the warm and sunlit air escaping in their breath.

What could you say to a dim man who stood and cried because he couldn't build what he wanted? Because the world had given him nothing to be happy over? Because he was alone?

'Dai . . . ?' Patty's voice, low and troubled in all their silences, 'Come down to the café with me, come on and we'll sit and talk. You want to do that?'

'No,' he said. He looked at all of them. He didn't want to sit with them, not ever, not ever again.

In the autumn, when the chance of this project had first come to Ruth and she'd been stolen away, the whole of herself stolen by the first thought of it, it had been for Lennie's sake that she'd imagined it, and rehabilitation had been the word she'd used. She'd believed that. Sitting on their bed, he'd told her how it felt to watch Ynys-morlan collapse. The day of Eirian Meredith's funeral, it had been. Trying to hold a ceremony that was meaningful inside its barriers, he'd taken hold of her son and somehow efforts at calming him had broken loose themselves.

And what was the meaning of the project now; how was today any different to that morning?

To put the pain you felt into something beautiful, that had been the aim. She'd told Charlotte she believed it was wrong to let that pain out, just ugliness, anger, misery. Dai's statue wasn't beautiful. It struck her with the pain of all those nights, as they'd lain beneath this pretty house's daytimes – this pretty house, now being recreated. How much did we have to control what we released? In the traditions of that funeral, or in creativity, something had evolved to give voice to what you felt. But it continued to evolve. You saw your own weakness as you expressed it, and you hid it. All the way to its extreme the voice grew. Until the words you used were masks, just like silence had been.

She looked at Emyr now.

Why was Dai's statue ugly? Barbed and angry, bewildered and chaotic with all the months he'd spent after that funeral: broken glass, objects shoving out of concrete? It was only sorrowful.

The last part of the conversation that passed across her kitchen table, under the noise of reconstruction in the other rooms, Ruth would remember many times as the project drew towards its end. How Emyr had looked at her, believing the completion of Ynys-morlan was a goal more important than any other. How, in that, he'd seemed almost to lose himself. She'd remembered days as she had looked at him, so long ago that they were no more now than casts of dry summer in her mind: Charlotte Weyland's garden, when it had not been Charlotte's but had owned its own walls, and how she'd gone with Emyr and his friends. A little boy who talked older; thought he knew it all because no one else his age wore glasses. A sweet sort of arrogance. She'd seen it pushed under the surface when his mum, her aunt, had stood next to him.

Ruth would remember, through the last four weeks, how Emyr had moved away from her that day, though she'd found no arguments that she could articulate. He didn't know her really, or what had become of her marriage, her life. A little boy, she saw, grown up. He raised his eyes and she didn't understand what was haunting him either. It had seemed to balance on his choice. They'd been close once. That day a door shut between them. He hadn't wanted to make the decision, she had seen, and yet he had.

She'd heard the sounds of rebuilding. She'd wondered how the project could do this.

'It can't stand,' he had told her quietly, two days before she heard that Dai had left.

Mommy showed me what I have done. She was as crying but I couldn't tell her why. Maybe its not true and I dreamed it. Maybe this was all my fault and I shouldnt have done it. Maybe what happened on saturday was a dream but the picture makes me know its NOT a dream because it makes me REMEMBER it. I must look at the picture evry day and I will look at it now. It was NOT a dream bacuse I put my finger on the writing. it was cut in.
mommy said I am taking this away and she showed me my toy horse and she said I am taking this as well bacuse you dont deserve it and your behavure is horrible. Mommy took the musical box that is old and that I love and I am sorry because of and she was saying i shouldnt have done it bacuse when she was a girl it was her musicalbox. Iam horrible like she saysbut it wasnt a dream. i have NOTdone this because Im not me.

'Do you want to hear a story about right and wrong?' Gwen asked. Her voice shook here, where the wind drove the shadows quick as leaves. 'You won't want to hear it, I think.' She had driven here, an expression on her face seen by no one. 'You should hear it, though. I don't know what to think,' she said. 'I don't know what to think of anything any more.'

Parked between the vacant caravans, their windows admitting no light until it was the tourist season's sun, she looked at Tom, standing with paint and brush beside his own, where he'd been working as she drove in. The smile had blown across his face. Her words fell to nothing but her own breath.

'Will you come for a walk?' she said. 'I've been sitting in town, I've been – will you come for a walk with me?'

'What happened?'

'I'll tell you . . .' There was a silence before he put the paint can down, looking in her eyes. He saw a change, like something had fled from her. Her hands shifted on her bag.

They walked out of the site through its unmarked lanes, past each of the caravans' doll's-house gardens. Four weeks now until the gates were open for everybody else, and Barry had spent a few maintenance days here already. Next Monday, Owen would be back from Aber and these little roads, where Gwen's low heels clipped the quiet, would be brushed with the sounds of a lawnmower and his radio, too low to make out the songs.

He walked fast to keep her pace. Her arms were crossed tight and her gaze levelled out, levelled out, on no view but the dunes. As she told him it all, though, those dunes rolling nearer and then around them as they took to the boardwalk, her footsteps slowed gradually, as her voice did. His expression unchanging, he echoed her, 'My mum.'

'Everyone,' she said. 'Everyone. Bethan, Patty, John Griffiths. People standing there and watching. Me watching,' she said. 'Kate . . . On the pavement. Right by the side of the road. And it got worse. Couldn't even have said whose fault it was. I saw it all. Couldn't have said. Everyone's fault? Dai's?' The wind left them bare as they topped a run of steps, sun and shade lying with clear-cutting edges in the hollows of the sand dunes behind. 'I feel so empty,' she said. 'I feel so angry and empty and shocked . . . sorry . . .' she said. After a moment, she turned to look at him and saw everything she said reflected. 'Standing there . . .' Her voice was caught and ran away from her, 'and he's just saying over and over – you know what he's saying to them? – "My mum gave me this land," he's saying, "my mum gave me it." They couldn't leave it . . .' She looked out at the view before them. 'They didn't want to leave it,' she said. 'Not for the planning committee to deal with, not for a few days, and certainly not to let the thing stay. A bloody witch hunt . . .' she said. On her face there was a loss that left her void.

Out ahead, the dunes fell to flatness. The incoming tide was a distance from them that reached with nothing but sand, the palest yellow, this low sun pushing shadows from its tiniest ridges, lengths like fingers. She looked down at the shoreline. These people were her friends and her community.

'Guilt,' she said. 'I feel that.' But the memory of that afternoon, of Dai's house, her own voice in its musty rooms, seemed faded here, to this distance. Everything that she knew seemed faded. 'Where's the right and the wrong in it?' she said, blunt-toned. 'Five hundred people who want to regenerate this town and one man wanting to build some stupid, I don't even know what you call it. Sculpture? One who wants to build some sculpture. What do you think, Tom?' she said. She turned towards him again and he saw that her eyes were red, torn with more than pity or regret for Dai. And seeing that look? He felt loss just like it. Sickness, incomprehension that shifted, light enough to be thrown on this wind.

'What did she say to him, my mum?'

Memories, he had, of Siân's disgusted condemnation, when she'd come with Dai's crying ready for retelling in front of everyone who knew Gwen. He'd been shocked by that readiness. Then he'd had the shock knocked out of him, hearing her tell them, no forewarning for him, she was going to apply. He'd seen changes in her through the last two months that he couldn't ever have imagined. But he stood here with the story Gwen told him dropping through him till it could sink no further, and couldn't believe his mum had had a part. He tried to picture it and couldn't picture it.

'I can't remember,' Gwen was saying. 'I listened to it all – it's hard to pick who said what from the sight of it. They were all talking. Or standing and watching it, just like I was . . .'

'Bethan,' Tom said. He didn't cross his arms or move in the cold. 'Patty, like.'

She didn't answer. When she turned to him finally, all she said was, 'He was falling apart. Who wouldn't be? A crowd round you like that, who wouldn't be . . . ?' And then, as the disorder and the effort on her face fell apart as well, 'What's *"goodness"* then, what's *"right and wrong"* when everyone can stand together and do that . . . ?'

He didn't answer her. And the view certainly didn't, with all its tides coming in, going out, doing nothing.

After a long time, looking down at the sand that was scattered in the boardwalk's last stretch, he said, 'I couldn't tell you. I used to . . . used to listen to her, used to think she knew.' Then he laughed a little, raised his eyes and filled them up with all the coast. He thought of his mum's face and something in him – which he'd told himself was no longer there – seemed hollowed out.

'You know how I used to think of it?' she said. 'Helping others. But what's goodness when all the others are just as capable . . . ?'

'It's not,' he said. He remembered standing in the restaurant's new room, and Bethan asking him if he forgave her. How she deserved the happiness she'd got. How they all did. How it had seemed like doing the right thing meant nothing but sacrificing what you wanted yourself. In the caravan site, in the last few days of its empty months, he had been doing his own bit of renovation. Didn't know how to leave. Didn't know how to stay. Didn't know any fucking person in town but Gwen any more. Where's Rhys? Haven't got a fucking clue. Where's Bethan? Moved away and left some woman behind her – forgot to let her know that they'd been friends.

'Just as capable,' Gwen said, 'of hurting Dai . . .' The shortness in her voice gave no sympathy for herself, but over that hardened look, she was crying. 'I don't believe there's any such thing . . .' she said. With brutality for every hope she'd had; the peace she'd felt these last few days, and absorbed, despite doubts. 'Goodness?' she said. 'Should Dai get what he wants then? If it sticks out against the place that every single other person wants to live in. Should he get it anyway? Why? Just because he doesn't understand? But . . . like bloody jackals, they were. He's falling apart and they're still standing there telling him. "*Goodness?*" What is that?'

Marram grass made a low noise on the rises around them, pushed as easy as hair in the wind that came in off the sea.

'You know what it is?' she said. 'Justification, that's what goodness is. Whatever we want proven, that'll prove it. All my life . . .' she said, but she didn't even finish the sentence. 'You know what it is to me? I come to see you and we sit and we talk, I tell you, of course there's such a thing. It's right to look for it, I tell you. And why would I say that, I wonder?' She stared out, and that thin, shining line could not be a sea, surely. Not something so vast as a sea. 'Because I'm desperate to believe my work wasn't all for myself.'

He stood in silence, those nights receding from him as he heard her speak the truth.

'I hit that man,' she said. She nodded to herself. 'And then I sit with you and tell you that you should keep searching for something . . . something that I'd like to believe I've searched for.' Sadness broke away from the words Gwen said, as she remembered beliefs, connection in their few evenings, that had seemed to validate things she hadn't ever understood. 'How much easier, to prove something to yourself, when you've got someone else wanting to believe. I hit that man.'

'Everyone does wrong things –' He thought of Rhys on the last night he'd seen him; how he'd condemned him when he himself had been the one lying that he was sleeping with this woman.

'Wrong things?' Gwen said. 'What does that mean? Pleasing yourself, like Siân is?'

Tom remembered. *I don't want my mother hearing that.* And Gwen, as she'd sat beside him in the van: convincing herself? Just convincing herself she was in the right? 'Everyone does fucking wrong things, or the right ones wouldn't be so hard!'

'Pleasing yourself over other people? That what wrong means? And doing right is . . . pleasing others instead?' The tranquillity, the control she'd felt, seeing Ynys-morlan in the last week and knowing that she benefited nothing from the project, she saw again. 'Do you think it's wrong, Siân telling Dai he's got no right to build that . . . thing? Cruel,' she said. 'It's that. But she doesn't hurt people for the sake of hurting them.'

He didn't know any more. Morals had always been like walls with her, she'd kept everything she disliked out with them; and applying for the grant, she'd taken out the bricks right at the bottom. Fallen down piece by fucking piece, so he couldn't even recognize the person she'd used to be in all the mess that he saw now.

'She doesn't hate the world,' Gwen said quietly, 'wouldn't be cruel for no reason . . . How is it for her, I wonder?' Had she even asked, that last evening that they'd spent? No, she had not. Would Siân have answered? She didn't think so. 'How is it for her, to turn round now? After such a long time, make changes . . . her own son condemns her for.'

'No,' he said, staring at her as she turned.

'She must feel guilty.'

And if she hadn't been so sure, talking with her, that she would find the place where right had turned to wrong in her own life, maybe she would have seen it. Sitting there, glass in hand, as the day had faded from the panes of the window beside them, maybe she would have realized.

'She must feel guilty, Tom.'

'I don't condemn her! I don't fucking well understand her – I don't condemn her. She doesn't feel guilty . . .' He'd seen her, her self-righteousness. But precious things were tumbling: those nights with Gwen. Memories of his friends, just the feeling of being fucking young, pictures of the way his mum's house had been when it had been his too. Things, both sad and precious, all fucking needed and all falling. 'She doesn't believe in guilt these days.'

'Do you think that takes it away?'

Gwen's reddened eyes looking at him, the years between her and eighteen seemed as empty as this bay. She knew Siân. She had heard her voice from the road's other side. Brittle and empty it had been, with all its echoes left behind, of years when she'd made strengths of everything she didn't have. How had it been for her to cross the line, leave all that time behind?

Holding herself in with her arms, tears came out anyway as she said to Tom, 'There's no such thing as being a good person. Do you think it's good for me to drive out here? Do you think it's good for me to come and see you, in the middle of the night? You're eighteen years old and I'm convincing you of all the things I want to think – do you even ask yourself why you care so much for doing the right thing?' Sand was lifted in the wind and thrown out on to the dunes again. 'I've watched Siân . . . bring you up. I've seen her push you. Life's been hard for her – I've watched her teaching you how it's going to be hard for you as well.'

Mouth open for denials that wouldn't come, Tom stared at her pale face.

'I've watched her. She's a difficult person to earn respect from. Doesn't hurt if you're just her friend . . . She makes her choice. I've been going through town telling people – what a marvellous opportunity the project is. And I've been going to Dai Meredith's house and saying . . . anything I can to stop my own work going down with all the rest! Dai tells her, and it's easy for her to make her choice. Why shouldn't she leave – a lot of hardship – a lot of hardship behind? And you?' she asked him. 'The times when you did get her respect? Few times, Tom? They must have been few. By living just like she taught you. I saw it . . .' Gwen held herself because she could not hold him, crying fully now and not fully understanding why. 'What did those few times mean . . . when she left behind the things she taught you?'

The picture that came to Tom, as her expression seemed to crumble, was of leaving. That day with Rhys. Sun lying on the road to the site like it wouldn't ever get up again, and the short grass, yellow with two months of summer, flattened around him as he'd sat down, fluttering in the wind that never left this place. He was always walking. Or always swimming out to save that girl whose cards had stopped coming when she'd reached twelve. Always ready to smile in black and white for a picture *The Star* had published ten years ago.

'You can't think like that . . .' he said, but he couldn't hold on to his voice. 'You can't think, like, because there's reasons . . . *Everyone's* got reasons! You can't think . . .' He was losing it, voice and words. Was that all it was to him? To be a good person? 'You can't believe reasons make it meaningless! You wouldn't think like that if you were thinking straight! We've all got reasons! We've all got fucking reasons! It doesn't make what you want worthless! Gwen –' His hands moved out, but to hold on to what? 'Is that all you think of me then?' Standing in the new backyard, he remembered, how Siân had asked if he'd needed her money, and how he would've taken it if he could. *'Is that all you think of me?'*

'Tom –' She looked at him, with all the sand dunes behind him and his hair blown in his eyes as he shouted at her. 'Do you think it's looking to do the right thing that gets me driving out here? You're eighteen! How much harder – you tell me how much harder it's been – for you to have . . . any kind of relationship with your mother since I started seeing you!'

She nodded as he didn't answer her.

'Harder, a lot harder, yes. And the choices you make at eighteen, they're the ones you keep. You think, after my coming out here and seeing you, do you think, a year from now it'll be any easier for you and Siân? What you are at eighteen's a lot harder to break at nineteen, and at twenty-five . . .'

'It's not you,' he said, 'causing that.'

'Is it not?'

'What's the reason then? Why do you come?' And just saying it, the feelings that fled from him as he did so, he knew that she was right. He had left his mother in some place outside his reach on the first night he and Gwen had seen each other. She had stopped him wanting to close the gap he'd always seen when he'd looked at Siân.

His clothes billowed. His hand fell back to his side. Around them, grasses bent their thin necks as the far tide was blown slowly in. 'What's the reason?'

Gwen held her bag. 'I come to see you . . . because I think you're wonderful. Because I love seeing you. Because I love – you . . .That's the only reason.'

He stood in silence. She had given away the last trace of pretending to know herself.

'I don't care then,' he said. He moved up a step towards her. 'Other things – I don't care –' Awkward hands rising, shadow was caught in an expression that was devoid of things he'd held true for such a long time. And was she going to move away? Because it wasn't right?

The cold sun very bright, she couldn't see him properly. She felt his hands around her back. She dropped her bag and did not notice, because she was putting her own hands inside his coat, between the layers of jumpers and T-shirts. Because he was grasping a hold of her just as tightly as they stood with the view around them, with the sparks of light on a sea too far away to be made out, and as he held her, walking back along the pale road with their figures just little silhouettes in that thin sun.

And she did not go home. All that afternoon, into the evening, she did not go home. It was dark outside and he'd brought in the paint tin, the brushes, put them in a cupboard in the caravan's tiny kitchen space, and she stayed. All the vehicles' headlights letting dusty beams wander as they queued to leave at the other end of this long road, she was there with Tom. She'd never lain in a bed with any man except her husband and, though it took them long times to kiss, longer times to touch, though she started crying when he moved towards her clothes like he would try to take them away, still that was where she lay.

When they made love, long after all parts of that road had emptied, moving with the sides of their faces pressed against each other, eyes closed hard against everything else, it *was* abandoned. For, though they shut their eyes against it, everything else had left them behind.

*

The day of Dai's decision to leave Ynys-morlan ended. It drew down into night.

And when Gwen went back to her house? When she found Emyr waiting in their living room and he raised his face, the carriage clock on the mantelpiece telling them both that it was half past four in the morning of a different day, could she have hidden it from him?

'Where have you been?'

She stood in silence, make-up gone from her face as for years she'd not even let him see her.

'Only thing to ask really, isn't it?' he said.

He wiped his hands in a restless, almost organized way, on his knees. He nodded only for himself. She saw these things, and recognized them, and all the person lying under them. She didn't answer.

'Where have you been?'

As he had asked her once before, she remembered, on a night as wind-struck and cold as tonight; different only, in that it had been autumn then, and this was now a growing year.

'Gwen . . . ?'

'I can't tell you,' she said.

'Gwen!' But she left him, walking up the stairs to her bedroom, calling her name in a drier voice with the all passing seconds; left him, refusing to shout out the accusations that had gathered through the night, looking at an empty living room and a project that had seemed to him like a memorial for both of them.

The place in Emyr's imagination was full of empty houses. It was silent and clear and beautiful. In the next days, ghost sounds of her with another man came like echoes to walk between the buildings. But he'd always envisaged it as some ghost town. Lovelier because it was. This place had been for both of them but it didn't grow less beautiful.

She wouldn't tell him where she had been that night. Her manner, which he had tried to embody in the project, its faultlessness, its justice, fell away from her. She didn't sit with him in the evenings to listen to the project's progress. She took the ornaments away, one by one, hour by hour, in the few evenings she did spend in their home. By the time that he remembered that day in the sunlit car park, and the words that Rhys had shouted in his face, all Emyr's feelings were at war. There was anger, hurt. There was the need to find what she was hiding. The project, though, their elegy – his love for it didn't lessen.

When she was gone one of these days, he stole a box from the stack that lined the hallway. And he took it, on the passenger seat of the car, down through the winding, sun-splashed traffic, between the building sites' rows, all the way to the museum. He locked it there in the office. The restoration would be finished soon. And he stood and looked at the pictures Rhys had painted, spilling on to each other – hating each other, it seemed – and didn't let himself feel the edge of their loneliness.

Brush strokes, scratching pencil as he drew the outlines, the thin clutches of working light from the torches on the floor. A place growing clearer between the half-finished figures of Bethan and Tom, between the recreated graffiti. There was an internal place, full of feelings you couldn't control, and you gave it the name of your home.

The bus shelter was covered in stone cladding now. Tiny sea stones in a cobbled wall and the clean loveliness of fresh render covering the inside. Its roof was being slated so it could catch the sky in just the same shade as every other building here.

There'd been a place maybe in history where Lennie's beliefs wouldn't have become what they had done here. Perhaps – he stared at the photographs, copied them as well as he could do – perhaps Ynys-morlan had once been like that. The thought hurt him but it touched him. The town couldn't be that now, whatever Lennie's hopes were. Since listening to the man out on the shorefront, though, Rhys couldn't give up his need for that place. It had grown; was growing now. He couldn't give up the belief that this real town where he'd lived had robbed him of it.

The boy's voice in empty air, Emyr remembered. The boy's lies. Or truths.

'You want to talk about morals, Emyr?' Gwen said that week. 'You think I've cared more for my work than for you? Good motivations wouldn't have made that better!'

Calm had left her, the way she shook her head.

'Let's talk about Dai Meredith then,' she said. 'Let's talk about where I left the path, and what it did to him. Because it's no worse than what's being done now. He's being shoved out, do you realize that? I think "oppressed" is the word. There's no such *thing* as goodness, Emyr . . . there's only . . . there's only majority rule!'

Scrawled sketches, Emyr saw now, that ran into paintwork. Spray-paint. A group of men raking stones from a street that was filled with them.

It was goodness that he'd tried to embody in his vision for this town, and he'd cared for Dai. Those weeks when Dai had lived with them, he'd liked the man. But what they were building here could be – as Dai himself had wanted – flawless. Unmatched.

He looked at the wall. He remembered that day in the community centre's car park.

Thoughts of goodness gave out against the project's ideals; a quick and quiet little war.

While Rhys painted his leaving card on the wall, while Emyr sat listening to Gwen's footsteps as she left him in the living room, four a.m., Bethan couldn't sleep, tangled up under the covers she'd taken Dai into. Pierced by memories – of the man's face, of his body, open-mouthed – imagery full of beauty. What had she done to him?

Abused him. But she'd wanted it, more than him even. And not to hurt him, only to feel what it was like to be with him. The vivid colours that she'd tried to hold in real life were hollowed out. The things she'd wanted couldn't be real. What was real she didn't want. To be this person. What had she done to him? Hurt him, used him. What was he feeling now? Alone in his house and with nothing but confusion. This was what she'd done. Hating herself, reaching out anyway, this was what she had done.

All the truths Rhys had told her and all the loathing she felt for herself hadn't been able to stop the flights of those colours, though. Trying to wreck everything she had felt with Dai, to drag it back into the truth before the truth could do it for her, lying in this bed now, still the images grew brighter.

Of Dai's face. Of her dress. Hope. Despite what she'd done to him, the pictures were of hope. For herself, when she didn't know how they could be.

Did Dai love her now? Was he lying there, feeling it? She'd ground his purity down, taken everything she could get from it, left it empty. He might hate her now. And it still felt like his innocence survived. It must have. Inside her, it was breaking all other things.

She couldn't commit to the town. The same choice she'd had to face two years ago, and so fucking painful then it was a joke that it could come back. In effect, though, that was what the restaurant meant. She couldn't – no commitment that wasn't cold, grey, fraught by the sight of her mum like every year of Bethan's future could be found in the flatness of her eyes. Pat hadn't wanted Ynys-morlan to progress. Didn't want the town full of opportunity. The bitterness she gave out – Bethan could see it – it was loss. Confronted without warning by possibilities she must have given up on so long ago. Washed suddenly away by them, along with the life she'd made in their stead when she'd fallen pregnant at eighteen.

Across the street at night, Rhys sat in the Lion – almost completed now. A different place. He'd never spent an evening in the room where he stood, never spent a drunk hour. He would be there, looking through the faces, drinking bottled beer at half price from the boxes stacked behind the new bar, the walls still unpainted.

She watched the delivery of the stained-glass windows that week and, busy now with only details, the last little parts, Bethan would stand and see them installed. In a sunlit afternoon, new roofs almost finished on every house around them – without clarity as thoughts of Rhys and Dai ate her up – she would see the plastic slowly taken from the panes, surrounded now by painted walls, three-coated. See that peel-off covering drop on the floor and she would watch the men as they set the windows she'd designed into their places. In the project's final week of clamour, she'd see the colours – yellows, blues, deepest red – touch the restaurant's walls for the first time, and move with slow hands across them as the workmen turned their frames.

The last of all the windows were being fitted in Ynys-morlan. Brass hinges came in boxes, row upon row of them, separated by little card borders. Front doors arrived: a truck which stopped short, seeing the traffic-flow from a distance. In its bed, they stood against each other, no handles, no knobs, a wall of them.

Faxed maps that Emyr had sent out from his little study were checked by the driver, but didn't resemble what lay here in front of his windscreen. Looking for the concrete space where they'd been told to unload, they couldn't see it, or the seawall he'd drawn and labelled, or the sea.

From the backs of the landscaping company's van, bags of compost and grit and lime were taken and stacked on top of each other. They were sliced. Into the trench, they were poured, dark and fresh. A great circle when you stood at the edge. A little ring, if you looked down from above, in the midst of all the movement.

Bethan would hear of Dai's leaving from her mum. She didn't have the chance to say goodbye to him. The only person who saw him before he walked away from Ynys-morlan was Gwen Morgan.

It wasn't autumn and the daylight wasn't dying from the air. No

sense of time fading, as it had done last year, to touch the garden with
greyness and steal its memory away. When she went back to Eirian's
home, it was springtime there, as it was everywhere. And she didn't
know that he'd already packed bags. Dai's last hours, spent in silence,
lay closed behind the door.

The sun shone on it and didn't warm it, the wind blowing past it from the sea.

At its base, a smooth cube of timber blocks set around the concrete, then a looser shape, glass pieces that didn't fit against each other, set into the cement over objects you couldn't see. To the height of six feet maybe. Over your head, the two-by-two lengths jabbed out to cast shadows, timber hands, that would count Time like a sundial's, but not with hours or any other words that they'd invented. So many wooden fingers, and so many silhouettes, over the cold and ruined ground. And last, high enough that you had to step back to see, crane your neck, the smaller pieces of debris that he'd found in the old gift shop's stock.

Windmills, all their colours changing as they turned their faces with sweet, soft flicking sounds. Kids' toys, sunglasses, a beach ball and one of the little blankets his mum had used to stack by the ice cream counter, because people only buy blankets when they're cold. It hung, one end cemented in, its other too heavy to get lifted on the wind and dropping down almost to touch your face. The gutter's spiral held them in, its last end jutting at the only angle Dai had been able to bend it to.

The clocks in his home had struck two in the morning with their perfect choir chimes. A short walk from the single lit window in the Meredith house, on the empty mantelpiece in the Morgans' living room, like a little sentinel the carriage clock had chimed too. It didn't have any memory of Dai, or of that one morning in a wash of disconnected days that had begun the statue; a glance that had lengthened to minutes of staring as Dai had realized that crying came to him and left him with perfect regularity.

He'd left the dusty disarray of his house last night, walking through the quiet trees to see the town that spread itself before him; a thin and shining imitation of the stars. As if there were answers there.

He'd always felt he was a stranger. They'd proved to him that it was true. He'd used to watch them talk sometimes and wonder, only wonder at what was in their thoughts. Now, they were looking to build a different place, these people here. Really, the town that they'd had before had been a Newfoundland to him.

He had cried through the afternoon to this half-risen night. He'd sat with his watch, all the house's clocks round him, and tried to see if his tears still came with rhythm. Looking from one of their moon-faces to another. Over Bethan, his thoughts moving. Over the images of Siân and Patty on the sunlit street, their voices. Time's path a nest of snares. Every hope, when he thought of how he'd tried to follow It, came up against Bethan's words. So beautiful before and so ugly then – fucking ugly – dirty ugly – so cold, telling him his pillar couldn't be a part of Time's work. Crying, he'd stared from clock to clock, waiting for when the tears ebbed, to see.

Ten minutes. With the chimes and just the gentle, switching seconds. Ten minutes, he saw.

The way he'd changed, though: he looked at this and the thought came that he might be doing it himself. Without his knowing, without trying to, to prove that Time was with him. The way he'd changed, like Bethan's figure in the window to the person that had lectured him with Siân and Pat – there was no safety any more. Perceiving the room around him, he couldn't find any beauty, couldn't feel Time holding him.

He remembered that day, months ago, and saw it again. If he hadn't believed then, all the hectic intervening weeks might have looked empty of the future, just bewildering, and purposeless, as his mother's living room was now that none of the light bulbs worked. He'd always known he was a stranger here. It was only Time that had shown him otherwise. Holding everyone, he'd thought.

He didn't know what to believe, walking down to see Time's statue now. You could shout, ask It over and over to give you the things that you needed, make every move It showed you. You wouldn't be given them because of that. Time only had Its rhythm, that could hurt or take hurt away. It had no voice to tell you what you'd done wrong.

Dai moved between the first black buildings towards that circular valley; its roughened edge. Its pegs and ropes tipped their silhouettes as if the land was water and they were sinking. This would be Time's garden; round like every clock. Dai stood at its border and stared at what he'd built. Feeling the cold on his face, he saw its stretching arms.

He'd chased every desire that Time had given him and this was what he'd made.

It didn't look like Time. No splendour, no wholeness. It had twisted itself, thrust out stiff, broken clutches, cracked its skin into a jigsaw of glass. He stared and couldn't help but see. It wasn't a sculpture of Time.

He'd believed he was meant for Bethan. How you could see the months in her baby. The way she held everything that Ynys-morlan meant. He'd believed that in Time's project he'd a great part to play. It would have needed to be great, though, to bring him alongside everybody else.

What he'd built was not a statue of Time. In the night air, windmills turned and under the street lights were all yellow. Look at the blanket. Time didn't hold those memories precious, only you did that.

The fingers threw a thousand shadows. It didn't reveal what moved above people. It looked more like people themselves.

Where had his devotion led him, or trying to do what It meant? Only to this broken, half-finished spire. He remembered their closed-cupboard faces. Here it stood, with the power to ruin Time's wondrous labyrinth. How could his questions be that strong?

The blanket, shifting slightly in the wind, gold-shadowed. Dust on the glass pieces. Thoughts seemed like the holes across the street where the bench's foundations had been. He put his feet in them.

Time had no design.

It was wrong to think it, bad to. But he waited. Nothing happened. He stood like the statue. A short distance across the riven ground from it, in his mind and in his heart where Time lived, Dai asked it.

He didn't know if he only spoke to the sculpture or to Time Itself. He didn't know if one could be found in the other. If Time had a voice, It spoke with everything – with the trees moving, with people walking, in building work and babies – and then there were too many sounds for you to make out meaning.

He wanted to ask It what It was. He needed to know more than ever.

Houses lined the road behind him, with lovely shapes in the lamps' illumination, only scaffolds and their plastic coverings to draw a line between their appearance and the impression of home. Rubbish skittered, that Dai didn't see.

Look at it. His statue wasn't the shape of Time.

It was the shape of his own belief.

Its rusty limbs went out and up and they found nothing. There'd been days when the stacks of A frames had seemed to touch the sky and Dai had realized that could be done. But the sky had no solidity, no feeling at all. It couldn't be held on to. He stared at that blanket. When it touched your face, it didn't touch it with summer. It was cold and couldn't keep those days inside its little folds. It was wet and didn't smell of the gift shop any more.

Maybe there was no pattern to Time.

Six months almost since his mum had been taken. You didn't pass. You were stolen away. His house unchanged since then but for the dust you couldn't stop, like a layer between you and before that made the past dimmer every day.

Bethan's face. There, beside the seawall. He could have turned to see the place they'd stood together, no day there now. Her expression as he had told her about Time. Distance it had been. And sympathy, that he knew well enough how to recognize. And wanting, he'd seen. Sad and wanting to believe.

Emyr, as Dai had sat with him on the morning of the gift shop's demolition. His quiet answers as Dai had told him the same.

Yes, Dai. Yes, that's so.

But people lied. They mixed things up when nothing was clear anyway, like they didn't want the thinnest edge of clearness. People lied when they felt sorry for you, or when they got confused like he'd once done.

No one in Ynys-morlan believed but him, he knew it. And his belief had built nothing but this. His questions weren't unfaithfulness, he hadn't meant to sin, but they'd unravelled everything. Because of them, he'd been unable to hold on.

There might be no perfection in Time.

There was the sky and there was the land. Maybe there was no design. People and the lights of Ynys-morlan, all laced together – a reflection, it looked like, of something with more meaning. But maybe there was nothing more. And what you could see in children, the way they grew, what you felt when you thought about the future, or the beauty of the past once it was gone – maybe there was nothing more than these things. Maybe nothing made them whole.

Like a person leaving, it felt as he saw the sculpture. He stared at it on the barren soil and he saw this place around him. The seashore that lay behind him and, when he looked up, the sky.

A person, Time had been to him. But this place he saw was uninhabited.

He had built this, though. What did that mean? Nothing but the confusion he'd put into it? The thought seemed real, like the truth, but he didn't want to believe it.

There was something that unified the world. He gazed out over this town; saw what they had brought to life here, every one of them. He looked into his memories and, lies or not from Emyr, distance from Bethan or none, they'd been together in some way as he'd told them about Time.

Uninhabited, Dai saw, but maybe not abandoned. Not if Time had never held the place. Not forsaken then.

And at the edge of the floodplain, at the head of this street where the changing season came now with its warm night winds and fragile grass, the guardian Time had been to him was gone. There was only himself in all this new year. The thoughts he had were his alone. The smell of the air. The look of this spring.

Dai saw the statue he had made. It did reveal Time's shape. It was a lighthouse made of rubble. A watchtower by the sea. It didn't look like it could stand, but he had given it foundations. It was a sculpture of him.

'Dai?' Her voice was quiet at the door.

There was no answer. The sunlit yard was cold around her as Gwen stood, no car behind, and looked up at the house that she'd used to come to on Tuesdays, Thursdays and Saturday mornings.

Quiet and translucent in the open air: 'Dai? Are you here?'

She had thought first, standing at the gates and seeing it, that all the woman's efforts to draw endings down around her hadn't succeeded. But maybe Eirian had imagined this March: the garden's beds caught with daffodils, rising up around the untouched house. The curtains were drawn and the windows showed only cloudless blue. Gwen stood on a dead-weed path and birds sang.

It seemed, as she knocked once, as she heard a soft noise inside the house, that the sun which this year had brought, cold and still, was full of shame for all of them. It made its way down through the bare trees to lie, long shapes across the step. The house would slowly be buried. More gently, she thought, than Eirian had been.

'Dai,' she said. 'Dai?'

She heard the woman's voice in the last moment of silence.

Lying beside Tom after he had been inside her, perspiration drying on her as if her skin wasn't her own, and his eyes open, all her confusion and abandon had fallen to a picture of this place.

Why do you come here, Gwen?

In the distance, in place of any answer, there was the project's low and constant tone.

The door didn't open as on its other side, he spoke, his voice quieter than hers had been.

'Who is it there? Who is it? . . . I'm doing something now.'

'It's Gwen.'

'No,' he said. She heard him. Then, 'What do you want?'

She didn't know how to reply. 'Just to talk to you.'

She stood in front of Dai's home with no defence. There was an empty room inside her. Just this small stillness, that had gathered its scattered moments – of boxing her possessions, of talking with Emyr about a project she had no part in, looking at Ynys-morlan from that place on the seawall – into some kind of whole, as she had lain with Tom in what they called an afterglow. Only this. She came to give it to him. She didn't know any word that served as a name for the purpose. As he looked back at her from the doorway, slowly opening, wilderness seemed to move around her resolution like the springtime in this garden.

'Gwen.'

'Yes.' She tried to smile. 'How are you?'

'I'm good,' he said, 'thank you for asking,' as he'd used to, a long time ago.

He took in the way she stood, and the driveway behind her, empty of any car. A man who, with his dark skin and vague eyes and mad hair, had once looked back at you with the naïvety of a child but with none of a child's growth or curiosity. Gwen saw him after he'd stood, trying to defend what he had made, and what had replaced that naïvety seemed no more open. Sadness came to her, looking at it. There were choices, made already, where there had been none. In the branched sunlight across his face, they were of distance, she saw.

'I'm good,' he told her.

'Is that true?'

'Yes. It's true. I don't lie. I'm doing something at the moment. I'm busy.'

'Dai, I saw you yesterday.' He didn't nod or answer. As his innocence had been, the awareness she saw in Dai's eyes was a shade you couldn't touch. 'I came here in case you wanted to talk. Do you want to talk about anything? Because you know I'll listen.' But as he looked back at her, she heard what she'd said again, and how it was nothing more than a little piece of the past. He didn't know that. He had no reason to believe it any more. Perhaps it wasn't even the truth. 'I will listen,' she said. 'I would like to, if you have anything to talk about . . .'

'I don't. No.'

'Dai –'

He only stared at her.

'Dai, I'm sorry. I came to tell you – that I'm sorry.'

'Sorry for what?'

'For the last time I was here . . . And sorry that it was the last time. Sorry for a lot of things. I don't have any excuses to give you. I've regretted – I've regretted what I said, what I did. I should have come before, to tell you that.'

Dai looked at her on his doorstep. Three bags were sitting, down this short corridor, through the second always-open wooden door, on the floor there. His living room was swept with soft sun. He had never seen her – slight wind ruffling her hair, eyes with no words waiting in them – he'd never seen her like this. All his mother's things lay, in the hallway, in all the rooms, untouched since she'd been buried.

Gwen said, 'I saw everyone.'

He didn't answer.

She had seen them in the street, she had listened, and she had not gone to him. There'd been many things she could have said, and she'd said none. Maybe she hadn't even realized fully, until she'd stood here.

Dai Meredith would say nothing, and all your faults would come up in the places of the words he didn't use. Dai Meredith, who might have been a genius for all the insight that others' guilt afforded his silence.

Why do you come here, Gwen?

She heard the flight of a small bird behind her. 'I'm sorry,' she said. 'I'm sure – that everyone is. That's not just some speech. Do you understand? I'm sure everyone is.' Though she no longer believed that she spoke for them. There'd been a time when they'd stood behind her, all of Ynys-morlan's community. A strong wall at her back.

'Yes. Maybe. Probably she does feel bad.'

'Who?' Gwen said. 'Which?'

'All of you,' he finished, looking away. He heard the low exchange of the first clock in the hall. 'I can see how important the project is to everyone. I understand. Nobody just wants to make someone else feel bad, nobody likes that. People do things because it's important then they feel bad about them. But they do them anyway. And do you know?' he said. Her face was still as she listened, as though in stillness she could do nothing wrong. Dai didn't understand the way she looked. 'None of you know why it's even important,' he said. 'Like, no one believes it's for any reason.'

Emyr's study lay behind her, and she pictured it, all his papers with their tiny diagrams and their descriptions of the houses that stood, different every day, two miles away.

'Everyone believes that it's for a reason. You're not right in saying that, Dai. Different reasons for everyone, but . . . no one behaves the way they did, with you yesterday, unless they have a reason . . . one they think is important. The way I behaved with you . . .' she finished. She did not let herself look away. 'When I came here, when I came . . . the gift shop mattered a great deal to me. Maybe not as much as it did to you, but . . . still.'

Go and stand, Eirian had said, stand and look at it and ask yourself why you care. For the good, she'd thought. For work that had been moral. She might have laughed now.

'No one wants to hurt anybody else, just like you say, Dai. Sometimes, people are hurting themselves. They don't understand . . . how to mend it, they think they're making decisions . . . but they're just running. Do you understand? No one would try to hurt you. I know they're sorry.'

He looked at her for long seconds in the sun's stark reflections and then slowly he nodded, he took in what she said. He felt better. Feelings weren't meant to lead you anywhere maybe, but they still came in a rhythm. Sitting, he remembered on Gwen's cream sofa, her arm around him, staring at the world and not believing in his mother's death. He saw her now. Feelings came in harmonies, in circles.

And really this was the question there wasn't any answer to. The bags behind him in the living room were packed up with the things he'd gradually chosen. He'd leave this house. He'd decided in the early morning, walking out, away from Ynys-morlan as the traffic had begun to flow. He'd leave the town. This was the question: you saw the sky or the seasons, you felt changes – a great symmetry, that couldn't be. Maybe there was no pattern that united things, no shape to hold the world – except us. Just the way that people saw it.

He remembered now how Gwen had shouted. He said, 'It's hard to watch things just go away, when you made them.'

'Yes it is,' she nodded. 'It is.'

'Because you . . . you use . . . you make them out of *yourself*.'

'Yes,' she said.

'Thinking about them not being there is like . . . what you put in them, just away, just gone. Can't do anything about it.'

Gwen bit her lip, shook her head. The smile she gave to cover her sadness was bright and frail enough to make her look like a girl.

'You know what I think?' he asked her.

'What do you think, Dai?'

'When you make something . . . it's more than you,' he said slowly. 'It doesn't matter then, if it gets taken away, the gift shop or my . . . tower. It makes you change. Even if it's gone, it still did that, didn't it?'

She couldn't answer for a moment. She would have liked to believe so. All the doing, though, years of action, and these last weeks when she'd denied herself – she was no closer to understanding. No change had taken away the drought in her. Why did we have to strive, make things, build things? The need was so strong. As if we weren't enough on our own, or life wasn't. She'd thought it was morality that pushed her on, but right and wrong dissolved when you tried to see them. To work for others, for your community, seemed like nothing but handing the decision over. In nothing she'd made had she found comprehension. There was an empty room in her, always looking to be filled. But she had created it inside her home and, staring at it, had no longer felt stranded.

Standing here even now in front of Dai, knowing in her heart that it didn't mean anything, she was trying to do good still. Not for forgiveness. Not for success. There was a reprieve somewhere inside it, that was all.

'Do you blame them, Dai?' she asked him.

'No, I don't. I don't.'

She couldn't see if it was true or not. 'I wanted to tell you – I know maybe you won't want to hear it now but nonetheless I want to say it: I'm going to do everything I can to make sure that . . . what you've made doesn't get destroyed.'

His eyes darkened, and this door seemed to be guarded.

'I can't promise that it's going to make a difference, but I can promise my support. I believe . . . that everyone has as much right here as everyone else to see what they want in their home. I don't know – I have to admit it, I'd be a fraud standing here if I didn't tell you that I don't . . . understand everything the statue means. I don't believe, though, that that's what matters. I'm going to do everything I can, Dai. Do you understand? I want you to know that there's someone supporting you. I'm not trying to win . . . your approval. Just . . . that it would make it balance in some way.' Even as she spoke, though, it seemed what she was doing was for no purpose but her own redemption. In the quiet sunlight, in this garden, she remembered Eirian: *Maybe that even balances, being empty on both sides.* 'Dai, I'll do everything I can.'

Dai looked at her and he had lots of memories too, his mother's words about Gwen. There was guilt as he started to answer. He didn't know how to explain. 'Maybe it's better if you don't do that. Maybe it's better if it doesn't stay there, like.'

'No – don't let the things they said to you take away your confidence, Dai, whatever the reasons you had for making it, I'm sure they're as valid as everyone else's. I know they are.'

'It doesn't matter if it goes . . . People don't want it. I don't mind if they take it away.'

'Don't say that. Obviously you had a reason to make it. Even if . . .' and she tried to be careful, 'if you don't understand it yourself. Perhaps I haven't understood things that I've done. You had a reason, all reasons are as good as each other maybe.'

'I don't care.'

'No, Dai, you *must* care.'

'No,' he said.

She saw the truth in it. 'You *have* to care, Dai. Why wouldn't you . . . ?'

'I'm going away.' He nodded several times, waves that got smaller and became no movement at all.

'Going away? No. What do you mean?'

He shrugged, he couldn't hold her gaze. The decision had been a fragile thing as he'd walked back to his house. It hadn't grown any stronger. It wasn't really made out of reason and conclusion and choice, but only out of pictures.

'I want to go away,' he said.

'I don't think . . . Dai, I don't think that's a good idea. You don't have to leave, no one would want that, they didn't mean to hurt you. Listen to me at least. It doesn't mean you have to go.'

'I know I don't have to. I want to.'

She saw a different place lying behind his eyes. 'Can I come in? To talk?'

'You can come in . . . it won't change my mind . . .' But his face was hesitant, clouded.

She'd changed a hundred minds or more on a hundred different subjects through the years. She didn't doubt, as she looked at Dai, her ability to do so now. Her eye moving to the faded room behind him, the memories in it, it wasn't this she doubted at all.

'Let me in,' she said, though.

She followed him inside. Eirian's belongings, she saw. The woman who had never thrown a possession away, but had kept her son's grown-out-of clothes from the first ones until he'd stopped growing. The house was a storeroom of the past. Sounding between each dusty item, Gwen heard the dripping of some pipe or tap, climbing stairs with its notes.

They left the hall behind, where the open door's light stretched in, to clean memories from the air as far as it could reach; permit the sounds of the day. Gwen had time to wonder how any of the changes that she saw in Dai had come – this place untouched by anything but time.

It wasn't so different to the way her own home had been before she'd started packing her things away. And what was it that Eirian had told her? How she and Emyr and their home would fall into silence.

In the living room, Gwen saw the bags. She looked from them, over his shifting feet, to his face.

'You're ready . . .'

'Yes. Ready. Yes.'

'Dai –' She saw the books on the tables; Eirian's books. His own clothes, she saw, scattered on the floor in places, as if his life before his mother's death had been made of things so small that they were falling through the cracks. 'Dai –' But all she found was another guilt. When this was the time to start speaking. ' – I'm so sorry I haven't been here, I should have come, Dai.'

Here three times a week to help a woman who had hated her. Why? When she'd not come here for Dai? And she had thought her visits to Eirian good things. He had been living in this, sleeping in this. Any dreams must have moved through dust. Gwen remembered speaking firmly to the woman. She attempted to speak that way now.

'What would you do with this house, Dai?'

'I won't do anything . . .'

'Leave it here? Like this?'

'No one would rob it.'

In the silence her voice left, he didn't move, the bags beside him. Four hours deciding what to take. He'd gone through all the rooms and looked for things in them that he'd want, to remember. It had been hard to imagine. He looked at Gwen, as she stood so near to them and, in his eyes, was asking her not to talk.

'A house needs maintenance,' she said.

But it had had none while he'd lived here.

'Maybe I'll come back, like, to check on it. For maintenance.'

'It needs to be heated, needs to be lived in, Dai . . . There's the shops. The reason the gift shop came down in the first place . . . Will you just leave them then . . . ? After the work on them? Money? Planning? You need to hire shop assistants, Dai, organize the places. They'll become dilapidated. When you first decided – when you stood up at the meeting – and I know I came here and tried to convince you not to do it, but you stood up to me, you didn't listen – for a *reason*. Does that reason not matter any more? You'll just abandon it?'

'I can't do it. I can't do it, Gwen. Hire the people, sort out the stock and everything. I don't know how. I can't . . . I can't learn, like. I'm not . . . able.' But doubt came. She saw it.

'That's not true.'

'Yes it is.'

'Look at how far you've come. And you didn't think, back before, that you'd be able to do all this. Did you?' But it rang hollow, all of it, in these rooms where she'd once told his mother the same things that he said now. He shook his head and sadness came to her, to see him say it in return. 'The project . . . the project that you were the first person to apply for, Dai, its whole purpose was to *stop* the dilapidation, to get rid of the empty shops. Will you just leave them there, against all that?'

'Gwen –' he said, 'I never thought about the project. Emyr talked about it, I never thought about it, though. Did you know that?'

She couldn't answer.

'It was the shop.' Its blank windows, he remembered, and the sadness, and the guilt.

'The shop?'

'It's not my project,' he said.

'It's everyone's.'

But of course that was a lie. They saw each other, and it lay dim between them, though a mile away it was so loud that it seemed to encompass everyone, everything.

'We can work at having what you've built maintained. And then the project would be *yours*.' Other words she might have used seemed to disperse. 'How would you live, Dai?'

He didn't answer. He didn't try to cover the silence, no shuffling. It didn't scare him any more. There was always going to be a kind of silence between him and everyone else. Didn't mean they hated him; even if they shouted at him in the street, didn't mean they wanted to hurt him.

'For God's sake, where would you go? There are a lot of things . . .

there are a lot of things . . . that you don't understand.' Half-light made him look old. 'Ynys-morlan's not a bad place,' she began to warn him, 'and there *are* bad places in the world. Many of them.'

'I know,' he said.

'You could be hurt, leaving. Do you know that?'

'But I might not be. I might not.'

Something gave in her. It seemed as if that small good thing she'd come to do today was breaking; the last thing she had, after months of the falling that had begun here, in Eirian's bedroom.

'How would you live, Dai . . . ?'

'I'd go to the post office in Aberystwyth . . . I get the money every month, goes into my mum's post office number and I can take it out. I've seen her do it in Aber.'

'You're thinking of there at least . . . ?'

He nodded a lie. And one she saw. He looked at her from this house where she was a stranger and he was not. There was nothing left for him. In the town, in Bethan or his friends, in his statue. There was just this feeling that he'd found.

And what would she tell him? That he was simple and couldn't go away? He didn't look simple, but like the brightest part of this house. There was an empty place inside her and a crack gently trickled down its wall.

'I want to go,' he said.

'That matters, Dai, I know it matters . . .' And Gwen, who'd prided herself through more than three decades, every day until this last year, on doing the right thing, found herself now losing hold of it. '. . . Maybe that's all that does matter, I don't know . . .' she was saying. 'Maybe it is.'

Dai saw her: standing beside the window, small and upset between all these things she'd used to clear away.

She said, searching, quick and distressed, 'I'm going to write my phone number down. At least, in case you forget it, in case you want to come back, all right?'

'I know it.'

'You know it?'

He nodded.

She had no bag anyway, no pen and paper.

'You're going to go . . .' she said. 'Will you . . . will you be happy then?' As if it was a choice he could make. 'Will you take care of yourself? Will you call me? Will you be happy, Dai?'

She moved her hands again, wanting to hug him. She didn't hug him. Dai only stood there looking at her, no answer. He didn't know. But he was trying to smile, like the prettiness of the day outside was held in just not knowing.

At their fingertips the hedges showed slight green beneath the trees' bare branches. Gwen walked from the doorstep to the path and then the gate. She looked back, but that couldn't give you any answer.

The post office books were in the side pocket of the largest of his two bags and the pieces of identification that he needed to use. Lots of times he'd seen his mum do it in Aber. But once, and he remembered the day clearly, they'd gone to Clarech.

You took the bus to Aberystwyth, from the shelter where Rhys and Bethan had sat so many days, though he hadn't known her well enough then to pick her out from anyone else. You could take it from there or, if you walked on up this hill, away from the town and past the church, you came to another little bus stop, where this lane met the main road again. The bus you caught from here didn't touch on Ynys-morlan. It would take you right to Aberystwyth car park. It was a sunlit day. It was a nice day to take a bus. And there was Argos there and everyone would be walking. And beside that car park, underneath its red sign and missing letters, there was Aberystwyth train station.

He would turn three different locks, three different keys and take them and hold them as he saw the door. Unclouded shadow, his figure would be caught there. There were moments that looked like memories while you still lived them.

A small good thing, Gwen resolved that day, walking from Dai's home on to the lane. She would do anything she could for that sculpture. A small good room in her.

The morning had seemed to grow brighter round it, more empty, though. The morning had seemed to threaten it. A sky clear enough to touch everywhere.

She would put herself into protecting the thing. In these last days of the project, against the flow of other people's wishes, she would campaign.

In the cold air, just as she had gone from Siân's door – an evening, though, and not a day like this – she walked away. She moved between the still arms of the trees. In just exactly the same way, because that had been the night she'd gone home to remove her things from the shelves.

She saw her own shadow, long like winter. She heard birds, rising, alighting.

She stopped walking for a moment, captured by the similarity, but unable to put her finger on just what it was.

She'd returned from Siân's to remove all the things, little trophies really, that success had bought her. It was success that extinguished goodness, Siân had said; switched off the light in that little place – a bedroom, a living room – in her heart. She'd kept that light on; this project was for the community. And a harmony had come, all the objects gone from her own home.

How was it the same?

It was an image of Dai's statue which kept that empty space inhabited now. And she would give up her pride, tell anyone who'd listen: *the sculpture must stay*. Whatever she'd previously done to Dai, whatever they'd heard.

Not her possessions that she would sacrifice, but her dignity in their eyes.

She stood in the half-sun and the air seemed to hollow, it took a part of her. That little crack broke. It took the wall.

What she intended wasn't doing right. What she saw, it wasn't goodness.

It was absence. The absence of things she held dear. Pride. Respect. Belongings. It was the surrender of them. The abstinence – that was the vacant room.

A hole.

There was a hole in her.

She saw it.

His head moving down until it was just above her throat and his hair touching, as the movement was made, so slight, the underside of her jaw. Coming closer to her and his mouth touching her there. A kiss there, and her own, opening to air.

It was warm, the air in the caravan, always close.

He'd had friends once that were a world apart from this woman and all the things she meant to him. He didn't care, didn't fucking care. He loved her. And he wanted to show her that this was what you did with love.

So afraid, feeling that kiss, and still her own mouth was opening.

Gwen took the objects that were still left here, the cut-glass photograph frames, and one by one placed them into a half-full box. With slow movements she took them and, as if across an undiscovered ocean, watched herself.

Candlesticks, made in 1893. Bought in 1980 and bringing symmetry to their bedroom ever since. Lavender stems in fragrant oil. She remembered filling this house. Two months of piecing together each of these well-conceived spaces. Finding this cloth – it was a thick, peach-tinted gold – having the curtains made. Gwen reached up and, with this stillness that their home had always had, all around her now and unconfined, she took the curtains down, each hook. She looked at them in her hands.

He opened his mouth and, with the gentlest movement, he bit the skin of her throat. He bit it. Her hands were pressed against his back, as if that way she kept them away from the rest of his body.

She was moving, though. She was drawing them free. Into his hair.

His whole body above her, supported only by his arms, and his short movements, felt unclearly: his shoulders and back, the weight of his chest.

She stared down at the things she'd collected. She had felt a better person as she'd taken each away. More than that. She'd achieved something that had always seemed to run in front of her – no matter how she worked, no matter how she woke each day, more determined, desperate.

These things, they'd been so carefully selected. She'd brought them home and found their perfect places. But the harder she'd worked to make it all just so, the more bankrupt her moments of contentment had been.

These rooms, without their objects, were beautiful in the way she had always tried to achieve, filling them.

Those mornings of waking in one single sterile motion, Gwen remembered. All the things which weren't right and could never be made right rising up in her thoughts for the new day. It had been years. It had been many years.

She looked at her home now and saw what she had been striving for.

Why had she visited Eirian Meredith three days each week? Because the woman had hurt her, every time.

She'd never denied herself things in order to achieve goodness.

The lie, she saw. The clear and beautiful lie.

The denial itself had been the only reason. There had never been a goal.

Above her the walls were clean.

'We can't do this,' Ruth said.

They were now painting.

'I've been thinking, Emyr,' she said quietly. 'I've been feeling . . . frantic.'

Smooth and indistinguishable it rolled on: a dapple first, Dulux sunlight through new Dulux leaves. And then even, untraceable colour.

She said, 'We're in the last week now. I've been watching it move towards the end. I have to speak to you. I've been looking at Dai's statue.' His silence on the telephone line, a distance she spoke into: 'We can't do it.'

Yellow, they repainted. She would see no future in this house's rooms, or any change that might make her believe in one. That lovely yellow, of afternoons and calm. At nights, when he was gone, she stood surrounded by it. Ruth dragged herself forwards. Where, she didn't know.

There were plans, there were drawings and lists scattered over her kitchen table: there were pieces of a design that was all-embracing to her, and would soon be flawless as these rooms.

'I go out and look at it. They're constructing the flower beds in the garden there. I see the fountain.' Blankness, she saw; white morning sheets and never-ending days lying over them. 'You know why Dai's thing looks so ugly? Because it's the same. It's just like everything we've done.'

For a moment nothing.

'He's left, Ruth.'

She heard Emyr and she saw Dai's sculpture in her mind; she saw him leaving.

It was stirred together, all this noise, both from outside and from inside these rooms. In its fall, the roofing was completed in the street and the last cladding under every house's eaves, letters were arriving through doors, of new business grant approvals and premises assigned, there was the core-rattle of jackhammers: paving work edging its way down this street in its small, barricaded spaces, empty between all the milling mess apart from the Kango's huge sounds.

'That's not possible,' she told him.

She saw him leaving, though: the picture was of a road uncrowded and she believed it before he even spoke again. Dai's wandering feet and how he'd look out. A vivid kind of picture it was.

'He left yesterday. Gwen saw him before. He's abandoned the thing . . .'

She'd not stepped over the threshold of Emyr's study, where he sat constantly now, organizing, streamlining, creating; where lamplight fell on papers and his imagination. Quietly she'd told him.

She'd described Dai's house. And given no word on the actions that she thought her husband should take regarding the statue that the man left behind. And he'd asked no questions. Though she hadn't come to stand close to him, and so had not seen, he'd been very drunk by then.

'Where?' Ruth said. 'Gone where?' Her voice was blank as that place.

'Dai didn't tell her.'

Ruth saw the man, inert and gentle as he'd been six months ago. He'd changed it was true, but he couldn't leave. For moments Emyr continued, and Ruth didn't speak.

'I'm going to call the committee today, they'll be sending a representative within the week.'

'You sound – like you don't even care. My God. Why has he left?'

But Emyr was silent with the story he had heard, of many people in a crowded street, of all their voices. There'd been no blame in Gwen's face as she'd told him. But there was nothing in Gwen's face at all any more, except the memories, barely concealed, of someone whose name he didn't know.

'I didn't ask her.'

'What about his shops? They've almost finished the internal work . . . ? And why?'

'They're his. If he wants to leave them empty that's his choice to make. Let the work on them get finished. If he doesn't come back . . .'

Another pause before Emyr's voice returned. 'We'll cross that bridge when we come to it.' It should have been the most worrying part maybe – but his visualization of the finished town, the final morning, how the dawn would be – it had overtaken years of council pragmatism; superseded them.

His feelings had gone too, or so Ruth saw, off to some place they couldn't reach him from. He'd packed bags for them and sent them away.

'It doesn't matter why,' he said, 'as far as what he's left is concerned.'

Standing in her kitchen, an answer didn't come as she tried to find herself. Just a fumble of reactions. Guilt; the view of the road and its houses through this window. Worry, fear for him. And, rising through, another that had no feet on the ground, no tie to hold it down, it seemed: a sense of hope. It broke from everything, remembering Dai, and wondering what he might have gone to look for that he hadn't found here.

'For good . . . ?' she asked.

'That's what Gwen told me. Do you hear what I'm saying now?'

'No,' she said. 'No I don't hear it.' She'd woken up this morning, deciding.

Waiting to come, like a shape she knew and had never touched, there'd been a terrible pain. It had been awaiting since the project's first day maybe, when she'd watched the dry rot under the bedroom's walls exposed and for a moment had seen its face without façade.

The sculpture was so lonely; that was the ugliness in it. And the fact that he hadn't meant for its loneliness to show. Pieces of the old gift shop's stock jammed into concrete. Memories of his past, his mother maybe, and those girders rising out of their middle. A home broken down and stuck back together in random, reaching piles. When she saw it the images she had for Ynys-morlan, idealistic images, they seemed vapid as pots of tea and coffee and sugar set together like chattering friends in a house where the only voice was her own. When she saw the sculpture, thought of it being demolished, this project seemed like nothing but evasion.

'If he's left, that only makes it more important. It doesn't clear the way for us.' From Nia's room, Ruth heard the sounds of the men. Of rebuilding. 'Charlotte won't pay to have it demolished.'

'She's not liable to pay for it. It's not a permitted construction.' Far away, his hands were neatening his own plans, rearranging them in piles and empty, flexing.

'Who pays for it then? Who pays for it if it's knocked down?'

'Dai pays.'

'And if he can't be contacted?'

'The council pays. He'll be billed.'

The work went on. She could see it; every day a little closer to the exactness she had designed. '*Listen* to yourself . . .' she said.

'This is not a matter of anyone being to blame! Don't you talk to me like I'm in the wrong! You started this. It's not a free-for-all. He's left it behind, for God's sake!'

'Just listen to yourself.'

'Don't you talk to me like that, Ruth! You of *all* people!'

'I should have said it when we were face to face.' She could feel it coming. Not only sadness, something blacker. Something far more ugly. 'You used to have compassion. My God . . .' Like little reaching hands. She tried to hold on to her choice.

'How dare you,' she heard him say.

'It was his only idea! It's the one thing that he built himself! He made it!'

'*He left it!*' In his mind, he was picturing it too. Ugly enough, sad enough to see, but more – Emyr didn't understand, it seemed a betrayal, for Dai to make it and to leave it behind. It was a pathetic, desperate, ugly thing. But what Dai had felt for it must have been love.

'How can you?' she said. 'You've *headed* this project, Emyr! You know *just* what it means to . . . to make something! . . . This is someone who's never put his hand to any other thing in his life! And you know just how important it is! *How can you?*'

'Nothing has ever been as important to me, in my life,' he said, 'as this project.'

As he spoke, he knew: more than Gwen even. More even than her infidelity. It held the same emotions, this project, as loving her had done once. 'At this point,' he spoke quietly in his study, in his paperwork, his place without a view, 'I can say, yes, the completion of the project matters more than what Dai has left behind.'

'No, Emyr.' She shook her head. 'No,' she said.

As ugly as it looked to him, *as deep-down ugly*, it did to her. Seemed just as much to ruin Ynys-morlan. It was herself too that she was thinking of, standing here in the kitchen where they had sat together two days ago. She'd pitter-pattered around how they shouldn't, and when Emyr had broken down, she'd let it go. She'd looked into his face and seen the strain she felt herself, not even knowing what was making him so sad. Unable to speak to each other, the project hadn't brought them together. It had broken and neglected them.

It wasn't over yet, though. It wasn't finished yet. No person here had even seen the place that they were making. 'Emyr, it seems to matter more than anything else – I know it does, that the town should be perfect.'

Outside, in the public garden behind which Dai's statue stood, they were creating the rose beds. It was a carnival of work. It was a fantasy you could watch solidifying. She needed its perfection herself. This guilt, like that sculpture, was rising.

'Seems like nothing matters more. Nothing wrong. Not a mark. Not a flaw. Feels like the most important thing but if you get that statue taken down, do you know what it is, this project? This perfect project? It's dead,' she told him.

Her voice was loud in the home that Lennie came back to each night, belief in his eyes a little clearer, that they had a new future together here. She'd known for days now and all the work had circled round this choice: to knock it down made the place's beauty vacuous. It looked to her like a statue of everything that this project was meant to dredge away. But Dai had no hate in him. However it seemed, it was only a symbol of unhappiness.

The ugliness she saw when she looked up at it was her own. 'What have we been building then? A picture. A lie. You have what he's made torn down, all this work, it's just meaningless! It won't be any better place, it'll just look . . . perfect.' These five months, when that word had acquired a meaning it had never had before, all that time seemed to give way, and years before it. She looked at this room and she remembered a dream that had been blind enough, perfect enough, to hide in its bright mornings every night before.

'It could never be a lie to me,' Emyr answered. 'In my life, nothing's been less *dead*. Do you understand me?'

'Yes,' Ruth said. 'But if you have it taken down, you're making the project a screen. It's . . . *puerile*. Worse than just meaningless! It's hiding! It's just *silent!*' She couldn't explain to him how that would hurt. It would be worse than the pain that was coming now. Because this house would be remade completely, in a town where its lie spread out past the doorstep, over everything. '*Silent* . . .' she just repeated.

And Emyr put the phone down on her.

He left her looking at the kitchen window, only the sound of disconnection to hear.

In a house not far away from her, he put his hands over his face and held them there, where the images of Ynys-morlan remained anyway. Its marvellous spectacle, and the marks on that loveliness: Dai's statue and all the scribbles in the museum, that scarred the vista he saw.

Emyr had sat with yesterday's afternoon and his own pearl-toned reflection in the living-room window, another Scotch in another crystal glass. He'd taken all twelve from the packed box in the hall and he had used them up one by one.

He'd sat telling himself, at first telling himself, that it was right and that they had to knock it down. He'd got drunker, and at some point, he couldn't remember – he'd imagined Dai, sitting right in the chair beside him, where he'd watched TV so many days. All Dai's clothes and his face had been grey, and Emyr had talked to him, long shambling sentences that dragged each other's hands, and Dai had listened. He'd always been good at that.

'You know what that sculpture shows, Dai?' he'd asked, gesturing with his glass to the man's watercolour face. 'Shows how weak we both are. How bloody weak we both . . . I know what it's like. To feel that way? I know. Let me tell you. What I see when I look at that thing of yours: what it makes you, to respect something . . . *look up* to something, the weak person it makes you to care for something that doesn't care for you! No it doesn't.' Though Dai hadn't spoken. No, Dai was all empathy.

And when Emyr had begged him, he hadn't made objections, hadn't said he loved the thing or needed to keep it.

'You think time's beautiful?' Emyr had asked, 'then why would you want to spoil its . . . Eden, Dai, its *Eden* . . . with something that shows how you can't even understand it? How you just follow it, whatever, whatever it takes away! Something that shows . . . how powerless it's made you. What you've built, man? Isn't just a blot on the bloody landscape, don't you fool yourself and think that's all it is. I'll tell you . . . That statue, that bloody thing – it's the crack in the sky.' He'd laughed and Dai's listening face had made even his own laughter grey. 'The crack in the sky, Dai. And if you trained a telescope up on that bastard – I tell you, faint type, you know? Just next to it, there it'd be. Little stamp. Your very own name, right under "Designed and Commissioned by".

'You know what that sculpture shows?' His voice had bumped and wandered from word to word as the day had dissipated around him and left him sitting in dimness there alone. 'Shows the kind of needs . . . needs you can't have any respect for! Needs to make some . . . some stupid world where you'll feel safe, all small and safe . . . Shows what kind of helplessness . . . is under the love. That's what. Under all the devotion, the loyalty . . .'

When he had begged, Dai Meredith had agreed. Hadn't needed to answer to do that.

'Let the project be,' Emyr had pleaded. 'Let it be at least! Because there's something – I tell you, there's something worth *describing* in a love like that! There's a sacrifice, I swear to God – there's something fucking *noble* in a love like that! Let the project be. Don't show the . . . defencelessness, the . . . Dai, the weakness . . . Just let it say that . . .'

Dai had given no words at all. There'd been nothing in that room but twelve crystal glasses and a window that pictured an old man's tearful face.

Obscenities and bad drawings, overlapping, chaotic.

He would look at them as the workmen left and the evening came.

He didn't call the planning committee after speaking to Ruth that day. He finalized the details of the last slate delivery, a little supplier only ten miles away. The man had three-times overcharged them. He checked the progress of every single business refurbishment, that each window had been fitted. Done. That each door was being hung. Yes. That they would all be gone by this time next week. It could be so. He called the sandblasting company and reaffirmed their date, the same with that of the street lamp replacement crew. He spent the day speaking with men whose names were written down because he was no longer able to remember them, and replaying in the quiet after each conversation had ended, how Gwen had softly said as she'd turned away, that she couldn't tell him where she'd been.

He called to verify that the plaque which would stand in front of the museum's new collection would be delivered. He told himself he was working for this community; that the will to do right was what he had once – many years before, it seemed – loved in his wife. But he didn't call the planning committee over Dai's tower. The project's completion seemed threatened by his not doing so, but he couldn't bring himself to.

Emyr would see the mural Rhys had painted. His hands would be shaking, taking out a pen, a small piece of paper as he stared at it; trying to keep whole all the things that he needed, when they would not stay together, not even inside him.

A window, small-paned and perfect, that looked out on this town. A telephone and a dead line. Thoughts that stuttered, which overspilled, and Ruth sat down at the table with all strength gone out of her. Things she'd believed the project could wipe away, they rose.

The view changed like a trick of the eye and she was no longer living in the same street. Smooth slate roofs – the only part of this picture yet completed – topped the houses and the debris of traffic flowed. The people squeezed through any tiny hole that they could find, trying to go about their days. And the rest of the picture, the end that each unfinished part was reaching towards, what she'd called a vision, it shattered as she stared out, until it looked nothing but broken.

She couldn't see Dai's work from here.

Not long ago, Ynys-morlan had been fading. Things had happened here, bad things. She'd wanted to make a place where they couldn't happen again. But it was more than that. She'd wanted to make something good enough that she'd be forgiven. A town where people wouldn't feel like their futures had no hope. People felt that and they hurt others. Tried to get the feeling out. Maybe Lennie had needed to see his sadness on someone else's face, on hers, so he wouldn't be alone any more. Maybe he'd only wanted to blame her. She didn't know. But people felt hopeless and they hurt others or, one morning that looked no different than all the days that had passed before, they just left that place behind. She'd wanted to make a home where these things couldn't be.

How had this plan changed? How was it that she'd started making somewhere where even thoughts of these things were disallowed? Even their memories gone. She'd said this place would be *perfect*. A liberation of the hurt she'd felt, in something better. But the two aims weren't the same. And knowing that, throughout, it was the first one she'd chased, the idea of some flawless paradise that had seemed to offer forgiveness, not any better place, and never any real one, Ruth now let go of the vision that had led her here. To this new house in this new town.

Sitting at the table, she cried. Guilt came like bile; she shook her head and wouldn't let herself and then cried anyway. Guilt came up in her like a broken tower made out of the pieces of her home. Sitting at the table, the view before her, Ruth tore herself.

Just above the shadowline of her own row, they were laying in the fascia and barge boards on the houses opposite. Framing the gable windows and the eaves with sweet-cut, wooden outlines, while below the cement trucks slowly left, not to return.

Yesterday she'd ordered the lawn. Fifteen by fifteen for each garden. Three thousand nine hundred square feet. Another thirty by forty for the public garden. Miscellaneous areas at the roadside and spaces beside the seawall, seventy feet at least in length. Measurements had been taken by the public works crew and delivered to her, and on the telephone, she'd laughed and she'd told them, yes *that much* grass. Yes it's incredible. A stupid and incredible and fantastic thing. How could she not have loved this project?

Last night, Lennie had brought her primroses that he'd picked. He had pressed them into her hand. Leave me alone, she'd said, leave me alone, in a lot of different voices, a lot of times. She had cried at the start, by the end she'd been shaking and hiding her head in her arms. He saw promises in the project, and in this house. And it had felt to Ruth as she had watched him put the flowers in water himself, as she'd watched him stand them on this table, that she'd led herself through five months of creation, only to build what she'd been running from.

The sound of hammers, on the roof above her. Perfection only ever made the world mute. It couldn't express.

So Ruth looked out and saw the town, she saw its future, containing Dai's sculpture. Imperfect as though woven with a filigree of holes, through which the knowledge welled unchecked – of what she'd allowed here.

She wouldn't let the project be a mask to hide things under, and wasn't sure if she could live in Ynys-morlan without that mask.

What had she allowed?

She'd kept Nia here. Through it all, she'd kept her here.

Sunday 7 July nineteen sixty eight

its me thats diffrent not The Nursery. How do I know Im me? beacase a person only knows who they are when people tell them. They dont get BORNand know. and what I see now is how OLD everyting is. Like my

toys that arent mine. I was always asking how come I cant chose
toys and names for them. I always thouhgt the house was watching
me. it IS a big house and it IS scary somtimes. Now I know its
bacuse im not who im SUPOSED to be. Its looking atme becuse Im
not the one who should be walking ALLROUND it or touching it

From the sunlight into the shade of Charlotte's house, she pushed
Nia, and Charlotte raised her eyes from the girl to Ruth. Ruth looked
back, determination in her features, of something found, that seemed
to hold the loss around her together.

'I told Emyr he mustn't have it demolished.'

A little smile rose in response but it faltered. She saw the stress in
Ruth's expression. She saw the way Ruth stepped back from the
doorstep, leaving her daughter standing inside.

It had been three days since Ruth had phoned to talk about the
thing that Dai Meredith had erected. 'I don't know what to do,' she'd
said. 'It can't stand there. It can't just stay.'

And Charlotte had heard familiar tones and the past had gently
risen to the surface. In a great, oak-panelled corridor, the echoes of
her mother's voice had skittered from the polished surfaces. Mrs
Weyland had sat alone in bed and cried behind the East Suite's doors.

Now Ruth was nodding, 'I don't know if it'll stay. Building regs
and the committee, they'll be on to it anyway probably. But I told
him.'

Charlotte nodded too, a faint reflection. Like her own in candlelight.

'It's good . . . the right thing,' she told Ruth.

She saw the desperation that Ruth chose with, though. A little
flame travelled a circle around Charlotte's face, a girl aged decades
and stood here: unchanged, acquiescing.

'It's just a lie, isn't it? To give it my approval, knocking it down.
The whole project, prettiest picture in the world, just a lie then.'

'Yes . . .'

Charlotte saw her nod to herself like she needed confirmation, and
the hope she felt, and the doubt, just warred against each other. Ruth
looked lost in everything but this one choice. It *was* better. Each time

Ruth had spoken about the project, landscapes had filled her mind –
Charlotte had seen them – which in her eyes were only blank.

'Ruth, you know, you can think . . . that you're getting something
out, getting rid of it. You can . . .' Charlotte moved out on to the
doorstep herself. And she gestured, like the example was random,
'You can keep a diary,' she said. 'Could write all the time and it would
seem as if you were . . . communicating things . . . but really it would
just be a wall. Do you understand what I mean?'

Secrets that she couldn't have touched on, couldn't have forced out
once upon a time, they tried to push themselves out when she was
with Ruth now. A child's needs, that didn't feel constrained, as she
had done for years.

'You have to make decisions too,' she said to Ruth. 'You can't just
design or write or imagine . . . and think the things you make will
change your life . . .' But she could picture a home that was now being
fitted back together, which Ruth was still sharing with her husband.
She couldn't push Ruth. What would that make her?

'A fantasy, that's what I've wanted to make . . .' she admitted to
Charlotte, almost inaudibly.

'If that was true, then it isn't now . . .'

'No it isn't now.' She looked up, seeming fragile, older than she
had done, yet more real somehow. She had lost everything that was
definite in her and what was left, so uncontained, Charlotte thought,
must be the truth of her. A few feet away, untouched by Ruth, Nia
stood.

Charlotte saw the guilt between them and, because she saw no
crime, loved Ruth the more for it – heart going out to her. The
moments that her own mother had pushed her away, there had been
no guilt at all. Just the anxiety, the unreasoning need, which Charlotte
had never satisfied. In Ruth now, guilt was fraught, though. Charlotte
saw it and felt more compassion.

'It's not a fantasy, you're not hiding,' she told her quietly. 'Ruth,
you'll see it finished . . . and you'll forgive yourself. That's what it's
for, isn't it?'

Tears were coming but Ruth looked out through them. She seemed to see a narrow path. She didn't answer Charlotte. Couldn't answer. 'Will you take her?'

'Take her . . . ?'

'For the day, will you look after her? It's been busy. I can't – she's had tantrums, and I can't today. Just for a few hours?'

Nia stood between them, the outdoor light a cut across her face, playing with the shadow patterns which changed and spilled and turned under her hands, held out and hung in the cold air.

'Of course . . . I offered before.' When Ruth had responded as though stung.

'I can't manage her. She won't have tantrums with you.' There was a quiet stretch, neither of them spoke. 'She's been crying,' Ruth said.

Charlotte watched the girl. There was no sign of tears in her expression. Only in her mother's face. She stood for a moment, disabled as Ruth transferred toys, a beaker cup, two tangerines, to the telephone table, her hands far away from the girl.

Charlotte's voice was low, the birdsong behind Ruth light and empty. 'What began it?'

'I don't know what began it. They're finishing the rooms upstairs, so things are ready to be transferred back there, maybe . . . She got upset when the place was first changed round, maybe . . . She just started, I don't know.'

'She seems fine now.'

'Well she's here now. Not on her own with me. Seems fine now, yes of course.'

In the dust motes that the sunlight divulged, Nia seemed buried. Charlotte reached a hand towards her, almost touched her. She had those dark eyes, like Ruth's, but without any memory.

'Something happened,' Charlotte said.

'Nothing "happened", nothing has to "happen". She's not like it with you, why should she be? She just starts, you know. Starts off small, she'll push something, she'll get all interested in something, play with it, or it looks like playing, and then more and more. She –'

But Ruth turned away and didn't finish, just nodded again.

'Come inside . . .' Charlotte asked.

She stepped forwards and took Ruth's arm and for a moment the light fell on her also. Perhaps not even a moment, before Ruth shook free. She looked from the lower path up into Charlotte's face and Charlotte saw the tears that Ruth had tried to lay on her daughter, saw a laugh try to bubble through them; that awful mix that she had first seen on the night when Ruth had shown her the bruises.

'How many months?' Ruth said to her. 'I've been caught up . . . in how *right* it has to be. Had to be *seamless*. It can't be. You think really, and there's no such thing. A perfect place. What's that? It doesn't exist. How can something . . . as meaningless feel so important . . . you think it'll fix everything?'

She looked at Ruth. She had been afraid that Ruth would stare out over Ynys-morlan completed and see a place lying under wax. 'You've needed something . . .'

'Yes, that's how.' She nodded. The air was a chill touch against Charlotte's face.

'People need things, that's how. I'm no better,' she said.

She wanted Charlotte to love her; wanted Charlotte to hold and to forgive her. Ruth didn't believe she deserved these things, though. There were times when she knew she loved Charlotte, but she'd felt that for Lennie. She had no belief any more in what love was to her.

'I'm no different . . . What have I been trying to make?'

For a long moment no answer would come to her. She hugged Ruth on the doorstep, her eyes still open, and far off, in new-world yellows and greens, saw the mountains. She pressed her hand to Ruth's hair and stroked it before fear of rejection stopped her. From passion to anger, Ruth could tip without warning, crying to shouting or laughter. Charlotte nearly took her hand away – after a second, though, pressed her hold tighter.

'Somewhere better, not somewhere . . . perfect.'

'Dai's left,' she heard Ruth say. 'Did you know that?'

There was a space of silence before she spoke. Responses occurred to her and she abandoned them. What could she say? The project and the new place they'd embarked for – they weren't selfless. Really, they'd never been. And Dai Meredith had left now. The anxieties that Charlotte felt – old fears, of not being able to connect with anything without breaking it, any *where* – they were held suspended by the feelings she had for Ruth. Those old fears had only ever stemmed from love, and that, as they both knew, was never selfless either.

'You don't have to leave Nia here, not on her own. You've nothing to feel guilt over, Ruth – stay here with her.'

She didn't reply. She felt Charlotte holding her and, though she couldn't, she wanted to be delivered by the feeling. 'Do you regret it? Meeting me?'

'I don't regret it . . .'

'I love you.'

'Then *stay*.'

But she did not.

She left, hands shifting like rags, estranged from Nia and so desperate, never having been estranged before.

In the hallway, shadowed after the door had closed, the girl stood without moving.

Ruth drove, crying, wiping it away, berating herself, the trees passing like they were all one, a patina of sunlight cast across the road before her and the project still ahead.

On her own, Nia stood. The birds couldn't be heard. She looked up into Charlotte's face and made no sound. Charlotte had been working on interior designs before the knock had come; the plans for children's bedrooms. Now wordlessness filled her house as if Nia carried deafness with her rather than inside. 'It's all right,' Charlotte said, and her voice fell into it.

The vehicle came to a stop as Ruth lost hold of that path. Her hands rose up and she beat at herself with raining blows that couldn't get inside her to cause damage. A little storm behind glass – the day in stillness outside her car.

*

She looked at Nia, almost took a step forwards. Between the stone walls her eyes were grey. A toy face and Cupid's bow mouth, just like Ruth's. It wasn't Ruth, though, who Charlotte thought of. Her low heels made two sounds, towards her on the slate floor.

As if you might have shaken her, and she would not have known. She had drawn her body into silence too. The way in which Ruth had brought her, the way she'd gone, even these anxious things faded as Charlotte bent down and saw Nia; alone with her for the first time.

'How are you?' she asked.

She saw Nia's fingers fret in her jumper and then hang still as she didn't look around at the place where she'd been left, or the door that had closed behind Ruth. Charlotte reached but didn't touch her, afraid to touch her.

'Are you all right, Nia?' she said.

'I'll look after you today,' she said.

'You know me.'

A tightening of the muscles across Nia's face that passed for a moment of confusion. In the worry and the hope Ruth had left in her wake, this isolation that the girl had, it echoed, like Charlotte's voice.

'You know she loves you. Yes she does. Very much. You can't even imagine, can't even see. You're a lucky girl.' And then she did reach out and brushed Nia's fringe away from her eyes, and felt the girl stiffen – as if Charlotte could ever threaten her.

'No, no. It's all right.'

With her hand, she touched Nia's face. Cool skin and the softest feeling. She'd never been close to children, she had kept away. She stroked her hair just a little and her cheek again. She moved forwards so she could put an arm around her. So that she could hold her – very close, very tight, full of solace – and put her own face next to the girl's like there was no line between.

As she had planned to do alone, she went with Nia down towards the town. At first the girl wouldn't walk and only stopped every few feet, the coat that Ruth had brought her buttoned to the neck and an expression on her face of waiting. At first, she did pick her up. After ten minutes maybe, Nia began to walk with only her hand held. By the time that they came to the road, she had wandered on her own for a little while. She had stopped to look at a bird that landed on the lane in front of her. Charlotte had watched in a quiet so light that the sound of its feet could be heard.

She carried her through Ynys-morlan, though, where the heave of work around them pressed Nia against her neck and made her hang, a dead weight there again. The noise surrounding Charlotte wasn't a whisper for her even. The trucks and vans ground by without life signs.

The men climbed down from finished roofs. They left the scaffolds' upper platforms, on every building, empty. Sun lay there, the only thing unstirred by the wind, while below, in the shade they still cast – of poles and planks and bolts and rivets – the new windows of render-dirty houses now looked out.

An estate, Charlotte remembered, the gardens of which, high and closed by hedges, enshrining careful beds, had given way to meadows more yellow than green, and silent completely, through the windows she'd looked out from. Years of private tutoring and no child's voice but her own, and her own had never been childlike. Saturdays spent with the girl, Jennifer, Claudette, Sandra, Laverne, whoever was currently paid – or, if her mother was feeling well, the daytrips; little weekend masquerades. Often, through long afternoons and old, pale, drawn-out evenings, no voice at all in Hedera's rooms or corridors, except the underlying voice – a happy one, Charlotte had often imagined, bright and unafraid – which of course had never left the house.

Nia hid from the vehicles now, even soundless, cowered close.

Between the houses where new door frames were being fitted, where gable windows were trimmed with soffit boards, and the last slating work that covered their small steeples now completed smooth, dark roofs, Charlotte walked slowly, with Nia in her arms. She'd once felt like a stranger in this town. What she had created in her houses, though, or recreated, all those memories remade, they were little gifts. The home that she had grown up inside had never been her own. With the new ones Charlotte built, she was trying to offer it – cosiness, security, belonging, what was a sense of home? – she was trying to offer Hedera to Ruth and Nia, who she loved, and so maybe to herself again.

'You'll like it,' she said. 'Wait and see it finished.' Just a murmur, into the hair that was pressed into her shoulder. 'Wait till you can come out in the street here, when all the builders have gone and the traffic, you'll see . . .'

They walked by the park that Ruth had designed where, in foot-deep holes, they were laying fertilizer, and by Ruth's home then. Charlotte saw the windows but shade there made all the rooms only vagueness. By the garden where she'd first seen this girl, and on, the rest of the road that she would have walked that day, had Nia Lewis not been standing on the path.

Charlotte looked towards the houses she had bought.

'You wait and see,' she said again, and was glad, despite everything, despite the way that Ruth had left Nia, that she had had the chance to bring her here today. Builders worked, the people moved, the cars passed by these almost finished homes, Charlotte loved them. She didn't know whether Ruth could. Whether Ruth could stay. But she'd given part of herself to Ynys-morlan, as she had nowhere else.

She'd been afraid of coming today, to finalize the children's rooms. And now, with Nia bundled up against her, she did feel what she'd been scared of. Bereavement. But there was hope as well, like she'd kept the two apart. And she remembered lying with Ruth in a dawn, seeing her face, gradually discernible. Today they'd hugged, even if it had been brief – they'd just held each other – but Ruth had seemed to give back something real.

The children's rooms had been painted pale pink, as the nursery had been. They had views of the sea, not of meadows, but they were lined with long oak shelving, like the nursery. All the boxes, Charlotte remembered so many dolls and games and teddy bears that many had never been opened; the highest shelves always undiscovered. She had no memory of the day when she'd destroyed the toys. Just her mother afterwards.

In Ty Heulog, the children's room was an attic. Its long beams had been exposed. It had two windows, next to which she had ordered the beds to be set when they arrived. What did children want from their homes? She'd tried to look beyond Hedera – or to a time there before herself, tried to imagine – and so fill them. What did children love? How would she know?

She set Nia down. Undecorated wooden boards and the shaded slope of roof made a triangle room. It seemed the type a girl would like. Charlotte had thought so.

She watched her Nia stand there – just in the centre, wherever she was set down. Her eyes roamed up over the walls. So small, vulnerable. Too young to hold blame for anything. Charlotte had been young herself once, and she'd thought the blame was hers.

In this room where the sound of construction and traffic was muffled until it almost seemed remote, she watched Nia begin very slowly to move round the empty space. A few feet, before coming to a stop, not knowing what else to do. It must have been very large to her. She raised her eyes and looked up at the empty shelves. She had no curiosity. Touched nothing.

Charlotte stood and watched her as a knock came at the old, worn door that tomorrow would finally be removed. There were footsteps outside. She ignored them. Through the end of the day, through each of the houses, till twilight echoed with the last sounds of work outside, Charlotte and Nia explored. They sat together.

Through the boxes that were crammed in Lennie's study, where Nia's makeshift bed lined the wall, through their solid little memories. She took out every one, the framed photographs, the cushions and books, and carried them upstairs to where new rooms held the evening – palpably still, softly silent. There wasn't even any dust between their walls. For a moment, hands still, Ruth only looked around herself.

In her mind, she took a photograph of what she saw. She held it and watched it develop, the colours slowly growing till they were clear. She imagined hanging it in the kitchen, above the cooker. A little square that showed a space as yellow as meadow grass. And far away, in a different afternoon, in a pink pebbledashed house – just one in a row where they were all the same, all left behind – her mother came home from work and huffed her coat on to the chair. She stood listening for a moment, to see if her daughter was home yet. Somewhere far back and lost to Ruth, she turned from the quiet view outside her window and glanced at her child's drawings, little houses every one. And she saw it there between them. An empty room; one she recognized. Yellow, as she sometimes talked of painting it.

Lennie would close Nia's bedroom door. Emotions that looked so uncontained when he stood over Ruth, they weren't so rash, they weren't so desperate that he couldn't plan for them. He'd close her bedroom door. Why would he bother? She might sit with it open, and the air open, all between. If her back was turned or her eyes closed, she'd be protected.

Maybe Ruth's mother looked at that photograph and realized. Maybe she saw that vacant honey-coloured space and in it, years. Of trying to make it seem anything but empty; trying to prove that there was nothing wrong with this home, and that it hadn't deserved to be left behind. Maybe that afternoon, when Ruth came home from school and put her bag down, her mother would sit and talk with her. She would try to tell the girl that it hadn't been her fault. She would explain that there was nothing inside Ruth that was wrong, nothing that had made her father want to leave. She might attempt to convince her, she didn't need to give up the things she wanted, a future, a possibility of other places, to try to build this home into somewhere that he might have stayed.

Every day, brushing Nia's hair, a plait or pony-tail. This was what she'd done.

She wouldn't let the project be the same. It was her making of amends, her expiation.

Ruth rebuilt the rooms so she could see them. She walked up and down the stairs with all the boxes that were stored in Lennie's study, as other boxes had been once, when she'd been a child and a trespasser.

A fountain had been built, and rose beds, as a high tide had receded from the line of stone-clad walls. Rooms had been painted, B&Bs, and shops with no purposes yet, still-blank signs fitted above their doors. Traffic like an estuary, lorries leaving for the last time, vans that arrived for the first as the day's sun was reduced by early evening and somewhere, with the woman who'd shown her such care, with the woman she had kissed and let herself be kissed by, Ruth's daughter was sitting silent. Or crying maybe, kicking maybe, she didn't know; letting out in a flow all the feelings that Ruth was so scared to think of. The town where Lennie now believed they had a future, it grew and shaped itself, greyness came, and darkness.

She didn't go to Charlotte's house to bring her daughter home. When Lennie opened the door, a day's work behind him – another, all of which were leading forwards it seemed to him – the house that Ruth's father had walked out on one sunny, unmarked morning was empty again but for her.

In the evenings, on her own, Charlotte had started taking her keys and going through these homes. They had been lived in, different worlds, only two months before, their For Sale signs going dull out in their gardens.

As she wandered, rooms that were almost finished now were thrown off kilter by the work's fluorescent strip lights. Windows would have no places outside them, just her own reflection in their dark.

The paint, a stack between many other materials, was stored inside the kitchen at Ty Heulog. She saw rollers and brushes and trays. Soon an ash table would stand here. In empty rooms, she listened to the echoes grow, on the staircase, and with Nia again, in the children's bedroom.

The same pale pink walls. The same shelving. She loved the rooms. Sounds that had shifted through their afternoon together, the traffic and the grind, were now gone. Nia held the toy that Ruth had left her with, a little donkey. She'd tried to engage Charlotte in the silent toy game, where the toy slept and the toy awoke, then, under Nia's jacket, went to bed again. Charlotte put the pot of paint down on the floor between them.

She sat with her on the floor. Nia did nothing as she slowly prised the lid open and saw her own reflection in blue; didn't shift or play or even stare. Charlotte poured a little paint into the tray. She smiled at the silent girl. Something almost gave way. She saw a little dream – not Nia but herself. She saw a mother's desperation and fantasy; a little dream constructed with her features. In Nia they were all reflected, but with no wrong, no blame for Ruth. All these things – but Nia was still young enough to heal.

Outside, the wind made patterns. In this long-ago room, Charlotte smiled into Nia's eyes.

A dream, or a ghost maybe.

Because even with its headstone and its years of summer grass, the grave she'd found in the northern meadow when she'd been eight years old, it hadn't made an ending. Not one her mother would believe. In a way the burial had been incomplete, the grave open wide, and Charlotte had heard its voice, in all the rooms where she stayed silent. One of them must have been a ghost.

Where she sat now, trying to imagine a child's things, the families who might move here, the walls were uneven with age beneath fresh coats of paint and plaster. They curved and made their little worlds of shadow. Like many maps she had traced in the nursery once upon a time. Lost in them, she remembered.

She didn't know if Nia was watching as, after a moment, she put her hand into the blue. Gradually she held it up, wet and bright.

She smiled at Nia and felt memory emerge, bare as the girl smiled back. Hedera was here.

With her clean hand, she took Nia's and put it into the paint, whereupon the girl saw it and burst into a laugh that had no sound, was only movements and expressions. Air lay between her and the rest of the world.

They sat examining each other's palms before Charlotte moved towards the wall. She turned from Nia's face to the blank pink, and she reached out. She slowly made its print. In the strip lights and silence of a night that seemed to resonate, Charlotte saw it. In bright blue. Nights, she remembered, not wanting to touch anything.

It was vibrant and vivid on the wall here. She turned round and made gestures, silently encouraged, until Nia came forward to sit beside her. Nia reached out slowly, she looked to Charlotte to see if she was doing right. She put her hand on the wall beside the first print and, removing it slowly, Charlotte saw the girl look at it as she had done her own. She saw the silent laugh again.

Hollowed by it, Charlotte nodded to her. She took the girl's other clean hand and put that in the paint as well. All around the four walls. After some time Nia seemed to forget her, she did it without being shown. After some time, Charlotte was only sitting and watching as the little girl, kneeling down, immersed just in the surface of these walls and in the movement of her own hands, made the place belong to her, without even realizing. Just seeing the marks that she could make.

In the darkened street, Bethan Hughes stood and listened to the sound of next door's radio, the scuffle of a dog's feet in the quiet and the low steps of someone walking with it. Long pavements that were half completed, houses with new doors around her; an almost finished town beside a silent coast.

Bethan looked up at the stained-glass windows. The light didn't touch her face, blues and reds. They were beautiful. They were full of captured moments. She'd seen the long bar's lacquer finish slowly top-coated today. She'd watched the glass shelves set on their brackets behind it, their protective plastic peeled, left without fingerprints. The room she'd made was beautiful and she stared up now at the three tall windows and their falls of colour, trailing each other over the stone between – and there Bethan saw the words DAI HAS GONE. One for each pane of glass.

'He's left . . . ?' she'd said.

'Gwen came.'

'Left for where?'

'She didn't know,' Pat had told her.

She thought these things: that she was glad he'd got out of this godforsaken town, where experience filled people's faces with nothing but bitterness for the past, where she belonged and always would.

That the town wasn't like that any more; that what she saw now, looking up, made a mockery of cynicism.

She thought these things: that Dai must be in danger now, must feel like he couldn't come back, his home taken away and his hopes taken and all the little pieces of strength that he'd built into a person since his mother had died. She'd ripped them out of him. Forced the innocence in him down to match her. At ground level, where all innocence fell eventually anyway.

She had her arms folded around herself. She stared up at those three words, which would be written into everything she made. HE HAS GONE. She'd driven him away.

She told herself that she'd been forced to stay here. That she had chosen to stay. That she'd been abandoned two years ago. That she'd abandoned Rhys.

She had overseen the delivery of the restaurant's utensils, decorations; stacked them in the unused kitchen. White tablecloths in plastic wrapping, she'd placed them on top of each other, waiting for the hard furnishings. The kitchen's counters were chrome. They were unmarked. Knives and forks and spoons had come in boxes. Twenty-five white vases. Twenty-five candle lanterns.

Somewhere behind her, that statue had stood all day, its arms throwing out fifths of hours and quarter afternoons, that blanket hanging down out of it and showing what dreams really looked like.

The dress was gone. The dress was parcelled up and delivered.

The colours of the stained-glass windows blended and she was crying. This was how she stood, viewed from the rest of this street: her face forced up and her mouth forced shut. A young woman with long blonde hair who made men shout till they passed and saw her

825

face. A young mother with her twenty-month-old girl held as she slept, not by her, but by Patty.

Had Dai left with nothing but sadness?

She stared up, standing under one street lamp. They'd hold the rain sometimes, a thousand fading droplets, a corona, when she saw it through her window.

She wanted to believe that there were hopes out there for him; that the world outside this place was full of them. But it almost seemed like Ynys-morlan could be too. She'd stranded herself here, in the desert, but it wouldn't stop growing now; throwing out new green shoots to prove the failures that she felt inside were lies. A garden now, it left her tattered. All the innocent things in her were fantasies, pathetic, ugly, shams – she'd told herself the same thing every day since she'd had to sit down and make the choice between a new life – an undiscovered life – and her own.

All her dreams fantasies – she'd fucking proved it, she'd lived one, lived Dai's, and the truth had kept on grinding her down until she'd stained that night with her own reality.

But this place – these colours – they weren't fantasies. They'd made it, piece by piece, all of them.

The rain would fall sometimes and seem frozen in the halos of light. Bethan would look out at it from her window, an instant taken from the rest of time it would seem – so that young things couldn't even get older. You might walk round it, and see those drops, never falling. You might circle, where she stood now in its centre, and the rain would be unable to drift down.

The image of Dai bloomed, clear enough to cut. She saw nights when they'd lain together and she'd asked him questions just to hear the newness, the strangeness of his answers. She saw things that she hadn't chosen. Dai's memory seemed to flower as she stood in this incomplete, fairy-tale street – this reality – to leave her bitterness as nothing but tears, which in this light would never fall.

Rhys was leaving. One week. Not a lot of nights left. He'd go tonight and try again to finish what he'd started.

In the museum, the tarpaulin that had covered window holes had been replaced two days ago by glass. And he'd stood there, laughed at himself, pockets full of paints, as he'd touched the locks on the window frames.

But in the alleyway at the building's side, the office door had been left open. Not just unlocked, but ajar. And when Rhys had gone inside, expecting as he did every night now to find what he had done blank with three coats of white paint, it had not been. Staring back at him, like it had a secret.

Emyr drove: the dark and the trees' bare branches reaching through it. The museum ahead, Gwen behind him. In his mind, the words he'd written sounded over and over as if their rhythm brought clarity. And his hands on the wheel, they were firm. He had liked to think of himself once as a man firm but fair, and now he didn't like to think of himself.

Down towards the town, the project, that they might once have shared. There were beginnings in Gwen's eyes, though. There was someone else in the images behind.

Emyr drove. Towards Rhys? He did not know.

Stuck in the middle of one badly painted face, Rhys found it. And they were all badly painted. Men that didn't even look like fucking men. The figure that was nothing like Bethan's. In this still darkness, he looked at his drawings, the piece of paper in his hand, and hated all the things they couldn't say. Yes, he'd felt guilt. Stare it in the face and see it. Why not now? Two fucking years, yes he'd felt guilt. But the town had blamed him. When it didn't know, when it didn't have the right.

He took the photographs from his pocket and held them in his other hand.

He hadn't seen Lennie Lewis since the night he'd found him on the doorstep. Lennie had been full of hope, as he was now, walking in, to find his wife alone in the house. A brutal kind of hope, that rose stronger from the ground it had been battened down to – hope for the place he'd always believed was inside him, and for Ynys-morlan, like they could finally be the same.

They could never be the same.

He looked down at the photographs and loved them with a kid's love, when he wasn't a kid.

He hated the mural, the ways it could never express what he felt. Hated its crude, clumsy pictures and himself for believing in it. He hated the fact – as he turned, as he moved his torch over the museum's changing room – that thoughts like these only left him when he imagined saying goodbye to Ynys-morlan.

What kind of home made its people feel like that?

I want to speak with you, the note said. *Here. Eleven p.m. And we'll talk about why this wall hasn't been painted out yet.*

You could feel her absence. Strangest thing, because she was silent.

He walked in and knew Nia was gone, even before he saw Ruth standing there, in the doorway to his study, where their daughter now slept. Three weeks: he had discovered the ways she could wait for him, the things she could keep in store. He'd been burned up by her and he'd kept walking in through this door. He'd waited three years for these three weeks. Nia's absence, though. As if the house had been forsaken. Not silence but something far less close to you. And Ruth's face. What he saw was different as the front door closed behind.

His heart would beat, coming in down the garden path each evening. He couldn't feel it now.

She had moved half the furniture back. Beside her, the chest of drawers showed its oval reflection of the wall, the pictures still missing there. At the top of the stairs, he could see into Nia's bedroom, could see the desk that she'd returned to its place and Nia's bed. She must have struggled with it.

There'd been a lot of hope, seeing this house reform. Looking at the skeletons of its old arrangements now, that hope like Nia was not present.

'Where is she?'

'At Charlotte's.'

She touched her hands to her sides, the slightest gesture, like there was dust on her palms.

'You're going to pick her up?'

She only looked back at him and didn't need to answer.

Lennie was silent, stepping forwards, putting the tool box down. 'You don't need to take her away from here.' He stood still before her, hands as empty as if they were held up open-palmed. 'I can tell you that . . . There's no reason in the world why she shouldn't be here.'

'Sounds strange, doesn't it?' she said.

The carpet had been laid back down the stairs, a thin-pile river with no battening to keep it there. The feeling of this room seemed to grow clearer around the cadence of her voice. Only hearing her, he saw her past few hours. She'd been preparing for him.

'It sounds empty,' he said.

'Lonely.'

'Yes it does. Yes it does.'

Ruth came slowly from the doorway and shut the room away behind her.

Steps were difficult. Every movement. She sat down on the staircase, as she had done once before, arms resting on her knees, hands holding each other, and didn't look at him. Words were difficult. She wanted to hate him. Hate was like perfection, blank, and bright.

'This can't go on,' she said.

'You tell me where you want to go from here.'

'I had to take her away, you know that?'

'Why'd you take her?'

She looked up at him, at that sound in his voice, of readiness for anything she'd say. For a moment, the tears were gone and it was sickness. He believed in it all, all these nights. The feeling of breaking in this house fed something in him. These last weeks, he was newborn. She'd seen it.

'I can't trust myself with her,' she said.

'Explain to me. Tell me, Ruth.'

She stared out, trying to keep in her mind the decision she'd made today: Dai's statue and a vision, imperfect but better. 'Do you know that I'd be ashamed to explain? Do you know, the way I am, it makes me scared?'

He wanted to move forwards, touch her. He had tried that before and she'd not been ready. He was afraid if he didn't do it now, chances would be gone. In jeans and a work shirt, half her hair tied back, she'd left behind the person that she'd been when she'd entered this project. In the growth of it, had found no one new yet. There was nothing in her except change.

He did come forwards. 'You've nothing to be ashamed of.'

Eyes clear, she stared at him. 'I want to hurt myself. I get so that I can't stop. I can't trust myself with her. It's worse with her.' Like a reel, she gave them out, low-voiced. 'It's easier if I think about the things you've done. Or if I concentrate on what I'm making. Do you understand why I'm doing it?'

'The project?' he asked.

'I said I'd make something out of it, out of what I've . . . done. You feel these things – you know what I said? That I'd find a better way to express them than the way they wanted to come out. But I can't. I hate you. I look at you, I have to hate you, or me.'

'I know.'

Her saltwater gaze was held on him, unmoving. 'I can believe in what Ynys-morlan will be. It's . . . just staring at the bloody sun, though. It's a lie to do it. I know a lie. Three years in this home we've had. I know what hiding feels like. When I think of the project as anything less . . . just building work, that'll be over soon . . . no "grand vision" . . . it doesn't make up for what I've let . . . go on here. Doesn't make up for Nia's door being shut. It doesn't make up . . . for Nia's door ever being shut.' Very tight, her hands were holding each other as he waited, that expression on his face. So many times she'd seen it now.

She could have comprehended the abuse. But she couldn't comprehend his believing that this passion – or violence, which was really its name – was part of love. And that was the certainty in his eyes.

'Nothing I do, nothing real, could make up for the fact I didn't leave you.'

'You didn't leave me because you were scared. I've been the one who's made that.'

'I was scared of losing the idea that we were happy. How dare I?' she asked. 'How dare I?' It threatened to overspill. She stopped him in his tracks as he moved towards her. 'I don't love you. I don't love you any more. You wore it out, Lennie, all my love. It's not . . . it's not endless. It stops. Comes a point when you look at it and you don't know what it is any more. It's hate. I loved you, I loved you –' She had to stop herself. 'I imagine you touching me now or I think of us – kissing. I couldn't let you touch me, ever. I think of our bed, making love. I want to hurt myself.' She used the bland word again. It was water to the things she'd wanted to do.

She saw doubt and conviction, still conviction, tip to try and win against each other in his eyes. 'You have to give me the chance to show you.'

She carried on, disregarding him. The past threatened to brim over. And she would run. She had looked at the car keys all day, hanging up in the kitchen. She had thought about roads at night. The line of her gaze was a thread. 'I have to tell you and make you see that we're over. It can't make up for what I've done, but I still have to.'

Lennie walked the last steps to the staircase and he sat beside her. She didn't try to move away from him. In the hard light she didn't even turn her head. And so he put his arm, slowly, a slight touch and then more, around her shoulders. And he felt what was happening in her body.

For a moment, he almost took his hand away.

Still she hadn't turned. Her eyes were held on the floor where he'd been standing. He felt the shaking. Every muscle, across her back and in the curve of her neck, was taut. The whole of her, shaking, held. Held in.

'You can let me touch you,' he said. 'Look.'

She gradually turned, she swallowed. Ashamed, she'd said. The pictures of things she would hurt herself with and how. In her face, in her temples, the most tender parts. The images had a clarity in her mind which was unmatched. It was guilt. That was the name it had. She wished that there were better words, so that she could describe it to him and he could know what it was really like.

'Yes. You can touch me. That's how much – I don't respect myself. I hate myself. I'll let you.'

Lennie spoke very slowly. 'Hurts more than anything in the world – to hear you say you hate yourself. But if that's the truth, and I've done that, I deserve to hear it . . .'

'No,' she said. 'Because it's play, to say you deserve this and think . . . some kind of punishing yourself makes it right. You listen to me, and I hurt you. It's play. This is it. It's over, Lennie. There's no way to make it right.'

'I won't believe that –'

'I know you won't.'

'There can be a good ending. I know what I've done but listen, what we used to want – *we can create that*. I'm telling you so fucking listen to me. *I love you*. We can have our good ending, like. I'll make it.' He gave each word to her, whole. 'There's a way to heal it up, Ruth, I promise –'

She wondered how this house would look tomorrow night, every night from now on. And what he would be, when the project was gone and this place a town again.

Until now, she'd let herself believe in absolution.

She watched Lennie's face change as she spoke. He seemed to leave himself.

This silence, that wasn't Nia's.

'I've made love with Charlotte,' she said.

You looked to find yourself in the place around you, the parts you couldn't express.

Greatness, the depth of history, if that was what you felt. And a landscape, coast and plain and mountains, could be the home of those things. You cradled them, until the pictures were brighter than life. You hated life because it couldn't equal them.

Or redemption, if that was what you needed. And a town by the sea could be the canvas for something beautiful enough to make you clean.

'What?' he said, because he didn't understand.

'We're . . .' As the word failed to come, Ruth saw it clearly: how she herself didn't know what they were. 'We've made love.'

'No,' he said, small and simple, complete.

'The night you hit me . . . when I told you to . . .' small stones from her mouth, and she saw his head move slowly back and forwards, 'I called her and she came here, straight here. I was crying. You know how long I've covered them up, long sleeves. I showed her the bruises,' she said and as she spoke, that night came again and seemed to find a shape for the first time, reflected in Lennie's eyes. 'I saw her looking at me and I was . . . couldn't control myself, I was hating myself and I saw her look at me like she . . . cared for me, I tried to ruin it. I kissed her.'

'You don't know what you're saying, Ruth. You're in a state like you've been . . . in a state for months now, and it's my fault. You're lying.'

'No. We were upstairs.'

She heard him laugh and saw it move his face. His disbelief made it real.

'I kissed her and because she *does* care, she didn't run away. She cared enough . . . to kiss me and make it . . . stop it from being . . . I meant it to hurt her.'

'A dyke,' he said. 'A dyke? That's what you're telling me? Why do you want to lie? You don't have to any more. I know what I've done, you've showed me. Don't have to do this.'

And she could have said it, as she had done everything in these last weeks, just as he told her, to hurt him. She could've driven it into him. She wouldn't, mustn't do that now.

It made her innocent, to think only of Lennie's actions. She wasn't innocent.

In this silence, she tried to hold away from herself thoughts of the wrong that she had done alone.

'I took my clothes off to show her them.'

'Be quiet now . . .'

'We made love.'

'Be quiet now, don't –'

'I've been to her house and we've had . . . the night together. She's said she loves me. I don't know what that means, if that means any kind of future. I find it hard to think of any kind of future . . . but I know what it means, for you and me. I've told her I love her. I don't know if that's . . . if that's true or not. What would I compare it to . . . ? What would I compare it to?'

Lennie looked at his wife's face, sitting here beside him. His throat was empty – and his body, empty of anger. Empty of memories and of a home – the landscape that he'd made inside himself. A mountainous place, where his life meant something.

'You're fucking her.'

'Call it that. You can't ruin it.'

Only she could do that. Or make it real.

'That's why she's doing this? That's why . . . giving her money. Because she's a dyke. Because you're fucking her? That's why Ynysmorlan's . . . going through this project? Because . . . because you're saying you love her, because she's getting to put her hands all over you. That's what she's doing? Got your hands . . . got your hands all over each other? Making love . . . ?' His words ran on and didn't touch the disorder in his eyes. 'Got her fingers in you.'

She heard him speak things that had happened, clarity coming to the memories, which they hadn't had when she had lived them. In her mind as Charlotte had touched her, she'd been striking out at him, at their home and at herself, unable to bear love.

Lennie looked at her.

It seemed that there were things he should be saying.

He should be talking about the future, leaving her. He couldn't speak.

It seemed that there were things he should be feeling. Disgust, betrayal. He couldn't feel them. They'd been taken from him.

'You fucking bitch,' he said. His voice was quiet as this hollow house. 'You fucking bitch.' It had no vehemence. 'You do this to me?'

She saw him falling, inside the pupils of his eyes: vanished.

'Not to hurt you,' she said, and for the first time knew it was true. 'Because I want it.' As if she could carry that truth on through what she said now. 'Because she cares for me. Because I deserve that. It's fair. It's fair for me, after all this. It's right – that I should have it. I deserve it.'

'No,' he said.

'Yes I do. Yes.'

'No . . .' he said, but didn't feel it.

Pictures filled his mind, of them lying together, and he couldn't seem to understand them. What he knew – had always known – drained away.

They had believed for the first time in these last months, both of them, that the things they held in their minds' eyes and the lives they saw around them could be made one. The thought of it seemed to heal. Ruth finally let it go, and she took it away from him.

'Why would you want that? You want to fuck her? Why would you want that? What are you?'

'It makes me feel like I'm not spoiled by what you've done to me.'

Part of it was true, part was a wish. She came to images of the future, of happiness for herself, Charlotte and Nia. She felt a compulsion to destroy them. And making the commitment now, she didn't know if it could be real. She felt the urge to rob such images from herself. Could barely control the self-hate that was in her now her vision for this little paradise was gone.

'I loved you,' he said. 'You make that mean nothing. You make that dirty.'

'No . . .' she said. 'It's *not* dirty. It's nothing like dirty. Being with you has made me that. You don't even know, you can't even imagine, how it's different. I don't want to hurt you. Lennie, I don't want to hurt you any more. I want you to know what the truth is and see. I want you to open your eyes. Look at me. See me.'

'Go away, Ruth. Go and fuck her. You're a dyke. You're not my wife. I can't believe I ever loved you. You're not my wife –' But what he said wasn't in his eyes.

'No. No I'm not.'

He stared out. The things he'd been were shrinking. He had tried to kiss her, tried to touch her yesterday. He'd brought her flowers. The confusion and the tears on her face now, the desperation in her eyes as she looked through to him. He saw her. She was no stranger.

'I hate you. You do this to me? I don't know you.'

'No, not any more.' She didn't know herself. 'I'm going to stay here till the project's finished. I don't know what'll happen then. We'll use the last few weeks to make plans, where to go . . .'

'You love her,' he said.

Broken apart, their daughter absent, it seemed as though the past lay clear. And it was pity she felt for him. It ran to fill the holes that there had always been between them.

He only sat and continued to stare at her.

After a moment, seeing he wasn't going speak, she reached out and she picked up his hand with both of hers.

'Don't you touch me,' he said, 'get your hand off me, don't you touch me any more.'

But he didn't take it away.

Soft flashes in the darkness. Covered tools and the white, white, white of new things.

The display cabinets were under construction, both those which would be detached and those against the walls; diaphanous plastic lay in drifts over them. At the edges of the high, new-painted ceiling, in the final reach of the torch Rhys held, the wiring of inset bulbs hung down above the platform on which they had worked.

To finish the wiring, another three days. To finish the painting, another two. As Emyr drove, his gaze on a stretch of road that spilled and twisted out, he thought of the packages that had come to his home in the last three days; the photos and little objects that he'd unwrapped, stored in his study. Some had come unmarked, some with names. The exhibits reordered from Aberystwyth were on their way now, and this new collection was slowly building. The two boxes he'd so far taken from the stacks in their hallway sat locked in the museum's tiny office tonight.

No such thing as goodness, Gwen had said. Dai had left, she'd told him. His eyesore still stood.

Whatever she believed now, in the throes of some new relationship, she had been a good person. Her work here had been good – she'd proved that to him with every reaction of these last weeks. The questions that rose to him, he let them sift away behind as he drove on towards the museum.

Emyr Morgan. The last person, the last in this whole fucking town that Rhys wanted to see.

Men raking stones from the street, he saw, roughly copied on his wall. He glanced down at the note, the promise and the threat there. Didn't fucking care about either. There was nothing the man could offer him that would even reach towards the only thing he wanted. As the headlights of Emyr's car stretched on between the houses, though, Rhys stood there torn. He didn't want to stay. But why would he shy away from seeing the cunt? Not to stand his ground seemed like putting some faith into hopes he knew weren't real. There'd only ever be confrontations for him here. There was nothing left for Emyr to threaten.

Under the sodium lights, he was parking.

Rhys listened to the sound of the engine live and fall still. The torch in his hand was off. In the dark he sat.

Emyr stepped out and pressed the central locking remote. He smoothed his trousers. He looked at the museum's doors. Tall and set in the centre of old stone walls, they were oak, they were beautiful even at night, yellow shadows a lamina over the wood. His hands were still. He stood for a moment. And threats and promises seemed to flee, and leave only the memory of Rhys's ugly, careless face in autumn sun.

He looked around him – this museum, this entire street – he felt love for it, when that didn't seem possible. The town was his thoughts and designs, his beliefs laid out. Was him, though there was nothing that he loved in himself.

No such thing as goodness, Gwen had said. Did it make you want to abandon what you'd believed in, to begin a relationship with someone new? Yes, he supposed. Yes.

In the cold, he walked towards the door and saw no light beneath it. He heard the distant, muted noise of voices from inside one of these homes. And standing there, seeing himself dimly repeated in panes of new window-glass, Emyr remembered the night months ago, the beginning of all this, when the dogs had barked and he had gone to the front door to find Eirian's son. Their voices, his and Gwen's, must have sounded to Dai that night like the ones that he heard now.

He took the keys from his pocket and he let himself in.

Closed the door behind him.

He stood, feeling the shape of his own body in the dark. Heart beating, red. Warm breath in the cold of this space. No bulbs in this room that could yet be turned on. He stood, afraid to step forwards.

He had no torch with him, he realized. He felt his own hands in obscurity. He heard the quiet.

'Are you here, Rhys?'

'Yes.' Though he didn't know why. From his place by the wall, he had watched the door open and seen it close.

Solid-voiced after he had swallowed, Emyr said, 'Do you have light?'

Rhys pressed its button and the single torch shed its words across the floor. He saw the man standing there. Neat and sweet in his slacks and Barbour jacket. Hands in his pockets.

Emyr walked across the room towards him and stopped six paces distant. What was pounding in him did not show. He swallowed again, swallowed himself down. He wasn't sure if he could do this.

'What do you want, Mr Morgan?'

Twenty years of giving speeches. He had found that it was best never to sound as if you were answering. Two small figures with a tiny light on their faces that didn't stretch to touch the corners of this room.

'I think the question is, what do you want?'

'No,' Rhys said. 'It's not.'

'I come here each day and see that you've painted a little more. If you call it painting – this.'

He held his hand to the wall Rhys kept his back to, and Rhys didn't need to look; pictures that had left him with less hope each day that they'd ever be what he wanted. Pictures he'd tried to say something with, and failed.

'As you've seen,' Emyr said to him distinctly, 'it's been left, till tonight. Obviously you've been aware that that night was coming. So I think the question is, what do you want?'

'I don't want anything. Not one fucking thing. And if there was one I wouldn't take it from you.'

Emyr stood in silence. His face was pasty in the torchlight and Rhys didn't want to look at him, willed him not to speak but to turn and walk out in the dark. Yet he didn't go himself.

'So I can tell the men to go ahead with this wall tomorrow then.'

'You can tell them what you want. You could do that anyway.'

'Yes, that's true.'

They stood with the note, crumpled, somewhere on the floor between them. This high room, its white paint, dark-framed cases in the making and last wall of derelict, over-sprayed mess, it seemed to house both their pasts. Both unhappy.

'Put a lot of work into this . . .' Emyr said.

'I wouldn't call it work. You might.'

'What would you call it then? Art?'

'A way to pass the fucking time. Why'd you ask me to come? Say what you want and then fuck off.'

'Say what I want, and then *you* can "fuck off". Do you think you have any right to be here? I don't believe you do. I could have you taken off the property in ten minutes. I have the keys to the doors.'

'You've got the keys. That's right.' He moved to stand, pushing against this wall to get his body up, bringing the torch to waist height. He wouldn't stay. Not to listen to this.

'You've put an awful lot of work into it. Going to walk away just like that?'

He didn't answer. The things he'd drawn were gone anyway. In some way, they'd always been gone. The walls had always been this voiceless white. All these slung-together pictures, that was what they shared – they were never anything but lost.

'Well that doesn't surprise me. You've had a lot of practice.'

'That's right,' nodding again, 'that's right.' And he stepped across the floor to move past him, the sound of his own feet very loud, and in their echoes, low memories. Low self-loathing that he couldn't leave behind, whether or not he walked out through this door. Bethan shouting at him how little her future had been worth. Why he'd gone to her, just so he could tell himself that he'd been in the right, because he'd offered her the chance. The chance to forgive him. To leave the place he'd lost anyway. 'A lot of fucking practice. Yeah.'

'I can have it kept, Rhys. This whole wall. Has that occurred to you?'

He turned and stared at the man in one movement and thought he saw, in the pass of his torch over Emyr's face, some kind of excitement, barely held under those words. It faded to nothing in the light.

What did the boy see? Was it desperation? It must not be.

'I can have it kept. Everything you've done.'

'Don't try and push me and pull me with your little speeches. You can have any fucking thing you want. What am I meant to say to that? Huh? "Oh really? That's awfully kind of you, Mr Mayor. And what can I do for you in return?" You want something from me then you fucking tell me it.' The light bobbed and weaved in his hand, his heart beating. 'I'm not going to listen to your bullshit. You can give it to everyone else. You think I'm going to believe you?' he asked, staring through the dark and his own feelings. '*I can have it kept*. What makes you think I even want it kept? That occur to you?'

'No one makes something like this unless they want it kept.' Emyr's breath hung in mist on the thick air.

'Speak for yourself.' And Rhys held his hand out to a wall that couldn't be seen. 'I'm not like you. I'm not fucking interested in changing everything around me. You want to paint it out, fucking do it.'

'I'll give you my word,' he said quietly, 'that it will be kept. If you do something for me.' Silence. One last nod.

'Well there you have it. Something for you.'

'My word . . . do you understand that?'

'And who are you, like . . . that your word means anything to me? Some gentleman? You're no gentleman. I've seen you. Foul-mouthed as anyone! I've seen you.' He lost himself it seemed, only his words stayed tangible and he held on to them, though he didn't really even want them to be his. 'I've seen you. Know what you are? You're every fucking thing that's wrong with this town!'

Emyr was silent over the only denial he could have given. After a moment he said, 'I need something. Someone's word might mean nothing to you. It does to me.' And it had done once, a long time ago. He remembered when he'd prided himself on it. He looked back now and had no pride, speaking to this boy and hearing the lie come out; seeing it in the dark before his own face.

In silence, Rhys looked at him.

Evaluation, if the boy was capable of such.

In everything that was left of this town, though, it was some kind of small wonder that Rhys felt, hearing Emyr Morgan say so blatantly that he needed help. And though the rest of him was leaving now, was walking out this door to a road where he might regain some balance, there was a part of Rhys that felt satisfaction – he didn't want to feel it. But he wasn't walking away.

'What do you need?'

Emyr shifted, very slight. Around them, he felt the presence of all the unseen shapes that would make this room complete. Or would have done so, three days ago. When he'd still been able to believe that Gwen was with him in some way.

He'd had a dream – of a town full of beautiful buildings, somehow empty, of a street surrounded by the things they might have made together. A place that would embody his love. Love you gave to a good person, a dedicated, self-sacrificing angel; a woman who could not return it. How had he stayed with her? He had loved the work that had taken his place. Good aims. They had caught his heart. And what he had said to Dai in the past, let him believe, or the fact that Dai's sculpture now stuck up through his vision and he wanted to tear it down, those things didn't change the fact that it was goodness he'd loved in Gwen.

Emyr Morgan drew in breath, like even the air here was running from his grasp, and he spoke.

'My wife is sleeping with someone else.'

In some other time, Rhys might have smiled. He stood in a quiet that outweighed him. He'd thought he was beyond wanting to punish this town. There were things he'd found, maybe he wasn't capable of drawing them – but there were things that had changed him. Changed the way he'd wanted to take out his hurt on Ynys-morlan.

'My wife is sleeping with someone else. And I believe . . . I believe that it can only be the person you first told me of. She's no whore.'

In one torch's light, Rhys's eyes were slowly staring.

'She doesn't form relationships with people at random. If you believed she'd formed one with . . . the person you spoke about before, then that's who she's with now.' Evenings, long nights. 'I want to know who it is. As you can understand. I'll feel much better when I know. You can tell me. Or everything you said before was . . . hot air. I am putting myself –' at the dark floor, he glanced, and he heard his voice echoing as he raised his eyes again. He was saying this. To this boy. 'As you can imagine . . . I am putting myself in a position that no one . . . would . . . no one would envy me. I do not want to be standing here. I do not want to have to say this to you. I'm saying it despite these things, because I need, I *have* to know . . . and I am offering you the only thing I've got. You didn't do all this so you could see it painted out.'

Stifled silence. What else could he give? The atrophied silence of this room and its high shadows.

'Do you understand me, Rhys? Have you taken in the things . . . that . . . the things that I've said to you?'

'Yes. I reckon I have.'

'Then we understand each other.'

Rhys wouldn't say that. There was a terrible sadness that made its way inside him, standing in front of Emyr. There were thoughts of loneliness and pity. He saw Morgan adjust his glasses. He saw the man had nothing left but bluster now and mannerisms. Rhys's hands were empty by his sides as he thought of Tom, of everything he had lost since he'd last seen him. It cut, the sadness. Rhys couldn't look at him without the hate he'd felt for two years – not just for Emyr but for everything he was the peak of – and Tom's words that night, in this place, returned to Rhys as Emyr Morgan stared into his face.

Ignorant. Immoral, he had told Tom.

What did you expect? Tom had said.

Those hadn't been the worst things Emyr had told him, though. How he had no place here, that had been the worst. Because it was fucking true. Went right down in old wounds, and it had taken months since that, just to confess there were things, in these old photographs there were things that he needed from a home.

'You've got a problem now . . . And you think, like, think because you're hurting now you can ask me . . . to help you.'

It cut, because he looked at Emyr and hated him still. Felt the pity and *still* did. What had he done wrong in this town? What had he done? He hadn't wanted any fucking child. Ignorant. Immoral. Yes, he'd been those things. He'd fucking been them. But at sixteen years old. How old was Emyr? Old enough, standing in that car park, looking at him, old enough not to judge. Old enough to see, surely see that he didn't want this fucking life he had. That he'd never wanted it. Never wanted to be this person.

'To know . . . "would make you feel better"? You . . . you treat me like shit, Mr Emyr Morgan. You even realize that? You even realize, like . . . the things you've said to me? You want me to help you now?'

'I never tried to hurt you.' But the voice he spoke with was his no longer, it belonged to a man who hadn't done what Emyr had. 'I want . . . to offer you a deal. Not just ask for your help. This, this is what I've got to offer you.'

He moved his hand, but only slightly – any deal failing between them.

'My word on it.' Which had meant something once. Did he care for right and wrong? Dai had left. What would become of him outside Ynys-morlan? A vagabond on the streets? He wouldn't find a home. Did Emyr really care for morality? He wanted that fucking statue knocked down, eradicated like this sprawl of pictures. 'I need to know . . . I have to know, as you can understand. I . . . will promise that this stuff, it'll be kept . . .'

'I can hear the lie,' Rhys said to Emyr, quiet-voiced.

'No lie.'

But it was. Just falsehood. Had it been goodness that had let him love Gwen, while she'd worked through him, worked over him, ignored, disregarded him? When he'd sat in the gift shop's last morning and told Dai that the man's beliefs were true, had it been goodness then? He'd heard the things that Dai had said, he'd felt the echoes. He'd needed to look at Eirian's son and see a fool.

Rhys's mouth was dry, though, as he said, 'Fuck your word. I can *hear* you fucking *lie!*'

A hush, like water between them. They stood and faced each other, only this shallow dark around. He didn't believe the promise. And even if he had, if he'd wanted all the pictures kept, fucking displayed here, it was Tom's name that the man was asking for.

Their breath rose and fell in the fluttering light.

There'd been injustice, though. Rhys couldn't just let go of it. The image of Tom he'd tried to paint, leaving home, unable to leave, moving towards somewhere that had no end. It came up in him. He hated this man who looked so fucking pitiable now. Had this town in the palm of his fucking hand and he still reached out to hurt others, who would've loved to call it home.

Two years of being judged by Emyr Morgan's fucking 'word'. All their words.

He'd never give the man Tom's name or any other. But two years. Didn't he deserve some fucking amends? Like a simple step, he chose it. Like leaving confusion behind, and Bethan's reflection; all these images he couldn't draw.

'I don't believe you'll ever keep this.' He didn't gesture to the wall. Emyr looked at him.

'You want . . .' Rhys said, 'you want to know the name, like . . . then I don't want any promises from you. I want . . . You know what I want?'

Emyr shook his slow head. His gaze had been sure once, and was now indistinct, as he watched the beginning of a proposal to which he would answer yes. Anything, he realized.

'*You know what I want? . . . I hate you.*' For a moment what he felt escaped him, and he had to close his mouth and take himself in to make it simple again. 'I'll tell you what I want . . .' he said into the cold, 'and then you can say yes or no.'

There'd been three of them once. Tom was walking tonight. Bethan stood in the café, in front of these new windows that made the street into a Christmas tale. Tom was striding out. He'd used to go up and down this road. He was standing, looking at his mother's yard now where the cast-off things, the old things, had been kept before. At his back and to his left and to his right, this town – this town that Bethan saw – it was an alien country. What if you left, if you went off to Thailand or New Zealand, and you still felt lost? You didn't understand yourself any better, and the things you recognized were gone.

The wind moved, as it had always done. Blame that had no line.

Windows were half lit, he saw them. Underneath new slates. And the scaffolding that still covered this town, it held all three of them.

In a room Rhys couldn't see – walls that would shine when the morning's first light stole over them – he spoke words that grew harder. A voice that feelings left behind. He told the man to move towards the centre of the floor. He told him to stop there.

The torch's light placed a filigree on Emyr's shadowed face.

He moved and he stood still. Like everything was gone already, a simplicity came to him as well. In the safety of this half-dark, he let the last recent days reverberate. An empty house lay behind him, and before him, when that morning came.

Rhys's hands faltered and stumbled, but his voice didn't, moving to the place where he'd put the cans of paint and all the brushes. The sounds were soft touches.

'Stay there.'

A simplicity, Emyr thought, like the culmination of all these months, through which he'd fallen, each day a little lower than before – to finally follow the orders of this boy.

'Just stand still.'

A completeness, Emyr thought, something dawning. Some revelation in the quiet. He felt sick. He stood still as ordered. Would this boy tell him the name? He wasn't sure he believed it.

Dai had left. To what future? How could he have loved Gwen, if not for the strength of being good?

Rhys turned and looked at him. No pride in the man's face any more. Nothing to break down in him like there'd been that day in the car park, but still he couldn't hold in the words he had. When Emyr Morgan had still had his pride, Rhys'd never had the chance. Two years and he'd been lost. He deserved reprisal. Didn't he?

'Kneel down . . .' he said. 'That's what I want, like.'

'Kneel down?' Emyr asked.

'You fucking heard me!'

Cold white breath in the torch's light. Emyr moved his body slowly. Floorboards that would be stripped and polished in a week's time. His knees creaking, he wondered desolately, had she left the house already? Driven to that man's home? That boy's?

'You reckoned . . .' Rhys said, 'I'd believe you. Thought I'd just agree? So ignorant, yeah? And you, like. What are you then? *What are you?*' he said.

In the quiet, Emyr didn't answer.

Frustration was a tide in Rhys, desperate. No arrogance left in Emyr. '*What are you?*' His own voice echoed. Lost.

'I'm a liar,' Emyr said. The truth came, simple.

'You wouldn't have kept it!'

'No. I wouldn't.'

A liar. A man who'd lead Dai through all the little paths he'd wanted; the demolition, sending him to Siân. He had never cared for morals.

'A liar,' he reiterated.

Rhys didn't speak, hard hands caught round the things he held. The expression on his face unseen, the light showing only Emyr. 'What I want –' he said finally, ' – if they start painting it out tomorrow, like, all of it, I'll have done it anyway. What I want is a picture of you. Fucking – kneeling. Fucking kneeling here! Go on and put your head down.' He looked at Emyr as the man, illuminated, stared blindly back at him. 'A picture of you . . . and I'll know what it meant. Even when it's gone, I'll know.'

Only wordless quiet came back to him.

'You put your head down! Put it down!'

There was a moment. Emyr might have been looking towards anyone. In his eyes, there was only the stare of light. It shrank his pupils. But before he lowered his head, something was exchanged it seemed. Just sadness, that neither of them could control.

He wouldn't hear the name. He knew it.

But slowly, faltering, he did as Rhys told him. And Rhys held the torch, staring down at him, gripping the last anger he could find.

As the night moved, they seemed not to. Rhys drew him. Things he'd said to himself, alone, in anger, echoed in the sounds of Emyr's movements. The picture was the worst he'd done, his hands mixed up with the ebb of what he felt. In rough blocks of the wrong colours, he painted it in, all the others unfinished around it, names from the bus shelter, all the cunts and fucks and unhappiness. Obscenities.

He thought of Bethan. It seemed so long ago but it had never been behind him. He didn't know what he'd been offering her that recent night. What this place had taken from him, what she had taken, was a picture of himself that he could love.

Patty came down into the café's lower room, Chelsea finally sleeping upstairs, to find her daughter crying. Staring out, her back to the space into which the chairs and tables would be delivered tomorrow, there was the street's light around Bethan's figure. There was the inert air of this new, almost finished place, around the noises she made.

Pat stood in the doorway for a few long moments without saying Bethan's name. All the reasons were here – in the way Beth stood, and what surrounded her – and she didn't need to ask.

It had been a long journey to this. There'd been a lot of choices. And many had been made, just running, not looking back, or even to the future. She remembered, like an ending, watching Bethan tell Dai he couldn't build that thing. She stood and saw her now, love coming up, like it so often did, to make you sad instead of bringing any smile. She felt a barrenness, that you could know someone so well and still have so much to keep you apart from them. In this same room, that feeling had started. And she remembered that night as clearly as Bethan, more than two years and Chelsea's whole life ago.

'Is it the place?' she said.

'Is it the place?' No change in Bethan's figure as she answered. Maybe she'd known who was standing behind her. 'Yes,' she said, picking her way from word to word, they were all serrated, 'it's the place, it's me *in* the place . . . and everything else round those two, like.'

'Almost finished.'

'Yeah.' Her mother saw her nod. 'Almost finished.' She saw her put her arms about herself before she turned, like she needed protection, which really she should have looked to her mother for.

There was some make-up on her face, puffed up and tight as she met Pat's eyes. And it was a different place this room, than they'd sat in on that night.

She said to Bethan, 'You don't feel any different.'

'There's no difference to feel.'

The yellow shadows on Beth's face caught a smile too bitter for an eighteen-year-old. Though bitterness faded, Patty knew really, and didn't grow with the years like people thought.

'Are you sure that's true? To me, you seem different . . . maybe I'm not in a position to judge. But it's easy to bring up all your expectations, when you're looking at the end of something like this. It's easy to find something lacking there when you do. You know what I mean?'

'I didn't have any expectations.'

'You sure that's true?'

But Bethan only said again, 'I'm no different.'

'Beth . . . even if you weren't, that wouldn't be a bad thing. There was nothing wrong with you . . .' What welled up in her, she couldn't pass it to her daughter. In herself it was too painful and close. 'Nothing wrong with you then *or* now. It's easy to take something like this . . . and wager everything on it. You understand what I mean? But there was never anything in you that needed change. It's not a bad thing, if you don't feel any.'

Bethan saw a woman who'd made the same choices. They'd sat at the corner table, which had slowly become her table afterwards. Two years, watching everyone's daily routines. Dai's coloured-in crosswords, she remembered. His hot chocolate every day. Except this wasn't the same place. Everything was gone now. She hadn't known until she'd seen Ynys-morlan change, how much she wanted to change herself.

Patty moved up to her. Wooden floorboards now, and beams fixed to the walls around them that looked as if they'd always been there. Little brass shines in the corners; no plastic here any more. Patty walked across and stopped, in the shadows, a few paces from where Bethan stood.

A woman who'd made all the same choices, Bethan saw, and had never honestly told her daughter what they'd done.

'Talk to me,' her mum said.

'You don't want to hear anything I've got to say.'

'Just talk to me.'

'You know what I've got, like? I've got blame, that's all I've got.'

'Who do you blame?' And then she said quietly, 'You blame me.'

Resolve on Bethan's face dispersed. All things she could have told her: how she had stood in the window with Dai below. What she'd done with him. What she must be.

'I don't . . . like myself,' she said, through a hard clenched jaw.

Pat couldn't answer before she spoke again.

'I hate myself . . . Do you know that?'

'I know you've got no reason to –'

'That's not true, though.' The room was unspeaking. How they had sat here, Bethan remembered, and the voice she'd used then, that hadn't yet been her own. Short, bare sentences, which had taken her from school and exams and teachers, to this. Just one quick talk. And her mum had reached out, Bethan recalled, then withdrawn her hand. Confusion, sadness, had made her do it. Memories.

Bethan looked at her now and her voice burst like not one hour had passed since. 'I don't understand how you could've done it, you know that? I still, like, I look back and don't understand. I see you now, like, trying to make up for it. I see you letting me do this fucking restaurant and how bitter the project's made you, so fucking bitter, and I don't understand –'

'Tell me then,' Patty said. But there was nothing maybe to tell.

'I think, like . . . I think, if Chelsea came to me . . .' She didn't finish.

The room had been dark. And the television on upstairs. And across the table, Bethan had looked at her mother and had heard for the first time how fucking young, how naïve it sounded when she talked about the future. Going away with Rhys somewhere. And what then? Had she even known? The adolescence in her eyes must have been so clear to someone who'd been sixteen years past the same choice. It must have been so transparent.

'I'm going to keep it,' she had said. She'd seen her mum's face. There'd been fewer lines then, in these same shadows. 'I'm going to keep it . . . What else can I do?'

Ynys-morlan was a different place now. It was one of those places she could have gone and discovered.

'I don't understand,' Bethan said. 'I was young. You must've seen that . . .'

'Of course I saw it.'

Patty looked out to her. Didn't need the moment named.

Sitting here that night, her mother hadn't mapped out other places, other choices. 'I was so fucking young.'

'I know –'

'You know how I feel?' she said. 'I feel old . . . I've been thinking . . . I've been looking at you, asking myself . . . what it'd be like if Chelsea came up to me, if she was sixteen and she came up to me. If she was pregnant. You know? What I'd say if she asked me . . . about what else she could do. Other possibilities, chances . . . I would tell her – that there's lots of things. I'd tell her, anything. Anything.'

'Bethan –' Patty held out her hand, as once she'd drawn it back. How could you explain?

'Chelsea being young . . .' Bethan said, 'it's beautiful to me, like. It's precious to me. It must've been precious to you! I was a kid . . . I don't understand how you could've looked at me, and seen that last bit of innocence, and not told me . . . to keep it. How could you have done that? How?'

Patty's mouth open, words falling with no sound, all she was saying was, 'I did –'

'All these changes in town, like . . . and I've seen you so resentful. How does it look? Seeing all the stuff you left behind come back? How does it look, to make you bitter like that? You told me you were happy! You weren't happy! I see your face now – all the things you gave up, they're all coming back aren't they? You were never happy! How could you have told me to make the same choice . . . ?'

'Bitter?' Patty said. 'That's how I look . . . ? That's what you've been thinking? That I resent all this . . . Because I decided to stay here and have you. My God, Beth.' And then she did reach out and she took Bethan's hand, tight, desolate. 'You think you've got no innocence? You think the way you feel is because of that?'

What could she tell her; that she'd made love with Dai Meredith? That she knew how innocence felt, and how she felt herself after it?

Patty looked at her face, ripped and angry and full of sadness. The past welled up and filled her. 'All you've got is innocence,' she said.

'I'm old – fucking experience is what I've got –'

'You think you feel this way because you're experienced?' Patty held her gaze, hurting. 'You feel the way you do, Beth . . . because you've never experienced anything. Anything at all.'

In the silence that came from Bethan, some part of her was lost and lessened her.

'You feel the way you do . . . because all you've got is innocence.'

There had been a time, a place – there had been a summer – when none of these cares had been in their lives. Surely there had been a time. When the light of afternoon to evening had been the only change. Surely. There'd been a time when their memories had lived. Those thoughts – the tender quality of them – couldn't lie. There had been a time of innocence, which had left them now. Surely. It felt that way.

Bethan didn't speak, though. The things she knew wouldn't come to her, to say their pieces, defend themselves.

'When you asked me what you could do,' Patty said, 'and yes, you looked so young. Of course your being young was *precious* to me. I never regretted the choice I made.'

'How can you say that, when you've been so angry . . . ? All these opportunities, and you've hated it –'

'I do hate it.'

'*How can you say you don't regret it?* You've been watching, you've been looking out the window, seeing everything you sacrificed! I know you have! Everything you let me give up too.'

'I never wanted . . . maybe it seems unbelievable to you, maybe I should've known it would be different . . . I never wanted anything but to stay here. Does that sound stupid? Do you believe me? You talk about innocence. I looked at you – Bethan, I *saw* it. I tried to keep it. I tried to hold it in you. I *never* regretted what I did. There's no more innocence in the world than . . . staying where you grew up. Having your family there.'

She looked at Patty and could not answer her.

'When I stayed here, when I had you . . . that wasn't cowardice. It wasn't sacrificing anything.'

'You knew you couldn't do anything else,' Bethan said into the paint-deadened air. 'You looked at yourself and you knew you couldn't. So you stayed.'

'I wasn't thinking that! This project . . . doesn't look like a lot of choices I left behind. It looks to me . . . like a hundred other places I never wanted to see.'

'That's not true. How can that be true?'

'Because we're different.' She looked away from her daughter's eyes. 'You think having a child here is experience? It makes you old? What about an abortion, Bethan? What about an abortion at sixteen, and then going off to some other town, nothing but that behind you? Because it's that, it's that that sounds like . . . the sort of experience that makes you old.' On Bethan's hand, her own tightened, 'Because we're different and I – I should have told you to go away. You look at your baby, though, just like you said, when Chelsea gets to sixteen years old, you look at her, and try telling her to let go of the last bit of being young she's got. I never wanted to leave here,' she said. 'Do you believe me? There's no more innocence in the world than in Ynys-morlan. I thought that you'd be happy here . . .'

She said nothing. She saw Patty cry. She had been ready to speak, but said nothing.

'I'm *sorry* – if I let you make the wrong decision, I'm sorry. But look at you . . . *look at you*,' she said. 'You think it's experience that makes you hate yourself? Bethan – you're innocent of everything there is.'

He'd always been just what Emyr had called him.

He drew the mayor broken down. The man would never look at

him and tell him he had been wrong. The man would never tell him he was sorry. And even that word, if spoken, wouldn't have come from Ynys-morlan: from the place in the photographs that he'd almost destroyed. It would have come from this new-grown town Rhys didn't know. Ynys-morlan was gone. He thought of Bethan that night, crying nearly, telling him what her dreams had added up to. He took this moment with Emyr instead of the forgiveness he'd never have from this place – and couldn't give to it.

There were visions, there was a picture of himself inside and, if he didn't love it, he could still find strength in it. Of leaving, that picture was, of other places that might still hold the feelings Lennie's stories gave. And he thought of Lennie, still full of hope when he'd last seen him. Despite everything, believing in them. Though Rhys did not, like his friend he couldn't let the stories go. Images of grandeur in a lessened fucking world; of self-belief in the midst of obscurity.

'Tell me now,' Emyr said, standing, as Rhys turned off the torch.

The windows beside them were like a church's, high and thin, permeated by the new dawn, walls still dark around them.

'Fuck you. Fuck you . . .' he told him emptily, as Emyr had imagined he might.

No ending came for Rhys that night, just turmoil, that gathered with the slow touch of morning, to form a day where everything looked torn to him; where his feelings were white and desperate as the sky.

It was in that morning, while the workmen arrived in the street, their headlights still brighter than sunrise over the project's final day, it was in that hour that should have been quiet here, Dai Meredith's time, that Rhys went back to Tom.

Bethan slept with Chelsea in her family's living room, and Pat watched her go in the morning. The last restaurant furnishings were to be delivered today, and all its wiring completed. She wheeled the pushchair out slowly through the doorway as Pat looked down from the

window above, unable to see what expression might be on her face –
thinking of the sun, clear and pale across the street, and hoping it
would make the day look good to her.

Soon the road wouldn't be full of this traffic: trucks and vans. It
would be caravans, it would be day trippers and tourists. People would
arrive, the regular holidaymakers, and stop at the head of town,
maybe laugh. Patty didn't know really what they had ever thought of
Ynys-morlan, she didn't know what they'd think now.

The sun rose on timber and slate, on sea stone and the last scaffolding that still clung around it. Little wooden doors with their brass
hinges glittering so clear they could only be new. Little peaked,
windowed entranceways. Porches? You couldn't have called them
that. People's homes, that she recognized. Under the last of the work
you could still see their old shapes. The changes didn't look like
cladding any more, though – it seemed as if the buildings she knew
had stretched themselves, grown new outlines beneath the scraps of
broken render that men were still chipping from the walls. Filthy
walls, and these pretty, pretty houses. Like now they were shedding
their skins. Patty didn't even know any more, looking down with the
dust and the sunlight on her living room's windowpanes, what she
thought, or what she felt. The Ynys-morlan she knew, she'd been able
to stay young there. Patty Hughes. As bright as a morning-washed set
of cutlery. All her curls and her cute, tight little walk, with the business
she had loved, where she could stand each day and talk to everyone.
A grandmother really, though she'd never felt it. Never felt herself
grow older at all. It was part of the magic of home, she'd always
thought. She'd watched Gwen, and Siân too, make decisions that
she'd never been able to understand. Because they'd stayed as well.
She had believed, somewhere deep down, that no one ever wanted
to leave home. To do so was always a battle against what you really
needed. The struggle of it changed people's lives. And she'd believed
that they would have found happiness far closer, on their doorstep in
fact, if they'd admitted what she'd always known: there wasn't any
place where your dreams lived longer than the place where you'd
been born.

It had been true for her. She couldn't hold on to the belief any more, though, that it was true for others. And this street, that had been a whole acre from the coastline in her own grandmother's time – and how she'd liked to tell it – it was no longer her Ynys-morlan. What she'd told Beth, that night two years ago, had been the truth – from the top to the bottom.

She'd never regretted staying. In some way, the lives they kept here weren't real enough to be taken out of Ynys-morlan. Couldn't have survived the weathering of the real world. People still left their front doors unlocked here, and you couldn't ever feel small, never frightened, walking down the street. Not when you could put the name to every face.

She had come to this morning, when she'd seen Bethan's unhappiness like a picture of that sweet little dream twisted up. She saw her daughter step out through the door and into a new town. Home didn't mean to everyone what it meant to Patty Hughes. And the sea had come eventually, it had come anyway, to wash over her own. Recede, and leave this other place, with all its new little gleams between the last work, as clear and bright as if the street were still saltwater-wet.

There was the business, behind her as she stood at the window, and there was a day's work ahead, to finish whatever had been begun. She didn't know if Bethan would be able to stay here and be happy. She herself didn't feel like she could leave now.

The world was always full and always spilling over. For the first time Patty felt old. She looked down to see the town where she'd retire one day, and it didn't know her any more – her daughter pushing the pram off slowly down its street, through the industry and early sun.

His back to Ynys-morlan and the road that led out of it, where a queue of trucks and vans ate the first of the morning's quiet, Rhys had walked to the caravan site: nothing else ahead but dunes and the sky, still paling then, and here still silent.

They had used to walk out in the summer. Long before Bethan.

Twelve years old, thirteen maybe. Get off with all the holiday girls. He remembered one saying – the memory clear, left to rise alone out here in the stillness – 'Yes, but you *live* here.' The question, or whatever else had come before it, gone now. He remembered hearing some kind of magic. 'Yes, but you *live* here . . .' Where, as far as she'd known, it was always summertime.

Rhys looked at the site before him, almost ready for another summer now. Just the foot-gate unlocked. The car's entranceway beside it double-gated and with a padlock, he saw, to keep out this empty road that he was standing on.

On its other side, the car park was quiet tarmac, the office and the little shop blinded-down. Beside the fence he'd walked already, and seen them all, vacant, set apart from each other, unchanged in the growing light; sunshine or fluorescent lamps, didn't make any difference in these last few out-of-season days.

For a few minutes he didn't go in.

He saw, over the roofs of the first caravans, the tops of the swings and the slide in the playground, a gull there, perched motionless. In the dawn, Rhys's face was grey as well as he looked, and he was crying. The image of Emyr wasn't behind him, but everywhere. It was in all this soundless space. He was wiping his cold hand across his cold mouth, and he spat. A little circle on this cold ground.

Bethan wasn't behind him. Or the memories of walking here with Tom. It seemed to him like he'd never got older. He had been sixteen, or he'd been eleven, and what was different now? He came to the site, with all the words Emyr had said ready to be told again. More than ready. Like the place was tearing, the fucking sand dunes and the sky, when it was only him. Making or breaking to touch somewhere, Lennie'd said. And it seemed like he had done neither, though he had the memories – memories of both. They couldn't be real, for everything was changed now but him.

Sleeping between the others, he thought he'd find Tom's caravan, with the same uninhabited sky drawn across the windows. He'd thought that he would wake him up. The light behind Tom's curtains, though, could be seen from a hundred yards away. Well before the noise of Rhys's footsteps was edged with the music's sound.

Last night Siân had asked him to the house. He'd gone against his will. He'd gone because of the tone in her voice; the first time he'd seen her since Gwen had told him about Dai in the street.

The table had been laid, with a lamp from the living room brought in to stand beside the plates. The cable trailing out through the doorway, into the dark of rooms still disordered, it had shown the dinner set just for two.

'I would've picked you up,' she'd said, opening the door beneath the scaffolding.

'No need.'

'Silly night to walk,' she'd said. They had stood in the corridor, as awkward, both of them, as if this had never been his house.

No electrics in the kitchen yet. The lamp had shone on the two plates, on the serving mats, and across a newly painted room without decoration. He'd stood in the doorway and had not gone in. Without the washing machine or the fridge in their places, just the cooker and dark spaces on either side, it was the strangest mix of new and old. She'd looked at him from it all, nothing but resolution to cover the things she felt.

'Stacey not here?'

'No she's not. She's over at a friend's place tonight.' After she'd called to say she'd be away, Siân had telephoned him. 'What've you been up to then?'

'Nothing much. Nothing at all.'

'Been asking around for any new jobs?'

'No. I haven't done that yet.'

'Well I was talking to Madryn today. She's not filled the place – you know they've passed her application? It's a specialist food shop, or it will be anyway. Second place down from the Lion? She's not filled the post yet, someone to help her out.'

'Mention me, did you?'

'No I didn't. Not my place to do that, is it? I don't know where you want to work.'

'Not there.'

She'd nodded. 'Well I'm only telling you. Where might you want to work?'

'What does it matter?' he said, watching her face, turned away from him.

'I'm only interested,' and she'd looked back to where he still stood in the kitchen doorway, careful of the tightness, 'Will you not come in? Going to lurk in the door there?'

The room Tom saw was nearly twice the height it had been. There were exposed beams going up to the roof, stained dark between white paint. In the opposite wall, looking over the backyard, a small-paned window was nestled – in the light's reach, he saw the sea stone that held it and the new, wider sill. Like a cottage's room, it was. Outside, beneath the scaffolding still, the window had a little peak of its own.

'I'm interested in everything you're doing,' she'd said.

He hadn't answered her, memories of Gwen rising; all the things they'd done together. At the front door his mother had kissed him, and in the moment that her face had come close, so had a flash of Gwen. Siân was looking at him now and he didn't know what to say to her. What had he been busy with? He'd been making love with the woman who'd been his mother's best friend, all her life. In this shadowed, half-finished room, thinking of all the things Gwen had told him, it seemed as if he couldn't be much younger than his mum. And how did Gwen feel, he wondered, standing somewhere between the two?

Guilt, he had. Like it was written on the skin she'd touched. And thoughts of what his mother might have said to Dai that day, they moved free in the quiet that this guilt put between them.

'And you? What've you been up to?'

'Too busy with the house to be up to anything. And checking in on the Spar.'

He looked at the room.

'What do you think?' she said.

'What do I think?'

She went from the counter to the cooker as though she was in a friend's house, where it was always going to be brighter to clean or cook, wash up, whatever, than it was in your own. There was something small about her, in this place that wasn't hers yet. No brittleness as she turned, waiting for him to answer, except the brittleness of asking him.

'It's nice.'

'You think so, do you?'

'It's pretty, Mum.'

'Be nicer when there aren't wires hanging from the ceiling . . . I think it's pretty.'

'Good.'

He wished he'd been there, that day with Dai in the street, so he could've known what she'd said.

He was glad he'd come, though; seen her happy in this place. She was that at least. He sat and watched her move to the table, put herself down with little arrangements of the knives and forks. Lasagne, she served up, which she didn't really like and he did.

'You want to sit? I thought it would be nice if we got the chance to spend a little time in the new place together.'

He nodded.

'I didn't want you . . . not to see it till it was finished.' She didn't move to dish out the food, and he saw in her face, more plainly than in everything else, the gesture that she was trying to make. He wanted to show her the same. His words were all stalled, though. 'I want you to be able . . . to feel at home here,' she told him.

He could say a lot of things. That's nice, he could say. Thank you.

Days lay behind her. When she'd watched the compensation cheques handed out, and had gone down to the Spar's little toilet. When she'd stood beside all the others on the pavement with Dai. That afternoon wasn't out of her thoughts either.

And what Tom said, the food lying out before him, his mum only looking at his face, it was bare: 'It's been a long time since I felt at home here. It's not the building work. It's not the project.'

The little lamp cast unfamiliar shadows, on her face, on her still hands.

'I know that, yes.'

No such thing as right or wrong, Gwen had said. Months estranged, believing that he was searching for something. What had Gwen said? That his mother had always been hard to please. In this confusion, looking at her, all he could find was the truth.

'It's been you, like.'

Her voice was quiet, held. 'Well, I know.'

'Been nearly two years since I felt at home here. I mean it's not. Is it?'

'That's not true.' The resolution that she'd constructed, cooking, waiting for him to come, it seemed to threaten to break again into all the little pieces she'd built it out of. 'That's why I wanted you to come, Tom. So you can see that's not true.'

What would he say? That he saw nothing? And break even this gesture.

He'd lain in bed with Gwen. They'd kissed each other, they'd tried to make each other promises. He didn't feel young enough to be Siân's son, no more than he felt old enough to be Gwen's lover. He didn't know himself. And he must be lost then, because no one else here knew him any more. Wanting to think of this as home, all he could remember was his mother's condemnation of Gwen. And what had she herself then said to Dai, surrounding him in the street with that little crowd he'd been told of?

'Have they started opening up the site yet?' she asked him.

'They're . . . you know, they're getting ready.'

'Be people complaining about your music soon.' She raised her eyes and looked at his hesitation. He was just staring back at her. It had always been this fragile between them. And she had never understood it. 'You haven't been happy there,' she said.

'No, I haven't been happy there –' He looked out at her, this food untouched, and wondered if she even knew, had ever once worried that he was lonely.

'Tom,' she said, 'you remember when we talked about it? And you didn't know what you were going to do? If you were going to go away. Newport, you were talking about. And we thought it'd be a good place to stay while you made your mind up. Tom . . . for God's sake, I didn't know you'd still be there after nearly two years. I didn't know that.'

He said nothing for a moment. 'No, me neither.'

'I didn't know.'

And then nothing at all.

'You blame me,' she said.

'You asked me to move out.'

'I said maybe it would be a good idea – you weren't doing anything, you didn't have any plans. You were seventeen. I thought, to be somewhere on your own . . . would give you the chance to decide.'

He spoke as though the words weren't his. 'Or give you the chance to have a bit of peace.'

'No! Is that what you thought? That's what you still think!' She waved her hand over this table and then out, somewhere else, to memories maybe. He didn't know. 'You think I've always had myself at heart, not you. Think I've never even *tried* to do right by you . . . isn't it? Isn't that what you think? You know the truth of the matter, Tom?'

'No . . .' he said.

'The truth of it . . .' Siân looked at him, this new room around them, remembering the kitchen as it had once been and the air there, filled up by his crying. 'You want a lot,' she said, her voice falling. 'You always wanted a lot. Needed a lot. You know, when you were six you still wanted to be carried round? I never wanted you to move out! So I could have some peace . . . ? What does that mean? The house is empty! Stacey's off all the time. Think I want to rattle around in here?' She remembered him going: the way he'd packed his stuff so slowly, meaning in every little motion he'd had. She had wanted to drive him there and he'd wanted to walk. 'You were seventeen, Tom, not a plan in your head . . .'

'I didn't need a plan.'

'Of course you did! You need one now.'

'Well what does that mean? Never sat and talked to me, did you?

You never said that to me! All you said to me was how much you thought it would be a good fucking idea!'

'Because I'm a bad mother.'

'What am I supposed to say to that?'

'That's what you think. Wait till you have children, Tom. Wait till you have children, and I hope you're never in the situation where you have to bring them up alone.'

Gwen, he thought of, and all the questions of the future that came with that. Ones he was scared to answer. Gwen, who'd told him that the only reason he cared for right or wrong was because it had once won him his mother's favour. That couldn't be the only reason, though. Not something so small or from so long ago. Gwen had never felt it, had she? Been searching for it all her life and she'd never felt it. Getting to that girl, under the water. Knowing you were doing something that was truly good. Truly fucking good. You were touching the thing, he realized now, which would stay ahead of you every day after that moment. It would be shapeless.

'I don't think you were a bad mother –'

'What then? What do you think? What is it exactly, Tom? What is it . . . ?' she asked.

And what could he answer her with?

He pushed the plate in front of him away. He wanted to accuse her, shove right in her face what she and everyone else had done to Dai. How she didn't know him, how she didn't know her oldest friend. The only thing she knew was how to make herself feel better.

'I've got nothing,' he said. 'Do you know that? I've got no friends. I've got no home and I've got no fucking job. I've got no plans . . . do you know that? Nothing.'

Siân was silent, sadness slipping over her anyway.

'Tom . . . I know. I want to help. *Look*. I want to help.'

'I don't think you're a bad mother!'

'I'm sorry . . .'

What did he have? The belief that there were such things as values in the world. And for this belief, had given up his only friend, had lost all the respect that he'd once had for his mother. And where had it led him? Would Gwen leave her husband? She was never going to leave him. What would he even have with her if she did?

'What have I always wanted . . . ?' he asked. 'What have I always wanted that's too much . . . ?'

'You never wanted to grow up! You never wanted to go to school or . . . you didn't want to leave! Do anything but stay here with me. Do you think it would've been better if I'd just let you?' She stared at him, the features he remembered for so long as tight, unhappy, were different now. This guilt she felt, all her sadness over him, they were only lines across a younger face.

He wanted to be glad for her. He was lonely. Was that all there was to his beliefs?

'I wanted to ask you here . . .' Siân had said slowly, her hand moving out, awkwardly, 'so you could see the place, before it's finished.' In the light of the table lamp, touched over Tom's expression, she had thought of Dai. And of Gwen Morgan, as the woman had come to her doorstep yesterday; something she would not say now. She had no reason to think that Tom might have heard of what had happened in the street that day with Dai; she didn't need to mention how Gwen's brief conversation had run right over the threshold and into the house.

It had been the quiet in her voice, the emptiness. Right into her home they'd run, where shame and justification were kept in a bedside drawer beside an £8,000 cheque. Waiting to be opened when all this was over. Two little words, Gwen had said: Dai's left.

All over the house and in that room, boxes were piled randomly with the possessions which she waited to rearrange here. She remembered all these years – of unchanged rooms. She looked at Tom across the table with too much in her eyes because one night could never fix it all. 'I wanted to say to you that, if you want . . . so you can have a chance to make up your mind over everything, what you want to do . . . you could come back here maybe. You could come back and you could live for a while at home.'

In the midst of that new place, Tom had seen her. And all the things he believed in, they'd risen up. To spill out, it seemed, in front of her, as nothing more than sadness.

Rhys knocked on the caravan's door, pale and newly painted, the music something he didn't know. Dance music, beats overturning. There was no answer. Loud enough outside the caravan to drown out the noise of him calling. 'Tom? Tom?'

Slipping out between the other quiet vans, until it tapered to nothing between them on all the site's little lanes. Rhys stood before the door. Long seconds before taking the handle. He saw lamplight. 'Tom . . .'

But there was no answer. He stepped in.

On a mess of shit, that light lay. And on Tom, asleep in the middle of it. He was sprawled across the seat with his head against the window and the curtain half into his face. The caravan was bitter with fag smoke, the beers were gone and the music was still playing.

Rhys's memories and the feelings of this morning were a step behind him as he moved up towards Tom. He looked at the CDs scattered over the table and could've read the night before, just in the order they were lying. So you had your angry time, and you had your happy time, just listening to the music, then you went on to this shit and finally you passed out.

The curtains held this night in when it wasn't real any more. Feelings passed through him, the things he'd lost very clear here, and anger over them, but a softer feeling too: it made him seem less alone to stand in this van and look down at Tom's night.

Coming down on to the little room, the music fell on to itself, the bass, and on to itself. He reached out and slowly wound the volume back to a level where it kept out the sound of the waking gulls.

Tom's mouth was open and dried up. He was snoring. You could hear it now.

Not knowing if it was true, what Emyr Morgan believed his wife was doing, if this was the shit it had led Tom into – not knowing whether his friend had changed in a million ways or none at all – Rhys moved to the seat opposite. Said nothing. Reached out and touched a couple of things on the table. He looked at Tom for long moments, and didn't go near the curtains or the day outside, waiting for him to wake up.

Lennie had opened the door to see that white sky waiting, the queuing cars and these houses, once well known.

He hadn't left the doorway. He'd stood for a long time without even closing it behind him, the daybreak slowly penetrating. There was no voice in his head to tell him the right thing to do. He could walk forwards and out, as he had done every morning before, or he could sit here, see this morning grow with people and noise and final changes. Only sit here. Seemed to make no difference. No voice, only the quiet which had filled the house last night, of Nia's absence, and Ruth's words.

A long time without stepping out. A stranger to the place he saw and to the rooms behind. She and Charlotte. Making love. The words sounded foreign to him, he couldn't touch them.

He saw the money, Charlotte Weyland's money, in the shadowed angle of every roof that had not yet caught the dawn, in the lie of the land where a garden would be made today from these pegs and ropes, this earth turned over. The cars moved gradually as Lennie looked out. There was a slow motorway on his doorstep.

He stood with a tool box in hand, looking towards the job her money had bought him. And Ruth behind, asleep, or awake as he had lain, turning pages in his mind, drawing pictures on them of the things his wife had done. Anger had been far away from him. It had left him here, in this place that he'd once believed in; where his beliefs, through these last months of that woman's money, had seemed to gain a life and grow.

'How has she been?' Ruth would ask Charlotte.

The morning full by then, the three of them alone in Charlotte's kitchen, Ruth would stand in the doorway and would not come forwards. She would look from Charlotte's face to her own daughter's.

*

Lennie's breath trapped in mist, this stillness lay, with reflections of the coming sun, across the roofs of every waiting vehicle. His eyes touched the details of this place, his body and mind empty; his gut. He couldn't hear the gulls cry beneath the constant, breathing sound of the engines.

He could not imagine it. With the facts that she'd laid out before him, still he couldn't find a way to hold the story. Pictures he'd drawn in his mind, but they'd been vague with guesses. He could see them kissing. The pages were blank after this. He knew Ruth's body naked. He didn't know it, touched by a woman. He didn't know it.

Vehicles straining off from the flow to their places, beside houses, beside the seawall, into each waiting space. The first sounds of voices, he heard. He thought of walking out. He didn't do it. He listened to them. Words that couldn't be made out. Unfamiliar people, who called out to each other across a road that they'd soon say goodbye to. Leaving Ynys-morlan to him.

'She's been fine, Ruth. We've had a good time together.'

'Yes?'

Charlotte would nod, ' – yes.'

'What have you been doing?' Ruth would ask her.

There should have been questions but he found none. What could he ask? There was nowhere to reach out from, to understand. Making or breaking, he remembered saying, to really *touch* the world. There'd been years of commitment, they had been hollow and unreal. The feeling of that touch, after so long, had been fucking validation. This project, the last month with Ruth – he had believed, when they sat together, when she told him as she hadn't done in three years what she felt, even if those feelings were terrible, if they both cried over them, he had believed they were finding a love again. Or maybe for the first time.

He looked at the town this morning, where he'd lived all his life, and didn't understand what that feeling had become. He could find no home for it. It hadn't been a lie, not inside him. But he stared out at the road, these dark, new houses, and the conviction that it had been true rebounded from everything before his eyes. Ynys-morlan stared back at him and did not know him either.

While he'd been committing himself to her, she'd had pictures in her mind that he couldn't imagine: a woman's hands. Kissing her. Getting touched. Saying in the dark the sorts of things that normal lovers did. The sorts of things he'd said to her. Dyke, he thought. The word had no substance.

He could walk out. But what was the point? Where was he going now?

The sound of closing car doors in the rumble that began every day for Ynys-morlan.

The sound of machinery, coughing to life in the cold.

In the windows: that white sky, while in a distant house, Nia and Charlotte were still sleeping.

He found that he couldn't hate Ruth. The month she had dragged him through, it had changed him. He'd told her that. In the freezing dawn, his coat hanging loose and this knowledge disclosing itself across his face like this ground was being overturned, he found he couldn't even hate Charlotte Weyland. Incomprehension had stolen hate away from him.

Were they moving towards – what then? He didn't know a word for it. Marriage? The dyke version of marriage? A 'relationship'? Were they going to walk down this street, where nothing he remembered could be recognized, arm in arm? And what? With Nia between them? Just three happy girls.

Love needed something to make it vivid, for a person or a place. It needed something fucking volcanic. Did what they shared have that? *Could* it, like the nights he'd spent with Ruth? *Passion*. Violence you could call it, but it didn't come from the hands. From right inside it came; from under your own landscape. His old man had known – there was no love without it. Just convincing yourself. He remembered looking down at her, lashing out at her, and how the things he felt had still never been freed.

He was sorry. Standing here on their doorstep, sorry for everything that he'd done to her. But what he'd lacked in those three years, what he'd needed, wasn't false. Love had to have something. Or it was grey as the fucking roads he'd travelled for so long.

The place Lennie saw around him wasn't grey. He'd fallen in love with it – through the project. He'd found what it had always lacked. He had broken it down and remade it, and now, even with the truth in front of him, could not hate it. He couldn't understand what he gazed out at.

He couldn't understand.

'We've made love,' his wife had said. At first the words had made no meaning. Then they'd leached it out of every other thing, to make a sheen of mist across the view, as the noise of rebuilding began its final day.

'Hello.'

Tom opened his eyes and saw first the place where he lived, his face fluttered; he saw the night before all round him, and that it had ended.

'How are you feeling?'

Tom saw him.

On the other seat, these closed curtains behind, Rhys looked back and there was waiting in his face. Hope.

The smile that came up to Tom was grim and it was drunk and still it was funny. The night before seemed to fall into place round the sight of him sitting there. Tom just lay for a minute; just looking at him like this, just happy to see him sitting there.

'What are you doing here?'

Rhys shrugged.

They saw each other, the day not more than a touch beneath the curtains. Tom watched him ash, smoke, ash it again. He saw in Rhys's face, there was nowhere else for him to be. He saw someone – across the street in these last months, always turning away, he hadn't seen it – someone who wasn't young, not any more, not really.

The music fell and rose.

'Those my cigarettes you're smoking?'

After a second, Rhys gave another shrug. After a second, gave a laugh.

Outside there was no other sound but theirs, a mile of sleep and sand dunes before the town, and no one dreaming here. It seemed far enough, with Rhys opposite him, to let all the thoughts of change fade for a while.

'I'm glad you came . . .' he said. And wanted to tell him again.

'You know what time it is?'

'What time is it?'

'I don't know,' Rhys said.

Somewhere down this road, men were starting to take the scaffolding down so that all the walls still rendered could be chipped clean. On the rooftops, they were unbolting the first platforms.

'What happened last night?' Rhys asked him.

'Last night?'

'Last night.'

'My mother asked me to move back in.'

In the quiet of nearly two years, Rhys gave a tiny smile. The lamp's faintness still shone on the table and all the things the night had used. He looked at Tom, a picture of Emyr Morgan's kneeling figure behind him, to join every other thing he'd drawn, to join all the days, and there was only another blank morning ahead. He saw Tom smile as well.

'I'm glad you came,' he heard him say again. And then, 'I've missed you.'

'Missed you too. Fucking missed you too.' She'd asked him to go home. Maybe those last two years had never passed.

For a long time, Rhys didn't answer him. The words that came up to him weren't the ones that he should say.

'What did you tell her?'

'I didn't.' After a moment, he said, 'Did I never want to move away?' Other nights here, he thought of, and all the things he believed in while they lasted.

Rhys couldn't see any change in him. 'From her house or from the town?'

871

'From Ynys-morlan.'

'No . . .' he said, 'you never wanted to move away. Someone wants to leave then they do it, don't they?'

'Maybe they do.'

Rhys's smile was thin but it was still there. 'How are you then, Tom?'

'I'm shit. You?'

'Shit as well,' he said.

'Well, that's it then. At least you came.'

Rhys nodded, nothing else to say. The story he had to tell lay flat as the seabed in him. 'I missed you too,' he told him again.

As the day rose and the scaffolding's boards were piled slowly back in town, nothing changed here but the music.

'I spent last night with Emyr Morgan,' he said.

And here, the reaction came. Tom straightened in the seat. There was a moment, but all he did then was reach out to shake each of the cans. He found one, half full, across the table.

'You been ashing in this?'

He shook his head and watched Tom drink.

'It's true then . . .'

Tom didn't answer. He had pictures of the house in his mind where she and Emyr lived and he'd never been. He didn't need to ask for the story, only waited.

'I spent last night with him. He came to find me. Came to ask me for a favour. He told me his wife's sleeping with someone. Like I said to him before, when it wasn't true.'

There wasn't a nod from Tom, or a reaction of any kind, unless it was emptiness.

'He thinks . . . who she is, like, if she's sleeping with someone, it's the same person.' And hearing the words in his own voice, he saw the rift that must have come for Emyr Morgan. My wife is not a whore, he'd said. A huge fucking rift through his pastel-coloured world, and if Tom's was the name – as he saw it might even be – then that rift lay through Ynys-morlan. It was of generations, and nothing more. 'He came to ask for your name.'

'To ask you.'

He looked at Rhys as this story unfolded and saw what he had never thought of, any night. He'd imagined a house untouched by him, rooms that still felt like home to her, whatever she'd told him.

'He's in a bad way,' Rhys said.

'To come back to you asking favours.'

'To come back to me.'

Late talks with Gwen, the quiet bed they'd lain in, he remembered, asking each other what mattered in life. Tom tried to imagine Emyr telling Rhys these things, and could not. The beliefs Gwen had thrown into confusion on the last day they'd been together, the beliefs he'd looked at like a pie of fool's gold last night, as his mother had waited for an answer, they were parted by a rift as well now; opened up.

'I didn't tell him.'

'And he thought you would?'

'I didn't.'

'Only asked you? Like that . . . ?'

'Wanted to make a deal. Some kind of fucking deal. He's a liar,' he told Tom.

'What deal?'

And he himself had had lies ready. But he saw Tom now, imagining him with Gwen Morgan, all her jewellery and some little place in her eyes, some endlessly playing annual society dinner, where no one else could live. He didn't want to lie to Tom.

'I drew a picture, a few pictures, paintings . . . I wrote some things, like. Been doing it, nights, the last month. One of the walls in the museum.' But it was an old story now, wasn't it? He couldn't think of any way to tell Tom how it was different. The last four hours he had spent hurting someone, looking at him on the floor. 'I drew pictures,' he said.

'Pictures . . . ?'

'I wrote some stuff up, nothing. From the bus shelter, stuff people had written there . . . I was copying it up.'

Tom looked at him; remembered their last night.

'He tried to make a deal with me, wanted me to give him your name . . . Thought the best offer he could make me was to keep the stuff. Like I'd believe it. He's got the cases for the place being made up and he reckoned I'd believe it. Give him your name just for the chance –' But he hadn't really. Though he'd knelt and stayed kneeling, four hours, he'd known there was no chance. Moments of the music came and left, as he told Tom each of these things. Words became a little movie screen as Tom imagined. Gwen had told him nothing. Never said Emyr knew.

'Pictures.'

'I didn't tell him,' Rhys said.

'Pictures of what?'

'Of nothing. I didn't tell him, Tom.' They were finished with Emyr's image. They were finally whole with it in the middle. Inside the museum, they might have started painting white already now, and for all the things he had tried to draw, he'd rather have that wall blank.

'Tom –' he said ' – I'm sorry, I'm sorry for that night, like. I didn't mean it, do you understand that? I'd never hit you,' he said. 'I hit you. I'd never do that. I'm sorry for it –'

'It doesn't matter.' And there wasn't a snag in the words, they came easy. He didn't even know any more what he'd been trying to prove that night. That he had beliefs that made him different from Rhys? The beliefs of a little kid, he feared now. 'It doesn't matter . . .'

'I'm sorry, do you understand?' In this room that still felt like evening, he stared at his friend. In his own memories he now held the proof of everything this town had ever called him. And he asked, 'What are you doing, Tom? You're with her . . . ?'

'What am I doing? I don't know what I'm doing.'

'You're together . . . ?'

'You know what we are? You know what I am? I'm lonely,' he said. 'I'm so fucking lonely. And Mum asks me to move back in . . .' and he tried to laugh. 'I've been lonely for how long?'

Rhys didn't answer. Where are you? he wanted to say. Are you with me?

These the sort of fucking questions loneliness brought. As if places changed, miles and miles elapsed and you were in a different country – when it wasn't true. The sky never broke when you broke. And they had never even moved.

'I think I love her,' Tom told him.

'. . . And she says what to you?'

'She says she loves me.'

'You can't be lonely then.'

'She's nearly forty. You come and say to me, Emyr's . . .' but he didn't finish. 'I don't know what I'm doing. You know what you're doing?' He reached out and lifted the edge of the table and let it fall again, all these things settling right back in their places. 'You know what you want? I don't know what I want . . .'

He looked at Tom, something old and real and close drifting away from both of them. He wouldn't try to hold on to it, not with this picture of Emyr Morgan's bowed head in his mind. 'Does she make you happy . . . ?' was all he said.

'She makes me feel like I'm not on my own.'

And Rhys could remember that with Bethan.

'We're together. I think we're together.' And then he said, 'It's not wrong.'

'What would I care, if it is or not? I wouldn't care.'

'How does it sound to you?'

'I don't know what it's like . . .' If they lay together for long times or what they talked about. He didn't know what they might have shared. Did they speak about the future? It could seem like you wanted the same things, like you were both the same person, and it just hurt when you looked back and saw it had never been true. But Tom wasn't looking back. 'Will she leave him?' he asked.

'How would I know? She only comes to me out here.'

Rhys had thought the pictures he'd tried to paint were just frozen memories, and in some way had hoped not – had hoped that Tom was still living as he'd drawn him.

He saw him lift his hands.

'I have these things,' Tom told him, 'I have these things I think are true . . . they make me feel like I don't know anybody else, and I still think they mean something. Maybe they're not true,' he said. 'Maybe they're just bullshit.'

'What things . . . ?'

'Right and wrong.' Embarrassed just by the sound of the words, no understanding even of what they meant any more.

'Right and wrong, like.'

'Yeah . . .' What would he say, that he'd been searching?

To give to someone else and sacrifice what you needed, that wasn't anything noble. To give to a whole community, that didn't make morality when every person in that place could unite what they had against a man like Dai. What could he say? That he didn't know who he was without believing he was a good person? That he was scared now that his search was made of nothing but his own little needs? Come home, she'd said.

He didn't want to think his convictions could be just some fucking urge to please. They were pathetic if no more than that. He wanted to carry them into his life. He wanted to make a future with them.

Rhys saw him, in this evening light that didn't feel like a lie. He'd hoped he wasn't on his own, even after what he'd done to Emyr Morgan. He'd wanted forgiveness, he saw – and how Tom might tell him over and over that he had it, and it wouldn't feel inside as if he did.

'Right and wrong,' he repeated. Where did he stand in that? Above Emyr's kneeling figure. 'At least you care,' he said.

The way they sat here, it seemed like a picture of it could be kept and wouldn't look a lesser thing between the photographs he'd found: this van and these curtains drawn, something kept inside that otherwise would not have stayed. He'd looked through all the Ynys-morlan they were making and had seen nothing to give that feeling.

Far away, they were passing the scaffold boards down, level to level to the ground. They were opening the museum's doors. In the Shoreline Restaurant and Bistro, tables and chairs were being hauled through the doorway from one of the many trucks outside, and Patty, upstairs, had her hands on the box where she'd put all the old decorations.

Rhys said to Tom across the table, 'If you have things you think are true and you believe in . . . they're only bullshit if you don't make anything out of them. Got to use them. That's all.'

Patty was passing the Hollywood prints that Bethan had stared at each day, imagining she saw bitterness in Pat's choice of them; their little windows on glamorous worlds, smoky monochrome between the dry and ever-youthful aspidistras.

She was finding the picture with its faded Seventies' colours and the rounded edges they never put on photos now, of her and Siân and Gwen, all standing there at that spring wedding, feeling life ahead. How could it be, she wondered, when a photograph was meant to catch and hold a day, how could it be that you saw it years later and it had aged as well?

'They're not meaningless,' Rhys said to him. 'You can make them so they're not.'

In the caravan's quiet music, both of them distant from the houses where new roofs now had no iron poles to hold them, Tom listened to him, not knowing how that could be done.

Rhys thought of Lennie Lewis, who'd lost himself, as if into the museum's sepia photographs. All their shadows slowly growing so it seemed like they showed evenings, when the light on the figures, on their faces, must once have been a day's. It seemed to Rhys like he was leaving himself in those pictures too; that he had done already, with what he'd pushed Morgan to last night. There was no way he could love this little fairy town they'd built themselves, and he'd stopped the place from loving him as well. Really he wanted to leave himself in those old slow-taken shots; couldn't let go of the belief that their little vistas held somewhere better than this. A home, and some foreign country, all at once.

'Beliefs are only meaningless,' he said, 'if you sit, just going over them at night like, instead of building them into something . . .' And then he heard what he said, remembering what they'd built and were completing two miles down this road. He gave a quick laugh, looked up, and saw that Tom was hearing him. 'You've got them. You're lucky. Just use them,' he said.

As if years passed inside that little room, when it was not so, and they both changed. Eight o'clock in the morning and they still had the lamps on. A glow from outside, you could've seen it. But in here, a whole night. In here a hundred memories. Just like a photograph it was.

Ruth would see Charlotte turn towards Nia, who'd be reaching out and trying to engage the woman in her hands and all the games her hands could play.

'We've been doing all kinds of things. Some painting,' she'd hear Charlotte answer, 'we played some nonsense Scrabble . . .'

They had slept together. After making a bed for her in the study, Charlotte had come back down. She'd watched Nia's change after they'd returned from the houses: from excitement that had bordered on anger, to immobility, as if covered by cloth. She had come back down and found Nia in the study's corner, her hands over a face chewed up like paper.

They'd slept together, and Charlotte had never woken like that before.

'We did lots of things. She was upset once, at night, but it's been very good. It's been lovely . . .'

Ruth wouldn't answer, looking at them both. She'd woken in a house that was a part of her no longer. Its shadows had retreated into her alone, back where they had always belonged. 'Not so happy to see me, is she?' Nia's little face distracted, mist-covered. The only life in it coming when she turned to Charlotte.

'She didn't understand being left.'

'I had to leave her.'

The house had been empty when she'd woken. The day still opening, Garvey's men fifteen minutes from arrival. The house had been empty, and freedom had hung in its mute spaces.

She had thought of Charlotte. The rooms didn't even look like the pretence of a family's any more. She had thought of the way that Charlotte had looked into her face before touching her, every time. How she had asked with that look. She had touched the lines of her cheeks, her mouth, as they'd lain there on the floor. Ruth remembered how there'd been this feeling, this feeling of deliverance, just in those little motions.

This morning, she'd stood in Nia's bedroom before the first knock could come to the front door and had found herself closing her hands and eyes, her whole body up. Whatever she'd said to Lennie about punishment must have been a lie because she couldn't stop. She'd thought of how she and Charlotte hadn't slept but only talked or lain there without speaking at all. For a while that night it had seemed like no day would ever come. What she'd said to Lennie must have been a lie because she'd stood and looked at Nia's room this morning and had wanted to take these things away from herself.

When they'd been touching each other, in her mind she'd torn at that house, like love couldn't redeem her but only bring her justice. And afterwards, those memories had slept. She'd put them to rest with what they'd done. Was that Charlotte's purpose? At rest, Ruth had been free from them, and had lain next to Charlotte, thinking nothing but how she loved her.

Half an hour ago, she'd let in Garvey's men. With no words ready, she'd driven here.

Charlotte returned her gaze now, saw how she wouldn't step inside.

The project began its ending. The gesture which would make up for everything. Oak doors were earmarked with the houses' names, built to each aperture's specifications. They were hung on hinges that now projected the first sun as dapples on the builders' hands. Over the doorways of shops from which the scaffolding was being removed, they screwed long wooden signs, with handpainted borders. On gable windows and roof peaks, where the wind began, they set the ridge tiles with their finials.

The sculpture Dai had built stood behind Ruth's public garden and looked to her like the bare truth. Had Emyr called people? She didn't know.

She stared into Charlotte's face.

Nia's play made little sounds.

'I had to leave her,' Ruth said again, 'I had to talk to Lennie. She couldn't have been there.'

'About what?' She looked at Ruth, tried to make out in her face what she hadn't yet said. She didn't stand but remained at the kitchen table with Nia, where they'd eaten breakfast, where they'd looked at a picture book about India, letting Nia turn the pages. She hadn't known when Ruth would come, or if she would come at all.

She watched her take two steps, and not sit, not even come towards her daughter.

In town somewhere, Ruth thought, Lennie might be working. She could think of no reason for him to do it today, but what else was there? Perhaps he was only walking around. Perhaps he had left, she didn't know.

She put her hand on a chair's back. She looked at this pretty picture: Charlotte and Nia.

Remembered arranging flowers in Nia's bedroom. Remembered putting on blouse and cardigan over any marks, and in her daughter's room, grooming Nia's hair as her mother had her own.

'Ruth –'

But she said, 'I told him.'

She saw the hope rise up in Charlotte's eyes, though she was trying to make no expression.

'That you're leaving him.'

'Yes.'

She saw Charlotte almost stand and then only put her hand out on the table's surface.

'What did he say? He understood? That you meant it?'

'Yes, he understood.' Ruth didn't reach to take it.

And Charlotte stared at her, the morning she'd begun with Nia reforming itself round hope. The view she'd seen from her bedroom window while the child had kicked her legs on the bed behind: the far road and its stream of cars. Ynys-morlan like a painted map. And she tried to find the right words. When would she leave? Did she have things now? With her in the car? Clothes and Nia's toys? She saw Ruth's reserve.

'What did you say to him?'

'I said that we'd made love.'

Charlotte was as silent, the validation of Ruth's words at war with the expression she saw on her face. And with tangled fears of what a man like him might do after hearing such a thing. Just with the way that Ruth said nothing else.

'Talk to me. He was angry? He hurt you?'

'He wasn't angry.'

'Talk to me –'

But for a moment Ruth couldn't.

She felt sorrow for Lennie. Three months of shoving back at him the feelings he'd given her, unable to stop herself. And now she felt this pity for him. Hatred only for herself, the memory of soap bubbles like a little lost sea inside a bowl.

'What then? He must have . . .' but she had no idea what he must have done, or what this look on Ruth's face meant. She was afraid to know.

'He couldn't understand it. He said a lot of things but he couldn't even . . . get angry, I think. It was shock.'

'You're afraid of him?'

'No.'

'You said we'd made love.' The reality of it came into the room as Charlotte said the words herself. Took away the air, took away the distance. Through the window behind them, ivy undulated in seaweed waves.

She wanted to ask Ruth how it had been to tell him. The question was only stalling, though, when she knew what answer she was really looking for. They stood in the quiet as if unable to go on: the future as indefinite as unfinished homes and blank shop signs.

She said, 'You'll never regret it, Ruth. Whatever you decide to do. Telling him . . . it makes the project worthwhile, everything we've done, you see that?' her voice was as quiet as the project's end.

'Yes.' But all she saw was confession – or flight.

All she saw was this woman: pale and slim and self-possessed, a woman who easily hid her desperation. A dyke, Lennie had called her, but Ruth remembered the painful hesitation as Charlotte had tried to touch her. Ruth remembered kissing her that first time as if she could kill her with it. And the way that Charlotte had responded, slowly trying to change what Ruth had done, till it wasn't hateful. How afraid she'd been, Ruth remembered.

And she saw what she'd done to Charlotte in the last months: how that desperation had climbed up towards the surface till she was open, unable to conceal anything. They had changed into each other, Ruth thought bitterly.

She watched Charlotte begin and stop and then only say, 'I love you . . .'

At the table, Nia sat and shifted the last of breakfast round her plate like there was no conversation.

'I love you,' she told her again.

Ruth didn't respond.

'Do you love me . . . ?'

There was only woe, exposing itself under Ruth's features.

Distant from them, down this hill, men were beginning to pack the scaffolding on to its trucks again. A new place they had made. Could seem like a new world sometimes, when your needs were so twined up with it, a new land. A home – that would soon be revealed, and that could not make amends for her.

'Do you want to be with me . . . ?' she was asking Ruth.

She couldn't answer.

'Can you stay with me . . . ?' And she saw Ruth's tears starting. 'Are you . . . are you in love with me? Will you stay . . . ?'

Charlotte felt again – memory was not a clear enough word – the painted blue prints they'd put on the walls. Her own, a middle-aged woman's hands, and Nia's.

'I don't know,' Ruth told her. She wanted to say yes. But even as she saw Charlotte, thought about a future, she felt herself being moved farther away.

Lennie's face as they had sat together finally on the stairs last night, the feeling of his hand, for the first time these things were fading. Till she was distant from him as well; like nothing, she couldn't remember, though it had only been three years.

She stared at Charlotte across the space. She wanted to say yes.

'I can't even touch Nia.'

She had watched a hundred doors shut on her own daughter, allowed it, just to save a dream. A false, beleaguered, rotten little dream that had only been real in the eyes of other people. She didn't look at Nia now, though it hurt not to.

'Yesterday, couldn't go anywhere . . . anywhere near her.'

Slowly Charlotte nodded.

But Ruth couldn't tell her. She didn't know how to explain.

'I called Emyr . . . I told him this stuff . . . did everything I could. But do you know how it looks to me, what Dai's built? I hate it. I look at it . . . it seems to ruin everything. Do you know why . . . ? Even if the statue's allowed to stay, the project doesn't reflect . . . anything good in me. It ruins everything . . . because it looks like what I've hidden from. Used the project, to hide from.'

'That's not true, no. You haven't seen it finished yet . . .'

'I meant it to . . . communicate the way I felt, make that into something. Do you know the only ways I've been able to communicate what the last three years have been? By hurting him. Hating him.'

Charlotte shook her head.

Ruth said impotently, 'I've made him hit me over and over again. While he's been crying. I've gone . . . gone to the bedroom where he's been sleeping . . .' The tears were coming now and she hated herself for crying them. 'I've had sex with him, and kissed him, and let him touch me, so I can leave him after in the worst way that I can find. Make him lonely . . . Hurting him is the only way I've found to let anything out of me. What does that make me? An abuser, an abuser just like him, and hiding in the . . . idea that I can create some kind of perfect place? What does it make me? A coward. Two years and Nia upstairs. I'd be on the floor and asking myself if her door was shut. I can't touch her now . . . do you know that?'

'The project has meaning. What you've made more than any other part. It does . . . it does communicate it. I want to show it you. So that you see.'

'I stayed,' was all Ruth said.

'You've *left now* . . .' But the reaches of things Charlotte couldn't know lay between them like a lie. 'You've left him now.' The only thing she could find to say, hearing Ruth lay down so clearly these things that she'd feared all along. 'And you can't even see – you're so close to it all, Ruth – you can't see the things you've expressed. Little things. Look at the garden,' she said.

'You can't walk through it.'

'. . . *Everything* you've made. There was always going to be unhappiness in them. The garden's beautiful.'

'The garden's untouchable . . . I hide,' she said. 'Everything I've made, the beauty in it . . . it's just far off. A little flight of fancy . . . I hide, I always did.'

'No . . .'

'I never meant to hurt her, Charlotte.' Just like a lie, it stretched to fill the space. 'Never meant to hurt her. She's mine. I love her. Don't deserve her –'

It was frightening to see how she spoke and never looked at her child. 'You've got to forgive yourself . . .'

'But that's what this was all for. And I used it to run away.' Ruth looked at her as if she had no ways left to tell herself she deserved happiness. As if she had no words left at all – and without them, could only leave.

Charlotte got up, came close to her. 'I'll take you down to town, and I'll show you it and you'll have to see then just how much you've given it. How much it's not hiding. Because I can see.'

But she looked into Ruth's eyes and tried to find love in them, and she couldn't. Just saw herself, blankly reflected: someone to cover the holes in Ruth. Perhaps she didn't even care any more. Perhaps she wanted to fit the role.

'We're going to drive down, I'm going to show you what you've built , . . and what I've built . . . You haven't been running away! You've been *healing* . . . It's possible, to make something better . . . out of *sadness*.'

She looked. Pale eyes, something in them that wasn't free, even without her husband. Just a small and unreachable lie.

'There are houses, homes . . .' Charlotte said. 'I'll show them to you.'

In the tiny lane that trickled down towards Ynys-morlan, and here overlooked it, she parked the car. With Charlotte and Nia, she opened the doors and slowly stood.

Below, seen in shadows between the boards and the gradually dismantled poles, there were battered-render cottages looking out on to a long, straight road, all of them ready to be sandblasted clean. The scaffolds were coming down. You could almost see it.

'Look at it all,' Charlotte said. 'For God's sake, look. It's incredible. You made this happen. Your idea, your hope, your *work*, Ruth. You see that? See all of it?'

'It's so selfish . . .' Ruth said, disconsolation filling her voice. 'That's what I see.'

Charlotte held Nia. She had no answer. She'd never touched a place before this. Ruth had given her the right, she'd thought.

'Everyone was in favour . . .' Ruth told herself, 'I mean, they applied.' The words scattered and drifted, though. It was done. All you could ask was whether it had been for the right reasons. 'Maybe it's not possible . . . to set things right just by creating . . . anything, a family, a place, anything. Maybe you just can't heal through that. Maybe just thinking so is selfish.' If they wanted to, over time, perhaps they could change the town back. What could never be changed was the lie that she'd told: of happiness and beauty. While she'd kept Nia in pretty rooms.

Ruth looked out. It was spread below them on this flat canvas plain. And she didn't know if her project told those same lies.

'Come with me,' Charlotte said with urgency. 'Come down with me then. I want to show you . . . There are houses, that I've made.'

The windmills he'd planted, they rushed and stuttered.

Red, she saw, all three of them, and remembered how he'd used to fill in crosswords: squares and circles. On the ground, the timber shadows showed a quarter past fifteen.

Would he come back?

Gwen hadn't known where he was going, her mum had said. A person left that way, and you couldn't fill in the blank. A whole country of blank. A whole continent.

Bethan stood alone. In the pushchair Chelsea wriggled, her hat's brim flapped up and down, her face was snow and pink blush. She held Bethan's finger as her mum stared up at it, her world, with small, slow motion, overturning.

Behind her they were planting beds of roses. Into small concrete-filled holes, spaced every six feet, they'd set the posts of tiny wrought-iron fences that would delineate the flower beds from the grass. Three circles, growing smaller and deeper. In their centre, they were laying sea stones in piles over the fountain's little spouts.

You feel the way you do, her mother had said, because all you've got is innocence.

Behind her the road was now full of the metal teeth of jackhammers, and you could imagine the spaces in those noises, tiny gaps growing wider as they rose up from here. Separating, until there were miles of quiet sky between the fall of each.

They were taking up the pavements in ten-foot stretches. The ground underneath them was bare.

There's no more innocence in the world, her mum had said, than there is in Ynys-morlan.

Behind her the truck was parked from which they carried the roses, a flatbed. It held two hundred plants perhaps. They were nodding and dancing with each other. Arriving in one load, bought in one payment, they were fully grown and already in flower.

Behind her and on all sides now, they were taking down the scaffolding.

Tomorrow the houses would be bare for the first time in two months, you'd be able to see their new shapes, but not covered like this with the husks and chaff of render. And in front of her, Dai's sculpture still stood. Whose decision, she wondered?

Her memories, with this motion, overturned.

The blanket moved.

She had brought Dai up to her home and made love with him, showed him something he must never have seen before, and then had taken all the colours of that moment and had made them as ugly as she could, driven them into what she'd thought was the real world.

Why?

Because those were the feelings she was made of. She remembered seeing those two small blue lines and knowing it. Feelings of strength, but ones that didn't have hope in them. She didn't feel strong now, Chelsea's finger inside hers.

Her fantasies, of everything, a life outside Ynys-morlan, what she might've achieved, they'd been wrong. They'd been dirty in a way she couldn't have explained; visions of her future that should've seemed innocent. But innocence, it was something to be scared of. Because it opened up. She had been afraid two years ago. This same fear that she felt now. Innocence opened everything. She had been scared that what would show inside her was ugly.

What would her visions have been if she had had an abortion? If she'd left and in the life she'd made, just failed? She would have failed. Pictures like these they would've been: an overweight girl in a homemade ball gown, a retarded man who thought he loved her. Pictures like these: that girl in the window, and turning, like she thought she was in a music box.

She'd stayed and she'd kept the baby. She'd chosen to accept what she'd never be capable of. She'd chosen Ynys-morlan – and experience, she'd thought.

The windmills turned. In the cold air, she saw the truth. It was Ynys-morlan that was innocence. And the bitterness she'd felt – what innocence did to you. Bethan looked at it all. She saw the sculpture and, yes, it was ugly. It was a silly, ugly thing. But it was made of beautiful ideas.

Everything in her overturned.

Those vivid moments, making the dress alone, standing in the window for Dai – or in her bed with him, watching him move like water, unknowing. Those moments – what was bright in them, if not innocence?

The fact that they were first times? Could it be that? The restaurant she'd conceived of was almost complete and the town seemed different, another country. She looked at Dai's watchtower. Maybe there was nothing wrong with her. Maybe she wasn't old – and it was only that there were many things she'd never done. She saw the difference between innocence, which faded, and first times.

They were bringing out benches from trucks parked beside the road. Benches that were still wrapped in plastic, the sticky edges of it trembling in the wind.

Gwen had come and stood on Siân's doorstep. She had told her in a quiet voice, with no blame, that Dai had left. There had been a moment when they had looked at each other, and both of them had held the guilt – though Gwen had told him she was sorry.

In her yard, Siân sat on the stone-clad wall and watched the scaffolding taken from the roof, waiting to see if Tom would call. She looked at somewhere that held none of their past. She tried to see if that was a mistake.

There'd been hard times. She'd tried to make ideals out of the things that she'd gone through. Was that wrong? Was it wrong to abandon them? She couldn't help what she had believed in when Tom had been young, or that those beliefs had left her stranded. She couldn't help the fact that when she'd seen a chance to abandon them, she'd taken it. Now she saw Tom doing what she had then. Setting losses into concrete by making them his principles. It didn't look like she could change it. Perhaps for him the ideals were better, wouldn't make him lonely like they had done her.

If he could come back for a while, maybe he might tell her what they were, the things he wanted.

Ruth walked on her own. Charlotte couldn't place an arm around her. With her eyes staring on and through as they moved on to the pavement, still half shaded. Charlotte saw the effort it was taking her to hold it in.

Ruth was selfish: this project, this whole town, one image from her heart. And she herself was selfish: looking at her and thinking only of whether Ruth loved her or not. It seemed as though every person reached out to touch the world and couldn't help but try to drag what they needed from it. There was only Nia. And Nia never reached out.

She thought of the blue palmprints on the wall.

She thought of them, as though one single expression could make all the others good.

4 july Thrsday nineteen sixty eight

I wasn't alowed to go to the party. I am upstares with my locket its not mine. When I used to hold it and see there little pictures I could feel all three of us together and I could talk to them when I was looking at it. more than talking to the real them bacuse mommys so sad and always somwhere else. Daddy just has to go away always. when I had my locket I could say the things to them that made me sad or the things I want even thouhg I know its not real . its like they talk back to me when I open it.
But I think now its not mine. its yours. I used to feel the three of us together. me and mommy and daddy all together when I was holding it. thats why they gave it to me. but its not the three of us bacuse Im not there. even if I hold it   its realy you.

She would pack them away. Dear Charlotte. Dear Charlotte. She would put them in boxes. Two days ago, Emyr Morgan had come to her, the last person in a long list, the last front door, a mile from town.

'The exhibition will show . . . what it's meant, what it's all meant,' he had said. And Charlotte hadn't known him well enough to see the sadness. An idea like that, though, a heart for the project that had taken everyone's ideas and made them real, maybe you didn't need to know each other, didn't need to share a past.

*

Lennie hefted bags, threw broken remains, obscure shapes in their plastic, on to piles. At the always shifting roadside, he forced the piles down till they were crushed under the new bags. Work gloves over hurting hands, face down, eyes down, unseeing.

In the rubbish and the sweepings and dust, Ruth and Charlotte made love. He buried them. They rose again. And at every side, despite the gaze that he never brought up from the rubble, a new town began to show its face.

It seemed the world had split. Evenings in the last month that he had never known the like of. He had looked into Ruth's face, what had been false, becoming real, like he'd always known it should be.

In the house up on the hill, Ruth and Charlotte: discovering. Was she there now? And with his daughter? With his fucking kid, sitting in a room maybe where she wouldn't see the reality of what they did to each other.

Underneath the last of the scaffolds, the entranceways that had been built to replace what his old man had made, they were finished. Had their own little slate roofs, little gables. Had their own little fucking finials with their fucking figure-sculptures his wife had designed. A man or a woman? He'd looked at them in the van's back, passing them one by one to the bloke behind – who'd never see this town again when the scaffolding's final six feet were gone too. A man or a woman. It couldn't be made out.

Emyr moved the rest of the boxes from his hallway to the car, to the museum. Cases there, smooth lines across the room. Where he had knelt for four hours without getting up, men were sweeping, finishing, removing the plastic protection so these cases were revealed. In the dark their shapes had been obscure, under a moving torch. As the pale morning had filtered through these high windows behind him to make them blue, bright oblongs, he'd seen this room clarified around him. And in the daylight now, the boy gone and only his memories to remind him, Emyr saw the exhibition area, almost complete: the beautiful centre of this project that was now being deconstructed outside.

He oversaw the last of the other exhibits' deliveries. He unpacked the boxes from the car. Gwen's, and the others: cardboard boxes, old paper-ream boxes, shoe boxes and fat, padded envelopes. Handwritten and some hand-delivered to the house, they'd been pushed on to his study shelves, accumulated on the empty floor of their living room or spilled around the stack in the hallway that Gwen had made, intermingled. The house, its empty rooms, had become a working space. His mind was a working space.

He didn't look at Rhys's finished wall.

'You want to tell me what you want done about it, like? Because you're the one who likes handing out the deadlines and you're telling me, leave it, leave it.' Behind Emyr, staring at him as he worked, the foreman's face was a blend of contempt.

Emyr's mobile phone beside him rang three times during their conversation alone.

He turned. He still didn't look at the wall.

'I'm dealing with it.'

'You want to tell me how you're dealing with it? I'm finishing up here. You see this? This is a bunch of men sweeping up. This is the end of a job, I'm sure you've seen one before. So you want to tell me what you want done?'

Emyr stood slowly.

'No,' he said. He stood close to the man. 'When I tell you something, like, "I'll deal with it," this is what I want you to do: turn away, leave me alone, tell yourself it's being dealt with. Tell yourself it doesn't matter because you're about to leave, your work's being paid for and you have no position of responsibility. I am busy. Leave me alone please.'

He would paint the wall out himself. Tonight he was going to begin. It didn't matter what had occurred because this project was almost finished. The chaotic nature of these last days was about to be drawn together into the end which he'd been designing for so long. Many threads, many that seemed as if they couldn't be untangled, would fall into their places.

Outside they were revealing the town.

The street-lamp replacement would begin at eight o'clock, the road clear of all other traffic. The sandblasting would start its sweep at the town's end, half an hour ahead of the street-light crew.

Muffled in bubble-wrap plastic it came. Its long oak stand was beautifully finished, its brass plate yellow. Gleaming, even covered. The museum's collection was spread across the floor. Emyr carried the plaque from the delivery van himself, and placed it gently down inside.

Munday 1 stjuly
nineteensixtyeight

when I think about what I found its realy wierd but like evrything kind of is easier to understand. I thought that it was made for me first but it wasn't for me beacuse of the dates on it that were march 3 in nineteen fiftyone and augest 16 in nineteen fiftyfour so thats a long time before I was even born. And then I relised. I had to think realy hard about it but I DID work it out AND IT MADE EVRYTHING REALYSEEM RIGHT. MAKING SENSE. like how theres always been sombody missing here like thats how its alawys felt. So now it makes sense and I can SEE. like all the things I was suposed to know and look likeand I never did. bacuse I always knew it but I didnt UNDERSTAMD how the person who was missing could be me.

The sound never leaving, chasing itself: the skip trucks' alarms, passing Lennie. And the fall, and the jackhammers on the last parts of the pavements to be torn up, pieces of the place where he'd been young.

It had grown and gradually become what he'd talked about. The stories that he'd told Rhys – he had seen them become vibrant and dark and real as this work went on and Charlotte's money washed out over the town. Stories no longer. Behind his eyes, he'd seen them and they were whole.

Sunflowers. He remembered, and piled the debris, crushed it down. Into those stories, a kind of dawn was coming. He couldn't make it stop. A light, in which they didn't seem true.

The passion he had for her, the love he'd felt, these last weeks – she hadn't felt it. In her mind, she and Charlotte had been touching each other.

He couldn't reconcile the two.

As he took what had been the fabric of these homes, and was now rubbish, and as he threw it into the skip to be hoisted and driven away from Ynys-morlan, it seemed to him for the first time, that the story his father had told him, there was no place for it in the world.

A night was paling. He couldn't stop it. How could that story have unfolded, in a life where Ruth's adultery could be real? It makes me feel, she'd said, like I'm clean of all the things you've done to me. How could Lloyd's story be true, in a world where Ruth and her dyke relationship were the ending that same passion had brought?

Like there was a split in the world. Emptying the town's last remains and finding he didn't want to look up at the new avenue of Ynys-morlan, Lennie couldn't make it mend.

Sunday 30 june
nineteensixtyeight

I had the most AMAZING day today and I found the STRANGEST thing. So I thouhgt I would sit down and use my Diary that Daddy gave me and I have drawn it on the first page. I dont even know what to write first beacuse its SO exiting.
First of all Ill say about how mommy and Daddy went off to Boston yestarday so they could get all the things they need for the Rally Party on wensday and beacuse Cray was sick and couldnt go with them they took nannanancy insted. So it was just Claudy looking after me. and I can trick Claudy. Shes nice and shes pretty but she's NOT SMART. I went away. I went away ON MY OWN. I put the sadle on mayflower and I took her. I had the best day evergoing all the way to the top vally and the north pastures and that was when I found the AMAZING STRANGE THING. Right at the top of the medow before you get to the river its under the trees. its white. Its

STRANGE and FUNNY! My mom and Daddy have made my own grave. Its got my name on it and evrything. HOW FUNNY AND INTERESTENG isnt it! it has an anlge on the top of it and shes got these realy BIG ~ingsits realy old I coud tell that by all the grass. I ~as just standing there and I ~as just lAUhgING bacuse I nEVER HERED OF SUCH A AMAZING FUNNY THING!

They came to Ty Heulog. Like every doorway in Ynys-morlan's street, still shaded by the last overhanging boards.

She pushed the door slowly open for them. In her mind, where the thought of home had had no substance, there were pictures now. And she knew why she had kept them blank so long. She'd needed them. Underneath all the anger and hurt, she had wanted them to be hers. And surely that made her weak, no better defended than she'd been at eight years old. They were pictures full of promises.

They came into a small passageway, where skirting boards were being screwed into the walls, where a man swept dust and fragments into piles across the slate floor, and others' voices could be heard. For only a moment, they were looked at.

She led the two of them forwards into the place she'd made.

There were no doors inside. The entranceway to each room was an open arch, beams and clean space where the air moved between. There were no doors to close. Charlotte watched Ruth looking at them. She wanted to tell her but could only hope she'd see.

Charlotte stepped forwards to the living room's opening and raised her hand to it, let it fall. She watched Ruth come towards it slowly. Things had overturned – that she should end up here, showing Ruth something she'd thought she'd never love herself, and trying to make Ruth love it.

The fireplace, she showed her, and the hearth where people could sit. The evenings there might be, she tried to depict. The window ledges were wide, for books and dust, projects half finished. Paintings, jigsaws, whatever Ruth would like to do. Wooden floorboards that would catch the firelight. Winter evenings, cosiness. Images like the ones her own mother must have held so dear. How could you not love them, though? They went deep. They meant safety. They meant care and happiness.

Ruth walked vaguely, unclear expressions shifting across her face. She saw a little dream. A dream that had been tainted. But wasn't selfish, not in itself. Not wrong. She had wanted a home that was full of life. She'd wanted shouting children and footsteps and a father there, not an empty room.

A place without absences. And Nia had come, like absences made real.

'It's lovely.' Ruth's voice rusty. She thought of Charlotte's white stone house, empty in comparison to this. 'It's lovely . . .' And she said, 'I could never make anything like this. It's personal. I can see you . . .' She gestured to it.

'Look outside. You can't tell me that.'

She wanted to say to Ruth, like a little girl brimming over, what it meant to her. How hard it had been to conceive of. The part of her past that she'd had to touch again, and without hatred or anger, and how it had hurt. Seemed to make real every vulnerable, needy part of her. Those parts still very young. She would have begun to speak and been unable to stop, but she looked into Ruth's eyes and saw pictures of escape there. Pictures of running.

'I couldn't make this. It's so sweet, Charlotte, it's lovely . . .' She saw a dream that had been made rotten. In her own life, she'd turned it into a twisted parody of the things she'd wanted it to be. Her little arrangements, things set side by side like they could keep each other company and no loneliness would be allowed, not past her doorstep. All her cushions scattered on the sofa and chairs, to make perfect sitting places for the perfect days that never came. She had hidden behind the dream. Buried herself under her good ending.

Here in Ty Heulog, there were long oak bookcases and she could imagine rugs and armchairs and music, all those tiny meaningless things that seemed to make up a life, happiness. She felt Nia's touch at her leg and she started, everything in her jolted. She was wire-edged like this; had done it to herself. Once she'd had fantasies of being stronger than her mum had been. Free from the past. Instead she'd let herself become this person, pathetic, fragile. She had given herself this guilt.

Shut Nia's door. She remembered. I hate you, she remembered. I love you. He'd said one and then another, interchangeable. Looking down at her, he'd seen no difference. She had let herself become that.

Ruth put a flat hand to her mouth for a moment and blinked. 'I can't really, I can't do this –'

'Come up with me. Upstairs. Please come look at it.'

She turned to Charlotte and saw love in her face. She didn't know how Charlotte could feel that. She looked in the mirror and she didn't feel it. Looked into Nia's face and didn't see it there.

'I don't want to.'

Charlotte took hold of her light hand.

How many months of this project, Ruth had told herself that she wasn't building her hideaway home with all its tall tales of sweetness, not all over again. Refusing to focus on details, just refusing to focus. Looking only at the shapes of the street and the sky, like that made it true. The bigger the vision the more you could conceal behind it. How many people had she roped into her daydream? Could they ever be happy here?

They reached the stairs and she saw Nia's door, though there was no door. She saw a double bed and a room with yellow walls where in the mornings she woke and was still afraid. Already afraid. Even alone. She saw the scrubbing and dusting, hoovering, washing, polishing. She saw how what she made and maintained was not real.

'I don't want to –'

And Charlotte knew it was selfishness to push her, and more than ever with these words. But she couldn't stop herself; she had to try. 'Don't hide,' she said. When she couldn't understand what that meant to Ruth. In desperation she said it, 'Please come with me . . . don't run away.'

The door Charlotte had closed when only she and Nia had been here, it was gone. Its frame was sanded, stripped oak. The hinges were gone, and their holes were filled and varnished. It was finished, this room, but for belongings.

This pale pink that in Hedera, with the windows wide, had caught the air of another country. Ruth stepped to the entranceway and it was a blush, diffuse, reflected on her skin. Charlotte's hand moved out, touched Ruth's arm like she could will into her the understanding of what she'd tried to do. The colour of her childhood, shadowed there, across a face that broke apart.

Nia moved into the room without encouragement. Because it was hers, she had made it that. But Ruth stood and watched her and could not move as her eyes travelled over the lines of her handprints. Above the skirting boards, they danced.

'What do you mean by this?' Her voice was thick. She forced the words through as her hand signalled and fell. 'What do you mean . . . doing this?'

Charlotte took a breath. She heard the last of Ynys-morlan's debris falling. 'This is . . . this is what Hedera looked like. The nursery. None of them are exact, these houses, they each have different parts . . . that reflect . . . the way it used to be. There are some . . . where the light's just the same. In Seaview, the kitchen's much smaller . . . but the shape is like where I grew up.'

She saw how Ruth was shaking her head.

'I wanted to do what you said – put the past, you know, put it into something better. I wanted to . . . heal it. Started designing the interiors . . .' A blankness, she remembered, that she had felt first, just a sadness. 'I couldn't find any way to make them homelike – except to make what I remembered. I didn't want – to reconnect with it. I wanted to make something new. But I was trying to do what you'd talked about . . . express . . .' she lost the words in a voice that grew older and lost its hope. 'I wanted to show you that it's possible.' She saw distraught bewilderment in Ruth's expression, though. She saw something worse, desolation. It was rising. She had to finish now, though. She had brought herself to this room again, to all its raw memories. 'I never connected with my home, where I was young. You know? I never believed that I . . . was right for it. I wanted Nia to connect with these houses. With the town, or anywhere maybe. She's . . . so lost, Ruth. I wanted her to be happy. I watched her, and she *was*. So involved. I was watching her . . . it was so good to see. Can you see it?'

And in her mind, Charlotte saw the northern meadow above the house. Slow words took her, as her footsteps had once, towards the stone at the top.

'Like you said, Ruth, like you wanted to: it was a way to express it, that was better. A good ending.'

But that desolation had come full like a moon. The tears had dried over Ruth's face, as if they were wax, and her expression cracked now. She stared at the handprints that pattered above the skirting boards. She remembered washing the grey shapes away; the shapes that, when you looked closely enough, resolved themselves into pairs. Tiny pairs, a hundred times, more, where over and over again, three years' of days and nights, Nia had crouched low against the walls, low to the floor, and placed her hands.

She saw them, in bright blue. Like every wall might be an escape that Nia couldn't find.

Charlotte looked at her. The only words she had left were secret words: they had never been spoken and she couldn't give them to the woman who stood in front of her with despair written in the place that love might have been.

'It's a gift to you,' Charlotte said.

'A gift . . . ?'

'To show you, what you said is possible. We've made it, here.'

All over every wall, just the level where they would have been if Nia knelt. If Nia could've heard, where she would have placed her ear to listen.

'What've you done?' Ruth asked her brokenly.

'With Nia, last night, I –'

'Why would you want to do this? *This*. Why would you want to do this?'

'To show you . . .' How could she explain? Ruth shaking her head this way, glass passing over her face and splintering and reforming. She'd thought that it would show Ruth that the things she had believed forever ruined could be restored. Regeneration. That's what this project was for. In the muted noise, Ruth's hand moving, stiff and wild as she motioned to the walls, Charlotte tried to articulate these things.

'Ruth –' But there was horror across her face.

And into Charlotte's mind again came the things that Ruth had told her this morning; things done with her husband. The only ways she'd been able to communicate what she'd suffered. Bitter sex, violence of her own. And now the revulsion and fear there in Ruth's gaze. Tears and the same self-loathing that she'd shown that night, standing before Charlotte, covered with her bruises.

She reached towards Ruth.

'Don't touch me!' She shied, feet away. 'Don't *touch* me. *Let go of me.*' Though Charlotte had been too slow for her hand to even brush her.

'You thought this would look . . . good to me? Beautiful? It doesn't look beautiful to me. *Oh God* –'

Charlotte saw her through her own tears. Not a woman who had healed. Not a woman who, through healing, had found love. Just someone who'd been fleeing and was still. And everything that Charlotte had hoped she could be to Ruth now seemed depleted, it issued from her until she was left unfilled. A shell. As really she'd always been. As this very room, two thousand miles away, had made her.

She had rebuilt Hedera's memory. All around the walls, she saw the need she'd had, painted plainly. The need she'd finally admitted last night, watching as Nia reached out. In the night's silence, sadness had welled and flourished as she'd looked at Nia. She had seen clearly, in the place where the diaries' chaos had lain, that reach of the Atlantic. Just empty water. Just how lonely she had been.

Nia's laughter, she remembered. Silent.

She looked at Ruth's now, who was unable to see any beauty in what she'd tried to make. Unable to see Charlotte herself. Not a woman who was in love with her, just someone, like her mother, who was blind.

She was drawing towards a secret she'd never told. She wanted to lay it out, its skin naked, and tell Ruth the fears she felt. She wanted Ruth to allay them.

'Please see it?' she asked.

She said Ruth's name again, but Ruth would only look at the walls, at the handprints.

Like there'd been a hundred nights and unheard tears.

She did not know what she did. Nia was in her arms.

She heard Charlotte call out to her but she was running, and her voice was already far behind. She heard Charlotte asking her to come back but she took her daughter and, in the room that Charlotte knew so well, that she'd so perfectly recreated, left her alone.

Outside, the upper levels of the scaffolding came down.

They unbolted the joints. Slid poles free with metal sounds into the virgin air. Around the houses' chimneys, dressing the tips of their roofs, the first slates lay, immaculate.

Around Charlotte, the shades of Nia's palms danced. Little signs of an isolation Nia had finally seemed to emerge from, putting her hands in the paint and owning this room. The nursery had never been hers of course. The toys on the shelves, older than Charlotte had been, never her own.

Throughout the street, where the public works crew's barricades had forced passers-by into a stream around the slow-moving traffic and left, a trail through water, the pale of new pavement behind, everywhere the constant alarms of the skip trucks overlapped to fill the spaces between the project's last tidal noises. At the base of each building, final debris was poured.

The woman who stood here on her own and listened to it was nameless.

She'd looked into the mirror and asked sometimes, a lot of times when she'd been younger, what her name might be. In her diaries, there were lists of possibilities. She had never owned the one that she'd been given.

Charlotte Weyland had never left Hedera really, or Massachusetts. She had never written in any journal, or on any other page. Had never ridden out where she wasn't allowed to ride or discovered in long summer grass a secret, which would change the way her life grew. In truth she'd never had a life. Charlotte Weyland had died at the age of three years old. The woman who stood now in a recreation of her childhood home had never known her.

Worn but still beautiful, her name had been inscribed on the headstone. She had been unable to copy it properly; an eight-year-old's drawing. She'd looked back at it, taken the volume down and opened its bound cover, only once, and only in recent weeks. For more than thirty years this woman who'd never found another name but Charlotte Weyland, who'd never healed well enough to give herself another, had been unable to turn the pages and look back.

She stood here now, nameless still, in the midst of the project she'd created, and she heard Ruth run, taking Nia away too. She looked at the room and just cried. No sound really, just cried as she saw the shapes of Nia's hands.

Beside her a view, not of meadows, but of seawater.

She turned to stare out at it, in all its white spring glory. Continuous until it reached America's coast. She cried and lost the view and blinked the tears away to see it again – the ocean, which people said had no memory.

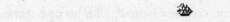

'I feel confused,' she said. 'And I feel . . . empty. Not bad though, not really that.'

Muted light lay across the bed, undisturbed by her voice.

'There are things that are . . . missing from me.' She gave a laugh that seemed to have no focus, like the sun and wind blowing everything round outside.

Tom touched her, as he'd kissed her that very first night when she'd still been Emyr's wife; when he did it, it felt as if he might be touching different planes than she saw in the mirror. That afterglow, she felt. It was a sense that you'd been changed by what you'd just done. It was a sense of renewal.

Here she lay, a mile or nearly two from Ynys-morlan and from Charlotte Weyland: a woman of not dissimilar age, a very young man's hand beside her breast, and a vacant room inside her, that was ready now. Here she lay, while the town's every site began to be deconstructed. His hand traced lines and Gwen couldn't have voiced to him how intimate that felt. An afterglow. The sense that, after these moments, everything else in your life might be altered.

He heard the story of what had happened with Dai on Dai's last morning in this town more completely than anyone else had done.

'I haven't known what to say . . .'

He lay next to her, silent, confused himself, with his own stories waiting. He listened to see if what she said would cast light on the things that had forced themselves into his life in the last night and morning. He kept close to her as he remembered Rhys's face.

'I haven't known.' She spoke with gradual openness. 'Do you know how many years it is that I've done doorstep rounds?' She didn't name a figure, though; counting years had become an activity she wanted to share with Tom far less than she'd done before. 'He didn't care. After everything they said to him – all the thought and time and work and love he'd put into that thing, it didn't make him want to defend it. There are these little hooks, I thought there were . . . little sharp hooks that join you to things you've done. I couldn't understand how they could just . . . give up their grip. He didn't care if it stood or got torn down. I remember the gift shop . . .' For a moment her voice trailed into a hole and she didn't see the window she was looking at, the half-drawn curtains that held the sun like cupped hands. 'I never needed it . . . loved it, as much as when I knew it was under threat. Like motherhood, maybe like that. And you strain to get those hooks dug in deeper, maybe your hooks in it, maybe its in you. But they'd just fallen out of him. He didn't care. No statement in it,' she said. 'He wasn't trying to abandon it. He just made it and then he left it behind.'

He listened to her. He looked at her beside him in the bed in a different way than he'd ever done. Because her husband knew. She hadn't talked about it, or hinted to him, but her husband knew.

In his mind he saw his mum asking him to come home. Beliefs, he saw, that had lost their meaning or seemed to, once she'd said that. Because the feeling of wanting to was a hand in him. He waited to speak.

'I've been and I've told Patty,' she said. 'I almost went to Ruth Lewis. Emyr, I told. I've been to your mother and I've told her.'

His eyes shifted, he went to speak but then did not. As he'd imagined maybe, as he'd not quite pictured, light fell into the memory of last night. And it had been very dark. It didn't matter maybe if Dai's leaving had been one of his mother's reasons. Maybe the offer was better that way even, meant more.

'I went and told them. Just like – all those years, petitions, funds. Everyone's hurt him, on my own I've hurt him. But the way he didn't care, if it stayed, if it just got demolished . . .'

He tried to imagine Siân listening, but he'd not even been able to imagine what she might've said to Dai that day in the street. He thought of the doorstep, new, the house, from which all the past had been dusted away. It hadn't been deeply rooted, like you would normally believe. He could imagine himself living there, though. It was a picture, as it had been in the back of his head for the last two years, that didn't have any goals or beliefs in it. Only a good picture. It didn't need them.

Rhys, a few hours gone – his expression – was clear in Tom's mind.

He'd left the van and, here alone, all his thoughts flying round, the place had seemed *fuller* than it had ever done. It had seemed to hold parts of the past – the piles of his stuff, the CDs, the tiny kitchen – and in the sun against the windows, its drifting sense of the coming day, the future too, which the place hadn't done since he'd moved here.

Gwen had come at noon, after the playschool had ended and the groups of kids and parents dissipated. She'd come and they'd kissed. And the rest. Afterwards, she'd begun to talk, raising herself in his bed when they'd lain without speaking for a while, and her husband's name had been in Tom's mouth before she'd said, 'All our talking . . . What've I been looking for, Tom . . . think for the first time I've realized.'

And then, because that had touched his confusion close, he'd been silent, the pieces of a decision lying inside him, like working parts that haven't been put together.

She said now: 'He didn't want me to try and get the sculpture maintained. I wanted to tell people it should be kept. I was walking home, just seeing how much I wanted to.' She remembered the spring air surrounding her, as if Dai's lack of care had left the very atmosphere deserted, displaced. 'It was right for him to go. His house was still full of . . . last year. Like every last year you could imagine. I thought of telling people how we should keep what he'd built. How we owed him that, even if he'd stopped caring . . . And how they'd react to my saying it, what they'd see. Full of myself. And pious. After shouting at him. A hypocrite. I wouldn't care. I'd be doing the right thing. And then I saw . . . why it seemed like right. *Because* they'd think those things . . .'

Her face, in which he'd seen that very first night – an autumn night when they'd still been deep in the heart of Ynys-morlan – the same needs he had been feeling for years, and the same loneliness, he saw now. What she said, though – they were not the same.

Her expression; it was unfastened and beautiful for a moment. Not old or young. He saw something in her eyes that was rising, which had been shapeless for both of them.

But not the same, he saw, not when you got down to the bottom of it. He remembered his mum's voice. He feared being a good person, or goodness itself, was nothing more than the peak of some great heap – some Dai-sculpture – built out of whatever rubble was in your life. He didn't want it to be something so senseless.

There was a pain in her eyes but he saw it was for memory, not for the future. Tom's hand shifted, would have tightened.

She was remembering Emyr asking her to prove her motivations had been good.

'We were wrong,' she said, 'or I was. I walked back from Dai's that day and saw it: it was denial. Denying myself – I don't know, their friendships maybe, or just pride. Like . . . denying myself a part in the project, before I saw what we could all do to a naïve, harmless . . . when I still believed goodness could be the same as the sake of the community.

'But it wasn't goodness at all. It hasn't ever been. What's good in working and never being satisfied? In not taking, like your mum did . . . something your community shares out? What's good in – denying yourself that community, just to defend a . . . a white elephant . . . regardless of what it is, just because it's what Dai's left behind?' She answered herself as the shifting curtain caught her gaze, so sunny out there. 'Nothing.'

Years of work, of overlapping goals that like waves never stilled. Years of sparseness in her home which she hadn't understood. A thousand possessions and sparseness had lain on the freshly dusted shelves between them. Nothing ever right, nothing ever *done*. There'd been no time when she'd believed in her achievements. Achievement should mean some end. She looked at Tom and his memories – skating there, dark eyes – she also knew they weren't the same.

Down deep, though, there it was, a shapeless thing. Or the lack of it. The reaching out, constantly. She wanted to draw everything she saw in his gaze into one, as if the person she had been all her life and the change she felt now could be reconciled by doing that.

Without words, she was looking at him.

Gwen Morgan, nearly forty years old, who had never made the

journey between childhood and adulthood. She'd replaced it with one choice, one bright and shining lie. Somewhere underneath, for twenty years, she'd still been a girl. She looked at Tom and saw the point where she had chosen. Saw it again, and perhaps could go back.

He'd made love to Gwen and kissed her all the time like he was losing her, but he didn't need to feel that way. He'd had no orgasm, he had been reaching too much for something else – to be closer to her maybe, to the things that had seemed so important when they'd shared them.

'I don't want to think,' she said, 'that denial is all it's been, for years. But I look inside myself and I can't find anything, which feels "good" . . . that doesn't feel like some sacrifice.'

'Or like it'll reward you,' he said. In his mind, he saw the wet and distant shapes of a girl's hands. He was silent a long time. So many feelings for his mother were tangled like those hands had been, guilt for the things he'd said to her and anger still, the way he'd missed her and, more than everything now, after Rhys had been here and they had sat together, the loss of realizing that his beliefs rose out of someone no older than he'd been when he'd swum after that little girl.

He sat up slowly and he looked at Gwen. Half-light caught her face. Her last days, as she'd retold them, left her expression bare in a way he'd never seen it before. She had said she felt confused. If that was so then confusion was light as air.

For a moment he looked at his hands. He raised his face again.

He didn't mention his mother's house or her offer.

He said only, 'Your husband went to see Rhys last night.'

Gwen turned.

'Rhys came to see me this morning.'

She looked at him and there were questions on her lips that withered away.

Looking at her carefully, these still-disassembled parts in him moving now, churning to life now, Tom told her the story – just like Rhys had. He left out nothing. He spoke without any questions in his voice. Gwen half lying, half raised on his bed, never moved her eyes.

She thought of Emyr, so disconnected now from everything except the project, like he believed they would finally come together, the town he was building at night in his study and the town that lay a mile away. He would finally be proven right.

She tried to imagine the scene Tom recited.

The Morgans had once been upstanding people, pillars of the community. They'd torn each other apart, this quiet little marriage that no one could have believed would ever come to harm. This quiet little man, who had been both evil and in pain, while no one knew. Not even she, completely.

And when he'd finished, after the silence had settled into the bed where they lay and he had nodded to himself, once, twice, and known there was really nothing else left to say, Tom asked her, 'Did you tell him? Was it you?'

'He knew anyway.'

She could not imagine Emyr's night. She wondered if the boy Rhys might be lying.

'You told him then,' Tom said.

'He asked where I'd been . . . I didn't answer.'

He looked at her. Pulled in two by the currents, he thought about how much he had held back from her, believing that she went home to somewhere that was unchanging. He thought about how hurt the man must've been, while he himself had been talking about right and wrong, lying here with Gwen.

Beliefs he thought of, that came from nothing more than small and unhealed wounds. He wanted to go home. But he wanted to be more than just the sum of the things he'd felt in the past. Maybe ideals only made you lonely when they reached back instead of onwards. 'I don't know if you want to be with me,' he said. 'Don't know what your . . . ethics, like, what they are now . . .' He showed her this place with one of his hands but really Gwen supposed he meant himself. She was looking back at him. 'I'm in love with you,' he said.

She smiled, a concession, tears in her eyes that had started with imagining Emyr, that now grew to encompass Tom and herself, Dai and the way of the world.

Tom didn't look at her as he said quietly, 'I want to tell him, about us. I want you to. And I want to go back home and see my mother, and tell her.'

Her lips opened slightly. There was this light on her. She'd hardly worn any make-up.

He remembered Rhys and felt, just saying it out loud, something lift in him that since last night had seemed small and needful, useless. Rhys's face had looked like a million lost chances, and he didn't want to be that himself. It hurt his heart to see it in Rhys. He himself didn't have to feel like Ynys-morlan had deserted him, though – or like his beliefs had only ever come from that.

Gwen covered her mouth for a long time.

He looked so young and when he kissed her she felt young too. Was that bad? It must be selfish. He had old eyes and when she looked into them, she saw her own mistakes, except they didn't seem like that, not in him.

She remembered Emyr asking and asking and her quiet. She thought of all this would mean. Emyr. Siân . . . And she saw how secret it was, what they were sharing here. She wet her lips, thoughts ranging through her, of this changing town during the last year, as though she had sat beside the sea and seen it all, unbroken, rapid.

What illusions could she have? He wasn't even nineteen. They could never stay together. But it seemed like there could be a while – a beginning – and they could share it maybe. There were things she could give him; there must be things. And if he wanted to leave her, anytime, a month from now, she'd let him do that, she would say it was the right thing. She told herself now. She would encourage him to.

She said quietly, 'I've been thinking that I don't want to stay in Ynys-morlan.'

Tom watched her face and didn't know how to respond.

'Go where . . . ?' he said. And then, 'You couldn't stay?'

'I could stay.' She saw herself walking down this street, holding Tom's hand. How she'd keep her head raised, she saw, and need to hold on all the time to feelings which she didn't want any more. 'I want to go, though. There are places we could go to . . . We could tell people, and we could leave.'

Tom didn't answer. He hadn't thought of other places. There was a wrench that came with thinking of them. There had always been. In his mind he saw his mother's house, and the street then, the town. Kids he saw, that had been ten-, eleven-year-olds when he had finished school. They walked around here now, Saturdays, Sundays, they looked the same as him. Clothes and boots, and the expressions on their faces. He didn't want to get washed away. And that was how they looked, those kids: like a slow tide rising.

He thought of telling his mother, and then leaving her. He thought of never living in that house again. 'Where would you want to go?' he said.

'We could find a hotel, just to begin with.'

Gwen pictured their rooms, always strangely empty. And a window, an indiscernible view. 'A hotel. Somewhere out of Ynys-morlan. We can just go fifty miles, it doesn't matter.'

'And then where?' He was afraid of how much that sounded like this site. Maybe he wouldn't feel stranded though, if he was further away from here.

'Anywhere,' she said. She imagined warm places.

'I don't know anywhere . . . that I'd want to go.'

'There's a road, in Spain,' she said, 'I went there. There's a road that runs along the coast. Perhaps fifty yards from it. Several hundred miles,' she said, 'it follows it.'

'I don't know. No,' he said.

'There's a bar I went to once.' She didn't give the memory a name. It had been their honeymoon. She'd been twenty-one years old. 'It looks out on the sea. They all do.'

It wouldn't be there any more, she thought. But you couldn't move forwards without trying to hold on to, or return to, the things that lay behind. She wanted to revisit that place. She wanted to make it what it hadn't been before.

'I can't go to some other country.'

'We wouldn't have to decide right away . . . I want the chance,' Gwen said then, 'that you've got.'

'What chance?'

'If you don't see it then you need to go.'

Tom didn't answer her. He didn't want to say goodbye to the people or the place. Not now, when it had changed so much and he no longer knew it. There were the chances, though, that Rhys had lost. Rhys could set off for wherever he wanted, but he'd never be able to leave this place behind. It couldn't forgive him. He couldn't forgive it. And Tom didn't want to be the same.

'A hotel?' he said, 'to start off? You'd want to go soon . . .'

'I'd want to go once I'd spoken to Emyr. Once I'd said a few goodbyes.'

He was silent.

'There's a road,' she said, 'all the way along the coast.'

He could picture it. In your head, things were always beautiful, though. He was scared they wouldn't be in life. He was scared of a lot of things. Of being young – and of not being young any more. He knew Ynys-morlan, he couldn't love anywhere like he did here, even changed, even unrecognizable. You didn't know yourself when you went somewhere new. People would ask you where you came from and you'd feel rootless, that place a million miles behind.

She looked at Tom, the covers spread almost over them. She was naked and almost unselfconscious. Like healing perhaps, these changes came before you saw them. And when you realized, they were already formed. 'I want you a lot,' she said. 'I love you, a lot.'

Warm places, she envisaged, waking up in the beginnings of their days. She wanted to go. It was afternoon, but she thought of mornings; the end of March, but it was a sunny season she saw. She wanted to stay awake all night with him, and to fall asleep like this. To fall asleep in the bed of summer . . . to fall asleep with the sunrise in the curtains and the somnolent buzzing of flies.

Distant from the town, where the skip vans were leaving in queues, carrying a rivulet of debris away, and where machinery was being hefted across doorsteps and back into dirty vans, those doors looking out from gradually dismembered scaffolds, render-filthy in the dust and dirt and the commotion – distant, where the wind blew between unoccupied caravans, Tom Humphries began to make two piles: things he'd take and things he wouldn't. The first one was small.

He moved CDs, clothes, books he didn't really need, unwillingly from the first pile to the second. His thoughts brimmed and turned each other over, and he made a pile for them, in his head, and told himself he'd leave that too. He picked up his phone and looked at it for long moments before trying Rhys's house.

Looking out of the window as Barry's distant voice told him to wait and called Rhys's name, Tom saw the Wendy-house gardens with their knee-high picket fences, the long lanes and short grass and all the unfilled moments of somewhere he'd known inside and out. The site's office was open. Gavin was moving out there. In less than a fortnight, the whole place would be unlocked and people would begin to bring in the new season.

Tom spoke to Rhys and, after two minutes' silence, looking again down at the phone, he dialled the café. Thoughts of goodbyes, like this wind-driven sky, were lonely and led towards no sure ground, none at all, and looked all the newer and more moving for it.

It was half past five, it was four hours after Gwen had left, when he took the caravan keys and locked the van, stepping out. That wind was cold. Thin, new-green grass was caught in its waves. Between the regimented silences of the site, he heard Gavin and Owen, far-off voices, and then the cut of a strimmer's engine. He looked at the road that led past the stranded community centre, grass-covered dunes around it, towards the edge of a town now less known to him than this remote island of a home. He took the keys and walked towards the site's gates.

Four hours after she had left. She'd gone back to the house to find, not only her husband gone, but every box she had slowly packed.

Where had he taken them? Images of the skips in town, and her things scattered, rose and buffeted her. They left her empty eventually, though, like these rooms looked as she finally stood in them, having walked the dogs for an hour along the hill. The first time she had known she was leaving. The living room, the kitchen and their bedroom, they were all distant, cold. Had Emyr thrown her things away like that? Did she care? Had she really been planning to take any of them?

Emyr's steam train prints hung along the hallway with all their little water-coloured pasts. Gwen walked through the house.

Years there had been, and if she could have gone back through them, the person she had been then wouldn't know her any more. Might look her up and down and turn away with fear and disapproval.

She stood in the doorway to his study and saw the chaos of a project which had become his life. It could have been hers too; once upon a time it would have been.

She waited hours, taking the few things she needed, but Emyr didn't come home. Not the correct term for it any longer, she thought, finding her identification, her financial papers, her store of letters and photographs. Ones that had been framed till a few days ago she had added to them, their frames placed into the boxes, the whereabouts of which Gwen no longer knew.

She looked at these few things collected, and thought of the only goodbye that she would say tonight after finding Emyr and speaking with him. She thought of Patty, as she had stood at this front door, Gwen telling her that she was fine, and to leave. Two days ago she had gone down to the café and told Pat that Dai was gone. And in the noise, Pat had given her a small smile, a mix of sadness and hope.

She would lie to Patty tonight. She'd say goodbye in a way that would allow them to share that; a way which would carry the possibilities – light as the quiet that had lain on the café's doorstep between them as they'd both envisaged Dai walking out – carry it onwards. She'd say goodbye with no honesty, but in a way that would still allow them to be friends.

She waited for Emyr and she waited, but he didn't return. In the empty house, on the cream-coloured sofa, she sat.

The road was gentle with the sand this wind had thrown across its edges, the dunes a cold, black-shadow line between Tom and the shore. Through this distance he saw the community centre, its car park, and the road's continuing reach towards Ynys-morlan's edge – just a shape there, just a silhouette there, in the daylight that was now failing.

To the west, above the dunes, the sky was red.

He walked slowly. He heard the first fingers of the work's noise. He saw the lines of the rooftops growing clear, and that they were clean of scaffolding. The sight cut their outlines into him – from this far away, they looked the same as they had always done. He thought of his mother, tried to imagine her face. Tried to set out his words.

Before Tom reached the first houses, the sprawl could be seen. Both sides of this road were hedged with vehicles, some empty, some with headlights blaring as they started, some waiting already to leave. On the dirt beside the tarmac, the first of them: a group of yellow road-crew machines with their slow lights turning in the twilight; men stood in ragged groups. He saw scaffolding that had been thinned until it was nothing more than climbing silver arms on the buildings' faces, hanging loose – and even this being taken down. They were stone cottages, they had little peaks and points. The windows, he saw, stared out from walls haggard with the remnants of before, and they were now being covered by boards. He came to the edge of the trucks and machinery. He got out of the centre of the road, along its verge instead, to make a way between the men. Heard their conversation in snatches, between the engines' growing drone. He walked with grey amazement brushed across his face.

The houses, these first houses, had front yards covered with lawn. Thick and new and green. You could see the lines that ran between the strips they'd been laid down in. A foot wide, each length of turf; you could see them. Older paths peeked out from the centre of each garden, leading on to new wooden garden gates. The craziest thing, to see grass like that, which wasn't fake – as it looked to be – but real and ready to lay down roots. Even as he walked in between these first buildings, they were dismantling the scaffolds' final frames, dull steel now blue-caught in the gathering darkness.

The last days hadn't shown it. Like really he'd believed they'd disassemble the project and Ynys-morlan underneath would be the same as it always had. Some part of him hadn't thought that it could change, even seeing it happen.

In the light's last minutes, though, Tom made out a different town. It looked as if it had risen up, new buildings dirty with the waste of pebbledash and paint, like it had been dragged to the surface. He saw the café, its big lower windows now curving bottle-glass panes and above them, casting colours with the bulbs behind, on to the road's opposite face, the stained glass of a restaurant above.

The craziest thing, to walk into the town where you'd grown up, to look all around you and be homesick. These last few months he'd felt abandoned but, like the shapes of the houses under all the work, it had been vague. Tom saw clearly what had been taken now, and what had been given to replace it. He'd never be able to go back to the place he remembered.

He looked up, the slowly reducing grind of this mess around him, to see lastly, with a foreign kind of stare, how the street lamps were unlit. Floodlights started with little shocks here and there. But like the land surrounding Ynys-morlan, like the sea on the other side of its long terraces, all the street lamps' bulbs were grey and gradually being lost into the coming night.

It was twenty past six when Gwen stopped waiting. She went to the car. Four years ago they had bought it – or more accurately, Emyr had bought it for her – at a reduced price. Like everything they'd bought locally after Emyr had been voted mayor. In the darkening driveway, as she stood with her coat hanging open, their Lexus looked like the last piece of normality, parked in the tender fall of the house's light. She could turn around, it seemed, and open the front door again, and inside would find Emyr sitting and reading, would find their living room cast with a little quiet music or television, broken only by the carriage clock's chime. A final pang, she felt, for a time when there'd been no confusion. She thought she would leave the car behind tonight as well.

Tom came to the gate of a garden that had never been there before.

He came to a lush little lawn where before straggling beds and old paving stones had been piled with the odds and sods that would stand in the rain every winter. Bicycles that had been grown out of, flower pots. Each year's shedding skin. It was the law of the natural world: life ended up in the yard when it was done with.

Cut away at one side for a new flower bed, that lawn was empty and waiting for any of those things.

Tom opened the gate, measured traffic eking out the road behind him and the spilling warning lights of machinery trailing, falling, trailing over again on the walls of the house he saw.

It was tall with its deep gable windows. Beside the door, three men, indistinct: fitting board over the last of these, as they were on the neighbours' places too now. It looked neglected with these wooden panes and detritus-covered stones. He turned once to see the others. All of them, neglected, somehow awful. Tom turned finally back.

A peaked house. A house he'd never seen, blank-eyed. All of them. Pretty cottages, full of heritage to the stranger's eye, battened down and dirty with that dry scum of render, as they waited for the sandblasting crew. He'd seen them gathering at the end of town, he realized. The yellow trucks. Tanks on the back, they'd had.

How would they do it? Sand and water, it would hit the walls and run off in a filthy wash right across this lawn they'd laid. He saw an image of the water's grey limbs, creeping out on to this grass. How would they do it – the question blank like all these new answers around him, just another blank joke – how, without ruining the lawn?

Still carrying the caravan keys in his cold hand, he looked at the edges of the boarded windows to see if he could find lights on behind. He ran through his words and he saw how pale and unprepared they were. The craziest thing, to stand here with this piece of news, to see the place where he'd used to live in the ghost of the shuttered building that stood now at the end of the path. To be leaving – to be leaving this way. He could come back to get more of his stuff, he told himself. But he told himself lies.

He had the key to this new place on his old chain. He listened to the men talking as he walked past them beneath the new porch, to let himself into a new hallway. The smell of cooking there, frying sausages, and the half-unpacked contents of his home.

For a moment, the town was outside.

He heard his mother's voice and shut the door.

He looked at the pictures leaning against the wall; ones that had used to hang in the kitchen. The sounds from the town were stifled by those boards.

She came around through the kitchen doorway and saw him standing in the hall. Pale-looking, set-looking.

'Evening,' he said.

She had a dishtowel in one hand and a face that was blushed-up from standing over the cooker. She had a smile that came. He moved between the boxes that were stacked against the walls and she wondered if it was an answer she saw in his face. It could have been that he'd come to say yes. He was the sort who'd look stern with that – as if asking for what she'd offered already. Tom had lost the ability a long time ago to ask her for anything with ease.

'Well, nice of you to come. Don't let me know, will you?' She smiled again. 'There isn't enough mash. We'll halve it up.'

'I wasn't going to eat, like.'

'I was only joking. Seen it all starting outside, have you?'

'They've got the boards up. Go out and look.'

'We're not meant to go out if we can help it tonight. Not meant to get in the way.'

'I walked through. I wasn't in anybody's way.'

'Come on in,' she said.

The house was muted: a little ship, hatches fastened down against the outside. Layers of home were settling slowly to cover what had been a building site. He followed his mother as she turned. He saw things set out that hadn't been on the shelves last night. He saw the loose wiring completed and covered, and the kitchen table, as it had been then, set for two. There was a scatter of normality. There was a kind of comfort.

'Stacey's here,' he said.

'Graced me with her presence tonight.'

'She's upstairs?'

Siân raised her face and looked at him from the cupboard where she was bent down, reaching out a third plate. A little stack, a fifth of the kitchenware, set inside the clean and empty place – lost in the space of it, they looked like.

'Yes, upstairs.'

His face was guarded. Siân saw the keys in his hand for the first time. She stood without taking out the plate.

There were no boards on the kitchen windows, looking out as they did on a backyard – nothing but shadow now and, somewhere, the sea. Newly clad in its little sea stones, there was no sandblasting to be done on this extension. There were peaked, cottage windows, Tom saw again. Under a blackening sky this house must have held like a keepsake the memory of what it had been.

'I wanted to talk to you.'

'Talk,' she said. She tried to look open, encouraging.

'You're eating soon?'

'Ten minutes . . .'

'You want to come – you want to come sit down with me? In the living room, like?'

He watched her nod slowly, begin to move, and didn't know how he could bring out the words he had. They seemed unreal as he stood here, surrounded by all these little possessions, unpacked and familiar. They couldn't be said here. Surely couldn't be said, when she looked better than she'd ever done. She was waiting to find out if he'd come back home. And as Tom watched her preparations gathering themselves together, saw her wipe her hands on the towel and glance at him, moving towards the living-room doorway, he saw with a brutality how different these two parts of his life were. Lying in bed with Gwen, he remembered. Looking at his mum's life-lined face now, they were pulled free from each other like skeins of wool – two different people it seemed.

Had he thought he could just make them a whole? He came into the room after her: drawn curtains and boards behind them, the cargo hold of this little ship with its open cardboard boxes, still full of her stuff. Siân sat on the sofa and looked at him as if ready. He wiped a hand across his mouth, did not sit for a moment.

No, he hadn't believed he could bring them together. Real sadness came to him for the first time that evening as he saw that the freedom he had felt today, packing his things, was the freedom of pulling the two apart.

She had no make-up on. Her short hair was pushed in awkward ways from cooking, running her hands into it. Her face, as it had been last night, was empty of a lot of the tightness he had thought, always thought, was the heart of her. Tom looked at her and saw the way that what she'd asked him last night had torn everything out into clarity: he'd lost the want, not admitted for two years, in the moment when she'd offered it to him.

'Don't be worried,' Siân said, 'you can tell me whatever you want, you should know that.'

What was left in him was regret. Resentment he couldn't lose. Love he couldn't quite feel. He looked at her and, in the quiet, asked himself if he did love her. He must do. It must be the reason for all these twists of feeling.

Engines. A constant sound round his quiet. He wanted her to know him. He couldn't change the identity of the person he'd fallen in love with. Or how his mother knew her. He looked at her steadily. Those engines, rising, turning, falling back.

'I'm going away.'

Siân heard.

He was telling her, 'I thought about what you said. I'd love to come back for a while, like, stay here. And I'm glad, means a lot to me, that you asked, and you said . . . all the stuff you said last night.' Awkward words and he didn't want them to sound that way. 'Made me realize, though, how much I want to go away . . . need to go. I'm going to do that . . .' he said. 'Rhys came to see me.'

She took a long breath as she looked at him, like that space was long enough to make sense out of what she felt.

'You know what you want. You know what's best for you. I'm glad . . . if that's what you've decided. Tom –' she reached out her hand as he came to sit in the chair beside her, but she saw him stiffen. 'Long as we're on good terms ... doesn't matter where you are,' she finished. 'You don't have to shy away from me.'

'I'm not "shying away from you".'

'I didn't think you would come back. But you're welcome.'

He looked at her: this wasn't true. She had thought he might. She was always lying to him and for no reason, just like this. Without talking now they watched each other and both thought the same. They were similar. How could it be that similarity lay between them, blocked like this, instead of making a bridge?

'I'm going away tonight,' he said. 'I'm going to come back and get some stuff but it won't be for a few days –'

Words tightened into silence in her mouth, outside the sound of some machine reared up and her gaze moved over him. 'What are you talking about, tonight? Where would you go "tonight"?' His hair was brushed roughly away from his eyes, and they held a lie, she thought, looking like an adult's. 'Set off into the sunset, is that what you're going to do? For God's sake! Not a plan in the world? Where?' she said. 'Where?'

'A hotel to start off with.'

'Oh Christ. And with what money? And to go where afterwards? Got a job ... ? Thought of that? My God, I wasn't asking you to make a decision in fifteen minutes! Offering you the chance to *work out* what you wanted ... Come off it, Tom. Just come off it. Or is this meant to make some point?'

'There's no point I want to make to you. Not everything's about you.' But confusion rose. What he said rang untrue. Staring at her as she continued, he suddenly said, 'I'm going away with someone else.'

Her voice came to a halt.

In the warm living room, where hidden boards held in this tight space everything that was so well known to them, Siân looked at her son and seemed to see the edge of a foreign place.

He had imagined calmness, room inside himself to tell her. A cramp passed through her expression and he said no more.

'You've got a girlfriend. You're going away with her? What: you've been planning? Knew last night, and didn't tell me. I haven't even met her, Tom.' A plain of distance seemed to come between them as she imagined unknown faces. 'Who were you embarrassed of then? Me or her? I haven't even *met* her . . .'

He was silent, that expanse, which would not break, straining out between them as he sat with no answer. She was shaking her head. In the kitchen, dinner was nearly ready and outside, they were starting to train their hoses on nearer buildings; he heard their far-off noises, like a falling hail.

She was seeing months, through which he'd hidden a stranger from her. Seeing a goodbye, come without warning. 'You make me sad,' she said.

'I didn't want it to be so fast –'

She nodded but didn't even look at him.

'I have to go away. All right?'

'What is this supposed to mean? Is this some punishment?'

'I'm not doing this because of you!' A bare shout in the little room. So alien here, the words could only sound like lies. 'Look at me, all right? Because I'm fucking . . . *I'm trying!* This is going to be hard. I don't want to hurt you –'

She did slowly as he said, lifted her face, and like a path before his words, she saw it.

'I know her.'

He swallowed. He nodded. 'You know her, yes.'

'I know her and you didn't want to tell me? You've been together how long, and you didn't want to tell me? Who?' Siân said quietly.

Tom saw this evening, like a night removed from the rest of life. He saw how months might go by and tonight would be untouched by them. An evening when recognizable voices and the smells of cooking, when the feeling of home held, instead of normality, a rift. He saw it clearly.

'I'm in love with her,' he said.

'Who . . . ?'

'And she's in love with me. You won't believe that. It *can* be true, though.'

'Tell me who. You've kept it from me till the night you go . . . tell me now.'

'I haven't been planning it, going. I just have to.'

Fear gathered itself up as he stalled and she tried to find names to fit this hole that lay revealed. She found none. For this expression he had – this hopelessness – she found none.

'I love you,' he said.

'What's going on?'

Siân lost her age in her moment of surprise; incomprehension. He saw it – just fall away from her. Lines around her eyes smoothed. Years became softer.

'I've been with Gwen. We're going away.'

He heard the work outside as she continued to look at him.

Her face and her body were still while beneath, there was something breaking, as if to leave her expression a façade. He saw things pass as, sitting near to him, she felt them deep inside her.

She went to speak. She did not speak.

An image came to her, of Gwen standing on her doorstep.

It was an image imbued with simple facts that you didn't even recognize: friendship, umbrage, just parochial history, knowledge. 'Gwen,' she said. She saw these facts suddenly: random things, which need not be true. An image with the background of a street that no longer existed outside.

Tom looked at her, only waiting. He'd had things to follow with, things to say. They'd abandoned him.

'Gwen,' she said. She couldn't make a coherent pattern. Nothing hard enough to hold on to and put into a sentence. Gwen sleeping with him. Her oldest friend, sleeping with him. Emyr Morgan, cuckolded. These images rushed. They did not form themselves into anything like the truth. 'Are you lying to me?' she asked.

'We were friends first, just talking.'

'You're not telling me this, really?'

'I said – I'm in love with her.'

'Sleeping with you? You've . . . been with her?'

'That's not what matters.'

'She's taking you away?'

She looked at her son and tried to imagine the woman she knew so well, with him, in bed with him, saying things to him while he lay there believing he was falling in love with her. She saw Tom's face and hands and they couldn't be touched by Gwen. She saw his face with all its earnestness and naïvety. His youth, that couldn't be touched by Gwen. There was a line in the world, between parents and children. Gwen was separated from him.

That sound drew louder as they sat there. Water – and sand, in its fall.

He remembered those feelings of freedom as he'd packed. He remembered two long, strange miles between. And those feelings must have lain there, like a trail still. They should rename this town, he thought. Like that would sever any sense of loss.

'You're in love with her?' his mum said. 'And you believe . . . she feels that for you. Gwen,' she said.

'I know she does.'

'You're a little kid then . . .' Siân said.

Gwen's face, and betrayal unseen, all this time unseen behind it. Emyr Morgan, like the background of that street, no longer real. It had been a lie for that woman to stand on her doorstep. Had she been silent there, lies would have been told. They had been, only when Gwen passed her on the road. It had been a betrayal for the woman to meet her gaze.

She looked at Tom and said quietly, 'You already have a mother.'

His mouth opened. But the words tripped, spattered out of him. 'That's not what it's like . . .'

'What's she been doing with you? What's she telling you? That she'll run away with you? She's been taking you to bed? And you've been trotting along, you've been hand in hand, little lamb after her? What are you trying to say to me, Tom? Doing this? This your slap in the face for me?' Her hands shook as she held them in stillness. 'You've proved nothing to me except that you're very young, and full of a lot of need . . .' Her face fell and her eyes fixed on the carpet. She saw Gwen, she saw a boy in Gwen's hands and he was her son.

'I don't want to prove anything to you.' Spoken, naked though, it sounded hollow. It shouldn't sound that way because it was true. He loved Gwen, independent of everything – everyone they knew. What they shared was protected – it was different.

'Who started it? Was it her, was it you that started it? What did you think, Tom? One in the eye for me? Did you?'

'You want to turn this round to be about you . . . ? You're so selfish! . . . See yourself in everything! She's nothing *like* you.'

Fear came up and bit a piece out of him, a blocking, blanked-out fear. He thought of making love to Gwen, when the edge of a dread had sometimes touched him like this. It would be tenderness he wanted. He would put himself inside her – feeling intrusive, feeling wrong. It would be tenderness, and sex with her wouldn't bring it. He'd never admitted, not at any point, that in some way he was afraid of making love to Gwen.

He shook his head as the muffled sound of machinery grew greater and in its volume, this room seemed to shrink. 'She's nothing like you, and you know why? Inside her, not everything's about herself . . . inside her, there's some honesty! She has beliefs, that mean something to her. She wouldn't drop them on the fucking ground just because a better chance came along!'

'You stupid fool. What do you think she's done? She's been married twenty years.'

Tom swallowed. Saw this. And rejected it.

'You think she didn't *believe* in that marriage?' she asked him, pictures of Emyr coming to her as she spoke – and of their wedding day, so long ago now, Tom's whole life ago – coming to her while she was unable to believe Gwen would even be unfaithful to her husband.

She did not know this woman. Siân's voice was cold but electricity ran underneath every word. 'It's a slight on me, I suppose: "drop them on the ground"–'

'She hasn't believed in her marriage, no,' he said. 'There was nothing in it for her to drop.'

'Unlike me? This the crime?' She held her hands out to this house

that, outside, could hardly be recognized. 'You look at her . . . and
you don't see my failings?' She nodded to herself but even while she
did so, her eyes were aging. 'I bet you're sick of seeing failings, they're
so stuck in your bloody eyes every time you look at me.'

'This has got nothing to do with you!'

The noise of his own voice left him empty.

'And don't, don't think,' he said, 'that what you've done is about
a fucking house . . . You dropped her. You heard what she did to
Dai, and you used it, to make the biggest fucking turnaround I've
ever seen in my *life*. It's not about a house! Everything that you've
ever said in your life, like. That's what you dropped! Everything
you ever told me.'

'And there's the crime,' Siân said quietly, seeing the separation both
their voices had already laid out. 'She's better than me, is she? You've
already *got* a mother, Tom,' she repeated, almost scornfully.

He stared at her. 'How would I have known that, the last two
years? She's not a fucking mother to me! But if I had needed one, I
tell you, I would've been fucked, wouldn't I? I wouldn't have known
where to look . . .'

'Because all you can see in me is the *fault!* Do you even *know* how
young you seem? Like a little boy, like a stupid, judgemental boy! I'd
love to know,' she said, 'what you would think of what I've been
through in the last twenty years. You don't know,' she said, 'you have
no clue what it's like, because you're a child. You go off with the one
you love. Now you imagine this, Tom. You go off with her, and you
start a life . . . you get yourself a home to have it in, and you get
yourself two babies to bring up with her there. Now imagine this,
Tom. Try to see,' she said, her expression becoming complex,
entangled as she held in all she could, 'try to see what it's like when
she dies. Because she dies. Very suddenly, it happens, so suddenly . . .
you don't know how to bridge the gap between the day before and
tomorrow. You look around you and there she is, in every little part
of your home and your life and it's impossible, it's just impossible,
that she can't be there any more. Because you love her . . . And you
have these kids. Try to see . . . Look at twenty years, bringing up

children that she never saw past childhood . . . have a good long look at that and tell me about the ways I've failed! Because I've failed, I know I have. I can see you telling me every day.'

He was crying but the things she said were not fair, the guilt. It had never been fair.

'Even when you talk now,' he said, 'you tell it like you feel it. You were stuck with me.'

He couldn't help himself, the child that had reared up last night in place of all his belief, hearing her asking him to come back home – he'd thought to make an adult out of that kid. That he could do it, and feel pride. But he couldn't help himself as he watched her face cramp up, bitterness and sadness, which she'd never spoken.

'And I can't believe you'd go through that,' he said, 'loneliness, like, and know how it feels . . . and for nearly two years, look at me, and see it, and do nothing.'

She shook her head, wordless, about to speak.

'I've been on my own out there! If you were so lonely too, why did you want me to go? Why did you see me every fucking week out there and not ask if I was OK? *Why'd you want me to go and live out there?*'

'You were seventeen! Not a plan in your head! I thought you'd want to . . . go on from there! I thought it would be a way for you to grow. You were, you are, you've always been this *mixture*. You want everything, and nothing satisfies you. You wanted to stay here and hang on and hang on . . . and you still couldn't stop judging me. This *mix-up*, Tom! You've got your hands out, asking, but you can't stop yourself from looking at me and seeing the wrongs! I thought it would be a way for you to grow!'

'I don't judge you . . .'

'You want to lie now?'

'Do you even see how much I've tried? Years, I've tried to live the way I thought . . . I thought was right by you! So yes, I'm a fucking child! And you've never even cared! I did everything I could to be what you'd *respect* . . . and you turned round, and you just dropped it all! Every rule . . . I tried to live by them! So don't you look – don't have that shocked look on your face – that I'd find somebody and love them because they really believe in the things you used to say!'

'That's what you think of her . . . ?' Threads, she seemed to try to catch, and she lost them all. 'She's said a thousand things, Tom. She's a person, my God. She's just the same as me . . . said a thousand things and then realized that they've just made her . . . made her unhappy. You don't think it's a crime for her to marry a man, to change her mind, to change everything? But it's a crime for me to change? It's always a crime for me.'

'You don't know her . . .' he said, 'and she's your best friend. You don't know me and I'm your son. You're hard to please! Do you *see* how you're hard to please? You had everything and it wasn't good enough for you. You judge! You're the one! If I've done it too then you know where I've learned it.'

The grind of mechanisms and the spill of their motors outside these boarded windows grew and ebbed, grew and ebbed like the sea outside. Yet for the first time, he felt a thousand miles from it. He'd never go back, to rescue anyone, or to try and live by this woman he saw in front of him, lonely and lost and still unable to reach out to him with an open hand. Roots he saw, that could only be cut.

'You had everything and you let it go. Because it wasn't good enough for you. Gwen never matched up to what she should. I never did it right. Tried and still couldn't do it right. You know why everything looks wrong to you? Because the world's been hard to you, and you think *everyone* should climb through the same shit . . . You built a wall, like, out of everything you were sad about, then you used it to measure everyone else against. And everyone else failed.'

Siân stared at him, silent in this room where boxes full of saucepans and dried foods were still stacked between the settees, where the television sat and looked out with its dull eye and the ornaments that were crammed on the shelves together waited for new months, when calm would come; redecoration maybe. She opened her mouth to speak but at that moment the noise that had been distant rose in full to strike against the stone of the house. In a road they couldn't see, the sandblasting had begun on these walls. Like a rain of stones it sounded. They looked at each other and could not have heard a spoken word. They could not have heard the footsteps – only six stairs, for she'd been waiting a long time, halfway down – as Stacey finished the short distance, coming to stand in the doorway.

He turned to see her there, a magazine hanging out of her hand. She had her hair down, and Tom had a moment, in this weather of noise, to think that it had grown longer. Different than when he'd last seen her. Another thought cast with the colour of leaving.

She turned to see one and then the other. He didn't know how much Stacey had heard. She only stood there for one short space of time, though, depression, blame on her face – and then turned away with a shake of her head, and left them alone again.

He looked at Siân. He could have spoken but she wouldn't have heard him. He could have told her again that he loved her. She stared back at him, and maybe she would've answered. Maybe she would have said the same in return and added nothing else.

Sand and water struck this house's face, as if the sea that he had swum out into a long time ago, trying to prove something, and once succeeding, rose itself now. He had left it behind. It came up while they stared at each other, and washed through the town. To reave the buildings, and leave them beautiful.

Lennie Lewis came home to a boarded house with no one living inside it.

He stood in the hallway, as he'd often done, with his coat in his hand. Once, there'd been a truck outside, these moments, and a lot of road behind. There was a town now, full of darkened work and final, grating noise. There was a road with boarded houses beside it and new lawns, green as the moon's cheese.

He listened and he did not hear them. He would walk through every room – though he stood motionless yet – and look inside to see that they weren't hiding. He would come down finally to the kitchen, with the knowledge that they'd gone to the woman who his wife now said she loved.

Perhaps they were kissing there, he'd think.

He'd think of killing. Images that held no bright colours in that instant, but were only banal, as it had been finally to strike Ruth, after two years of telling her that he loved her and seeing no love created with the words. As it had been before the project.

Outside, he would hear its sound. Falling lights wouldn't touch the rooms, because Garvey's men had secluded them. He would hear it, and love the sound of it, and wonder again how a love like that could fit with a world in which your wife left you for a woman. Despite its emptiness, he'd think of killing. He would go to the table, and there would find the letter.

Now, though, he only stood and looked at the hallway where once he'd picked her up and carried her over the threshold. He wondered if she'd taken bags, and if, as she had closed the door, the memory of her old man had returned.

Gwen had come to the museum in half-darkness. She'd had to leave the car and walk beside an impassable road. She'd looked at the boarded houses, looked at a crew of trucks which were replacing the street lamps; thin cranes and a clear sky fading to twilight. Seen the sandblasters. A growing noise had flooded Ynys-morlan's street, and it had come to her that she was leaving and that this sight – this crazy and impenetrable place – might be her last. The men were everywhere and vague, and all the buildings were blind. From somewhere she could hear the sound of sand-struck water on their stones.

Too strange to be an ending: standing here outside the museum's tall, wood-covered windows, looking at its door, unable to see a way inside. Too outlandish. Once upon a time this could not have been a part of her life. She was imagining Emyr's face. In her imagination, she was speaking Tom's name.

Behind her, tarpaulin and rope in gathering darkness covered the Lion's new wooden figurehead. If lights were being lit in there, you couldn't see. The café was faceless. New windows were hidden, and new floorboards behind, the oak counter and chrome stools beside it, small round tables like dancers across the room where the old ones had once been bolted down. And above, stained glass was covered. Bethan couldn't be made out there in the restaurant, arranging candles, unwrapping tablecloths and beginning to see what she had made.

Gwen stood, remembering the office door and not walking down the alleyway toward it. This building had been a garage once; repair shop. She remembered seeing photos: a tin sign hanging over a dusty road in a wind that would never catch it, a single pump and a vehicle beside it that would be called a classic now. After, in the Fifties and into the early Sixties, it had been a tiny cinema and theatre. Her mother had played parts in the productions there sometimes. Once, the role of Juliet. It was only the old exhibition of which Gwen held any image of her own, though: a high room of wood and dust, the town's early documentation unreadable under glass, a desk and chair, beside this door, where no one had sat in the years she could remember.

She walked through the tiny office into a very different place. The room was vaulted, white.

Things caught at Gwen's eyes as she saw him there: a wall of pictures beside which a stepladder stood, a strew of boxes, a profusion of them. Objects, strange objects in his hands. Things caught but dissipated, trailed from her, as she looked at Emyr's back. In the midst of it all, he bent over a cabinet. They lined the space in waist-high corridors. His shirt and tie were dishevelled, his hair wiped into little wafts, as it always was when he woke up. Like a small boy, she thought, as she often thought, making worlds with his toys that no one else could see. She stepped into the silence his hands had made in the hours since the builders had left.

Concentration, this solitude, had held him like deep water. He turned – thoughts of the boy, memories of last night – but it was Gwen that he saw in the doorway, and every memory he had. The discreet, inset lighting shone down on her face and cast no shadow, and he put down the things he held.

'What are you doing here?'

'I came to find you, to speak to you.'

'There have been a lot of nights when I've been at home. I'm working. I'm finishing something here. There are things, see, that I do.'

'I had to come now.'

He moved between her and the cases: dark wood and untouched glass. Those boxes were everywhere, she saw: multifarious bits of cloth for wrapping, polystyrene pieces that spotted the floor.

'Well then?'

But she said, 'The work's gone well here.'

Emyr looked down then raised his eyes again quietly, 'You've hardly spoken to me for the last week. You've hardly been at home to speak to me.'

'I know.'

'Tell me what you want to say then. Tell me, and leave me be.'

Irascible. She'd never heard him achieve full anger, she didn't think. Only that.

'I'm leaving, Emyr,' she said.

He blinked a little. His focus sharpened and then glazed again. Around them, silence moved, and the periphery of the work's noise. It slipped across glass. Thirty cabinets.

What were you to believe in?

Lennie walked the rooms. From the hallway, where the furniture had been replaced. Tomorrow it would look just like this. Tomorrow or the day after that, or any day, or any evening. Ruth was gone for good. He could smell it in the air. Her house had been abandoned.

Past the kitchen, where the letter lay, unread, unseen. He walked the staircase that had been bare for weeks now, untacked and rolled and stored by him when the project had begun. She would sell the house, out from under him. He felt the floorboards buckle and slip away and he was standing on air. What was he to believe in? The story she'd told him as they'd sat on these wooden steps, it breathed here now. Ruth had been crying. Yes, he could hear that. In the muffled scrape and groan of the blast-cleaning in the road, you could hear anything. She'd kissed Charlotte Weyland. She'd kissed her first. To ruin everything, she had said.

He came to his daughter's bedroom door and, after a moment, passed it by. Should he think about things like 'access' now, like 'custody'? Moving through the age-warped, cottage corridor, he imagined a courtroom, which he'd never seen, a judge in battle dress. He tasted the word *lesbian* and opened his mouth to let it fall down to the floor a hundred times. He opened their own bedroom door.

He saw himself and Ruth in bed there. Saw himself, and he was kissing the side of her face. There were apologies, there was devotion in his kisses. He saw himself holding her and stroking her hair after they'd made love – in him there was a care that had felt, after the shit had first begun, after the first times shouts had turned to bruises, so desperate and perfect that it had seemed to lie like the salt of perspiration on his skin.

What he had done to her, three years of their marriage, was a bad crime. He'd known it every moment that they'd lived it, but he knew it intimately now, after the months she'd spent telling him, intimately. What he'd done to her was a river, blocked and forced from its course till it ravaged the ground, made it useless.

Had she stood here tonight before leaving? Maybe she'd just run. He knew where Charlotte Weyland's house was. Easy route, a mile, no more, to ask these questions.

What was he to believe in? A misguided river. Three years. A head full of stories and vividness; a life full of motorways and a hometown to come back to that looked closer to death every day.

He'd told her. Ynys-morlan's dying, he'd said.

She'd waved a wand. Charlotte Weyland's.

There was a plywood view through the window, that made a perfect mirror.

Did you say water was an evil thing because it flooded and drowned? The project and the way that it had changed Ruth had made those stories into life. Since the night that she'd told him to hit her, and he'd hit her, there'd been no violence in him. His hands had been full of renovation work, regenerating, rebuilding. He'd taken structures that his old man had built – down to their bones, and seen the little marks once put there. He'd remade parts of this town himself. He'd come all those miles, and reached the shore.

Had she thought of good endings, standing here today?

After three years of being in pain, put there, by the man she'd chosen to marry, Ruth Lewis had packed maybe one bag and had taken her daughter, to go to the house of a woman she believed she loved. He would have liked to have sat with his old man and told him the story. He might've cried – could not imagine crying now. He might have asked how it could be.

Hate from Ruth, he understood. That she would leave him, though. He'd seen in recent weeks how they'd shared each other for the first time. They'd taken a pound of flesh from each other and exchanged them and in the moments, quiet moments after – she'd been crying or he had – then they'd partaken of each other. Comprehended.

Lennie thought about weapons. He thought about prison, about the future, as outside the sandblasters made their slow way down the street, eventually to reach this house. He could even understand that she'd leave. If comprehending wasn't enough for her to heal the scars he'd given. The project's single spring had been a season of growth and breaking. Perhaps it had been too much for her to heal in, though she had brought it on. Yes, that he could've understood.

But this was the truth: as they'd been sharing those moments, she'd had a woman in her heart and in her thoughts of sex. When he'd been out there in the street that was hidden by these boards now, putting into the foundations of the place every regret and passion she gave him, she'd been taking her clothes off with that woman. They'd been giving each other pleasure.

The project's Ynys-morlan had been a place of fractured rock and beauty. He'd finally realized. He'd seen how love – a love he'd always believed in – was made, not just of good things but of sadness. It was grim and great. He'd finally realized: what it was his father's face had always held.

And while he'd felt this, Ruth hadn't been there, in the place he'd come to love like he'd always believed that he could. No, she had been living in a separate world.

The room was hollow. The room was naked. It looked like it was already for sale.

Lennie thought about the kid as he closed the bedroom door and the deafness that had been – what? – an easier thing? Than attempts to connect? Yes. He'd felt trapped for three years. In the last months, he'd looked at Nia and loved her. Needed her, in a way that he'd never imagined. He'd seen a future. Now, he must see that differently.

He walked the rooms and looked for them when he knew they weren't here. To Nia's room. The ever-closed, thankful door.

He opened it and looked inside.

She had gone down to the garden. There, where her mum's rose bushes had been and were no longer, where the green green grass of home lay instead, she had bent over on the path. Turf like a carpet. She'd pulled it up by the corner and put her hands into wet ground, had churned them there. She'd gone back through this hall that seemed empty to Lennie – but it had been full to her. Up the staircase that lay at his back now, ready to catch him if he should fall. She'd put her own palmprints on to the walls.

A lot of times.

Perhaps a hundred. Maybe one for every time that he'd hit her and this door had been shut. What a funny sight to see: out there on the path as the evening began with a clear sky. While the night's work crews started and the street-lamp replacement cranes slid into that high air. A woman bent over the peeled corner of a lawn, muddying her hands there, like she was washing them.

Lennie turned and stumbled on the stairs. He opened the door to the lounge, to see its normality and nothing more; the chaos of every empty room. He opened up the study that had been his. He went to the kitchen door – a look he was not aware of, of fear, on his face – and there, as he set it to opening, he saw the letter. Lying calmly on the table, as he walked in with slower feet.

Behind them, Emyr and Gwen's home was vacant: a hundred nights in the quiet dark that must have lain there now.

Did she feel a wrench? She'd loved the place once, each tiny part in its own specific way. It was just that it had never made her happy. It was just that she had always seen the spaces in between. She had used it wrongly.

Leaving. Emyr watched her say it, took in the words gradually. He saw all those little differences in her, which together made the end of them: how her stance had changed and the look inside her eyes. For the first time since he'd closed the door behind the builders, the project left him.

'When?' he said.

'I've taken a hotel room.'

'Now.'

'Now,' she told him, 'yes.'

It couldn't come like this, surely. With only a few words, with no weeks in which to try and heal the rifts, no weeks for final pleading. Would he have pleaded with her? He didn't know any more.

They looked at each other and neither was crying. It left her bereft, that eighteen years should come to that. There must be a thousand things that they hadn't said; must be, for she had known him once and could not feel it now.

'Why?' he said.

'You know why. Months . . .'

'That's not why.' How he'd asked her these last nights, and

how the silence had been drawn across her face in the same lines that had once made her pious. 'You're leaving because you've found someone to go with. Isn't that the truth? Isn't it? When did you both decide?' he said. He heard the accusations come from him before he could even feel anything. 'You waited, to tell me? Till the last possible moment.' Hearing it, and blank inside, this room did not seem real.

'No – I didn't wait. I wouldn't do that. I decided today.'

'Tell me,' he said.

'Emyr –'

But his expression was void, no resentment or self-punishment, only realization as he asked her again. 'He's young, isn't he? He's the same boy. He's "the kiss".'

She mouthed something soundless and then looked down.

'Well don't be ashamed, Gwen. If you're leaving with him, you can't feel that way.'

She raised her eyes.

'Yes, he's young. He's eighteen. He's eighteen years old and we're going to a hotel, tonight. Is that what you want me to say?'

The words came out and lay bare. She listened to them and couldn't believe that they were hers. Emyr looked at her and she saw the shame of it, which had once, that first night, made her run from Tom's place back to her home and pick up every thread like she could hold them together around the hole that kiss had made.

'I came to tell you, Emyr, but I don't know what to say . . .' She remembered today's tender afternoon, visions of a sunlit somewhere, a place where she would be freer than she'd been here. 'What should I say? Should I tell you I'm sorry?'

He gritted his jaw. 'Don't say that, no. It's your choice. I don't think I need that.'

She only nodded, watched him.

'So you tell me, he's eighteen years old? You tell me how that happened, Gwen. You tell me, how you can do that. And live with yourself. You're a funny person. You're a funny, lie of a person. Do you know that? Do you see yourself?'

'Yes.'

It had come out of her, and now she must be leaving, because there was no way back.

'You tell me how you can sleep with an eighteen-year-old boy. Doesn't it . . . make you feel like you're wishing yourself into a fantasy land, doesn't it –' Emyr broke off. He cleared his throat. He shook his head and she saw tears then, behind his glasses, like ice in this light. 'You're leaving.'

'I'm going away . . .'

'And where?' he asked, as Siân had done. And Gwen had no better answer for Emyr.

'I don't know yet . . .'

He barked a laugh. In this calm room, it echoed strangely. 'You're leaving me. Well, who would have thought? These last months maybe, you know, I could have told, that it would happen. But before, eh? Who would've imagined it? Not me.'

'Not me either.'

'For a child.'

'Not a –'

'Fucks like an adult though, does he?' He turned his face away and hid from her what was happening there. He pushed a hand out, like that could wipe it away, and he had never said it. 'You want that, do you? A boy? And he wants you, now. At forty. He wants you.'

'He wants me . . .' Beginnings, she had thought of. She couldn't push her imagination past them, because there was nothing past them. She stared at Emyr and the emptiness filled her, the fears which, when she was lying with Tom, seemed not to matter. When she was alone? Far later? Would it matter then?

'You're a fool,' he said.

'Maybe, yes.'

'You're an adulterer.' It seemed like a tragic, comic, old-fashioned word as he said it – and why not? To her he was old-fashioned. To her he was old news. Emyr looked at Gwen, memories of the night that he'd passed here and of the boy's face, grey in the torchlight, were painted in his gaze it seemed. The museum's exhibits surrounded him like a gathering of silences; these boxes, which she had not yet really seen.

'You won't stay to see it finished even.'

'No, I won't.'

'What happened to you?' he said.

'Everything . . . fell apart.'

'That's strange, because I was there. You broke it, I think. Everything, you broke it.'

She remembered the night, when she'd still thought of this town as hers, standing in Eirian Meredith's house and hearing again the words the woman had said, which could never be taken back. She had died. She couldn't apologize, or explain.

'Everything just fell apart . . .' she said. She remembered standing on the beach before Tom had been there, thinking to herself that it was the middle of the night and she had not seen that time for years. 'There were things . . .' she tried to tell him slowly, to tell herself perhaps, for the first time. She couldn't understand how the ground had split to leave her life in halves. 'There were things that people had said to me. A lot of – cruel things. You know I was used to that. I've heard the jokes, heard all the little stories . . . second hand. For a long time, used to drive me on. For a long time, I thought, jealousy – and then there was a night. I don't know, Emyr. I don't know . . . There was a night when I listened to them all again, thought of them, and they all seemed true . . .'

He saw her and was blank, unbelieving. Even now.

'I didn't feel any different, than any day. But I was crying, I couldn't stop it.' She shrugged a little. 'I was sad . . . just the same as any day.'

There was bitterness in his eyes then, and acceptance. 'I wasn't sad,' he said.

'I felt a loss, Emyr, you don't know what that's like? I looked at myself . . . and I was old,' she said simply. Cold humour. 'I looked at myself and I was old and there were a lot of things . . . I'd never felt.'

'Never felt.'

'No.'

'And do you feel them now?'

What could she tell him? That she did? That, when she lay with Tom or even sat and spoke with him, she could believe in possibilities? Could she tell him yes, and that she was scared those hopes were lies? She had to chase them.

He saw it all, and she needed to tell him nothing. He saw a thousand days when he'd given her kindness and support, when she'd been angry or embittered or alone, and he had gone to her. He'd held her and told her he loved her. He saw the feelings written all over her, which that kind of care had never brought her. It was clear as anything. And yet he asked her, asked her again. 'You feel them now?'

'Yes,' she said. 'Yes, Emyr, I do. I'm sorry . . .'

'Sorry for what? Sorry for feeling it? Or sorry for sleeping with him? Sorry that you were lying to me, saying you loved me? Sorry you wouldn't tell me where you'd been or . . . which, Gwen? Sorry for everything . . .'

She nodded.

'What a sickening thing to be told,' he said. 'That your wife is sorry for her marriage to you. What a worthless thing.' He nodded to himself, turned away in the museum's bland and perfect lighting. Looked for a moment at the wall which would be white by tomorrow, and then away from that as well, as its colours filled his eyes and merged together.

She hadn't really noticed it, or anything that was here.

'Maybe I made the wrong decision a long time ago,' she said, 'before we even met – maybe I should have known better than to start out on the road.'

'Of what, Gwen? The road of what?'

She couldn't answer him.

'Your life? You made it, woman. You spent years making it, my God, every little part of it. And you tell me now, what? It was wrong?'

'A fool, Emyr. Isn't that what you said?'

'A lie of a person, I said.'

He turned around to see her again, and wanted not to recognize her, but knew every line. So well that each new change was a fault in the look of her.

'There was a time, we would've been doing this together. Stupid to talk about that, I suppose. Say it anyway. Why not? We would've worked late, gone home, you know . . . we would've sat and talked about it all in bed. Tomorrow morning, driven down here. Maybe walked, you know? Seen it finished . . .'

She tried to imagine that. She was glad, glad it was no longer her.

And he said, 'I look at you, and I can't even see a tug. No regret . . . no regret in your face. Don't even know how that can be. You don't understand, Gwen, do you? What I – what I'm even trying to say. Try to see it,' he said. 'You love someone and you're happy with someone . . . two decades. How about that? A whole life. And you're getting old? You think you're the only one? I look in the mirror, Gwen. Face of a man there . . . who's not just *old* . . . but being left behind. And I hate him. For being so weak as to . . . keep with you, keep loving you. I wish I'd never made myself into him – and if I had the chance to do it all again . . . marry you, just exactly the same? I still would. I still would.' He looked at her as if he couldn't understand himself.

Gwen saw that man he spoke of and she was sorry.

'I believed in us,' he said. 'But to you, it was something . . . to grow out of one day.'

She wanted to deny it but she'd come too far to lie to him. Had come with only one reason – to tell the truth. It seemed, the hardness of it, like she must never have done an honest thing before.

'You were never in love with me.'

'I still . . . love you.'

'No!'

He shouted without warning, and small filaments rose in Gwen, of fear, for she'd never seen that look before.

'Don't you say that! You want to coddle me? You were never in love with me! You weren't capable.'

'Maybe not . . .'

'You were too dried up with yourself and your life and all your *work*, your *work*, you couldn't have been in love with anybody! You didn't have the space in your *schedule*. Isn't that the truth?' He stared out at her and hurt her though he didn't want to. 'Don't think that I'm so naïve, not to understand why you were with me! There were a lot of opportunities it gave you.'

It came with a wrench – she saw it. He'd told her the same before but never with such hatred. And she had to ask herself if it was true. The answer left her naked, and afraid. She remembered what he had asked her at this project's outset: to prove her ambitions had ever been for anything more than her own sake.

How could you explain, that ambitions like those weren't a search for satisfaction? But in a way, for unhappiness. How could she explain that, for the longest time, she'd felt some purity, some kind of triumph, in the emptiness of walking always and never reaching any goal.

'Emyr,' she said, 'I always . . . appreciated . . . the support and the love and kindness . . . I appreciated you.'

He looked at her vacuously. 'What a word,' he said.

'The work we did together . . .'

'Yes, the work.'

Standing in between the half-filled cabinets, where other people's memories gathered together, and together made something that didn't seem lost, his eyes wandered. Over glass and through it.

A memorial, he remembered.

'You're the first person to see this,' he said. 'You know that?'

She looked around slightly, she recognized the things which had arrived at their home every day during the last few weeks. Their address repeated over and over in different hands, she saw. She had asked him and had not been told. She saw the cabinets.

Little ornaments, she saw, letters, soft shock coming up in her as she realized what this exhibition was – and turned to him again.

'These are from people in town . . . ? This is the collection?'

'They're contributions.' It lay all around him, defenceless. 'People have sent them for the last month or so. If they didn't understand at first, didn't like the idea . . .' He nodded.

He watched her move closer to the glass.

'This is what you've been doing.'

Emyr wanted her to understand. She would look over what he'd made. It's beautiful, she would say. And she'd be saddened, terribly saddened by it.

Her eyes were pale and distant. There were photographs.

Lying on dark-grey velvet, they were carefully spaced; Gwen saw faces she knew. Pictures perhaps thirty years old: a couple standing on the doorstep of a house which no longer existed outside. There were letters. She went with slow feet towards a cabinet. The 29th of *March*, she saw, *Dear Claire, I'm so happy the move has gone well and you're enjoying the new house. Things are the same as always here.* Twenty years old. It must have been. She stopped, a hand on the glass, as she came to stand over a fan of prints. Images of old movie stars.

She looked up at Emyr and he looked back without speaking, readiness in his face.

'They're from the café.'

'Pat brought them round today.'

'Why? Why did she bring them round? What kind of exhibition – ?'

Gwen looked down at the prints again then and she saw it. Smaller beside them, a photograph in which she stood herself. She stood, married for the first day. She stood with her two oldest friends beside her, though they didn't look so old.

She went to speak and didn't speak.

'What do you think?' he said.

They looked alone and lost, like they'd drawn together under the bald light for company. She tried to imagine Patty's thoughts, bringing these here; couldn't understand what it might've been underneath the bright, defiant person she knew so well, that would *give* this away, give out, and let go of these possessions.

It reached into Gwen as she looked down at them, to touch thoughts of Tom and the change she'd come here to make – to show a past which would not change.

'What do you think?' he asked her again.

She turned. 'It's . . . it's very sad.'

'I've been sad recently.'

'I don't understand . . . why you've done it.'

'What does it look like?'

One cabinet had been given over entirely to a dress, that, laid out in this way, seemed like Sleeping Beauty, gone.

Emyr had found the box that afternoon, left outside the museum's door.

There was a miniature house made from seashells, that she recognized, that brought dusty memories, but that she could not place.

'It looks . . . it looks morbid to me, Emyr,' she said.

As her friend had at first. 'It's a memorial,' he said. 'There's nothing morbid about memory . . . Why should so much change, and not be remembered?' Patty had changed her mind.

Gwen looked around at the place where he'd been in the hours when she'd left their house empty. She saw clearly for the first time the wall on her left-hand side and some small confusion passed over her face as he watched her.

So immersed in what she'd come to say, she hadn't been aware of it.

A crowd of pictures, a deluge of them. Colours that dripped down and through them, words, swear words that clung between.

'That'll be gone by tomorrow,' he said.

She turned to him and opened her mouth to ask him who had done it and why, but the question didn't come, or anything else, because Gwen saw the boxes that lay between the cabinets where he'd been working when she'd walked in. The hallway in their house was empty. She saw her missing things.

Like little pieces of their last heartbroken weeks together: realization gathered. It rose and it formed the shape of this museum, and she saw it, what this exhibition was.

Her gaze tugged towards him.

'No . . .'

Had she meant it to come strongly? It was lost in the quiet. She tried to clear her throat.

'No,' she said. 'Put them back. They're not yours.'

He watched that realization. The place had been weeks in the making, but the concept had grown far more slowly, reached far further back. Emyr's face was devoid of any expression, because all he felt was scattered here.

'Put them back, Emyr!'

He didn't answer her. He was crying a bit, motionless, soundless.

'You've got no right! My God, what are you doing here . . . ? What is this place? You can't put my things in a museum! What's *wrong* with you . . . ?'

The tears came on. He opened his mouth but had no answer that wasn't already lying in the silence here. All he had left was this. A memorial, but not for her. Just for him, and for these other people, everyone who would come and see their own past and their neighbours'. A lot would come, strangers would. It was full of sweetness and sorrow and loss. In every contributor's face he had found these things, and none of them had even seen it completed yet.

He remembered the boy Rhys, in the darkness. He remembered the moment when he had finally got down, and knowing the boy would never tell. Some change had come, with no one here to see it but them, some chemistry in this empty room. He'd thought of Gwen, and of this project. The balance had finally tipped.

He hadn't wanted the boy's name any more. He'd seen himself and, kneeling, had admitted.

Gwen looked at him.

She suddenly saw someone – who had fallen so far away from her that she could no longer understand him. Yet she saw everything she knew. The little boy, the man, with his endless quiet concentration and the tiny reverent place it would make. Gwen thought of the steam engines which still stood on their shelves. The chief planning officer and the mayor, she saw. All the funny pomp and self-belief in that. A lifetime working on Ynys-morlan she saw.

She didn't glance around her again. She saw the product of all these familiarities. But turned to stone, like things in fairy tales, left alone for centuries.

'What are you doing here? What do you mean to say by this?'

'It's a memorial.' He had no other word. He would have liked to describe it to her so clearly that the pictures it conjured in him would touch her too, reach up in her and let her know how he had felt, not just for months, but for years. 'A tribute . . .'

'It's awful, Emyr. It's . . . it's a funeral. You've been unhappy? You want to dig your heels in and . . . *engrave* that here? It's self-absorption . . . it's . . . masochism.'

He swallowed tightly, to hear those words. He searched in his throat and heart for the way to show her.

'What do you mean it to say . . . ?'

She was leaving, and he'd have no other chance.

'I mean it . . . as a way to describe . . . I started it, it began . . .' He looked at her and now images of their home rose, how she had slowly purged it of personal effects. And he'd felt no loss. 'It was a way of describing what it's like to be with you,' he said.

Gwen uttered quietly, 'Wallowing . . .'

'It's a way of describing what it's like to love someone who's committed . . . to doing good work. Someone who has a vision, that takes up everything, so that they don't see you. Every day, they wake up and the first thing, you can see it, the first thing and the only thing they think of is what they need to do.' Every morning, he'd been left there. 'Somebody who's only with you because it facilitates what they need . . . And you don't care, because you love their goals. You love the fact that they want to make the world better, even if it's just the little place where they live. And you love . . . how they do it. That drive, that leaves you on your own every day . . . you love it in them.'

She saw their bedroom and the apricot air, she remembered plans laid out across their table in the kitchen; thought of them now as though some map had always lain there, a chart of this, and she had never seen it.

'It's an empty thing, that feeling. You didn't see me? Didn't matter. You realize that? I love this town . . . I love it, maybe even more than you. To see you working for it, to live like that . . . it's an empty, beautiful thing. It's a sacrifice,' he said.

He could see how strange it sounded to her, and the tiny reflections in her eyes of the things she recognized. She looked at him with that recognition, and incomprehension, blending together there like the colours of a sky.

'Saw you packing everything away. You've got a . . . strength, always have had. You could do it, lose everything, get rid of it all to get back . . . get back to the way you used to be. I watched you, I thought . . . remembering what mattered. All your goals.'

She looked at him, the questions recurring, as he'd asked her to prove, that morning at the project's outset, that those goals were selfless. It came to her that it had mattered to Emyr more even than it had to her.

And she'd believed she was doing just that, ridding herself of success's little pay-offs. For a while there'd been that composure, a purity inside her. Whatever they'd shared before, for a while, it had re-grown. Not love, but together they had made some whole.

'I went round. Door to door, you know. I wanted to build a collection which would . . . go around your things. I'd decided to take them . . .' Guilt crossed his face and it was smoothed away. Perhaps it was more, perhaps it was shame. 'I asked for contributions and they came. Slowly. People saw what it meant. A centrepiece. A project like this, it deserves a centrepiece. It ought to have something to hold the meaning of the whole project.' He thought of Dai. 'The era,' he said. 'And to me – this whole project ought to have been ours. You know that,' he said.

She looked at him, wordless.

He held his hand out to the cases. 'It's meant to look . . . futile. They're meant to be lost, all these things. They're beautiful that way. They're sacrifices . . . I can't describe it.' He presented them to her again, gesturing: all the elegant cabinets that gave them context. And knowing the words he used were incoherent, needing her to have some kind of understanding anyway, he said, 'Like a church. Loving someone like you. It's inside me, reaches up. It's untainted . . . it's . . . unfilled, like a church. I wanted to make something, to describe it.'

'And all this?' Gwen said. 'Everyone's things? What does it mean to them, Emyr? Or is it only for you?'

'Everyone here has lost something. We've rebuilt this town. We've remade it. We've all got a past . . . that we can't touch any more. It's about building, Gwen – outside, it's about building. And in here, it's about what's been left behind.'

The room's quiet was delineated by the muted sound of that blast-cleaning. They held each other's gazes, bisected.

Someone had once said that love was not to stare rapt at one another but to look in the same direction. There'd been a time when they'd looked far. They'd not been able to walk the distance. And Gwen saw the difference between them now, drawn clearly with these hundred little, lost things.

'It's wrong, that you should be like this, Emyr. I'm sorry . . . I'm sorry.'

'No. You belittle it.'

'It wasn't goodness,' she said. 'I never . . . tried to improve anything, except myself, I think.'

'Not even love,' he said. 'It wasn't even loving this place.'

'Not even that.'

'Not goodness.'

How she had told him, he remembered, that what he planned to do with Dai's statue showed beyond doubt that he cared nothing for right or wrong, just as she didn't.

'I've been sleeping . . . I've been going to a boy young enough to be my son. I've been letting him . . . fall for me. Disconnected, he is, from everything. Family and friends his own age. And I've asked him to leave with me, and he's said yes.'

He didn't want to know but he let the words trickle from her because his own mouth was hollow and he could find no way to stop her. The boy had had no face to him, no family or past. You couldn't grieve that way. Even feel anger. Maybe it was better.

'No,' he said, 'you were never a good person. And I believed . . . that you were noble. I kept thinking . . . you went off, kissed him, this boy. You wouldn't . . . you wouldn't save the place where we were married, when you only had to . . . only had to tell people what you really thought about the demolition. Let them think whatever they wanted about our marriage . . . tell them, and know you were proving something to me. That what we had was more important than their *ideas* of what we had. You went to Dai,' he said, as she listened without answering. 'You went and you slapped him in the face rather than let anyone know I'd arranged it without your knowledge. And I kept on believing . . .' He gave a laugh with nothing in it but his exhaled breath, 'I kept believing.'

She was silent.

'Do you know what love is to me?' he said. 'I had great respect . . . great, for you. But I see now, what I respected was a lie. For me as well. Love is security . . . It's . . . safety, you know? Love is being held . . .' he said. 'It's no different than Dai. Did he ever talk to you? Did he ever tell you about his "Time"? Love is looking at someone, or looking up at the sky . . . and seeing something more important than yourself.' The shadows left his eyes for a moment and he was only seeing her, seeing someone he had needed. Who, for a while, had been his. 'That's what you want. Smallness. That's how it feels and I stayed – I stayed with you. I loved it,' he said. 'I thrived on it.'

'That's what you think . . . ?'

'I listened to him talk about it once. We sat . . . in the morning, it was. He told me everything he thought. He told me . . . that his mother had died for a reason. He told me that the reason was this project. "Time's come here," he said. It was . . . the sweetest thing. It was the sweetest, saddest thing. Beautiful, you know? And such a lie. Such a great big lie he managed to cover everything in the world with it.' A grey defeat was drawn on Emyr's face as he thought of the last week when he'd battled with the need he felt to knock down what Dai had made. 'Look at his sculpture,' he said, 'and you see it. His great belief, his Time. A stack of rubble. It was the sweetest thing, hearing him describe it, and it was sickly. Convincing himself. He would've given anything he had, everything . . . and he would've felt his *love* for "It" more strongly – would've felt his *connection* to it grow. Beauty in being small. You know, Gwen? Do you even understand?'

Gwen gazed out at him. Perhaps she'd always known these things. Maybe you knew, waking up with someone, eating, reading with them, the close things that they did not know themselves. Maybe the knowledge came slow in you, like a tide filling footsteps in the sand.

She shook her head slowly. She said, 'You want to knock it down . . .'

'What does it mean, Gwen? You tell me! You look around this town. Go and take a look because you're leaving! It should have been ours, and well, it wasn't. Only mine. Only my memorial. What am I remembering? Not a lifetime loving someone because they were driven to do good. A lifetime,' he said finally, 'of loving someone, only because they were driven.' A few steps from her, rumpled, middle-aged, he stood. His eyes were baleful. Something was visible in him that had never been, and he seemed to hold it out. 'What's the sacrifice then . . . ?'

She had nothing to answer him with.

'It's not for any good reason. It's only because . . . because the sacrifice feels good.' His expression lost solidity, there was just this grief in his face. 'Releases you from everything because it makes you feel . . . safe.'

What he described, what was embodied here – a piercingly calm room with beautiful, untouchable exhibits – it was not so distant, she realized, to what she had felt for years now. Married, living together, they had fitted without a line.

The air here was empty, full of clarity, as it had been on that recent spring day. The noise of machinery on the other side of these walls, it moved like a breeze across the glass.

'What's the sacrifice then?' he said,

'It's some kind of . . . it's some kind of stupid asceticism,' she answered. 'That means nothing.'

'Yes.'

They stood between the cabinets. The strangest picture, they must have made. As the sandblasting outside this room took away the last remnants of the place she'd known, as the street lamps out there were replaced, and boards taken down from clean houses, their two lives lay here, unpicked and arranged to be viewed.

She'd taken them down from the curtain hooks and the mantelpiece. He had put glass covers over them, and invited everyone to contribute; he had designed a plaque so that visitors would know the meaning.

'I came to tell you, because you asked me, if you want to know . . . who I'm leaving with,' she said to him.

Beside, unseen by her amid the other pictures, Emyr was kneeling down and he was begging for the name. Some chemistry had occurred when this room had had no lights on, though. Confusions had grown simple. He'd cared for the name no longer. He had knelt.

There was a simplicity. It reached up through you, as a church's windows would.

'You know how Dai used to talk? You remember? He changed so much, like . . . so much, and I don't think anyone saw it. Used to tell people all the time: "I don't know about that, don't really know about it." You do that, I think . . . when you don't believe that the person you're talking to can understand what's really in your mind.'

'Do you want me to tell you, Emyr?' she asked again.

'I don't know,' he said. 'I don't really know about that.'

There was a feeling – not love maybe but so close. Of giving up everything, watching it dissipate, as though it touched something up there which you could never see. There was a safety. At its farthest horizons, it was some kind of reverence. At its closest, just devotion. Just that.

'I came here to do it,' she tried to say, 'to be honest with you. For us to be honest, between us.'

'I don't really know,' he told her.

He thought of this eighteen-year-old man and wondered who he was. Not in the name but in everything under it. He missed Gwen in every part of his life, in all the simple things. He would go to bed and she would not be there. He wondered if this eighteen-year-old man could ever know her the way that he did now.

'I want to tell you!' she said. 'Do you want to know?'

He cried two tears, that ran and left his face, and then he didn't cry again.

She saw him as if he was fading. His shirt and tie a useless mess, understanding in his eyes, which had never been there, as if he'd always remain in this room.

'Don't really know about that,' he said quietly.

He made no point with his voice, there was only sadness. When the person you were talking to wouldn't understand, he had said, or when you were scared they wouldn't.

She knew she did, though. Very deeply. Very well.

And so she didn't tell him. She left Emyr. Slipped out through the side door, and out of their life together. She left the museum, without uttering Tom's name – or anything more about him than that he made her feel like she needn't always be the person she'd been before. She left her boxes of things. To be seen in cabinets, if she and they were to go separate ways, and that was what lay ahead for them.

She came to the alleyway's tiny exit and stood there, seeing Glen Partington's house, the one that had been Mrs Pryce's, seeing Siân's. They were illuminated by a warning bulb's flashes. They were invisible and then they were dark shapes. She saw the light spill out from the windows of houses far down this road, that were clean, men crawling over their blurred shapes to take down the first of the boards. She pressed her hands against her cheeks as she saw all this, surreal and unfathomable. One under each eye, to block tears.

And he looked over the museum's room, once it was empty of her. He looked at the workmanship – of the highest calibre. He looked at the various things that people had donated. It had been an incredible thing, this project. It was an opportunity that came once in a lucky man's lifetime. Throughout all the unhappiness of the last autumn and winter with his wife, he believed that he had seized it.

He sat down on the floor and went through the boxes again, to pick out the important things; not special things in particular. Some of them very ordinary, some beautiful or sad. The sadness that Emyr felt, though it seemed inescapable as that light shone on down and the sandblasters' water finally struck against the building, it was not quite so. He'd lost Gwen, but then really he had lost her a long time ago. Maybe just a season. Maybe years. It was himself that he felt grief over, and the things that he'd discovered inside. Because he loved the project, just as he'd loved her, just exactly the same. And if, in the last months, it had called for some kind of sacrifice, he would have given it – whatever.

But what he had made here was a eulogy. The town would go on. The advertisements would be seen here and there in the broadsheets where they'd been booked. People would come, to visit or to buy – a little house by the seashore, amid heritage. But it was a memorial. For him, it was. He had written an ending, in this beautifully crafted, discreetly lit room. It was a memorial, but now he didn't want it to die.

This was what Bethan saw: boards removed from the other side of the stained glass. Wide round tables that fanned across the space of this room that had once been three. The ill-defined face of a man. Through the glass, he was red. Through the glass, there was the slow revolution of alarm lights, as his arms reached. Balanced high on a ladder she couldn't see. There was the muffled crash of that thin board, falling.

She saw the candles that she would blow out in a moment, flickering their reflections in the multicoloured window as if the flames were caught underwater. Behind her was the black lacquer bar that, on her drawings, had been filled in with Chelsea's pencils. Reflections on its sides as well, like it was still a drawing and the faulty patches of her colouring-in had been transferred unchanged.

This was what she saw as she put her coat on: the planes of that man's face, made bizarre, unrecognizable. A room that had succeeded in every way she'd meant it to; that had grown more real and beautiful as she'd been falling with Dai. It had lost none of the vividness it had had in her imagination. She'd thought only lack of experience gave that vividness. It had been the old Ynys-morlan, though, its familiar shops, its pebbledash and boredom, its normality, that had been innocent.

This room was beautiful because she'd never seen it before. A first time, as her night with Dai had been.

Bethan blew the candles out. Years she saw, in the sudden darkness, when she'd been cynical, dead-feeling – and innocent.

She felt afraid now. She never would have, before. She felt vulnerable. The last time she remembered feeling that, she'd been standing and staring into the mirror at a body that didn't look pregnant. Imagining an abortion and all the opportunities, the hundred thousand million incredible opportunities that had awaited her after one.

She felt exposed, walking to the restaurant's stairs and down. Unprotected, as she saw the board taken from the front door – it left a square of night in its small window. She felt hope – that was the weak spot – as she turned and viewed the room, its little bistro tables, and left a straight smile behind, the sea ahead.

Rhys waited there.

Wouldn't have come, if not for Tom. Wouldn't have spent a single minute outside of his folks' house till he walked to the bus and caught it out of here.

Rhys stood and looked at the black sea as machinery overran Ynys-morlan's street behind, waiting to say goodbye to the friend who was finally leaving before him. He could not shake off, let fall on these stones he saw, what he'd done to Emyr Morgan.

The stars were bitter. He wasn't crying any more, though water and salt and sand ran in streams down the faces of these buildings.

He was holding images, very close to him: some past, some town, some place. It was full of life there. Transcendence. He'd never known it, but perhaps the Ynys-morlan where he'd grown up had been a bridge back – and he'd not realized.

The last remnants were blasted from the buildings. He didn't turn. Didn't glance.

Tom would come very soon and Bethan too. So that he could look in her face and see reflections of what he'd proven last night: there was nothing but hate to leave behind him.

Some old harbour, Rhys imagined. Some history. It was the craziest thing, the last night of this project. The craziest thing, to see the town you knew boarded, and to feel grief – though you knew you'd hated them – to feel grief, for nothing but houses.

Ynys-morlan was gradually, grindingly completed under the mask of night, and many of its inhabitants were going away. Gwen was walking the road, edging past men who looked at her as if she was the stranger here. Between the two gatherings of machines, the clear stretch of the street a dry seabed between them, she had to stop and to wait her steps in the moments when the warning lights didn't fall.

Perhaps ten yards from the café, where light now unfolded on to the pavement, trailed in colours from above, she came across

Bethan. Perhaps in the unsteady illumination, Bethan couldn't see her face.

Because her face had tears on it and the girl only stopped in her walking; stared for a moment. And with no question in her gaze.

It was a look of stillness, between all this strange noise. Gwen had a moment to think that she looked older, and to wonder if her own age and all the wisdom she should have owned with it had left her.

She remembered running errands for this girl, after her child had come.

'Are you all right?'

'Yes,' Bethan said.

Their voices were almost lost.

'My God, it's mad,' Gwen saw her say.

There was the fall of a window's boarding.

And Bethan just told her, 'I've got to go . . .' and passed by her, touching Gwen's arm as she did so.

So that she came to the café empty-handed, stone-beaten. She stood outside for long minutes and, though she glanced back, couldn't make out the museum, only Bethan Hughes's figure as she wandered her way down the pavement, to somewhere else.

Bethan was staying and for the first time the thought of it was pale, as if opening.

But some were leaving. Many were.

Ruth Lewis was moving away: halfway up the lane between the town and Charlotte's house, she had sat, parked for two hours while she cried. In the passenger seat, Nia's face was hidden by her lifted knees, as Ruth started the engine that had long gone cold and began to drive again.

She had opened the wooden front door. There had been a hallway. A little staircase with an oak banister and pink carpet risers, old beams forming arms above, to hold the shadows in. It had seemed as if it wasn't she that stood there.

Disconnected, it might've been someone looking in from the doorstep who hadn't seen the house for years. Anyone. A nondescript man, ageing, summers that had been spent in a different place now gone from his face, and with no trace left.

He would have seen a long and perfect row of pictures. Wildflowers. Jacob's ladder and ragged robin, petals in no wind. He would have looked down, she thought, and seen a welcome mat.

She wandered into the hallway with his hands. She put them on the kitchen door and saw a place where the fall of evening light lay on an oilcloth. Into the living room, he would have looked and, closing its door again, seen his own face in the oval of the mirror. Would have opened this last door and seen a new man's room.

Lives lay unchanged, he might have thought.

Ruth had walked into her house. He would have been calm. Would have always been a calm man. You had to be, to kiss your wife goodbye for the day and not come back. He would have seen, as he looked around, that that day had not yet ended.

Calm and regretful, she visualized.

She had not been calm.

Now she parked outside the house and the headlamps, dying off, left Charlotte Weyland's driveway in the darkness.

There'd been the flicker of orange reflections in the wing mirrors as they'd sat in that lay-by, Ynys-morlan behind. Now there were trees. Ruth watched their shadow stems bend and their bare branches; almost leafing, when in the daylight they could be seen. There was a wind up here.

She opened the car door and stepped on to the gravel. Behind her, head in her knees, Nia didn't move. Her hair was a curtain across her face. At first, she'd pushed gently at Ruth's crying shoulders. After a long while, the pushes had become shoves and tiny slaps and, at the end, Nia's hands had beaten like sand and water, trying to make her look up. Then this.

Ruth crossed the silent driveway, to the car's other door. Was that the sound of the work? Very distant, could she hear it? Her eyes were white and in the sweet night air, she was looking at the glass across her daughter.

She opened the door and she dragged Nia out – a hard ball, picked up whole. A heavy ball of little bones. She stood here, holding her, with the sun gone, and the evening and the winter. Only the new year, growing wide around her until it was a wasteland of horizons.

The doorstep lamp illuminated itself. She stood in a half-mess of work clothes, loose hair unwashed and pushed behind her ears. In the back of the car, there was a suitcase. She was not sure what was in the suitcase. She remembered the garden, and how lawn had peeled back. She remembered writing. The recollection of Lennie's face had been dim to her.

Nia's hands clambered up around her neck and held on to her there, where Ruth could not feel them. What she had done – the project or whatever you wanted to call it – lay below, under completion, as she knocked.

She wouldn't let herself see it finished. Nia was an embryo in her arms and down there, her beautiful, almost-grown garden swept out to fill a coastline. Nia was a quiet, broken bag.

The door opened, to a house which she'd seen in the grey of afternoon, in the blue light of a morning, and filled with music – a house that had once been closed down, to walk around, like a sleeping stone troll – and which had come back into Ruth's life with its memories stretching forwards from her, as hopes.

The old door opened, and Charlotte held it. She looked at Ruth and at the child.

She looked at the car, hurriedly parked, hurriedly to move on. Its doors were still open in the dark. She saw the mess that crying had left on Ruth's face. Perhaps she saw two hours of stillness in which a project that had meant everything to Ruth, everything she could imagine, had been nothing more than the soft flashing of some far light, turning round, falling, lit again in her rear-view mirror.

Charlotte pushed her gaze aside and stared at the ground.

'I'm sorry,' Ruth said.

They stood together, with leaving between them, and a spring they could not achieve. There was no healing to be seen in Ruth; a few long seconds when it seemed as if they understood each other.

This was a lie, though. For Charlotte had told her nothing, and the first thing that Ruth said after their silence was utterly unexpected; like a fissure it came across the clean night.

'Take her away from me.'

She put Nia down on the doorstep like a little gift, which stumbled and found its legs.

Lennie told the empty house that the letter's words weren't true. The house, which had never been his, responded that they were. It told him in Nia's voice, that for three years he'd been blind.

His fingers traced the letters and when he looked up they were traced over his vision. His hands shook. Look at this rock of a man with his hands shaking. He read the letter again. *This is what we've done*, it began, and then it told a simple tale that ended, not with Charlotte Weyland's house, but with a road Ruth didn't know.

A cautionary tale. One that ruined. One that scratched the eyes out of the pictures he had held so close since he was so small, and made them blind as well.

Once, a man had driven away from this little cottage. He'd made Ynys-morlan into a memory and first put the silence in these walls. The house had no thoughts, though, or heart. As Ruth had let the letter drift down on to the table, she had seen the many years of believing that in some way it lived. Whether to be blamed, or to be made beautiful, like a substitute.

The house hadn't said goodbye to her. Nor she to it, but she'd gone crying, as she had taken her ghosts out into the street and stood with them, while the sandblasting had begun.

Charlotte had asked her father with innocent voice, perhaps one year after finding the grave, perhaps less – the exact date would be recorded – where the choice of her name had come from. Who had chosen, and what the alternatives had been.

Her father had replied with only one stumble, only at the beginning. Looking back on the moment, Charlotte would see that that stumble had been the breach of four years. From her own birth, back through grief, one year now hard to remember, and the three previous, of unnoticed happiness, as the real Charlotte Weyland had grown from an infant to fulfil her life.

She would think later that there must have been diaries – an era of volumes – in that single falter. She would wonder how he'd managed to pass them by.

He'd told her how, if she had been a boy, her name might have been Tristan. Andrew had been considered, but Tristan had been the one that both of them had truly chosen. And that Jacintha, for a girl, had also 'done the rounds'.

It hadn't answered her question, for he'd not been thinking of her at all. She'd wanted to look into the names – see if she could find some recognition of who she was in one of them. She hadn't thought of it exactly this way. Building her defences to ask, she'd thought only, I'm an Alice. I'm Victoria.

She had seen in her father's expression, though, that at the time of her own birth there had been no alternatives to 'do the rounds'. When her mother had been screaming, her father holding her hand, they had already known.

'Your mother's always loved the name Charlotte,' he'd told her kindly. And so it had been her daughter's, for three years.

It had also been her second child's. And this girl had never understood, because Charlotte Weyland had been a real person, with a future and a home; the very finest luck can bring. This girl had wandered through them, wondering if she was meant to mimic what Charlotte would have done. No, she had never understood. And she had written, sometimes just hating, sometimes with questions, more rarely with a quiet documentation of the life that had not been hers. She had written; tried to understand.

It was abandoning them, to have your child in your arms and see only the past. How could you look down – she was your daughter – how could you look down without seeing her at all? Surely there was a bond, that grew like vines, and abandonment – desertion of that kind – was impossible.

*

'No, Ruth,' she said.

'Take her.'

Charlotte shook her head, though she did not feel it. 'You selfish woman . . .' she said. Her breath misted, though it wasn't winter any more.

'I'm going to leave,' a voice that lay on tears. 'I'm going to the car now. I'm going to walk to the door and shut it and drive away. I'm not going to let her come with me.'

'Then you are a horrible person.' She looked at Ruth's face in the harsh lamp's light. She saw with pale comprehension the distance that had always lain between Ruth and the girl she'd now taken her hands away from. From whom, with hands now free, she was totally separated. She looked at Ruth and saw no mother.

She had loved this woman. She'd touched her hair and face, like she could draw hope out from Ruth that way and make it real. She'd realized what she was herself, because of the touch. And everything, everything re-evaluated, wavered on whether Ruth was in love with her too, or whether, once again, she was nothing but a crutch.

Love retreated from Charlotte and dug its hands into the centre of her, to hide.

'Take her away, Ruth! You want to leave, before you've even seen it finished . . . want to leave like this, with no words to me, then you take your daughter with you! She's your goddamn child and you take her wherever you go!'

Tears ran over her face as she stared out at Charlotte and did not see her.

'I can't take her.'

'You *selfish* woman!'

'I can't take her anywhere with me.'

'Have some strength! I'm in love with you,' she said. 'I *was* . . . Have some goddamn strength! You come here with all the things you need and you shout at me! Every time – every time, and now you come here with Nia. You're a *coward* to stand here! I can't believe you'd do it!'

After finding her feet, Nia had given them up and sat down between them on the step. She'd covered up her face again and Charlotte remembered her half-laughter as they had sat in Ty Heulog's bedroom. She saw, these pictures gradually clearer, that coy voice that Ruth had always used for her daughter, the fussing hands, which then fled.

'Please.' Her dirty, lovely face was held together by her words. 'For her sake I'm saying it. I don't care how it looks to you. I'm sorry to say goodbye this way. You take her away from me now.'

'*You take her away!* My God, you horrible . . . *uncaring woman!* And you expect to *heal*? To change? Look at you, *you act like a hateful child!* Use your daughter, *your three-year-old daughter*, to hurt yourself! Do you understand how selfish you are . . . ? Do you understand? You have no excuse! He can hit you, Ruth. He can do the worst things . . . you can't use your child like this! You're worse . . .' she said. 'You're worse.'

Ruth heard these things that she had told herself, and recognition welled up and trickled from her eyes and slipped from her mouth. 'I'm not trying to punish myself.' The air was cold but she didn't feel it. Behind, the trees were shifting. 'I told you, for her sake. I'm not lying . . .'

'*How can you do this?* I hate you . . .' Charlotte said. With those hopes, of years, all pulled apart, she felt that hate. 'I've given and you've taken. You crowd yourself in with your own little hurts and you *use* them! That's what you do . . . *Look down at her –* ' But Charlotte herself did not look down to where Nia sat on her cold doorstep. '*User . . .*' she said. 'You think you hate yourself? *You give yourself the reason!*'

Ruth tried to keep any control. At her sides, her hands were still. At the coast behind her now, it was almost complete: all the pretty houses and beautiful ideas of reshaping sadness into renewal.

She had not come here to speak. She had written it down because she couldn't say the words. With the last of her will, she looked at Charlotte's face and saw someone who would take Nia. Of course she would take her. Whatever she said in hatred now. Seeing the last of it, Ruth turned away.

Charlotte chased across the doorstep, took hold of Ruth's clothing.

The collar of her shirt and held her, shook her. Ruth moved like washing in the breeze. A few steps from the car, they stood that way.

'Look at yourself! Turn around and face your goddamn life! Pick up your daughter! Horrible woman!' she said, tears of her own coming up, bitter. 'Bitch!' she said, into this face, which she had kissed. 'Selfish bitch! No you don't run away! Once! Always done it, haven't you? You want to hide for years and come crying to the only person who'll listen? You want to come here and dump your tears on my doorstep every time I see you? *Not your daughter!*' Words she'd never used. Images were blurring, homes that she had recreated paling, until she was standing on the great curving steps, the half-moon steps that stranded you as you looked towards Hedera's doors. '*Not your fucking daughter, Ruth! Look at her!*'

And Ruth looked.

She turned her head from this place where Charlotte held her; where her car waited. She saw Nia. Had made herself as small as possible. Just like Ruth herself, she was, in miniature. Trying to find a little corner, that maybe everything would stay away from. Ruth looked at her, mouth open, no sound escaping.

She turned and saw Charlotte's face. She believed that she loved her. If a person was capable of love when they hid everything. It had striven for the sky when Charlotte had touched her body, like it could reclaim happiness. It had made her want to put her arms round the woman and comfort her, when it was she herself who wanted comfort.

'Do you think I could keep her?' Charlotte asked. 'If you ran away, do you think any court would let me? She'll go to your husband, Ruth! Will you leave her with him?'

She could feel the trees curling, many branches, all their stems. Her face was wet and cut by this wind. 'I'll come inside, Charlotte . . . and I'll tell you, and then you won't question me. You'll shut a door between me and her . . . You'll say to me, it's better, if Lennie has her.'

Charlotte looked at her, spring's last cold night outside this house. It made the world seem cruel enough to blame. There should have been a bond, parent and child, which could never be broken. But it seemed all ties could break. She couldn't comprehend any world where this was true.

'Yes,' she said. 'You come inside. You bring your daughter with you.'

Lennie knew where the house was, the one that had been empty so many years. He could make his way up there by foot, he could collect his daughter. He thought of seeing the woman's face and all the anger and the lack of understanding that had filled him these last twenty-four hours, it would fall silent, to nothing, as he took Nia.

This is what we've done.

And how would the girl look? Would she look different? Would he see his guilt, right there in her eyes?

There was a split in the world and his side of it was a dream. It must have been, since he'd been young. Sunflowers, that had broken the night into multicoloured stars and made his home a place of majesty. They must be lies, however beautiful and vivid; however they had seemed real to him. Because a world in which this letter could be true – it wasn't any place where violence and greatness touched.

He stood at the table. He left the kitchen slowly but when he came to the front door, it would not give. While he had walked the rooms, they'd shut him inside and they'd boarded the door so he would stay that way.

Lennie had to open the window in his study – the one that had once looked out on the flagpole. Had to push his body through it. He'd meant to come to the road, look back at this house and then out to Charlotte's; and to go there. But he just saw that space of ground. He stood immobile, the window open behind him, the curtains rising to touch his back in this wind.

He saw a lie, buried deep down there. He saw nothing but earth.

What would he do at Charlotte Weyland's house, where Ruth had left their daughter? Would he look into that woman's face and claim he had the right to take the girl? Did Charlotte know?

He could not believe that.

He could not believe, for three years, Ruth had been silent to him, then told another.

He was full of rubble. He heard the machinery. And he was crying tears that held no light's reflection. The street lamps his father had told him about – they had gone out, Lennie saw as he looked upwards.

They sat opposite each other on the sofa.

Ruth had picked Nia up, manoeuvring herself around the tight arms and legs, to lift her. She'd carried her in. Charlotte had remembered a biblical story. Two mothers claiming and a baby torn in half. But they had stood with their hands held away, as if to touch her was for ever.

They sat opposite each other. Ruth stared out.

Charlotte saw, nebulous in her expression, something she had waited months to see. She had been hoping then. She was hoping no longer. All the things she had felt for Ruth, confused and wonderful and desperate, they had crested as she'd stood in the rooms that she'd recreated and had told Ruth they were a gift. Those emotions had almost been demolished; Charlotte had seen her clear. A desolate woman, years from love, who only needed her.

She saw now – a calm had settled, Ruth's dirty face dry – some baseline there. Some kind of acceptance, from which you could only move upwards.

Nia lay huddled up in the chair as Ruth began to speak.

For a little while Charlotte forgot what she was feeling. Abhorrence seemed to trail away from her and uncertainty rose instead into the air. A little while. She forgot Hedera, Massachusetts. She heard a history, a long parable, with its roots in Ynys-morlan, which made the past a fragile thing.

'Should never have tried for good endings,' Ruth said, her voice quiet. She would tell it. 'It was the good endings, you know . . . it was all the days wandering round this place and imagining. You're too young to realize . . . that you're desperate. And you're so young, you can't know desperate feelings . . . bring on desperate choices. Don't they? I was so sure . . . I was going to leave. Always knew I'd leave – the house, this town. Everything. And then she died.'

She stared out at Charlotte, and Charlotte saw there was no self-punishment in her expression. It brought the sunken movement of fear, to see it. The girl on the night-dark doorstep. *It's for her sake.*

'I was looking after her . . . Mum, you know, looking after her . . . I –' Her voice was low but it filled the room because out here, there were no machines. There was no project. The closest house was almost a mile away, and a vacant church the only building nearer. Ruth's tones drifted through the corridor here, and below the conservatory's cold glass. They would have been faintly heard inside Charlotte's study, where a closed door hid the shelves.

Ruth's gaze must have been hollow. It was queer to speak. For a long time now, there had been demons. But this room, and she herself, seemed empty, starting to tell it.

'You know, I had people say to me, after some time, you know, respectable time . . . that it does funny things to you when your parents die. Not just the bereavement . . . things you don't notice? Maybe it did that to me. Because I wanted to stay. I wanted – I thought about how hard she'd worked, to get rid of him. Like she'd mourned him for years and she'd finally got over it. Admitted he wasn't dead, and she didn't need his things, and he'd never come back for them.'

Charlotte looked at her and saw days, long-past days, wandering through the garden, when the weeds had only shown their fingertips between the herringbone bricks. Charlotte looked at Ruth and told herself she hated her, but feared it wasn't true.

'You think the world runs, like it has to bring happy endings. I didn't want to run away, when she'd worked . . . What goes around comes around. You think it's true. You miss them, you grieve for them, you miss them so much . . . something has to be made out of it. You feel that . . .'

She did not look at her daughter. Charlotte saw it through the course of minutes. Not one glance. Bereavement was the word for what she felt herself.

'He's lovely, so many ways –' she said. 'There's ways that he's –

more beautiful . . . you can think that a stupid word but it's right . . .
more beautiful than any other person I've ever met. I wasn't blind.
He didn't . . . talk easily to me. He had a temper. He had a kind of
loneliness. I would've shied away, I would have, but he loved me. He
loved me. I wanted that. Never had it . . . He talks sometimes, he'll
be drinking but it doesn't matter, he speaks sometimes, he tells you
the things he cares about . . . they catch you up.' A knot touched her
face. 'They carry you off.'

Was he thinking of them? A mile away? Charlotte wondered.
Conjuring ugly words for what she and his wife had done. He didn't
know maybe that for Ruth it had not been real. Had Ruth told him,
really, that she loved her? No easier way to end a marriage, Charlotte
thought. But she saw the tears in Ruth's eyes and the bitter thoughts
that moved through her were lies.

'I loved him, Charlotte. I couldn't show him – he'd look at me and
I'd get scared, I'd get so blocked up. I thought he'd leave me. Wasn't
one day, not one, when I didn't believe he was going to leave. I loved
him. I loved him,' she said again, as if that were an excuse. Ruth
looked at her. She had never said it to Lennie with a voice that
sounded as real.

The tears were useless and wouldn't fall. Even writing him the
letter, even up to that very moment, when she'd thought of the past
a kind of madness had come. It was the only name for it, madness. A
guilt like this. Because it moved your body for you, let words spill
from your mouth that you didn't want to say. It destroyed, and burned
down, and created nothing, and it was you.

You looked down at two hands. They were yours.

'When someone pulls you up to them, they bring you right up to
their face and they say to you . . . "I've waited for you all my life. I
could never love anyone else. You were meant for me." When they
do that . . . you love them for it. Can you understand?'

She looked at Charlotte, saying nothing of years. She'd tried to
imagine herself with a husband – a little girl, walking round this
derelict garden. She'd been unable to make any story where the man
who loved her didn't leave. She didn't mention how she'd always

believed that Ynys-morlan was to blame. Flawed in some way just like her.

She sat there, this woman who'd been sweetness and light when Charlotte had first met her, who had created herself from little bits of femininity like pieces of bright cloth, and who'd stood in a bare bedroom with Charlotte, stripping herself, skin and clothes and hair, until there was nothing left but loathing. Charlotte remembered being kissed with some morning rising unseen in the windows here. She wondered if she had seen who Ruth was. Maybe she only wished it.

Ruth looked back at her, eyes full of deprivation. She couldn't ask for understanding.

'We'd go to sleep, he'd hold me. Isn't it a stupid thing? Do we think things like this make a life . . . ? He held me like that. When I couldn't . . . couldn't even give it back to him. "I love you," he'd say. I wouldn't know how to answer, be scared to answer. He had this passion in his eyes . . . and I couldn't believe it was real.'

While Ruth sat there, dry-voiced, the river in Lennie was spilling out again. He was walking out to the spot where the flagpole's foundations had been, past a garden that was now completed. Rose bushes would have shone, every one of them yellow – but there were no street lamps and the stars weren't bright enough.

He was looking down, and he was speaking under his breath. There was this wind, so that he couldn't hear it. He was cursing and swallowing. He was saying this piece of earth was nothing but empty. Telling it how it had always been a lie.

He'd believed it, because it had made him feel greater. More than he was. More than his life added up to. He'd believed it, because it had been the start of him. Right down inside, all things had grown from it. He was nothing without it, he had known.

Lennie was crouching down on the ground, then was kneeling, pulling up earth that was already disturbed and throwing it away from this place.

A lie, his father's story. It had always been. There was beauty in it but the beauty wasn't real. There was passion and it was false. Because he'd seen now, understood now, the pallid, terrible things that this kind of passion really made. A morning was coming and he could not stop it. Did not want to any more.

Charlotte's lips were parted like empathy escaped from her that way, when she could not let it show on her face. She saw Nia on the step again, maybe she made herself see it. She saw this woman saying she'd drive away.

'We got the pregnancy. I tried for it –' she started. Her expression scattered: as if in the blustering dark outside, was gone. 'I shouldn't have had a baby with him. I wanted one. A family. I had these ideas . . . how it would be. Is it wrong to want to prove you can have a family? Be happy? I didn't believe I could. I wanted to prove it . . . I didn't want him to leave!' she said, as though Charlotte's silence-stricken face gave back all the hateful things she'd told herself; nights, while he was sleeping. 'Whatever it was like. It was wrong, lots of ways . . . But I didn't want him to leave me behind, just get in the car . . .' There were images, as there always had been, of drying: water to earth, earth to sand. There were images of what Ynys-morlan was, and she herself, which she'd never shed. 'I was desperate,' she said. 'I was desperate for him to stay.'

The story lay motionless in Charlotte; layers on top of the last.

She remembered times that Ruth had said loving things, and they'd not been blocked. She said nothing, these memories passing in the breath between her words.

For the first time then Ruth dropped her eyes. The words she had said already seemed to lie without moving in the air around her. Nia huddled in that chair a few feet away, in a slumber or some other stillness. Her mouth opened to speak and she did not. After moments, she said, 'She used to cry. When she was a baby, she used to cry all the time.'

'Gwen . . . ?'

Patty saw the tears. Through all the recent months, the strange stories she'd heard, the way Gwen had been absent from the project and from Ynys-morlan almost, retreated, there'd been nothing that might have lessened the shock of this. In the doorway, she stood. Her face was bare, her expression cast like gravel. She was crying. Through all the years really, there'd been nothing to prepare her for it.

'I hear her sometimes,' Ruth said. 'Squalling away. When the house is empty, I can hear it.'

A great distance seemed to lie between Charlotte and Ruth's figure, head lowered. There were strands, though, Charlotte couldn't help it: stretched through the fear that she felt and still unbreaking. She remembered Ruth, in a dawn, gradually falling into sleep. Lying and holding her, she'd kissed her lightly many times, with thankfulness, and not to wake her.

Ruth's hands lay dead in her lap. They were still dirty. She looked at them. Under the grass, there'd been only the same earth, wet and so easily revealed.

The café was lifted, straight from some London dream. A mosaic of abstract sand and sea was stretched across the wall where once, a month ago, two months, no more than that, there'd been shelves with nylon roses and the Hollywood prints Gwen had seen tonight. Bette Davis here, beside the door, looking down on the space where a delicate round table with wrought-iron legs now filled one window corner. Room for four to eat, or five, in the summer sun that would tumble in. Rita Hayworth had hung opposite, where new paint now gleamed in a pretty, secret light.

'Come inside, my God. What's wrong . . . ? What's happened?'

She stepped over the threshold, numb. She looked at the lovely oak bar, the tall stools and, behind, a rack of antique bottles. Whose ideas had these been? Patty's? They had been realized so quickly. She couldn't understand what had happened. Down this street behind her, little parts of the place she'd known, telling parts, were lying in a museum.

She walked across oak floorboards.

Patty was still sitting at a table, covered by figures – books that her hands still rested on. She moved as if to stand but Gwen walked through the room. That blank inability to grasp fading slowly to some understanding, wan like a morning, of what Emyr had been doing with his exhibits.

It wasn't only the change in the place, it was who had succumbed to it. Or flown with it perhaps, taken it up and just flown with it. And why.

Patty looked older, as her daughter had done, seen only in a few moments. Something was gone from her, Gwen saw, some bright edge. And what showed beneath it looked sadder, far more real.

This place she'd made, Gwen thought – it had stolen the spring right out of Patty, to be painted across the walls instead.

Open-eyed, Pat was staring at her.

She took hold of another chair's back and she pulled it to her. She sat and felt a relief. Behind them, bottle-glass windows looked out on a street that was too dark to be seen.

Where was Tom? she wondered. Was he still coming to her?

Pat reached out slowly and touched her friend's hand.

'Emyr and I . . . we are leaving each other,' she heard Gwen say.

'Yeah, well, I can see now why we're not meant to be out tonight. Had to walk most of the way on the beach.' Her footsteps trailed back there to prove it, shapeless in this wet sand. She'd crossed the road beside Ellen's Bed and Breakfast, where a new sign had hung in the crazy revolution of orange or the trail of flashlights. In a wrought-iron bracket, it had been shrouded; some canvas thrown over it, loosely roped. And Bethan had stood and looked at it, hearing all the noise for several moments, just hearing it all and smiling with disbelief – an expression only strangers had seen.

She had thought of staying. She had thought of a restaurant, that was beautiful to her, full of dreamlike pictures that hadn't evaporated. They'd not shown ugly, or stupid, grotesque, because out here, where madness ruled OK tonight, Ynys-morlan was waiting. Under the light of a morning, it wouldn't be full of age and broken windows, memories of dreams, wouldn't reveal her stained-glass windows as some stupid flight of fancy. When tonight was over, the town would still be full of wonder.

She had walked through the little alley. She'd put her hand on cobbled walls. She had come past gardens, where withy screens could almost be made out in the light that fell only from rear windows. These two rows of houses that held their backs to everything except each other, across the road – they'd had their eyes closed across the street now, and the only views they owned, even hidden in darkness, were of the mountains or the sea.

That sea was quiet tonight. It seemed to lap up on the sand and tickle stones, while in the street, water blasted and rasped clean. She couldn't tell really. Those windows' lights didn't reach. In the quieter seconds between the muffled whine of the hoses, though, it sounded sweet and calm.

From that spot where she'd come to the beach, all the way here, her footsteps trailed.

She had seen their figures. She had seen Rhys turn away.

They stood together now, only looked at each other. For Bethan, like years had gone by. Rhys's face was hollow, shadowed. Tom's, she saw, had the smallest smile. She could make out sadness there but more besides. And her own, though she didn't know it, could only feel its edges, held the sort of defencelessness neither of these boys, or men, had ever seen on her.

'It's a weird fucking evening out,' Tom said quietly.

He looked from one of them to the other, just half seen beneath this clear-skied night, and could make out the changes in them anyway. It might be his last sight for a while.

The sea gently overspilled itself.

On the other sides of these houses, the sand battered everything.

She couldn't see Rhys's eyes in the half-dark. Come with me, he remembered saying. Come with me tonight. But he looked at Bethan now and saw that it couldn't have been her he'd tried to save. She looked beautiful. He no longer knew, no longer knew what it might have been.

And she felt naked, just that one glance. Like a girl who'd never left this town.

Tom sat down on the sand between them.

Because he was going away from Ynys-morlan, because he'd be someone else if he came back and their past would've drifted off into the sea like a great piece of land, broken loose. After moments, just watching, they sat down next to him. Rhys and then Bethan in the soft sand.

The boards had loosened. First, Siân had seen the man's hands in her living room's lamplight. They had crept around the edges, pressed right up to the glass. It had been hard to hear; maybe she'd made out the scrape of the tacks pulled free. She'd retreated from the window as it had fallen away, imagining that man looking in – his unknown face, his unknown life – and she herself caught like a butterfly.

He'd turned away, though.

He'd turned and carried the board and had left her, staring out through the glass into a road where, if you walked, you walked between hulking machines. Their yellow sides she saw, and their operators' shadowed figures, the dark snake of hoses across tarmac. And the road was painted, black and then illuminated, in a constant cycle.

She looked uselessly for Tom.

Behind her, Stacey sat in silence. The television was dusty nothingness. She stared at it. She'd swapped no words with her mother. She hadn't told Siân how much she had heard, nor had she asked: anything, how Siân was. Her brother leaving – it seemed to lie in the dust. There was a lot of dust here at the moment. There'd been too much going on for her mum to clean. In that dust and the open boxes, her brother leaving – that fact seemed to show its edges, just in the little bits and bobs that stuck out, not yet unpacked.

She didn't look up at first when Siân left the room. Maybe she'd gone to the kitchen, to turn the stove off on a dinner they wouldn't eat. Maybe she'd done that already and she was going to the bathroom, to lock the door, and deal with the stuff she felt there. She only raised her head – turned around on the sofa – when she heard the front door open and close.

She sat a moment. She opened her hands up to the ceiling, as if to ask what could be done. Then she rose up, she went to the window and saw her mother on the pavement: trying to find a way across the street as if it were an ice floe and she could see no sure footing.

Stacey saw her glance from the street – across. A lot of times, she saw her do it.

She'd heard Tom say Gwen Morgan's name. She didn't believe it. It was a lie. But in the café there, where the boards had also been taken down and rounded, small-paned windows were filled with the shapes of their own light, in the café there, the door was open wide, and Gwen Morgan was standing just outside it.

Stacey didn't believe it, though. It was a lie.

Look at the woman, almost sixty or something.

'Emyr and I are leaving each other.'

The man who'd loved her like a given sacrifice. He'd had bluff and composure, he'd had good manners and an overbearing mother once; a man with a rare laugh that came out puffing steam. He'd used to close his eyes when they'd made love. He'd never looked at her. And she had wondered, when he'd been only feeling, moving, his eyes shut that way, what version of her he had seen; if it was the woman she'd always tried to be.

Patty's sight of Gwen – it broadened. Her eyes grew wide with it. And her sight of this place, alongside. Months when Gwen had hardly come into town and never into the café here, they were now reviewed, colourless questions rising to encompass them.

'I went to the museum this evening,' Gwen said.

She saw Patty's curly hair, bundled up and spilling down. She saw the lines around her face and the careful, light make-up. In the months when her daughter had fallen pregnant, the final months, when Bethan had put on all the weight, Pat had taken to wearing no make-up at all. She could build her face up until it was doll-beautiful. She'd not built it at all during that time. Memories rose like they'd been stored in the ground that outside was so broken and churned.

'I went to the museum. I saw there . . . Emyr was working . . . he had all the pictures you used to have hung up in here. He said you took those to him. Is that true? Why did you do that?'

But Patty only looked through her words and said, soft-struck, 'You're leaving each other . . . ? After twenty years . . . ?'

'I saw them there,' she tried to say.

'What are you talking about, Gwen?'

'The pictures. Humphrey Bogart and Marilyn Monroe, you know the ones I mean.'

She shook her head, in still and gentle air. 'Why do you want to ask about those . . . ?'

'I'm leaving,' she said.

'No.'

'I have a room booked. I might come back to take some things. I don't know.'

'What's happened? You tell me! You're leaving? You've got enough time to talk?'

She sat silent and Patty's face seemed very precious. All her expressions, which were so well known. She didn't want to feel like they were dear in the same way as those things in the museum. She said, 'It's been months, Pat. It's been years. I have time to talk . . . I don't want to talk about that, though.' She thought of Tom's expressions and how precious they also seemed. She was afraid, terribly afraid, and full of hope. There had been things that for a long time, she'd never felt. She wasn't used to them. It was like this shattered ground. 'I want to talk about us,' she said. 'Just want to talk about you, and me. About the past.'

Gwen's hand was cold underneath hers. Pat looked at her and took moments to catch up, as if the waves were moving fast and Gwen was far ahead.

'You came to this decision together?' she asked.

'We were . . . brought to it.'

The words fell like raindrops on a cloudless day. Patty tried to re-evaluate but it had been many years since Gwen had been anyone but Emyr's wife. She looked at her with pity, though she didn't seem to need it. She was crying, her face was naked, but she looked different.

Like a girl. She tried to think of the past but outside the project was ending. The crew replacing the street lamps advanced and filled the road with their cranes and their flooded light. In here, she had been only sitting. She had been looking at the place she'd created, not out of choice but for Bethan. She'd been thinking of Beth's tears the night before and of her silence today – an open silence, occasional smiles, that seemed to have no stones in them – and she had been telling herself that, though she felt sad, as if the world was moving on when she had only inertia left, despite these things, it had been worth it.

She liked the place. This place, this room. Couldn't love it maybe, as she had when it had all been hers. But she'd been thinking of how those smiles flashed up, lit Bethan's face and made the resemblance between her daughter and Chelsea more real.

'The past,' she said, and gave a quirk of a smile.

'The past, you know . . .' Gwen said. In truth, though, she asked because she could not remember so clearly herself. She wanted to be reminded. Without guilt, without any thoughts of Tom or the future – for a little while, just reminisce. 'Why did you take them to the museum?' she asked. 'They're not old . . . They're not just memories. He's got them in cases now. He's got the photograph, my wedding day, the one that hung up here. Why?' she said.

Patty shrugged. She would have looked away but the moment between them was new, and a last moment too. She gestured with the lightest fingers, not even raised from the top of Gwen's hand. 'Why do you ever clean out the cupboards? Make an ending, and a new start, you know . . .' And then she said, 'It's all changed. My God, has it all just changed. I feel old, Gwen. I'm not so good at moving on . . .'

'That's not true, Pat. You've always been good, at just that.'

'You're leaving,' she said. 'You and Emyr, going separate ways. My God . . . You're the one moving on then.'

Gwen swallowed and didn't answer; stillness fell after Pat's voice, like confirmation, as she saw this new place and her friend, an unchanged person. After a night when the changes had rung loud in the street, through all the shock and realization that had come as she had stood with Emyr in the museum, for the first time now, Gwen felt the hope again fully – the hope that had seemed so new as she had lain with Tom. Full of summertime. She was leaving. She was glad to be leaving. She had no destination in her mind and when you thought about that, it was a freedom.

The things you were, they weren't set in stone. The past became a foundation, not a weight.

She saw Pat starting to cry. 'It's all right,' she said. 'There's no need for that.'

But she didn't know, Patty thought. She didn't know.

Through a bottle-glass window, out on a new pavement, from the dark of a moving night Siân looked in. She couldn't hear the words but she could see Patty's face. There was none of the truth written there. The goodbyes they were saying were easy. They were sad and sweet and they were lies. She stood out here, where the noise that was only an edge to those two women seemed to hold the world and shake it, and she wanted to go inside and let that truth run out and ruin everything. But she missed them. Bereaved by what Gwen was taking, stealing away, still she wanted to be sitting in there. She wanted none of this to have happened and to be sitting, talking, sharing whatever they said.

She put her hand on the doorknob. She lifted it away, afraid of the bell that no longer rang, or even hung above.

She had been robbed. In many ways, she'd been betrayed. She had tried – just in days perhaps, but she had tried – to find out what Tom needed and give it to him. It had been too late for trying, though. He'd already found something, which would only take them further from each other. It would take him across a distance she couldn't even step out into. She looked at Gwen's back in the little café's new, hushed light. A distance she couldn't even understand.

She could not let it go, without reaching out in some way. Without acting. She wasn't that sort, and wouldn't be changed, robbed of the ways she knew herself as well. Siân moved once again to take hold of the door, and push it open. And she stepped into the room.

*

They sat together, three of them on a dark beach, all with secrets.

They asked each other what they'd be doing this time next year. Some of the answers were lies. But the sea tried to cover unspoken words, cover them with its little kissing sounds. It washed on like it must love these stones, this sand, to come back every day.

'It's cold,' Bethan said.

Rhys nodded. For a moment he managed to hold her gaze. And Tom was quiet, only seeing them both. They didn't have to say anything really, because the changes were too complex and too wide to tell without great stories. And they didn't want to swap stories here. They only wanted to look at each other and see the things that remained the same.

She walked in and they stared at her with their shocked and different gazes.

She made no introduction, didn't even say their names.

'You know . . .' she said, 'you know why she's going? That's why you're sitting here, isn't it, you're saying goodbyes? D'you know who she's going with? She's taking my son away.'

Gwen looked at them in the sand-struck silence. She opened her mouth but too late to ask Siân not to tell. She looked at the woman, with whom she'd once been a child. She wanted to tell her not to end it this way, but the words had been spoken and every moment that had grown here between herself and Patty, they all lay breached, they lay and showed empty insides.

'She's taking my son away . . . she's leaving her husband for him and she's taking him from me.'

'No,' Patty said. One small and disbelieving word.

She looked from the face of one friend to another and saw the truth in their eyes. The clocks stopped running forwards and turned themselves and headed backwards, to steal away years – that had been filled with love, and with difficulty, for all three.

'That's what she's doing . . .' Siân said, but her gaze was on Gwen herself. 'How can you do that? How can you do that?' It was the only question she owned.

Gwen sat and could say nothing, but only feel the silence drift. Those clocks ran back. She was a young wife and then a girl with her fiancé. A girl full of needs that she thought were right.

And Patty only stared at her, divested by the shock, of everything.

She tried to hold the truth of it, thought of Bethan, and could not.

'How could you do that, Gwen?' Siân asked her. 'To me, not some stranger, to me.'

'I didn't want to . . .' she started to answer. There was nothing else inside her, though, she felt nothing else that she could say.

Shock. Which took the months Patty had been through, turned them inside out, easily as a fucking jumper. Tears were coming up to Gwen's eyes. They stood framed here, this pretty little café, this London dream, like an old photo torn in three.

The shock came from something far deeper than morals. Maybe it was because Gwen had never had children. But, with Bethan, Tom was so young. He was a child. And to Gwen, there must be no difference between.

The clocks' hands mocked them. They were three girls making an elaborate lunch, and laying a table with the perfect things, for no one but themselves. They were pretending to be wives. They were discussing the jobs their husbands would have, and the homes that they would make themselves.

All of them had spent these last months discovering that a great part of their lives had ended. They'd spent them trying to cope with that, trying to find ways to shape the next piece, just ways to understand it.

But to Gwen Morgan there was no line between herself and an eighteen-year-old boy.

It took the years they'd shared or spent alone and dissolved them, until they were just passing moments. She was leaving with Tom. It took Patty's feeling of age and pulled its fibres apart, till it meant nothing. And Siân's sense of simple confusion filled the last seconds that they shared.

Plaster and pebbledash fell in wet pieces, the water washed it on to new lawns where its whiteness would show the next morning, and the morning after, till rain came to eradicate its traces.

Their inability to understand filled those seconds, replacing the past and hollowing that passage of time, which was fundamental, which engendered hopes and fears – made long-gone things irretrievable, and was the heart of loss.

Ruth sat in Charlotte's home, a few feet away from her, and didn't look up at her face. Her hands were white in her lap. They were her own. They did not look that way, she thought. It was an unearthing, every time you saw what you had done.

'I can't remember the first day that she didn't cry. I've tried to look back, you know, and find it. Face it. It must've come and gone without me noticing . . . perhaps, after a week, I started realizing, sixteen, eighteen months she must have been . . . I got scared, that she might be ill. He said to me, if she was ill, she'd shout it out.'

She couldn't remember what fights might have come and gone around that time.

Charlotte watched her speak, the shelves of her study lying behind her, boxes ready there and waiting to be sent away, but their volumes still dusted with the memory of blame. She watched her speak, and she felt the nights they'd shared together – like this story was a great wide space, rugged grass, no people, and those times of love lay on its other side.

'I don't know how long it was before I started . . . properly realizing. These things take a while, you know? That your daughter's deaf, that your daughter's gone deaf, it's not the first thing that comes to you. Or if it is, you tell yourself it's not the right one. And then you know, she was twenty months . . . babies don't cry at that age, not all the time. They make other noises. I started seeing – how she wasn't making other noises. She'd smile sometimes, laugh. Just . . . soundless. Just like a bubble,' Ruth said. The gentle astonishment in her own voice – as if it could strike her in such a way, after more than two years – it seemed to rise like a bubble also through this unmoving air.

'Lennie was worried too, like. He seemed worried too. We talked about it. I didn't . . . I didn't know what sort of things might cause deafness, when she hadn't had any bad diseases, I'd never even seen her take a knock, you know, a hard enough knock . . . and I never left her with him. Maybe you wonder . . . how you can stay with someone when you don't trust them so that you can leave your baby . . . But doubts, worries, they lie so low. You're not aware. You could go out to the shops, leave her there on a Sunday and you don't think about the reason you don't go. It wasn't . . . it wasn't that I thought he'd ever hurt her. He was . . . he was starting to hate me, I think. He loved me too, and that just made the hate worse.' She shook her head as if she couldn't understand these truths. 'I didn't trust him with me . . .' she said. 'But I never thought he'd hurt her. It's just – unconscious, when someone hurts you . . . it's just unconscious, you can't change it, that you don't trust them with the things that are . . . precious, in your life . . . and she is precious.'

Ruth raised her face and Charlotte saw that she was holding now, a lot of tears, a well of tears which would not stop if they began, behind this voice that she used like a rope, drawing herself from word to word.

'She is the most precious thing I've ever had. Don't think –' Her sentence broke into splintered images. Nia on the doorstep here. And outside, the car doors were still open and the spring wind made the empty seats cold. It was better. It was for Nia's sake. 'Don't think that I don't love her.'

But the words were useless.

'It was my fault,' Ruth said, and over that masquerade of control, tears slipped out and ran as she stared at Charlotte, 'as much as his. Maybe more than his. Maybe it was all my fault, because I stayed.

'She wasn't developing. She wasn't playing with things . . . and she wasn't starting to make any noises . . . I booked the tests. We sat and talked about it and I was scared and he was scared, to know. You understand? Who wants to know? But I made the date . . . I booked it.'

She looked at Charlotte.

'I never took her,' she said.

Charlotte's mouth softly opened as she heard the words.

'I never took her for them.'

Her mouth opened and her wide eyes – they gently tried to close.

Nia lay unmoving. Perhaps really asleep.

'Cochlear echo test,' Ruth said. She sounded a name, the reality of which she did not know. 'I never took her.' For a few moments, she just said the same thing over and over again. And a long-ago night was formed in tiny pictures, caught in the reflections as tears ran out and her face was only a shell beneath. 'We fought . . . the night before. Or Lennie fought, that night, evening, he hit me around . . . he hit me around,' she said. But to say that didn't hold the sounds she made when she was pushed from place to place or held down on the floor. To say that didn't hold the fact that she'd screamed, a lot of times. Or that she'd pleaded with him or that he'd shouted over and over how he loved her and how he couldn't understand why she didn't love him back. A useless thing, he'd shouted at her. It was a useless thing to love her. 'It's the fear of it, it's not even how much it hurts, when he's got his hand up . . . you see his face, he's a monster. You can't say his name and have him stop. You can't touch that person you love . . . he's not there. I didn't mean to . . . shout out so much. It's the fear of it.'

Tears ran. It was only this guilt that held her together.

'We fought,' she said. 'He went out, he left me. I went upstairs. I wanted to see Nia. I thought I'd get into bed with her . . . I went into the room and she wasn't in bed.' She remembered, how the street lamp's light had streamed in through the curtains to touch the empty sheets where Nia should have been. 'I went in and she was on the floor at the end of the bed. Her clothes all rucked up, her nappy . . . I went to see why she was sitting there. She was crying,' Ruth said, quiet-stricken. 'I saw her. She was crying.'

She looked at Charlotte and in the tears that ran and ran, those reflections would play on always: how she had gone and seen that, how she had slowly realized, how she had been afraid to touch Nia and, when she'd reached out, Nia had tried to scramble away from her hands. And the minutes then. Sitting across the room from one another, Nia with her face hidden away, all balled up, and she only staring back at her daughter, and realizing. Realizing.

Lennie hadn't known, because Lennie had been out.

'She wasn't deaf,' Ruth said. 'She'd heard. If she'd heard, and she'd been silent and she was, she was, always silent . . . if she could hear but she never cried any more and hadn't started making sounds . . . it was . . . it was just a layer. Like a barrier.'

She had seen it in the bedroom, in the thread of the streetlight: a quiet little shell that Nia had been living inside. For how long? A few months perhaps. Perhaps longer. At what age does a child start to realize, or if they don't realize, to feel afraid of the sounds that come when the door is shut?

Ruth had been afraid. The fear had come like snow, slowly building, slowly settling, as she'd remained there on the floor. She had been afraid of her marriage, and the love that had borne – this child that had been made from her desperate good intentions and her husband's frustration. She had been afraid of beatings – which she could forgive – but which could not be understood or forgiven by Nia. Lennie and Ruth Lewis. She'd seen the sum of them: she had seen a two-year-old who was trapped behind glass.

'Deafness . . . is incurable,' Ruth sounded the words. 'But a girl who's hiding . . . a girl who's just scared and doesn't make any sound . . . you can bring that child out, you can make her better,' she uttered softly. 'You can make her well.'

She had gone to hug her. All that night she had hugged her and they'd fallen asleep, after a long, long time they had, and when Lennie had come home and found their own bed empty and opened the door to Nia's room, he had believed that they were finding solace. He had felt estranged from both of them.

'I didn't take her for the tests. The morning came . . . I didn't put her in the car. We sat in the kitchen and I talked to her . . . I talked to her a lot. She smiled. I played with her. I could have taken her. The nurse would have seen her. I'd given the history. I'd said already . . . that it'd been months. She would have looked at Nia and asked herself why a hearing child had been silent for months and I . . . I . . . She would have looked at us. I could've dressed nicely, I could've smiled and talked to her, but she would've looked at me and seen. A battered wife. That's the term, isn't it? That's the term. That's what they use.

She wouldn't know what it meant to me, to have my family. Only
. . . what he'd done. She wouldn't have seen that Nia – Nia would get
better, she'd get all right, if things between us got better, if it was safe
for her. I just had to make it safe. I kept the house – a safe place.' She
was justifying herself and she must not do that, couldn't stop herself
trying. This was how she hated herself. At night, these justifications
came up to her mind and they overran each other and she lay, she lay
still. She heard herself saying that doctors couldn't do for her daughter
what a happier home would. And that it would be that soon. 'The
nurse wouldn't have understood . . . how it might have got better,'
she said.

The tears streamed, quick as passing months could. The seasons
left her, and spilled on to her hands, when she had talked to Nia, every
moment that they were together, talked and talked and talked over
Nia's silence and waited for a sound in response.

'I was afraid,' she said. 'Can you understand? Can you understand
that? Can you?'

Disabled, Charlotte looked back at this woman she had fallen in
love with. Could give no answer. Her silence was two thousand miles.

'I was afraid. I was afraid of what I'd made. I thought – one morning
she'd laugh and the sound would just come out. She'd forget to hide.
I'd tickle her . . . I'd play a game with her. She'd laugh out loud. I was
afraid to leave, Charlotte . . . I was afraid to step out of the house and
look back at it, and see what it had all become – see what I'd done,
what I'd made. When it might get better . . . if he got . . . happier, we
got happier, she might speak. *She could have done –*

'– When he got angry, I tried not to make any sound. I think . . . I
hated myself . . . I think, after a while, I wanted him to hurt me. I was
trying to make her better. But I wasn't leaving. I wasn't leaving him.
I was afraid for it to be over and I'd be the one who'd made this . . .
I'd never be able to heal it if I left him. I'd never be able to make it
right.'

Charlotte's head was shaking. For how long? For a year? Ruth had
stayed that way. More. It must have been more. She had woken every
morning, and picked up broken things, and cleaned the house and

loved the house and loved her daughter who didn't make any sound
that day but might tomorrow. Or that evening. Or in a moment's time.

'She hasn't spoken,' Ruth said. The face broke, the guilt that held
it, every feeling. And there was only anguish left, her voice full of
earth. 'She's three . . . she hasn't spoken . . . she hasn't laughed. I've
talked to her, Charlotte. Kept talking to her, every day. I've *left* him.
It took me . . . it took me a long time but I've left him. I won't be
with him any more.' The words fell between her sobs, her shoulders
heaved and she looked out at Charlotte and Charlotte could not move
to touch her, this person that she needed; loved. 'I've left him now
and I'm sorry . . . It's too late now. I can't have her now. How can I
touch her? I've let her live this way . . . I've done this.'

She saw someone who had first come to her, full of coquettish
laughter, and tears that had bubbled out afterwards as though the two
were one. Someone who had no friends, none to understand, none
who'd seen anything but the sweet cottage picture that had once been
a dream. That had become a trap. The small jokes, the appealing
smile, the constant voice which ran like a fountain over rocks you
could not see. And when at night Ruth had gone home, she had talked
to Nia in the kitchen and hoped for any sound.

Ruth stared out and palmprints dimmed her vision; a hundred tiny
grey palmprints, or bright blue, or made of soil. A thousand palmprints
placed along a wall where Nia had set her ear to listen. Ruth had
realized. Night after night, she must have. That grey shading, a
thousand marks. Waiting for the noises that dominated her and
terrified her and held her whole life.

Charlotte saw the self-loathing, the madness that let Ruth cry or
scream or run from her, when she was trying to understand. She
could not have understood. Charlotte saw a woman now, crying for
an aspiration and for what she'd made it into. No she could not have
understood. Her hands were empty things, as they'd been as she'd
walked Hedera's corridors and looked into its rooms. She didn't own
them as she saw Ruth clearly for the first time: reality came in pieces
to remake the shape of a face that she had kissed.

On the settee, covering her mouth, where the sobs came anyway,

Ruth was bent over. She was holding herself while her daughter slept or did not sleep – right in this chair, beside them.

And Charlotte, whose body did not feel like her own, was crying without knowing it. There had been many years, when she hadn't been able to cry. Maybe years – and she had always needed another woman really, just in order to make sense of herself. She had written, tried to express. Not entries, never a journal, but letters. A close-telling of the life she had never been able to believe was hers. Letters with no destination. Missives to her sister, who was gone.

Dear Charlotte, Dear Charlotte.

She'd wanted her. In truth, what she'd needed more than anything was the company of Charlotte Weyland, who might have understood. And all that loss, those years of picturing a female face that was not her own, that had come to rest on Ruth. To live in Ruth's blue eyes. Charlotte saw it now.

Ruth raised her head. Brutal hours leaving, throwing things into a bag and keeping her hands, always, away from Nia, they returned and she let the truth run out. 'Tell me – if what I've done . . . tell me, can I keep her? How can I keep her? How can she be with me? Please,' she said, and as she spoke the word, it came clearly, like some new coastline, seen from far away: she did not want to leave Nia, nor did she want to leave this place she'd built. She didn't want to leave this woman, who'd cared for her and made her forget things in the moments when they'd kissed. 'Tell me . . . could you forgive that? No one could forgive that. Could you . . . ?'

Words shook in Charlotte and were not said.

She saw a terrible cruelty, but a terrible mistake. It seemed, in these stretching silent instants, that a love she'd believed she had understood, since she had been a child, a mother's love, turned now, and showed her a side that she had never seen.

Ruth asked her, 'You couldn't, could you forgive me – ?'

And she took Ruth's hand. Took it brutally when she didn't want to be brutal. Pulled her from the seat like a loose and half-made thing. She looked into Ruth's face and saw a woman who had sacrificed her daughter for some dream. But a woman who had lived and lived on every day, spoken a hundred thousand words to Nia, waiting for her to heal. She pulled Ruth's hand, unable to make a word, and Ruth was repeating herself over and over. Charlotte was dragging her through into the corridor, her own hands like china, pushing her into the study. And Ruth stood there, not seeing the shelves around her. Not seeing the volumes. More than thirty volumes whose years were marked in gold.

Charlotte opened her mouth but Ruth's expression was scattered, unable to understand, just staring back. And she pulled from her left-hand side, the first in the highest row, and it fell to the floor like nothing. Just an object. Nothing that could hold what she had felt since that day, one single day in an American summer, that had shown her a white marble grave.

Charlotte bent down and, on the floor in front of Ruth's prone figure, she scrambled like a child among the pages. And she pulled it free and held it. The only thing that she had taken from Hedera. The only thing that remained, a photograph. She pushed it towards her.

'You know who that is?' she said. 'You know who that is?' She hated Ruth. She hated Ruth and loved her. Really those feelings had always been the same.

Ruth stared down, her gaze featureless, like Nia's.

In black and white, on a long lawn – on a picnic blanket – a mother and daughter sat. She looked down at the photographed girl. Nia's age, she saw, small and blue-eyed.

'It's you,' she said.

'No. No, it's not. That's Charlotte,' she said. 'That's Charlotte Weyland.'

Ruth raised her eyes, diffuse. The little girl in the photograph looked out at a world she didn't know. 'Not *you*? What do you mean, *Charlotte Weyland*? Then who are you . . . ?'

'I'm no one. I'm her sister,' she said. 'I was born . . . I was born three years after she drowned. I was given her life, because she couldn't live it any more. My mother was . . . she had a little dream. Just like yours. Must be a precious dream, must be beautiful . . .' But she knew it was. Months she had spent discovering it. Unable to deny it any more. She had sat with Nia and they'd put their hands against the wall and she had seen, it was a dream that you couldn't desert. She'd tried. Years she had tried. 'There was a hole in it, though. There was a hole, she had . . . she had a dead child. And when she was given a chance, to fill that hole, she did. When she gave birth to me . . .' Charlotte's hands rose and fell and did not touch Ruth. 'Just like you,' she said. 'She let me go on . . . not knowing. *Just like you have! You want me to forgive you . . . ? You don't even know what it means, to ask for that . . . you couldn't know . . .*' But she saw it from the other side now. And she cried, because the wrongs that had been done, they weren't evil, but only full of sadness, full of desperate final hope. '*Could I forgive you? Yes I forgive you –*'

As she had always needed to. As she had never written or admitted in her latest night thoughts. As she had told herself she never would. The picture shook between them. It was the child in you, forgiveness.

'You take . . . look what you take away from me! Yes I forgive you! I forgive you! I love you. Yes . . .' she said. She put out a hand that did not reach Ruth. 'Yes,' she said. She moved forwards, so that it touched her. 'Yes . . .'

The words cracked – they left a world behind her. She thought of Nia, of doctors, treatment, she didn't know. Good endings. They weren't the reasons behind her answer. But you couldn't condemn love, just because its hope was uncontrolled.

'Yes . . .' she said to Ruth. It slipped from her as easily as water.

What they had created stretched along this coastline, buildings in the distant darkness that hadn't yet been seen. The scaffolding was gone. Roofs which could only be made out, a sweep, densely shining when floodlights tracked across them, they reached into the wind, unconfined.

The early night had passed, the earliest morning was coming. March was over.

Where sand had now driven the stones clean, the houses' boards were being taken down.

*

You could see the gouge marks from his fingers. Filled with the turn of the warning lights as though with liquid, draining from them into dark again. Lennie Lewis made a trench, the width of two hands around the flagpole's foundation. He stared down at it, still lodged in this ground: a block of decades-old concrete, scarred by years, which he could only feel as he ran his hand over its surface – too black here, too hard to see.

Had there been some comfort through the last two years in his daughter's deafness? It was an easier thing, estrangement, when the child could not be heard. He loved her. When she had been missing from him – eight hundred miles away and driving home – then love for her had caught his heart. Standing with her, he'd been unable.

If he'd ever looked, truly looked into her eyes, would he have seen unformed sounds flicker there?

This is what we've done.

He had believed Ruth. He'd believed himself. At first, the violence that had come from him had seemed to hold as much passion – black passion, wrong passion, yes, but *still* – as much as it had pain. Until the last months, he hadn't known what it had really done to his wife.

Lennie Lewis dug. He moved the soil in handfuls to the pile he'd built behind him. Above, the trees soughed and grieved. He remembered how that violence, that at first had seemed to take the love he felt for Ruth and each next morning make it bloom – in remorse, in tenderness reaffirmed – how it had dried, become a husk. Till last autumn he'd looked at her and shouted at her, and the word 'love' had meant nothing, and the word 'hate' had refused to hold his feelings or carry anything away.

Till last autumn, when the project had come.

As Rhys stood on the beach and watched Tom say goodbye without remorse, Lennie scored the deeper earth with his filthy hands. Rhys's face was full of unspoken words, and there were pictures in his eyes that he'd tried to paint. That, as he'd turned from Emyr Morgan to the wall again and drawn him, had sealed themselves, completed, and kept him there inside them. Weren't they meant to leave you? When you'd finished them, weren't they meant to leave you free?

He watched Tom talk about how it felt to be going away, and he asked himself if he'd managed to make anything. Making or breaking, Lennie'd said. He wondered if the pictures were already gone.

And Emyr, who had completed the exhibits, set them all in perfect places, looked up at the wall that Rhys had covered. He had taken the wrapping from the plaque and had set it in its oak stand, in its brass bracket on the floor. He walked to the stepladder and took the lid off a paint tin. He stirred it, in thick and shining ropes. He was crying.

The trees bowed their heads over Lennie.

Three feet down into the earth now and he had to widen the trench. He moved around it with the throw of the lights on his forehead, on his shoulders as he bent. In darkness then and lit again as the sand-blasting crews made their way towards the house that his wife and daughter had left empty.

She had sat behind that door, a little three-year-old girl. She'd sat hearing, listening, she'd sat and played, she'd made a world with her toys where everything was peaceful and the seasons never changed. Downstairs, her mother had been screaming.

It seemed so bare. How could he have believed Ruth? It seemed so clear.

At the table she'd sat, like their silence made real, and he had never seen her. Yes he remembered how the violence had dried until there was nothing inside it. And how this project had begun.

While his wife sat unseen by him, and the story poured from her mouth, Lennie dug this earth, that had been dear to him.

The project had come. He'd seen how, through years, he had only believed and never felt, never truly known. He'd heard stories that had embraced him and reared him up into the air – where the stars wheeled now in great, disordered cycles as Lennie raised his face – he had loved them, but they'd been someone else's. Never his. Till this project had come. He'd torn down and he'd rebuilt. He'd found a different light, his own, to fill Ynys-morlan's night with. Had understood. For the first time, remembered his father and known, if they could have looked at each other now, they would have been equal.

All this, all this had happened.

But the story was a lie.

There was no place for this passion in the world. It seemed to make greatness but that greatness was false. The truth that he'd read in Ruth's letter brought a morning, an ashen, desperate morning, and he saw that passion for what it was. It only created pain. There was no love in it. It couldn't have made the marriage he remembered, his father and his mother so close to each other until the day the cancer had finally taken him away; half the man that he'd once been. That passion had muted a three-year-old child, until she hid away from the world behind her brown eyes, it couldn't make a marriage – it couldn't make a love. The story was a lie.

Questions rose in him that had never come. Had his father expected him to believe he had hidden murder for decades from his wife? That he had told a son but not her, who he was closer to than anyone? Imagine those lies true – how would his mother have looked at his father, the secret finally revealed? What would their love have been then? The story had no power to create, only destroy, only that.

He cleaved the ground. He pulled it away from the concrete, tainted by a lie. That legend had made a world in him where meaning was written in visceral colours, in touch and taste stronger than anything he'd ever known. Were those feelings lies? They must be lies. They must be.

It was the colour of Nia's skin, the bare truth that he saw. It bleached the life from everything he'd believed in. He'd made that girl. He'd made her silence, for she could hear, she could hear, and the door he'd closed had hidden nothing except the reality of what she was.

This was what his grand love had made. His father's story had never held truth.

There was no greatness. He had loved this ground. But there were no foundations laid here. Lennie wept and couldn't see the tears or his own hands in the ever-turning light. He was sorry.

To think that your history was buried in the earth, it gave your home meaning. You looked at the mountains then, you saw their shapes like remembrance. You were not alone. Without beliefs, it could feel like you made no imprint on that place. The things you did, they faded. You died and they were gone.

And now he saw this was the truth.

The wind touched Lennie and moved past him. Throughout the night he dug, to prove the myth false. To finally make a great enough cut in the ground that he could take hold of the edge of the concrete, pull it upwards. Separate it from his home.

The blast-cleaning came to an end and the last of the water streamed down, round the windows, trickling over their sills, over the shapes of stones that hadn't been seen for a hundred years, to drip on to new lawn. It made tiny tributaries through the grass, still in darkness, while the sky above grew lighter.

He was a huge man, at the end of his strength by the time he set his hands into the edge there. He grieved for the things that he'd believed and for the truth, which that faith had created.

Charlotte held Ruth through the night. Nia was sleeping beside them. At some point, Ruth must have slept too because she woke with a cry and looked around – to see all the lamps still lit.

Rhys and Bethan and Tom sat together on the beach for a long time. They looked out and sometimes saw things to be happy for, and sometimes things to be sad. Bethan was thinking of many days when they'd been here together, somewhere on the long stretch of sand that took you from one headland to another, and she was remembering a sense of hopelessness. She had looked at the future and had seen no opportunity. She'd seen herself failing – all the different paths she'd imagined – and she'd chosen to stay. She had thought that this town was the end of every line. But opportunity had followed her back. Made its way here from whatever town or city she might have lived in, wound along all those roads, and set up camp in Ynys-morlan.

She saw the sky growing lighter.

Rhys held his knees beside them.

A long night, when he wished and his wishes weren't fulfilled. He'd made little hills and mountains in the sand here, and drawn a road that turned its way between them and led down to nothing, the edge of all the rest, where the beach was blank again.

Tom looked at them sometimes. Only glad he'd brought them out here, though it hadn't been a night of easy talking, or old stories, or even smiles. In the building noise, while he'd been standing further down this beach alone, waiting for the time to come, he'd looked out at the sea and felt some kind of happiness, which couldn't leave him now, even with the complications he saw written in their eyes.

He'd stood there. Used to do it a lot, at a younger age. He'd used to have nightmares, where he swam out, and swam, and that girl's hand slipped through his fingers. Over and over, he was unable to grasp hold of it. In the minutes while he'd waited, though, and looked out and seen the black water moving, the girl out there had begun to swim herself, and she'd come all the way back to this shore and climbed out here and looked at him. She'd been fifteen years old and as good a swimmer as he was.

They stood up on the sand as the morning came and it slipped under their feet. In the silence that settled after the work, the sea could be clearly heard as they said quiet goodbyes, and as Tom left them there – walked slowly away, the end of the sand not far in front of him.

'You're going too,' Bethan said. 'A week, or something, from now?'

Rhys met her eyes as, somewhere else, Lennie turned the concrete foundation over.

There was dawn coming and the tips of the trees, if he'd looked up, for the first time could have been seen. His back was broken with the work and, staring down, he found himself giving out, till he was sitting on the ground. There was dirt everywhere. In the forming light, as Ruth and Charlotte walked out, Nia carried on Ruth's shoulder, the houses around him were almost visible. He didn't take his eyes from the hole, though.

There he sat, at the border where Ynys-morlan met the road. There he sat, hidden by the trees and their lowest, swaying twigs. He looked down into the earth and he saw, wet and filthy there, the remnants of clothes.

Lennie bent and reached into the hole. He moved his hands through the mud, he drew one out, with a hard thing in it that could not be a stone. Rubbing it in his shirt, he saw it: a belt buckle. It was dull in this vague light.

And when he stretched, and excavated – a bent shape in the growing dawn – there were more things to be found. He looked up at the sky with them laid out beside him. In the east there was morning. The night still filled the west and he made out a star there, two, now fading. He saw a split in the world. He saw a line.

The wind blew, and he felt it clearly.

Ruth and Charlotte found the car with its doors still opened, and everything cold inside. Ruth touched the seat, the night still lying there in that chill, though the morning was rising above them, beyond the trees. Her face was stained as she looked up at Charlotte, and if there was no future in either of their eyes then maybe one lay between.

Rhys was looking at Bethan. He could find nothing to say. He didn't want to know the morning here. She saw black pupils, the words they'd used against each other nothing but sea air now.

'Rhys –' In the quiet of the beach, though, Bethan gave up, and she leaned forward and she kissed him. Just for a moment he felt the touch of her, as soft as the first warm breath of summer. Then he was looking at her face again. And she said slowly, 'I'm happy. I'm glad . . . I'm glad to be staying here.'

He stared at her, incredulous, her hair shifting, the sand blown in rivers round her feet. She had a big old coat on and somewhere new in her face.

'I'm glad to be staying,' she said again. 'D'you see? D'you see what I mean?'

His mouth was open but he said nothing to her. Yes, he saw

what she meant. And he saw a town he had driven himself apart from. He saw a hatred that he had proven, and a clutch of pictures, a handful of beautiful, imaginary pictures, that were all he'd carry away.

He looked at her and almost gave no answer, these things shifting as if they might not be real, for a moment, might not be real at all, and then taking her hand and holding it, just for a moment, small and familiar there, he told her thank you.

She had this big coat on, and a future in her face.

He walked away, along the beach, through a little alley with cobbled walls where the night still hugged the stone, and out, into this street he was leaving behind. There'd been truth in her eyes as she'd said it and, staring around him at these half-seen houses, he seemed to miss Ynys-morlan more, feel closer to it, need it more. He could still see the shape it had had before, a ghost. If she'd forgiven him, if that had been her meaning, still he didn't want to be what he was. A vandal here, in a pretty town.

The first light showed gulls wheeling. Making or breaking, Lennie had said. With the memory of Emyr, painted everywhere, right here on the pavements that showed a gradual white beneath his feet, he knew which he had done.

Rhys walked away as Lennie only sat and remembered. He made decisions, the only ones that were left to him, and he was thinking of the boy. It would be a week before Rhys left and Lennie would see him go.

He would talk to him in the last evening they spent, when his hands would still have the stains of what was on them now.

They'd sit in the Lion, where everything was new and neither of them would speak words about it as they looked around them, but would talk of other things – feeling, in a way they hadn't expected, like they could say what they needed to, surrounded by a place they didn't know.

Lennie would have a chance to tell Rhys, two days before he went to the bus stop, bags in hand, that Rhys was nothing like him. With an expression that was a faded year to the one which he wore now, he would say to Rhys that the boy should not look at him and think they were the same.

Now the grass was moving. Now he only saw the world, and a rift, that he could not explain.

In the Lion, he would look into Rhys's face, look deeply, and tell him to be free of the things which he had never been free of.

'We're not the same,' he'd say. 'You're eighteen. We're not the same.'

Rhys would turn away, and then look back at Lennie Lewis. Half of him wouldn't want it to be true. But the other half would believe it, and let go of something that for a long time had seemed like all he owned.

Now, the sky was light enough to touch each windowpane.

Emyr Morgan walked out into it, the museum finished behind. Rhys would pass it in his last days there and he'd look in through the window: all the cases, he'd see, and be unable to make out the exhibits inside. He'd see his wall.

The figure of Bethan would be looking back at him, big and out of shape. The one of Tom beside the road with the sun Rhys had tried to put, and the shadow, on his face. He'd see the words from the bus shelter.

Emyr's face was tired and old, and nothing like this town, as he stepped out on to the street. He looked at the businesses and the homes and the new pavements. He loved it. He didn't want it to be a memorial. He didn't want it to be nothing but a eulogy.

He stepped into a gathering day. He had lifted his hands, he'd been biting his lip, crying; he had tried to paint it out. But he'd thought of Gwen and of the new look in her eyes. A good mayor, a good planner, he saw the place that he was responsible for and cared for it more than anything. There should be many mornings, from this one, on and on. And white paint, white rooms and lighting, they were lifeless things.

He'd tried at one point, early in the project, to estimate how much of that thirty-three million pounds they'd used. He'd not been able.

He wanted the coming mornings to seem uncountable. He'd slowly taken the brush away from what Rhys had made.

Gwen parked in front of the house she'd shared with him, and there they waited for the taxi. She went in. While Tom stood outside in the cleanest, earliest part of the day, she took one last look. She walked to Lucky and Baby's little sleeping room, and woke them up. She sat and fussed with them, cried helpless, silly tears over them, and then she closed them in again, easily asleep already, for the last part of the night.

She left the front door wide open and, as they packed their few bags into the taxi's boot, the driver stared at it. He was grumpy and hadn't slept well. He liked the late shifts better.

When they got inside, he turned around and motioned at them, this middle-aged woman and this young man.

'You've left the door,' he said. He pointed to the house.

The lights were on inside the hallway, and she could see one painting there.

'That's fine,' she said. She rearranged her hands in her lap.

'Well, what do you mean, "that's fine"? It's open, for God's sake.'

She raised her eyes and said again, 'That's fine.'

And he looked from one to the other of them, and his face wore a strange expression.

After a moment, he said, 'But . . . dogs'll get in . . .'

She thought for a moment that he meant hers, but they were in already. He meant wild dogs, she saw. Roaming dogs of some kind. As if there were a pack just waiting at the treeline.

'They'll get in . . .' he said, because he couldn't find another reason to close the door.

Emyr looked out.

Behind him, the museum's doors stood open too. The building would hold a hundred things. The flag that Lloyd Lewis had once planted into the ground would be given by Lennie to lie under glass. The red dragon endlessly clawing, the green earth would be an unchanging line and the white sky above always untouched. Against the wall, so many of them that their own case would be necessary, many volumes of a journal would stand, where dust could never gather. Bound in matching leather, numbered with their years, they would have made their way across two thousand miles of ocean to come into this room; the same body of water that you saw across the street, washing up and ending its travel here.

Beside them, resting close to Bethan Hughes's velvet dress, an £8,000 cheque would be set out. Siân Humphries would send it in the post, not to Emyr, but to the museum itself, unsure of whether it would be delivered – sent out from her house, which stood opposite, to a depot in a different town, categorized and brought back by the post van, to a building with no letter box. Unsure, slipping it into the envelope. If maybe it wouldn't just fly off, like some little bird, never to return.

Emyr's plaque stood beside the cabinets. Rhys's paintings stretched behind, and his obscenities, and his little copied pictures of the photographs, as if that plaque had been commissioned just for him.

Looking in through one high-reaching window, a smile would touch Rhys's face, and fade and come again. An evening it would be. He'd almost be able to make out the tiny, sun-shaded features of men raking stones. And the photos, wrapped up carefully and stored in a book inside his bag, wouldn't seem like they were stolen any more. Not so much like captured things, his hand resting on the canvas, sitting and waiting under the kind of bus shelter Bambi would've used, if Bambi had ever got tired of skipping.

Now, outside the doorway, Emyr Morgan stared up. And in the last moments of twilight, he saw new street lamps flicker into life.

Wrought iron, they were. They stuttered against a morning sky as the crews restored the electricity. A few minutes, they shone there, and he looked at them. A small row of moons, that winked out – ready for the beginning of the day, and for the start of the season.

Quarter to six in the morning. There were people here. He heard low voices. He saw them.

*

Ruth and Charlotte drove the mile and a half to Ynys-morlan's edge, sleep-caught, to see for the first time what they'd built. They came to a stop at the edge of the town and parked in the wide space where the lane ended and the main street began, to see a morning that should have been empty.

A car drove past them.

Ruth looked and saw Gwen Morgan there. Some young boy in the seat next to her, a new place painted on the window-glass between them, embroidered across their faces.

It was the strangest thing. She got out of the car, Nia sleeping now, curled in the back – and Charlotte opening her own door. It was the 1st of April. April Fool's Day, curiously enough. It couldn't have been later than half past five a.m., Ruth thought, and there were people here. She was white as she turned from that passing car's tail lights, now fading, and stared out, and saw the town.

The road opened between pale stone cottages. Their front doors were unmarked oak, shaded by the peaks of their little entranceways – delicate peaks, where climbers would grow when years had come and gone, clematis and roses, honeysuckle. Smooth pavements laid the way from every front garden and out, into this street. You could've stood there, turned there, and seen the shine of new brass, doorknobs and hinges, like tiny coins splashed everywhere.

Masonry that hadn't been seen by her generation, or her mother's, perhaps even further back, now blended to meet the sea-stone curves of softly cobbled walls. Two rows of houses, seeing each other for the first time: gabled houses, with windows arching like a dovecote's. Little L-shaped houses with purple lustre on their slate roofs and the painted wood of hand-cut fascia boards peeking out from under eaves. Little perfect houses like she'd wished for when she'd been ten years old, but not wishes. Things made solid. Things made real.

From here, the perched lines of their wicker screens could be seen, still, in this newly windless part of the dawn. But they would sigh, they would chatter and sigh when the sea breeze came to thread between their weaves. The sound would carry over lawns, between the finials that stretched their closed eyes upwards, between the sun-brushed windows and out, to move wherever it wanted in this air.

Far down the road, the Lion's new woodcut stared out like a Jack-in-the-green, over tarmac that had no lines yet. A long and curving bar in there, with not a fingerprint on its surface, the room filled with the dusky quiet of a pub's day. Of its first. And across the street, the stained glass of the Shoreline Restaurant was waiting for the light, passing over, to push through on to tablecloths, white, and vases, white, and mosaics of every kind of colour – more than you'd find inside the greatest dressing-up box in the world.

New signs swung from their iron-vine brackets on the walls of Bed and Breakfasts, where net curtains shaded the coming April light to make a latticework on the floor of each new room.

It was beautiful. Maybe beauty was only symmetry, or the touch of some old memory – reflected, half-caught, almost kept. Maybe beauty was nothing in itself, but when you were surrounded by it, it could give you happiness. And you could speak with it. As Ruth had said months ago, and not believed since, you could express the saddest things through it, and mend them somehow. She looked out and saw the proof she'd made. It needn't be escape. To her right-hand side and below, the garden curled its circles around a fountain. Little hills and valleys of sea stone, where fresh water would run and trap the summer in rivers. And behind, on a slight rise above the arcing flower bed, Dai's sculpture cast over the grass the shadows of nought o'clock.

She couldn't see them, just the glints, but there were windmills there.

And the blanket, hanging down, would be holding the dew: a little atlas, a whole world, in its fibres.

There were people. Charlotte made out each one of them; a tiny smile found her. There were people, on doorsteps. Maybe ten or fifteen. She could see curtains opening.

She could pick out the houses she had recreated – there the roofs, like steepled hands. She could imagine, though she could not see, the rooms inside them, the little pieces of Hedera, which had survived death and travel and change, which had still remained, now growing brighter. Long-limbed shadows, she could picture, retreating on the ash tabletop and, upstairs, sun painting Nia's hands in a brighter blue.

Ruth looked out over what they'd made.

It felt like the wrongs you did, the mistakes you made, couldn't ever be redeemed, but maybe building things could heal the world. You gave love when you made something. Perhaps everything could be redeemed through that.

She had built the place really where once, a long time ago, her father had arrived and set up home. She had built the place where all children spoke and love wasn't a battle against sadness. There was grass as green as in memory, there was a garden full of the strongest roses, yellow, as the walls had once been around her. Water and render-dust ran down garden paths and made its way to the drains. Her mother would have stood, hands on hips, but the place around her would have been no ground for the expression on her face: growing a little lost, Ruth saw her on that path, befuddled by the dawn. Unable to see a failure, anywhere. Looking from the buildings up to the sky.

Shadows were cupped in every angle but they were draining. All down to Dai's sundial silhouettes. Free-standing, there it was. And every other building here. Free-standing. A lovely view, a beautiful view. Ruth shook her head as she stared out.

She'd never seen this place before. She wouldn't run from it. It was her home. She had never seen it but she knew it so well. She looked down at the open street and the air seemed to prick through the pores of her skin. She wept internally. She saw the long and curving sea-stone wall, where the surf might touch you in the air if the wind was blowing in towards the land. She saw the new shops, their blank signs showing – canvas taken away from them now. She knew it all, in the shapes of the houses; one wall behind another. The Ynys-morlan where she had grown up lay beneath this town, as if its photograph was indistinct there. Doorways and yards, spaced just as they'd always been, but each pale colour clear as the coming year.

The strangest thing to see them wandering: the figures of people who were foreigners here. In the back seat of the car – as Ruth put her hand on the bonnet for steadiness, as she felt Charlotte's already there – Nia lay between their coats, opening brown eyes, and seeing condensation like treasure on the windowpane.

It stood beside the coast, a long and gently curving settlement. And because it was a sunny day, there was nothing between Ynys-morlan and the sky.

Emyr Morgan's plaque remains:

IN 1999 YNYS-MORLAN UNDERWENT A
REGENERATION PROJECT.
THIS COLLECTION IS COMPILED OF CONTRIBUTIONS
FROM THE COMMUNITY AND REPRESENTS
THEIR FEELINGS ABOUT ITS CHANGE.

Acknowledgements

Without these people I never would've made it home dry: Patrick Walsh, Nick Dickman, Jules Newman, Edward Lowe, Chris Boross, Sarah Cefai, Anna Reynolds, Scarlett Thomas, Eileen and Kenneth John Lowe, Steve and Harriet, Dee, Jo, Mina, Wayne, Blake and all at the house of dreams and parties that ended so sadly – Gareth and Isabel, Rosie, Dave Bones, Alicia, Lennie, Emily, Michaela, Petra, Pani, Carla and everybody else who's out there creating new dreams and parties every day. Thank you for helping me – and for making the world outside Newfoundland just as beautiful.

Thanks also to She Ra, the best dog ever.

Most of all, thanks to whoever keeps leaving all the feathers around.